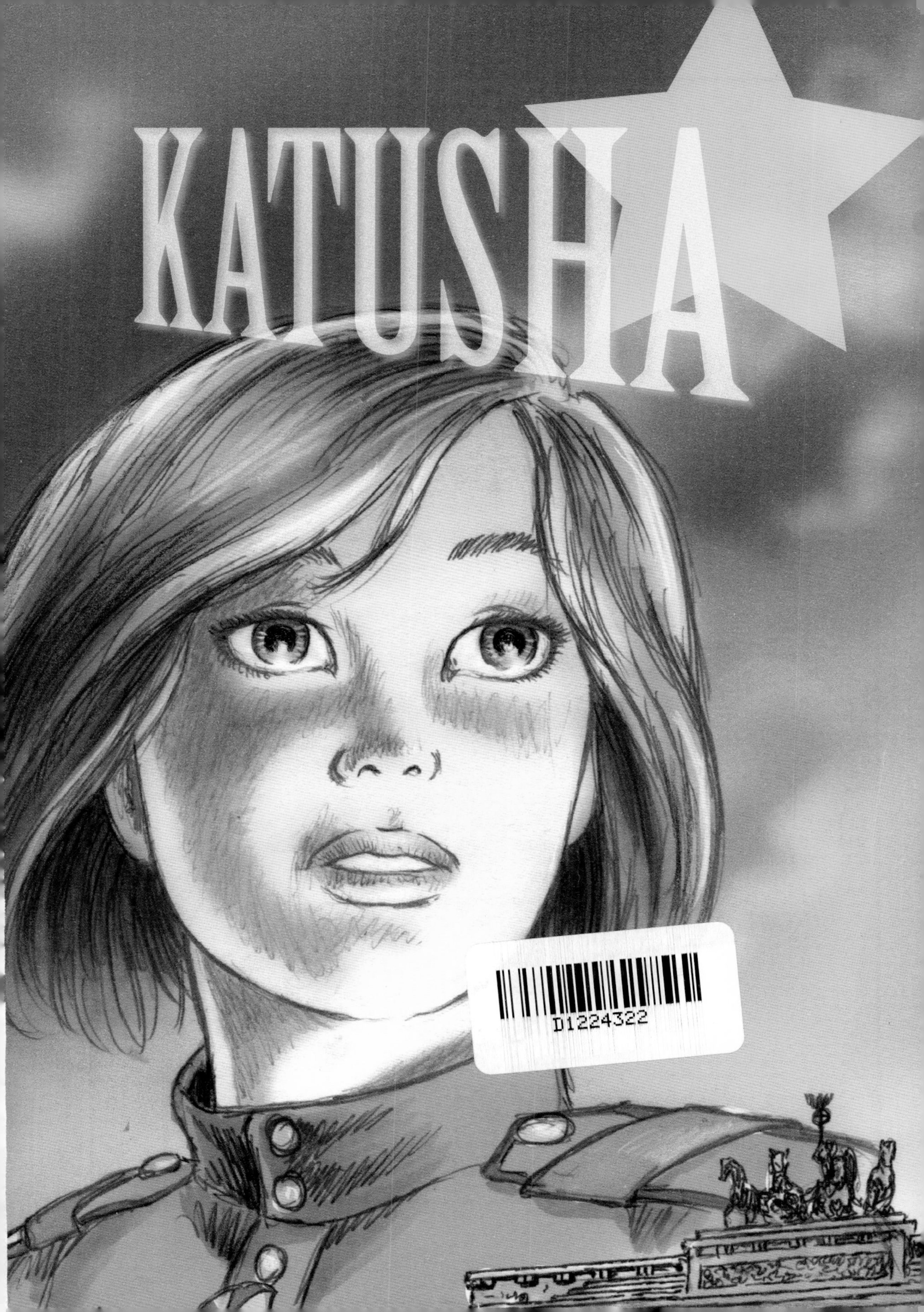
KATUSHA

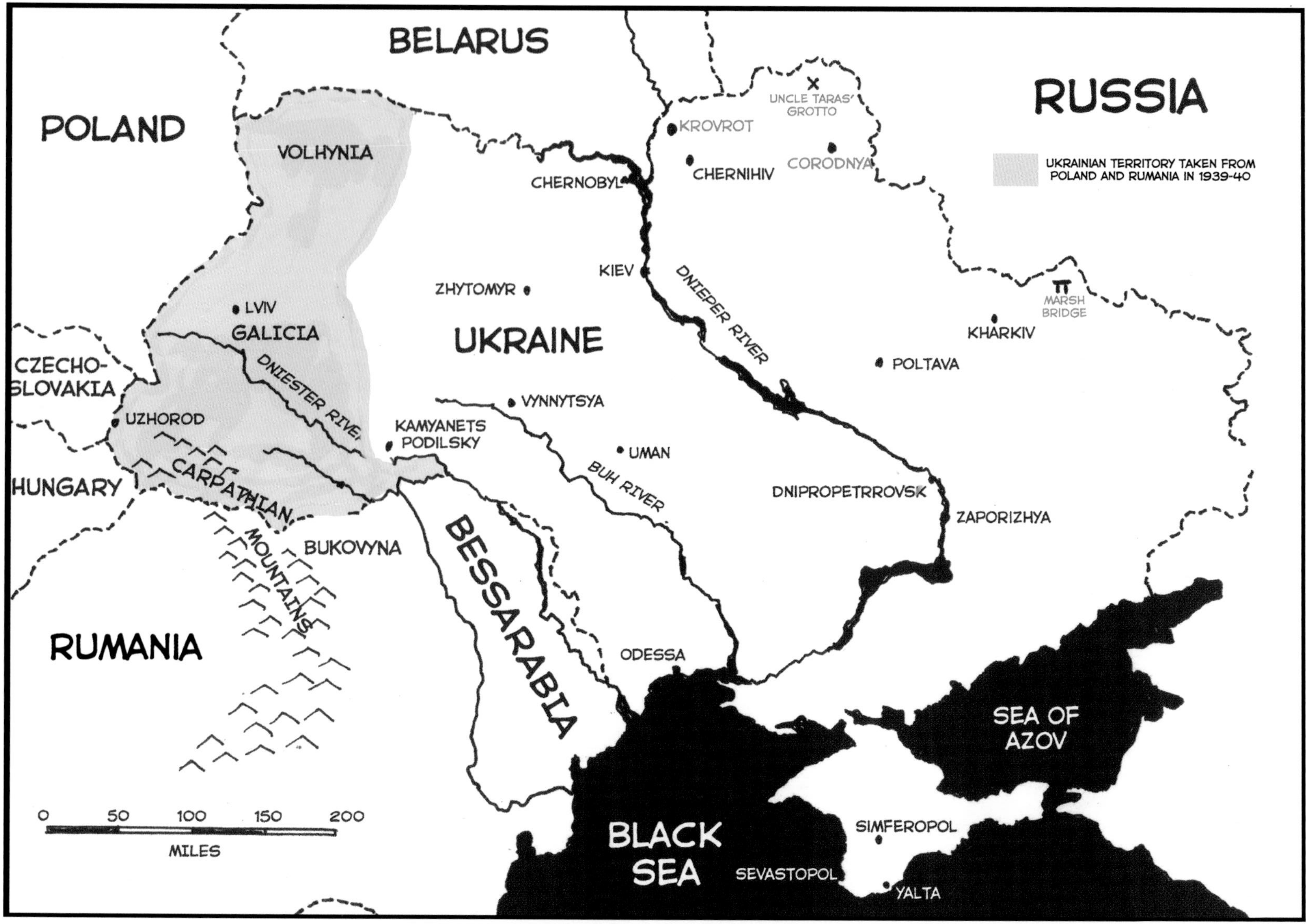

BELARUS
RUSSIA
POLAND
UKRAINIAN TERRITORY TAKEN FROM POLAND AND RUMANIA IN 1939-40
UNCLE TARAS' GROTTO
KROVROT
CHERNIHIV
CORODNYA
CHERNOBYL
VOLHYNIA
KIEV
ZHYTOMYR
DNIEPER RIVER
MARSH BRIDGE
KHARKIV
POLTAVA
LVIV
GALICIA
UKRAINE
CZECHO-SLOVAKIA
DNIESTER RIVER
VYNNYTSYA
UZHOROD
KAMYANETS PODILSKY
UMAN
HUNGARY
CARPATHIAN
MOUNTAINS
BUH RIVER
DNIPROPETRROVSK
ZAPORIZHYA
BUKOVYNA
BESSARABIA
RUMANIA
ODESSA
SEA OF AZOV
0 50 100 150 200
MILES
BLACK SEA
SIMFEROPOL
SEVASTOPOL
YALTA

SOVIET UKRAINE, 1941

KATUSHA

GIRL SOLDIER OF THE GREAT PATRIOTIC WAR

WAYNE VANSANT

DEAD RECKONING
Annapolis, Maryland

Jessamine County Public Library
600 South Main Street
Nicholasville, KY 40356
859-885-3523

Published by Dead Reckoning
291 Wood Road
Annapolis, MD 21402

Edge of Darkness and *The Shaking of the Earth* © 2013 by Wayne Vansant
On Wings of Thunder © 2019 by Wayne Vansant
Dead Reckoning is an imprint of the Naval Institute Press, the book publishing
division of the U.S. Naval Institute, a non-profit organization. All rights reserved.
With the exception of short excerpts for review purposes, no part of this book may
be reproduced or utilized in any form or by any means, electronic or mechanical,
including photocopying and recording, or by any information storage and retrieval
system, without permission in writing from the publisher.

Library of Congress Cataloging-in-Publication Data
Names: Vansant, Wayne, author, artist.
Title: Katusha : girl soldier of the Great Patriotic War / Wayne Vansant.
Description: Annapolis, MD : Dead Reckoning, [2019].
Identifiers: LCCN 2018042460 (print) | LCCN 2018051228 (ebook) |
    ISBN 9781682474396 (ePDF) | ISBN 9781682474396 (ePub) | ISBN
    9781682474259 | ISBN 9781682474259(pbk.) | ISBN 9781682474396 (ebook)
Subjects: LCSH: Women, Ukrainian—Comic books, strips, etc. | World War,
    1939–1945—Comic books, strips, etc. | Ukraine—History—Comic books,
    strips, etc. | Graphic novels. | GSAFD: Historical fiction.
Classification: LCC PN6727.V38 (ebook) | LCC PN6727.V38 K38 2019 (print)
    | DDC 741.5/973—dc23
LC record available at https://lccn.loc.gov/2018042460

Susan Barrows—Copy Editor and Computer Support
Maryam Rostamian—Design and Composition

♾ Print editions meet the requirements of ANSI/NISO z39.48-1992
(Permanence of Paper).
Printed in the United States of America.

27 26 25 24 23 22 21 20 19   9 8 7 6 5 4 3 2 1
First printing

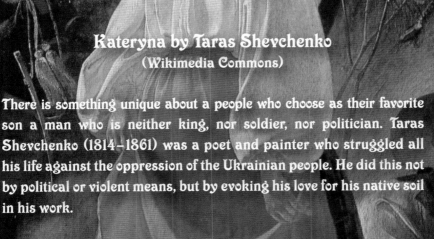

Kateryna by Taras Shevchenko
(Wikimedia Commons)

There is something unique about a people who choose as their favorite son a man who is neither king, nor soldier, nor politician. Taras Shevchenko (1814–1861) was a poet and painter who struggled all his life against the oppression of the Ukrainian people. He did this not by political or violent means, but by evoking his love for his native soil in his work.

This led to his imprisonment and the strictest supervision of his work. But despite this, more than 800 of his paintings and engravings survive today, and his writing played a major role in the development of the modern Ukrainian language.

Shevchenko's most famous painting is Kateryna, which tells the story of a Ukrainian girl who is seduced and abandoned by a Russian cavalry officer. This tragic allegory is a recurring theme not only in Shevchenko's work, but in popular Ukrainian ballads and folk tales, and gives us clear insight into Ukraine's hard and troubled history.

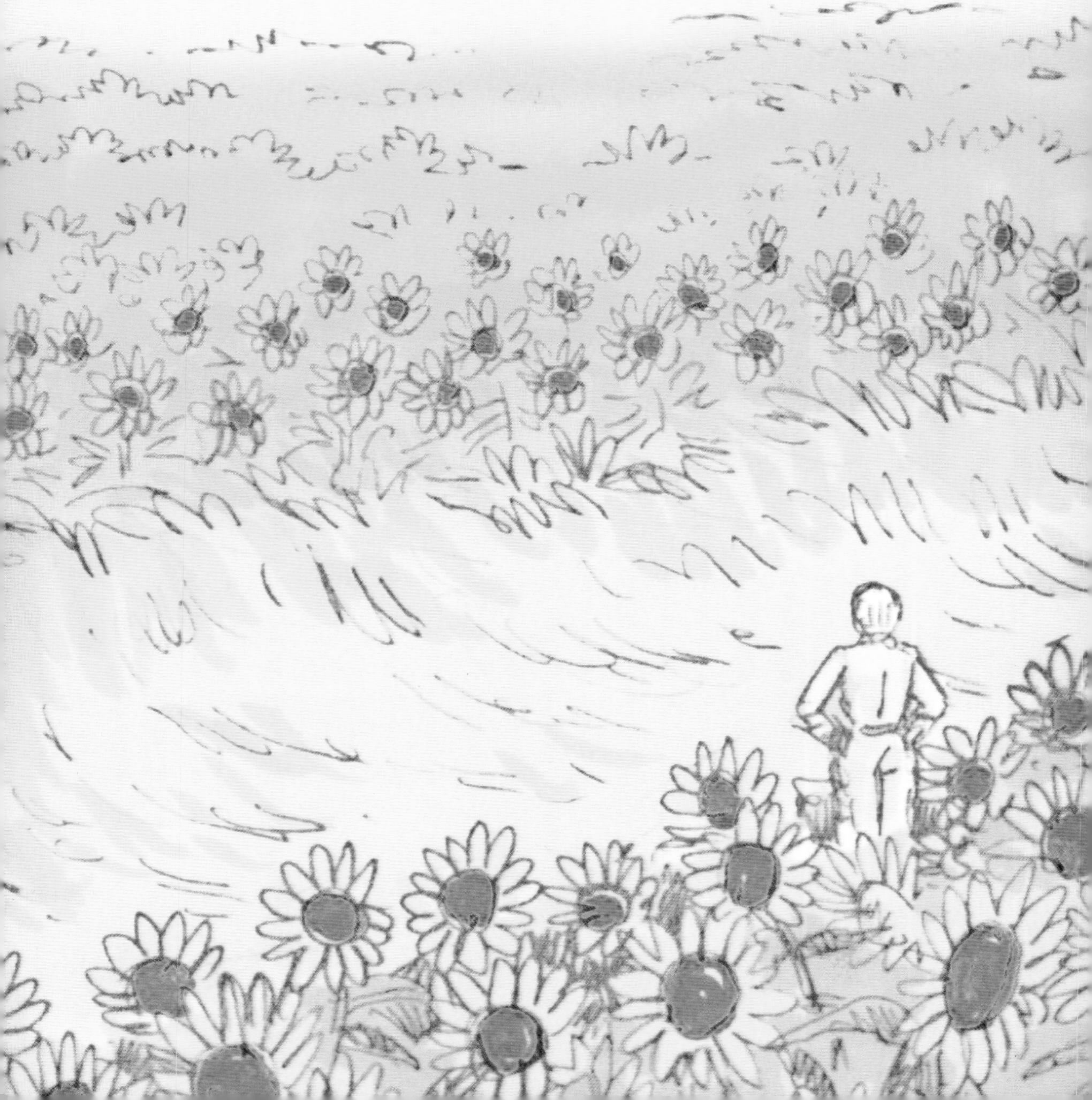

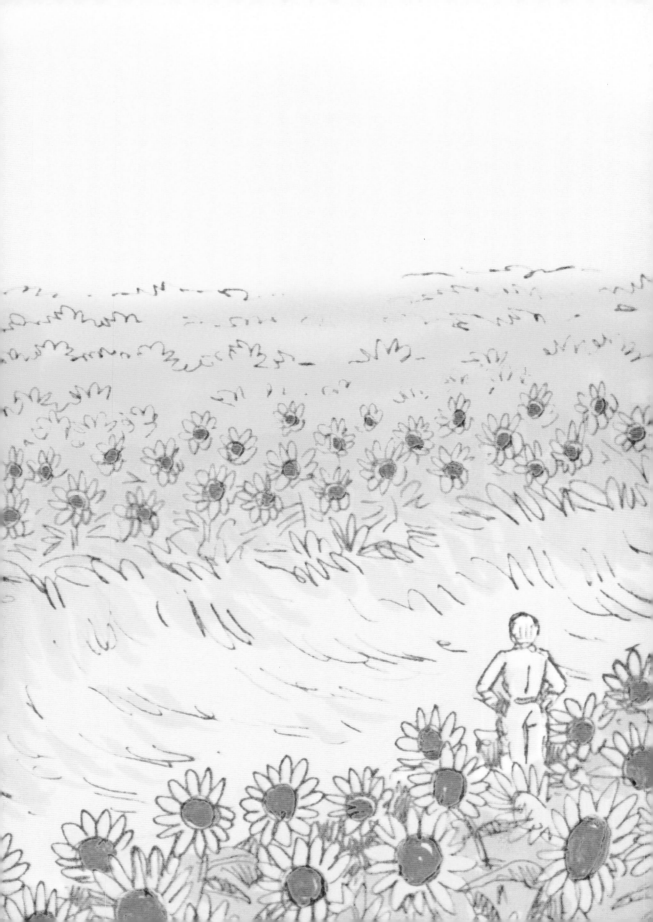

Contents

Foreword by Larry Hama ix

BOOK I ★ EDGE OF DARKNESS

1. Life on the Edge 9
2. The Pilgrim 34
3. Behold the Beast 61
4. Forks in the Road 88
5. The Mark of Cain 119
6. Thunder & Darkness ... 151

BOOK II ★ THE SHAKING OF THE EARTH

7. Not One Step Back! 186
8. Fiery Chariots 216
9. Arena 244
10. Lamentations 275
11. The 13th Commandment · 304
12. Harvest at Prokhorovka · 334

BOOK III ★ ON WINGS OF THUNDER

13. As Clear as Tears 367
14. Otomstite 402
15. A World of Crows 437
16. Ledgers of Revenge 476
17. Lily among Thorns 509
18. Remember Me 543

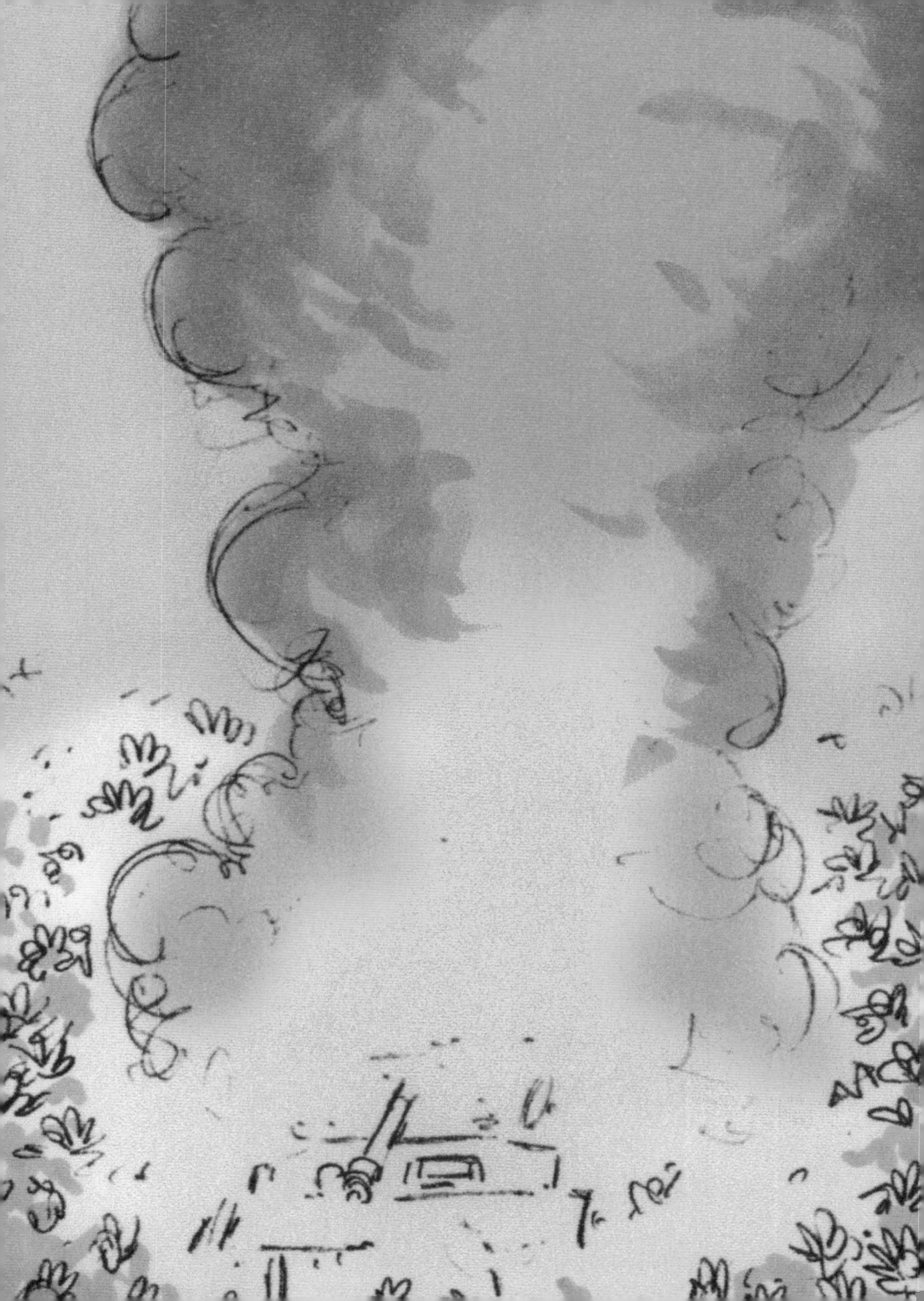

Foreword

Military historical graphic novels run the risk of being either too melodramatic or too dry. The creators who can deliver action-packed adventure often take substantial liberties with historical accuracy, tactics, weapons, and equipment. The creators who are sticklers for reality feel compelled to burden us with altogether too much information, delivered with the passion of a laundry list. Striking an appropriate balance is more difficult than most editors think.

What Wayne Vansant has done with *Katusha* is extraordinary in that he gets it all right. He gives us characters we can care about and identify with and allows us to see history through their eyes. He doesn't "fake" the guns, tanks, and period vehicles. They are correct for time and place, and he knows the difference between an MG-34 and an MG-42. The uniforms are meticulously researched with the right badges and insignia. There is a completeness to the world he recreates for us, and that completeness makes the narrative come alive.

The story is told in the first person, in the words of Katusha, a young Ukrainian girl. The narrative is more or less an illustrated diary of her transformation from a schoolgirl in Kiev to a partisan fighter hiding out in the forests, and then on to recruitment into the Red Army. She is not a cut-out maquette doing turns to fulfill the needs of a plot, but a fully realized character. You meet her family, her school friends, the people in her neighborhood, and they all stand up and walk around believably in this carefully crafted reproduction of a time before most of us were born.

The history comes alive because Wayne Vansant puts you in the thick of it. You don't see the overview of major battles, you see what the protagonist witnesses herself, and all of a sudden the event becomes personal instead of a remote account full of statistics and analyses of tactics. The deaths of fictional characters we have come to know gives form to cold numbers. A glimpse from the sidelines of a battle can tell us more than a plan-of-attack diagram. The visual "acting" of the drawn characters conveys the drama of the situations better than mere prose.

No, it's not just "another comic book."

Read, enjoy, learn.

Larry Hama
August 13, 2018

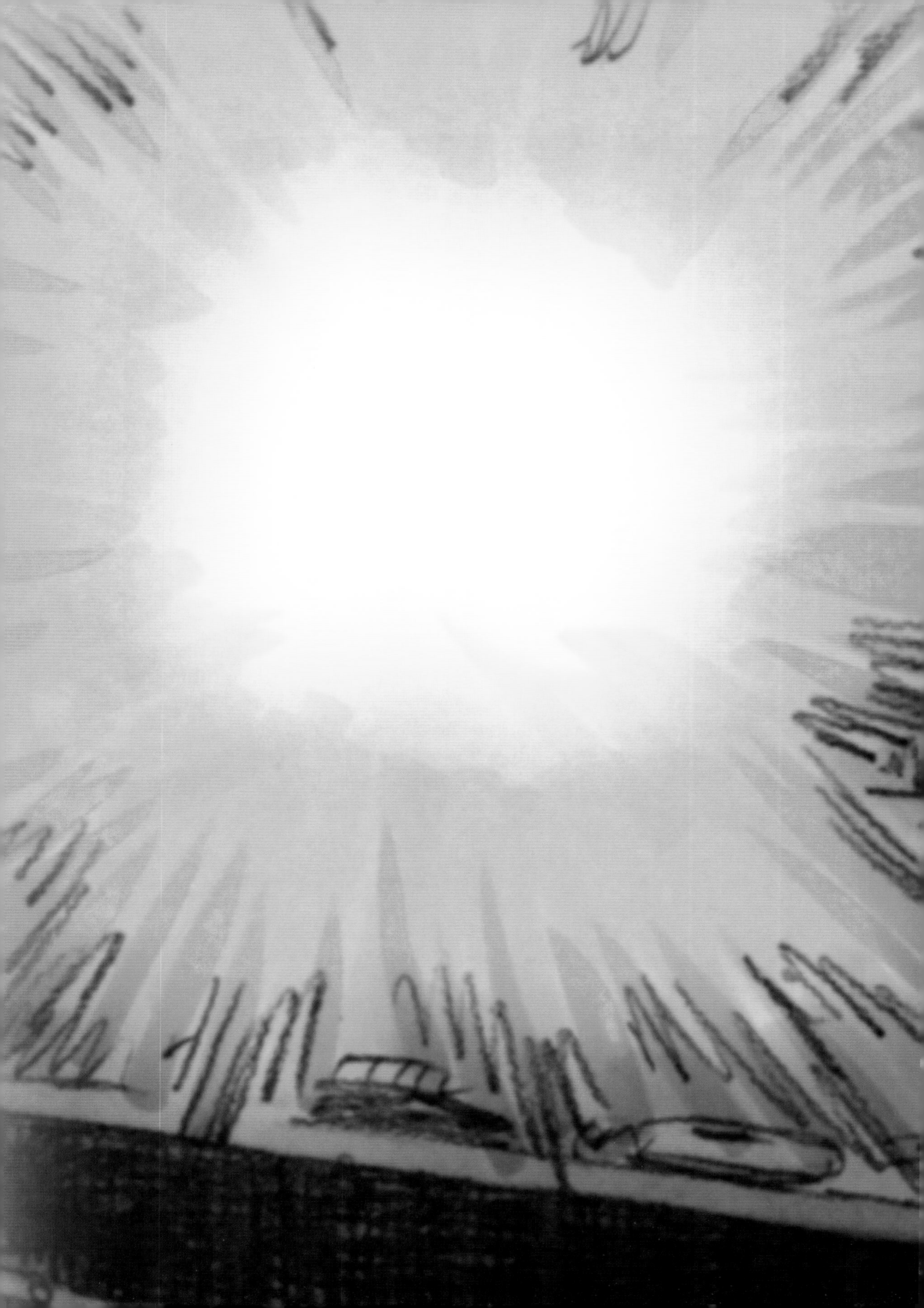

Book I

Edge of Darkness

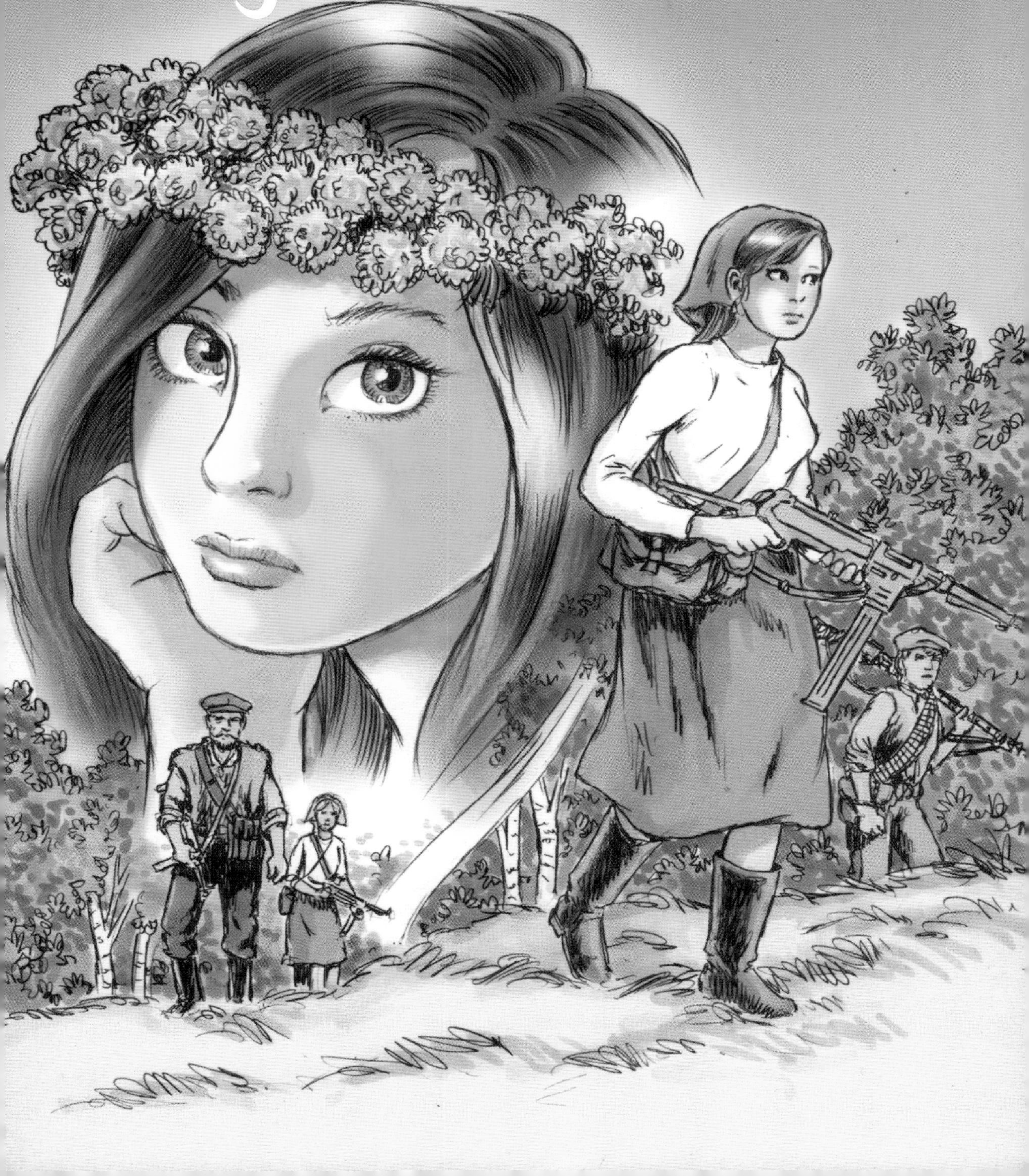

OPERATION: BARBAROSSA
NAZI GERMANY'S INVASION OF SOVIET RUSSIA

FROM *JUNE 22, 1941,* THROUGH *MAY 9, 1945,* THE PEOPLE OF RUSSIA, UKRAINE, AND THE OTHER NATIONS OF THE FORMER SOVIET UNION FOUGHT THE BLOODIEST WAR IN THE HISTORY OF MANKIND.

DURING THIS TIME, THOUSANDS OF CITIES AND TOWNS WERE DESTROYED. FARMLAND, FOREST, AND NATURAL RESOURCES WERE DEVASTATED. AND *27,000,000* SOVIET CITIZENS DIED.

NO ONE WAS SAFE. INNOCENCE COUNTED FOR NOTHING. THE VERY YOUNG AND THE VERY OLD SUFFERED AS MUCH, IF NOT MORE, THAN THE SOLDIERS IN THE FIELD.

IN THIS CONFLICT, SOVIET WOMEN FOUGHT--AND SOMETIMES DIED--BESIDE THEIR MEN. THEY SERVED AS FIGHTER PILOTS AND SCOUTS. SOME WERE MACHINE GUNNERS AND COMMUNICATIONS EXPERTS. OTHERS WERE MEDICS AND SNIPERS...

...AND SOME--LIKE ME-- RODE THE WEAPON THAT, MORE THAN ANY OTHER, WON THE WAR ON THE EASTERN FRONT-- THE TANK.

MY NAME IS *EKATERINA ANDREAEVNA TYMOSHENKO,* AND THIS IS MY STORY.

GERMANY, SPRING 1945. THE SOVIET FORCES OF THE *1ST UKRAINIAN FRONT* WERE CHARGING FROM THEIR BRIDGEHEAD ON THE NEISSE RIVER-- AIMING FOR THE NAZI CAPITAL, *BERLIN!*

BUT THEIR ADVANCE WAS NOT WITHOUT *OPPOSITION!*

ENTERING ONE NAMELESS VILLAGE, THEIR PROGRESS WAS OBSTRUCTED BY A 68-TON TIGER TANK.

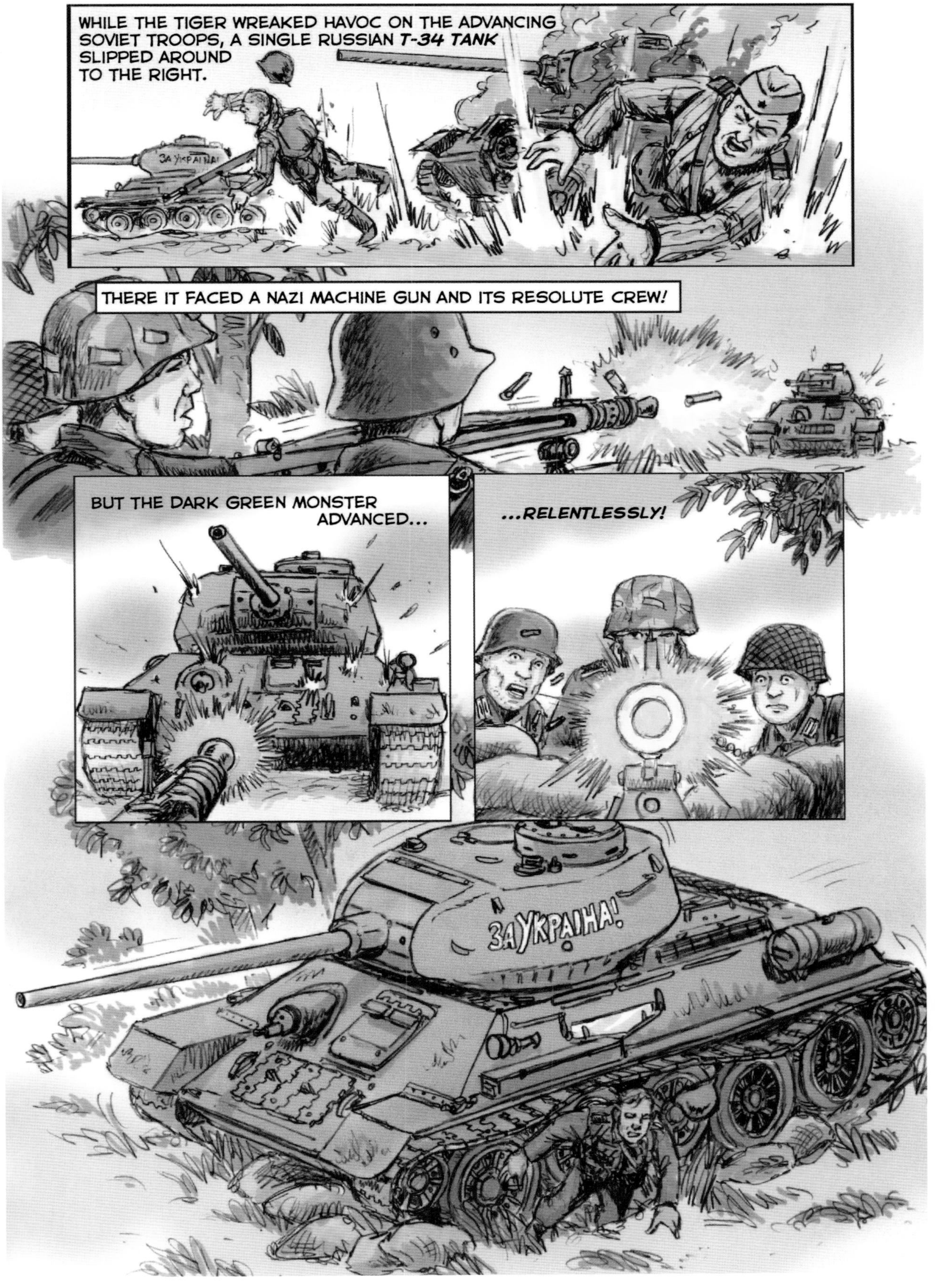
WHILE THE TIGER WREAKED HAVOC ON THE ADVANCING SOVIET TROOPS, A SINGLE RUSSIAN *T-34 TANK* SLIPPED AROUND TO THE RIGHT.
ЗА УКРАЇНА!
THERE IT FACED A NAZI MACHINE GUN AND ITS RESOLUTE CREW!
BUT THE DARK GREEN MONSTER ADVANCED...
...RELENTLESSLY!
ЗА УКРАЇНА!

NEARBY, AS GERMAN SOLDIERS HASTILY LOADED UP A TRUCK WITH SUPPLIES AND EQUIPMENT NOT TO BE LEFT FOR THE ENEMY...

WHAT'S THAT NOISE--?

HRM...?

YAAAGH!!

MEIN GOTT!

THE DEVIL IS HERE!

6

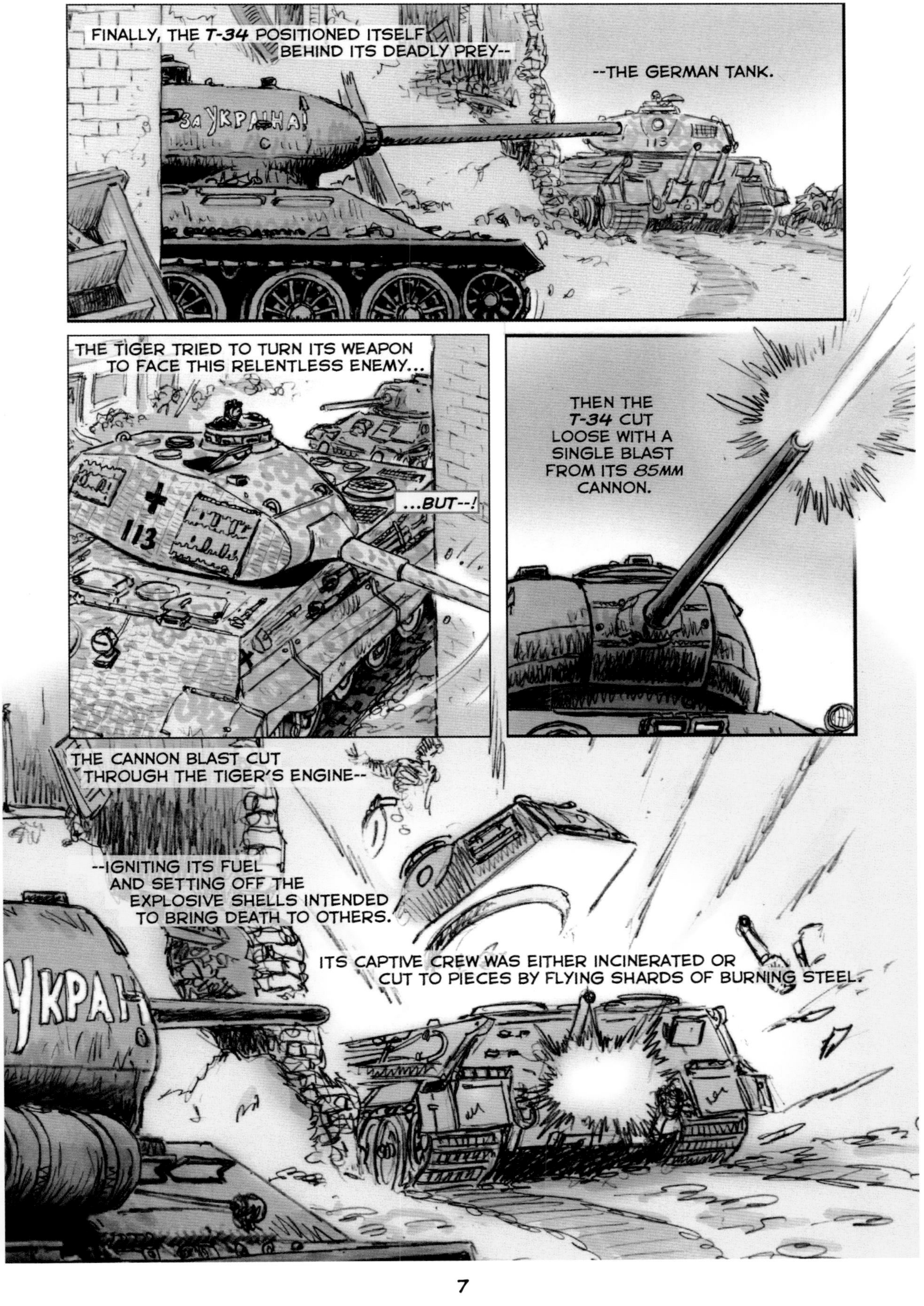

FINALLY, THE *T-34* POSITIONED ITSELF BEHIND ITS DEADLY PREY--
--THE GERMAN TANK.
THE TIGER TRIED TO TURN ITS WEAPON TO FACE THIS RELENTLESS ENEMY...
...*BUT--!*
THEN THE *T-34* CUT LOOSE WITH A SINGLE BLAST FROM ITS *85MM* CANNON.
THE CANNON BLAST CUT THROUGH THE TIGER'S ENGINE--
--IGNITING ITS FUEL AND SETTING OFF THE EXPLOSIVE SHELLS INTENDED TO BRING DEATH TO OTHERS.
ITS CAPTIVE CREW WAS EITHER INCINERATED OR CUT TO PIECES BY FLYING SHARDS OF BURNING STEEL.

FINALLY, THE RUSSIAN JUGGERNAUT'S *HUMAN* COMPONENT BEGAN TO REVEAL ITSELF...

GREAT JOB, LITTLE TYMOSHENKO!

YOU SURE *SAVED* US THERE!

HEY, KATUSHA! I GOT A MESSAGE FOR YOU FROM *COLONEL NOZDRIN!*

HE SAYS YOU HAVE WON ANOTHER DEGREE IN THE *"UNIVERSITY OF BATTLE"*...

...AND THAT *TARAS TYMOSHENKO* WOULD BE *PROUD* OF YOU.

THOSE WORDS FILLED ME WITH PRIDE, AND I *SMILED.*

AND THEN I THOUGHT OF *UNCLE TARAS*...

...AND I WANTED TO *CRY.*

LIFE ON THE EDGE

UKRAINE MEANS EDGE OR BORDERLAND. IT IS FOR THIS REASON THAT IT IS OFTEN CALLED THE UKRAINE, AS IF IT WERE A BORDERLAND BETWEEN RUSSIA AND CENTRAL AND WESTERN EUROPE. ALTHOUGH THROUGH MUCH OF OUR HISTORY WE HAVE BEEN DOMINATED BY OUR GIANT EASTERN NEIGHBOR, UKRAINIANS ARE NOT RUSSIANS, NOR ARE WE EVEN A TYPE OF "LITTLE RUSSIANS." WE HAVE OUR OWN DISTINCT LANGUAGE AND CUSTOMS. WHILE WE ARE A SLAVIC PEOPLE AS ARE THE RUSSIANS, WE HAVE FREQUENTLY PAID A CRUELLY HIGH PRICE FOR THESE CULTURAL DISTINCTIONS, AND FOR OUR LOCATION.

MY STORY BEGINS WITH MY GRADUATION FROM MY TENTH AND FINAL YEAR IN SCHOOL.

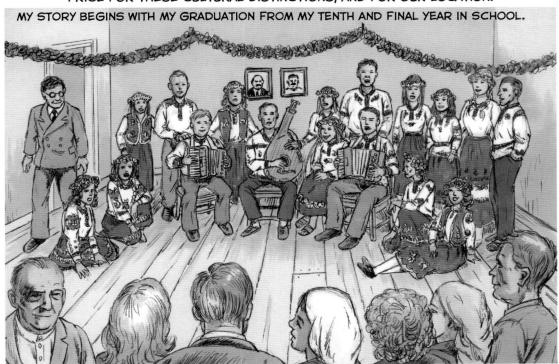

IT WAS SATURDAY, JUNE 21, 1941. THAT YEAR, THERE WERE 37 GRADUATES OF THE ZALIZNYCHNY SCHOOL ON THE SOUTHWESTERN OUTSKIRTS OF KIEV. GRADUATION, TO US, WAS A GREAT DIVIDE BETWEEN WHAT HAD COME BEFORE AND WHAT WOULD COME AFTER.

LITTLE DID WE KNOW HOW TRULY GREAT THAT DIVIDE WOULD BECOME.

THIS WAS MAMA. FOR A GIRL OF SIXTEEN LIKE ME, MAMA WAS THE CENTER OF MY WORLD.

AH! SO SWEET...

MY, YOUR GIRLS HAVE SUCH LOVELY VOICES, ELENA...!

"...AND *MILLA*, A STRONG ALTO."

"EKATERINA, A SWEET SOPRANO..."

IT DIDN'T TAKE A GENIUS TO TELL THAT MILLA AND I WERE NOT REALLY SISTERS.

PAPA WAS A FINE, QUIET MAN WHO WORKED HARD TO PROVIDE FOR HIS FAMILY. HE SELDOM INDULGED IN VODKA AND NEVER BEAT US.

WELL, HOW ARE THINGS IN *KHARKOV*, *ANDREY*? WE DON'T GET TO SEE YOU ENOUGH THESE DAYS.

OH, VERY *BUSY*--I HAD TO GET PERMISSION TO COME SEE MY GIRLS GRADUATE!

MY SISTER *NATASHA* WAS THE REAL BEAUTY OF THE FAMILY. BECAUSE SHE HAD MARRIED A MINOR BUREAUCRAT IN THE *COMMUNIST PARTY*, SHE FELT SUPERIOR TO THE REST OF US.

AH, IT'S *NATALYA!* AND SASHA.

OH...WHAT A *QUAINT* LITTLE GATHERING...

SHE MADE ME MAD WITH HER DISAPPROVING LOOKS...

BUT MAMA--BEING *MAMA*--WAS WISE AND GRACIOUS.

WELCOME TO OUR HUMBLE CELEBRATION.

VASILY, MY FIFTEEN-YEAR-OLD BROTHER, WAS ALSO THERE.

VASILY! LEAVE SOME FOR THE OTHERS!

HE WAS NOT A GOOD STUDENT AND WAS ALWAYS IN *TROUBLE*.

ZHENYA GERSTEINFELD WAS MY BEST FRIEND. HER PARENTS WERE TEACHERS AT OUR SCHOOL.

ZHENYA! WHY--I CAN'T BELIEVE IT!

FATHER GETS THE CREDIT--

WHO BUT A *TEACHER* WOULD THINK OF GIVING A SIXTEEN-YEAR-OLD GIRL *RADIO VACUUM TUBES?*

--IT WAS *HIS* IDEA!

TO ONE OF MY *BEST* STUDENTS!

THANK YOU, MISTER GERSTEINFELD! IT REALLY *IS* A PERFECT GIFT.

IT REALLY *WAS*.

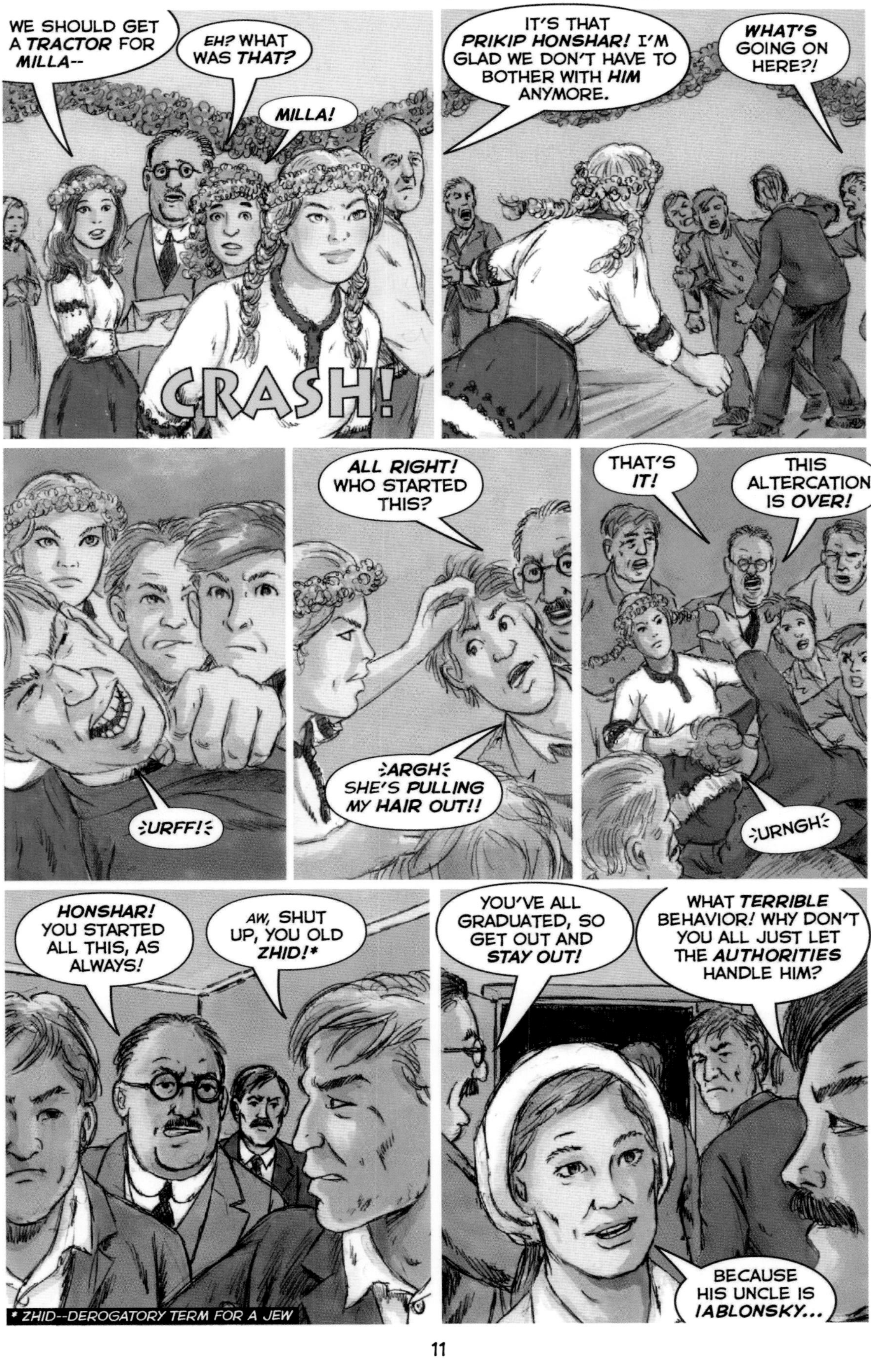
WE SHOULD GET A TRACTOR FOR MILLA--
EH? WHAT WAS THAT?
MILLA!
CRASH!
IT'S THAT PRIKIP HONSHAR! I'M GLAD WE DON'T HAVE TO BOTHER WITH HIM ANYMORE.
WHAT'S GOING ON HERE?!
URFF!
ALL RIGHT! WHO STARTED THIS?
ARGH SHE'S PULLING MY HAIR OUT!!
THAT'S IT!
THIS ALTERCATION IS OVER!
URNGH
HONSHAR! YOU STARTED ALL THIS, AS ALWAYS!
AW, SHUT UP, YOU OLD ZHID!*
* ZHID--DEROGATORY TERM FOR A JEW
YOU'VE ALL GRADUATED, SO GET OUT AND STAY OUT!
WHAT TERRIBLE BEHAVIOR! WHY DON'T YOU ALL JUST LET THE AUTHORITIES HANDLE HIM?
BECAUSE HIS UNCLE IS IABLONSKY...

...OF THE *NKVD!*

THE *SECRET POLICE.* YES--

OH.

WE LIVED IN A SOCIETY IN WHICH EVERYONE FELT THE EYES FROM ABOVE-- AND DREADED THE SUDDEN KNOCK ON THE DOOR.

THINGS CALMED DOWN, AND WE BEGAN TO SING AGAIN. THEN, AS THE NIGHT WORE ON AND THE LOCAL OFFICIALS LEFT, WE SWITCHED FROM *RUSSIAN* TO *UKRAINIAN...*

WE SANG "*LITTLE GREEN OAK,*" AND THEN "*OH, MOUNTAIN, MOUNTAIN,*" AND FINALLY, "*OH, I LOVED AND CHERISHED.*"

WE LEFT A LITTLE AFTER MIDNIGHT, WALKING QUIETLY DOWN THE DESERTED STREET.

MY SHOES WERE PINCHING MY FEET, SO I TOOK THEM OFF AND WALKED BAREFOOT ON THE SMOOTH, COOL COBBLESTONES.

PAPA HAD GONE TO WORK FOR THE STATE RAILROAD WHEN I WAS JUST A BABY.

HE WAS ABLE TO CHOOSE WHERE WE LIVED, WHICH WAS UNUSUAL IN OUR SOCIETY. HE PICKED KIEV'S *ZALIZNYCHNY* DISTRICT, BECAUSE IT WAS PART OF THE CITY, BUT STILL HAD DIRECT TIES TO THE COUNTRYSIDE.

MAMA? ARE WE *WORKERS,* OR *PEASANTS?*

WELL, YOUR PAPA SAYS WE'RE *WORKER PEASANTS...*

BUT I THINK WE'RE *PEASANT WORKERS...*

TCH...MAYBE WE'RE A LITTLE BIT OF *BOTH.*

KATUSHA, DON'T START WORKING ON THAT RADIO. IT'S *LATE*. GO TO BED.

YES, MAMA--

--BUT I'D LIKE TO READ A LITTLE FIRST, JUST TO UNWIND.

THAT'S FINE. GOOD NIGHT.

BOOKS--A SOURCE OF JOY AND FEAR... WHAT IS ACCEPTABLE TODAY COULD GET YOU SENT AWAY TO PRISON TOMORROW.

FOR THAT REASON, BOOKS WERE SELDOM KEPT OUT IN THE OPEN.

THAT'S WHY MAMA KEPT HER BIBLE HIDDEN AWAY WITHIN A CRACK IN THE WALL BESIDE THE STOVE.

WELL... THERE'S ALWAYS *TOLSTOY.*

WAR AND PEACE.

I LIT A CANDLE AND SAT GENTLY ON THE EDGE OF THE BED, TRYING NOT TO DISTURB MILLA...

SHE WAS ALREADY ASLEEP, AS ALWAYS. MILLA WAS ALMOST AS QUIET ASLEEP AS SHE WAS AWAKE.

PAPA ALWAYS REFERRED TO MILLA AS MY "BIRTHDAY PRESENT."

AND SHE REALLY WAS.

13

PAPA FOUND MILLA ON A RAIL SIDING NEAR *ZAPORIZHZHYA*...THE POOR LITTLE THING WAS DIGGING THROUGH ROTTING GARBAGE, SEARCHING FOR FOOD.

IT WAS MY SEVENTH BIRTHDAY WHEN PAPA BROUGHT HER HOME--*APRIL 15, 1932.*

SURPRISE, KATUSHA! LOOK--!

I'VE BROUGHT YOU HOME A NEW SISTER!

I REMEMBER SHE WAS SO DIRTY YOU REALLY COULDN'T TELL THE COLOR OF HER HAIR-- BUT THAT DIDN'T BOTHER ME.

WOULD YOU LIKE TO SHARE MY BIRTHDAY?

UHHH, WHAT'S A BIRFDAY?

I HANDED HER MY LITTLE PATCHWORK DOLL MAMA HAD MADE FOR ME. SHE LOOKED AT IT STRANGELY FOR A MOMENT--

--AND THEN SHE *BIT IT.*

LET'S GET SOME FOOD INTO THIS EMPTY LITTLE STOMACH!

NO, SILLY! IT'S NOT TO EAT--!

MAMA SCRUBBED HER CLEAN IN OUR OLD WOODEN TUB. THE LITTLE GIRL'S SKIN TURNED FROM BLACK-BROWN TO A ROSY PINK AND HER HAIR THE COLOR OF FLAX.

AH--THAT'S MUCH BETTER!

GIGGLE

SHE FINALLY *SMILED*...BUT SHE SAID LITTLE. SHE LOOKED AT US WITH WIDE EYES--

--BUT IF YOU LOOKED DEEP WITHIN THOSE EYES, YOU COULD SENSE AN ECHOING *SADNESS.*

WE GREW UP TOGETHER--WELL, *SHE* DID MOST OF THE GROWING--AND IT WAS AS IF SHE HAD ALWAYS BEEN PART OF US. WE WERE ODD TWINS--ME, JABBERING ABOUT ANYTHING THAT CROSSED MY MIND--SHE, LISTENING INTENTLY, RESPONDING NOW AND THEN WITH AN *"IS THAT RIGHT, KATUSHA?"* OR *"I DIDN'T KNOW THAT!"* OR *"UH HUH..."* OR JUST ONE OF HER SOFT, SWEET SMILES...

LOOKING BACK, I THINK I CAN SAFELY SAY THAT MILLA WAS PROBABLY OLDER THAN WE THOUGHT-- PERHAPS SEVERAL YEARS OLDER.

WE NEVER KNEW--AND DUE TO SOME UNSPOKEN TRAUMA, SHE HERSELF DIDN'T SEEM TO KNOW.

IN SCHOOL, SHE WAS NOT AS BRIGHT A STUDENT AS I WAS, BUT HER HARD WORK MADE AN IMPRESSION ON EVERYONE...

MILLA'S REAL TALENT WAS UNDERSTANDING MACHINERY. BY THE TIME SHE WAS FOURTEEN, SHE COULD DRIVE TRUCKS--AND TRACTORS!

I SLIPPED INTO BED BESIDE HER, OPENED THE BOOK RANDOMLY, AND BEGAN TO READ. I KNEW THE STORY, OF COURSE, SO I READ PURELY TO SAVOR THE BEAUTIFUL WORDS...

"Pierre was right when he said one must believe in the possibility of happiness in order to be happy, and now I do believe in it..."

"Let the dead bury their dead: while one has life, one must live and be happy."

HMMM...

I SOON DRIFTED OFF TO SLEEP, LETTING THE CANDLE BURN DOWN TO A SWIRL OF WAX.

SUNDAY, JUNE 22, 1941. OUR NIGHTS ARE SHORT THIS TIME OF YEAR. THE FIRST LIGHT OF DAWN HAD APPEARED IN THE EAST AROUND *3 AM.* BY THE TIME THE SUN SHOWED ITSELF 45 MINUTES LATER, MAMA HAD DRESSED AND WAS HEADED DOWN THE STREET TO *MRS. BOSHYK'S* HOUSE. SHE AND MY MOTHER, AND SEVERAL OTHER WOMEN, GATHERED TOGETHER SECRETLY EVERY SUNDAY MORNING TO PRAY.

IT SEEMED SO STRANGE TO ME THAT THEY HAD TO DO THIS. AFTER ALL-- WE LIVED NEARLY IN THE SHADOW OF *ST. NICHOLAS CHURCH.*

BUT LONG AGO, ST. NICHOLAS HAD BEEN LOCKED UP AND BOARDED OVER BY THE GOVERNMENT...

MR. BOSHYK HAD BEEN ITS ORTHODOX PRIEST. BUT THAT WAS ABOUT THE SAME TIME HE'D DISAPPEARED INTO THE SOVIET PRISON SYSTEM...

LONG AGO.

I WAS BUSY FIDDLING WITH MY CURRENT TOY,-- AN OLD RADIO PAPA HAD FOUND NEXT TO THE TRACKS, JUST AS HE HAD MILLA. AS I SET IT UP ON THE KITCHEN TABLE, I FELT ANXIOUS...

WOULD THE VACUUM TUBES WORK?

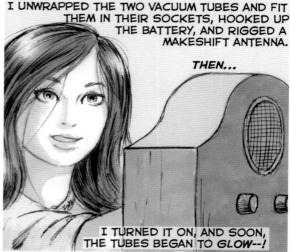

I UNWRAPPED THE TWO VACUUM TUBES AND FIT THEM IN THEIR SOCKETS, HOOKED UP THE BATTERY, AND RIGGED A MAKESHIFT ANTENNA.

THEN...

I TURNED IT ON, AND SOON, THE TUBES BEGAN TO *GLOW*--!

IT CRACKLED! I BEGAN TO SEARCH THE AIRWAVES... WHAT I WAS LOOKING FOR WAS *MUSIC!*

I SHOULD BE GETTING SOMETHING...MAYBE IT WAS *TOO EARLY...?*

HMMM, NOTHING...

--WAIT!

WAS THAT A VOICE? OR JUST STATIC?

BUT *NO*-- THAT *WAS* A VOICE... AND IN *RUSSIAN!*

SHORT, STACCATO PHRASES, THEN...

...A GASP--?

--A SHOUT!

--A CRY FOR HELP!

AT *3 AM* ON THE MORNING OF *JUNE 22, 1941,*
NAZI GERMANY INVADED
THE SOVIET UNION.

OVER *6,000* ARTILLERY PIECES BOMBARDED
RED ARMY DEFENSES, SUPPLY DUMPS, AND
BARRACKS ALL ALONG THE BORDER.

THEN, SPREAD ACROSS A
FRONT *1,700* MILES WIDE--

--3.5 MILLION GERMAN SOLDIERS
ADVANCED INTO SOVIET TERRITORY.

THEY WERE SUPPORTED BY A POWERFUL AIR FORCE
AND TANK UNITS--

--ALL OF WHOM HAD BEEN TRAINED AND BLOODIED IN
THE FIERCE CAMPAIGNS IN *POLAND, BELGIUM,* AND *FRANCE.*

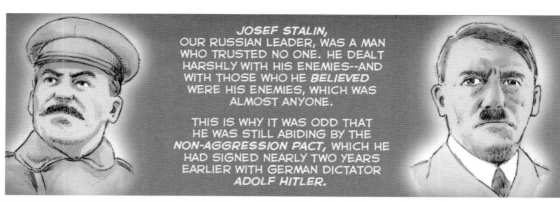

JOSEF STALIN, OUR RUSSIAN LEADER, WAS A MAN WHO TRUSTED NO ONE. HE DEALT HARSHLY WITH HIS ENEMIES--AND WITH THOSE WHO HE *BELIEVED* WERE HIS ENEMIES, WHICH WAS ALMOST ANYONE.

THIS IS WHY IT WAS ODD THAT HE WAS STILL ABIDING BY THE *NON-AGGRESSION PACT*, WHICH HE HAD SIGNED NEARLY TWO YEARS EARLIER WITH GERMAN DICTATOR *ADOLF HITLER*.

THIS PACT GUARANTEED THAT STALIN WOULD NOT INTERFERE WITH HITLER'S INVASION OF *POLAND*--THE BEGINNING OF *WORLD WAR II*.

STALIN ALSO TOOK ADVANTAGE OF THIS FRAGILE PEACE BY INVADING *EASTERN POLAND* AND *FINLAND* AND OCCUPYING THE BALTIC STATES OF *ESTONIA, LATVIA,* AND *LITHUANIA*.

DESPITE THESE VICTORIES AND TERRITORIAL GAINS, THE RED ARMY WAS UNPREPARED TO FACE THE INCREDIBLY PROFESSIONAL GERMAN ARMY.

WITHIN THE FIRST FEW HOURS OF THE INVASION, THE *LUFTWAFFE*, THE GERMAN AIR FORCE, DESTROYED MOST OF THE RUSSIAN PLANES AS THEY SAT ON THE GROUND.

BY THE END OF THE FIRST DAY, THE GERMANS HAD ADVANCED FIFTY MILES INTO RUSSIAN TERRITORY.

BECAUSE OF STALIN'S 1937 PURGE OF THE RED ARMY, FEW FRONTLINE OFFICERS HAD THE ABILITY OR THE WILL TO LEAD IN THESE DIFFICULT CIRCUMSTANCES. MANY OF THEM APPROPRIATED VEHICLES AND HEADED FOR THE REAR--

--LEAVING THEIR MEN IN THE FIELD TO FEND FOR THEMSELVES.

SOME OF THESE UNITS KEPT FIGHTING ON, REGARDLESS--

--BUT IN THESE SITUATIONS, THEIR EFFORTS WERE HOPELESS.

STILL OTHERS HAD NO INTENTION OF FIGHTING.

AFTER THEY HAD SUFFERED TWENTY YEARS OF PURGES AND MAN-MADE FAMINES AND BAD TREATMENT BY THE COMMUNISTS, IT DIDN'T SEEM WORTH THE EFFORT.

HOWEVER, THERE WERE BATTLES IN WHICH SOVIET SOLDIERS FOUGHT HARD AND FOUGHT *WELL*.

AT *BREST*, THE SOVIET DEFENDERS HELD THE BORDER FORTRESS FOR MORE THAN A MONTH AS THE MAIN BATTLE LINE MOVED HUNDREDS OF MILES TO THE EAST.

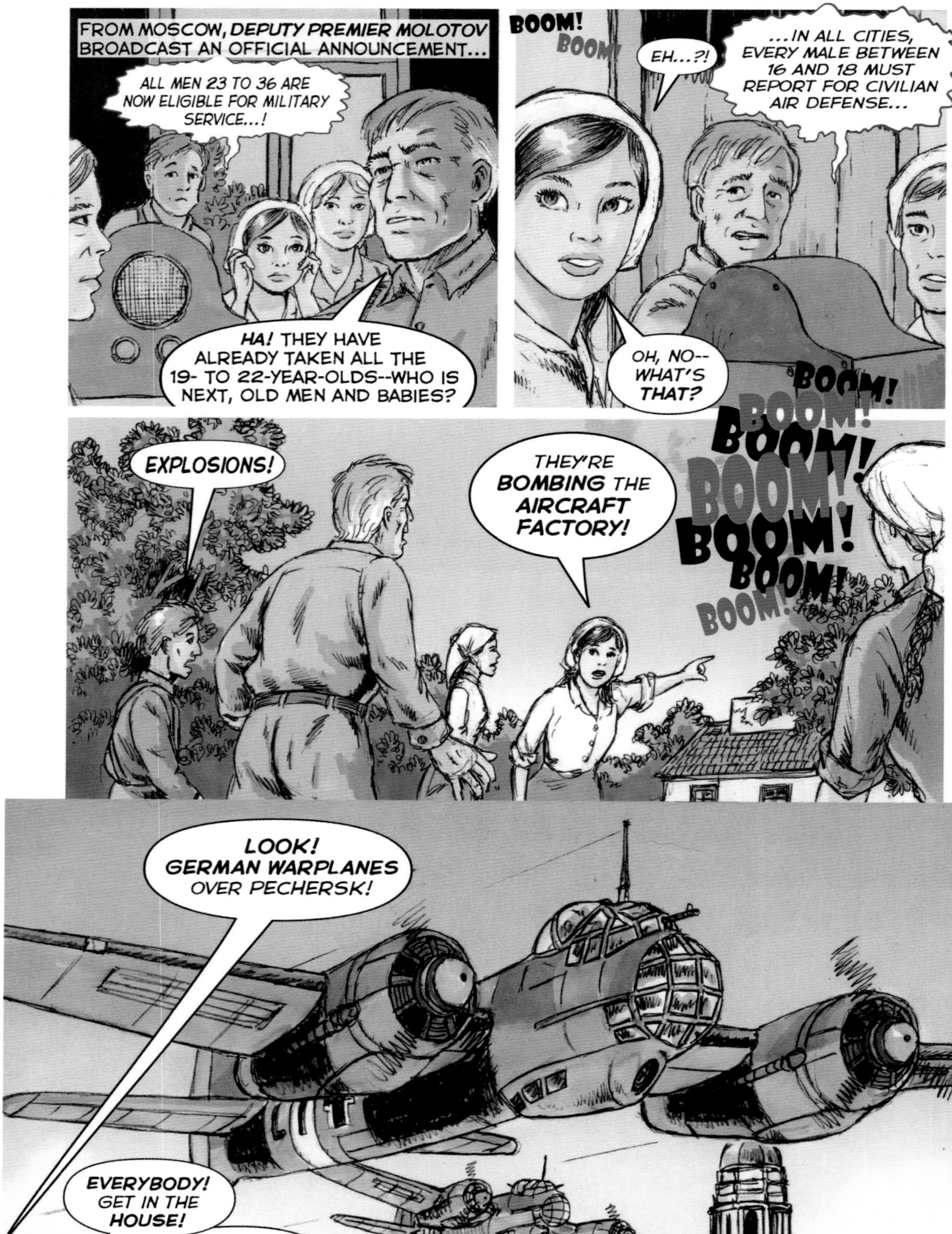

FROM MOSCOW, DEPUTY PREMIER MOLOTOV BROADCAST AN OFFICIAL ANNOUNCEMENT...
ALL MEN 23 TO 36 ARE NOW ELIGIBLE FOR MILITARY SERVICE...!
HA! THEY HAVE ALREADY TAKEN ALL THE 19- TO 22-YEAR-OLDS--WHO IS NEXT, OLD MEN AND BABIES?
BOOM! BOOM!
EH...?!
...IN ALL CITIES, EVERY MALE BETWEEN 16 AND 18 MUST REPORT FOR CIVILIAN AIR DEFENSE...
OH, NO--WHAT'S THAT?
BOOM! BOOM! BOOM! BOOM! BOOM! BOOM! BOOM!
EXPLOSIONS!
THEY'RE BOMBING THE AIRCRAFT FACTORY!
LOOK! GERMAN WARPLANES OVER PECHERSK!
EVERYBODY! GET IN THE HOUSE!
SHH, ELENA. THEY'RE FAR TOO BUSY TO SHOOT AT US.

THEY WON'T BOTHER WITH US. NOT *YET*.

NOW WE KNOW WHAT IS GOING ON. KATUSHA, YOUR *RADIO* CERTAINLY CAME IN HANDY.

ALL RIGHT-- I WANT US ALL TO STAY CALM.

WE ALL HAVE OUR JOBS TO GO TO TOMORROW-- MILLA TO THE *PYROHOVA* FARM, KATUSHA TO THE TELEPHONE POST...

AND ELENA, I'M SURE TODAY THEY'LL BE NEEDING YOU AT THE AIRCRAFT FACTORY. VASILY, YOU GO WITH MAMA TO HELP.

DON'T WORRY, PAPA-- YOU KNOW WE *ALL* WILL.

I GUESS I'D BETTER GET AN EARLY TRAIN BACK TO *KHARKOV*. I'M SURE THAT THEY WILL HAVE USE FOR ME THERE...

OHH, ANDREY..! *MUST* YOU GO--?

YES, I *MUST*-- BUT I THINK IT WOULD BE ALL RIGHT IF YOU ALL SAW ME OFF FIRST.

BY LATE AFTERNOON, PAPA WAS ON THE TRAIN BACK TO *KHARKOV*. I HAD AN AWFUL, SICKLY FEELING... WE HAD NO WAY OF KNOWING WHEN WE WOULD SEE EACH OTHER AGAIN.

GOODBYE, PAPA...

GOODBYE!

GOODBYE, ALL...

...TAKE CARE OF EACH OTHER!

21

THAT NIGHT, KIEV WAS COMPLETELY BLACKED OUT.

IF THE AUTHORITIES SAW ANY LIGHT SHOWING FROM A DWELLING, THE ENTIRE HOUSEHOLD WOULD BE ARRESTED BY THE *NKVD*. THE PEOPLE WERE CARRIED OFF, TO NOBODY KNOWS WHERE.

NONE OF US SLEPT WELL THAT NIGHT. EVEN MILLA TOSSED AND TURNED.

LATE IN THE NIGHT, I HEARD A SOUND LIKE SOFT SOBBING...

I WASN'T THE ONLY ONE WHO HAD HEARD IT.

VASILY SAT UP AND LOOKED INTO THE DARKNESS.

I COULD TELL MILLA'S EYES WERE OPEN.

I QUIETLY SLIPPED OUT OF BED AND TIPTOED TO THE DOOR...

I COULD SEE A FIGURE IN WHITE, KNEELING BY THE STOVE--

IT WAS *MAMA*.

SHE HAD TAKEN HER BIBLE FROM ITS HIDING PLACE.

SILENTLY, I WATCHED AS SHE HELD IT IN BOTH HANDS, THEN PRESSED IT TO HER FOREHEAD...

WE HAVE CALLED UPON THEE, FOR THOU WILT HEAR US, O GOD.

KEEP US AS THE APPLE OF THINE EYE. HIDE US UNDER THE SHADOW OF THY WING...

...FROM THE WICKED THAT OPPRESS US, FROM THE DEADLY ENEMY WHO COMPASSES US ABOVE.

ARISE, O LORD... CAST HIM DOWN; DELIVER OUR SOULS FROM THE WICKED.

22

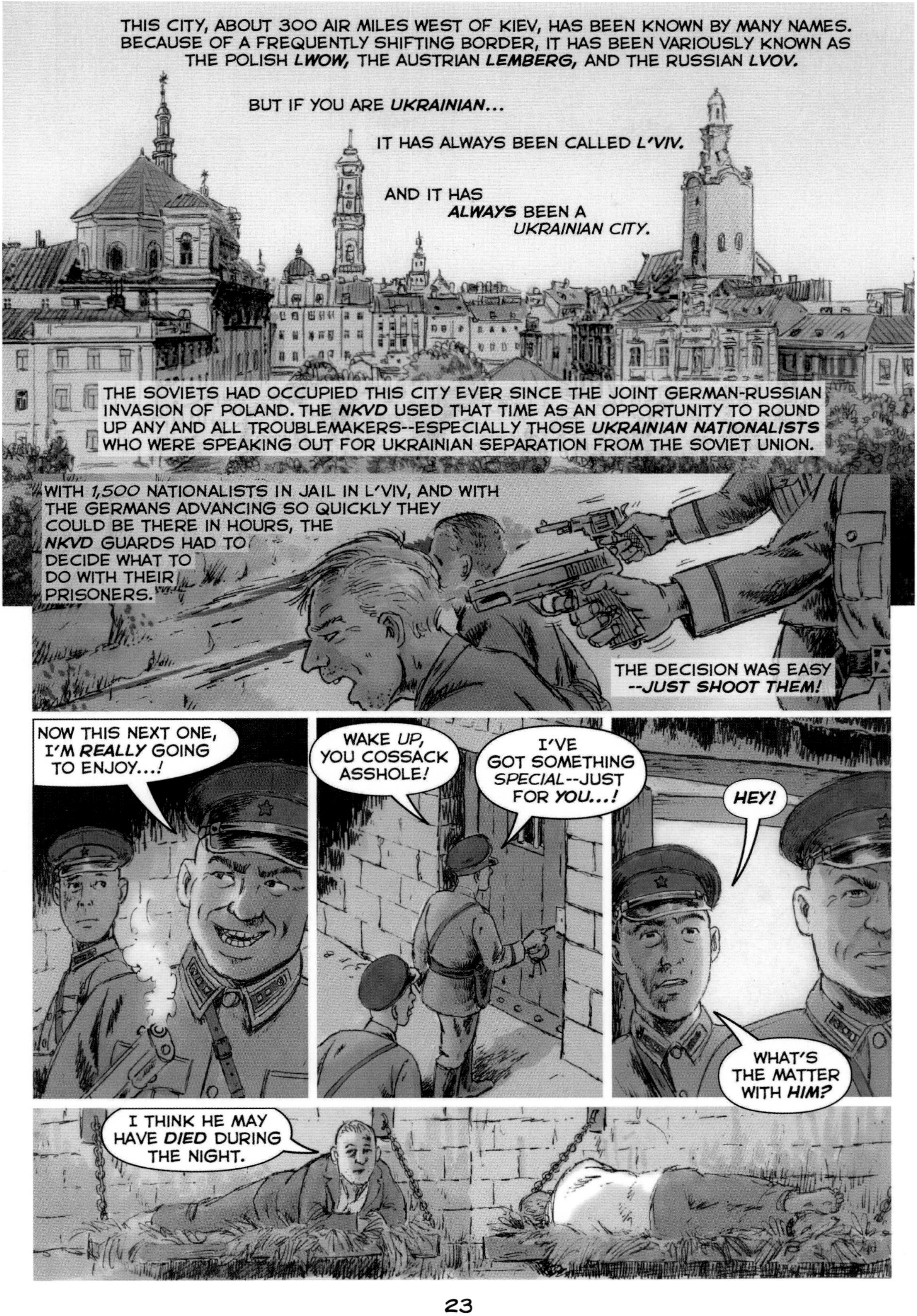
THIS CITY, ABOUT 300 AIR MILES WEST OF KIEV, HAS BEEN KNOWN BY MANY NAMES. BECAUSE OF A FREQUENTLY SHIFTING BORDER, IT HAS BEEN VARIOUSLY KNOWN AS THE POLISH *LWOW,* THE AUSTRIAN *LEMBERG,* AND THE RUSSIAN *LVOV.*
BUT IF YOU ARE *UKRAINIAN...*
IT HAS ALWAYS BEEN CALLED *L'VIV.*
AND IT HAS *ALWAYS* BEEN A *UKRAINIAN CITY.*
THE SOVIETS HAD OCCUPIED THIS CITY EVER SINCE THE JOINT GERMAN-RUSSIAN INVASION OF POLAND. THE *NKVD* USED THAT TIME AS AN OPPORTUNITY TO ROUND UP ANY AND ALL TROUBLEMAKERS--ESPECIALLY THOSE *UKRAINIAN NATIONALISTS* WHO WERE SPEAKING OUT FOR UKRAINIAN SEPARATION FROM THE SOVIET UNION.
WITH *1,500* NATIONALISTS IN JAIL IN L'VIV, AND WITH THE GERMANS ADVANCING SO QUICKLY THEY COULD BE THERE IN HOURS, THE *NKVD* GUARDS HAD TO DECIDE WHAT TO DO WITH THEIR PRISONERS.
THE DECISION WAS EASY *--JUST SHOOT THEM!*
NOW THIS NEXT ONE, I'M *REALLY* GOING TO ENJOY...!
WAKE *UP,* YOU COSSACK ASSHOLE!
I'VE GOT SOMETHING *SPECIAL*--JUST FOR *YOU...!*
HEY!
WHAT'S THE MATTER WITH *HIM?*
I THINK HE MAY HAVE *DIED* DURING THE NIGHT.

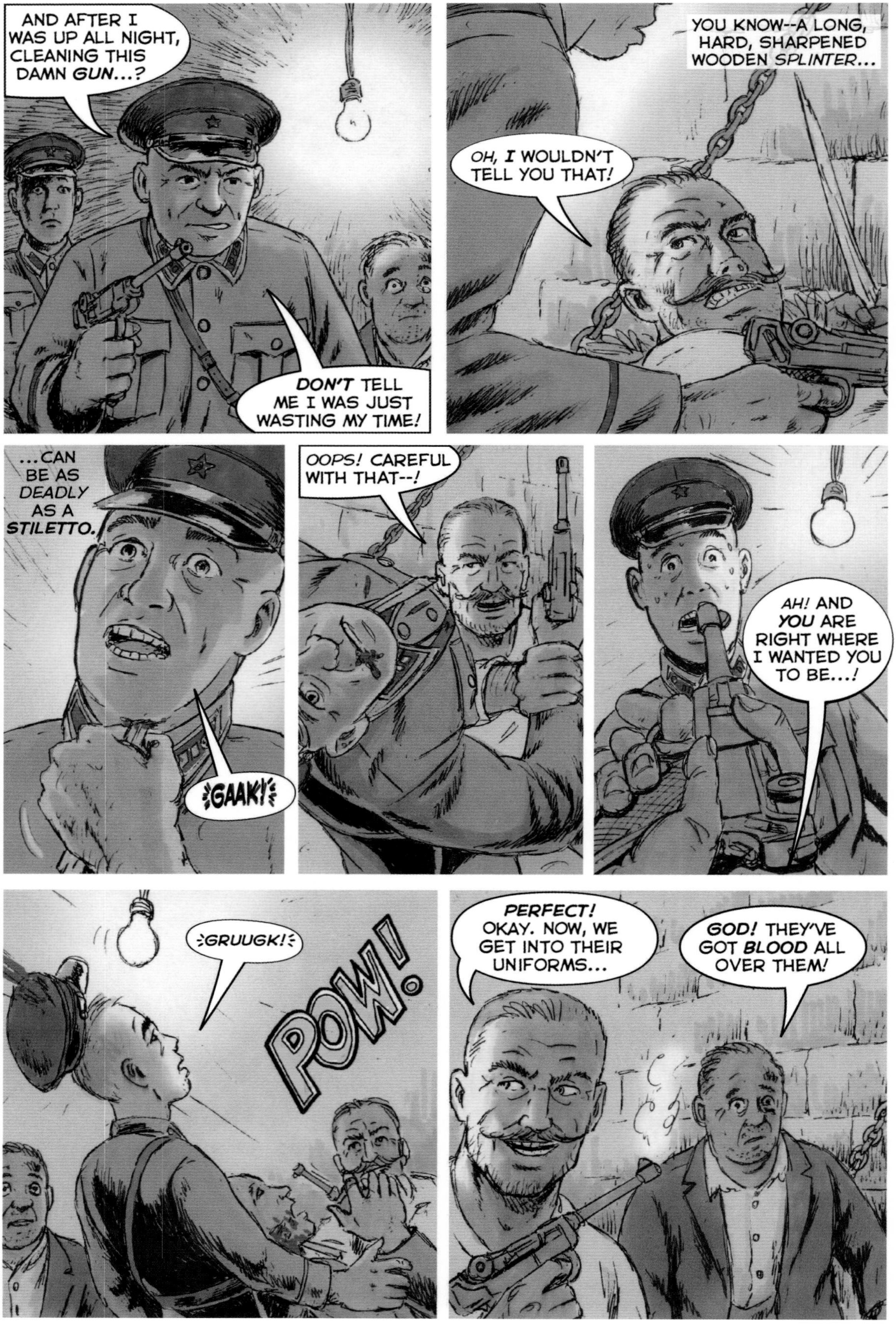
AND AFTER I WAS UP ALL NIGHT, CLEANING THIS DAMN GUN...?
DON'T TELL ME I WAS JUST WASTING MY TIME!
YOU KNOW--A LONG, HARD, SHARPENED WOODEN SPLINTER...
OH, I WOULDN'T TELL YOU THAT!
...CAN BE AS DEADLY AS A STILETTO.
GAAK!
OOPS! CAREFUL WITH THAT--!
AH! AND YOU ARE RIGHT WHERE I WANTED YOU TO BE...!
GRUUGK!
POW!
PERFECT! OKAY. NOW, WE GET INTO THEIR UNIFORMS...
GOD! THEY'VE GOT BLOOD ALL OVER THEM!

WELL, *SURE* THEY HAVE-- THEY'VE BEEN SHOOTING PEOPLE ALL DAY. TRUST ME, SYDIR...

...NO ONE WILL NOTICE.

I'M SURE GLAD FATSO CAME FOR US--NOW I HAVE MY *GUN* BACK, *AND* A NEW PAIR OF BOOTS.

LET'S SEE WHO *ELSE* WE CAN BREAK OUT...

AND JUST AROUND THE CORNER...

SAY YOUR *PRAYERS*, YOU GALICIAN DOG--!

HE'S SAYING THEM FOR *YOU*, CHEKNIC!

AAGH!!

OH, *GOD!* THANK YOU, *TARAS!*

AH, THINK NOTHING OF IT, *FATHER ZAPOLYE...*

GRAB THEIR *GUNS.*

IF YOU'RE GOING WITH *ME*, YOU MAY HAVE TO PUT ONE TO USE.

25

MY FIRST WEEK WITH THE TELEPHONE SERVICE WOULD HAVE BEEN UNEVENTFUL HAD IT NOT BEEN FOR THE FACT THAT IT WAS THE FIRST WEEK OF THE WAR.

FOR ONE THING, *NKVD* AGENTS WERE THERE, LISTENING IN TO THE CONVERSATIONS OF BOTH THOSE SUSPECTED OF BEING DISLOYAL TO THE STATE, *AND* OF ORDINARY PEOPLE--ONE AND THE SAME TO THE *NKVD*, WHO SUSPECTED EVERYONE.

EVEN SO, I WAS ABLE TO GATHER THE TRUE STORY ABOUT WHAT WAS HAPPENING AT THE FRONT--AND HOW *SERIOUS* THE SITUATION WAS.

EAVESDROPPING, I HEARD THE NEWS THAT THE GERMAN INVADERS HAD ATTACKED THE SOVIET UNION IN *THREE GREAT COLUMNS...*

ARMY GROUP NORTH HAD CUT THROUGH THE BALTIC STATES OF LITHUANIA, LATVIA, AND ESTONIA, DRIVING TOWARD THEIR OBJECTIVE, *LENINGRAD.*

ARMY GROUP CENTER STEAMROLLED ACROSS BELORUSSIA TOWARD SMOLENSK. IN JUST FOUR DAYS, THEY HAD PENETRATED *175 MILES!*

AT SMOLENSK, *300,000* SOVIET SOLDIERS WERE TAKEN PRISONER.

HAHA! HERE IS AN INTERESTING *COINCIDENCE!*

NAPOLEON HIMSELF ALSO CAPTURED *VILNA* ON THIS SAME DAY IN *1812!*

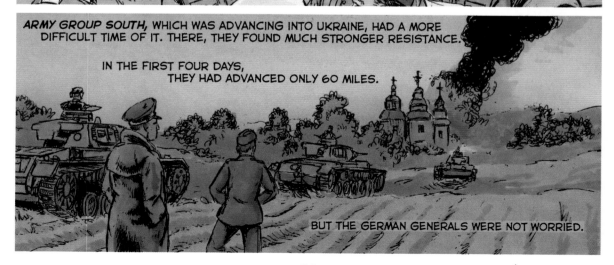

ARMY GROUP SOUTH, WHICH WAS ADVANCING INTO UKRAINE, HAD A MORE DIFFICULT TIME OF IT. THERE, THEY FOUND MUCH STRONGER RESISTANCE.

IN THE FIRST FOUR DAYS, THEY HAD ADVANCED ONLY 60 MILES.

BUT THE GERMAN GENERALS WERE NOT WORRIED.

BUT SOVIET RESISTANCE WAS LESS OF A CONCERN FOR THE GERMANS THAN WAS THE APPEARANCE OF THE NEW SOVIET *T-34 TANK*.

THE *T-34* TANK WAS THE VEHICLE THAT WAS BEING PRODUCED IN THE TRACTOR FACTORY BACK IN *KHARKOV* WHERE PAPA WORKED.

THE *T-34* WAS A SIMPLE, ROBUST DESIGN WEIGHING IN AT JUST 26 TONS. IT WAS CREATED WITH REVOLUTIONARY SLOPING ARMOR AND A POWERFUL DIESEL ENGINE. ITS TRACKS WERE WIDE-SET FOR BETTER WEIGHT DISTRIBUTION, SO IT WOULDN'T SINK INTO SOFT FARMLAND.

BUT WHAT REALLY ALARMED THE GERMANS WAS THAT THEY DID NOT POSSESS A GUN CAPABLE OF DESTROYING A *T-34* FROM THE FRONT.

WHEREVER THE GERMAN ARMY CAME UP AGAINST A *T-34*, ITS ENTIRE ADVANCE WAS TEMPORARILY HALTED.

THE *T-34'S 76MM* GUN, THE LARGEST OF ANY TANK GUN AT THAT TIME, WOULD TURN THE *PANZERS** INTO SCRAP METAL.

* *PANZER*--GERMAN WORD FOR *TANK*.

THE GERMANS WOULD HAVE TO BRING UP THEIR *88MM* OR *110MM* ARTILLERY TO DEAL WITH THIS NEW MENACE.

BUT THE *T-34 TANK* WASN'T THE ONLY GAME-CHANGING ELEMENT...

THE SOLDIERS OF THE RED ARMY WERE BEGINNING TO TOUGHEN UP AND OVERCOME THE INITIAL SHOCK OF THE INVASION.

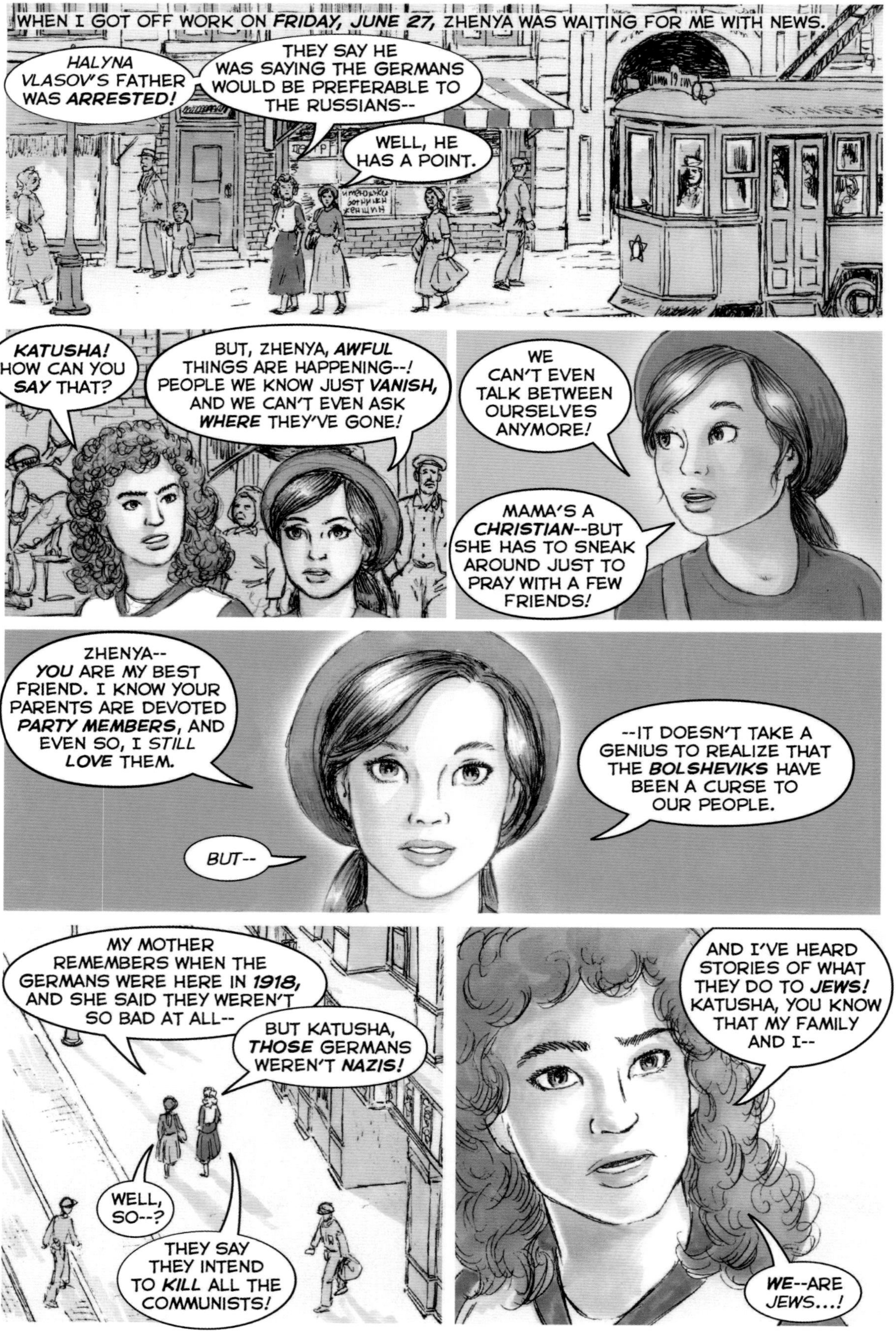
WHEN I GOT OFF WORK ON FRIDAY, JUNE 27, ZHENYA WAS WAITING FOR ME WITH NEWS.
HALYNA VLASOV'S FATHER WAS ARRESTED!
THEY SAY HE WAS SAYING THE GERMANS WOULD BE PREFERABLE TO THE RUSSIANS--
WELL, HE HAS A POINT.
KATUSHA! HOW CAN YOU SAY THAT?
BUT, ZHENYA, AWFUL THINGS ARE HAPPENING--! PEOPLE WE KNOW JUST VANISH, AND WE CAN'T EVEN ASK WHERE THEY'VE GONE!
WE CAN'T EVEN TALK BETWEEN OURSELVES ANYMORE!
MAMA'S A CHRISTIAN--BUT SHE HAS TO SNEAK AROUND JUST TO PRAY WITH A FEW FRIENDS!
ZHENYA-- YOU ARE MY BEST FRIEND. I KNOW YOUR PARENTS ARE DEVOTED PARTY MEMBERS, AND EVEN SO, I STILL LOVE THEM.
BUT--
--IT DOESN'T TAKE A GENIUS TO REALIZE THAT THE BOLSHEVIKS HAVE BEEN A CURSE TO OUR PEOPLE.
MY MOTHER REMEMBERS WHEN THE GERMANS WERE HERE IN 1918, AND SHE SAID THEY WEREN'T SO BAD AT ALL--
BUT KATUSHA, THOSE GERMANS WEREN'T NAZIS!
WELL, SO--?
THEY SAY THEY INTEND TO KILL ALL THE COMMUNISTS!
AND I'VE HEARD STORIES OF WHAT THEY DO TO JEWS! KATUSHA, YOU KNOW THAT MY FAMILY AND I--
WE--ARE JEWS...!

NEAR *ZHYTOMYR*, ABOUT 90 MILES WEST OF *KIEV*...

HELLO, FRIEND! HAVE YOU WORKED WITH THE RAILROAD A LONG TIME?

YES, I HAVE--NEARLY 17 YEARS!

DO YOU KNOW OF A RAILROAD MAN NAMED *ANDREY TYMOSHENKO*, LIVES AND WORKS IN *KIEV*...?

OH, YES--VERY SKILLED MACHINIST. NO LONGER WITH THE RAILROAD, THOUGH.

NO?

NO.

THEY SENT HIM TO WORK IN THE TRACTOR FACTORY IN *KHARKOV*, BUILDING TANKS.

BUT I HEAR HIS *FAMILY* STILL LIVES IN KIEV--IN THE *ZALIZNYCHNY* DISTRICT.

YOU MEN HEADING FOR KIEV?

WELL, YES...

...BUT OUR TRAVEL DOCUMENTS ARE NOT EXACTLY IN ORDER.

THAT IS NO MATTER HERE-- WE HAVE NO *CHEKA** ON THIS TRAIN.

CHEKA--OLD TERM FOR THE *NKVD, DATING* FROM 1917 AND LENIN'S FIRST SECRET POLICE, THE *CHEKA.*

MY STOKER'S BEEN TAKEN FOR THE ARMY...

YOU THREE CAN WORK FOR YOUR PASSAGE.

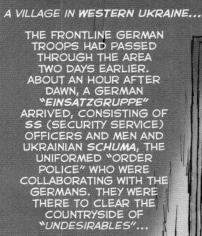

THE FRONTLINE GERMAN TROOPS HAD PASSED THROUGH THE AREA TWO DAYS EARLIER. ABOUT AN HOUR AFTER DAWN, A GERMAN *"EINSATZGRUPPE"* ARRIVED, CONSISTING OF SS (SECURITY SERVICE) OFFICERS AND MEN AND UKRAINIAN *SCHUMA*, THE UNIFORMED "ORDER POLICE" WHO WERE COLLABORATING WITH THE GERMANS. THEY WERE THERE TO CLEAR THE COUNTRYSIDE OF *"UNDESIRABLES"*...

I AM LOOKING FOR THE MAN WHO IS IN CHARGE OF THIS COLLECTIVE FARM.

THAT WOULD BE *ME*, SIR--

WITHOUT FURTHER WORDS...

...THE GERMAN OFFICER SHOT HIM IN THE FACE.

THE GERMANS AND THE *SCHUMA* THEN COMBED THROUGH THE VILLAGE, FORCING PEOPLE FROM HOMES AND WORKPLACES...

THEY TOOK SPECIAL CARE IN SURROUNDING THE JEWISH DISTRICT AND GATHERING ITS PEOPLE IN THE TOWN SQUARE.

THE MENTALLY HANDICAPPED SON OF THE LOCAL BAKER WAS TAKEN.

A WOMAN ADMITTED HER SON HAD BEEN DRAFTED INTO THE RED ARMY.

SHE WAS ARRESTED AS A *"PARTISAN."*

A *ROMANY*--A GYPSY-- WAS ARRESTED AS HE BURNED THE WASTE FROM AN OUTHOUSE.

THE VILLAGERS WERE MARCHED TO THE NORTHWEST END OF TOWN TO AN AREA WHERE WORKERS HAD DUG AN ANTI-TANK DITCH FOR THE RED ARMY.

THERE, THE GERMANS HAD ALREADY SET UP TWO *MG-34 MACHINE GUNS*...

THE VILLAGERS WERE THEN ORDERED TO UNDRESS--OLD MEN, WOMEN, AND CHILDREN...

AND *THEN*...

FINALLY, *KIEV!* WHERE ARE *YOU* HEADING OFF TO NOW, SYDIR?

I'M GOING TO TRY TO MAKE CONTACT WITH THE *ONU.* *

WELL, BE *CAREFUL*, MY FRIEND.

AND HOW ABOUT *YOU*, FATHER?

* *ONU*--ORGANIZATION OF UKRAINIAN NATIONALISTS.

I HEAR THE LITTLE VILLAGE OF *GORODNYA* IS IN NEED OF A PRIEST...

AH, YES! I KNOW THE AREA WELL.

GO WITH *GOD*, FATHER.

BLESS YOU, TARAS.

IT WAS SUNDAY MORNING, *JUNE 29.* THE WAR WAS ONE WEEK OLD. MAMA WAS BACK FROM PRAYERS AT MRS. BOSHYK'S, AND MILLA AND I WERE WORKING IN THE GARDEN. I LOOKED UP TO SEE A LARGE, DUSTY, WELL-TRAVELED MAN STANDING AT THE GATE...

AH, YOUNG LADY...

...WOULD YOU KINDLY GRANT A WEARY TRAVELER A SMALL SIP OF WATER FROM YOUR WELL?

WHY, CERTAINLY!

LET ME DRAW IT FOR YOU...

AS I TOLD YOU EARLIER: THERE ARE THOSE DAYS THAT MARK A GREAT DIVIDE BETWEEN ALL THAT HAS COME BEFORE... AND ALL THAT SHALL COME AFTERWARD...

...AHH! HOW REFRESHING!

"AND LET IT COME TO PASS, THAT THE DAMSEL TO WHOM I SHALL SAY, 'LET DOWN THY PITCHER, I PRAY THEE, THAT I MAY DRINK'; AND SHE SHALL SAY, 'DRINK, AND I WILL GIVE THY CAMELS DRINK ALSO.'"*

"YOUR CAMELS"...?

* GENESIS 24:14

I LOOKED ALL AROUND THE STRANGER--AND EVEN UP THE ROAD BEHIND HIM...

UHHH...

...I DON'T SEE ANY *CAMELS.*

THE STRANGER SUDDENLY THREW HIS HEAD BACK AND LAUGHED UPROARIOUSLY. MY FIRST THOUGHT WAS THAT HE WAS *MAD.* BUT AS I LOOKED INTO HIS LEATHERY FACE, WITH ITS RED WHISKERS AND OUTRAGEOUS MOUSTACHE...

THEN I SAW SOMETHING VERY FAMILIAR, AND VERY COMFORTING, IN HIS PALE BLUE EYES...!

...AND SUDDENLY, I COULD TELL THAT MY LIFE WAS ABOUT TO TAKE A VERY DRAMATIC TURN.

SUNDAY, JUNE 29, 1941.
THE WAR WAS JUST A WEEK OLD.

NAZI GERMANY'S *OPERATION BARBAROSSA*
HAD CUT DEEP INTO THE TERRITORY
OF THE SOVIET UNION.

THE *PANZERS* WENT INTO AND AROUND RED ARMY UNITS, CUTTING THEM OFF FROM THEIR SUPPLIES AND COMMAND STRUCTURE. FROM THE SKIES ABOVE, THE GERMAN LUFTWAFFE WOULD STRAFE AND BREAK UP ANY ORGANIZED CONCENTRATION OF MEN AND MATÉRIEL. THE RESULT WAS TENS OF THOUSANDS OF LOST AND DEMORALIZED MEN WHO HAD LITTLE RECOURSE BUT TO SURRENDER.

COMRADE STALIN WOULD ADD HIS OWN MEASURE OF HELL TO THIS SITUATION WITH HIS *ORDER NO. 274.*

THIS ORDER STATED THAT ALL THOSE WHO SURRENDERED WERE TO BE CONSIDERED *TRAITORS* TO THEIR COUNTRY AND WOULD BE TREATED AS SUCH IF THEY RETURNED.

THIS STATUTE NOT ONLY DEMANDED PUNISHMENT FOR THE SOLDIER-- BUT FOR HIS *FAMILY* AS WELL.

THE PILGRIM

EVEN IN TIMES OF GREAT EARTHSHAKING EVENTS, THE LIVES OF MOST PEOPLE ARE MARKED BY THE MOST MUNDANE OCCURRENCES. WE REMEMBER THOSE AFFAIRS OF MAGNITUDE BY PLACING THEM NEXT TO THE LITTLE INCIDENTS THAT MAKE TINY FOOTNOTES OF MEMORY IN THE LIVES OF ORDINARY PEOPLE. PERHAPS GOD LOOKS DOWN UPON THE FACE OF THE WORLD AND PLACES THESE UNIMPORTANT HAPPENINGS--UNIMPORTANT TO ANYONE BUT OURSELVES-- NEXT TO THESE EPISODES OF PROMINENCE SO WE WILL BEST REMEMBER THEM...

...OR, PERHAPS, HE DOES IT THE *OTHER* WAY AROUND.

HAHA! HAHAHA! HAHA!

MAMA! *MAMA!*

EVERYONE CAME RUNNING. MILLA EMERGED FROM BEHIND THE HOUSE WHERE SHE'D BEEN TYING BEANS, AND VASILY RAN OUT FROM THE BARN WHERE HE'D BEEN SHARPENING IMPLEMENTS...

MAMA CAME OUT OF THE HOUSE WITH A PARING KNIFE IN ONE HAND AND A HALF-PEELED POTATO IN THE OTHER...

AND *WHAT* IS ALL THIS *NOISE* ABOU--

⸝GASP!⸝

THE STRANGER QUIT LAUGHING AND RESPECTFULLY TOOK OFF HIS HAT.

HELLO, *ELENA...!* YOU HAVEN'T CHANGED.

THE *PRODIGAL BROTHER* HAS *RETURNED.*

TO OUR GREAT SURPRISE, MAMA DROPPED HER KNIFE AND POTATO AND THREW HER ARMS AROUND THE NECK OF THIS RED-WHISKERED WILD MAN!

CAREFUL, YOU'LL *CRUSH* ME--!

AH! TARAS-- IT REALLY *IS* YOU!!

MAMA?!

KATUSHA, THIS IS YOUR FATHER'S OLDER *BROTHER*...

...YOUR *UNCLE* TARAS!

UNCLE TARAS! I'D HEARD HIS NAME MENTIONED ONLY A FEW TIMES. I NEVER KNEW WHAT HAD HAPPENED TO HIM.

...AND THIS IS *VASILY!*

HELLO, UNCLE TARAS, SIR.

MILLA, COME HERE.

THIS IS MY DAUGHTER, *LUDMILLA.*

WELL...I DON'T SEE THE FAMILY RESEMBLANCE--

--BUT IT IS VERY FINE TO HAVE SUCH A FLAXEN-HAIRED *BEAUTY* IN OUR FAMILY.

MILLA'S FACE TURNED CRIMSON--AND SHE BROKE OUT IN A BIG SMILE SUCH AS I HAD NEVER SEEN.

WHY, YOUR HAIR IS AS *BRIGHT* AS THAT RADIANT *SMILE...!*

35

BEFORE WE COULD ASK ANY QUESTIONS ABOUT WHERE HE HAD BEEN AND WHAT HE HAD BEEN DOING, *UNCLE TARAS* JUMPED RIGHT INTO THE HOUSEHOLD CHORES WITH THE REST OF US.

ALTHOUGH HIS FACE WAS LINED AND WEATHERED, HIS EVERY ACTION DISPLAYED A ROBUST, YOUTHFUL ENERGY.

WHEREVER HE'D BEEN, NO DOUBT HE'D BEEN PERFORMING HARD LABOR, MAKING HIMSELF INDISPENSABLE TO THOSE AROUND HIM.

AS HE WORKED, *MILLA* WATCHED HIM WITH AN AWED FASCINATION THAT WAS VERY UNLIKE HER.

HAHA! WHEN YOUR SISTER *NATALYA* GETS HERE, SHE WILL GASP WHEN SHE SEES *UNCLE TARAS!*

HOW LONG HAS IT BEEN SINCE YOU SAW HIM LAST, MAMA?

MY GOD, KATUSHA--! IT HAS BEEN *TWENTY-SEVEN* YEARS!

CLUCK! CLUCK! ⸴GACK!⸴

"WE GREW UP IN *KROVROT*, WHERE YOU WERE BORN. WELL, YOUR FATHER'S FAMILY WAS THE POOREST FAMILY IN THE VILLAGE.

"HIS FATHER, *DEDUSHKA TYMOSHENKO*, WAS BY FAR THE *MEANEST MAN* IN THE TOWN.

"HE WAS AN OLD DRUNK WHO BEAT HIS KIDS AND TRADED WITH THIEVES. EVEN THE LOCAL *GENDARMES* WERE AFRAID OF *DEDUSHKA TYMOSHENKO.*"

"ONE INDIVIDUAL WHO TOOK SPECIAL INTEREST IN THE WELFARE OF TARAS AND YOUR FATHER WAS A ONE-ARMED FORMER CZARIST CAVALRY OFFICER NAMED *SEMEN KALASHNIKOV*... HE WAS A MAN OF PROPERTY WHO LOOKED OUT FOR THE COMMON PEOPLE. IN THE LOCAL *DUMA*, HE WOULD FREQUENTLY ADDRESS CONCERNS OF LOCAL PEASANTS.

"SEMEN WAS ALSO EXTREMELY RELIGIOUS, BELIEVING HE HAD A MORAL RESPONSIBILITY TO HELP THOSE LESS FORTUNATE.

"HIS WIFE, A FORMER SCHOOLTEACHER, MADE IT HER MISSION TO TEACH THE *TYMOSHENKO BOYS* HOW TO *READ*.

"ONE DAY, DEDUSHKA CONFRONTED SEMEN AND DEMANDED THAT KALASHNIKOV NO LONGER CONCERN HIMSELF WITH ANOTHER MAN'S SONS...

"SEMEN SIMPLY PRODUCED A BIBLE WITH A SILVER CROSS SCREWED TO ITS COVER. WITHOUT SAYING A SINGLE WORD, HE DROVE THE OLD BRUTE AWAY LIKE A *VERDILAC!**

*SLAVIC TERM FOR *VAMPIRE*.

"THEN ONE MORNING, DEDUSHKA'S BODY WAS FOUND AT THE BOTTOM OF THE TOWN WELL. EVERYONE CONCLUDED THAT HE'D FALLEN IN WHILE DRUNK. NO ONE SEEMED TO NOTICE THE BLOOD-COVERED *ROCK* LYING ON THE GROUND NEAR THE WELL, OR THE FACT THAT THE BACK OF DEDUSHKA'S HEAD WAS VERY OBVIOUSLY *BASHED IN*.

"MAYBE NOBODY *WANTED* TO NOTICE."

"SEMEN AND OTHER VILLAGERS HELPED THE BROTHERS TO ORGANIZE AND WORK THE NEGLECTED FARM. THE BOYS HAD NO FEAR OF HARD WORK, SO WITH A LITTLE ADVICE AND COLLECTIVE KNOWLEDGE, THE PROPERTY VISIBLY IMPROVED IN NO TIME.

"THE BROTHERS WERE AMAZED AT THE KALASHNIKOVS' FINE HOUSE, THEIR EXTENSIVE LIBRARY--AND EVEN MORE AMAZED BY THEIR *KINDNESS*."

"THEN CAME *AUGUST 1914*. ALL OF EUROPE SHOOK FROM THE MOVEMENT OF GREAT ARMIES. THE CALL WENT OUT: '*YOU ARE NEEDED, MEN! RALLY TO YOUR COUNTRY! TAKE A MAN'S PART!*'

'FOR **RUSSIA**! FOR **BELORUSSIA**!'

'FOR **THE UKRAINE**! FOR THE **CZAR**!'

"SEMEN WAS CALLED BACK INTO SERVICE AS A MAJOR ON THE IMPERIAL STAFF. HE TOLD THE TYMOSHENKO BOYS THAT THEY SHOULD COME WITH HIM, SO THAT THEY COULD GET A MUCH BETTER POSTING THAN IF THEY WAITED TO BE CALLED INTO SERVICE.

"THE PEOPLE OF *KROVROT* AGREED TO HARVEST THEIR FARM'S CROPS FOR THEM AND SHARE THE PROFITS.

"SO, ON A CLEAR MORNING IN *AUGUST 1914*, THE THREE OF THEM WENT OFF TO WAR...

"YOUR FATHER WAS THE ONLY ONE WHO CAME BACK."

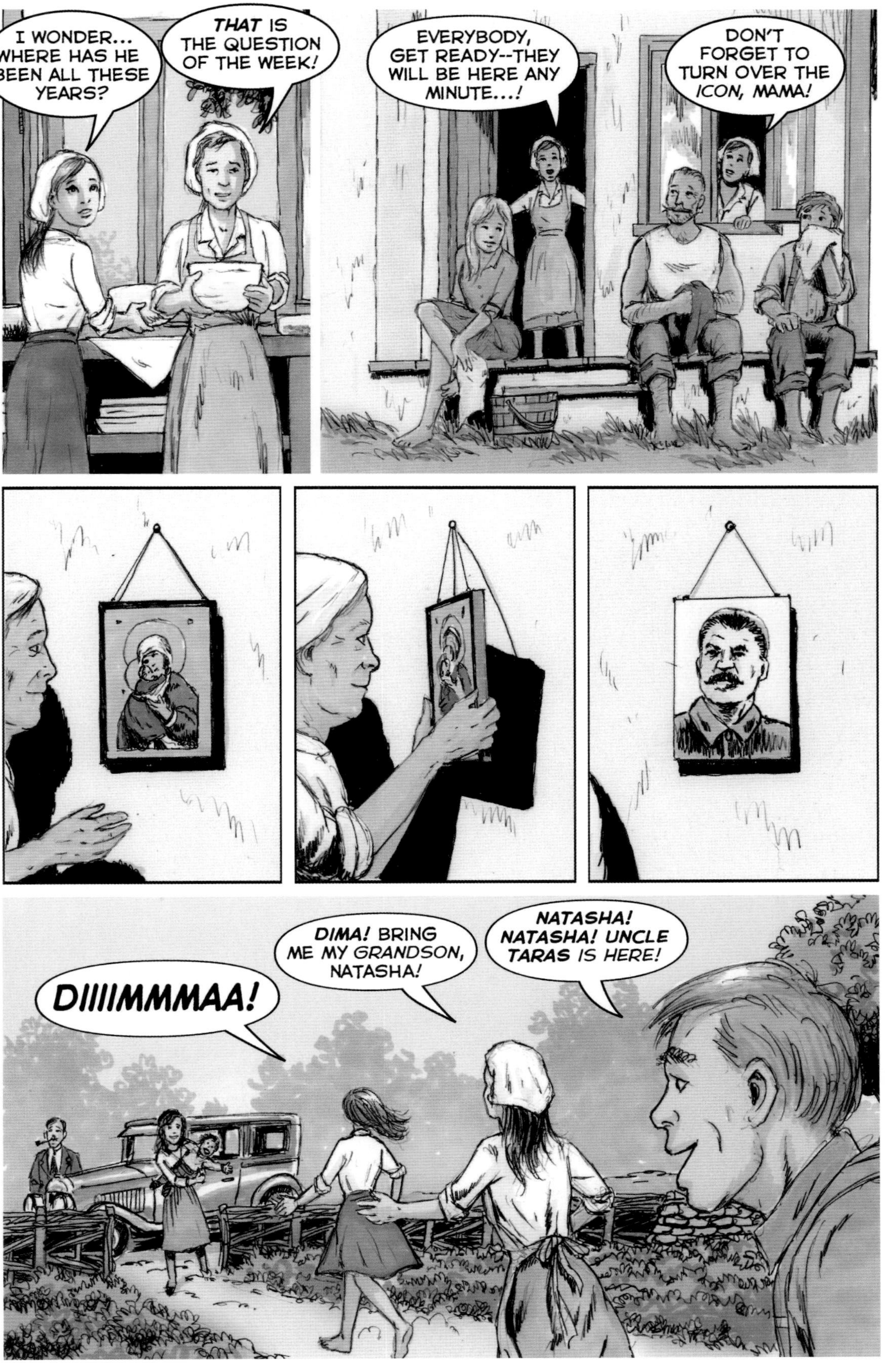
I WONDER... WHERE HAS HE BEEN ALL THESE YEARS?
THAT IS THE QUESTION OF THE WEEK!
EVERYBODY, GET READY--THEY WILL BE HERE ANY MINUTE...!
DON'T FORGET TO TURN OVER THE *ICON*, MAMA!
DIIIIMMMAA!
DIMA! BRING ME MY *GRANDSON*, NATASHA!
NATASHA! NATASHA! UNCLE TARAS IS *HERE!*

DON'T YOU JUST *LOVE* UNCLE TARAS' MOUSTACHE? I THINK HE LOOKS DASHING, LIKE *BOHDAN KHMELNYTSKY.**

WHO?

*17TH-CENTURY COSSACK MILITARY LEADER.

UNCLE TARAS WAS THE FOCUS OF THE MEAL. HIS SUDDEN APPEARANCE FASCINATED US, AND WE WERE CURIOUS WHERE HE HAD BEEN.

SASHA WAS JUST *SUSPICIOUS.*

WHAT HAVE YOU BEEN DOING ALL THESE YEARS? WHERE HAVE YOU BEEN? HOW DID YOU LIVE?

WELL, NOW--LET'S SEE...

...I'VE SERVED AS A SEAMAN IN PORTS ALL OVER THE WORLD.

I'VE TRIED MY HAND AT AGRICULTURE--MY *ROOTS,* YOU MIGHT SAY. I'VE PLANTED AND HARVESTED COTTON, RICE, TOBACCO, ORANGES--

--AND EVEN TENDED A RICH LADY'S GARDEN IN A PLACE CALLED *HOLLYWOOD.*

I'VE LABORED IN THE GOLD MINES OF *AUSTRALIA, MEXICO,* AND *KOLYMA...*

KOLYMA!

THAT MADE OUR EYES POP OUT. THAT WAS THE GOLD-MINING PRISON IN *SIBERIA.*

PEOPLE WOULD WHISPER: "KOLYMA MEANS *DEATH!*"

I'VE ALSO BEEN A HIRED SOLDIER IN *SOUTH AMERICA, CHINA,* AND IN *SPAIN...*

SPAIN--?! WHICH *SIDE* DID YOU FIGHT ON?

OH... FIRST ON *ONE* SIDE--

--THEN ON THE *OTHER...*

WHAT *I* CAN'T UNDERSTAND IS HOW YOU GOT FROM L'VIV TO KIEV WITHOUT A *PROPISKA*--

--AND WITHOUT BEING *STOPPED* BY ANYONE!

* SOVIET INTERNAL PASSPORT REQUIRED FOR TRAVEL.

YOU KNOW, I WAS WONDERING THE SAME THING...

I GUESS THE *NKVD* WAS TOO BUSY WORRYING ABOUT THE GERMANS.

THE SUMMER WORE ON, AND WE HEARD REPORTS OF THE GERMANS GETTING CLOSER AND CLOSER. UNCLE TARAS BECAME AN IMPORTANT MEMBER OF THE FAMILY, FIXING UP OUR HOME, WORKING IN THE YARD, AND BUYING THINGS FOR OUR PANTRY, LIKE CANNED AND PRESERVED FOODS.

41

EARLY THE NEXT MORNING, THE BUNDLE WAS DISCOVERED BY PEOPLE GOING TO WORK.

THE VOICE FROM INSIDE INFORMED THEM HE WAS *NKVD,* AND DEMANDED TO BE *RELEASED IMMEDIATELY.* HIS REQUEST WAS HONORED...

...BUT NOT UNTIL *AFTER* A FEW BRAVE SOULS HAD TAKEN A FEW BOLD WHACKS.

SOMETIMES, MOSTLY AT NIGHT--

--WE THOUGHT WE COULD HEAR THE RUMBLE OF CANNON IN THE WEST.

AS THE GERMANS ADVANCED, MANY UKRAINIANS *WELCOMED* THEM AS LIBERATORS FROM THE GODLESS COMMUNISTS.

COMRADE STALIN'S SPEECHES BECAME LESS AUTHORITARIAN AND MORE PATRIOTIC.

COMRADES! CITIZENS! BROTHERS AND SISTERS! MEN OF OUR ARMY AND NAVY! I AM ADDRESSING YOU, MY FRIENDS!

--OUR PEOPLE MUST KNOW NO FEAR IN THE FIGHT AND MUST SELFLESSLY JOIN OUR PATRIOTIC WAR OF LIBERATION AGAINST THE FASCIST ENSLAVERS...!

I WAS TALKING TO PRIKIP HONSHAR THE OTHER DAY...

HE SAID THE GERMANS WOULD HAVE *JOBS* FOR BOYS MY AGE--

WHAT ARE YOU DOING, TALKING TO THAT RUFFIAN--? BESIDES, YOU WILL BE BACK IN *SCHOOL* IN SEPTEMBER--

⸢AUUGH!⸣ I'M *TIRED* OF SCHOOL!

UNCLE TARAS, YOU'VE BEEN TO GERMANY--WHAT DO YOU THINK ABOUT THEM?

WELL...THEY'RE GOOD SOLDIERS. THEY'LL PROBABLY GET HERE...

BUT AS FOR OTHER THINGS ABOUT THEM--

--I JUST *DON'T KNOW.*

THE MAIN SOVIET LINE OF DEFENSE WEST OF KIEV WAS BUILT ALONG AN ANCIENT RIDGE CALLED *THE SERPENT'S WALL.* BUILT BY AN UNKNOWN PEOPLE BEFORE RECORDED HISTORY, THE RUSSIANS HAD DECIDED IN THE 1930S THAT IT WOULD BE A PERFECT POSITION TO ADD PILLBOXES AND GUN EMPLACEMENTS.

HOWEVER, JUST AS DID THE FRENCH IN THE *MAGINOT LINE* THE SUMMER BEFORE, THE SOVIETS FORGOT TO BUILD A STRONG BACK DOOR.

ALTHOUGH THE GERMAN ADVANCE HAD BEEN DRAMATIC, IT WAS ALSO COSTLY. BY LATE AUGUST, THE THIRD REICH HAD SUFFERED *440,000 CASUALTIES...*

...INCLUDING *94,000 DEAD.*

NOW, WITH RUSSIAN RESISTANCE GROWING STRONGER, *HITLER* THREW A MONKEY WRENCH INTO HIS OWN GENERAL STAFF'S PLANNING MACHINE.

HE ORDERED THAT THE ADVANCE ON *MOSCOW* BE TEMPORARILY *HALTED...*

...WHILE THE BULK OF GERMAN FORCES WERE TO BE USED IN THE CAPTURE OF *KIEV* AND *UKRAINE.* THE HIGH COMMAND PROTESTED STRONGLY, GOING SO FAR AS TO SEND *COLONEL GENERAL HEINZ GUDERIAN,* ARCHITECT OF *BLITZKRIEG* TACTICS, BACK TO GERMANY--HOPING TO CHANGE THE *FÜHRER'S* MIND.

IT *DIDN'T* WORK.

GUDERIAN FLEW BACK TO SMOLENSK, TURNED HIS PANZER GROUP SOUTH...AND BEGAN TO HEAD FOR *KIEV.*

THEN, ONE EVENING IN AUGUST, MILLA AND I WERE GOING TO MEET UNCLE TARAS AT THE *BESSARABSKY MARKET.* WE'D JUST SPOTTED HIM WALKING ALONG THE STREET, WHEN...

WHA--? HE TURNED AWAY. BUT I *KNOW* HE SAW US...!

HE DID! MILLA--

--*THOSE* MUST BE THE MEN WHO'VE BEEN FOLLOWING HIM!

SUDDENLY, ONE OF THE MEN RAN UP BEHIND UNCLE TARAS--

--AND *STRUCK* HIM...!

THEN A BLACK VAN--WHAT WE CALLED A "BLACK RAVEN"--PULLED UP, AND A GROUP OF MEN PILED OUT TO JOIN THE FRAY!

AFTER A TERRIFIC STRUGGLE, THE MEN FINALLY SUBDUED UNCLE TARAS.

WE COULD ONLY WATCH HELPLESSLY WHILE THEY DRAGGED HIM INTO THE BACK OF THE TRUCK AND *DROVE OFF!*

UNCLE TARAS!

HUSH, MILLA--!

--LET'S GO GET *MAMA*...!

NOT WAITING TO CATCH A TRAM, WE RAN HOME LIKE DEER.

MAMA! UNCLE TARAS HAS BEEN *ARRESTED!*

OH, I WAS *AFRAID* SOMETHING LIKE THIS WOULD HAPPEN...!

HE WAS TOO FREE WITH WHAT HE SAID, AND TO *WHOM*...!

WE HAD BETTER GO SEE WHAT *SASHA* CAN DO.

WE HAVE BEEN WATCHING YOU, **TARAS TYMOSHENKO!** OUR FILE ON YOU IS VERY THICK, GOING BACK TO *1917...!*

TO ADD TO THAT, HERE YOU COME SNEAKING IN WITH **NO PROPISKA.**

WELL, NOT WANTING TO BE ON THE WRONG SIDE OF THE LAW, I TRIED--

:-OOF!:-

NOW, THAT *COULDN'T* HAVE HURT *THAT* MUCH! I'VE TOLD *SERYOZHA* HERE TO PULL HIS PUNCHES.

NO--IT WASN'T BAD AT *ALL...*

THANK YOU, SERYOZHA--YOU ARE A *TRUE* GENTLEMAN.

I'VE ORDERED HIM TO GO EASY ON YOU--YOU BEING AN OLD MAN.

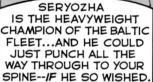

SERYOZHA IS THE HEAVYWEIGHT CHAMPION OF THE BALTIC FLEET...AND HE COULD JUST PUNCH ALL THE WAY THROUGH TO YOUR SPINE--*IF* HE SO WISHED.

SO...*YOU* ARE THE ONE I HAVE TO THANK FOR THIS FINE TREATMENT...

WELL, THEN, TYMOSHENKO-- IF YOU *ARE* TRULY GRATEFUL... *NAME* ALL THE *BANDERITES* WHO CAME TO TOWN WITH YOU.

OH, YES, YES...BUT WHAT IS *YOUR* NAME? I KNOW THAT MY FRIEND HERE IS SERYOZHA, BUT--

--WHO ARE *YOU?*

I AM COMRADE GUDZ!

AH! VERY *GOOD!* YOU SEE, I WANTED YOUR *NAMES*--

--SO THAT I COULD **PISS** ON YOUR **GRAVES!**

WE WENT TO SASHA AND NATASHA'S APARTMENT OVER ON BANKIVSKA STREET. MANY OF THE PARTY OFFICIALS LIVED IN THAT AREA.

WHERE *IS* EVERYBODY?

NATASHA! SASHA? LET US IN!

WHO IS--OH!

:WAAAAA...!:

--EH, *MAMA!* UHH-- SASHA'S NOT HERE...

THAT'S FINE. LET US *IN*, NATASHA...

UNCLE TARAS HAS BEEN *ARRESTED!*

EH--YES, I KNOW. SASHA TOLD ME. I ASKED HIM *WHY*, AND, *UH*...

OH, DIMA, WHAT'S THE MATTER--?

:WAAAA...!:

NATASHA!

LOOK--! IT'S *NOT* WHAT YOU *THINK*...!

AAH! MY LITTLE NATALYA--! WHAT HAPPENED--?!

UHH...

BUT *MAMA UNDERSTOOD* IMMEDIATELY...!

WHERE IS HE, NATASHA? WHERE IS *SASHA*--?!

MOTHER, IT'S *NOT* HIS FAULT! I QUESTIONED HIM ABOUT UNCLE TARAS--

AND IS *SASHA* BEHIND THAT--? *WELL*, IS HE?

NATASHA! TELL ME--!

MOTHER, ALL THIS IS *NONE* OF YOUR AFFAIR! SASHA HAS RESPON--

--DID HE DO IT?

--DID YOUR HUSBAND *DENOUNCE* YOUR FATHER'S BROTHER?

47

WE WERE UNABLE TO GET CLOSE TO SASHA'S OFFICE IN THE *DUMA BUILDING*-- THERE WAS TOO MUCH *ACTIVITY.*

WE WATCHED FROM THE SHADOWS AS *NKVD* MEN AND RED ARMY TROOPS BUSILY UNLOADED TRUCKS ALL UP AND DOWN *KHRESCHATYK BOULEVARD.* IT SEEMED EERIE THAT SO MANY COULD WORK IN SUCH *SILENCE.*

I WONDER WHAT COULD BE IN ALL THOSE BOXES THEY'RE CARRYING INTO THOSE BUILDINGS?

SSSH! THEY MIGHT HEAR US--!

WE DECIDED TO LIE IN WAIT ALONG THE ROUTE SASHA TOOK ON HIS WAY HOME...

AH--! *THERE* HE IS...!

BUT--*WHY* IS HE GOING INTO THAT APARTMENT BUILDING...?

WHY, THAT LITTLE *WEASEL*--!

IT WAS SEVERAL HOURS BEFORE SASHA CAME OUT-- AND WHEN HE *DID,* WE WERE *READY!*

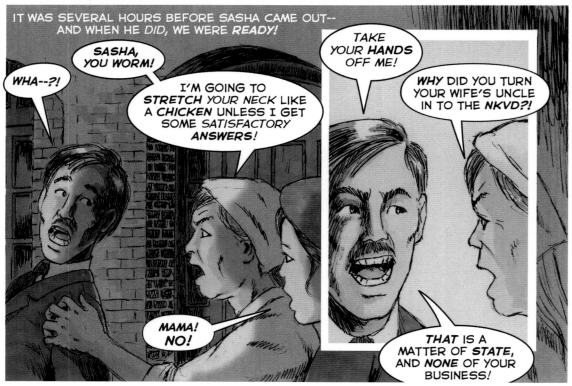

WHA--?!

SASHA, YOU *WORM!*

I'M GOING TO *STRETCH* YOUR NECK LIKE A *CHICKEN* UNLESS I GET SOME *SATISFACTORY ANSWERS!*

MAMA! NO!

TAKE YOUR *HANDS* OFF ME!

WHY DID YOU TURN YOUR WIFE'S UNCLE IN TO THE *NKVD?!*

THAT IS A MATTER OF *STATE,* AND *NONE* OF YOUR BUSINESS!

SASHA TRIED TO SQUIRM AWAY, BUT MAMA HAD A FIRM GRIP. SHE'D SEE TO IT THAT HE FACED THE MUSIC.

I DON'T CARE IF THE ORDER CAME FROM THE *POLITBURO*--!

LET GO OF *ME*!

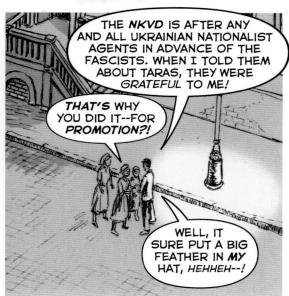

THE *NKVD* IS AFTER ANY AND ALL UKRAINIAN NATIONALIST AGENTS IN ADVANCE OF THE FASCISTS. WHEN I TOLD THEM ABOUT TARAS, THEY WERE *GRATEFUL* TO ME!

THAT'S WHY YOU DID IT--FOR *PROMOTION*?!

WELL, IT SURE PUT A BIG FEATHER IN *MY* HAT, *HEHHEH*--!

WITH THAT, MAMA GAVE HIS THROAT A GOOD SHAKING. I'D NEVER SEEN HER SO ANGRY!

WHAT ABOUT MY DAUGHTER?!

WHAT ABOUT *NATALYA*?!

:WUGGA-GLAK!:

:KOFF: WHAT *ABOUT* HER?

YOU UKRAINIAN PEASANTS ARE IGNORANT SWINE FIT ONLY TO SERVE YOUR RUSSIAN MASTERS!

SO *THAT'S* WHAT YOU THINK OF US? LET ME TELL YOU ABOUT *UKRAINIAN BLOOD*...!

COSSACK BLOOD ALSO FLOWS IN OUR VEINS! AND *YOU* HAVE BITTEN OFF MORE THAN YOU CAN CHEW BY *BETRAYING TARAS TYMOSHENKO!*

IF YOU *HARM* MY DAUGHTER *AGAIN*, SASHA, YOU WILL HAVE TO DEAL WITH *ME*!

SHE HELD HIM IN HER GRIP FOR A LONG, COLD MOMENT. THEN FINALLY, MAMA LET GO OF SASHA'S COLLAR.

AS HE SLUNK AWAY INTO THE DARKNESS...

...HIS GLARE DRIPPED WITH *HATRED.*

AS THE RED ARMY LINE MORE OR LESS HELD TO THE WEST OF KIEV, THE GERMAN PINCERS MOVED FROM THE NORTH AND SOUTH BEYOND THE LEFT BANK OF THE DNIEPER. AUTHORITIES IN MOSCOW BEGAN TO REALIZE THAT UKRAINE MAY BE LOST, AND THEY BEGAN TO TAKE SEVERE MEASURES.

THEY'RE CLOSING THE AIRCRAFT FACTORY AND SHIPPING THE MACHINERY TO THE *EAST!*

WHAT ABOUT THE CANNED FOOD IN THE CANTEEN?

YES! OUR *FAMILIES* CAN BENEFIT FROM THAT!

ALL OF YOU--*HALT!* PUT THAT FOOD BACK, *NOW!*

WE HAVE BEEN ORDERED TO *DESTROY* THIS FOOD, SO THAT IT WON'T FALL INTO THE HANDS OF THE GERMANS!

WELL, *I'LL* HELP MAKE *SURE* THAT WON'T HAPPEN!

AND SO WILL *I!*

--!!

OW!!

50

IN SOME TOWNS THE GERMANS REACHED WITHOUT DOING MUCH DAMAGE, THEY WENT FROM STORE TO STORE WITH THE LOCALS, TAKING WHAT THEY NEEDED. THE GERMANS TOOK CAMERAS AND RADIOS, WHILE THE CIVILIANS TOOK FOOD.

THE CHILDREN TOOK TOYS.

BUT THE SOVIETS HAD NO INTENTION OF LEAVING ANY FREE GIFTS FOR THE GERMANS. ANY INDUSTRIAL INFRASTRUCTURE OR MACHINERY THEY COULD NOT TAKE WITH THEM, THEY *DESTROYED*--AND THEY MADE SURE UKRAINE'S AGRICULTURAL BOUNTY REMAINED OUT OF THE REACH OF THE THIRD REICH...

JUST LIKE NAPOLEON'S ARMY HAD SEEN A CENTURY BEFORE, THE GERMAN FORCES FREQUENTLY WERE GREETED BY *SCORCHED EARTH!*

ON THE AFTERNOON OF *AUGUST 17,* SOVIET MILITARY ENGINEERS BLEW UP THE CENTER SECTION OF THE *DNIEPER DAM.* NO WARNING WAS GIVEN TO THOSE DOWNSTREAM.

THE RESULTING WALL OF WATER DESTROYED TOWNS AND VILLAGES, FARMS AND LIVESTOCK, THE SOUTHERN DISTRICT OF *ZAPORIZHZHYA*--

--AND HUNDREDS, MAYBE THOUSANDS, OF *CIVILIANS.*

SOME BELIEVE THAT AS MANY AS *20,000* RED ARMY SOLDIERS *DROWNED.*

IT WAS ONE EVENING IN EARLY SEPTEMBER...

WE HADN'T HEARD A WORD ABOUT UNCLE TARAS, AND NOT MUCH MORE FROM NATASHA. ALL OF OUR JOBS HAD BEEN DONE AWAY WITH, SO WE HAD NO MONEY COMING IN. STILL, WE HAD PLENTY OF FOOD ON HAND, AT LEAST FOR THE TIME BEING--

I HEAR *NIKOLAI KOVCHENKO* HAS HAD TO BE REPLACED ON THE LENINGRAD PHILHARMONIC--

IT SEEMS HE'S JOINED THE *ARMY.*

WELL, I HATE TO BE THE BEARER OF MORE BAD NEWS...

--AND AT LEAST I STILL HAD *MY RADIO.*

...BUT THE AUTHORITIES HAVE ORDERED THAT ALL *RADIOS* ARE TO BE *TURNED IN* TO POLICE HEADQUARTERS.

OHHH, NO!

THAT'S *RIGHT.* DO IT TOMORROW.

BUT IT'S *MINE!* I WORKED HARD ON IT...!

KATUSHA, DO AS I SAY!

I DON'T WANT ANOTHER MEMBER OF THIS FAMILY IN *NKVD* CUSTODY!

I WAS SO MAD! MAD AT MAMA, THE GOVERNMENT--*EVERYBODY.*

I WAITED UNTIL MAMA AND MILLA HAD GONE DOWN TO JEWISH STREET TO GET SOME MILK...

...AND AS SOON AS THEY WERE OUT OF SIGHT...

...I RAN INTO THE BARN AND HID THE RADIO IN ONE CORNER, WRAPPED IN STRAW.

IT WAS THE FIRST TIME THAT I'D EVER DISOBEYED MAMA--

--UHH...

...WELL--THERE WAS THAT *OTHER* TIME.

BY THE END OF THE FIRST WEEK OF SEPTEMBER, THE DEFENDERS OF KIEV KNEW THEY WOULD BE THE VICTIMS OF ANOTHER OF THE *WEHRMACHT'S* HUGE ENCIRCLEMENTS. THE SOVIET COMMANDERS ON THE SPOT REQUESTED PERMISSION TO *WITHDRAW.*

"NOT A STEP BACK!" STALIN ORDERED. *"HOLD OUT--AND, IF NECESSARY, DIE!"*

THIS DIDN'T STOP COMMUNIST CIVILIAN OFFICIALS FROM DESERTING THE SINKING SHIP.

THEY FLED THE CITY BY TRAIN, CAR, BOAT, PLANE, ON HORSE, AND ON FOOT.

MAMA, I THINK I SEE *NATASHA* COMING UP THE ROAD!

DIMA IS WITH HER-- AND THEY'RE *WALKING...?!*

NATALYA! WHAT'S GOING ON? WHERE'S *SASHA?*

HE'S *GONE...!*

HE'S LEFT KIEV--HE DIDN'T EVEN TELL ME HE WAS *GOING...!*

HE JUST LEFT THIS *NOTE.*

53

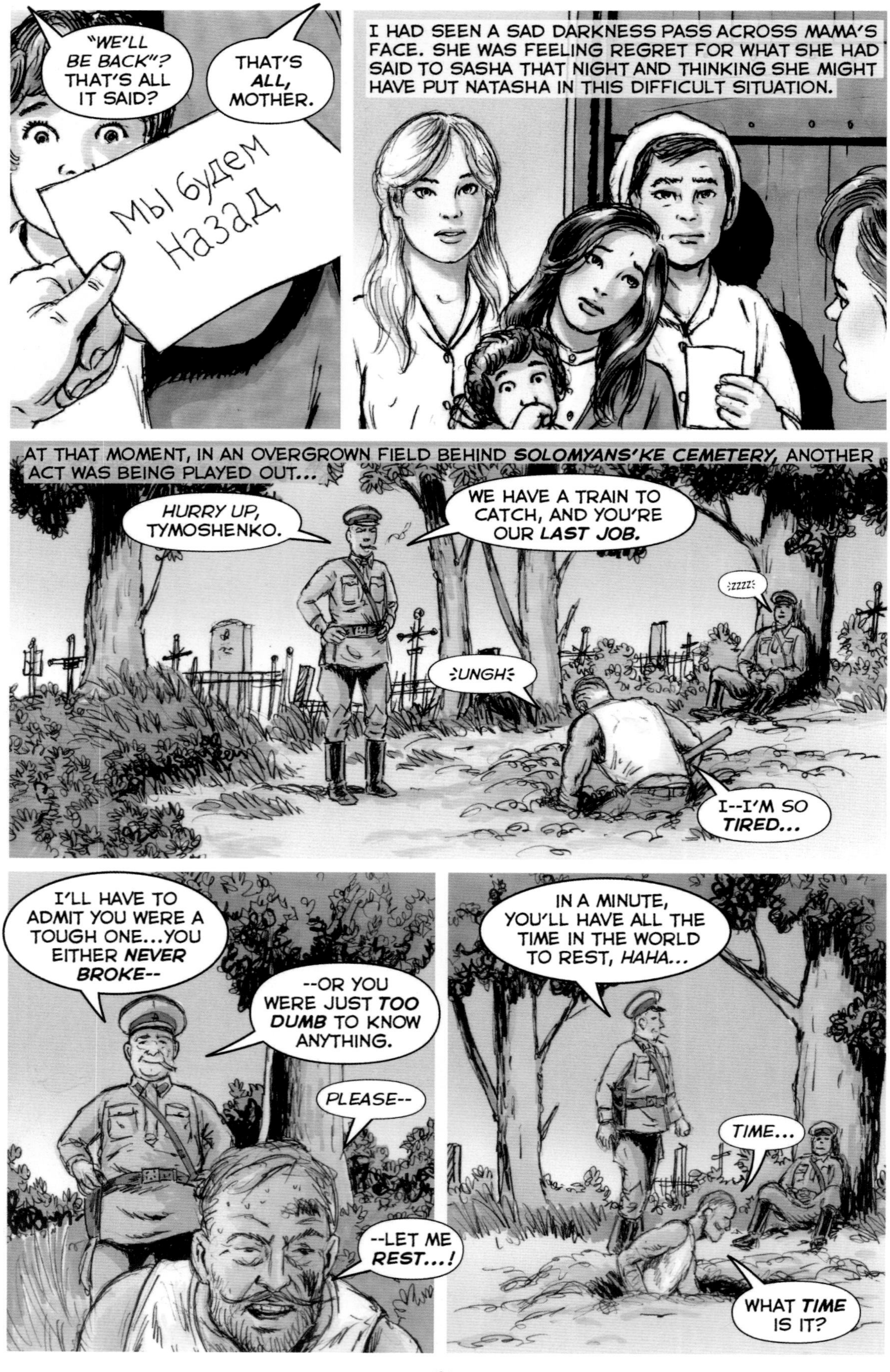
"WE'LL BE BACK"? THAT'S ALL IT SAID?
THAT'S ALL, MOTHER.
Мы будем назад
I HAD SEEN A SAD DARKNESS PASS ACROSS MAMA'S FACE. SHE WAS FEELING REGRET FOR WHAT SHE HAD SAID TO SASHA THAT NIGHT AND THINKING SHE MIGHT HAVE PUT NATASHA IN THIS DIFFICULT SITUATION.
AT THAT MOMENT, IN AN OVERGROWN FIELD BEHIND SOLOMYANS'KE CEMETERY, ANOTHER ACT WAS BEING PLAYED OUT...
HURRY UP, TYMOSHENKO.
WE HAVE A TRAIN TO CATCH, AND YOU'RE OUR LAST JOB.
ZZZZ
UNGH
I--I'M SO TIRED...
I'LL HAVE TO ADMIT YOU WERE A TOUGH ONE...YOU EITHER NEVER BROKE--
--OR YOU WERE JUST TOO DUMB TO KNOW ANYTHING.
PLEASE--
--LET ME REST...!
IN A MINUTE, YOU'LL HAVE ALL THE TIME IN THE WORLD TO REST, HAHA...
TIME...
WHAT TIME IS IT?

IT SCARCELY MATTERS TO *YOU*, BUT IT'S A LITTLE AFTER THRE--

--EEAGGH!!!

~AGGA-GAAA!!~

~zzSNUK!~ WHUH--?

~URGHK!!~

AH, WELL, GUDZ-- SORRY THIS'LL BE MORE *CROWDED* THAN YOU'D PREFER...

~GNAAGH--!!~

--BUT I JUST DON'T HAVE THE TIME TO DO BETTER FOR YOU.

YES, I'M AFRAID IT'LL BE A LITTLE TIGHT...BUT YOU'LL BE HAPPY TO KNOW IT'S STILL UP TO CURRENT *NKVD* STANDARDS.

~AAH!~ NOOo--!!

WELL, AS THEY SAY IN IRELAND, "*MAY YOU BE IN HEAVEN...*"

BUT *NO*, YOU DON'T BELIEVE IN *THAT*...

WE WERE WORKING IN THE GARDEN IN THE COOL OF THE EVENING. MOTHER, NATASHA, AND I WERE CHIT-CHATTING, AND VASILY WAS PLAYING WITH DIMA. MILLA WAS QUIET, HAVING GROWN QUIETER SINCE UNCLE TARAS HAD BEEN ARRESTED.

SUDDENLY...

WELL, LOOK AT ALL THE BEAUTY!

I CAN TELL THAT THE WOMEN RULE HERE.

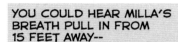

YOU COULD HEAR MILLA'S BREATH PULL IN FROM 15 FEET AWAY--

--THEN EXPEL IN A PURR OF JOY.

SHE RUSHED TO TARAS AND THREW HER ARMS AROUND HIM.

⋇OOF!⋇ IT'S WONDERFUL TO BE MISSED!

TARAS...!

WHAT HAPPENED TO YOUR FACE?!

OH, A FEW DISAGREEMENTS WITH THE LAST GOVERNMENT...

THAT NIGHT, MILLA INSISTED ON COOKING BORSCHT, AND SHE OUTDID HERSELF. HER FACE BEAMED WITH HAPPINESS.

WE ALL WISHED PAPA HAD BEEN THERE... AND NATASHA SEEMED A LITTLE SAD, BECAUSE OF HER SITUATION.

MAMA, MILLA IS VERY FOND OF UNCLE TARAS, ISN'T SHE?

YES, SHE IS. NOW, YOU MUST REMEMBER--THERE IS NO REAL FAMILY RELATIONSHIP BETWEEN THEM AT ALL.

AS I SAID BEFORE, MAMA IS SO *SMART*.

ON *SEPTEMBER 15*, THE GERMAN FORCES OF GUDERIAN AND KLEIST MET AT *LOKHVITSA*, CLOSING A RING AROUND THREE SOVIET ARMIES AT KIEV.

NEARLY *ONE MILLION MEN* WERE TRAPPED WITHIN THE ENCLOSURE, MAKING IT ONE OF THE GREATEST ENCIRCLEMENTS IN MILITARY HISTORY.

THE NEXT DAY, MOSCOW GAVE ITS COMMANDERS PERMISSION TO WITHDRAW. IT WAS *TOO LATE*.

THE FORCES INSIDE THE RING STRUGGLED TO BREAK THROUGH THE ENCIRCLING TANKS AND INFANTRY, THEIR EFFORTS SET AGAINST A SOUNDTRACK OF STALIN'S SPEECHES, BLARING OUT FROM SPEAKERS STRUNG IN THE TREES...

OUT OF FOOD AND AMMUNITION, MOST HAD NO CHOICE BUT TO *SURRENDER*. SOME *650,000 RUSSIANS* WALKED INTO GERMAN CAPTIVITY.

THE GERMANS ALSO CLAIMED TO HAVE CAPTURED 3,718 PIECES OF ARTILLERY AND 886 TANKS.

HITLER CALLED IT ONE OF THE GREATEST VICTORIES IN HISTORY--AND UP TO THAT TIME, IT PROBABLY *WAS*.

THURSDAY, SEPTEMBER 18, WAS A TIME OF MUCH CONFUSION AND EXCITEMENT ON THE STREETS OF KIEV.

HAPPY, SMILING FACES WERE MIXED WITH ANXIOUS, SERIOUS ONES...

...AND THAT EVENING, THE FOUR BRIDGES ACROSS THE DNIEPER WERE BLOWN UP BY SOVIET FORCES!

LATER, WHEN I HEARD THE NEWS, THIS SEEMED TO ME A LITTLE RIDICULOUS, SINCE THE GERMANS NOW HELD BOTH BANKS.

I DIDN'T SLEEP WELL THAT NIGHT. I GUESS THE FUTURE HELD TOO MANY QUESTIONS...

THE DAYS WERE GETTING SHORTER ALREADY, AND WHEN THE SUN ROSE BEFORE SIX THE NEXT MORNING, I NOTICED THAT VASILY WAS ALREADY UP AND OUT OF THE BEDROOM.

I FOUND UNCLE TARAS UP, TOO, SITTING ON THE FRONT PORCH.

GOOD MORNING...

HAVE YOU SEEN VASILY?

YES. HE WENT WALKING DOWN TO THE MAIN ROAD.

I THINK HE WANTS TO BE THE FIRST TO SEE THE GERMANS.

DO YOU THINK HE WILL BE ALL RIGHT?

I THINK SO.

THE GERMANS DROPPED LEAFLETS TO SAY THEY WOULD NOT BOMB THE CITY...

...THEY ALSO SAY THERE'S NO REASON TO HIDE.

UNCLE TARAS, I'M SO GLAD AFTER ALL THESE YEARS YOU'VE ENDED YOUR PILGRIMAGE AND HAVE BECOME PART OF THE FAMILY...

"ENDED" MY PILGRIMAGE?

KATUSHA, MY PILGRIMAGE ISN'T OVER YET. A PART OF MY PILGRIMAGE HAS BROUGHT ME HERE-- THAT WAS *ALL*.

NO, IT *HASN'T* ENDED...

...AND NEITHER HAS *YOURS*.

WE EACH FACE OUR OWN PILGRIMAGE. YOUR FATHER AND MOTHER BOTH DO--NATASHA AND VASILY HAVE THEIR PILGRIMAGES AHEAD OF THEM...

...*MILLA* MOST ASSUREDLY DOES.

THIS PILGRIMAGE IS CALLED *LIFE*.

AND *NO ONE* KNOWS HOW IT WILL *END*...

VASILY WAS FIRST TO SEE THE GERMAN ARMY AS IT CAME UP THE LONG, DUSTY ROAD.

THIS WAS TRULY A REMARKABLE ARMY...

...AN ARMY THAT, TIME AND TIME AGAIN, HAD BEEN SUCCESSFUL AGAINST SUPERIOR NUMBERS.

THEIR RANKS INCLUDED HIGHLY EDUCATED MEN AND THOSE RIGHT OFF THE FARM. BUT THEY ALL HAD THIS IN COMMON:

THEY WERE *GERMAN,* AND THEY ALL TOOK GREAT PRIDE IN THAT FACT.

THEY HELD AN ABSOLUTE FAITH IN THEIR LEADERS, BOTH POLITICAL AND MILITARY, FOR THEY HAD ENJOYED UNBROKEN AND MIRACULOUS SUCCESSES UNDER THEIR DIRECTION.

BUT BEHIND THIS CONFIDENCE WAS A DARK CLOUD OF *CONTRADICTION.* IN ITS MUNDANE FORM, IT SHOWED AS OVERDEVELOPED *PRIDE.* AND AT ITS *WORST--*

IT WAS A DEEP-SEATED AND UNREASONABLE *HATRED* FOR ANYTHING OR ANYONE THEY CONSIDERED LESS WORTHY AND LESS PRIVILEGED THAN *THEMSELVES.*

BEHOLD THE BEAST

THE *PECHERSK LAVRA*, OR THE MONASTERY OF THE CAVES, HAS STOOD OVER KIEV SINCE 1051.

BUT ON *SEPTEMBER 19, 1941*, A HUGE FLAG WITH A GLARING SWASTIKA WAS UNFURLED FROM HIGH ATOP THE CHURCH'S BELL TOWER.

IT COULD BE SEEN FROM ALL OVER KIEV.

THE WARY POPULATION DRIBBLED OUT ONTO THE *KHRESCHATYK* TO GAUGE THEIR NEW MASTERS. BOTH SIDES HELD BACK, ANXIOUS AND UNCERTAIN. FOR A LONG, TENSE MOMENT, THE TWO GROUPS STARED AT EACH OTHER, SULLENLY SILENT...

A FEW ON BOTH SIDES TRIED INVESTING FRIENDLY GESTURES AND LITTLE SMILES, BUT IT FINALLY FELL TO THE CHILDREN TO BREAK THE ICE.

I REMEMBER SEEING A LITTLE JEWISH GIRL COME UP TO ONE OF THE GERMAN SOLDIERS AND OFFER HIM THE GIFT OF BREAD AND SALT...

THE GERMANS SMILED AND ACCEPTED THE GIFT--AND PEOPLE BEGAN TO RELAX.

THERE WAS A SOLDIER WHO CALLED OUT TO ME IN WORDS I UNDERSTOOD ONLY ENOUGH TO LAUGHINGLY CORRECT...

HEY, GIRL-- MISS...!

BOLSHEVIK, FINNISH, UKRAINA!

"UKRAYEENA"!

JA, JA! "U-KRAY-EENA"! GO WALK, SPAZIEREN, BITTE!

I HAD NO IDEA *WHAT* HE COULD BE SAYING--

--BUT I FELT MAMA'S HAND *TIGHTEN* OVER MINE.

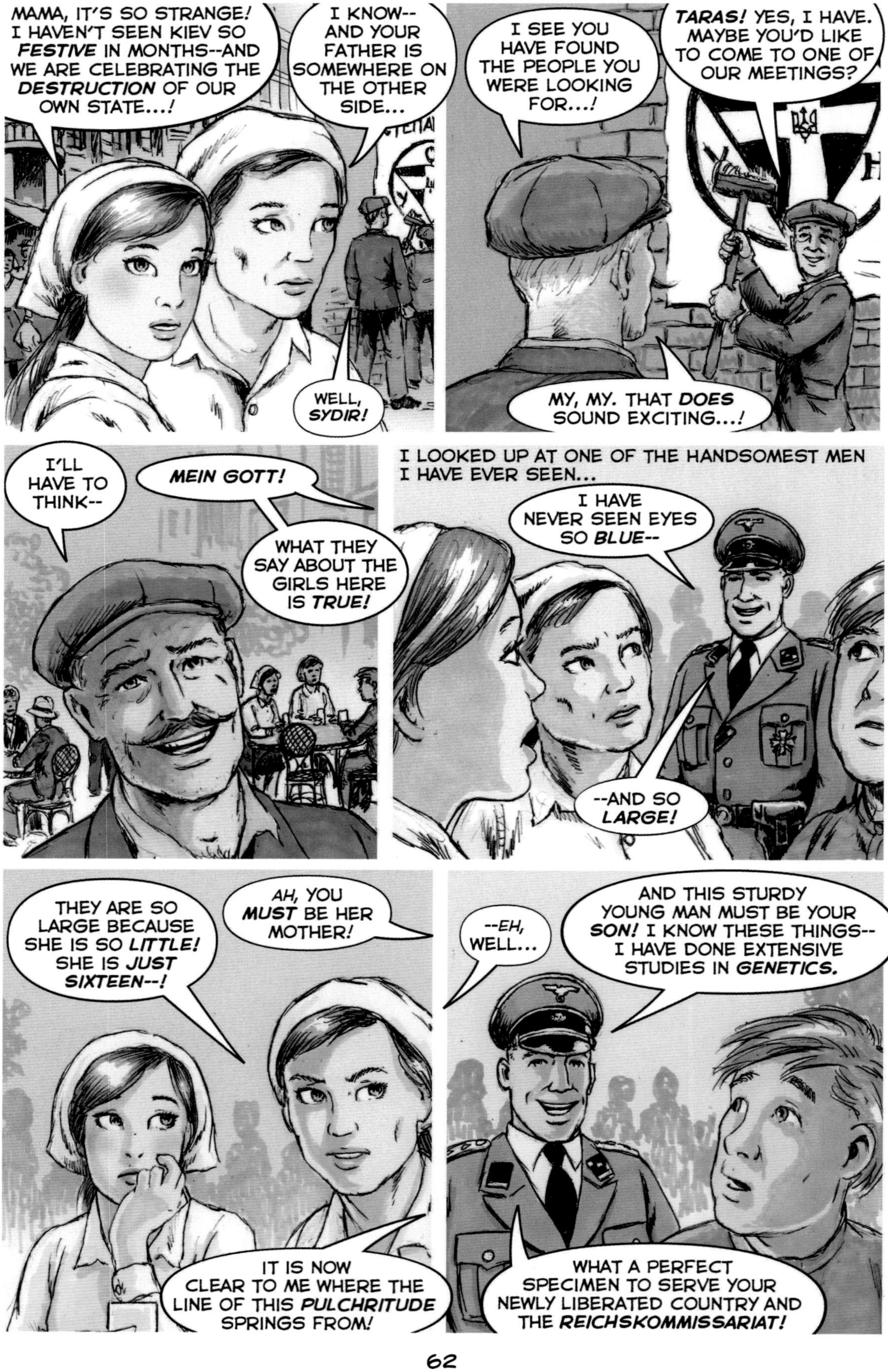
MAMA, IT'S SO STRANGE! I HAVEN'T SEEN KIEV SO *FESTIVE* IN MONTHS--AND WE ARE CELEBRATING THE *DESTRUCTION* OF OUR OWN STATE...!
I KNOW-- AND YOUR FATHER IS SOMEWHERE ON THE OTHER SIDE...
WELL, *SYDIR!*
I SEE YOU HAVE FOUND THE PEOPLE YOU WERE LOOKING FOR...!
TARAS! YES, I HAVE. MAYBE YOU'D LIKE TO COME TO ONE OF OUR MEETINGS?
MY, MY. THAT *DOES* SOUND EXCITING...!
I'LL HAVE TO THINK--
MEIN GOTT!
WHAT THEY SAY ABOUT THE GIRLS HERE IS *TRUE!*
I LOOKED UP AT ONE OF THE HANDSOMEST MEN I HAVE EVER SEEN...
I HAVE NEVER SEEN EYES SO *BLUE*--
--AND SO *LARGE!*
THEY ARE SO LARGE BECAUSE SHE IS SO *LITTLE!* SHE IS *JUST SIXTEEN--!*
AH, YOU *MUST* BE HER MOTHER!
IT IS NOW CLEAR TO ME WHERE THE LINE OF THIS *PULCHRITUDE* SPRINGS FROM!
--EH, WELL...
AND THIS STURDY YOUNG MAN MUST BE YOUR *SON!* I KNOW THESE THINGS-- I HAVE DONE EXTENSIVE STUDIES IN *GENETICS.*
WHAT A PERFECT SPECIMEN TO SERVE YOUR NEWLY LIBERATED COUNTRY AND THE *REICHSKOMMISSARIAT!*

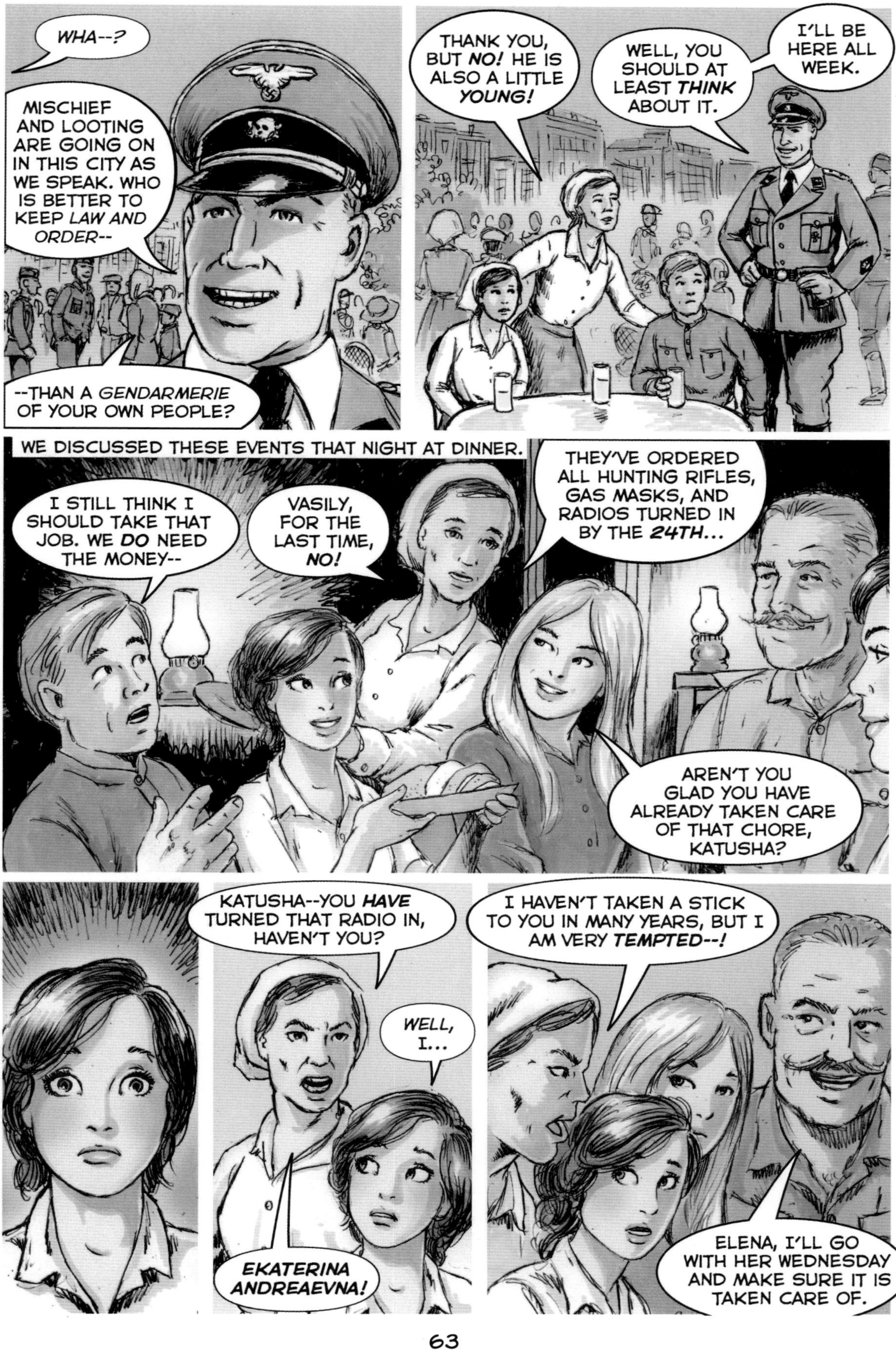
WHA--?
MISCHIEF AND LOOTING ARE GOING ON IN THIS CITY AS WE SPEAK. WHO IS BETTER TO KEEP LAW AND ORDER--
--THAN A GENDARMERIE OF YOUR OWN PEOPLE?
THANK YOU, BUT NO! HE IS ALSO A LITTLE YOUNG!
WELL, YOU SHOULD AT LEAST THINK ABOUT IT.
I'LL BE HERE ALL WEEK.
WE DISCUSSED THESE EVENTS THAT NIGHT AT DINNER.
I STILL THINK I SHOULD TAKE THAT JOB. WE DO NEED THE MONEY--
VASILY, FOR THE LAST TIME, NO!
THEY'VE ORDERED ALL HUNTING RIFLES, GAS MASKS, AND RADIOS TURNED IN BY THE 24TH...
AREN'T YOU GLAD YOU HAVE ALREADY TAKEN CARE OF THAT CHORE, KATUSHA?
KATUSHA--YOU HAVE TURNED THAT RADIO IN, HAVEN'T YOU?
WELL, I...
EKATERINA ANDREAEVNA!
I HAVEN'T TAKEN A STICK TO YOU IN MANY YEARS, BUT I AM VERY TEMPTED--!
ELENA, I'LL GO WITH HER WEDNESDAY AND MAKE SURE IT IS TAKEN CARE OF.

ON THE AFTERNOON OF **WEDNESDAY, SEPTEMBER 24,** VASILY, UNCLE TARAS, AND I WENT DOWN TO THE *KHRESCHATYK* TO TURN IN MY RADIO WHERE THE GERMAN FIELD COMMAND HAD SET UP SHOP IN A FORMER HOTEL AT NUMBER 1 SVERDLOV STREET.

CAN YOU BELIEVE THIS *MOB* OF PEOPLE? WE'LL BE HERE *ALL DAY!*

WELL, THAT IS *ONE THING* THE *BOLSHEVIKS* HAVE MANAGED TO DO...

THEY HAVE TAUGHT PEOPLE HOW TO STAND IN *LONG LINES.*

WELL, IF IT ISN'T THE *UKRAINIAN ROSE!* ALLOW ME TO BE OF ASSISTANCE.

LET ME ESCORT YOU AND YOUR PARTY TO THE FRONT OF THE LINE.

AND YOUR *BROTHER*-- HAS HE THOUGHT ANY MORE ABOUT JOINING THE *SCHUMA?*

YEAH--SEE IF YOUR *MOTHER* WILL LET YOU COME OUT TO PLAY, *RUNT!*

HONSHAR!

IT WAS ABOUT TWO IN THE AFTERNOON. WE WERE ONE HUNDRED YARDS FROM THE OLD *DETSKII MIR* TOY STORE, RIGHT NEXT TO THE GERMAN HEADQUARTERS.

SUDDENLY...

WHA--?!

WITHIN SECONDS, MORE MINES EXPLODED IN THE TOY STORE AND THE HOTEL--
TEARING TO BITS BOTH GERMANS IN THE BUILDING AND PEOPLE IN LINE!

THE BLAST OVERTURNED GERMAN TRUCKS PASSING BY ON THE STREET--

--KILLING OR INJURING THE SOLDIERS INSIDE!

THEN THE ROOFS AND UPPER FLOORS OF THE BUILDING COLLAPSED--

--CRUSHING AND BURYING CIVILIANS IN THE RUBBLE!

THIS ACT OF SABOTAGE IS MONSTROUS!

WE KNOW WHO IS RESPONSIBLE-- AND WE WILL TAKE THE APPROPRIATE MEASURES!

THAT'S IT, KATUSHA! I'M NOT COMING HOME WITH YOU--!

I'M GOING TO JOIN THE SCHUMA!

NO--VASILY!

COME BACK!

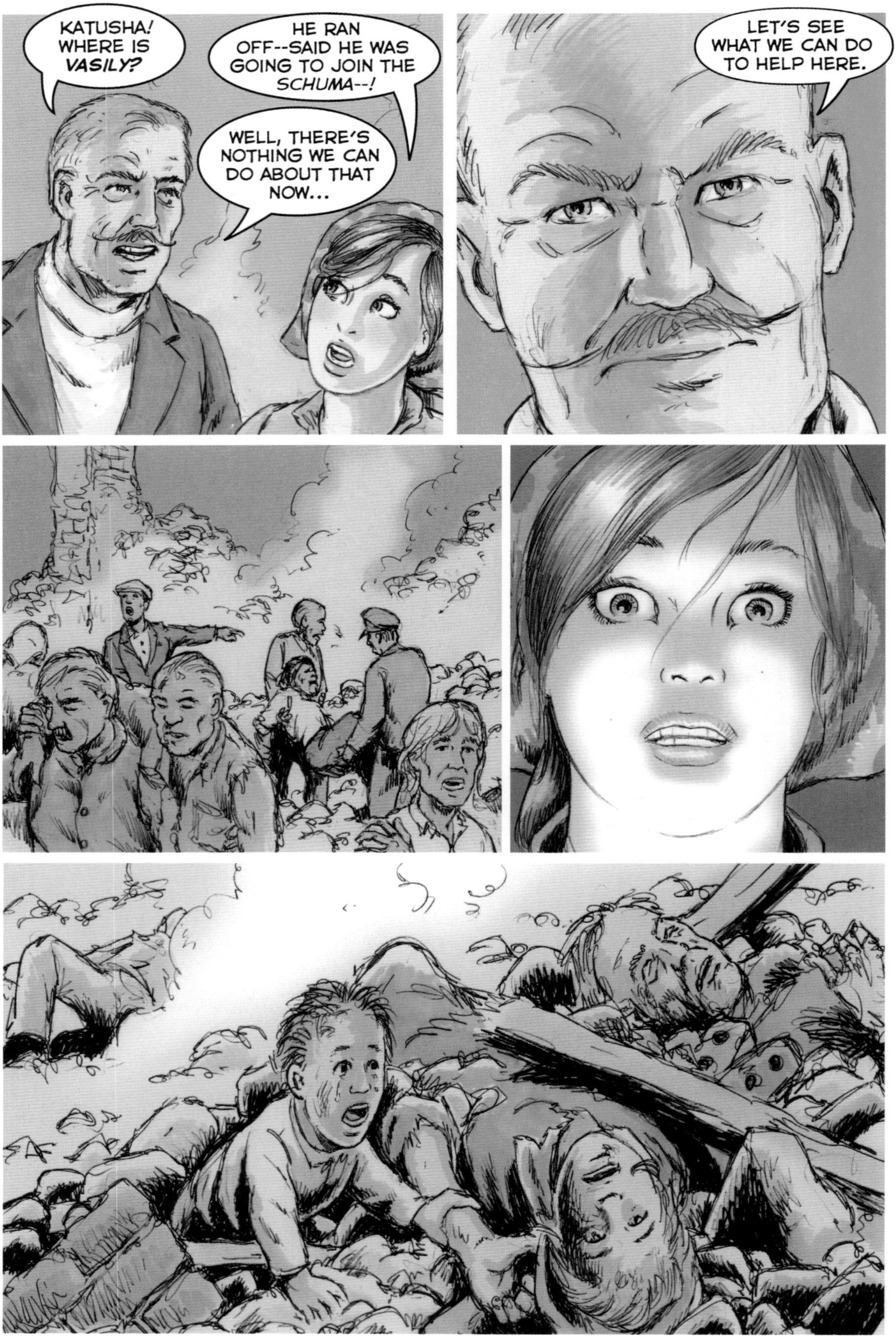
KATUSHA! WHERE IS VASILY?
HE RAN OFF--SAID HE WAS GOING TO JOIN THE SCHUMA--!
WELL, THERE'S NOTHING WE CAN DO ABOUT THAT NOW...
LET'S SEE WHAT WE CAN DO TO HELP HERE.

IN THE NEXT FEW HOURS AND ON INTO THE NIGHT, *EXPLOSIONS* ROCKED THE CENTER OF KIEV AS *MINES* LEFT BY THE *NKVD* TORE APART HOTELS AND PUBLIC BUILDINGS.

SINCE THE FORMER COMMUNIST GOVERNMENT HAD DESTROYED THE WATER-PUMPING STATIONS BEFORE THEY FLED, FIGHTING THE FIRES THAT FOLLOWED WAS ALL BUT *IMPOSSIBLE*.

WELL, WE BROUGHT THE RADIO BACK--BUT NOT *VASILY*.

IT'S NOT THE FAULT OF EITHER OF YOU. VASILY IS STRONG-WILLED.

NOW I PRAY THAT MY SON IS JUST *STRONG*.

THE FIRES BURNED ON FOR FIVE DAYS AND NIGHTS.

HUNDREDS OF GERMANS AND AT LEAST AS MANY KIEVANS WERE KILLED IN THE BOMBING, AND 25,000 PEOPLE WERE MADE HOMELESS...

...ALL AS A RESULT OF STALIN'S *SCORCHED-EARTH POLICY*.

THE GERMANS BEGAN TO CRACK DOWN ON ALL SORTS OF ACTIVITIES...COMMUNISTS WERE TRACKED DOWN AND *SHOT.*

NATIONALIST GROUPS, WHICH AT FIRST HAD BEEN TOLERATED, WERE NOW *ARRESTED--* AND SOMETIMES *EXECUTED.*

WELL, *SYDIR--* I'M SORT OF GLAD THAT I *DIDN'T* MAKE YOUR MEETING.

THE ROUNDUP OF THE *JEWS* BEGAN IN EARNEST. WORD WAS PUT OUT THAT JEWS WERE RESPONSIBLE FOR THE MINES AND FIRES, AND MUCH OF THE POPULATION ACCEPTED THIS.

ON *SUNDAY, SEPTEMBER 28,* ALL JEWS WERE ORDERED TO PACK UP AND ASSEMBLE AT THE CORNER OF MELNYK AND DEHTIARIVSKA STREETS--

--FOR "RELOCATION."

MANY KIEVANS HATED JEWS--AND AS USUALLY HAS BEEN THE CASE THROUGHOUT HISTORY, THEY PROBABLY COULD NOT EXPLAIN *WHY.* THEY WEREN'T SAD TO SEE THEM GO...

SO LONG, *ZHID!*

STILL, THEY WEREN'T PREPARED TO FIND OUT LATER WHAT HAD *REALLY* HAPPENED TO THEIR NEIGHBORS.

LATER, WHEN TARAS AND MILLA WENT INTO THE CITY TO PICK UP NEWS, THEY FOUND THE POPULATION TENSE AND THE GERMANS SERIOUS.

THE LEVITY OF THOSE FIRST DAYS AFTER THEIR ARRIVAL WAS GONE AND FORGOTTEN.

THE HOUSEHOLD CHORES DONE, I SPOKE WITH MAMA AS WE DID OUR NEEDLEWORK...

69

"AS YOU PROBABLY REMEMBER, TARAS AND YOUR FATHER BOTH FOLLOWED *SEMEN KALASHNIKOV* INTO MILITARY SERVICE DURING THE FIRST WORLD WAR...

"YOUR FATHER, WHO WAS ALWAYS MECHANICALLY INCLINED, WAS ASSIGNED TO A MACHINE-GUN ORDNANCE COMPANY...

"...WHILE TARAS BECAME A COURIER ON GENERAL BRUSILOV'S STAFF, WHERE SEMEN SERVED AS A PLANNING OFFICER.

"FROM THE VERY BEGINNING, THE WAR DID NOT GO WELL FOR RUSSIA. WE WERE A 19TH-CENTURY PEOPLE FIGHTING A 20TH-CENTURY WAR.

"THE COMMON SOLDIER SUFFERED TERRIBLE HARDSHIPS, WHICH FROM THE FIRST DAYS NURTURED *REVOLUTIONARY FEELINGS.*

"YOUR FATHER WAS BADLY WOUNDED IN THE SUMMER OF 1916. WHEN HE RECOVERED, HE WAS SENT TO A MACHINE-GUN BATTALION IN *ST. PETERSBURG.*

"HE FOUND IT FILLED WITH *RADICALS* AND *BOLSHEVIKS.*

"THEY WERE SO REBELLIOUS THAT THE GENERAL STAFF FEARED THAT SENDING THEM TO THE FRONT WOULD LEAD TO A MUTINY."

"THEN CAME THE *FEBRUARY REVOLUTION OF 1917*.

"THE GREATEST PART OF SOCIETY ROSE UP AGAINST THE GOVERNMENT AND FORCED THE CZAR TO *ABDICATE*. A PROVISIONAL GOVERNMENT WAS FORMED UNDER *KERENSKY*.

"*DEMOCRACY* WAS BORN IN RUSSIA...

"IT WOULD BE *MURDERED* IN ITS CRIB.

"THE PROVISIONAL GOVERNMENT MADE A BIG MISTAKE BY NOT WITHDRAWING US FROM THE *GREAT WAR*.

"BY 1917, MILLIONS OF RUSSIANS HAD DIED-- AND THE PEOPLE DESPERATELY WANTED *PEACE*.

"*VLADIMIR LENIN*, LEADER OF THE BOLSHEVIK PARTY, RETURNED FROM A 14-YEAR EXILE TO PROMISE THE PEOPLE:

PEACE!

LAND!

BREAD!

"OF COURSE, *NOT ONE* OF THESE PROMISES WAS EVER FULFILLED.

"ON THE NIGHT OF *NOVEMBER 7, 1917*, THE CRUISER *AURORA* OPENED FIRE ON THE WINTER PALACE IN SAINT PETERSBURG...

"THE *BOLSHEVIK REVOLUTION* HAD BEGUN!

"IN AN ALMOST BLOODLESS COUP, THEY GAINED CONTROL OF THE CITY AND BEGAN THEIR *SOCIAL REVOLUTION*.

"AND YOUR *FATHER*, AS PART OF THE MACHINE-GUN BATTALION, WAS CARRIED ALONG INTO HISTORY."

"WHEN THE REVOLUTION REACHED THE FRONT, WHOLE RUSSIAN UNITS REVOLTED, SHOT THEIR OFFICERS, AND DESERTED THEIR POSITIONS. THE GERMANS POURED THROUGH THE GAPS, ADVANCING EAST.

"AND NEXT IS WHERE THE STORY TAKES AN UNSURE TURN...

"SOME TELL HOW KALASHNIKOV AND TARAS HALTED A RETREATING UNIT OF DESERTERS. SEMEN URGED THEM TO RETURN TO THEIR ASSIGNED POSITIONS...

"...BUT HIS OBVIOUSLY REFINED SPEECH CAUSED THE MEN TO MISTAKE HIM FOR A MEMBER OF THE CZAR'S WEALTHY BOURGEOISIE.

"DRIVEN MAD BY MISGUIDED RAGE, THE REVOLUTIONARIES SWARMED THE TWO MEN AND OVERCAME THEM. THEN THEY STRIPPED KALASHNIKOV AND TIED HIM TO A TREE...

"WHILE TARAS, TIED UP AND HELD CLOSE BY, WAS FORCED TO *WATCH*--

"--AS THE SOLDIERS SLOWLY *TORTURED* KALASHNIKOV TO *DEATH!*

"THAT NIGHT, TARAS MANAGED TO SLIP HIS KNOTS, STRANGLE A GUARD, AND ESCAPE-- TAKING WITH HIM KALASHNIKOV'S BODY.

"TARAS BROUGHT HIM BACK TO KROVROT AND BURIED HIM IN OUR LITTLE CEMETERY...

"ONE ACCOUNT HAS IT THAT HE BURIED HIS FRIEND AND MENTOR IN A SECLUDED PLACE, SO THAT THE REVOLUTIONARIES COULD NEVER DESECRATE HIS GRAVE."

YOU SAID THE STORY "TOOK AN UNSURE TURN"?

YES. BECAUSE *SOME* SAY SEMEN KALASHNIKOV LED A WHITE ARMY UNIT IN THE CIVIL WAR--

--BUT *OTHERS* SWEAR HE WAS A UKRAINIAN GUERRILLA LEADER...

"...OR THAT HE USED HIS BAND TO RAID SUPPLIES FROM BOTH THE GERMAN AND RED ARMIES TO FEED HUNGRY PEASANTS.

"THEY SAY HE WAS FINALLY CAPTURED AND CARRIED OFF INTO EXILE IN *SIBERIA*.

"I REMEMBER HIS WIFE BACK IN KROVROT *GRIEVING* TO *DEATH*.

"YOUR FATHER, BECAUSE OF HIS TALENT WITH MACHINERY, WAS ASSIGNED TO TROTSKY'S WAR TRAIN, RUSHING FROM BATTLEFIELD TO BATTLEFIELD DURING THE CIVIL WAR...

"THERE WAS NO NEWS OF TARAS. MANY BELIEVED HE WAS *DEAD*."

JUST BEFORE DARK, TARAS AND MILLA RETURNED HOME.

WELL, THE HONEYMOON IS OVER...

THE GERMANS HAVE *CHECKPOINTS* EVERYWHERE, AND THEY HAVE TIGHT CONTROL OF WHO COMES IN AND WHO LEAVES THE CITY...

...AND NO SIGN OF *VASILY.*

WE ALL WENT TO BED EARLY, BUT I'M SURE THAT NONE OF US SLEPT...

IT WAS ABOUT *11 PM* WHEN WE ALL HEARD FOOTSTEPS OUTSIDE AND A LIGHT KNOCK ON THE DOOR.

DON'T WORRY. THE *NKVD* HAS A LOUD KNOCK...

...AND THE GERMANS DON'T KNOCK *AT ALL.*

IS THAT *YOU,* VASILY?

YES! AND A FRIEND.

WHO IS IT?

ZHENYA!

KATUSHA, THEY *KILLED MY PARENTS...!*

⟩SOB⟨---MY WHOLE *FAMILY* IS *DEAD...!*

AS MILLA, NATASHA, AND I TRIED TO CALM DOWN ZHENYA AS BEST WE COULD, UNCLE TARAS AND MAMA TALKED WITH VASILY...

MAMA, I'M SORRY I RAN OFF TO JOIN THE *SCHUMA*. I SHOULD'VE LISTENED TO YOU...

I'M JUST GLAD YOU'RE HOME, AND *SAFE*.

WHAT *HAPPENED*, VASILY?

THEY TOLD US TO KEEP THE JEWS IN ORDER...

"WE WERE TO LEAD THEM TO TRANSPORT FOR THE RESETTLING. I THOUGHT IT ODD THAT WE WERE HEADING AWAY FROM THE RAILROAD TRACKS--BUT I SUPPOSED TRUCKS WOULD BE WAITING ELSEWHERE, OR SOMETHING...

"THE PEOPLE WERE VERY MUCH AFRAID.

"SOME WERE CRYING AND PRAYING OUT LOUD--OTHERS WERE TRYING TO CALM THEIR CHILDREN, TELLING THEM THERE WAS NOTHING TO WORRY ABOUT. YOU COULD TELL BY THEIR DRESS WHETHER THEY WERE RICH OR POOR, EDUCATED OR PEASANT...

"AS WE NEARED THE OLD RAVINE, I COULD HEAR *GUNSHOTS* FROM UP AHEAD. I WONDERED-- WERE SOME MAKING TROUBLE, AND THE SHOTS WERE TO HERD THEM BACK INTO THE LINE? BUT THE FIRING *INCREASED*--

"--AND THEN I HEARD WHAT SOUNDED LIKE *MACHINE-GUN FIRE...!*

"IT WAS THEN I FELT *FEAR* FOR WHAT I HAD GOTTEN MYSELF INTO."

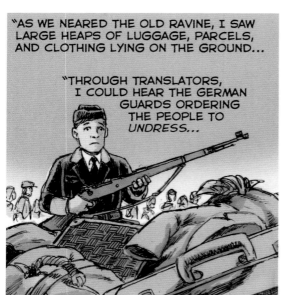

"AS WE NEARED THE OLD RAVINE, I SAW LARGE HEAPS OF LUGGAGE, PARCELS, AND CLOTHING LYING ON THE GROUND...

"THROUGH TRANSLATORS, I COULD HEAR THE GERMAN GUARDS ORDERING THE PEOPLE TO UNDRESS...

"THEY MADE THEM THROW THEIR CLOTHING ON THE TOP OF THE PILES THAT WERE ALREADY THERE. THEN, THEY DIVIDED THE PEOPLE INTO *TWO LINES*--

"--*MEN* IN ONE LINE...

"...AND *WOMEN* AND *CHILDREN* IN THE OTHER.

"IT WAS SO *HORRIBLE*, MAMA! IT SEEMED AS IF ONCE THIS NIGHTMARE HAD BEGUN, IT COULD *NOT* BE *STOPPED*...! THE POOR PEOPLE DID THEIR BEST TO RETAIN SOME SORT OF DIGNITY, DESPITE THEIR DISCOMFORT IN BEING NAKED IN FRONT OF US...

"I REMEMBER A GIRL WHO LOOKED ME RIGHT IN THE EYE AND THEN POINTED TO HERSELF AND SAID--

TWENTY-ONE YEARS OLD!

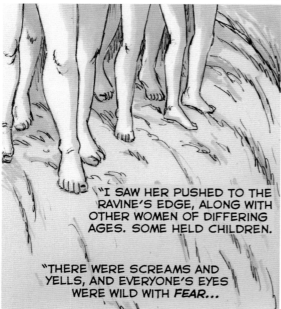

"I SAW HER PUSHED TO THE RAVINE'S EDGE, ALONG WITH OTHER WOMEN OF DIFFERING AGES. SOME HELD CHILDREN.

"THERE WERE SCREAMS AND YELLS, AND EVERYONE'S EYES WERE WILD WITH *FEAR*...

"... AND *THEN*--

"--THE MACHINE-GUN FIRE *TORE INTO* THEM...!"

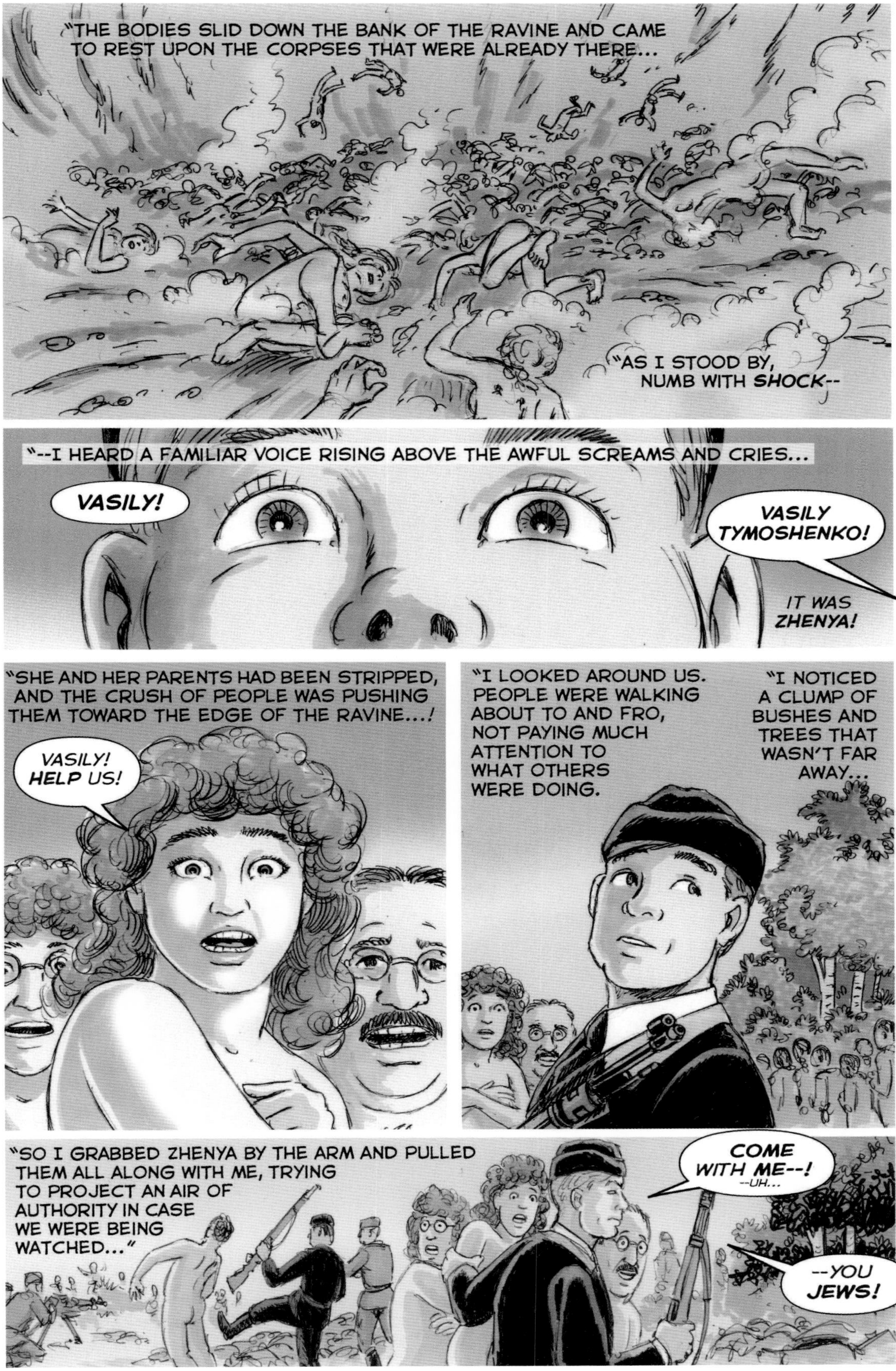
"THE BODIES SLID DOWN THE BANK OF THE RAVINE AND CAME TO REST UPON THE CORPSES THAT WERE ALREADY THERE...
"AS I STOOD BY, NUMB WITH SHOCK--
"--I HEARD A FAMILIAR VOICE RISING ABOVE THE AWFUL SCREAMS AND CRIES...
VASILY!
VASILY TYMOSHENKO!
IT WAS ZHENYA!
"SHE AND HER PARENTS HAD BEEN STRIPPED, AND THE CRUSH OF PEOPLE WAS PUSHING THEM TOWARD THE EDGE OF THE RAVINE...!
VASILY! HELP US!
"I LOOKED AROUND US. PEOPLE WERE WALKING ABOUT TO AND FRO, NOT PAYING MUCH ATTENTION TO WHAT OTHERS WERE DOING.
"I NOTICED A CLUMP OF BUSHES AND TREES THAT WASN'T FAR AWAY...
"SO I GRABBED ZHENYA BY THE ARM AND PULLED THEM ALL ALONG WITH ME, TRYING TO PROJECT AN AIR OF AUTHORITY IN CASE WE WERE BEING WATCHED..."
COME WITH ME--! --UH...
--YOU JEWS!

"AS I PULLED THEM AWAY, I LOOKED BACK AT THE RAVINE--AND MY GUTS HEAVED. GUNSHOTS ECHOED AS AN ENDLESS LINE OF BODIES SLOWLY TUMBLED DOWN, DOWN ONTO THE PILE BELOW.

"SOME WERE DEAD-- OTHERS WERE TOO WOUNDED TO FLEE...

"FOR ALL, THEIR LAST FEW MINUTES ON THIS EARTH WERE AN EXCRUCIATING *TORMENT.*

"WALKING PAST THE HEAPS OF CLOTHING, I QUICKLY GRABBED A FEW THINGS SO THEY COULD COVER THEIR NAKEDNESS. SO FAR, WE'D BEEN EXTREMELY *LUCKY...*

"BUT RIGHT THEN, I *HEARD* HIM--!

HEY, RUNT--!!

"--IT WAS *HONSHAR!*

--JUST *WHAT* DO YOU THINK YOU'RE UP TO--?!!

"HE WAS THE SAME BULLY HE EVER WAS--NO SURPRISE TO ME.

"WHETHER *CZARIST, COMMUNIST, FASCIST--*

"...A BULLY IS A *BULLY.*

"HE CAME CHARGING AT US. IT WAS CLEAR HE INTENDED TO TAKE CHARGE OF THE CAPTIVES.

"SO I SWUNG THE BUTT OF MY RIFLE AGAINST HIS JAW, AS *HARD* AS I *COULD*--!!

"--AND I FELT *BONE CRACK!*

"THEN HE SLID TO THE GROUND WITH A *THUD...*

"...OUT COLD.

"BUT SUDDENLY, A *VOICE* RANG OUT IN GERMAN--!"

WAS IST LOS HIER?!

EVERYBODY, RUN!!!

78

"NOT ONLY DID *WE* BEGIN TO RUN, BUT OTHERS AROUND US--CLOTHED AND NAKED--SAW THEIR CHANCE, *TOO!*

HALT! HALT!

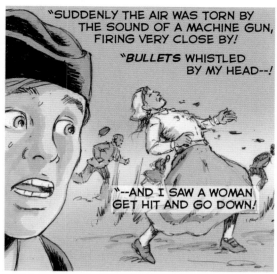

"SUDDENLY THE AIR WAS TORN BY THE SOUND OF A MACHINE GUN, FIRING VERY CLOSE BY!

"*BULLETS* WHISTLED BY MY HEAD--!

"--AND I SAW A WOMAN GET HIT AND GO DOWN!

"I SHOT A GLANCE BACK OVER MY SHOULDER, TRYING TO PINPOINT THE SOURCE OF OUR TROUBLES...

"IT WAS A *GERMAN GUARD!*

"HE HAD A VERY DEADLY LOOKING WEAPON--AND HE WAS *FIRING AWAY!*

"THE BULLETS RIPPED INTO MR. AND MRS. GERSTEINFELD! THEY FELL TO THE GROUND, *LIFELESS--!!*

"I WAS GLAD ZHENYA HAD RUN AHEAD OF US, SO SHE DIDN'T SEE IT HAPPEN. *OHH*, IT WAS AN *AWFUL* THING TO SEE...!

"I TURNED AND RAISED THE RIFLE THEY HAD GIVEN ME--BUT ALL I COULD THINK OF WAS HOW I'D *NEVER* FIRED A GUN IN MY LIFE...!

"I AIMED AS BEST I COULD IN THE GERMAN'S GENERAL DIRECTION--!"

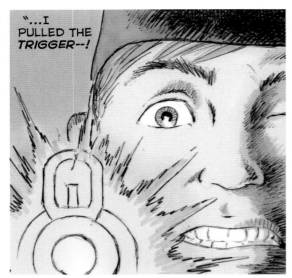

"...I PULLED THE *TRIGGER*--!"

"--AND A *FIRING SQUAD* COULD NOT HAVE DONE BETTER!"

"BY NOW, GUNFIRE WAS COMING FROM EVERY QUARTER."

"MOST OF THOSE WHO HAD TRIED TO MAKE THE DASH TO SAFETY WITH US NOW LAY BEHIND ON THE GROUND, BLEEDING..."

"AHEAD OF ME, I SAW ZHENYA RUN TOWARD THE TREES. I FOLLOWED HER."

"WE RAN THROUGH FIELDS, OVER FENCES, ACROSS PEOPLE'S BACKYARDS..."

"LUCKILY FOR US, WE SAW NO ONE--"

"--AND NO ONE SAW *US*."

"I TOOK TWO BEDSHEETS FROM A CLOTHESLINE SO THAT ZHENYA COULD COVER HERSELF."

"...AND I THOUGHT THAT SHE WOULD CRY *FOREVER*."

"WE FINALLY FOUND A CULVERT TO HIDE IN. IT WAS THERE THAT ZHENYA ASKED ME WHAT HAD HAPPENED TO HER *PARENTS*."

"I TOLD HER..."

FOR A FEW MOMENTS, UNCLE TARAS SAT THERE IN SILENCE. THEN HE SPOKE...

VASILY, WHEN YOU SIGNED UP WITH THE *SCHUMA*--

--DID YOU GIVE THEM YOUR ADDRESS?

NO--THEY WERE TOO RUSHED.

THIS *HONSHAR* FELLOW YOU BANGED UP--DOES HE KNOW WHERE YOU LIVE?

HE'S NEVER BEEN HERE, BUT I'M SURE HE'D KNOW HOW TO FIND OUT.

OKAY. I THINK IT'S TIME WE ALL TOOK A TRIP.

A TRIP? *WHERE?*

KROVROT. HOW LONG HAS IT BEEN SINCE YOU'VE SEEN YOUR *MOTHER*, ELENA?

LET'S START *PACKING.* GATHER ALL THE CANNED FOOD WE CAN CARRY.

CHECK THAT EVERYONE HAS GOOD BOOTS, AND STURDY CLOTHES--NOTHING FANCY. WHAT WE DON'T HAVE, WE'LL JUST HAVE TO *BUY.*

"BUY"? USING *WHAT?*

OH, NEVER YOU MIND...

KATUSHA, MILLA--I NEED YOUR HELP IN THE *BARN.*

THERE'S *SEVEN* OF US... *EIGHT*, WITH DIMA. AND HE'LL HAVE TO BE CARRIED. HMM... UNCLE TARAS, COULD THE WHEELBARROW BE OF ANY USE?

PROBABLY NOT--TOO UNWIELDY.

NOW, WHERE IS MY *LUGER...?* --AH, *THERE* YOU ARE...!

...AND *SHH*--! LOOK WHAT *ELSE* I HAVE HERE--!

WHY, *UNCLE TARAS! LOOK* AT ALL THAT *MONEY*--!

HAHAHA! SO--

--YOU REALLY *DID* ROB THE *REICHSBANK!*

HAVE I *EVER* LIED TO YOU?

HOW ABOUT MY RADIO?

GOOD IDEA! IT WILL HELP KEEP US INFORMED.

DESPITE THE TERRIBLE THINGS THAT HAD JUST HAPPENED AND ALL THE DANGERS WE FACED--I WAS FEELING *EXCITED!*

WE WERE GOING ON A *GREAT ADVENTURE!*

WE TRUSTED UNCLE TARAS' EXPERIENCE AND INSTINCTS AND DID AS HE INSTRUCTED US.

ALL RIGHT, WE'RE ALL PACKED. NOW EVERYONE GET SOME *SLEEP*--WE'LL HEAD OUT AROUND THREE IN THE MORNING.

WE'VE GOT A LONG WAY TO GO.

BEFORE WE WENT TO BED, MAMA TOOK A LITTLE LOOK AROUND OUR SIMPLE HOME FOR WHAT COULD BE THE LAST TIME.

I SAW LITTLE *TEARS* IN HER EYES...

...AND I FELT MY HEART *BREAK* FOR HER.

I'M GOING TO SLEEP IN THE BARN WITH THE DOOR OPEN, SO I'LL BE ABLE TO HEAR ANYONE WHO COMES UP TO THE HOUSE--

I'LL COME *WITH* YOU.

--EH?

WELL...?

...WHY NOT?

IT WAS QUIET, AND WE SLEPT AS BEST WE COULD...BUT SOMETIMES--

--WHEN THE WIND WAS RIGHT...

...WE COULD HEAR *GUNFIRE* STILL GOING ON AT *BABI YAR.*

A GERMAN TRUCK CAME UP OUR DIRT ROAD.

IT SLOWED DOWN, AS IF ITS DRIVER WERE LOOKING FOR SOMETHING...

THEN, IT *STOPPED*--

--IN FRONT OF *OUR HOUSE!*

MAMA HAD ALREADY WOKEN US UP, AND WE'D GATHERED TOGETHER OUR PARCELS...

...WHEN SUDDENLY, MILLA CAME RUSHING IN!

TARAS SAYS EVERYONE *OUT* THE *BACK DOOR!* QUICK!

AND *CUT* THAT *LIGHT!*

A GERMAN SERGEANT GOT OUT OF THE CAB AND WALKED TO OUR FRONT GATE.

THE DRIVER ALSO GOT OUT, BUT STAYED BY HIS VEHICLE.

TWO MEN GOT OUT OF THE BACK. ONE WAS A GERMAN SOLDIER...

THE OTHER WAS *PRIKIP HONSHAR,* HIS HURT JAW TIGHTLY WRAPPED.

THE DRIVER SMOKED A CIGARETTE WHILE HE WAITED BACK AT THE TRUCK, WATCHING AS THE THREE OTHERS CALMLY WALKED UP TO THE FRONT DOOR. THE MEN APPARENTLY FELT NO PANGS OF CONSCIENCE IN FULFILLING THEIR MISSION...

WE RAN OUT INTO THE BACKYARD, HIDING BEHIND THE BARN, THE OUTHOUSE, TREES--ANYTHING LARGE ENOUGH TO CONCEAL US...

THE SERGEANT LED THE WAY INTO OUR LITTLE HOME WITH A QUICK, VICIOUS KICK.

THEY SQUINTED TO SEE ANYTHING IN THE PITCH-BLACK FRONT ROOM...

THEN--THEY HEARD A MAN'S VOICE.

WELCOME.

...AND THAT WAS THE *LAST* VOICE THE TWO GERMANS EVER HEARD.

KRAW! KRAW! KRA KRAW! KRAW!

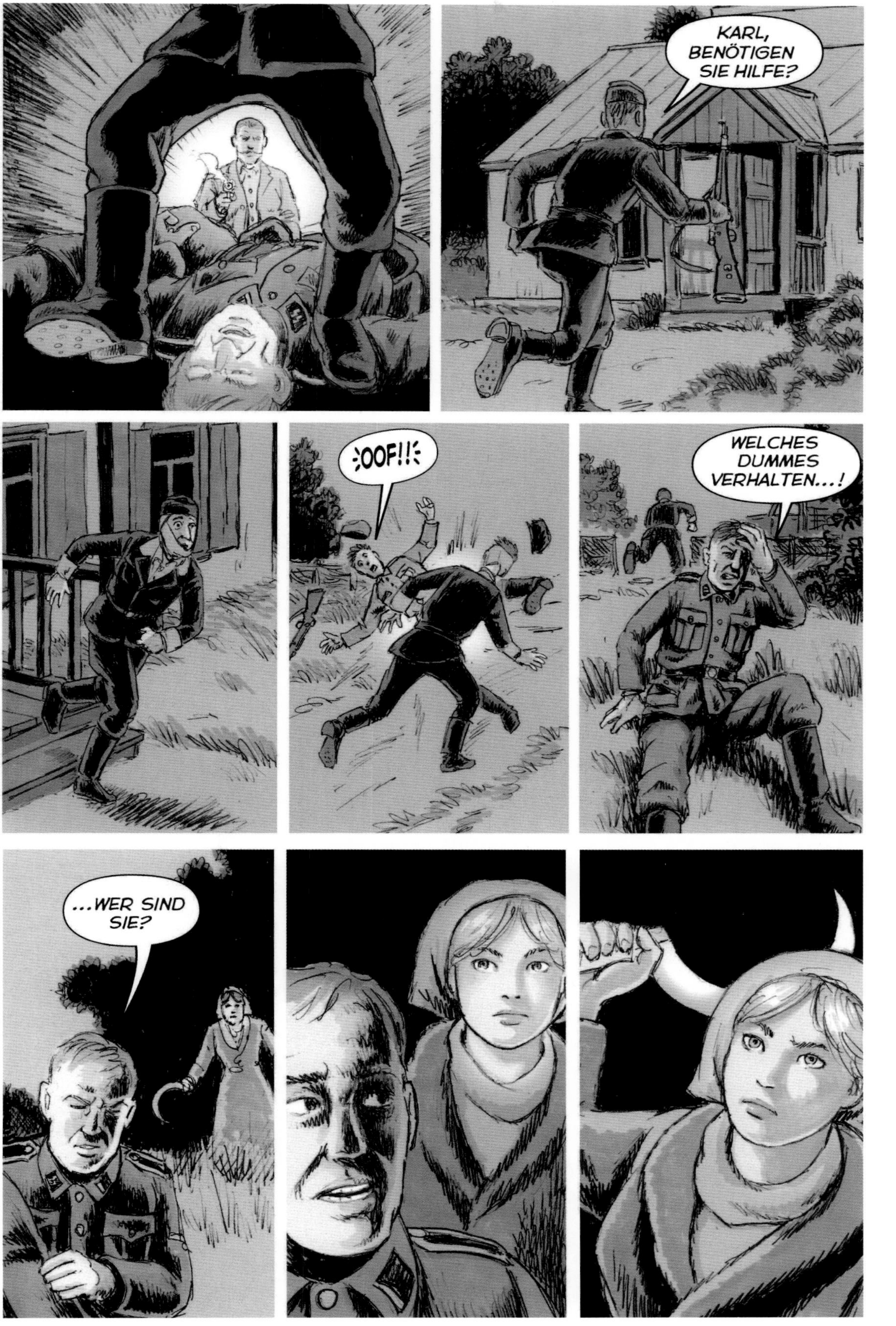
KARL, BENÖTIGEN SIE HILFE?
OOF!!
WELCHES DUMMES VERHALTEN...!
...WER SIND SIE?

I REMEMBER HEARING FIVE SHOTS FIRED--AFTER THAT, THERE WAS COMPLETE SILENCE. NO LIGHTS CAME ON, NO ONE CAME TO THEIR DOOR. PERHAPS A DOG BARKED FAR AWAY.

I THINK MAYBE THE COMMUNIST SYSTEM HAD TAUGHT PEOPLE TO MIND THEIR OWN BUSINESS. IT CERTAINLY WORKED WELL FOR *US* THAT NIGHT.

THE SCENE HAD BEEN A *SHOCK* TO US, BUT UNCLE TARAS KEPT US MOVING.

STRIP OFF THEIR TUNICS! WIPE OFF WHAT BLOOD YOU CAN.

WE'LL USE THE UNIFORMS AS DISGUISES--

HEY, THERE ARE SOME CANVAS TARPS IN THE BACK OF THE TRUCK...

GREAT! WE'LL USE THEM TO WRAP THE BODIES UP--WE'LL PUT THEM IN THE BACK OF THE TRUCK AND DUMP THEM AWAY FROM THE HOUSE.

NOW, SOMEONE GET A *MOP.*

HA! GOOD GERMAN MAPS! THESE LITTLE MARKS MAY SHOW US THEIR OUTPOSTS...

MILLA, CAN YOU DRIVE THIS TRUCK?

SURE!

HOW *FAST* DO YOU WANT TO GO?

EVERYBODY ELSE--IN THE *BACK* OF THE *TRUCK!*

WELL, MILLA, TAKE US TO *KROVROT...*

...OR AS *FAR* AS WE CAN GET IN THIS BUGGY...!

THEN, WE LEFT OUR HOME BEHIND.
AS IF TO ILLUSTRATE OUR SORROW, IT BEGAN TO *RAIN...*

TUESDAY, SEPTEMBER 30, 1941. THE CONQUEST OF UKRAINE WAS COMPLETE, AND THE GERMAN ARMY WAS ON THE MOVE AGAIN. THIS TIME, THE GERMANS WERE MOVING AGAINST THEIR MAIN OBJECTIVE--*MOSCOW.*

IN THE NORTH, THEY HAD ALREADY REACHED *LENINGRAD*, ENCIRCLED THE CITY, AND LAID SIEGE TO IT. THEY HAD COMPLETED THE SUBJUGATION OF *BELORUSSIA* AND HAD TAKEN *MINSK* AND *SMOLENSK.*

ALL THAT REMAINED TO DO WAS THE CAPTURE OF *STALIN'S LAIR.* IMAGES OF GOLDEN SPIRES BECKONED THEM ON, LIKE SHRIVELED, ICY FINGERS.

BUT GENERAL HEINZ GUDERIAN WAS *WORRIED.*

A COOL BREEZE HAD BEGUN BLOWING FROM THE NORTH AS THE LEAVES ON THE TREES TURNED FROM GREEN TO GOLD AND ORANGE. ALREADY THE FIRST CHILL DROPS OF THE AUTUMN RAIN PELTED THEIR GRAY-GREEN HELMETS...

...AND WITH THE RAIN, GUDERIAN COULD ALMOST FEEL THE EARTH DISSOLVING BENEATH HIS FEET.

FORKS IN THE ROAD

WE GOT RID OF THE GERMAN BODIES IN A CULVERT HIDDEN BY HIGH GRASS, THEN DROVE AS QUIETLY AS POSSIBLE TO WHERE THE NORTHWESTERN EDGE OF KIEV FADED INTO THE COUNTRYSIDE. THERE, A ROAD HUGGED THE RIGHT BANK OF THE DNIEPER AS IT SNAKED NORTH TOWARD THE BELORUSSIAN FRONTIER. WE HAD BEEN ON THE ROAD FOR MOST OF THE DAY WHEN UP AHEAD, UNCLE TARAS' SHARP EYE SPOTTED THE TAIL END OF A GERMAN CONVOY--LUCKILY *BEFORE THEY* SAW *US*.

WHEN THEY PULLED OVER TO REGROUP, WE RECONNOITERED FROM ATOP A HILL. UNCLE TARAS SIZED UP THE SITUATION...

*AH, GOOD, GOOD...*THIRTEEN VEHICLES, ALL OPEL BLITZES JUST LIKE OURS.

THIS RAIN WILL HELP A LOT. VASILY, COVER OUR TRUCK'S IDENTIFICATION TAG WITH SPLASHED MUD...

...AND KATUSHA, CUT A SMALL HOLE IN THE BACK CANVAS SO YOU CAN PEEK OUT.

WH·150425

WHAT ARE WE GOING TO DO, UNCLE TARAS?

WE'RE GOING TO JOIN THAT TRUCK CONVOY.

UNCLE TARAS INSTRUCTED MILLA TO HIDE THE TRUCK AND LIE IN WAIT ON A WINDING, HILLY ROAD, WHERE STEEP GRADES AND HAIRPIN CURVES WOULD MAKE THE GERMANS MOVE SLOWLY...

...WIDENING THE GAPS BETWEEN THE VEHICLES AND MAKING THEM LOSE SIGHT OF EACH OTHER.

HE WATCHED INTENTLY AS THE FIRST ELEVEN TRUCKS PASSED, TIMING THEIR APPEARANCES AS THEY CAME AROUND A BLIND CURVE--

--THEN UNCLE TARAS LEAPED BACK INTO THE TRUCK'S CAB, BARKING OUT INSTRUCTIONS TO MILLA...!

WAIT TILL THE NEXT TRUCK PASSES, COUNT TO *FIVE*--

--THEN PULL OUT ONTO THE ROAD, *AS FAST AS YOU CAN!*

MILLA PUT ALL HER WEIGHT ON THE GAS PEDAL, AND OUR TRUCK SHOT OUT ONTO THE ROAD--

--BEFORE THE TRUCK BEHIND US OR THE TRUCK IN FRONT OF US COULD SEE!

THROUGH THE LITTLE HOLE I HAD CUT IN THE FLAP, I COULD SEE THE TRUCK BEHIND US COME AROUND THE CURVE AND START UP THE LONG GRADE.

IT *WORKED*, UNCLE TARAS!

WE'RE RIGHT IN BETWEEN THEM...!

GOOD! HOPEFULLY, NUMBER 12 WILL THINK WE ARE *NUMBER 13*...AND NUMBER 13 WILL THINK WE'RE *NUMBER 12.*

WE RODE ON THROUGH THE NIGHT, FEELING SOMEWHAT SAFE IN OUR SITUATION--

--BUT ALL OF US WERE READY TO *ACT*, IF NECESSARY.

WE RODE ALONG WITH THE CONVOY, UNTIL...

THEY SEEM TO BE BEARING TO THE NORTHWEST-- BUT *WE* NEED TO BE HEADING BACK TOWARD THE RIVER...

MILLA, SPEED UP TO GET MORE DISTANCE FROM *NUMBER 13*, BUT WITHOUT GETTING US TOO CLOSE TO *NUMBER 12*.

THE NEXT ROAD WE SEE TO THE *RIGHT*, CUT THE LIGHTS AND TAKE IT.

AH! THAT LOOKS LIKE A GOOD PLACE UP AHEAD.

ALL RIGHT...

...*WAIT* FOR IT--!

--*NOW!*

HA!

GOOD--THEY'RE CONTINUING ON AS IF WE WERE NEVER PART OF THEIR LITTLE GROUP.

WE RODE ALONG A NARROW, ROCKY PATH UNTIL THE ENGINE BEGAN TO SPUTTER...

OUT OF GAS?

I DON'T THINK SO...

BUT IT DOESN'T MATTER. IT LOOKS LIKE WE'VE RUN OUT OF *ROAD*.

OKAY. PULL OVER INTO THE UNDERBRUSH.

THIS IS AS FAR IN AS I CAN GET...

IT'S ENOUGH. I'LL CUT SOME BRANCHES TO HIDE US.

WHAT'S ALL THAT UP THERE?

I DON'T KNOW.

I'LL GO OVER AND CHECK.

I'LL TAKE A LOOK AROUND. EVERYONE STAY WITH THE TRUCK...

...AND TRY TO GET SOME *REST* WHILE YOU CAN.

FINALLY DAWN CAME, AND THE RAIN STOPPED. A STREAK OF GOLD CUT ACROSS THE GRAY SKY...

BUT--

WHERE ARE NATASHA AND DIMA?

THEY WENT OUTSIDE. DIMA WAS FULL OF ENERGY AND GETTING RESTLESS.

I'LL *BET* HE WAS.

THAT WAS WHEN I BECAME AWARE OF AN ODD METALLIC SCENT IN THE AIR... A SMELL THAT I CAN ONLY DESCRIBE AS "BRONZE/GREEN."

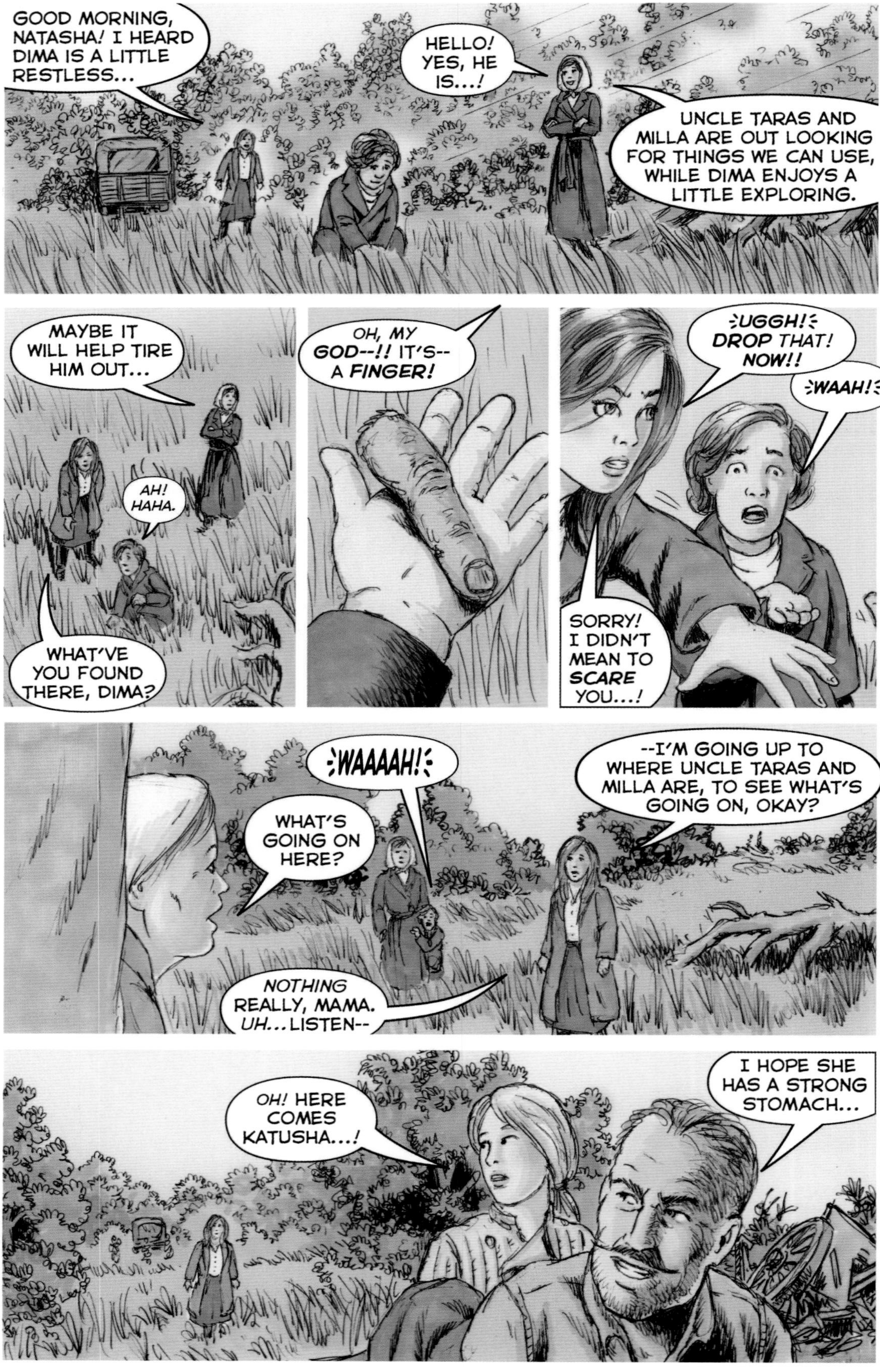
GOOD MORNING, NATASHA! I HEARD DIMA IS A LITTLE RESTLESS...
HELLO! YES, HE IS...!
UNCLE TARAS AND MILLA ARE OUT LOOKING FOR THINGS WE CAN USE, WHILE DIMA ENJOYS A LITTLE EXPLORING.
MAYBE IT WILL HELP TIRE HIM OUT...
AH! HAHA.
WHAT'VE YOU FOUND THERE, DIMA?
OH, MY GOD--!! IT'S-- A FINGER!
UGGH! DROP THAT! NOW!!
WAAH!
SORRY! I DIDN'T MEAN TO SCARE YOU...!
WAAAAH!
WHAT'S GOING ON HERE?
--I'M GOING UP TO WHERE UNCLE TARAS AND MILLA ARE, TO SEE WHAT'S GOING ON, OKAY?
NOTHING REALLY, MAMA. UH... LISTEN--
OH! HERE COMES KATUSHA...!
I HOPE SHE HAS A STRONG STOMACH...

SO... *THIS* WAS A *BATTLEFIELD.*

IT SEEMS STRANGE TO ME NOW THAT I WAS SO *SHOCKED*, BECAUSE IN THE MONTHS AND YEARS TO COME, SCENES SUCH AS THESE WOULD BECOME *EVERYDAY OCCURRENCES.*

I REMEMBER NOTICING THE WAY THAT NO TWO OBJECTS SEEMED TO HOLD ANY RELATIONSHIP TO EACH OTHER...

...THAT EVERYTHING WAS TURNED AND TWISTED AND THROWN UP RANDOMLY, WITHOUT ANY SHOW OF CARE.

BUT THE SADDEST THING WAS THAT THE OBJECTS THAT NOW SEEMED TO BE THE LEAST VALUABLE AND LEAST RECOVERABLE WERE THE REMAINS OF OUR *FELLOW HUMANS.*

THEY LAY AMONG THEIR EQUIPMENT, WHICH WAS STILL HARD AND GOOD--AND THERE, SLOWLY WASTED AWAY...

...MINDING THEIR OWN BUSINESS AND TRYING NOT TO BOTHER THOSE OCCASIONAL PASSERS-BY-- EXCEPT WITH A LITTLE GLASSY, VACANT *STARE...*

...TO REMIND US ALL HOW THEY WERE ONCE LIKE *US.*

WHAT DID YOU FIND, UNCLE TARAS?

THESE HANDY LITTLE WHEELED CARRIAGES MADE FOR HAULING THE *MAXIM GUNS!*

SEE? YOU CAN GUIDE IT WITH ONE HAND.

UNCLE TARAS SEEMED TO BE PERFECTLY COMFORTABLE IN THIS SETTING, AS FAMILIAR AMONG THE CASTOFFS OF WAR AS I WOULD HAVE BEEN IN OUR OWN FRONT YARD.

THESE ARE *USEFUL*--WE'LL MAKE A CART FOR DIMA TO RIDE ON, AND THE OTHERS WILL CARRY OUR FOOD AND SUPPLIES...

MILLA, TOO, DIDN'T SEEM BOTHERED BY ANY OF IT.

‹AAGH!!›

--OHH, WHAT IS *THAT?*

I BELIEVE *THAT* IS A MAN WHO HAS BEEN RUN OVER BY A *TANK.*

PRIKIP HONSHAR WAS NOT ONLY A SCHOOL BULLY--HE WAS ALSO A SNITCH. AS SOON AS HE'D FLED INTO THE NIGHT, HE TOLD THE FIRST GERMAN SOLDIERS HE FOUND WHAT HAD JUST HAPPENED AT THE TYMOSHENKO HOUSEHOLD.

BUT *SS OBERSTURMFÜHRER HARTMUTH PULZER* HAD ALSO EARNED A REPUTATION IN SCHOOL--FOR TENACITY AND THOROUGHNESS.

AS A YOUTH, *PULZER* HAD YEARNED TO BE A WELL-RESPECTED LAWYER LIKE HIS FATHER, WHO HAD BEEN KILLED IN THE *GREAT WAR...*

BUT THE SOUL-CRUSHING POVERTY AND HUNGER THAT HAD MARKED THE *WEIMAR REPUBLIC* GAVE YOUNG HARTMUTH SCANT OPPORTUNITY FOR SUCH ASPIRATIONS.

THEN, JUST IN TIME, THE *NAZI PARTY* SEIZED POWER...

...PROVIDING THE AMBITIOUS PULZER OTHER OPPORTUNITIES-- SUCH AS BEING MADE THE *COMMANDER* OF THE *EINSATZGRUPPEN.*

IF YOU CANNOT GET AN *EDUCATION*--ACQUIRING A USEFUL DEGREE OF *AUTHORITY* WILL DO FOR YOU JUST AS WELL.

AND, IF YOU CANNOT *REPRESENT* THE LAW--YOU CAN AT LEAST *ENFORCE* THE LAW.

AND, IF YOU CANNOT COMMAND *RESPECT...*

...THEN, AT THE VERY *LEAST*--

AH--! WELL, IF IT ISN'T MY LITTLE *UKRAINIAN ROSE* HERSELF...!

--YOU CAN EXACT...

FEAR!

OH, YES... I SHALL HAVE *NO* TROUBLE REMEMBERING *YOU*--!

UNCLE TARAS KEPT US MOVING ALONG AT NOT TOO HARD A PACE--BUT AFTER A WHILE, AS WE GOT TOUGHER, IT WAS AS IF WE PUSHED *HIM* ALONG, MAKING FUN AT HIS TOO-FREQUENT CALLS FOR A BREAK. BUT PERHAPS THAT WAS JUST HIS WAY OF ENCOURAGING US.

WE AVOIDED CONTACT WITH VILLAGES AND ANY POPULATED AREAS AS WE TRAVELED. EVERY NIGHT, WE SLEPT IN THE WOODS.

AT FIRST, THE FREQUENT RAINS DRENCHED US...

BUT AFTER UNCLE TARAS TAUGHT US HOW TO MAKE SHELTERS, PUTTING UP WITH A LITTLE RAIN BECAME *EASY.*

UNCLE TARAS WAS ALWAYS AT THE FRONT ON THE ALERT FOR TROUBLE, WITH MILLA AT HIS SIDE. VASILY TOOK UP THE REAR, KEEPING AN EYE OUT FOR ANY TROUBLE THAT MIGHT BE TAILING US.

FINALLY, WE REACHED THE DNIEPER. WITH THE DAM DOWNSTREAM DESTROYED, THE RIVER'S LEVEL HAD DROPPED, AND ITS CURRENTS HAD BECOME DANGEROUSLY SWIFT.

WE'LL CAMP HERE TILL DARK--

--THEN TRY TO FIND A WAY ACROSS TONIGHT.

ONCE WE GET TO KROVROT, WHAT *THEN,* UNCLE TARAS?

JUST *LIVE.*

WE'LL STAY OUT OF THE WAY OF BOTH THE GERMANS AND THE RUSSIANS UNTIL WE SEE WHICH WAY IT'S GOING TO GO.

WE FOUND A FISHERMAN WHO HAD A BOAT BIG ENOUGH TO CARRY US ACROSS, AND HE ACCEPTED THE JOB--FOR AN EXORBITANT AMOUNT OF *REICHSMARKS*...

IT MIGHT BE CHEAPER TO BUILD A *BRIDGE*.

THAT NIGHT, WE CROSSED THE GREAT RIVER WITHOUT INCIDENT...

...THEN WE CELEBRATED ON THE LEFT BANK BY COOKING THREE FISH WE HAD CAUGHT ON THE WAY ACROSS.

THREE DAYS LATER, WE REACHED *KROVROT* IN THE EARLY EVENING.

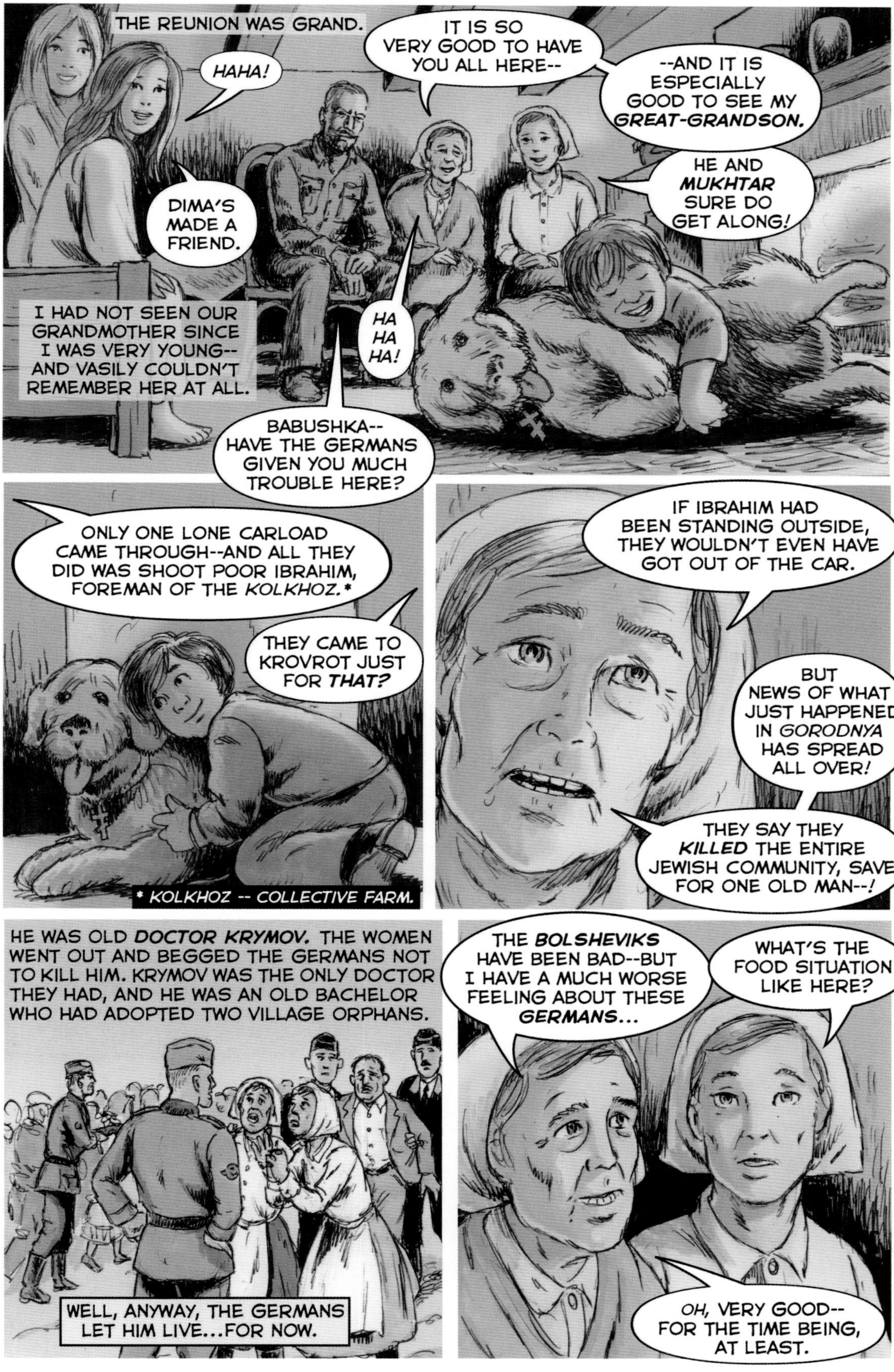
THE REUNION WAS GRAND.
HAHA!
IT IS SO VERY GOOD TO HAVE YOU ALL HERE--
--AND IT IS ESPECIALLY GOOD TO SEE MY GREAT-GRANDSON.
HE AND MUKHTAR SURE DO GET ALONG!
DIMA'S MADE A FRIEND.
I HAD NOT SEEN OUR GRANDMOTHER SINCE I WAS VERY YOUNG-- AND VASILY COULDN'T REMEMBER HER AT ALL.
HA HA HA!
BABUSHKA-- HAVE THE GERMANS GIVEN YOU MUCH TROUBLE HERE?
ONLY ONE LONE CARLOAD CAME THROUGH--AND ALL THEY DID WAS SHOOT POOR IBRAHIM, FOREMAN OF THE KOLKHOZ.*
THEY CAME TO KROVROT JUST FOR THAT?
* KOLKHOZ -- COLLECTIVE FARM.
IF IBRAHIM HAD BEEN STANDING OUTSIDE, THEY WOULDN'T EVEN HAVE GOT OUT OF THE CAR.
BUT NEWS OF WHAT JUST HAPPENED IN GORODNYA HAS SPREAD ALL OVER!
THEY SAY THEY KILLED THE ENTIRE JEWISH COMMUNITY, SAVE FOR ONE OLD MAN--!
HE WAS OLD DOCTOR KRYMOV. THE WOMEN WENT OUT AND BEGGED THE GERMANS NOT TO KILL HIM. KRYMOV WAS THE ONLY DOCTOR THEY HAD, AND HE WAS AN OLD BACHELOR WHO HAD ADOPTED TWO VILLAGE ORPHANS.
WELL, ANYWAY, THE GERMANS LET HIM LIVE...FOR NOW.
THE BOLSHEVIKS HAVE BEEN BAD--BUT I HAVE A MUCH WORSE FEELING ABOUT THESE GERMANS...
WHAT'S THE FOOD SITUATION LIKE HERE?
OH, VERY GOOD-- FOR THE TIME BEING, AT LEAST.

"AS THE GERMANS GOT CLOSER, THE WHOLE AGRICULTURAL SYSTEM FELL APART. THE RUSSIANS BEGAN TO SHIP ALL THE HEAVY EQUIPMENT TO THE EAST...

"...AND SUPERVISION OF OUR WORK WAS AS LAX AS I HAVE EVER SEEN IT.

"SO, AS IS USUALLY THE CASE, MOST OF US SPENT MORE TIME ON OUR *DACHAS.**

* *DACHA* -- A COUNTRY COTTAGE, OR SMALL PLOT OF LAND SET ASIDE FOR PERSONAL USE.

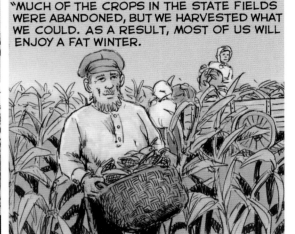

"MUCH OF THE CROPS IN THE STATE FIELDS WERE ABANDONED, BUT WE HARVESTED WHAT WE COULD. AS A RESULT, MOST OF US WILL ENJOY A FAT WINTER.

"BUT NOT EVERYONE HAS BEEN SO LUCKY. AT FIRST, THE GERMANS SAID THEY WOULD DO AWAY WITH THE COLLECTIVE FARMS. BUT IN SOME PLACES, THEY NOW CALL THEM 'COOPERATIVES,' AND THE PEOPLE WORK UNDER THE WHIP OF A GERMAN OVERSEER.

"TO ME, A RAT UNDER ANY OTHER NAME STILL SMELLS LIKE A RAT.

"ALSO, IN GORODNYA, THEY ARRESTED TWELVE YOUNG PEOPLE BETWEEN 14 AND 17-- AND SHIPPED THEM OFF TO GERMANY AS SLAVE LABOR!

"IN TIME, THEY WILL PROBABLY DO THE SAME THING HERE."

I COULD TELL THAT ALL THAT BABUSHKA HAD TOLD US BOTHERED UNCLE TARAS. I AWOKE ONCE DURING THE NIGHT TO SEE HIM STILL SITTING THERE...

...STARING HARD INTO THE FIRE, AS IF HE EXPECTED AN ANSWER TO BE SOMEWHERE IN THE FLAMES.

THE NEXT DAY, WE WENT DOWN TO THE VILLAGE CEMETERY. WE FOUND THE GRAVE OF MY MOTHER'S FATHER, WHOM I HAD NEVER MET. BUT SINCE MOST OF THE PEOPLE BURIED THERE WERE PEASANTS, MOST GRAVES WERE POORLY MARKED--IF INDEED THEY HAD EVER BEEN MARKED.

I HEAR THEY NOW HAVE A PRIEST IN *GORODNYA*.

I HAVE HEARD THIS, TOO.

THERE WERE GRAVES OF YOUNG AND OLD. SOME PLOTS WERE SO BADLY NEGLECTED IT WAS ALMOST IMPOSSIBLE TO BE SURE THERE WERE ANY GRAVES THERE AT ALL.

AND ON THE FAR END, OVER NEAR THE WOODS, WAS A PLAIN GRASSY MOUND. THIS WAS A **MASS GRAVE**, CONTAINING THE VICTIMS OF THE TERRIBLE *FAMINE OF 1932-33*.

THEN WE FOUND THE GRAVESITE OF **SEMEN KALASHNIKOV.** IT WAS MARKED ONLY IN THE SIMPLEST WAY, WITH THE GRAVE OF HIS WIFE BESIDE HIM...

HE WAS A MAN OF EDUCATION AND PROPERTY, SO IT IS SAD THAT HE ENDED UP LIKE THIS--

--BUT THEN AGAIN, IT IS PRECISELY *BECAUSE* HE WAS A MAN OF EDUCATION AND PROPERTY THAT HE IS EVEN HERE AT *ALL*.

OLD FRIEND, IT WAS YOU WHO TAUGHT ME THAT BECAUSE WE ARE *MEN*, WE MUST MAKE CHOICES. I REGRET TO SAY THAT I HAVE NOT ALWAYS CHOSEN WELL...BUT I SEEK NO SYMPATHY. I CHOSE MY OWN OPTIONS, AND ONLY I SUFFERED FOR IT.

BUT NOW, I MUST MAKE DETERMINATIONS FOR MY FAMILY...

HELP ME CHOOSE WELL, OLD FRIEND.

THE PLAIN OF *VYAZMA*,
130 MILES WEST OF MOSCOW...

FIVE SOVIET ARMIES STOOD READY
TO STOP THE GERMAN ADVANCE.

AS THEY HAD DONE BEFORE, THE GERMAN ARMY SIMPLY ENCIRCLED THE
OPPOSING FORCES, TOOK THE HIGH GROUND, AND BEGAN TO
POUR ITS HEAVY ARTILLERY INTO THE POCKET.

DESPERATE TO BREAK OUT OF THE TRAP, WAVES OF
RUSSIAN INFANTRY THREW THEMSELVES AGAINST THE GERMAN LINE...

...BUT THE GERMAN INFANTRY UNITS WERE READY FOR THEM.

WHEN THE RUSSIANS DREW CLOSE ENOUGH TO THEM, THE GERMANS REALIZED AN ASTONISHING FACT...

ONLY ABOUT ONE IN FOUR OF THE RUSSIAN SOLDIERS CARRIED A *RIFLE!*

THE REST OF THE TROOPS HAD BEEN FORCED TO TAKE PART IN THE ATTACK *WITHOUT ARMS!*

WHENEVER ONE OF THEIR ARMED COMRADES IN THE FRONT ROW WAS CUT DOWN BY ENEMY FIRE--

--AN UNARMED SOLDIER BEHIND HIM WOULD PICK UP THE FALLEN MAN'S WEAPON AND CONTINUE THE ADVANCE!

AS THE ASSAULT PROCEEDED, THE SOVIETS ADVANCED INTO MARSHY GROUND, SLOWING THEIR ATTACK AND MAKING THEM EASY TARGETS FOR THE GERMAN GUNNERS.

AT *VYAZMA*, THE SOVIET ARMIES LOST *150,000 MEN.*

WAS THERE *NOTHING* THAT WOULD STOP THE GERMAN DRIVE TOWARD MOSCOW?

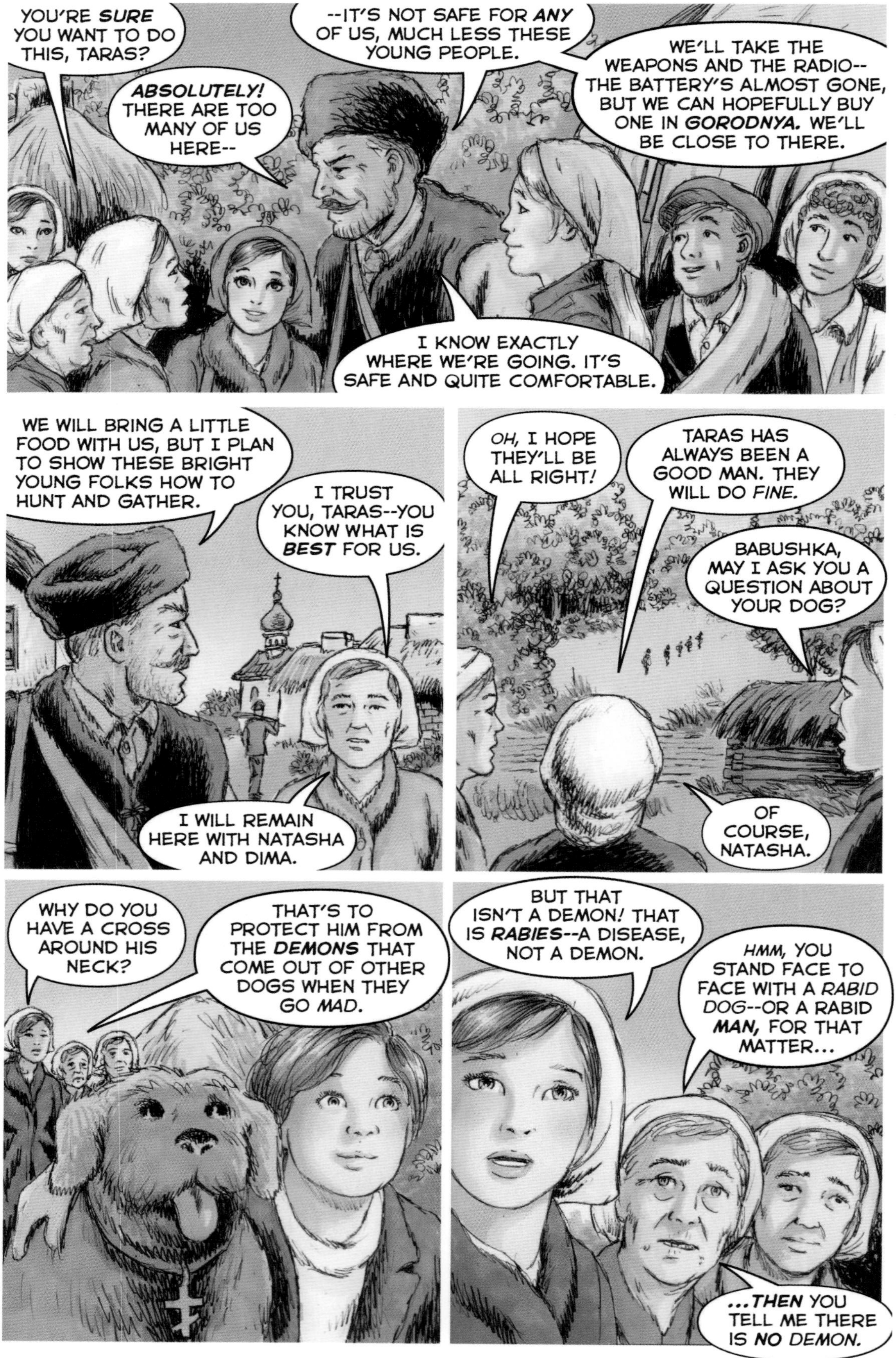
YOU'RE SURE YOU WANT TO DO THIS, TARAS?
ABSOLUTELY! THERE ARE TOO MANY OF US HERE--
--IT'S NOT SAFE FOR ANY OF US, MUCH LESS THESE YOUNG PEOPLE.
WE'LL TAKE THE WEAPONS AND THE RADIO-- THE BATTERY'S ALMOST GONE, BUT WE CAN HOPEFULLY BUY ONE IN GORODNYA. WE'LL BE CLOSE TO THERE.
I KNOW EXACTLY WHERE WE'RE GOING. IT'S SAFE AND QUITE COMFORTABLE.
WE WILL BRING A LITTLE FOOD WITH US, BUT I PLAN TO SHOW THESE BRIGHT YOUNG FOLKS HOW TO HUNT AND GATHER.
I TRUST YOU, TARAS--YOU KNOW WHAT IS BEST FOR US.
I WILL REMAIN HERE WITH NATASHA AND DIMA.
OH, I HOPE THEY'LL BE ALL RIGHT!
TARAS HAS ALWAYS BEEN A GOOD MAN. THEY WILL DO FINE.
BABUSHKA, MAY I ASK YOU A QUESTION ABOUT YOUR DOG?
OF COURSE, NATASHA.
WHY DO YOU HAVE A CROSS AROUND HIS NECK?
THAT'S TO PROTECT HIM FROM THE DEMONS THAT COME OUT OF OTHER DOGS WHEN THEY GO MAD.
BUT THAT ISN'T A DEMON! THAT IS RABIES--A DISEASE, NOT A DEMON.
HMM, YOU STAND FACE TO FACE WITH A RABID DOG--OR A RABID MAN, FOR THAT MATTER...
...THEN YOU TELL ME THERE IS NO DEMON.

THE FOREST WAS REALLY BEAUTIFUL THAT AUTUMN--AND UNCLE TARAS LED MILLA, VASILY, ZHENYA, AND ME INTO IT DEEPER THAN ANY OF US HAD EVER BEEN.

WE MOVED NORTHEAST TOWARD BELORUSSIA, INTO AN OLD HARDWOOD WILDERNESS BROKEN BY ROCKY HILLS.

UNCLE TARAS KNEW HOW TO LIVE OFF THE LAND, HOW TO FIND AND MAKE SHELTER, AND WHERE TO FIND FOOD WHERE NONE SEEMED TO BE...

I KNOW OF 52 PLANTS YOU CAN EAT DIFFERENT PARTS OF...

HE WAS CAREFUL TO SHOW AND TELL US EVERYTHING HE KNEW.

CAN WE EAT *THESE* MUSHROOMS, UNCLE TARAS?

YES...

...BUT ONLY *ONCE.*

AFTER THREE DAYS IN THE WOODS, UNCLE TARAS BEGAN TO LOOK WITH A FAMILIAR AND WARM EXPRESSION AT THE LANDSCAPE AROUND HIM ...

YES, I THINK THAT THIS MAY BE *IT*...

DO YOU *SEE?* HERE IS THE RIVER--

--BUT UP OVER THERE, SEE A STREAM THAT SEEMS AS IF IT IS FLOWING OUT OF THOSE ROCKS...?

NOW--WE NEED TO *CLIMB* UP THERE.

WHEW! I MIGHT BE GETTING TOO OLD FOR THIS...!

NOW, VASILY...PUT DOWN YOUR RIFLE AND EVERYTHING YOU'RE CARRYING--

--AND TIE THIS ROPE AROUND YOUR WAIST.

WE'LL KEEP THE SLACK IN THE ROPE BY WRAPPING IT AROUND THIS TREE...

NOW, BEGIN TO WALK SLOWLY ACROSS THE GROUND THERE...

THAT'S RIGHT...

YES...GO RIGHT ACROSS THERE...

UH-OH!

I THINK THE GROUND'S GETTING KINDA SOFT HERE--!

LOOK OUT! THE GROUND IS GIVING WAY--!

≶--OOH!≶

HOORAY!

VASILY HAS FOUND IT!

HAHA, YES! YOU DID IT!

I HAVEN'T BEEN HERE IN NEARLY 20 YEARS, AND WE WERE STILL ABLE TO FIND IT!

FIND WHAT?

WE WENT BACK DOWN THE ROCKY HILL ON THE FAR SIDE FROM THE RIVER. THERE WE FOUND WHERE THE STREAM DISAPPEARED INTO THE EARTH AT THE BASE OF THE HILL. WE DID A LITTLE DIGGING, MAKING A LARGE ENOUGH OPENING FOR US TO CRAWL INTO.

AN ELECTRICAL TORCH WE'D FOUND IN THE GERMAN TRUCK LIT OUR WAY INTO AN EXPANDING STONE HALL...

OH, MY GOODNESS...!

AS YOU CAN SEE, IT'S NOT REALLY A CAVE--THIS IS JUST A LITTLE CANYON THAT HAS ALMOST CLOSED OVER.

WHAT WE HAVE HERE IS *SHELTER*--WARM IN WINTER, COOL IN SUMMER-- COMPLETE WITH ITS OWN FRESH WATER SUPPLY!

THE STREAM FORMS THREE POOLS BEFORE IT EMPTIES INTO THE RIVER...

THE FIRST IS FOR OUR DRINKING WATER AND FOR COOKING--THE SECOND IS FOR WASHING UP...

...AND THE LAST POOL IS FOR "PERSONAL BUSINESS."

GOOD--THERE'S NO SIGN OF ANYONE HAVING BEEN HERE FOR THE LAST 20 YEARS. I'M PROBABLY THE LAST MAN ALIVE WHO KNOWS IT'S HERE.

UNCLE TARAS, IF WE BUILD A FIRE, WILL ANYONE SEE THE SMOKE?

THE SMOKE FROM A SMALL FIRE WILL BE SUCKED RIGHT UP TO THE CEILING AND THEN DISSIPATE THROUGH THE TREES. YOU'D HAVE TO BE STANDING RIGHT UP THERE AT NIGHT TO SEE OUR LIGHTS.

IF WE CAN GET A FRESH BATTERY FOR THE RADIO IN GORODNYA, WE CAN RUN AN ANTENNA UP THERE AND GET PRETTY GOOD RECEPTION...

THAT WOULD BE WONDERFUL!

SO, WE ALL MOVED INTO UNCLE TARAS' GROTTO AND SET UP HOUSEKEEPING...

A FEW DAYS LATER, UNCLE TARAS, ZHENYA, AND I HID OUR WEAPONS IN THE WOODS AND WENT INTO GORODNYA.

UNCLE TARAS WENT TO BUY WINTER CLOTHES.

IN THE MEANTIME, HE SENT US ON TO THE VILLAGE CHURCH TO MAKE CONTACT WITH A PRIEST HE KNEW...

KATUSHA--? I'VE NEVER BEEN INSIDE A *CHURCH* BEFORE...!

OH, IT'S JUST LIKE A *SYNAGOGUE*--

--EXCEPT WITH A LITTLE BIGGER BOOK.

FATHER ZAPOLYE?

YES, MY CHILD...?

SUDDENLY WE HEARD A LOUD SOUND AS SOMETHING HARD HIT THE FLOOR. WE LOOKED DOWN--AND SAW A *REVOLVER* HAD FALLEN FROM BENEATH THE PRIEST'S ROBES.

EXCUSE ME... BUT THESE ARE VERY DIFFICULT TIMES--

I'D SAY THEY ARE.

THEN...

TARAS IVANOVICH!

EXACTLY!

I SEE GORODNYA IS TO YOUR LIKING, MY FRIEND!

EVIDENTLY, IT WAS--HE HAD MOVED RIGHT IN WITH THE FORMER PRIEST'S WIDOW AND WAS ACCEPTED BY EVERYONE.

PYOTR HERE HAS SCOURED THE AREA FOR JUNK LEFT BY THE ARMIES...

AH!

HE HAD NO BATTERIES, BUT HE FOUND A HAND-CRANKED RADIO GENERATOR IN THE GARBAGE...

IT'S PERFECT. BETTER THAN A BATTERY!

BE CAREFUL IN THE VILLAGES AROUND HERE. THE GERMANS PATROL THE AREA REGULARLY.

WHAT ARE THEY LOOKING FOR?

OH, THE SAME THINGS-- COMMUNISTS, JEWS, PARTISANS... THEY SHOT TEN PEOPLE IN BIRKI FOR GIVING FOOD TO SOME ACCUSED PARTISANS.

ON OUR WAY BACK TO THE GROTTO, SNOW BEGAN TO FALL...

I'M GLAD WE BOUGHT THE VALENKIS*. WHEN THE SNOW DRIES, WE'LL PUT THEM ON.

THIS WEATHER WILL MAKE IT MUCH EASIER FOR US TO HUNT RABBITS AND SUCH...

...BUT IF WE ARE NOT CAREFUL, IT CAN MAKE IT EASIER FOR OTHERS TO HUNT US.

* VALENKIS--HOMEMADE FELT BOOTS, GOOD FOR COLD, DRY WEATHER.

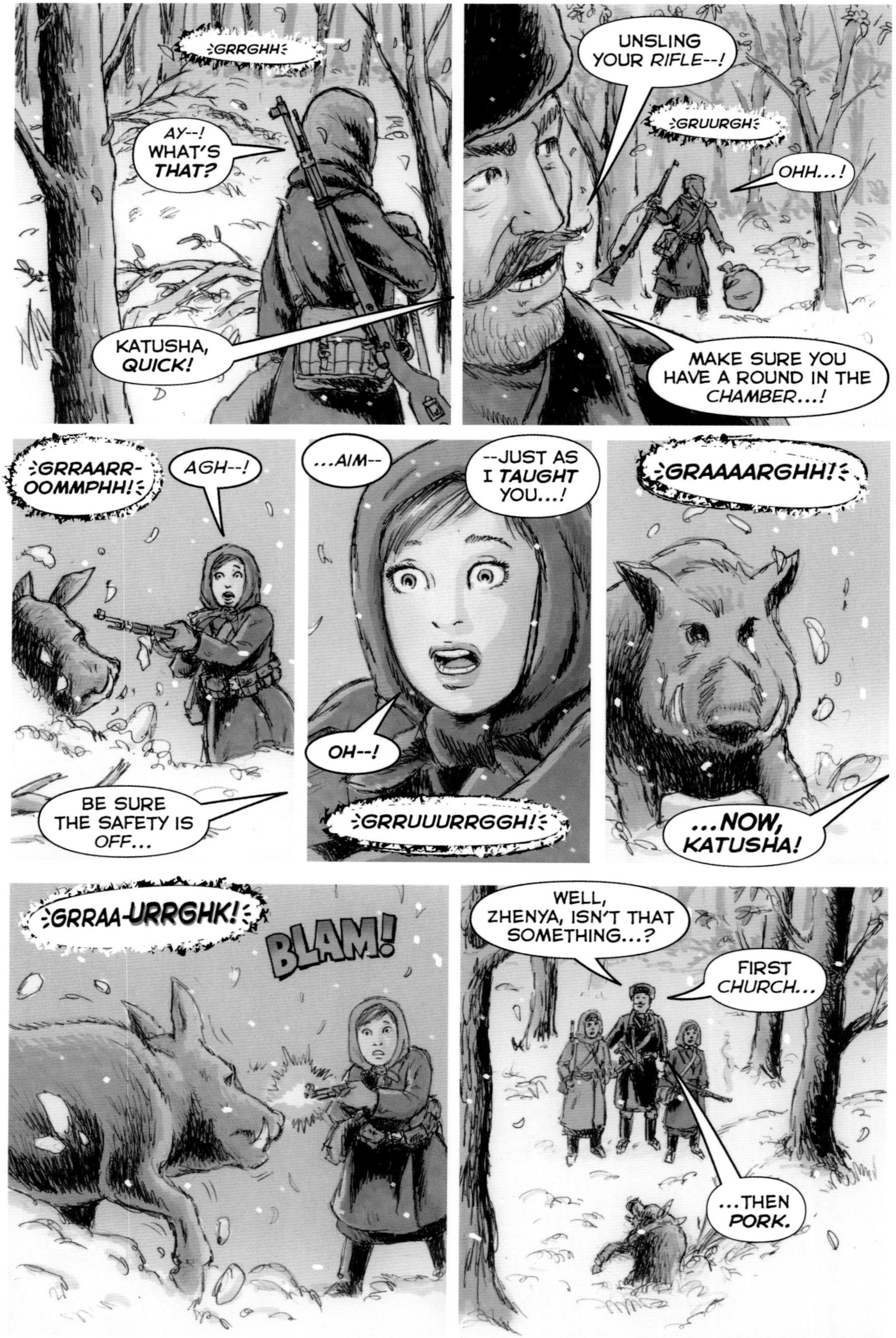
GRRGHH
AY--! WHAT'S *THAT?*
KATUSHA, *QUICK!*
UNSLING YOUR *RIFLE*--!
GRUURGH
OHH...!
MAKE SURE YOU HAVE A ROUND IN THE *CHAMBER*...!
GRRAARR-OOMMPHH!
AGH--!
BE SURE THE SAFETY IS *OFF*...
...AIM--
--JUST AS I *TAUGHT* YOU...!
OH--!
GRRUUURRGGH!
GRAAAARGHH!
...NOW, KATUSHA!
GRRAA-URRGHK!
BLAM!
WELL, ZHENYA, ISN'T THAT SOMETHING...?
FIRST CHURCH...
...THEN *PORK.*

THE PRIEST IN GORODNYA WAS RIGHT--THE GERMANS WERE VERY THOROUGH IN HUNTING THEIR CHOSEN PREY.

IS THERE ANYONE HERE IN CHARGE WHO CAN SPEAK FOR ALL?

A MAYOR, PERHAPS--OR MAYBE AN ELDER...?

WELL, I'M AS ELDERLY AS ANYONE HERE, SO I GUESS *I* WILL PASS AS AN ELDER.

VERY GOOD, MOTHER. TELL ME, ARE THERE ANY *COMMUNISTS* IN YOUR TOWN?

WELL, NO...

WE *DID* HAVE *ONE* MAN WHO CALLED HIMSELF A COMMUNIST...THAT WAS *MONIDZE.* BUT YOU *KILLED* HIM WHEN YOU CAME THROUGH THE *FIRST* TIME, IN *1918.*

WHAT ABOUT *JEWS?*

NO, WE HAVEN'T HAD ANY JEWS... NOT SINCE THE *CZAR* RAN THEM OUT, OH--

--ABOUT 50 YEARS AGO...?

AND *PARTISANS?*

OH, WE'VE HAD *LOTS* OF THOSE!

THEY GAVE THE *BOLSHEVIKS* FITS!

YES! WHEN WAS THIS?

LET'S SEE... I'D SAY IT WAS MORE THAN 20 YEARS AGO-- IT WAS DURING THE CIVIL WAR.

HA!

THANK YOU VERY MUCH, MOTHER.

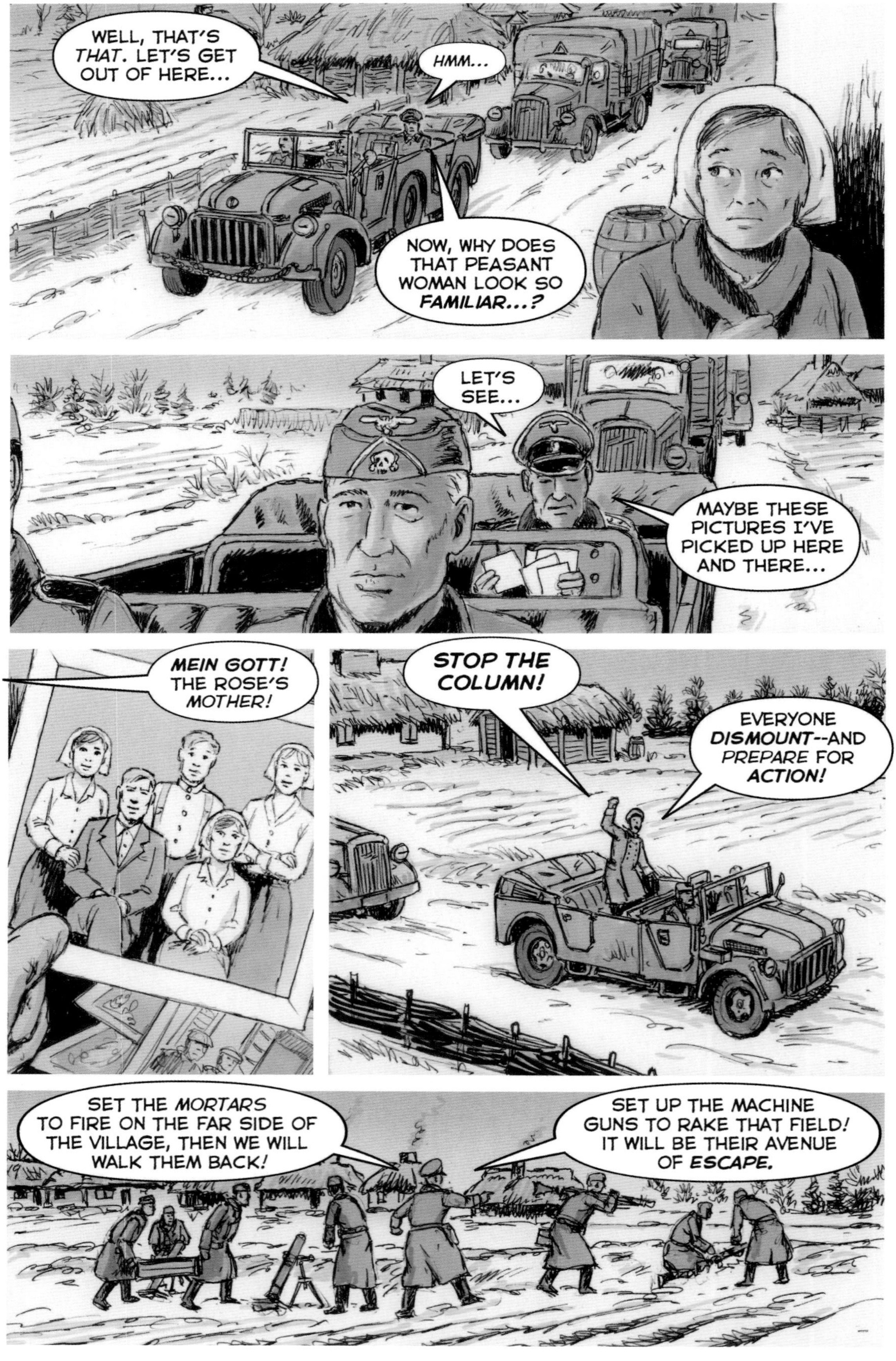
WELL, THAT'S THAT. LET'S GET OUT OF HERE...
HMM...
NOW, WHY DOES THAT PEASANT WOMAN LOOK SO FAMILIAR...?
LET'S SEE...
MAYBE THESE PICTURES I'VE PICKED UP HERE AND THERE...
MEIN GOTT! THE ROSE'S MOTHER!
STOP THE COLUMN!
EVERYONE DISMOUNT--AND PREPARE FOR ACTION!
SET THE MORTARS TO FIRE ON THE FAR SIDE OF THE VILLAGE, THEN WE WILL WALK THEM BACK!
SET UP THE MACHINE GUNS TO RAKE THAT FIELD! IT WILL BE THEIR AVENUE OF ESCAPE.

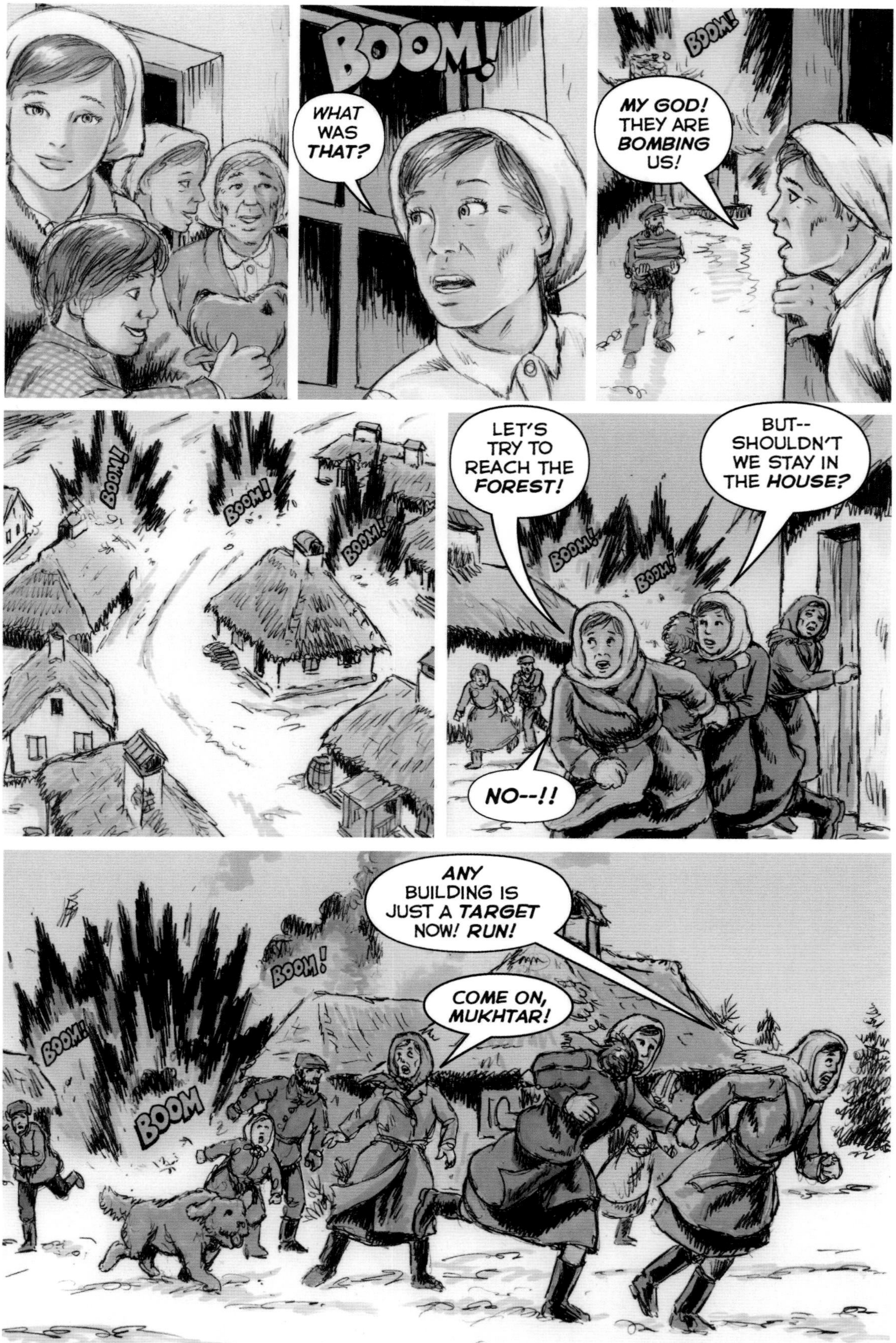
BOOM!
WHAT WAS THAT?
BOOM!
MY GOD! THEY ARE BOMBING US!
BOOM!
BOOM!
BOOM!
LET'S TRY TO REACH THE FOREST!
BUT-- SHOULDN'T WE STAY IN THE HOUSE?
BOOM!
BOOM!
NO--!!
ANY BUILDING IS JUST A TARGET NOW! RUN!
BOOM!
COME ON, MUKHTAR!
BOOM!
BOOM

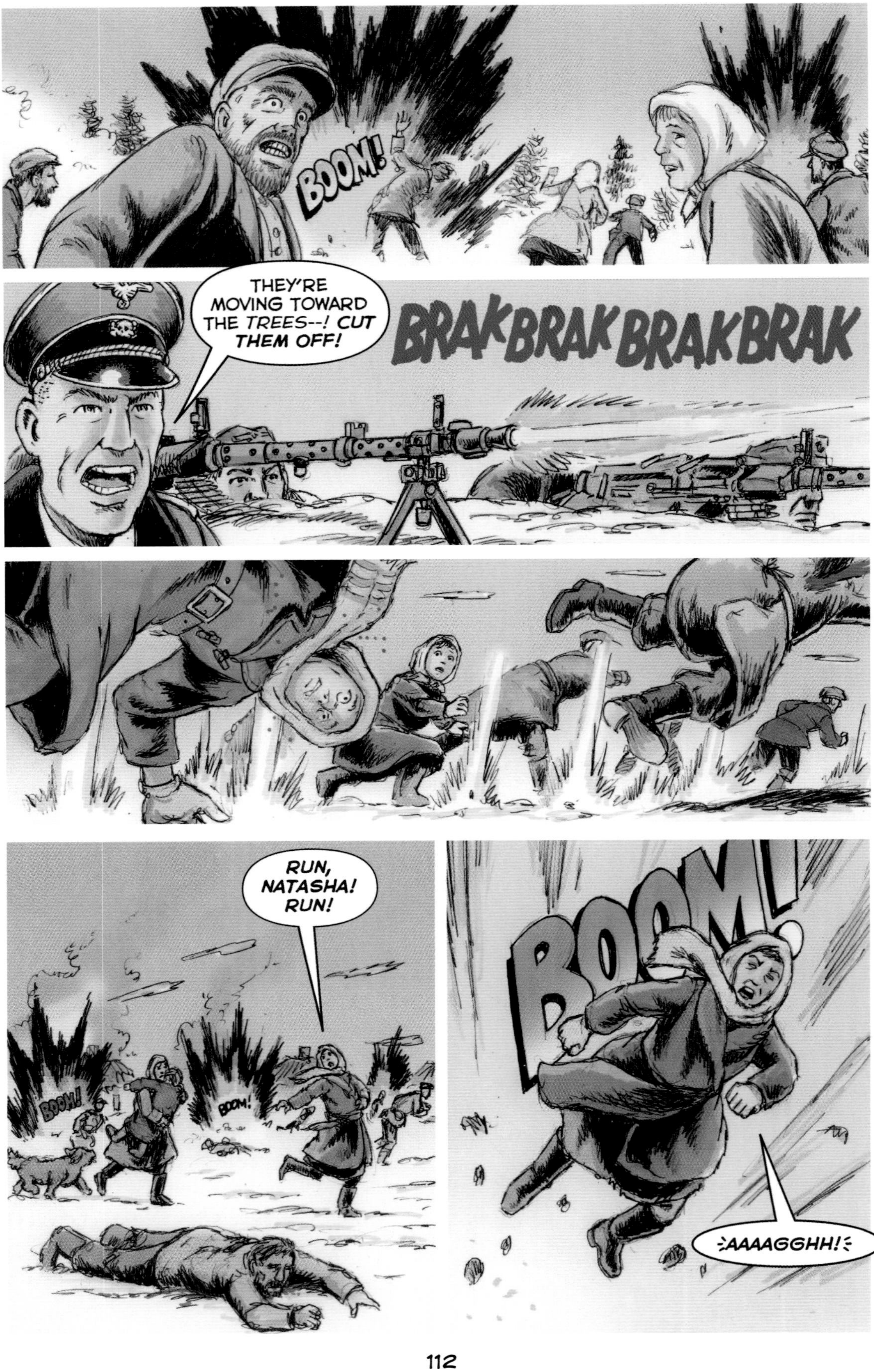
BOOM!
THEY'RE MOVING TOWARD THE *TREES*--! *CUT THEM OFF!*
BRAKBRAKBRAKBRAK
BOOM!
BOOM!
RUN, NATASHA! RUN!
BOOM!
AAAAGGHH!

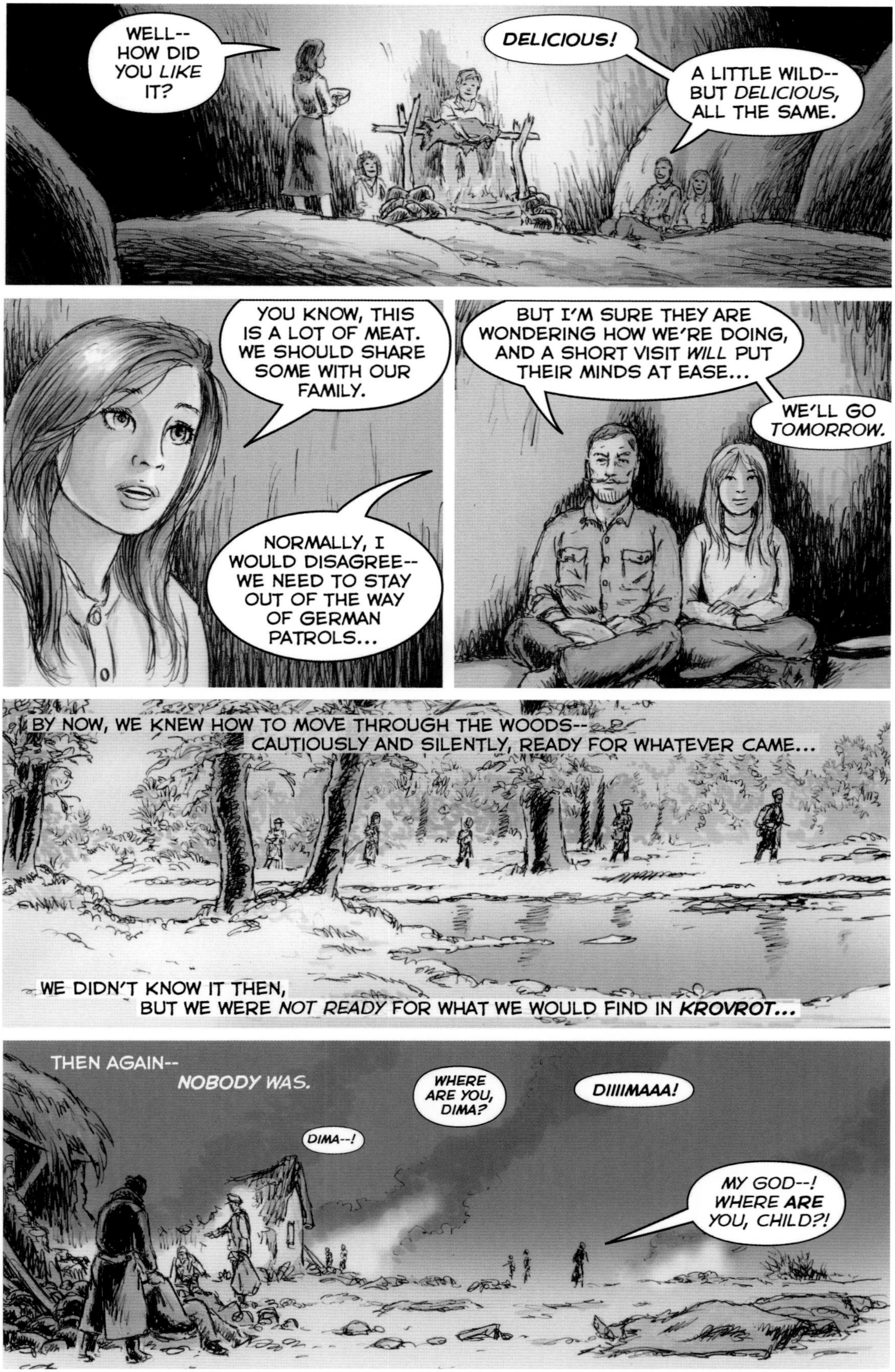
WELL-- HOW DID YOU *LIKE* IT?
DELICIOUS!
A LITTLE WILD-- BUT *DELICIOUS*, ALL THE SAME.
YOU KNOW, THIS IS A LOT OF MEAT. WE SHOULD SHARE SOME WITH OUR FAMILY.
NORMALLY, I WOULD DISAGREE-- WE NEED TO STAY OUT OF THE WAY OF GERMAN PATROLS...
BUT I'M SURE THEY ARE WONDERING HOW WE'RE DOING, AND A SHORT VISIT *WILL* PUT THEIR MINDS AT EASE...
WE'LL GO *TOMORROW.*
BY NOW, WE KNEW HOW TO MOVE THROUGH THE WOODS-- CAUTIOUSLY AND SILENTLY, READY FOR WHATEVER CAME...
WE DIDN'T KNOW IT THEN, BUT WE WERE *NOT READY* FOR WHAT WE WOULD FIND IN ***KROVROT...***
THEN AGAIN-- *NOBODY WAS.*
DIMA--!
WHERE ARE YOU, DIMA?
DIIIIMAAA!
MY GOD--! WHERE **ARE** *YOU, CHILD?!*

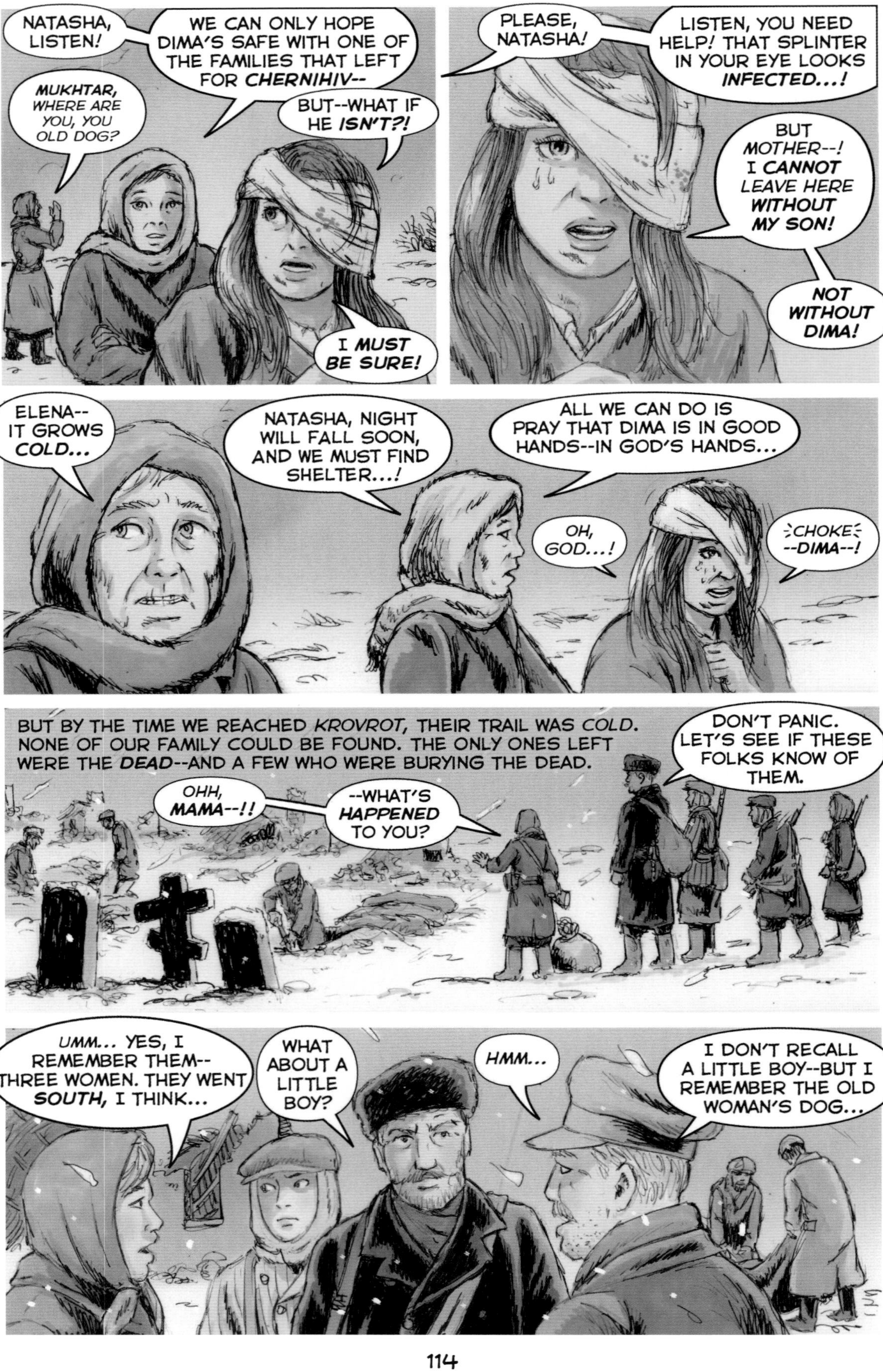
NATASHA, LISTEN!
WE CAN ONLY HOPE DIMA'S SAFE WITH ONE OF THE FAMILIES THAT LEFT FOR CHERNIHIV--
MUKHTAR, WHERE ARE YOU, YOU OLD DOG?
BUT--WHAT IF HE ISN'T?!
I MUST BE SURE!
PLEASE, NATASHA!
LISTEN, YOU NEED HELP! THAT SPLINTER IN YOUR EYE LOOKS INFECTED...!
BUT MOTHER--! I CANNOT LEAVE HERE WITHOUT MY SON!
NOT WITHOUT DIMA!
ELENA-- IT GROWS COLD...
NATASHA, NIGHT WILL FALL SOON, AND WE MUST FIND SHELTER...!
ALL WE CAN DO IS PRAY THAT DIMA IS IN GOOD HANDS--IN GOD'S HANDS...
OH, GOD...!
CHOKE --DIMA--!
BUT BY THE TIME WE REACHED KROVROT, THEIR TRAIL WAS COLD. NONE OF OUR FAMILY COULD BE FOUND. THE ONLY ONES LEFT WERE THE DEAD--AND A FEW WHO WERE BURYING THE DEAD.
DON'T PANIC. LET'S SEE IF THESE FOLKS KNOW OF THEM.
OHH, MAMA--!!
--WHAT'S HAPPENED TO YOU?
UMM... YES, I REMEMBER THEM-- THREE WOMEN. THEY WENT SOUTH, I THINK...
WHAT ABOUT A LITTLE BOY?
HMM...
I DON'T RECALL A LITTLE BOY--BUT I REMEMBER THE OLD WOMAN'S DOG...

VASILY AND I CRIED OPENLY. MILLA'S EYES REMAINED STRANGELY DRY--BUT THEY BURNED WITH ANGER.

I MUST HELP THESE GOOD MEN WITH THEIR GRIM WORK...

EH...?

WELL, IF IT ISN'T *TARAS TYMOSHENKO.* I'VE NOT SEEN *YOU* IN MANY YEARS...!

WHY, IT'S OLD *MRS. BELSKY!*

WHAT ARE YOU DOING DOWN THERE?

OH...?

...JUST WAITING TO *DIE.*

ONE OF THE NICE MEN DUG THIS GRAVE FOR ME. COULD YOU PLEASE COVER IT UP FOR ME, IN A LITTLE WHILE?

AH. SO, TELL ME--WHY WOULD YOU WANT ME TO DO THAT?

BECAUSE I HAVE SEEN SO, SO MANY PEOPLE *DYING*...IN THE *FAMINE,* THE *WAR,* THE *REVOLUTION*...!

ALL OF MY FAMILY, AND EVERYONE ELSE I EVER LOVED, THEY HAVE ALL BEEN *GONE* FOR SO *LONG*...!

EH, I'LL JUST LIE HERE AND LET THE *COLD* TAKE ME... AND I ASK YOU--WHAT IS SO *WRONG* WITH *THAT?*

IT SEEMS TO ME A VERY *NATURAL* DEATH.

THE BASTARDS HAD *UKRAINIAN POLICEMEN* WITH THEM! THERE WERE ABOUT FORTY OF THEM--ALL UNDER THE COMMAND OF A GERMAN NAMED PULZER--

PULZER, DID YOU SAY--? *HARTMUTH PULZER?* HE WAS THE HEARTLESS PIG WHO WAS RECRUITING FOR THE *SCHUMA*--!

ZHENYA'S EYES GREW COLD AND HARD...

HE WAS AT *BABI YAR!*

I WANT TO *REMEMBER* THAT NAME!

I WANT TO REMEMBER IT *TOO*, ZHENYA. TODAY HAS MADE A FEW THINGS VERY *CLEAR* FOR ME.

I'VE NEVER KEPT SECRET WHAT I'VE THOUGHT ABOUT THE *BOLSHEVIKS*...

I'VE LOST MUCH TO THEM--BUT ENEMIES AND FRIENDS MAY *CHANGE*.

TODAY, I'VE LEARNED WHO MY *REAL* ENEMY IS--FOR *NOW*, ANYWAY.

IT'S GETTING *DARK*, UNCLE TARAS.

SHOULD WE BE HEADING BACK TO THE GROTTO--?

EH?

AH, *YES*, YOU'RE RIGHT-- WE SHOULD.

BUT--I'VE GOT ONE THING TO DO *FIRST*...

I NEVER SAW *KROVROT* AGAIN.

LIKE MANY, MANY VILLAGES DESTROYED IN THOSE DAYS, IT NEVER ROSE AGAIN. THE FEW STONES STILL STANDING TOGETHER WERE EVENTUALLY CARTED AWAY FOR USE ON OTHER BUILDING PROJECTS ELSEWHERE, AS MEMORY FADED...

FINALLY, ONLY THE *CEMETERY* REMAINED.

SOON, IT WAS OVERTAKEN BY THE WEEDS AND THE NEARBY FOREST, MAKING THIS TINY COMMUNITY THAT HAD LIVED FOR MORE THAN 300 YEARS--AND THE LIVES OF THE PEOPLE WHO HAD LIVED HERE--SEEM TRIVIAL.

UNLESS THEY WERE ALREADY AWARE OF *KROVROT*, THE FEW PASSERS-BY WOULD NEVER HAVE NOTICED ITS PRESENCE.

BUT *SOMETIMES*...

PERHAPS SOME TRAVELER MIGHT NOTICE *SHADOWY APPARITIONS*--

THERE, AT THE EDGE OF THE FOREST...

THE GHOSTLY FIGURES OF A *SMALL BOY,* PLAYING WITH AN *OLD DOG.*

BY *MID-NOVEMBER, 1941*, TEMPERATURES HAD DROPPED DOWN LOW ENOUGH TO FREEZE THE MUDDY RUSSIAN ROADS, ALLOWING THE PANZERS AND TRUCKS TO MOVE AGAIN.

THIS CHEERED THE GENERALS IN THEIR HEADQUARTERS...

...BUT IT DID NOT CHEER THE MEN IN THE FIELD.

THIS JUST ADDED TO THEIR HARDSHIPS. THEIR REQUESTS FOR OVERCOATS AND WINTER BOOTS WERE MET WITH NERVOUS LAUGHTER AND VAGUE PROMISES.

STILL, THEY PUSHED ON--TAKING A TOWN HERE, CROSSING A RIVER THERE, EVERY STEP BRINGING THEM CLOSER TO THEIR OBJECTIVE...

...BUT EVERY STEP STRETCHING THEIR SUPPLY LINES FARTHER AND FARTHER AWAY FROM GERMANY.

WITH EACH STEP, IT GOT *COLDER*...

...AND THE SNOW GOT *DEEPER*...

...SLOWING THEM *DOWN*...

...LIKE SOME OLD FILM BEING PLAYED ON A PROJECTOR GRADUALLY DRAINED OF ITS POWER.

THEN ONE DAY IT HAPPENED--EVERYTHING SIMPLY *FROZE.*

THE WATER IN THEIR CANTEENS FROZE.
THE OIL IN THE SUMPS OF THE TRUCKS FROZE.

...EVEN *MEN* FROZE!

THE PANZER'S TRACKS FROZE TO THE GROUND,
THE BOLTS OF RIFLES FROZE SHUT...

ANY DELIBERATION ON ADVANCE OR AMBITION SIMPLY CHILLED TO A COLD, CLEAR CRYSTAL AS THE VERY THOUGHTS OF PAST AND FUTURE SEEMED TO IMMOBILIZE IN MIDAIR. MOST OF THE GERMANS HAD NEVER EXPERIENCED ANYTHING LIKE THIS.

ANY MEMORIES OF FAITH OR LOVE OR PATRIOTISM WERE QUICKLY REPLACED BY A DESPERATE AND ALL-CONSUMING DESIRE FOR *WARMTH.*

IT ALL SEEMED SO *CLOSE...!* ONE BATTALION HAD REACHED *GORKY,* A SUBURB OF THEIR PRIZE, AND ANOTHER REACHED THE RAILWAY STATION AT *LOBNYA,* JUST 10 MILES AWAY.

GENERAL FELDMARSCHALL *VON BOCK,* RIDING AT THE HEAD OF HIS ARMY, RAISED HIS FIELD GLASSES...

...AND SAW THE SPIRES OF THE *KREMLIN* RISING IN THE DISTANCE.

THIS WAS THE FIRST AND LAST TIME HE WOULD EVER SEE *MOSCOW.*

THE MARK OF CAIN

IT WASN'T ONLY AT THE GATES OF MOSCOW THAT GERMAN SOLDIERS WERE SHOWING SIGNS OF SUFFERING AND FRUSTRATION. PRIMITIVE ROAD CONDITIONS THROUGHOUT THESE EASTERN LANDS KEPT GERMAN SUPPLY LINES IN A CONSTANT STATE OF FLUX. EVEN THOSE FEW THOROUGHFARES WITH BETTER DRIVING SURFACES WERE POORLY MARKED ON THE INVADERS' LESS-THAN-UP-TO-DATE MAPS...

PICK IT *UP*, SEPP! IF YOU LOSE SIGHT OF KREEGER, WE'LL HAVE TO SPEND THE NIGHT IN SOME LICE-RIDDEN SHACK!

HEY--I CAN SEE THE DAMN ROAD ALREADY! AND DON'T CALL ME "SEPP"!

HOW CAN YOU SEE THIS ROAD? IT HARDLY QUALIFIES--

LOOK, THERE'S THE *DITCH*, THERE'S THE *EMBANKMENT*... ANYTHING THAT'S IN BETWEEN *THAT* IS ROAD!

FLOOR IT, DAMN YOU! HE'S PASSING OUT OF SIGHT...!

CAN YOU STOP *WORRYING* FOR ONE SECOND?

WE'LL CATCH UP ON THE OTHER SIDE-- THIS HILL IS A LITTLE HARD TO MAKE.

TEE HEE HEE!

ALL RIGHT, SMARTASS! *WHERE* DID HE GO--?

WELL--HE HAD TO'VE CONTINUED ON DOWN THE ROAD, TO THE *RIGHT*... UH, *RIGHT*--?

I THINK WE SHOULD STOP AND ASK DIRECTIONS.

DO *WHAT*--?!!

"STOP AND ASK DIRECTIONS"?! OF *WHOM?* IN WHAT LANGUAGE WOULD YOU SUGGEST?

WELL, I SUGGEST WE STOP AND ASK *HER*--!

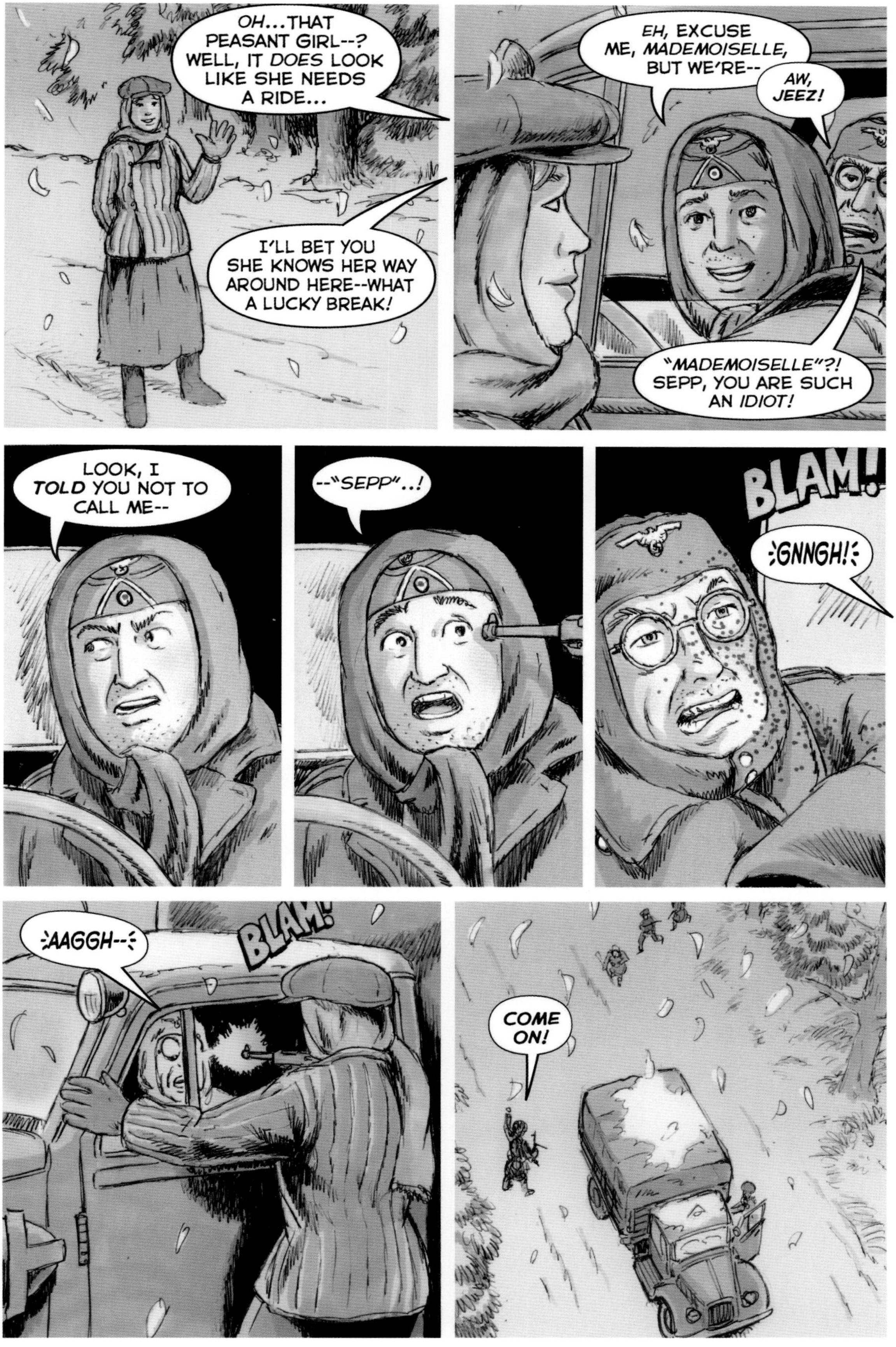
OH...THAT PEASANT GIRL--? WELL, IT DOES LOOK LIKE SHE NEEDS A RIDE...
I'LL BET YOU SHE KNOWS HER WAY AROUND HERE--WHAT A LUCKY BREAK!
EH, EXCUSE ME, MADEMOISELLE, BUT WE'RE--
AW, JEEZ!
"MADEMOISELLE"?! SEPP, YOU ARE SUCH AN IDIOT!
LOOK, I TOLD YOU NOT TO CALL ME--
--"SEPP"..!
BLAM!
GNNGH!
AAGGH--
BLAM!
COME ON!

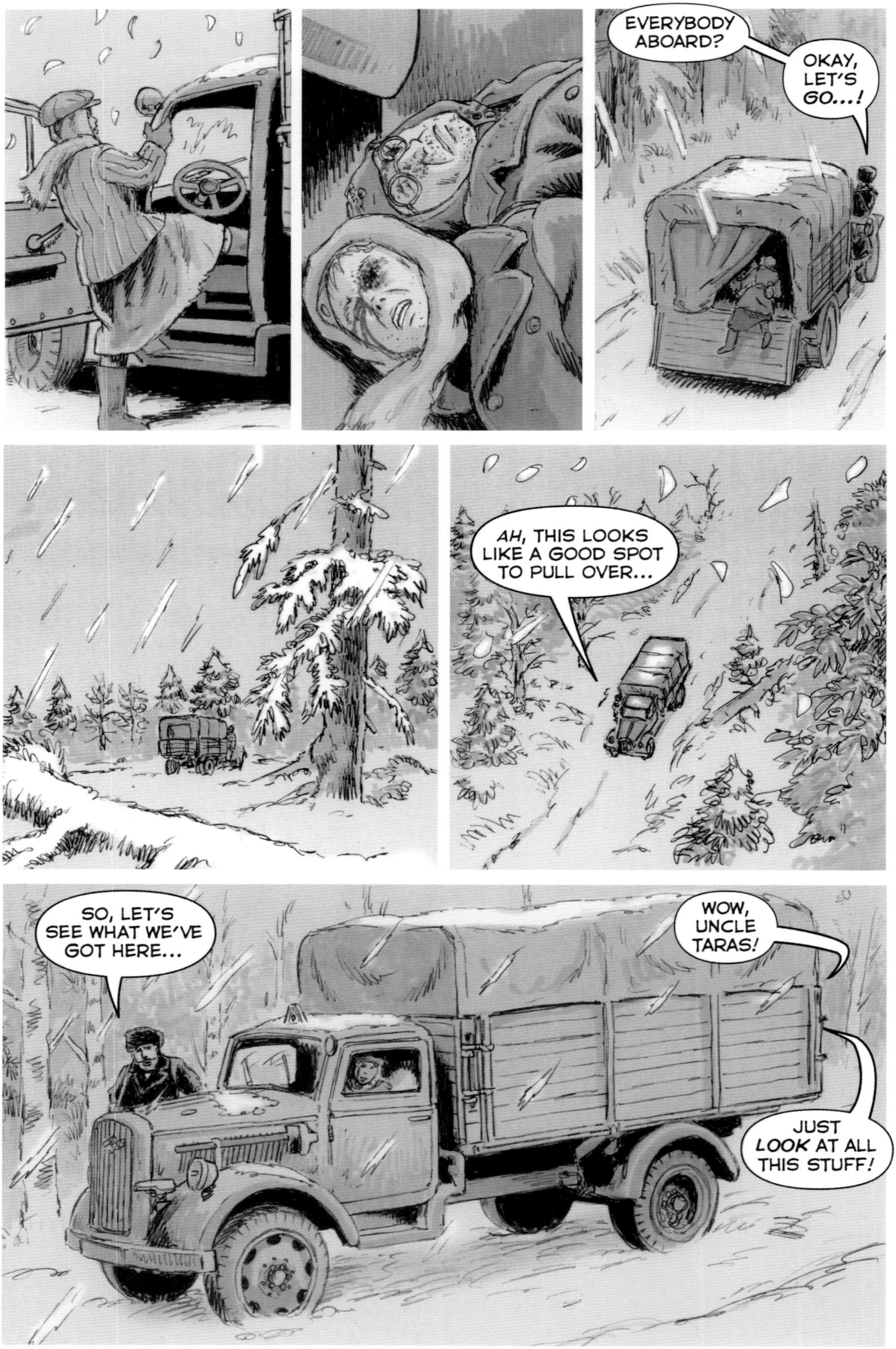
EVERYBODY ABOARD?
OKAY, LET'S GO...!
AH, THIS LOOKS LIKE A GOOD SPOT TO PULL OVER...
SO, LET'S SEE WHAT WE'VE GOT HERE...
WOW, UNCLE TARAS!
JUST LOOK AT ALL THIS STUFF!

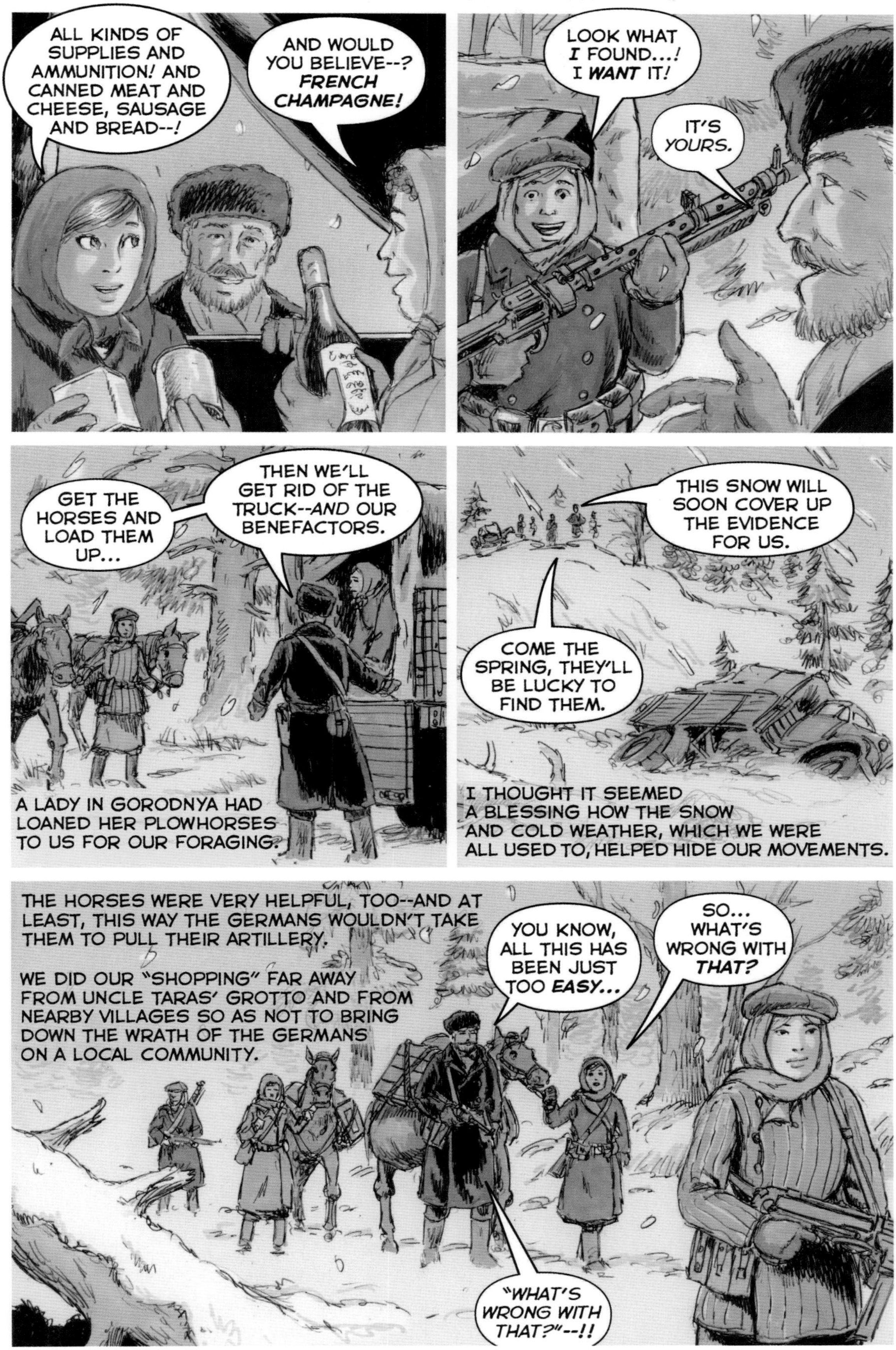
ALL KINDS OF SUPPLIES AND AMMUNITION! AND CANNED MEAT AND CHEESE, SAUSAGE AND BREAD--!
AND WOULD YOU BELIEVE--? FRENCH CHAMPAGNE!
LOOK WHAT I FOUND...! I WANT IT!
IT'S YOURS.
GET THE HORSES AND LOAD THEM UP...
THEN WE'LL GET RID OF THE TRUCK--AND OUR BENEFACTORS.
A LADY IN GORODNYA HAD LOANED HER PLOWHORSES TO US FOR OUR FORAGING.
THIS SNOW WILL SOON COVER UP THE EVIDENCE FOR US.
COME THE SPRING, THEY'LL BE LUCKY TO FIND THEM.
I THOUGHT IT SEEMED A BLESSING HOW THE SNOW AND COLD WEATHER, WHICH WE WERE ALL USED TO, HELPED HIDE OUR MOVEMENTS.
THE HORSES WERE VERY HELPFUL, TOO--AND AT LEAST, THIS WAY THE GERMANS WOULDN'T TAKE THEM TO PULL THEIR ARTILLERY.
WE DID OUR "SHOPPING" FAR AWAY FROM UNCLE TARAS' GROTTO AND FROM NEARBY VILLAGES SO AS NOT TO BRING DOWN THE WRATH OF THE GERMANS ON A LOCAL COMMUNITY.
YOU KNOW, ALL THIS HAS BEEN JUST TOO EASY...
SO... WHAT'S WRONG WITH THAT?
"WHAT'S WRONG WITH THAT?"--!!

HERE IS WHAT'S *WRONG*: THREE TIMES NOW, WE HAVE ATTACKED GERMANS, AND EACH TIME, THEY NEVER KNEW WHAT HIT THEM--BUT THEY HAVE BEEN SUPPLY AND TRANSPORT MEN, NOT USED TO FIGHTING.

...BUT WHAT IF THEY HAD BEEN READY? WHAT IF NEXT, THEY ARE *COMBAT TROOPS?*

I'M NOT SURE WE ARE *READY* FOR *THAT.*

I WAS AFRAID I KNEW WHAT HE HAD MEANT...

IT WAS *I* WHO HE BELIEVED WAS NOT READY... AND I KNEW *WHY.*

MY, MY! I HAVEN'T EATEN SO MUCH SINCE AT MAMA'S LAST EASTER...!

OOH, THIS CHAMPAGNE MAKES MY *HEAD* SPIN--!

HAHA! WAIT AND SEE HOW IT FEELS TOMORROW MORNING...!

ALL RIGHT, EVERYONE...I HAVE SOMETHING TO SAY.

TOMORROW MORNING, WE WILL START PLANNING AND TRAINING TO *ATTACK* A GERMAN MILITARY TARGET.

I BELIEVE THAT OUR BEING ABLE TO DEAL WITH SUCH AN EVENT IS NECESSARY FOR OUR *SURVIVAL.* WE ARE LIVING IN THE MIDDLE OF A *WAR*--A WAR THAT'S ALREADY HAD A STRONG EFFECT ON US ALL.

AT PRESENT, WE HAVE NO IDEA WHAT THE *OUTCOME* WILL BE--

--AND EVEN THOUGH WE HAVE NOT YET COMPLETELY CHOSEN SIDES, SOONER OR LATER WE WILL BE FORCED TO DO SO. IF WE DON'T, THEN WE MIGHT HAVE *BOTH* SIDES COMING AFTER US.

LATER, AS EVERYONE PREPARED FOR BED, I APPROACHED UNCLE TARAS IN PRIVATE.

UNCLE TARAS...? IT FELT LIKE YOU WERE TALKING DIRECTLY TO ME TODAY.

I GUESS I *WAS*, KATUSHA. I WORRY FOR YOU--FOR YOU ARE THE ONLY ONE OF US...

...WHO HAS NOT YET *KILLED*.

BUT--IN ALL OUR FIGHTS, I HAVE *ALWAYS* FIRED MY WEAPON!

YES! YOU LOAD AND FIRE LIKE AN EXPERT... BUT YOU NEVER *HIT* ANYTHING!

MY DEAR NIECE--YOU HAVE A GOOD HEART.

ZHENYA DOES FINE--SHE IS AVENGING HER PARENTS.

VASILY IS A WILD YOUNG BOY. SO FAR, HE IS ENJOYING THIS ADVENTURE.

MILLA...IS *DIFFERENT*. THERE IS SOMETHING IN HER-- I'M NOT SURE WHAT. SOME PEOPLE ARE JUST BORN KILLERS...

I PRAY SHE IS *NOT* ONE OF THEM.

BUT I AM AFRAID THAT EVEN WHAT WE HAVE JUST WITNESSED IN KROVROT HAS NOT HARDENED YOU.

KATUSHA, I HAVE SEEN MUCH OF THIS WORLD-- AND I HAVE SEEN *MUCH WAR*.

YOU DO NOT YET REALIZE WHAT WE ARE GOING TO HAVE TO DEAL WITH...

I HAVE KNOWN OTHERS JUST LIKE YOU, AND THEY ARE SOME OF THE FINEST PEOPLE I HAVE EVER KNOWN. BUT THE SAD THING ABOUT THEM IS--

--THEY USUALLY *DON'T SURVIVE*.

THEN UNCLE TARAS BADE ME GOODNIGHT AND WENT ON UP TO THE LEDGE THAT HE AND MILLA SHARED.

HE CALLED IT THE "*PENTHOUSE*"-- WHATEVER THAT MEANT.

SOON, EVERYONE WAS ASLEEP.

EVERYONE BUT *ME*, THAT IS...

I WAS ALONE WITH MY THOUGHTS.

THE NEXT DAY, UNCLE TARAS BEGAN TO DRILL US. HE EXPLAINED "MUTUAL SUPPORT FIRE" AND "MOVING BY ECHELON," AND TAUGHT US HOW TO SPOT SMALL FOLDS IN THE GROUND TO USE FOR CONCEALMENT OR PROTECTION.

SAY A GERMAN IS FIRING ON YOU FROM THAT TREE...

ZHENYA-- *WHERE* WOULD *YOU* TAKE COVER?

RIGHT HERE.

I'D STAY LOW IN THIS DEPRESSION, CRAWL OVER TO THERE, AND THEN--INTO THE WOODS.

THE MACHINE GUN VASILY HAD TAKEN WAS A GERMAN *MG34*. IT CAME WITH A PACK THAT HAD HEAT-PROOF GLOVES, A SPARE BARREL, AND A MANUAL IN GERMAN.

THIS IS VASILY'S WEAPON, BUT ALL OF US SHOULD KNOW HOW IT OPERATES. *ZHENYA*, I WANT YOU TO BE HIS ASSISTANT--

HEY, *I* COULD DO THAT--!

NO, KATUSHA.

I HAVE *OTHER* PLANS FOR YOU.

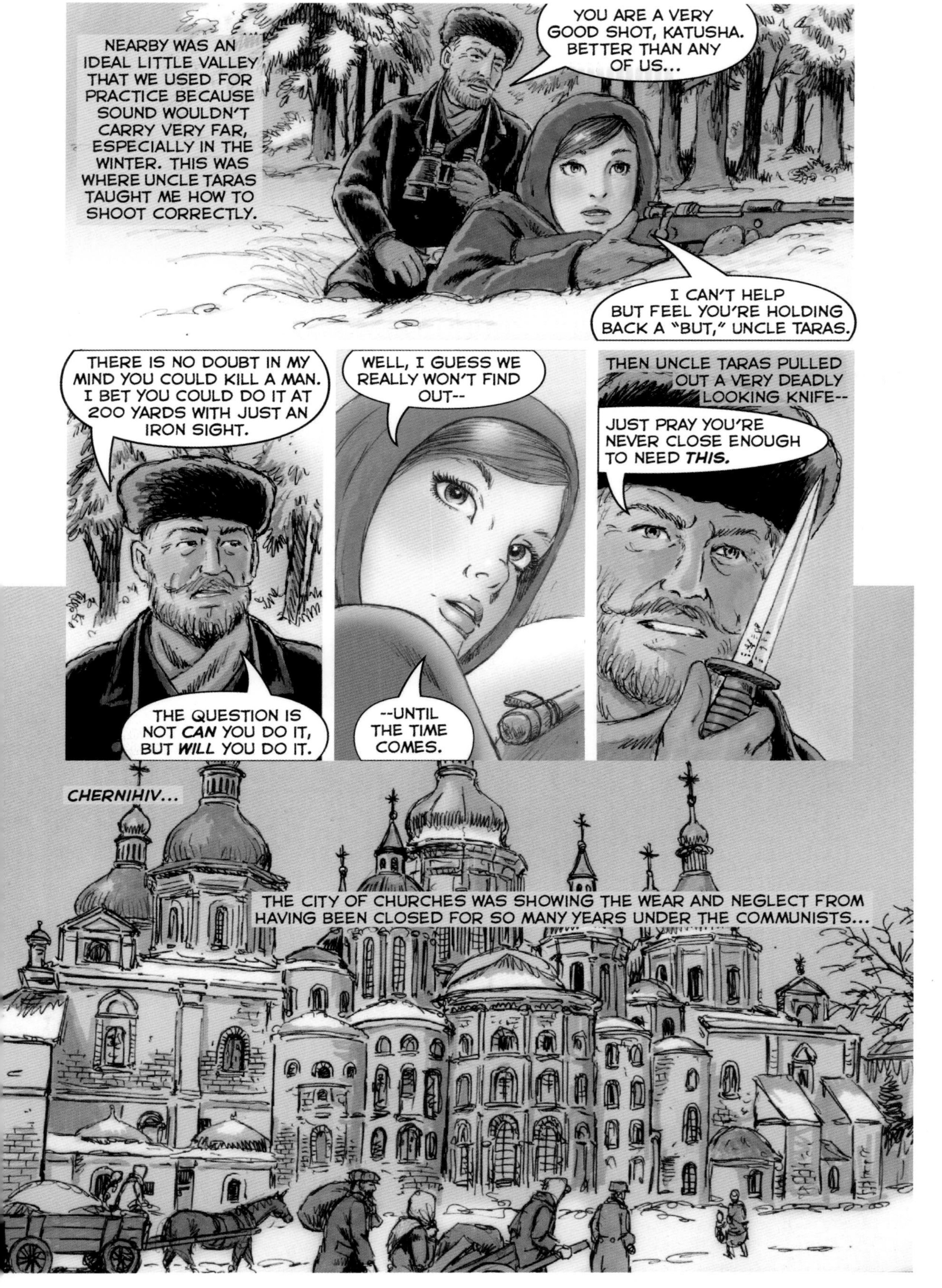
NEARBY WAS AN IDEAL LITTLE VALLEY THAT WE USED FOR PRACTICE BECAUSE SOUND WOULDN'T CARRY VERY FAR, ESPECIALLY IN THE WINTER. THIS WAS WHERE UNCLE TARAS TAUGHT ME HOW TO SHOOT CORRECTLY.
YOU ARE A VERY GOOD SHOT, KATUSHA. BETTER THAN ANY OF US...
I CAN'T HELP BUT FEEL YOU'RE HOLDING BACK A "BUT," UNCLE TARAS.
THERE IS NO DOUBT IN MY MIND YOU COULD KILL A MAN. I BET YOU COULD DO IT AT 200 YARDS WITH JUST AN IRON SIGHT.
THE QUESTION IS NOT *CAN* YOU DO IT, BUT *WILL* YOU DO IT.
WELL, I GUESS WE REALLY WON'T FIND OUT--
--UNTIL THE TIME COMES.
THEN UNCLE TARAS PULLED OUT A VERY DEADLY LOOKING KNIFE--
JUST PRAY YOU'RE NEVER CLOSE ENOUGH TO NEED ***THIS.***
CHERNIHIV...
THE CITY OF CHURCHES WAS SHOWING THE WEAR AND NEGLECT FROM HAVING BEEN CLOSED FOR SO MANY YEARS UNDER THE COMMUNISTS...

A NUMBER OF CHERNIHIV'S CHURCHES HAVE BEEN OPENED FOR NO OTHER REASON THAN TO PROVIDE SHELTER FOR THE THOUSANDS OF REFUGEES MADE HOMELESS BY THIS LATEST WAR...

ELENA! WHERE HAVE YOU BEEN?

GETTING US SOMETHING TO EAT, MAMA. HOW IS NATASHA'S EYE?

NOT GOOD-- IT'S TOO *PAINFUL* TO OPEN.

WHAT'S THAT YOU GOT THERE?

LOOK, I MANAGED TO FIND THIS OLD TIN *SKILLET!* AND GUESS WHAT, MAMA...!

I THINK I'VE FOUND ME A *JOB!*

THE GERMANS HAVE OPENED A SLAUGHTERHOUSE. THEY SAID THEY WOULD HIRE ME!

THAT WAS WHERE I GOT THIS BOTTLE OF *COW'S BLOOD...!*

I'M GOING TO MAKE US A NICE OMELET--

YUCK! I *CAN'T* EAT *THAT!*

BUT... WE *HAVE* TO FILL OUR STOMACHS, NATASHA--!

I WONDER...IS MY *DIMA* HAVING ANYTHING RIGHT NOW...?

IS--IS SOMEONE *FEEDING* HIM--?

--FEEDING MY *DIMA?* OHHH, MY DIMAAA...

WE'RE LUCKY WE FOUND THEM, THIS FAR OFF THE BEATEN PATH...

YES. BOTH MEN HAD BEEN SHOT IN THE FACE AT CLOSE RANGE--

--AND THEIR CARGO WAS PICKED CLEAN OF *EVERYTHING*-- WEAPONS, AMMUNITION, FOOD, MAPS...!

WHAT IS THE NAME OF THE CLOSEST VILLAGE?

CLOSEST TO *HERE? NONE!* NOT FOR 20 MILES. WHY?

THE *FÜHRER* HAS ISSUED STRICT ORDERS IN DEALING WITH PARTISANS.

FOR EVERY MURDERED GERMAN SOLDIER--*TEN* HOSTAGES WILL BE EXECUTED.

I CAN'T BELIEVE IT. *OBERSTURMFÜHRER*--WHEN WE FIRST CAME THROUGH THIS COUNTRY, THE PEOPLE SEEMED GLAD TO SEE US.

I HAD THE IMPRESSION THAT WE COULD WIN THEM OVER--

SERGEANT! WE ARE NOT HERE TO "WIN THEM OVER." WE ARE HERE TO *CONQUER* THEM.

THESE SLAVS ARE *NOT* OUR EQUALS, AND YOU SHOULD REMEMBER THAT.

IN THAT CASE, SIR...

MY MEN AND I REQUEST TO BE SENT BACK TO THE *REAL* FRONT, TO FIGHT OUR *EQUALS*-- THE "IVANS."

SERGEANT, YOU WILL BE SENT BACK TO THE FRONT...

...WHEN I AM *FINISHED* WITH YOU.

I TRUST THAT IS *CLEAR.*

MY RADIO KEPT US ABREAST OF THE LATEST NEWS, BUT WE GOT THE LOCAL GOSSIP WHENEVER WE SLIPPED INTO GORODNYA TO SEE *FATHER ZAPOLYE.* ONE NIGHT, WHEN UNCLE TARAS AND I STOPPED BY THE FATHER'S HOME...

IT'S OFFICIAL NOW... GERMAN FORCES HAVE BEEN STOPPED IN FRONT OF MOSCOW, AND THE RED ARMY IS PUSHING THEM BACK.

WELL, THAT'S STILL A LONG WAY FROM STALIN STROLLING DOWN THE STREETS OF BERLIN.

BUT THEY SAY THE GERMANS ARE WAGING A SIEGE AGAINST *LENINGRAD,* AND THAT ITS PEOPLE ARE *STARVING--!*

WHO DO YOU THINK WILL *WIN,* FATHER?

WELL, AS YOUR UNCLE WOULD TELL YOU, THERE IS NO LOVE LOST BETWEEN MEN AND THE *BOLSHEVIKS...*

...BUT *THESE* FASCIST DEVILS WANT TO ENSLAVE OR MURDER US. THEY ARE A MUCH MORE *IMMEDIATE* PROBLEM.

JUST YESTERDAY THEY TOOK AWAY *EIGHT MORE* YOUNG PEOPLE TO GERMANY --AS SLAVE LABOR!

LAST WEEK, A YOUNG WOMAN WAS BY TO SEE ME, "TO PRAY FOR A SICK FRIEND," SHE SAID--

--BUT SHE LET IT SLIP THAT A PARTISAN GROUP IN THE NORTHEAST IS LOOKING TO COMBINE WITH OTHER GROUPS.

*HMM...*FOR THE TIME BEING, FATHER-- JUST PLAY DUMB TILL WE LEARN MORE ABOUT THEM.

HOW HAVE THE GERMANS REACTED TO THIS PARTISAN ACTIVITY?

WELL, THEY ARE HUNTING DOWN JEWS AND *COMMUNISTS*-- AND SOME UKRAINIANS ARE HELPING THEM...! GERMAN TROOPS SENT BACK FROM THE FRONT FOR A REST ARE OFTEN PRESSED INTO THESE SEARCHES.

YOU SHOULD WATCH OUT FOR THEIR PATROLS ON YOUR WAY BACK.

WE WERE ON OUR WAY BACK THROUGH THE COLD, DARK FOREST TO THE GROTTO, WHEN UNCLE TARAS SUDDENLY STOPPED...

KATUSHA...

...DO YOU *SMELL* ANYTHING?

AHHH...

SMOKE, MAYBE?

WE CREPT UP THROUGH THE WOODS TILL WE OVERLOOKED A LITTLE VALLEY.

WELL, LOOK WHAT WE HAVE HERE...!

THERE BELOW US...

...WERE FOURTEEN GERMAN SOLDIERS, HUDDLED AROUND A ROARING CAMPFIRE.

THEY REALLY LOOK COMFORTABLE.

HMM... NO SENTRIES POSTED...

LISTEN, GET BACK TO THE GROTTO AND GET EVERYBODY UP. YOU REMEMBER WHERE WE DUMPED THE TRUCK?

YES, SIR.

THAT LITTLE VALLEY THAT CUTS OFF TO THE SOUTH--SET UP AN *AMBUSH* ON THE EASTERN SIDE OF IT, THEN WAIT FOR ME.

...BUT--

NOW, GO!

I'M GOING TO RUN THESE FELLOWS AROUND FOR A WHILE...

I RAN LIKE MAD!

THINGS WERE HAPPENING JUST TOO FAST--I DIDN'T KNOW WHAT TO DO!

I SIMPLY HOPED I WOULD FIGURE IT OUT BEFORE I GOT TO THE GROTTO.

I HAD NOT GONE FAR-- WHEN I HEARD GUNFIRE ERUPTING BEHIND ME...!

KRAK! KRAK! KRAK! KRAK!

UNCLE TARAS HAD BEGUN THE SHOW.

--A SHOW IN WHICH EACH OF US HAD A CRUCIAL ROLE TO PLAY!

EVERYBODY UP!! *GET YOUR* WEAPONS *READY--!*

--UNCLE TARAS HAS *DEADLY WORK* FOR US!

AS WE SCRAMBLED THROUGH THE ICY WOODS, I FELT THE WHEELS OF MY BRAIN TURN AS I TRIED TO RECALL EVERY WORD OF UNCLE TARAS' LESSONS...

LET'S GO THIS WAY, FROM THE HIGH END.

...LIKE THIS ONE HE TAUGHT US, ABOUT HOW ENTERING A VALLEY THROUGH ITS MOUTH WOULD LEAVE DAMNING FOOTPRINTS IN THE SNOW FOR THE GERMANS TO SEE.

IT WAS STILL QUITE DARK WHEN WE BROKE FROM THE TREES INTO THE OPEN. I SENT MILLA AROUND THE RIM TO A POSITION NEAR THE ENTRANCE.

ONCE THE GERMANS ENTERED THE VALLEY, SHE COULD SHUT THE DOOR BEHIND THEM.

VASILY AND ZHENYA SET THE MACHINE GUN UP HIGH ON THE EASTERN WALL.

...FROM THERE, THEY COULD SWEEP THE WHOLE VALLEY.

I WENT TO THE HIGH SOUTH END OF THE LITTLE VALLEY, AND FOUND A PERFECT SPOT BEHIND SOME FALLEN LOGS.

FROM THERE, I COULD SEE FROM ONE END OF THE VALLEY TO THE OTHER.

FROM WHERE I WAS, I COULD SEE VASILY AND ZHENYA AT THE MACHINE GUN.

THEIR EYES WERE GLUED ON ME FOR SOME REASON...

I WAS WONDERING *WHY*...

...THEN THE REASON FOR THIS *HIT ME* LIKE THE COLD WINTER WIND!

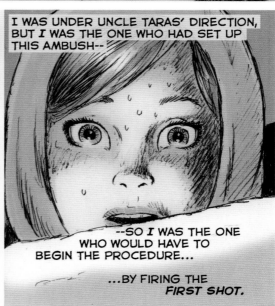

I WAS UNDER UNCLE TARAS' DIRECTION, BUT *I* WAS THE ONE WHO HAD SET UP THIS AMBUSH--

--SO *I* WAS THE ONE WHO WOULD HAVE TO BEGIN THE PROCEDURE...

...BY FIRING THE *FIRST SHOT.*

DESPITE THE COLD, I BEGAN TO *SWEAT.*

WITH NO TIME FOR ANY REAL EMOTIONAL PREPARATION, I WAS QUICKLY APPROACHING THE MOMENT I FEARED THE MOST.

THE PALE SUN BEGAN TO GLOW IN THE EASTERN SKY.

SUDDENLY, I SAW A FIGURE STEP OUT OUT OF THE SNOW-COVERED FOREST AT THE OTHER END OF THE VALLEY--!!

FOR SOME REASON, I'D THOUGHT--AND HOPED--THAT UNCLE TARAS WOULD BE THE FIRST ONE TO SHOW UP AND TAKE CHARGE...

...BUT HERE WAS A *GERMAN!*

MORE CAME OUT OF THE WOODS, CLEAR TARGETS IN THEIR GRAY-GREEN COATS BEFORE THE WHITE SNOW. SOMEHOW, TARAS HAD MANAGED TO TRICK THEM INTO ENTERING THE VALLEY AHEAD OF HIM.

OH, UNCLE TARAS HAD TRICKED US ALL, I THOUGHT, ALMOST ANGRY--LIKE THE WAY HE LEFT EVERYTHING UP TO *ME*...

...BUT THEN, ANOTHER THOUGHT RAN THROUGH ME LIKE A CHILL--!

--WHAT IF UNCLE TARAS IS *DEAD*--?!

OH, GOD! OH, GOD!, I BEGAN TO PRAY--*WHAT* IS GOING TO *HAPPEN* TO US?

I COUNTED THE MEN AS THEY CAME INTO THE VALLEY...

ELEVEN.

BUT...UNCLE TARAS SAID THERE WERE *FOURTEEN!* WHERE WERE THE OTHERS?

I PUT THESE THOUGHTS OUT OF MY MIND.

I HAD TO CONCENTRATE ON THE TASK AT HAND...

IT SOON BECAME CLEAR ELEVEN WAS ALL THAT WERE COMING. THE LAST OF THE GERMANS WAS AT LEAST 200 YARDS FROM WHERE THEY HAD COME OUT OF THE WOODS.

THEY WERE ALL THERE. THE FIRST GERMAN WAS NOW ABOUT 50 YARDS AWAY, AND MOVING AT A RATE THAT MADE IT CLEAR NONE OF THEM KNEW OF OUR PRESENCE.

I TOOK CAREFUL AIM AT THE LEAD GERMAN...

I TOOK A DEEP BREATH...

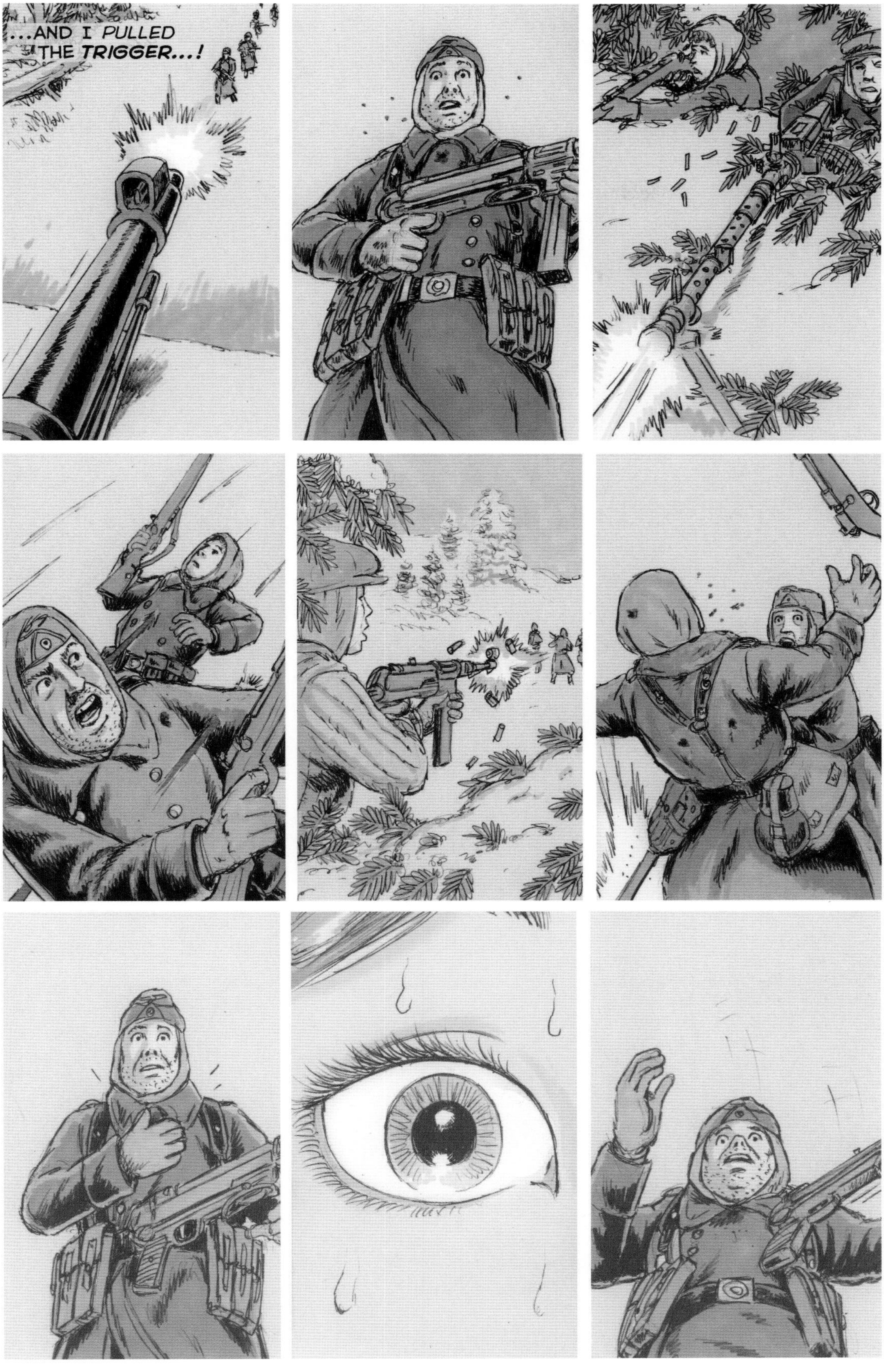
...AND I *PULLED* THE ***TRIGGER***...!

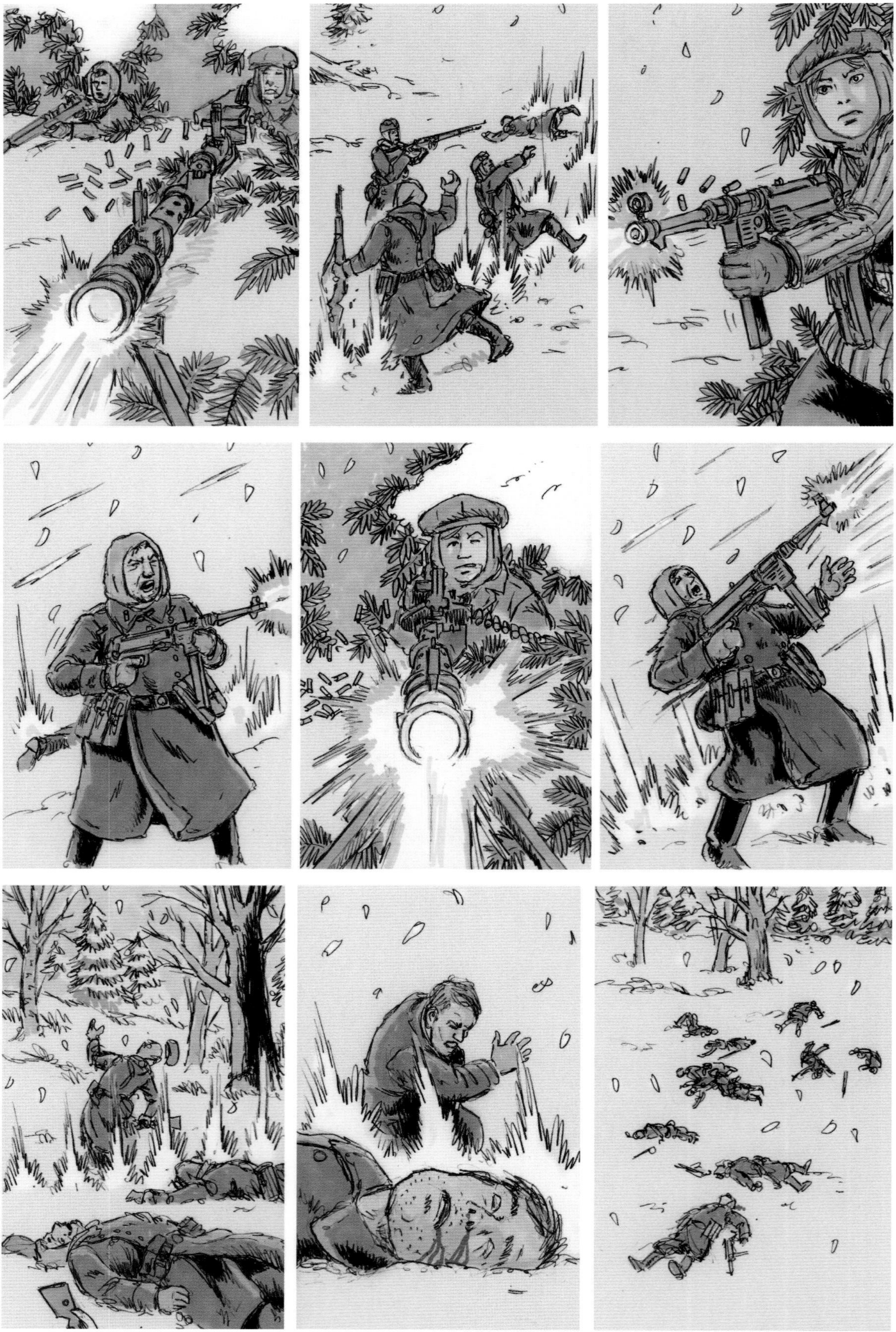

SUDDENLY, THE FIRING WAS *OVER*.

A FRESH SNOW BEGAN TO FALL ON THE STILL, GRAY FORMS...

...AND THE SILENCE WAS DEAFENING.

THEN UNCLE TARAS STEPPED OUT OF THE TREES, AS CALMLY AS HE WOULD HAVE WALKED IN OUR FRONT DOOR...!

GET THE AMMUNITION AND WEAPONS--AND ANY USEFUL ITEMS LIKE BOOTS AND OVERCOATS.

WHAT DO WE DO WITH THE BODIES?

NOTHING. THE SNOW WILL HIDE THEM TILL SPRING.

WELL, KATUSHA...?

HE'S *YOURS*.

ANYTHING OF HIS YOU WANT, YOU HAD BEST GET IT NOW.

AT FIRST, THE COMMENT *SHOCKED* ME--

BUT THEN, I FELT MY SHOCK SLOWLY BUILD INTO A SMOLDERING, NUMBING *RAGE*...

I THINK I'VE TAKEN ALL OF HIS THAT I CAN.

AFTER OUR SUCCESS, EVERYONE SEEMED IN A FESTIVE MOOD THAT NIGHT--EVERYONE EXCEPT ME.

I EXPECT THAT YOU ARE ANGRY WITH ME, KATUSHA...

NO, UNCLE TARAS, I'M NOT ANGRY--JUST A LITTLE DISAPPOINTED ABOUT HOW THINGS ARE GOING.

I MEAN--SO FAR, MY LIFE SURE ISN'T TURNING OUT THE WAY I HAD THOUGHT IT WOULD...!

NOT WHAT YOU THOUGHT, *EH?* WHAT *DID* YOU EXPECT OUT OF LIFE, KATUSHA?

OH, I DON'T KNOW-- A JOB, A HUSBAND, A FAMILY...SOMETHING LIKE THAT...

THAT SEEMS SO COMMON-- SO *ORDINARY.* NOT MUCH TO ASK FOR...

BUT ONCE, ALL *I* WANTED WAS TO STAY IN KROVROT, WORKING THAT LITTLE FARM...

REALLY? THAT DOESN'T SEEM LIKE *YOU*...!

PERHAPS-- BUT IT WAS NOT TO BE.

INSTEAD, LIFE SENT ME DOWN A ROAD I NEVER INTENDED TO TAKE.

OH, I SOMETIMES GOT TO CHOOSE WHICH FORK I FOLLOWED--BUT WITHOUT EVER KNOWING WHERE MY PATH WOULD REALLY LEAD ME...

THERE ARE THOSE SIGNS WE CANNOT READ-- THE MESSAGES WE DO NOT UNDERSTAND.

I CAN'T REALLY COMPLAIN, FOR SO OFTEN I HAVE BEEN REWARDED IN GREATER WAYS THAN I'VE BEEN PUNISHED. I'VE LEARNED TO ACCEPT THOSE BLESSINGS I'VE RECEIVED AND NOT YEARN FOR THE GIFTS THAT I FEEL HAVE BEEN DENIED ME.

THERE ARE REASONS WE ARE GIVEN SOME THINGS AND REFUSED OTHERS...BUT THE *GREATEST MYSTERY* OF MY LIFE--

"--IS RIGHT HERE... IN THE FORM OF *MILLA.*

"I'VE BEEN ALL OVER THE WORLD, KATUSHA-- I'VE KNOWN MANY WOMEN. BUT I HAVE NEVER REALLY *LOVED* UNTIL NOW. IT'S LIKE ALL THE BAD ROADS AND ALL THE HARD TIMES HAVE LED ME *HERE*--AS IF ALL THE EVENTS OF HISTORY HAVE CONSPIRED TO BRING A BATTERED OLD WANDERER LIKE ME TOGETHER WITH AN ANGEL LIKE *MILLA.*"

DURING THOSE EARLY WINTER MONTHS OF *1942,* WE HEARD ON THE RADIO HOW THE RED ARMY, REINFORCED BY SIBERIAN DIVISIONS, HAD DRIVEN THE GERMANS BACK FROM THE GATES OF MOSCOW. BUT WE ALL UNDERSTOOD WHO WAS THE REAL VICTOR IN THIS FIGHT--IT WAS "GENERAL WINTER."

WE ALSO UNDERSTOOD NOW HOW STRONG THE GERMANS WERE. COME SPRING, THE *WEHRMACHT* WOULD BE ON THE MARCH AGAIN.

THE UKRAINIAN WINTER WAS WANING, BUT STILL FRIGID. SOON WE WOULD LOSE WHAT PROTECTION THE HARSH WEATHER AFFORDED US. TO BE SURE OF OUR SAFETY, WE REGULARLY PATROLLED THE REGION AROUND UNCLE TARAS' GROTTO.

IT WAS ON ONE OF THESE PATROLS THAT ZHENYA AND I FOUND *FATHER ZAPOLYE* WANDERING ABOUT THE COLD WOODS...

AH! OVER *HERE--!!*

PRAISE GOD--! I AM *FOUND!*

TARAS, IT WAS ONLY BY DIVINE PROVIDENCE YOUR GIRLS FOUND ME! I WAS TOTALLY LOST--I'D HAVE FROZEN TO DEATH!

WHAT WERE YOU LOOKING FOR OUT HERE, FATHER?

ACTUALLY, I WAS LOOKING FOR *YOU,* TARAS--

THE *GERMANS* ARE LOOKING FOR YOU, *TOO...*

...BUT IT IS NOT BECAUSE OF *THEM* THAT I CAME...

BECAUSE THE **GERMANS** STEAL WHATEVER THEY WANT AND TAKE EVERYONE OVER FOURTEEN BACK TO GERMANY TO WORK--

--MANY FLED TO THE **FOREST**. MOST HAVE NOT FARED WELL...THEY GET CAUGHT, OR THEY STARVE. THERE ARE ALSO RED ARMY SOLDIERS HIDING IN THE WOODS--

--LEFTOVERS FROM LAST SUMMER'S BATTLES. THEY'VE NOT FARED WELL, EITHER.

STALIN'S CALLED FOR A **GENERAL UPRISING**. HE'S SENT SPECIAL TROOPS BEHIND GERMAN LINES TO ORGANIZE AND LEAD A PARTISAN WAR...

CAN YOU IMAGINE WHAT A WAR LIKE THAT COULD COST INNOCENT PEOPLE?

IT COULD MAKE THIS WAR WORSE THAN IT ALREADY IS. BUT TARAS--**YOU** HAVE THE ABILITY TO LEAD MEN AND TO CONTROL SUCH A SITUATION.

REALLY? WHAT COULD **I** DO?

PEOPLE ARE SAYING THAT **SEMEN KALASHNIKOV** HIMSELF HAS RETURNED TO THESE WOODS, MOVING LIKE A GHOST AGAINST THE GERMANS...! **TARAS**--

--THEY ARE TALKING ABOUT **YOU**.

SEMEN KALASHNIKOV! UNCLE TARAS' OLD MENTOR AND COMMANDER FROM THE FIRST WAR. HIS NAME SENT CHILLS UP MY SPINE!

THERE IS A **RED ARMY OFFICER** FROM AN ARTILLERY BRIGADE WHO'S BEEN HIDING OUT IN THE DEEP WOODS SINCE AUTUMN, WITH SOME 70 OF HIS MEN...

...AND HE WOULD VERY MUCH LIKE TO **MEET** YOU, TARAS.

TARAS SAT SILENTLY IN THOUGHT FOR A FEW MINUTES. THEN HE SPOKE...

WELL, AS THE OLD SAYING GOES... *"THE ENEMY OF MY ENEMY IS MY FRIEND."*

LET'S GO MEET THESE NEW FRIENDS.

140

UNCLE TARAS WISELY DECIDED TO CHECK OUT THE PARTISANS' CAMP FIRST WITHOUT MAKING A COMMITMENT. HE CHOSE ME TO ACCOMPANY HIM ON HIS FORAY, POSING AS A HOMELESS GIRL AND HER "ELDERLY" FATHER. HIDDEN PISTOLS WERE OUR SOLE WEAPONS.

AS WE TRUDGED THROUGH THE SLUSHY, FROZEN MESS, I COULD SEE THE FIRST TINY SPRING BUDS PEEKING THROUGH THE SNOW-- ALONG WITH *SOMETHING ELSE*...

SEE HIM?

OH, YES, I SEE HIM. NOT VERY GOOD, IS HE?

HOLD IT RIGHT *THERE*, POPS.

OH, MY GOD! *A BANDIT!*

WHOA! TAKE IT EASY, OLDTIMER!

I WON'T HURT YOU.

GOT ANY FOOD ON YOU?

BUT--

--WE WERE HOPING *YOU* COULD GIVE *US* SOMETHING TO EAT...!

OH. MORE OF *THOSE.* WELL--

--GO ON *IN* AND SEE WHAT THEY GOT...

HMM... THIS BUNCH DOESN'T SOUND VERY PROMISING.

I SHOULD SAY NOT-- LOOK!

THEIR CAMP WAS A HAPHAZARD SHAMBLES OF POORLY CONSTRUCTED ENCLOSURES. HYGIENIC DISCIPLINE WAS NONEXISTENT, AND THE PLACE STANK OF HUMAN MISERY.

UNCLE TARAS...!

THESE PEOPLE NEED HELP.

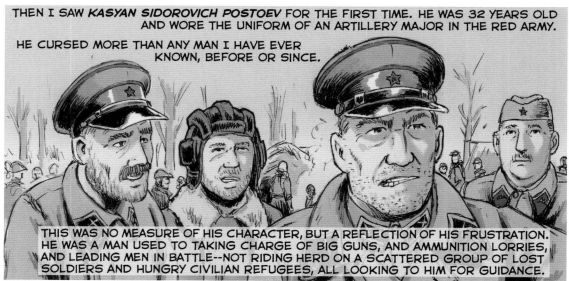

THEN I SAW *KASYAN SIDOROVICH POSTOEV* FOR THE FIRST TIME. HE WAS 32 YEARS OLD AND WORE THE UNIFORM OF AN ARTILLERY MAJOR IN THE RED ARMY.

HE CURSED MORE THAN ANY MAN I HAVE EVER KNOWN, BEFORE OR SINCE.

THIS WAS NO MEASURE OF HIS CHARACTER, BUT A REFLECTION OF HIS FRUSTRATION. HE WAS A MAN USED TO TAKING CHARGE OF BIG GUNS, AND AMMUNITION LORRIES, AND LEADING MEN IN BATTLE--NOT RIDING HERD ON A SCATTERED GROUP OF LOST SOLDIERS AND HUNGRY CIVILIAN REFUGEES, ALL LOOKING TO HIM FOR GUIDANCE.

WE APPROACHED *MAJOR POSTOEV* AS HUMBLE PEASANTS...

EXCUSE ME, MY LORD. HAVE YOU A BIT OF FOOD FOR A TRAVELER AND HIS DAUGHTER...?

SORRY, MY FRIEND--WE'VE ONLY A LITTLE *KASHA*, AND EVEN THAT IS IN SHORT SUPPLY.

HMM, THAT'S ALL YOU HAVE, *EH?* WELL, PERHAPS *THIS* WILL FLAVOR UP YOUR PORRIDGE...

WHAT IS *THAT--?*

CORNED BEEF. THREE CANS, IF IT'LL DO YOU ANY GOOD...

GOOD GOD! HOW'D YOU MANAGE TO GET IT OFF THE GERMANS?

OH, PEOPLE WILL GIVE UP EVERYTHING THEY HAVE...

...WHEN THEY ARE *DEAD.*

JUST *WHO* THE *HELL ARE* YOU?!

I'M *SEMEN KALASHNIKOV*...AND I UNDERSTAND YOU'VE BEEN LOOKING FOR ME.

142

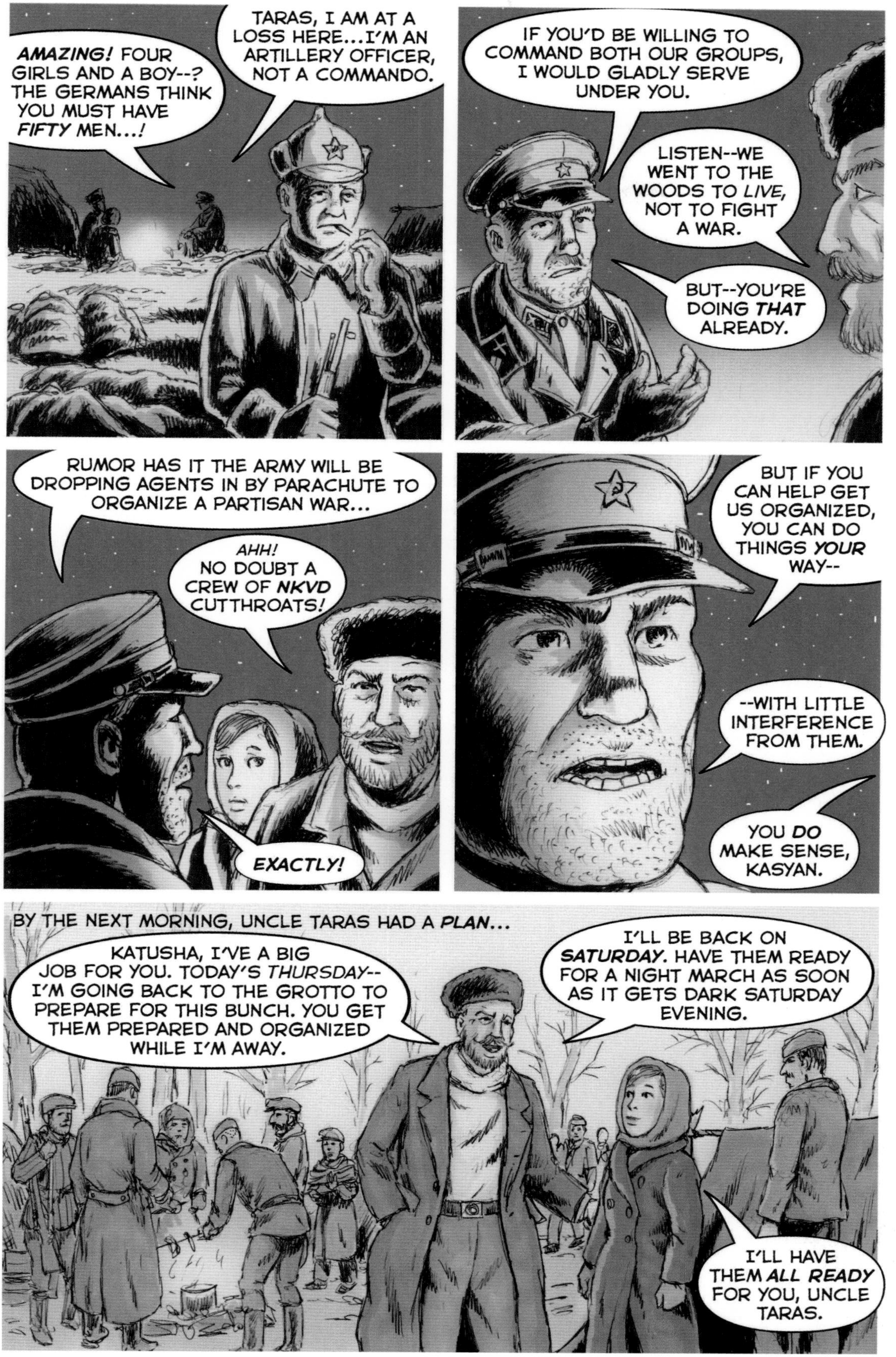
AMAZING! FOUR GIRLS AND A BOY--? THE GERMANS THINK YOU MUST HAVE FIFTY MEN...!
TARAS, I AM AT A LOSS HERE...I'M AN ARTILLERY OFFICER, NOT A COMMANDO.
IF YOU'D BE WILLING TO COMMAND BOTH OUR GROUPS, I WOULD GLADLY SERVE UNDER YOU.
LISTEN--WE WENT TO THE WOODS TO LIVE, NOT TO FIGHT A WAR.
BUT--YOU'RE DOING THAT ALREADY.
RUMOR HAS IT THE ARMY WILL BE DROPPING AGENTS IN BY PARACHUTE TO ORGANIZE A PARTISAN WAR...
AHH! NO DOUBT A CREW OF NKVD CUTTHROATS!
EXACTLY!
BUT IF YOU CAN HELP GET US ORGANIZED, YOU CAN DO THINGS YOUR WAY--
--WITH LITTLE INTERFERENCE FROM THEM.
YOU DO MAKE SENSE, KASYAN.
BY THE NEXT MORNING, UNCLE TARAS HAD A PLAN...
KATUSHA, I'VE A BIG JOB FOR YOU. TODAY'S THURSDAY-- I'M GOING BACK TO THE GROTTO TO PREPARE FOR THIS BUNCH. YOU GET THEM PREPARED AND ORGANIZED WHILE I'M AWAY.
I'LL BE BACK ON SATURDAY. HAVE THEM READY FOR A NIGHT MARCH AS SOON AS IT GETS DARK SATURDAY EVENING.
I'LL HAVE THEM ALL READY FOR YOU, UNCLE TARAS.

THE JOURNEY TO THE GROTTO WASN'T AWFULLY FAR, BUT I KNEW IT MIGHT BE A HARDSHIP ON SOME OF THOSE LESS FIT.

...AND HOW OLD ARE YOU, MOTHER?

I MET A LADY DOCTOR NAMED ALEXANDRA KIRILOV. WITH HER HELP, WE CHECKED UP ON THE HEALTH OF ALL THOSE THERE.

WE EXAMINED THE OLD...

I SAW YOU WITH SEMEN KALASHNIKOV IN THE CIVIL WAR! HE WAS A GREAT LEADER...

...THE YOUNG...

...AND HOW MANY FINGERS ARE YOU?

...AND THE LAZY...

IS IT FAR?

I'M A TANKER 'CAUSE I HATE TO WALK.

...AND THERE WERE THOSE WHO WERE TRAVELING FOR TWO.

I'M EXPECTING IN AUGUST. PLEASE--

--DON'T TELL MY FATHER.

I PREPARED THEM FOR THE MOVE TO THE GROTTO. ALTHOUGH I WASN'T QUITE SEVENTEEN AT THE TIME, MAJOR POSTOEV HAD COMPLETE TRUST IN ME.

WE MUST TAKE SPECIAL CARE IN BEING VERY QUIET AT ALL TIMES.

THOSE CHILDREN WHO CANNOT BE CARRIED MUST HAVE A PIECE OF ROPE OR CLOTH TIED AROUND THEIR WAISTS, SO THAT THEY STAY CLOSE BY...

THAT FIRST NIGHT IN KASYAN'S CAMP WAS COLD AND CLEAR. I LAY OUT AND LOOKED UP AT THE STARS, WONDERING WHERE MAMA AND PAPA AND NATASHA AND DIMA WERE...

I KNEW ALSO THAT UNCLE TARAS HAD RETURNED TO THE GROTTO, SO THAT HE AND MILLA WOULD HAVE A COUPLE OF NIGHTS OF RELATIVE PRIVACY BEFORE IT GOT TOO CROWDED.

I, OF COURSE, UNDERSTOOD--

BUT IT MADE ME FEEL A LITTLE *LONELY* THAT NIGHT.

IN *CHERNIHIV*...

MAMA! I FOUND US SOME BETTER CUTS AND A LITTLE FAT...!

AH, YES! ALONG WITH THIS HANDFUL OF DRIED BEANS I GOT US, THAT WILL DO NICELY.

UH-- WHERE IS *NATASHA?*

SHE WENT OUT WALKING--AGAIN...

ELENA, I'M WORRIED THAT POOR GIRL IS GOING TO DRIVE HERSELF *MAD* WITH GRIEF OVER DIMA--!

WELL, MAYBE SHE'LL RETURN BEFORE THIS IS READY. *NOW*--

--WHERE HAS THAT *KNIFE* GOTTEN TO? I NEED TO CUT UP THIS MEAT...

WAR IS A LONELY TIME FOR *ALL*. PEOPLE HAVE BEEN UPROOTED FROM THEIR HOMES AND OFTEN DRIVEN FAR AWAY FROM THE PLACES THEY KNOW AND THE PEOPLE THEY LOVE. THOSE WHOM WE CALL *"THE ENEMY"* ARE JUST AS SUSCEPTIBLE AS WE ARE.

OF ALL THE DESOLATE, CRAPPY PLACES WE COULD'VE WOUND UP IN, THIS HAS GOT TO BE THE *ULTIMATE...!*

WELL, IT'S DEFINITELY *NOT* PARIS.

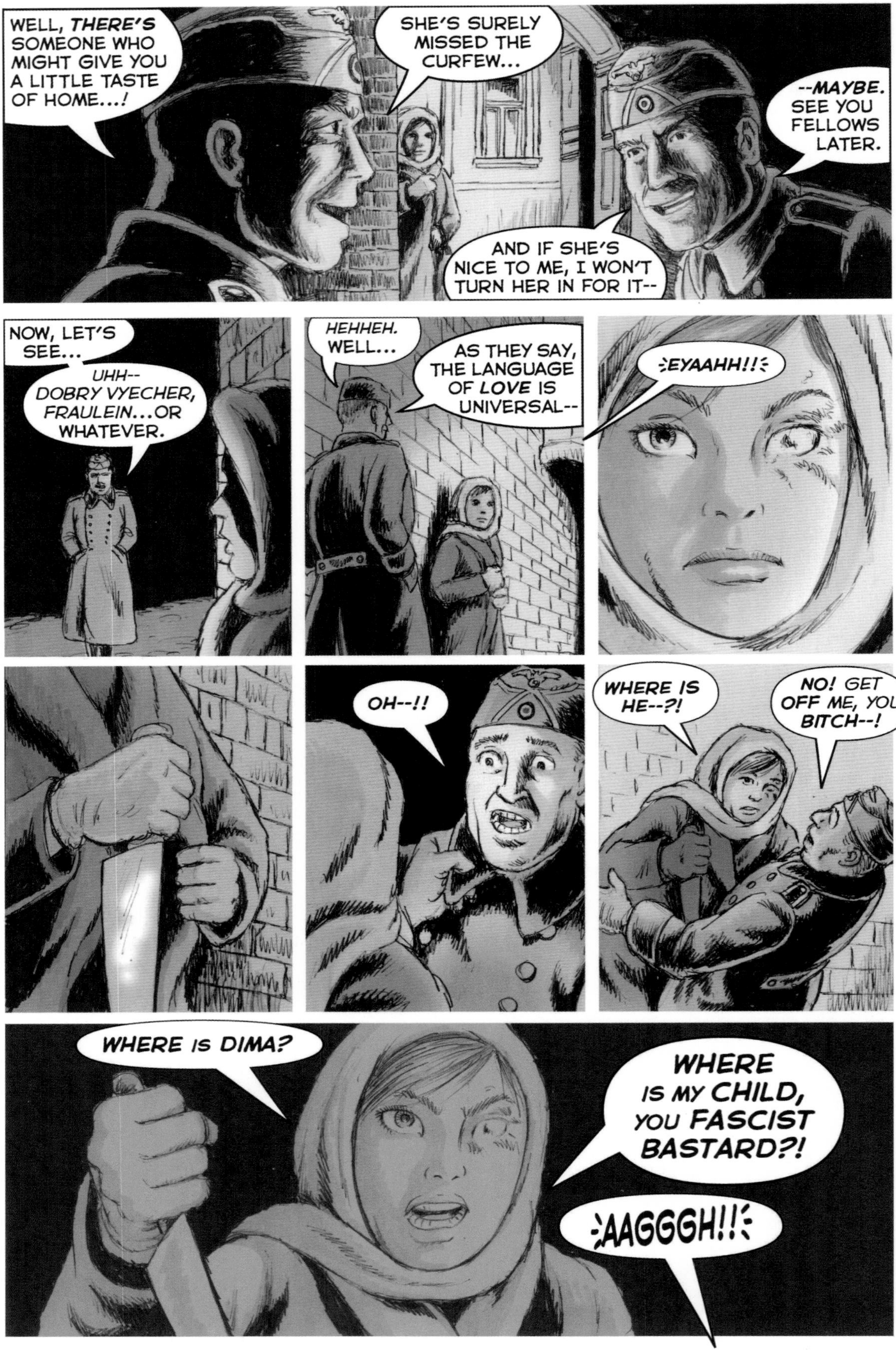
WELL, THERE'S SOMEONE WHO MIGHT GIVE YOU A LITTLE TASTE OF HOME...!
SHE'S SURELY MISSED THE CURFEW...
--MAYBE. SEE YOU FELLOWS LATER.
AND IF SHE'S NICE TO ME, I WON'T TURN HER IN FOR IT--
NOW, LET'S SEE...
UHH-- DOBRY VYECHER, FRAULEIN...OR WHATEVER.
HEHHEH. WELL...
AS THEY SAY, THE LANGUAGE OF LOVE IS UNIVERSAL--
EYAAHH!!
OH--!!
WHERE IS HE--?!
NO! GET OFF ME, YOU BITCH--!
WHERE IS DIMA?
WHERE IS MY CHILD, YOU FASCIST BASTARD?!
AAGGGH!!

SPRING, 1942. FROM MURMANSK ON THE BARENTS SEA DOWN TO SEVASTOPOL SOME 1,800 MILES SOUTH ON THE BLACK SEA, THE ICE WAS BEGINNING TO CRACK AND MELT.

IN *LENINGRAD*, THEY BEGAN THE GRISLY TASK OF DIGGING OUT THE THOUSANDS OF FROZEN BODIES IN THE STREETS AND YARDS. THOSE WHO HAD SURVIVED THE DEADLY "HUNGER WINTER" BURIED THEIR FALLEN NEIGHBORS WITH A NOD OF GRIEF--AND WITH A DEEP, QUIET SIGH OF CHEER THAT THEY WERE NOT YET AMONG THEM.

IN THE GERMAN TRENCHES 75 MILES WEST OF MOSCOW, THERE WAS ALSO GRIM GRATITUDE. THEY, TOO, FELT LUCKY TO SEE AND FEEL THE FAINT GLOW OF THE REBOUNDING SUN.

THE GERMANS HAD UNDERESTIMATED THIS UNYIELDING, IMMENSE LAND...

THEY HAD UNDERESTIMATED ITS SIZE, THE SEVERITY OF ITS WINTERS, AND THE FLINTY RESOLVE OF ITS PEOPLE.

BUT THE *WEHRMACHT* HAD BECOME THE MASTER OF ALL OF EUROPE.

THESE PROUD MEN IN GRAY-GREEN WOULD NOT BE OUTDONE BY THE SWEEPINGS OF ASIA AND AN IDEOLOGY OF LUNACY. *OPERATION BARBAROSSA* WOULD BE RELAUNCHED WITH THE BUDS OF SPRING.

WE ALL STUMBLED ON THROUGH THE NIGHT, WEAVING THROUGH THICK PINEY WOODS AND ACROSS ICE-COLD STREAMS. WE CROSSED ROADS THAT WERE REGULARLY PATROLLED BY THE GERMANS AND PAST HOUSES WHERE PEOPLE WOULD TURN YOU IN FOR A POTATO.

THERE WERE GRUNTS AND GROANS AND AN OCCASIONAL CURSE WHEN SOMEONE DROPPED SOMETHING, FOR IT WOULD THEN BE LOST FOREVER IN THE DARKNESS.

THERE HAD ORIGINALLY BEEN 79 MEMBERS OF KASYAN POSTOEV'S CAMP. A DOZEN OF THOSE HAD DECIDED TO RETURN TO THEIR HOMES RATHER THAN MAKE THE MOVE.

OF THESE, 51 WERE MORE OR LESS OF FIGHTING AGE-- THAT IS, MEN OR WOMEN BETWEEN 14 AND 75.

ALL OF THEM WERE AT A BREAKING POINT. SOME WERE SICK OR INJURED. SOME HAD SOULS LACED WITH HATRED FROM HAVING WITNESSED THEIR FAMILIES AND FRIENDS SAVAGELY MURDERED BY AN INVADER WHO LOOKED UPON US AS BEING LITTLE MORE THAN DRAFT ANIMALS.

SOME WERE OLD AND HAD TO BE CARRIED. IN ALL FAIRNESS, AND CONSIDERING THE PRACTICAL NATURE OF SUCH AN ENTERPRISE, THEY SHOULD HAVE BEEN LEFT BEHIND.

BUT OLD MRS. DARENSKY WAS A FINE COOK WHO COULD TURN A BUCKWHEAT STEW INTO LIGHT, TASTY *BLINI*...

AND NOW, TO ME--SUCH A TALENTED PERSON WAS A MILITARY NECESSITY.

AND THERE WERE THOSE WHO WERE VERY YOUNG...

DON'T BE AFRAID, TOLYA...

TOLYA'S MOTHER HAD COME TO KASYAN'S CAMP VERY SICK--SHE'D DIED ONLY THREE DAYS AFTER HER ARRIVAL. NOT A SOUL KNEW WHERE THE CHILD'S FATHER WAS--NOR EVEN HIS LAST NAME.

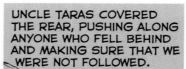

≥MRFM...≤

HERE, LITTLE ONE-- I'LL CARRY YOU.

MILLA TOOK THE LEAD, HER SHARP EYES PIERCING THE DARKNESS FOR ANY TROUBLE.

UNCLE TARAS COVERED THE REAR, PUSHING ALONG ANYONE WHO FELL BEHIND AND MAKING SURE THAT WE WERE NOT FOLLOWED.

I MOVED UP AND DOWN ALONG THE COLUMN TO CHECK HOW EVERYONE WAS KEEPING UP AND TO GIVE ENCOURAGEMENT WHEREVER NEEDED.

LITTLE TOLYA SHIVERED, BUT NOT FROM THE COLD...

MA-MA...?

IT'S ALL RIGHT...

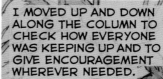

I WAS ONCE AFRAID OF THE DARK...

I WAS AFRAID OF THUNDER, TOO.

HALT! IS IT FRIEND OR FOE?

IT WAS VASILY'S REASSURING VOICE.

WE ARE *FRIENDS*, BROTHER.

THEN-- ADVANCE, SISTER!

WOW! YOU CERTAINLY BROUGHT ENOUGH OF THEM WITH YOU, KATUSHA--!

THERE ARE SOME 67 OF THEM, ZHENYA--MAN, WOMAN AND CHILD...

...BUT WE SHOULD COUNT THEM, JUST TO BE SURE.

WHOA--! IT *USED* TO BE VERY ROOMY IN HERE...!

WELL...THERE GOES THE OLD NEIGHBORHOOD!

HEY--WHAT'S WITH *FATHER ZAPOLYE*...?

HE'S ALL *DRESSED UP*...?

HOW LONG HAS IT BEEN SINCE YOU'VE SEEN A *CALENDAR*, KATUSHA...?

THUNDER & DARKNESS

IT'S *EASTER SUNDAY.*

IN MY YEARS SINCE THAT DAY, I HAVE SEEN MANY FABULOUS CHURCHES...

I HAVE SEEN *SAINT ANDREI'S* AND THE *DORMITION CATHEDRAL OF THE CAVES.* I HAVE SEEN THE MANY GOLDEN DOMES OF *CHERNIHIV.* I HAVE EVEN SEEN *SAINT BASIL'S* ON RED SQUARE...

...BUT NEVER, *NEVER* HAVE I SEEN A MORE BEAUTIFUL EASTER SERVICE AS I DID THAT MORNING IN UNCLE TARAS' GROTTO.

ONE WOMAN SAW HER HUSBAND WHO'D LEFT FOR WORK THAT MORNING JUST AS HE HAD FOR 17 YEARS. THERE WAS A CABINETMAKER WHO'D ALWAYS SMELLED OF VARNISH, AND A FREIGHT HANDLER WHO HAD A BAD BACK. THERE WAS A LADY WHO LOVED TO GOSSIP, AND A TAILOR WHO ENJOYED TELLING JOKES. THERE WAS A SCHOOLTEACHER WHO HAD ALWAYS BEEN FAITHFUL TO HIS WIFE, AND A DOCTOR WHO HAD CHEATED MOST OF HIS PATIENTS. THERE WAS AN ACCOUNTANT WHO MISTRUSTED MOST PEOPLE, AND A BLIND BEGGAR WHO COULD PLAY THE BANDURA SO WELL THAT PEOPLE WOULD WEEP TO HEAR IT...

...AND THERE WAS A GIRL WHO COULD NOT FIND HER SON.

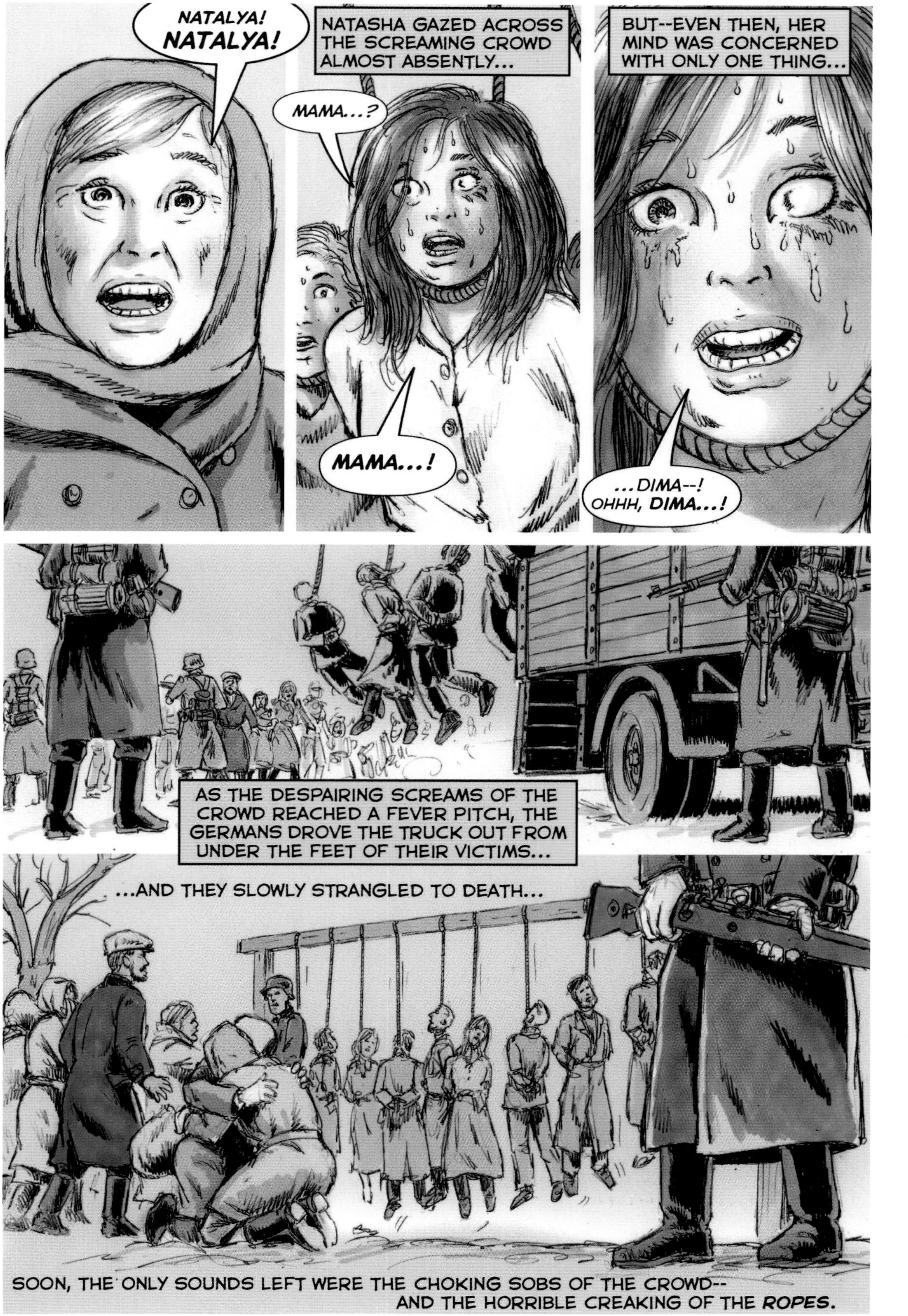
NATALYA! NATALYA!
NATASHA GAZED ACROSS THE SCREAMING CROWD ALMOST ABSENTLY...
MAMA...?
MAMA...!
BUT--EVEN THEN, HER MIND WAS CONCERNED WITH ONLY ONE THING...
...DIMA--! OHHH, DIMA...!
AS THE DESPAIRING SCREAMS OF THE CROWD REACHED A FEVER PITCH, THE GERMANS DROVE THE TRUCK OUT FROM UNDER THE FEET OF THEIR VICTIMS...
...AND THEY SLOWLY STRANGLED TO DEATH...
SOON, THE ONLY SOUNDS LEFT WERE THE CHOKING SOBS OF THE CROWD--
AND THE HORRIBLE CREAKING OF THE ROPES.

MEANWHILE IN THE GROTTO, EVERYONE HAD SETTLED DOWN WITH A SYSTEM TO MAINTAIN HEALTHY CONDITIONS AND SECURITY.

ASSISTED BY SEVERAL PERMANENT HELPERS, MRS. DARENSKY TOOK OVER AS CHIEF COOK. OUR MEALS MAY HAVE BEEN MEAGER, BUT AT LEAST THEY WERE TASTY.

MAJOR KASYAN POSTOEV RETAINED COMMAND, WITH UNCLE TARAS AS HIS CHIEF OF STAFF. KASYAN ALWAYS TOOK TARAS' ADVICE AND LEARNED INFANTRY TACTICS AS TARAS TAUGHT THE OTHERS.

THERE! YOU SEE HOW ILLARION'S GROUP ADVANCES, WHILE DEMENTY'S PEOPLE ARE PROVIDING COVERING FIRE--?

TO RELIEVE CROWDING AND UPGRADE OUR SECURITY, WE BUILT FOUR OUTPOSTS A NUMBER OF MILES FROM AND SURROUNDING THE LOCATION OF THE GROTTO.

THESE WERE DUG INTO THE GROUND AND MADE TO BE ALMOST INVISIBLE.

EACH OF THE OUTPOSTS WOULD BE MANNED BY THREE MEN AT A TIME...

THESE MEN WOULD PATROL THE TERRITORY AROUND THE OUTPOSTS, AVOIDING CONTACT WITH ANY LOCALS AND THE GERMANS.

OUR WAR AGAINST THE GERMANS WASN'T JUST A WAR OF REVENGE--IT WAS A FIGHT FOR SURVIVAL. WE ATTACKED THEM FOR FOOD AND WEAPONS, RANGING FAR AND WIDE TO MAKE OUR HOME BASE HARD TO PINPOINT. WE KNEW THE VILLAGES CLOSE TO OUR OBJECTIVES WOULD SUFFER IF THE GERMANS BELIEVED THEY HAD AIDED US--SO WE TRIED TO LEAVE MISLEADING EVIDENCE TO CONFUSE OUR PURSUERS...

STALIN HAD CALLED FOR A PARTISAN WAR TO BEGIN AGAINST THE INVADERS, BUT HIS GOAL, AS MUCH AS FIGHTING THE GERMANS THEMSELVES, WAS TO TERRORIZE SOVIET CITIZENS. THIS GAVE BANDIT GROUPS FREE AUTHORITY TO STEAL AND MURDER AS THEY WISHED.

MY HUSBAND TOLD THE MEN THAT WAS THE LAST OF OUR FOOD--BUT THEY TOOK IT AND OUR MILK COW...

...AND THEN WHEN MY HUSBAND TRIED TO STOP THEM--*SOB* THEY *HANGED* HIM--!

KASYAN, I'M TAKING MILLA AND TWO OTHERS. I INTEND TO TRACK THESE BANDITS DOWN AND GET THIS LADY'S COW BACK.

THAT SAME NIGHT, THEY DISCOVERED THE GUILTY "PARTISANS" AS THEY CELEBRATED THEIR SUCCESS.

THIS IS THE ROPE YOU HANGED THE OLD MAN WITH. SADLY, IT ISN'T LONG ENOUGH TO HANG ALL FOUR OF YOU AT ONE TIME...

...SO, WE'LL JUST HAVE TO DO IT IN *SHIFTS.*

THIS PARTISAN WAR SERVED TO MUDDY THE WATER AS TO JUST WHO THE "ENEMY" WAS. IN WESTERN UKRAINE, WHICH HAD COME UNDER SOVIET DOMINATION IN 1939, MANY OF THE INHABITANTS OPENLY SUPPORTED THE GERMANS--

--EVEN VOLUNTEERING FOR THEIR ARMY.

IT IS TO MY SHAME THAT I TELL YOU THAT MANY UKRAINIANS AND POLES HELPED THE GERMANS IN THEIR WAR AGAINST THE JEWS.

WHEN MILLA LED A SMALL GROUP OF OUR PEOPLE AGAINST A GERMAN SUPPLY BASE, THEY WERE AMBUSHED BY A NEW BAND OF PARTISANS...

WHOEVER THEY WERE WITH, THEY WERE WEARING WHITE ARMBANDS WITH THE ST. GEORGE'S CROSS ON THEM...

AH! THOSE ARE THE PARTISANS LED BY *BROSISLAW KOMINSKI.* I'VE HEARD HE HAS 1,400 WELL-ARMED MEN WITH HIM!

THEY SAY HE FIGHTS AGAINST THE COMMUNISTS--

--AND ALSO FOR THE ORTHODOX CHURCH.

HMM! HE SOUNDS LIKE A MAN AFTER MY OWN HEART...!

THESE EVENTS WEIGHED HEAVILY ON UNCLE TARAS...

GOOD AND EVIL, RIGHT AND WRONG--THEY DON'T EASILY PRESENT THEMSELVES, DO THEY, KATUSHA?

NO, THEY DON'T, UNCLE TARAS.

IN MOSCOW THAT SPRING, *MARSHAL STALIN* CALLED HIS GENERALS AND DEMANDED THAT THEY PLAN A MAJOR OFFENSIVE.

WE *CANNOT* JUST REMAIN ON THE DEFENSIVE, SITTING ON OUR HANDS AS WE WAIT FOR THE GERMANS TO STRIKE *FIRST*...!

...WE *MUST* STRIKE ON A BROAD FRONT AND PROBE THE ENEMY'S INTENTIONS!

THERE WILL BE THREE OFFENSIVES: IN THE *NORTH*, TO LIFT THE SIEGE OF LENINGRAD...

...IN THE *CRIMEA*, TO SUPPORT OUR FORCES AT SEVASTOPOL...

...AND OUT OF THE *IZYUM SALIENT*, OUR FORCES WILL DRIVE NORTHWEST TO RECAPTURE *KHARKOV.*

SOVIET INTELLIGENCE HAD ANOTHER WRINKLE:

WHY NOT TEST THE METTLE OF OUR PARTISANS?

WHY NOT ENLIST *THEIR* AID IN THESE MIGHTY OFFENSIVES?

BYELOV, BREAK OUT THE RADIO AND SEE IF YOU CAN CONTACT OUR *GHQ*--

--THEN WE'LL TRY TO MAKE CONTACT WITH THE PARTISANS.

UHH... CAPTAIN GLUSKOV, SIR--?

--I THINK MAYBE THEY'VE *ALREADY* MADE CONTACT WITH US...!

IN THE GROTTO, SILENCE GREETED THEM...

IN THE NAME OF THE *PEOPLE'S COMMISSARIAT OF INTERNAL AFFAIRS*--I HEREBY *TAKE COMMAND* OF THIS PARTISAN BAND...!

*UHH...*COMRADE, WE WERE JUST ABOUT TO ENJOY A *MEAL...*

WHY DON'T YOU AND YOUR MEN HAVE A SEAT AND *JOIN* US?

RIGHT! I'M SURE THAT YOU'VE ALL COME A *LONG WAY* TODAY--

--AND IT JUST SO HAPPENS THAT WE HAVE THIS CASE OF *FRENCH CHAMPAGNE* WE LIBERATED FROM THE GERMANS...!

LATER THAT NIGHT...

I AM AFRAID CAPTAIN GLUSKOV HAS A VERY LOW TOLERANCE FOR DRINK...!

WHAT DO YOU THINK OF HIS *PROPOSITION*, TARAS?

¿ZZZK...?

BLOWING UP A RAILROAD BRIDGE ACROSS A MARSH EAST OF KHARKOV? THAT'S SOME 150 MILES FROM HERE, AND IN OPEN COUNTRY...

HOW WOULD WE DO IT?

BREAK UP INTO SMALL GROUPS-- TRAVEL BY NIGHT, HIDE OUT IN DAYTIME...

HIS MAPS SEEM TO BE VERY GOOD. IF OUR TIMING IS CORRECT AND NO ONE RUNS INTO TROUBLE--*IF! IF! IF--!*

IT WOULD BE A GOOD WAY TO REALLY GET BACK INTO THE WAR...

WELL--WHAT DO THE LADIES THINK?

DOES IT REALLY MATTER? WE GO TO THE *WAR*--

--OR THE WAR COMES TO *US*...

IT WOULD REALLY BE *SOMETHING*, WOULDN'T IT?

ALL RIGHT!

MY HEART WAS RACING WITH EXCITEMENT--! BUT IT ALSO BEAT WITH *FEAR*...

SO--WE WILL EXPAND OUR HORIZONS-- AND TRAVEL FAR AFIELD!

WHERE SHALL IT TAKE US?

YES! *WHERE?*

THE FIRST THING UNCLE TARAS DID WAS WEED OUT THOSE TOO OLD, TOO YOUNG, OR UNFIT FOR THE MISSION.

HOVAN, OLD FRIEND, I'M TRUSTING YOU--

--STAY BEHIND AND GUARD THE CAMP WHILE WE'RE GONE.

THEN WE GATHERED THE EQUIPMENT THAT THOSE WHO WERE GOING WOULD CARRY...

HERE, KATUSHA-- SOMETHING WITH A LITTLE MORE *FIREPOWER*.

THE RED ARMY MEN HAD THEIR OWN IDEAS AS TO HOW THE MISSION SHOULD BE CARRIED OUT, BUT UNCLE TARAS HAD ADDED A FEW ANGLES OF HIS OWN.

THE BRIDGE RUNS ALONG A SERIES OF 24 PILINGS THAT CROSS SMALL ISLANDS AND PENINSULAS. IT WOULD BE IMPOSSIBLE TO BLOW UP *ALL* THE PILINGS...

BUT BLASTING THESE *KEY ONES* WILL CAUSE THE GERMANS THE MOST TROUBLE TO REPAIR.

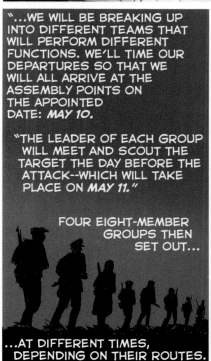

"...WE WILL BE BREAKING UP INTO DIFFERENT TEAMS THAT WILL PERFORM DIFFERENT FUNCTIONS. WE'LL TIME OUR DEPARTURES SO THAT WE WILL ALL ARRIVE AT THE ASSEMBLY POINTS ON THE APPOINTED DATE: *MAY 10.*

"THE LEADER OF EACH GROUP WILL MEET AND SCOUT THE TARGET THE DAY BEFORE THE ATTACK--WHICH WILL TAKE PLACE ON *MAY 11.*"

FOUR EIGHT-MEMBER GROUPS THEN SET OUT...

...AT DIFFERENT TIMES, DEPENDING ON THEIR ROUTES.

I, TOO, SET OFF WITH MY GROUP--UNCLE TARAS AND MILLA AND THE RED ARMY MAN NAMED *BYELOV.*

ALSO COMING ALONG WITH US WAS A YOUNG FARM GIRL NAMED *ALLA VARRENIKOV.* THERE WAS AN OLD RAILROAD MAN, *ROMAN MASOV*--AND AN ILLITERATE ORPHAN NAMED *YURIY HRYTSA.* BESIDE US ALL WAS *FATHER ZAPOLYE*--HE'D BEEN MOST INSISTENT WE'D NEED BOTH HIS GUN AND SPIRITUAL GUIDANCE.

WE WERE TO TRAVEL BY NIGHT--AND HIDE OUT AND SLEEP DURING THE DAY.

VASILY AND ZHENYA'S GROUP REVOLVED AROUND THEIR GERMAN MACHINE GUN. THE RED ARMY SOLDIER *NYEUDOBNOV*, A WEAPONS EXPERT, WENT WITH THEM-- HE AND VASILY DEVELOPED A NATURAL FRIENDSHIP.

THE *NKVD* CAPTAIN WENT WITH KASYAN'S GROUP. THEY WERE TO MEET UP WITH YET ANOTHER THREE PARACHUTISTS WHO'D BRING AND SET THE EXPLOSIVES.

WE KEPT A LOW PROFILE THE ENTIRE JOURNEY, TAKING CARE THAT WE MADE NO HUMAN CONTACT.

BUT--ONE THING THAT WE *DID* NOTICE BOTHERED US GREATLY...

WHAT LITTLE THE PEOPLE HAD THAT WASN'T DESTROYED BY THE SOVIETS WAS NOW BEING TAKEN BY THE GERMANS. BUT EVEN AT A DISTANCE, I COULD SEE--

MOST OF THE PEOPLE WERE *STARVING*.

WE TRIED TO AVOID ALL ROADS AND RAIL TRAFFIC, BUT WE COULDN'T HELP BUT COME IN CONTACT WITH SOME OF IT. FROM WHAT WE SAW, IT WASN'T JUST THE RED ARMY THAT WAS PLANNING AN OFFENSIVE--

EVERYWHERE, WE SAW LONG COLUMNS OF GERMAN TRUCKS AND TANKS, ALL HEADING *EAST*.

JUST AFTER MIDNIGHT ON MONDAY, MAY 11, WE ASSEMBLED WITH THE OTHER GROUPS AT THE APPOINTED SPOT. THE MOON WAS A WANING CRESCENT.

THERE WOULD BE *NO MOON* THAT EVENING WHEN WE MADE OUR MOVE.

THE LEADERS MET. WHILE THEY WENT OFF TO RECONNOITER THE BRIDGE, THE REST OF US FOUND A PLACE TO SLEEP FOR A BIT IN AN ABANDONED BARN.

I TRIED, BUT I JUST COULD NOT *SLEEP...!* I KEPT THINKING THAT I'D BEEN IN FIGHTS BEFORE, BUT NOTHING LIKE THIS. I WASN'T EXACTLY *FRIGHTENED*--BUT I WAS AWFULLY *UNCOMFORTABLE* WITH THE IDEA OF *DYING* AT THE AGE OF SEVENTEEN...

MILLA! *MILLA!* WAKE UP!

MMM--? WHAT *IS* IT...?

MILLA, I WAS *WONDERING...*

...WHAT'S IT *LIKE?*

WHUH--? WHAT'S *WHAT* LIKE?

WHAT'S *IT* LIKE?

"IT"? WHAT IS *IT?*

HAVE YOU LOST YOUR MIND, KATUSHA?

YOU KNOW! IT!

WHAT YOU AND UNCLE TARAS DO WHEN YOU'RE ALL ALONE...*IT!*

OH, *THAT--?*

THAT'S *IT!* YES! WHAT'S IT LIKE?

OH, IT'S *NICE*--VERY NICE...!

163

WELL? CAN'T YOU TELL ME ANY MORE THAN *THAT?*

KATUSHA! WHAT DO YOU WANT TO KNOW?

WELL-- *EVERYTHING!*

LISTEN--I'M GOING BACK TO SLEEP. IF YOU *REALLY* WANT TO FIND OUT ABOUT *IT*, GO GET SOMEONE AND TRY *IT* OUT FOR YOURSELF...!

GOOD NIGHT!

UGH!

I DON'T THINK I COULD DO *THAT*...!

THAT NIGHT, OUR GROUPS GATHERED FOR THE ATTACK--BUT NOT ALL WAS GOING ACCORDING TO PLAN.

YAROSLAW HAS DISAPPEARED! HE WASN'T VERY HAPPY WITH OUR MISSION...

TCH! I SHOULD HAVE LEFT THAT UNRELIABLE DOG BEHIND!

IT'S TOO LATE--WE'RE COMMITTED NOW...

WELL... LET'S *DO* IT!

"IT"!

EVEN THOUGH WE WERE WADING THROUGH ICY MARSH WATER, I FOUND MYSELF SWEATING AS WE APPROACHED THE ISLAND. UP AHEAD WERE SERVICE FACILITIES FOR THE TRAINS AND A SMALL CONTINGENT OF GERMAN TROOPS.

VASILY'S GROUP SET UP ON A LITTLE COVE.

FROM THAT POINT, HE HAD A CLEAR FIELD OF FIRE BETWEEN HIM AND WHAT HE FIGURED WAS THE BARRACKS. HE COULD ALSO SEE THE LONG, SKINNY DIRT ROAD THAT RAN TO THE SOUTHEAST.

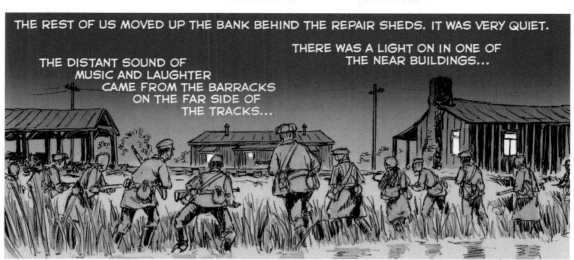

THE REST OF US MOVED UP THE BANK BEHIND THE REPAIR SHEDS. IT WAS VERY QUIET.

THE DISTANT SOUND OF MUSIC AND LAUGHTER CAME FROM THE BARRACKS ON THE FAR SIDE OF THE TRACKS...

THERE WAS A LIGHT ON IN ONE OF THE NEAR BUILDINGS...

LOOK! IS THAT A TANK?

YES, IT'S ONE OF OURS--A *KV-1*, NO DOUBT CAPTURED AND USED FOR DEFENSE.

IT HAS A *76MM* GUN. I CAN FIRE THAT!

MILLA'S EYES GLOWED.

I BET I COULD *DRIVE* IT!

"IT"?

THEN-- KASYAN LET OUT ONE SHORT BREATH ON HIS WHISTLE--!

≶TWEET!≶

--AND SUDDENLY, AS ONE MAN, OUR HUNCHED FORMS LIFTED UP AND SPRINTED FORWARD! THE ONLY SOUND WE MADE WAS THE RUSTLING OF GRASS AND THE SOFT POUNDING OF OUR WORN SHOES ON THE PACKED SOIL AS WE RAN...!

A SINGLE GERMAN WALKED OUT FROM A CORNER OF THE REPAIR SHED, CARRYING A BUCKET...

HE HEARD OUR NOISE AND SAW OUR MOVEMENT, BUT HE COULD NOT SEE WELL ENOUGH IN THE DARKNESS--

BEFORE HE COULD FIGURE IT OUT, HE'D BEEN HACKED TO PIECES WITH AN OLD IMPERIAL CAVALRY SWORD.

SEVERAL MEN PEELED OFF AND ENTERED THE SHEDS. THEIR JOB WAS TO FINISH OFF ANY OTHER GERMANS WHO WERE UNLUCKY ENOUGH TO BE WORKING LATE.

OTHER MEN WENT SEARCHING FOR ANY TELEPHONE WIRES COMING FROM THE SHEDS OR ON THE POLES ABOVE. ALL WERE QUICKLY CUT.

THE REST OF US CONTINUED ON AND TOOK PRONE POSITIONS ALONG THE TRACKS FACING THE GERMAN BARRACKS.

AND THERE WE WAITED...

RIGHT AWAY, GLUSKOV'S MEN WENT TO WORK PLACING CHARGES ON THE SIX NEAREST BRIDGE PILINGS. TORCHES AND LAMPS WERE LIT TO GIVE THEM LIGHT. WE WERE HERE NOW, AND IT WAS ONLY A MATTER OF TIME BEFORE THE GERMANS KNEW IT.

FINALLY, SOMEONE IN THE BARRACKS STIRRED. AN UNARMED SOLDIER CAME TO THE DOOR, SCRATCHING HIMSELF AND YAWNING...

HA! THE SIGHT OF US *REALLY* WOKE HIM UP!

HE BOLTED BACK INTO THE BARRACKS. TWENTY SECONDS LATER, OUT CAME THREE GERMANS WITH GUNS...

...WE CUT ALL THREE DOWN IN AN INSTANT!

THEN VASILY OPENED UP WITH HIS MACHINE GUN, SPRAYING THE BARRACKS WITH BULLETS LIKE A FIREHOSE...

THE REST OF US, LYING PRONE BEHIND THE RAILROAD TRACKS, ALSO OPENED FIRE ON THE BUILDING.

IN ABOUT FIFTEEN SECONDS, IT WAS ALL OVER.

ONE OF OUR BRAVEST (AND MOST CURIOUS) MEN WENT OVER TO CHECK THINGS OUT...

HIS GRISLY TALLY WAS *SIXTEEN* DEAD GERMANS-- MOST OF THEM STILL CLAD ONLY IN THEIR UNDERWEAR.

WITHIN TWENTY MINUTES, ALL THE CHARGES WERE SET AND READY...

THAT'S IT....!

EVERYBODY! NOW--MOVE TO THE EAST END OF THE STATION!

TWEEEEEEEEEEE!!

WHAT'S THAT--?!

THERE'S A TRAIN COMING!

GLUSKOV, BLOW THE BRIDGE--AND LET'S GET OUT OF HERE!

NO--I CAN'T!

WHAT?!

BOMBING THE BRIDGE ISN'T ENOUGH! MY ORDERS SAY IF A TROOP TRAIN ARRIVES-- TAKE IT OUT, TOO!

ARE YOU MAD?!

THE TRAIN'S VIBRATIONS COULD SHAKE OUR DETONATORS LOOSE!

I'LL SET IT OFF AS SOON AS THE TRAIN COMES INTO VIEW--!

WELL, GOOD LUCK--

--AND GOODBYE!

THE EXPLOSIVES WERE SET SO THE CHARGES FARTHER AWAY WENT OFF FIRST, ENSURING THAT THE EXPLOSIONS WOULDN'T DISTURB THE WIRES CLOSEST TO THE FIRING MECHANISM.

IF GLUSKOV HAD TAKEN THE TIME TO CONSIDER THAT, HE MIGHT HAVE MADE OTHER PLANS...

...BUT HIS FASCINATION AT SEEING THE TARGET HE WAS ABOUT TO DESTROY WAS JUST TOO GREAT FOR HIM TO LOOK AT THE SITUATION WITH A CLEAR HEAD.

THE SIXTH PILING SHATTERED, SETTING OFF MUNITIONS CARGO IN THE LAST TWO CARS. THIS, AIDED BY THE EXPLOSION OF THE FIFTH PILING, SENT TROOPS IN THE NEXT THREE CARS-- OR AT LEAST PIECES OF THEM--RAINING ACROSS THE MARSHLAND.

CLICK

THE EXPLOSIVES ON PILINGS FOUR AND THREE BLASTED WITH STUNNING VIOLENCE, SENDING FIVE *PANZERKAMPFWAGENS* INTO THE WATER.

HOWEVER, THESE WERE THE LAST EXPLOSIONS TO OCCUR ON THE BRIDGE, SINCE THE FORCE OF THE BLAST HAD SHAKEN LOOSE THE CHARGES ON PILINGS TWO AND ONE.

THE SHOCKWAVE FROM THE BLAST ALSO CUT LOOSE A CHAIN SECURING ONE OF THE THREE REMAINING PANZERS, WHICH STAYED IN ITS PLACE AS THE TRAIN SPED BY.

IF GLUSKOV WERE REHEARSING HIS REPORT ON THE SUCCESS OF HIS MISSION, IT WAS NO DOUBT A VERY SHORT ACCOUNT...

THE WHIPPING CHAIN ENDED ANY POSSIBILITY OF REWARD AND ADVANCEMENT.

WHAT WAS LEFT OF THE TRAIN ROLLED PAST US, ITS BRAKES SCREECHING. IT SLOWED AND CAME TO A HALT SOMEWHERE IN THE DARKNESS SEVERAL HUNDRED FEET PAST THE REPAIR SHEDS...

...THEN WE HEARD THE ROAR OF POWERFUL ENGINES AND THE GRIND OF STEEL TREADS!

IN THE DIM LIGHT OF THE BURNING BRIDGE, WE SAW PANZER TROOPS EXPERTLY DISMOUNTING THEIR STEEDS FROM THE FLATCARS.

I STOOD THERE IN SHOCK AS THE THREE TANKS PULLED OUT--

--AND THEIR DEADLY GUNS BEGAN TO SPIT LIKE ANGRY DEMONS!

EVERYONE RUN! INTO THE *MARSH!* GET *AWAY* AS BEST YOU CAN!

THEN A MAN, GARBED IN THE BLACK UNIFORM OF AN EVIL SOCIETY, CAME UP OUT OF THE TANK'S TURRET. THE MAN FIRED HIS *PISTOL* INTO THE AIR, AND IN A MERE INSTANT...

... IT BROUGHT DOWN THE *FULL MOON.*

IN THIS UNNATURAL LIGHT, WE WERE EXPOSED LIKE BUTTERFLIES ON THE SCIENCE TEACHER'S BLOTTER. THOSE WHO WERE OUT WADING THROUGH THE MARSH MADE PERFECT TARGETS AS THEY STRUGGLED AGAINST THE CHEST-DEEP WATER...

...AND WHENEVER THE ARTIFICIAL MOON WOULD BEGIN TO FLICKER AND GROW DIM-- THE ANGRY MAN IN BLACK WOULD JUST FIRE ANOTHER STAR INTO THE INFLAMED HEAVENS.

MILLA! KATUSHA! DOWN! TRY TO GET BEHIND SOMETHING SUBSTANTIAL!

BUT BYELOV WAS SUDDENLY OFF AND RUNNING--

--TO WHERE, I HAD NO IDEA.

BUT WHEREVER IT WAS--

MILLA, TOO, WAS SUDDENLY UP AND RUNNING IN THAT DIRECTION!

LUDMILLA!

NO! GET YOUR ASS BACK DOWN HERE--!

--OH, HELL...!

COME ON, KATUSHA.

IT WAS SOON CLEAR THAT BYELOV AND MILLA HAD BEEN HEADING FOR THAT TANK WE'D SEEN EARLIER.

MILLA, YOU USE THE HATCH BELOW...

THE REST OF YOU COME IN THROUGH THE *TURRET*.

SO, TARAS--HAVE YOU EVER LOADED A SLIDE-BREECH GUN BEFORE?

NO, BUT I'M A QUICK STUDY.

GOOD. OKAY-- USE THE ROUNDS WITH BRASS CASINGS AND BLUE ARROW-SHAPED TIPS...

WRAWRAWRAWRAW ROW...WWRROOPPP!

HEY!

JUST LIKE THE TRACTOR ON THE COLLECTIVE FARM!

THINK YOU CAN DRIVE THIS THING OKAY, MILLA?

SURE!

KATUSHA, YOU'LL BE OUR EYES UP TOP!

OKAY...

≥OW!!≤

OOPS! SORRY...

OKAY! AND HERE WE GO...!

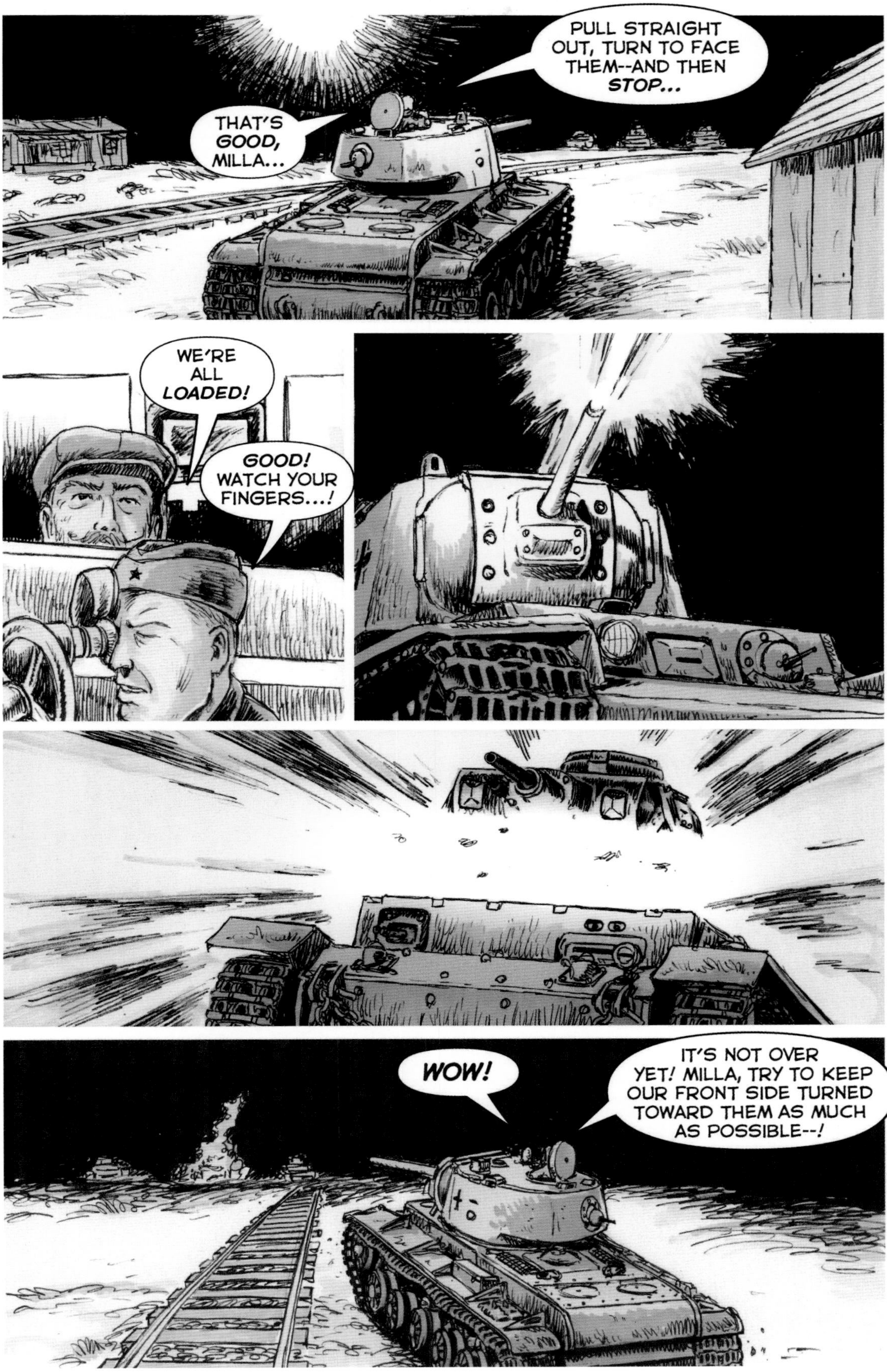
PULL STRAIGHT OUT, TURN TO FACE THEM--AND THEN STOP...
THAT'S GOOD, MILLA...
WE'RE ALL LOADED!
GOOD! WATCH YOUR FINGERS...!
WOW!
IT'S NOT OVER YET! MILLA, TRY TO KEEP OUR FRONT SIDE TURNED TOWARD THEM AS MUCH AS POSSIBLE--!

THE NOISE INSIDE THE TANK WAS *DEAFENING--!!*

I FELT LIKE I WAS INSIDE A GIANT BELL SOMEONE HAD JUST RUNG!

DON'T WORRY...AS LONG AS OUR FRONT IS TO THEM--

--THEIR 50MM GUNS CAN'T PENETRATE OUR ARMOR!

I LOOKED OUT THE TOP JUST IN TIME TO SEE *KASYAN* RUN UP FROM A DITCH AND JAM A LONG METAL ROD INTO THE TRACKS OF ONE OF THE *PANZERS--!*

--AND WITH A LOUD, GRINDING SHRIEK, IT JOLTED TO A *HALT!*

KASYAN TURNED AND RAN FOR COVER. BUT THE GERMAN OFFICER IN BLACK--

--THE ONE WHO HAD BEEN SHOOTING THE FLARES INTO THE NIGHT SKY--

--CAME BACK UP IN THE TURRET, THIS TIME WITH A DIFFERENT PISTOL...

--AND--!!

I WAS SUDDENLY GRIPPED WITH A WHITE-HOT *ANGER* THAT I DIDN'T RECOGNIZE.

ALL I COULD THINK WAS THAT *KASYAN* HAD SEEMED LIKE A FINE MAN...!

MILLA REACTED IN A SIMILAR FASHION... —

...AND THEN, AT HIGH SPEED, SHE DROVE US TOWARD THE REMAINING *PANZER*...!

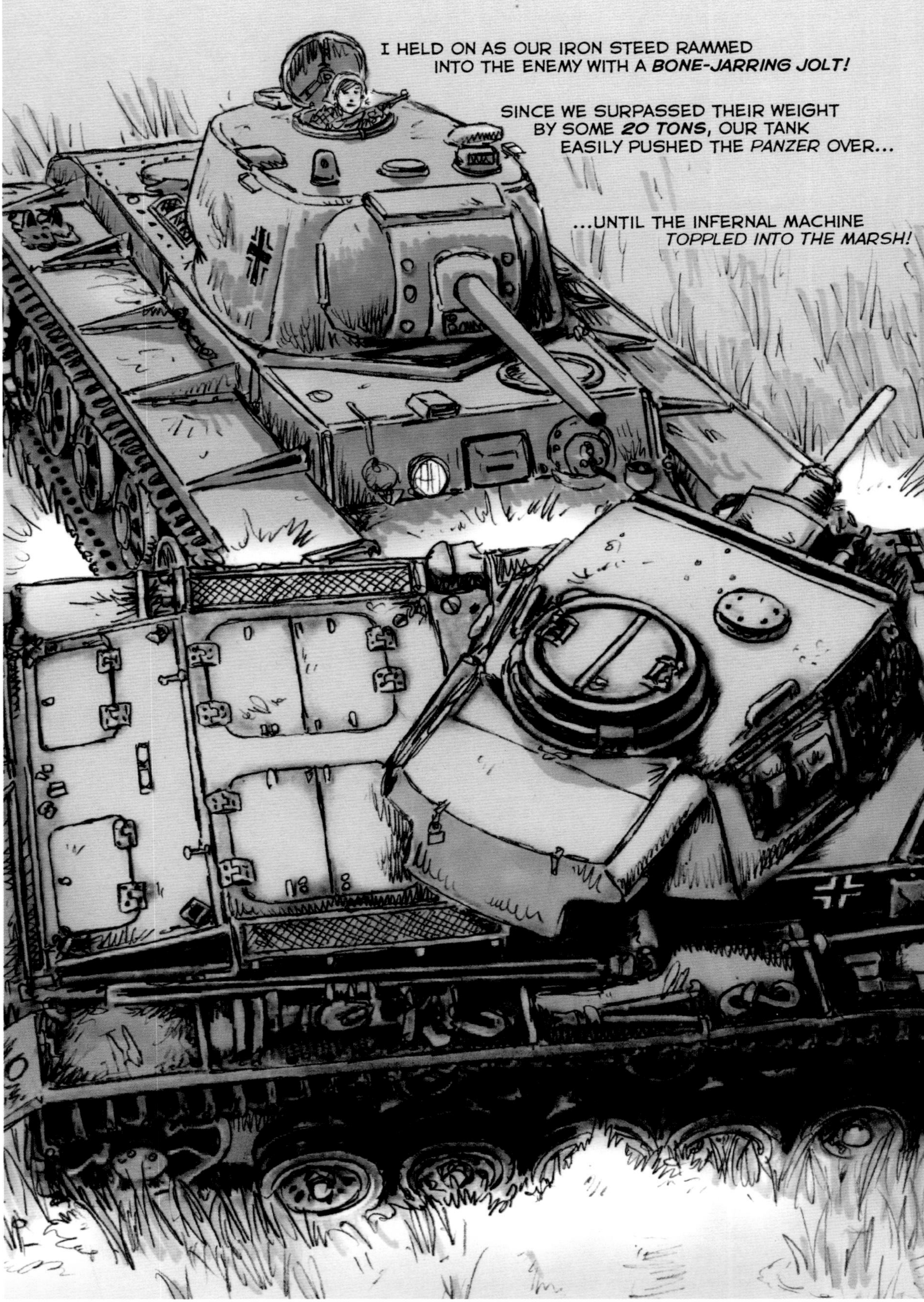
I HELD ON AS OUR IRON STEED RAMMED INTO THE ENEMY WITH A ***BONE-JARRING JOLT!***
SINCE WE SURPASSED THEIR WEIGHT BY SOME ***20 TONS***, OUR TANK EASILY PUSHED THE *PANZER* OVER...
...UNTIL THE INFERNAL MACHINE *TOPPLED INTO THE MARSH!*

AS WE PILED OUT OF THE TANK, THE PINK GLOW IN THE EAST MEANT WE'D RUN OUT OF DARK. JUST THEN, WE WERE DRAWN TO ANOTHER QUARTER--

HEY!

EH--?

IT WAS VASILY--CALLING FROM HIS MACHINE-GUN POSITION ON THE OTHER SIDE OF THE MARSH...!

LISTEN! GERMAN VEHICLES COMING DOWN THE CAUSEWAY ROAD!

YOU'D BETTER GET GOING!

YOU, TOO! HEAD WEST--WE'LL HEAD EAST, AND THEN COME AROUND WHEREVER WE CAN...!

GOOD LUCK!

WE HAD NO IDEA HOW MANY OF OUR PEOPLE HAD GOT AWAY--BUT OUR DEAD WERE LYING EVERYWHERE...

...AND OUR BLEEDING HAD NOT YET STOPPED...!

LOOK OUT!

THEY'RE FIRING MORTARS AT US!

BYELOV--!!

BYELOV WAS BADLY TORN UP. HE WAS ALIVE BUT COLLAPSING LIKE AN EMPTY TUBE--!

HE'S NOT SO HEAVY--!! WE'LL CARRY HIM--!

KATUSHA... NO...

...I'M SORRY.

HE WAS A GOOD BOY...

177

I STUMBLED ON, THROUGH ICY, COLD MARSHES AND DOWN DRY, DUSTY ROADS,
NUMB TO MOST OF WHAT WAS GOING ON AROUND ME--
BUT MY MIND WAS *REELING.*

I KEPT ASKING MYSELF...

WHAT'S A GIRL OF SEVENTEEN DOING HERE, IN A *WAR--?*
--CARRYING THE IMPLEMENTS OF MURDER
AS SHE WOULD A PURSE TO MARKET,
OR A PAIL OF SOUP TO A SICK FRIEND?

DEEP WITHIN ME, I FELT A RANGE OF EMOTION
THAT REACHED EVERY EXTREMITY AND DIGIT...

I FELT BOTH JOY AND GUILT THAT I WAS YET ALIVE.

I FELT GREAT CONFUSION ABOUT THIS CAUSE
THAT I WAS SERVING.

AND I REGRETTED THAT I HAD NOT LISTENED
MORE CLOSELY TO MAMA WHEN SHE HAD
SPOKEN OF WHAT GOD EXPECTED OF US.

BUT MOST OF ALL...

I FELT *ASHAMED.*

OUR MISSION WAS AN APPARENT SUCCESS.
BUT STALIN'S OFFENSIVE, WHICH WE WERE FIGHTING TO AID, WAS *NOT.*

BEGINNING ON *MAY 12,* THE SOVIETS HAD MADE
GOOD PROGRESS TOWARD *KHARKOV....*BUT ACTUALLY, THEIR PROGRESS WAS *TOO* GOOD.

... IT WAS A *TRAP!*

AFTER FIVE DAYS OF GOOD FORTUNE,
GERMAN FORCES CLOSED IN BEHIND
TWO SOVIET ARMIES AND BEGAN
TO CHEW THEM UP.

THE *STAVKA* ADMITTED LOSSES OF 5,000 MEN KILLED AND 70,000 MISSING, WITH SOME
300 SOVIET TANKS DESTROYED...

...AND ANOTHER 200,000 RUSSIAN SOLDIERS
FELL INTO GERMAN CAPTIVITY...!

IT WAS BEGINNING TO LOOK AS IF THE RED ARMY WOULD
NEVER WIN A DECISIVE BATTLE AGAINST THE GERMANS.

AS WE MOVED ON, ANY MOVE TOWARD THE WEST WAS BLOCKED EITHER BY NATURAL BARRIERS OR GERMAN ACTIVITY.

SO WE KEPT HEADING *EAST*, ACROSS BARREN STEPPES AND SCORCHED FARMLAND...

SURELY WE'LL BE ABLE TO TURN BACK EVENTUALLY...!

I DON'T KNOW...

MAYBE THIS IS THE BEGINNING OF *MY* *SECOND* CIRCLING OF THE GLOBE...

AT LEAST I HAVE BETTER COMPANY THIS TIME.

I WOULD LIKE THAT--TO SEE THE *PACIFIC OCEAN*... AND *AMERIKA!*

I WOULD JUST LIKE TO SEE *MAMA'S SMILE*...

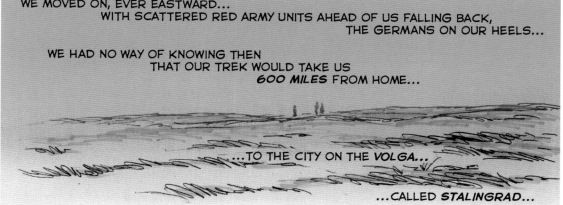

WE MOVED ON, EVER EASTWARD...
WITH SCATTERED RED ARMY UNITS AHEAD OF US FALLING BACK,
THE GERMANS ON OUR HEELS...

WE HAD NO WAY OF KNOWING THEN
THAT OUR TREK WOULD TAKE US
600 MILES FROM HOME...

...TO THE CITY ON THE *VOLGA*...

...CALLED *STALINGRAD*...

Book II
The Shaking of the Earth

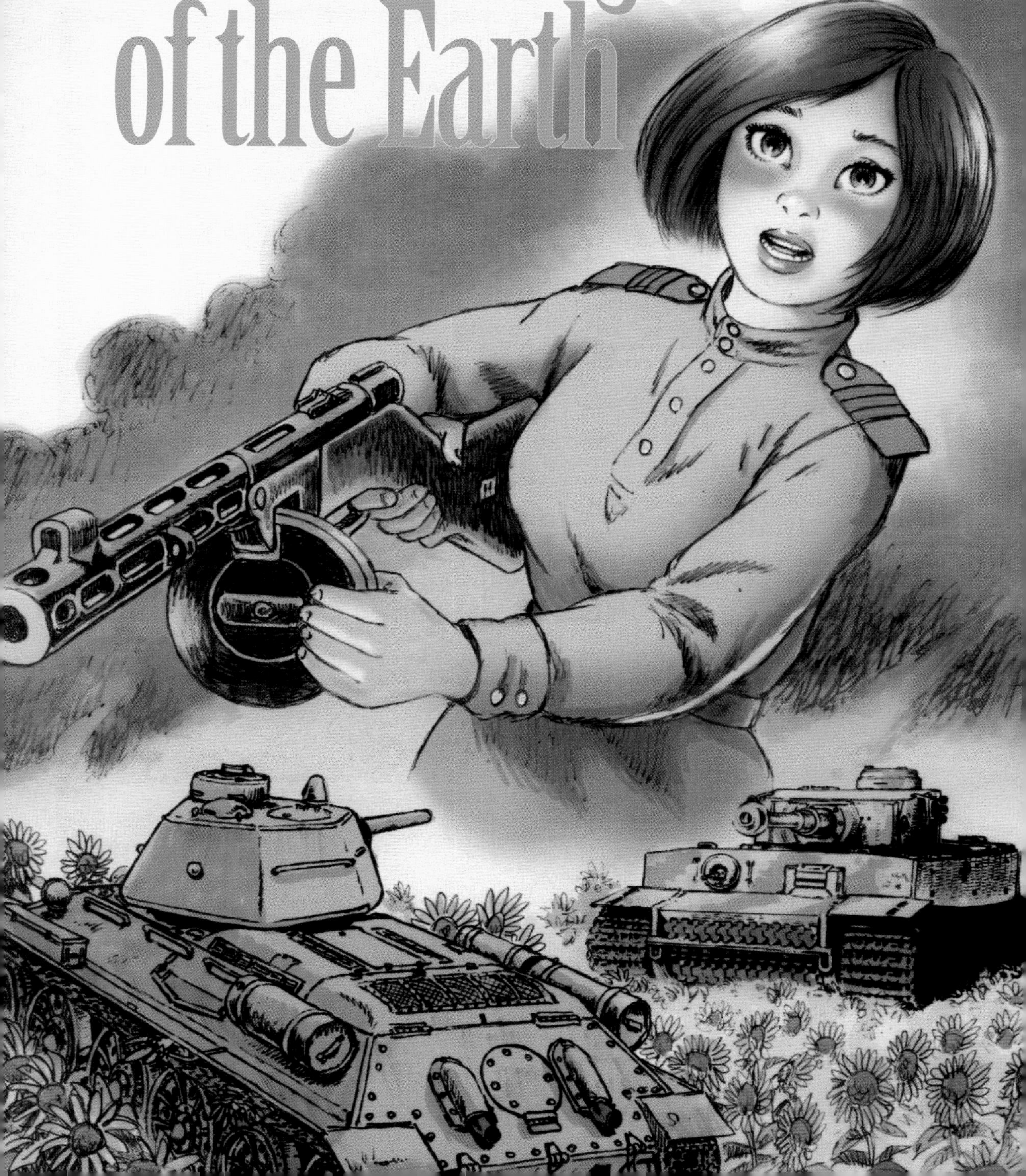

THE EASTERN FRONT
SOUTH WESTERN RUSSIA
1942-1943

JULY, 1942. INSIDE THE BEND OF THE *DON RIVER*...

VOR DER KASERNE VOR DEM GROSSEN TOR STAND EINE LATERNE, UND STEHT SIE NOCH DAVOR, SO WOLL'N WIR UNS DA WIEDER SEH'N...

HITLER'S NEW OFFENSIVE, *OPERATION BLUE*, WAS CUTTING ACROSS SOUTHERN RUSSIA.

BEI DER LATERNE WOLL'N WIR STEH'N, WIE EINST LILI MARLEEN, WIE EINST LILI MARLEEN...

ARMY GROUP A WAS MOVING SOUTH, TOWARD THE CAUCASUS AND THE OIL FIELDS OF THE CASPIAN SEA...

UNSERE BEIDEN SCHATTEN SAH'N WIE EINER AUS, DAS WIR SO LIEB UNS HATTEN, DAS SAH MAN GLEICH DARAUS UND ALLE LEUTE SOLL'N ES SEH'N...

AT THE SAME TIME, *ARMY GROUP B* WAS MOVING EAST, TOWARD THE VOLGA...

WENN WIR BEI DER LATERNE STEH'N, WIE EINST LILI MARLEEN, WIE EINST LILI MARLEEN!

183

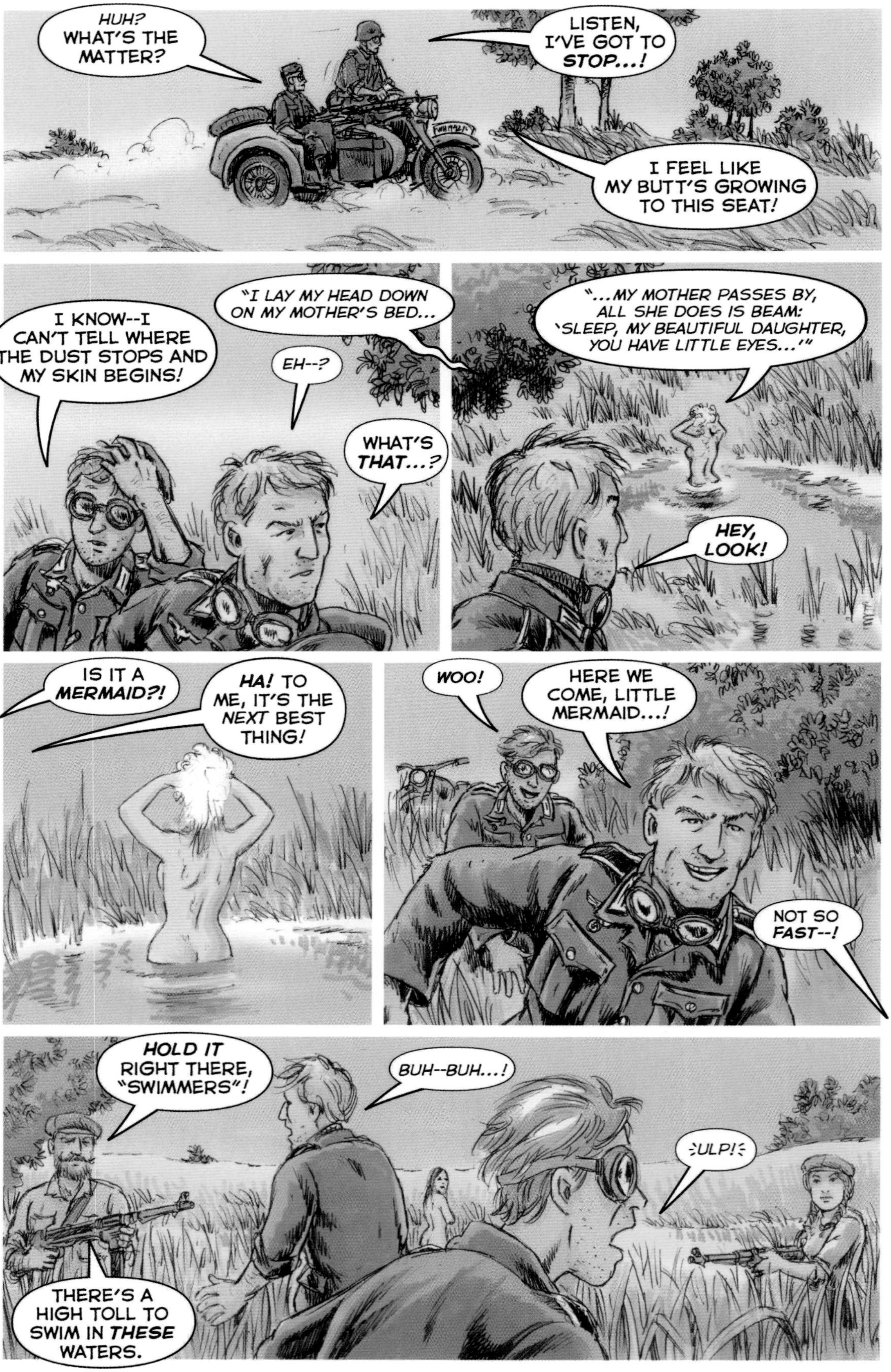
HUH? WHAT'S THE MATTER?
LISTEN, I'VE GOT TO STOP...!
I FEEL LIKE MY BUTT'S GROWING TO THIS SEAT!
I KNOW--I CAN'T TELL WHERE THE DUST STOPS AND MY SKIN BEGINS!
"I LAY MY HEAD DOWN ON MY MOTHER'S BED...
EH--?
WHAT'S THAT...?
"...MY MOTHER PASSES BY, ALL SHE DOES IS BEAM: 'SLEEP, MY BEAUTIFUL DAUGHTER, YOU HAVE LITTLE EYES...'"
HEY, LOOK!
IS IT A MERMAID?!
HA! TO ME, IT'S THE NEXT BEST THING!
WOO!
HERE WE COME, LITTLE MERMAID...!
NOT SO FAST--!
HOLD IT RIGHT THERE, "SWIMMERS"!
BUH--BUH...!
ULP!
THERE'S A HIGH TOLL TO SWIM IN THESE WATERS.

WELL, THAT WENT ALL RIGHT--BUT NEXT TIME, *YOU* BE THE DECOY, MILLA!

I KNOW-- NEXT TIME AROUND, WE'LL LET *TARAS* BE THE BATHER!

OH, YES! :HEE HEE HEE..!:

UH-HUH. HA, HA.

OKAY, LET'S HIT THE ROAD...CAN YOU DRIVE THIS THING ALL RIGHT?

OF COURSE!

OH, YEAH...

I ALMOST *FORGOT* ABOUT YOU TWO...!

I TURNED MY HEAD. I KNEW THAT YOU DARED NOT SHOW MERCY TODAY TO SOMEONE WHO WOULD SURELY *NOT* SHOW MERCY TO YOU TOMORROW.

I UNDERSTOOD THIS PERFECTLY...

...BUT I DIDN'T HAVE TO *LIKE* IT.

185

NOT ONE STEP BACK!

AS WE MOVED EASTWARD, WE RAN INTO MORE AND MORE RED ARMY UNITS. ALL WERE TIRED, HUNGRY, AND DISILLUSIONED. NONE OF THEM TRIED TO CHECK UP ON US, AND WE WEREN'T BOTHERED WITH SECURITY MATTERS UNTIL WE REACHED THE DON RIVER CROSSING AT NIZHNIY-CHIRSKAYA. BY THEN, OUR MOTORCYCLE HAD LONG SINCE RUN OUT OF GAS AND HAD BEEN ABANDONED.

...AND I'M AFRAID WE HAVE NO IDENTIFICATION ON US...

UKRAINIAN PARTISANS, EH? I'D SAY YOU WERE FAR OUT OF YOUR TERRITORY--THE TITLE NO LONGER FITS.

IF YOU'RE EXPECTING HARASSMENT FROM ME, YOU CAN FORGET IT...

THE "BOSS" HAS PUT OUT THE WORD--NO ONE IS TO BE ALLOWED TO PASS THE VOLGA.

"NOT ONE STEP BACK!" HE HAS ORDERED.

HE SEEMED LIKE A PRETTY GOOD FELLOW...

ESPECIALLY FOR AN *NKVD* MAN.

LOOK AT THIS!

WHAT IS IT, UNCLE TARAS?

IT'S A CAMEL, KATUSHA.

HE'S A RATHER UGLY CREATURE.

I THINK HE'S CUTE.

SO MUCH FOR BEAUTY.

CCCROOOKOH!

UUGGHH EEE!

THAT NIGHT, WE SLEPT IN A LITTLE SHACK BESIDE THE ROAD OWNED BY AN OLD WOMAN WHOSE DAUGHTER HAD RUN AWAY LONG AGO. MILLA'S AND MY PRESENCE HELPED SOOTHE HER BROKEN HEART, AND SHE FED US A THIN MILLET SOUP THAT TASTED WONDERFUL...

UNCLE TARAS, DO YOU THINK WE'LL EVER GET TO GO HOME AGAIN?

OF COURSE! I CAME HOME AGAIN, DIDN'T I?

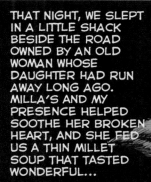

I KNOW, BUT, WELL, THAT TOOK MORE THAN TWENTY YEARS AND I DON'T WANT TO BE, YOU KNOW...*OLD!*

HA! SO THAT'S IT. WELL, MAYBE THE GERMANS WILL PUSH THE RUSSIANS BACK AS FAR AS THEY WANT, AND THEN MAKE PEACE. MAYBE THE GERMANS WILL TAKE *ALL* SOVIET TERRITORIES. WHO KNOWS? MAYBE STALIN WILL WIN! EITHER WAY, LIFE WILL BE HARD, BUT IT ALWAYS IS.

187

WE MOVED EAST ALL SUMMER, AND AS WE WENT, THE ROAD BECAME MORE AND MORE CROWDED. THE PACE ALSO BECAME MORE FRANTIC, BECAUSE THE GERMANS WERE CATCHING UP WITH US. "MEDDERS" STRAFING THE ROADS BECAME AN EVERYDAY EXPERIENCE. BUT WHEN WE REALIZED WE WERE WITHIN RANGE OF THEIR HEAVY ARTILLERY, WE KNEW THAT THE ROAD HAD ALMOST COME TO AN END...

...AND THE ROAD CERTAINLY WAS WELL MARKED.

Сталинград

STALINGRAD.

...ORIGINALLY CALLED *TSARITSYN,* IT WAS RENAMED IN *1925* TO HONOR OUR ILLUSTRIOUS LEADER. IT IS A CITY OF HEAVY INDUSTRY AND SHIPPING, WITH RAIL CONNECTIONS TO EVERY POINT ON THE COMPASS!

THIS LOVELY CITY OF PARKS AND BROAD STREETS IS HOME TO 500,000 CITIZEN WORKERS--

UH-OH--!

OH, *NO!* I HEAR IT, *TOO-!*

IT WAS *SUNDAY, AUGUST 23,* A DAY THAT I WILL NEVER FORGET. AS THE SUN ROSE OVER THE VOLGA, WAVES AND WAVES OF JUNKERS AND HEINKELS CAME TO MEET IT.

ON THIS DAY, THE MODEL CITY OF *STALINGRAD,* WITH ITS TALL, WHITE APARTMENT BUILDINGS AND LONG, TREE-LINED BOULEVARDS...

...WOULD BECOME A *HELL ON EARTH.*

188

THE GERMANS BOMBED NOT ONLY THE INDUSTRIAL TARGETS, BUT *EVERYTHING*. ALL OF THE ABLE-BODIED MEN HAD GONE INTO SERVICE--IT WAS A CITY OF OLD FOLKS, WOMEN, AND CHILDREN, LEFT WITH NO OPTION BUT TO HIDE IN THE SLIT TRENCHES THEY'D DUG IN THEIR GARDENS, IN CELLARS, OR IN THE RAVINES THAT RAN DOWN TO THE RIVER...

STALIN HADN'T ALLOWED AN EVACUATION--HE BELIEVED HIS SOLDIERS WOULD FIGHT MORE FIERCELY FOR A *LIVING* CITY THAN A *DEAD* ONE.

WHEN THE HUGE PETROLEUM TANK ON THE BANKS OF THE RIVER WAS HIT, A COLOSSAL *FIREBALL* ROSE 1,500 FEET INTO THE AIR.

FOR DAYS, THE ANGRY COLUMNS OF BLACK SMOKE COULD BE SEEN FROM TWO HUNDRED MILES AWAY...

IT WAS *WHOLESALE OBLITERATION*. ENTIRE NEIGHBORHOODS DISAPPEARED AS THEIR BUILDINGS, STREETS, AND PEOPLE MERGED INTO A NIGHTMARE OF CHARRED RUBBLE.

INCENDIARY BOMBS FELL ON THE WOODEN HOUSES OF THE SOUTHWESTERN PART OF THE CITY, TURNING THE DISTRICT INTO AN EERIE GRAVEYARD OF STONE AND BRICK CHIMNEYS.

PERHAPS AS MANY AS *40,000* OF ITS CITIZENS *DIED* IN THIS OPENING BOMBARDMENT.

NEAR US WERE *37MM* ANTI-AIRCRAFT GUNS-- MANNED BY YOUNG GIRLS, MANY OF THEM NO OLDER THAN I WAS.

LET'S GIVE THEM A HAND!

AT LEAST WE CAN PASS THEM AMMUNITION.

HOW CAN WE HELP?

THE AMMO BUNKER'S RIGHT THERE. IF THERE ARE ENOUGH OF YOU, YOU CAN PASS IT LIKE A BUCKET BRIGADE.

AH! THERE WE GO, ALL *DONE!*

NO MORE TARGETS FOR NOW. *NOW*, WE GET A *BREAK!*

I DON'T THINK SO! DON'T YOU HEAR THAT *NOISE--?*

THAT SOUND WAS ONE I'D HEARD BEFORE--AND DREADED HEARING AGAIN. OUT OF THE SMOKE EMERGED GERMAN *PANZER IV*s!

THE *16TH PANZER DIVISION* HAD ARRIVED AT STALINGRAD.

THE BATTERY COMMANDER, WHO'D TAUGHT SCHOOL IN STALINGRAD BEFORE THE WAR, REACTED QUICKLY...!

KEEP THAT *AMMO* COMING!

CRANK THOSE *GUNS* DOWN TO ZERO DEGREES--AND *OPEN FIRE--!!*

THE *37MM* ROUNDS FAILED TO PENETRATE THE ARMOR OF THE TANKS UNLESS THE RANGE WAS ALMOST *POINT BLANK.*

THEY COULD, HOWEVER, KNOCK OFF A TRACK OR EVEN OPEN A HATCH, IF LUCKY.

DESPITE ONLY MINOR SUCCESSES, THE GIRL GUNNERS KEPT AT IT...

...EVEN WHEN THE GERMAN GUNS WERE TAKING THEM OUT AT A GREATER DISTANCE.

THE GERMAN TANKERS WERE *STUNNED* TO REALIZE THAT THE GUNS WERE MANNED BY YOUNG GIRLS...!

I SUPPOSE THEY'D NEVER HEARD THE OLD MYTH OF THE *SARMATAE* OF THE LOWER VOLGA, A RACE OF FEMALE WARRIORS WHO WERE SAID TO BE DESCENDED FROM THE *SCYTHIANS* AND THE LEGENDARY *AMAZONS.*

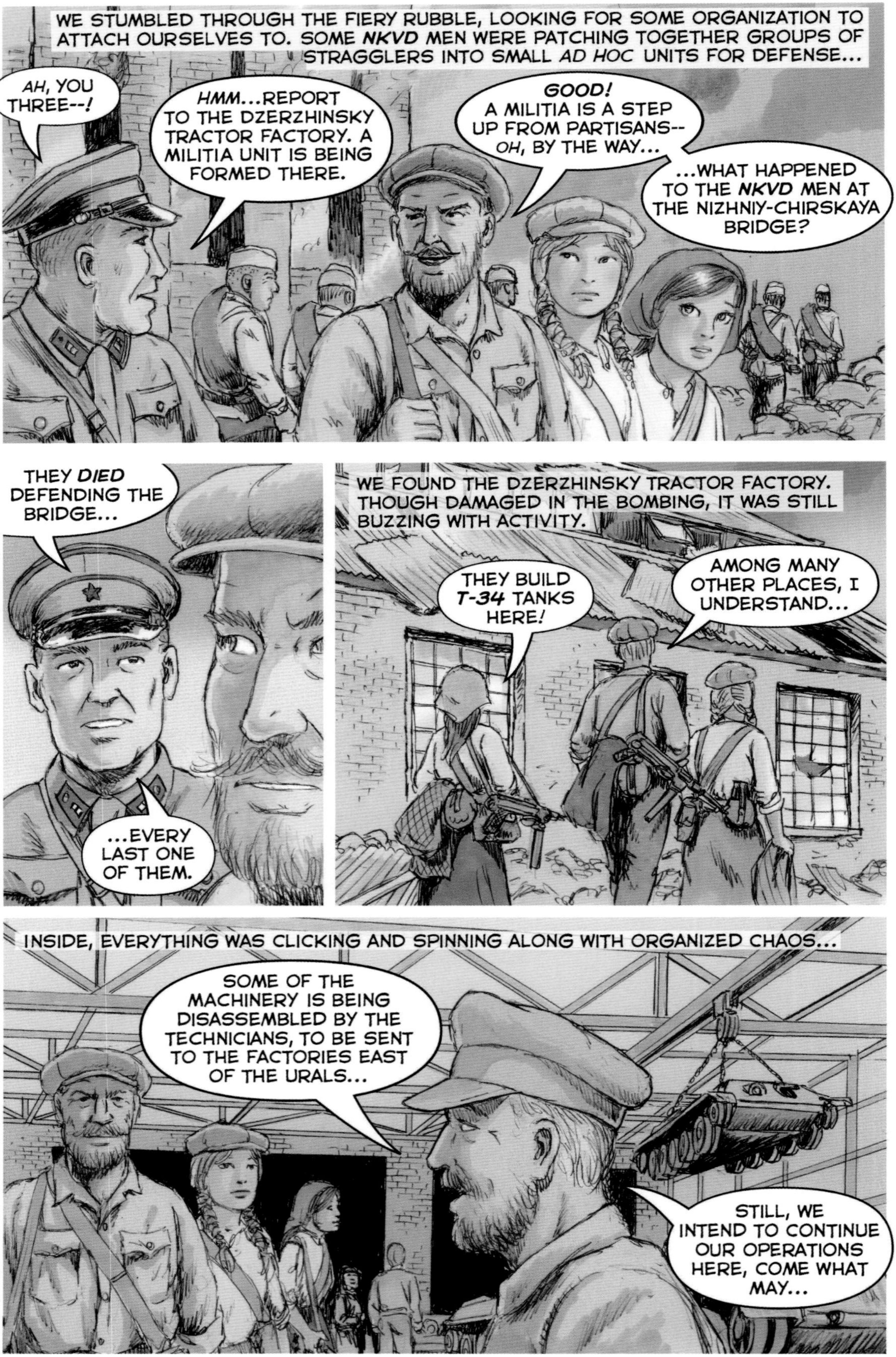
WE STUMBLED THROUGH THE FIERY RUBBLE, LOOKING FOR SOME ORGANIZATION TO ATTACH OURSELVES TO. SOME NKVD MEN WERE PATCHING TOGETHER GROUPS OF STRAGGLERS INTO SMALL AD HOC UNITS FOR DEFENSE...
AH, YOU THREE--!
HMM...REPORT TO THE DZERZHINSKY TRACTOR FACTORY. A MILITIA UNIT IS BEING FORMED THERE.
GOOD! A MILITIA IS A STEP UP FROM PARTISANS-- OH, BY THE WAY...
...WHAT HAPPENED TO THE NKVD MEN AT THE NIZHNIY-CHIRSKAYA BRIDGE?
THEY DIED DEFENDING THE BRIDGE...
...EVERY LAST ONE OF THEM.
WE FOUND THE DZERZHINSKY TRACTOR FACTORY. THOUGH DAMAGED IN THE BOMBING, IT WAS STILL BUZZING WITH ACTIVITY.
THEY BUILD T-34 TANKS HERE!
AMONG MANY OTHER PLACES, I UNDERSTAND...
INSIDE, EVERYTHING WAS CLICKING AND SPINNING ALONG WITH ORGANIZED CHAOS...
SOME OF THE MACHINERY IS BEING DISASSEMBLED BY THE TECHNICIANS, TO BE SENT TO THE FACTORIES EAST OF THE URALS...
STILL, WE INTEND TO CONTINUE OUR OPERATIONS HERE, COME WHAT MAY...

WHILE TARAS TALKED TO THE WORKER, I WANDERED AWAY INTO THE HUGE FACTORY THAT RATTLED AND CLANKED WITH ACTIVITY. IT WAS NOT A MODERN PLACE LIKE DPECHERSK OR BANKIVSKA, BUT ITS SENSIBLE DESIGN AND DEDICATION TO PURPOSE REPRESENTED A CERTAIN KIND OF BEAUTY.

I THEN NOTICED A MAN WHOSE *BACK* SEEMED SOMEHOW FAMILIAR TO ME...

?

PAPA...?

EH--?

AH!!

IT WAS A MOST JOYOUS AND UNEXPECTED REUNION, ESPECIALLY BETWEEN MY FATHER AND UNCLE TARAS. THEIR PURE AND UNINTERRUPTED LOVE FOR EACH OTHER WAS SO OBVIOUS IT WAS ALL I COULD DO TO KEEP FROM CRYING AND SPOILING THE EVENT.

PAPA'S SUPERIORS, WHO OBVIOUSLY MUST HAVE RESPECTED HIM A GREAT DEAL, LET US USE AN EMPTY OFFICE IN A CORNER OF THE FACTORY. THERE WE TALKED AND CAUGHT UP UNTIL LATE AT NIGHT.

PAPA WAS CONCERNED AND UPSET ABOUT HOW OUR FAMILY HAD BEEN SCATTERED FAR AND WIDE. BUT CONSIDERING THE TIMES, HE WAS STILL GRATEFUL IT HAD TURNED OUT AS WELL AS IT HAD. HE WAS GLAD THAT WE HAD THUS FAR PREVAILED, AND HE HOPED THAT OUR APPARENT GOOD FORTUNE WOULD SEE US THROUGH.

AS WE SPENT THIS TIME TOGETHER, HE SEEMED TO DETECT THE CONNECTION BETWEEN TARAS AND MILLA. AT FIRST, HE SEEMED AS IF IT BOTHERED HIM A BIT--BUT I COULD SEE HIM GRADUALLY REACH A QUIET ACCEPTANCE.

MILLA AND I HAD FINALLY BECOME SO TIRED FROM OUR JOURNEY THAT WE JUST HAD TO SLEEP.

THE LAST THING I REMEMBER BEFORE CLOSING MY EYES WAS UNCLE TARAS AND PAPA TALKING QUIETLY AND VERY SERIOUSLY IN A CORNER OF THE ROOM...

THE FIRST THING I NOTICED AS I AWOKE THE NEXT MORNING WAS THE SOUND OF SMALL-ARMS AND ARTILLERY FIRE IN THE DISTANCE.

‹YAAAWN›

‹SIGH› ALREADY AT IT, I SEE...

WHERE'S PAPA?

HE WENT TO SPEAK WITH A POLITICAL OFFICER WHO OWES HIM A FAVOR.

HE'LL BE BACK SOON.

BY THE TIME PAPA GOT BACK, WE WERE ALL UP AND MUNCHING ON SOME MOSTLY UNMOLDY BREAD. PAPA WAS CARRYING A BROWN ENVELOPE AND WORE A LOOK OF SATISFACTION...

ALL RIGHT!

WE ARE GETTING YOU GIRLS *OUT* OF STALINGRAD!

I WAS IMMEDIATELY CURIOUS... BUT *MILLA'S* EXPRESSION--?

--PURE *SUSPICION.*

WELL, YOUR FATHER AND I TALKED IT OVER LAST NIGHT, AND IT MAKES *SENSE.* THE FIGHT HERE IN THE CITY IS GOING TO BE BAD, AND IF THE GERMANS MANAGE TO *TAKE* STALINGRAD AND CUT THE VOLGA--THAT WILL JUST ABOUT FINISH THE WAR FOR *US.*

FOR THE TIME BEING, WE WOULD LIKE TO THINK THAT THE BOTH OF YOU ARE *SAFE.*

THE SENIOR POLITICAL COMMISSAR HERE OWES ME ONE--HE'S ALSO UKRAINIAN. HE'S PROVIDED ME WITH ALL THE TRAVEL PERMITS AND INTRODUCTIONS THAT YOU'LL NEED-- BECAUSE YOU GIRLS ARE GOING TO *CHELYABINSK...*

...TO ENTER THE *TANK-DRIVING SCHOOL.*

THE IDEA GAVE ME A RUSH OF EXCITEMENT--! BUT WHEN I LOOKED OVER AT MILLA TO GAUGE HER REACTION, HER EXPRESSION WAS ONE OF HURT...EVEN *BETRAYAL.*

SILENTLY, SHE TURNED AND STRODE OUT OF THE ROOM.

UNCLE TARAS WENT RIGHT AFTER HER...

PAPA, I THINK YOU DESERVE AN EXPLANATION ABOUT--

KATUSHA, I HAVE ALL THE EXPLANATION I NEED. LUDMILLA IS A GROWN WOMAN...

...AND SO ARE *YOU.*

THAT EVENING, PAPA AND UNCLE TARAS SAW US OFF AT THE RIVER DOCKS, WHERE A FERRY WOULD CARRY US ACROSS THE VOLGA. IT WAS A VERY DIFFICULT PARTING FOR ALL OF US, FOR OUR FAMILY WAS FRAGMENTING YET AGAIN.

THE CROSSING WOULD BE MORE DIFFICULT YET. AN ATTACK WAS IN PROGRESS.

GERMAN ARTILLERY AND PLANES RAINED DOWN A CONSTANT BARRAGE OF HORRIFIC DESTRUCTION.

A BARGE LOADED WITH WOUNDED WAS HIT AND SUNK RIGHT BESIDE US!

WHEN WE REACHED THE OTHER SIDE, I LOOKED BACK ACROSS AT THE CITY--AND WENT NUMB WITH HORROR. STALINGRAD FLASHED AND ROARED LIKE HELL ITSELF, THE FIERY LIGHT REFLECTING ON THE RIVER'S SURFACE MAKING THE VOLGA LOOK LIKE *BLOOD.*

WE WALKED SEVERAL MILES TO WHERE WE WERE TO CATCH OUR TRAIN. APPARENTLY OUR PAPERWORK WAS IMPECCABLE, SINCE EVERY *NKVD* MAN WHO SAW IT WENT ALL WIDE-EYED AND POLITELY PASSED US RIGHT THROUGH.

WE RODE IN A CATTLE CAR PACKED WITH ALL TYPES OF PEOPLE...

BUT NO UNIFORMED SOLDIERS WERE AMONG US. THEY'D ALL BEEN LEFT BEHIND FOR THE FIGHT TO *DEFEND STALINGRAD*.

IT IS FARTHER FROM STALINGRAD TO CHELYABINSK THAN IT IS FROM STALINGRAD TO KIEV--MORE THAN 700 MILES. MILLA AND I HAD TRAVELED FARTHER IN THE LAST YEAR THAN WE HAD IN ALL OUR PREVIOUS YEARS...

...NOT THAT THERE HAD BEEN THAT MANY YET.

AFTER THREE DAYS' TRAVEL, WE REACHED *CHELYABINSK* DURING THE NIGHT. SECURITY WAS TIGHT...

THE *NKVD* OFFICERS WANTED TO TAKE OUR WEAPONS--BUT ONE LOOK AT OUR PAPERS, AND *THEIR* EYES GOT LIKE SAUCERS AND THEY LET US PASS, *ARMED*.

ALL THIS WAS BEGINNING TO BE SUCH A FAMILIAR ROUTINE WE'D STARTED TO WONDER--WHAT *WAS* IT ABOUT THE SIGNATURE OF THIS *"NIKITA SERGEYEVICH KHRUSHCHEV,"* ANYWAY?

THEY PUT US ON A TRUCK WITH A GROUP OF RECRUITS FOR THE TANK SCHOOL, AND WE HEADED FOR CHELYABINSK...WHICH PROVED TO BE LESS OF A TOWN THAN IT WAS A HUGE INDUSTRIAL DISTRICT OF MUDDY STREETS LINED WITH ROUGH-HEWN BUILDINGS OF RAW LUMBER AND RUSTY SHEET METAL. EVERYTHING WAS NEW, ALL OF IT HAVING BEEN THROWN UP QUICKLY WITH AN EYE TO IMMEDIATE SERVICE...

THERE WERE WAREHOUSES AND MACHINE SHOPS AND WORKERS' HOUSING AND LAUNDRIES, ALL LIT BY THE RED GLOW OF THE ENDLESS FACTORIES THAT THEY SERVED.

WITHIN A YEAR, THE SMALL CITIES OF THIS REGION WOULD GROW TOGETHER INTO AN INDUSTRIAL COMPLEX 60 MILES LONG--KNOWN TO THE OUTSIDE WORLD AS *TANKOGRAD.*

THE TRUCK PULLED UP IN FRONT OF A LONG, SQUAT BUILDING, WHERE WE WERE GREETED WITH SHOUTED CURSES FROM A WOMAN SERGEANT.

SHE DIRECTED US INTO A LONG HALL, WHERE WE STOOD IN A ROW WHILE A PALE POLITICAL OFFICER LED US IN RECITING AN OATH TO DEFEND OUR *MOTHER RUSSIA...*

THEN A KISS OF ALLEGIANCE TO THE FLAG-- AND WE WERE OFFICIALLY PART OF THE *RED ARMY.*

THEY GAVE US BAGS SORT OF LIKE GRAIN SACKS FOR ANY PERSONAL ITEMS WE WISHED TO KEEP. MILLA AND I STUCK OUR WEAPONS IN THESE TO MINIMIZE THE CURIOUS LOOKS WE WERE GETTING.

РОДИНА-МАТЬ ЗОВЕТ!

EACH OF US WAS THEN ISSUED OUR EQUIPMENT:

* ONE RAIN CAPE;
* ONE PILOTKA CAP;
* ONE LEATHER BELT;
* ONE WOOL GREATCOAT;
* TWO WOOL GYMNASTIORKA SHIRTS;
* THREE PAIRS OF WOOL FOOT CLOTHS;
* ONE PAIR OF COTTON TANKER'S COVERALLS;
* ONE PAIR OF WOOL PANTS WITH PADDED KNEES;
* THREE SETS OF COTTON UNDERSHIRTS AND SHORTS; AND
* ONE PAIR OF BLACK JACKBOOTS.

OF COURSE, MY BOOTS WERE TOO LARGE--AND MILLA'S, TOO SMALL.

WE WERE LED TO A SHOWER ROOM WITH A CONCRETE FLOOR.

THE WATER WAS BARELY LUKEWARM, BUT WHAT A BLESSING IT WAS...!

IT FELT GREAT TO WASH OFF A FEW HUNDRED MILES OF DIRT.

AHH...!

WHEN IT CAME TO THE BARBER'S CHAIR, MILLA BACKED OFF...

TARAS LIKES MY HAIR LONG-- I'LL JUST BRAID IT.

I LONGED TO BE MORE ACCEPTING OF CHANGES IN MY LIFE, SO I PUT MYSELF AT THE MERCY OF THE BARBER. I COULD TELL HE WAS PROUD OF THE RESULTS.

I SMILED IN GRATITUDE... BUT DEEP INSIDE, I *CRIED*.

THEY THEN DROPPED US OFF IN FRONT OF A SIMPLE WOODEN BARRACKS THAT SEEMED TO BE FLOATING IN A SEA OF MUD.

UNFORTUNATELY, IT WAS LATE WHEN WE GOT IN, SO WE WERE ASSIGNED THE LAST TWO BUNKS AVAILABLE.

WE WALKED INTO A SOLID WALL OF NOISE AS EVERYONE WAS GETTING UP FOR THE DAY.

NEVER HAVE I HEARD SO MUCH CURSING FROM THE MOUTHS OF WOMEN...! WITHIN MOMENTS, I HAD HEARD GOD'S NAME BLASPHEMED IN EVERY LANGUAGE AND DIALECT OF THE SOVIET UNION.

WE WERE LINED UP OUTSIDE AND MARCHED TO BREAKFAST...

...SOMETHING MILLA AND I WERE *NOT* VERY GOOD AT.

IT SEEMED ODD TO ME HOW EVERYBODY COMPLAINED ABOUT THE FOOD. I THOUGHT BREAKFAST WAS PRETTY GOOD--PORRIDGE, MEAT, AND BREAD WITH BUTTER.

SO...YOU'RE THE *TYMOSHENKO SISTERS*, EH?

YOU SURE DON'T *LOOK* LIKE SISTERS...

WELL, WE *ARE*.

HEY, YURI! WHAT DO YOU THINK WAS IN THOSE *AWFUL* SAUSAGES--?

:UGH: *BOOTS*, DEFINITELY. *OLD* ONES.

WORD IS YOU TWO SHOWED UP PACKING GERMAN WEAPONS--!

THAT'S TRUE.

WHERE WE'RE FROM, IT *COULD* BE A BAD IDEA TO GO *UNARMED*...

THINGS ARE GETTING *UNPREDICTABLE*--

HOO! WOULDJA LISTEN TO THAT HICK *ACCENT?*

HAW HAW!!

YEAH--LOOKS LIKE WE'RE SHARIN' BUNKS WITH A COUPLE OF "*TUFTIES*"!*

I'M MARUSYA POZHARSKY.

OH, AND *DON'T* MIND THEM.

* RUDE TERM FOR A UKRAINIAN

MARUSYA, I WAS WONDERING. ALL THE OFFICERS ARE EATING TOGETHER-- EXCEPT FOR THAT ONE MAN OVER BY THE WINDOW...

...WHY IS HE SITTING THERE ALL BY HIMSELF?

OH--THAT'S *CAPTAIN RAMSKOV*. HE TEACHES TANK-TO-TANK TACTICS...

YOU'LL MEET *HIM* LATER.

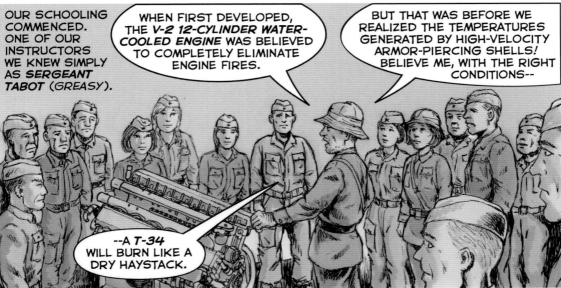

OUR SCHOOLING COMMENCED. ONE OF OUR INSTRUCTORS WE KNEW SIMPLY AS *SERGEANT TABOT* (GREASY).

WHEN FIRST DEVELOPED, THE *V-2 12-CYLINDER WATER-COOLED ENGINE* WAS BELIEVED TO COMPLETELY ELIMINATE ENGINE FIRES.

BUT THAT WAS BEFORE WE REALIZED THE TEMPERATURES GENERATED BY HIGH-VELOCITY ARMOR-PIERCING SHELLS! BELIEVE ME, WITH THE RIGHT CONDITIONS--

--A *T-34* WILL BURN LIKE A DRY HAYSTACK.

THE FOUR-STAGE TRANSMISSION WAS SO UNRELIABLE THAT A COMMON SIGHT WAS A *T-34* WITH A SPARE TRANSMISSION CHAINED TO ITS ENGINE DECK!

THE ANSWER WAS THIS MUCH MORE RELIABLE FIVE-STAGE TRANSMISSION. AT TIMES, HOWEVER, THIS ONE CAN BE DIFFICULT TO SHIFT.

ON A LONG MARCH, YOU'LL NEED THE HELP OF THE ASSISTANT DRIVER/BOW GUNNER.

I NEVER COULD HAVE MADE IT THROUGH THAT SCHOOL--

--IF IT HAD NOT BEEN FOR *MILLA.*

SHE HAD A CLEAR AND NATURAL UNDERSTANDING FOR MACHINERY THAT I DID NOT.

SHE MADE CHANGING OIL SEEM AS SIMPLE AS MILKING A COW...

...CLEANING AIR FILTERS JUST LIKE CHURNING BUTTER...

...REPLACING BRAKES LIKE SLIPPING ON A NEW PAIR OF SHOES...

...AND LUBRICATING PARTS JUST LIKE...

...LIKE...

...WELL, *YOU KNOW.*

THAT NIGHT, ALMOST AT "LIGHTS OUT"...

TYMOSHENKO TWINS...! CAPTAIN KOVCHENKO IS OUTSIDE AND REQUIRES YOUR PRESENCE!

"TWINS"-- *VERY* FUNNY.

SO...WHO IS KOVCHENKO?

WAITING FOR US OUTSIDE WERE THREE MEN. WHICH OF THEM WAS CAPTAIN KOVCHENKO WAS OBVIOUS--HE HAD THE LOOK OF A MAN NATURALLY BORN TO LEAD.

FLANKING HIM WERE A TALL, SKINNY SERGEANT AND A POLITICAL OFFICER WITH A DISAGREEABLE-LOOKING EXPRESSION ON HIS FACE.

COMRADES TYMOSHENKO-- IT HAS BEEN BROUGHT TO OUR ATTENTION THAT WHEN YOU ARRIVED HERE AT THE SCHOOL, YOU BOTH CARRIED WEAPONS OF ENEMY MANUFACTURE. PERSONAL WEAPONS ARE *NOT* ALLOWED IN THE BARRACKS--

--PARTICULARLY *GERMAN* WEAPONS.

COMRADE CAPTAIN, JUST WEEKS AGO, WE WERE PARTISANS. HAVING THOSE GUNS CLOSE BY MEANT OUR *SURVIVAL*. WITHOUT OUR WEAPONS--WE'D HAVE *DIED* A DOZEN TIMES OVER.

WE COULDN'T SLEEP A *WINK* WITHOUT THOSE GUNS BESIDE US.

THIS TIME, THE CAPTAIN SPOKE IN MILDER TONES...

COMRADES, WE'RE A *LONG* WAY FROM THE FRONT LINES.

THERE'S NO PLANE IN EXISTENCE THAT CAN BOMB US HERE. YOU ARE PERFECTLY *SAFE*.

FINALLY, I YIELDED.

VERY *WELL*, COMRADE CAPTAIN.

WE WILL GIVE YOU OUR WEAPONS.

MILLA AND I WENT INSIDE...

...AND CAME OUT BEARING A COLLECTION OF GUNS, KNIVES, GRENADES, AMMO...

VERY GOOD, COMRADE TYMOSHENKO. I TRUST YOU NOW FEEL ALL RIGHT ABOUT THIS.

HONESTLY, COMRADE CAPTAIN--

--I NOW FEEL *NAKED.*

WITH THIS LAST COMMENT, THE CAPTAIN LOOKED UP AT ME FROM UNDER HIS BILLED CAP...

...AND *SMILED* WARMLY.

HE THEN TURNED-- AND WALKED AWAY...!

EVEN IN THE MOONLIGHT, I COULD FEEL MY FACE GLOWING *SCARLET.*

WE WENT BACK INTO THE BARRACKS AND RIGHT INTO BED.

I DIDN'T SLEEP WELL THAT NIGHT...

...BUT IT HAD NOTHING TO DO WITH NOT HAVING A GUN BESIDE ME.

THE FINAL CLASS OF THE DAY WAS CAPTAIN RAMSKOV'S TANK TACTICS CLASS. MILLA AND I WERE THE LAST INTO THE ROOM, AND THE ONLY SEATS LEFT WERE UP AT THE FRONT.

THE CAPTAIN WAS WRITING ON THE BLACKBOARD--AND I COULD NOT HELP BUT NOTICE RIGHT AWAY THERE WAS SOMETHING *DIFFERENT* ABOUT HIM.

THEN...

...HE *TURNED AROUND.*

STUDENTS...!

...I LIKE TO BEGIN THIS CLASS WITH A QUESTION:

HOW MANY OFFENSIVE WEAPONS DOES THE *T-34* TANK POSSESS?

THREE, COMRADE CAPTAIN! A *76MM F-34 MSIN GUN* PLUS TWO *DT MACHINE GUNS*--WITH A TOTAL OF 2898 ROUNDS, ONE MOUNTED IN THE BOW AND ANOTHER CO-AXIALLY IN THE TURRET!

VERY GOOD! IS THERE ANYTHING ELSE?

YES, COMRADE CAPTAIN!

A *PPSH-43 SUBMACHINE GUN* IS ON BOARD IN CASE THE CREW MUST ABANDON THEIR TANK.

TRUE...

BUT YOU HAVE OVERLOOKED TWO OF THE *T-34'S MOST LETHAL* WEAPONS...

...THE TANK'S *TRACKS!* *NOTHING* CAN APPEAR MORE FEARSOME TO INFANTRY MEN THAN THE TANK'S DEADLY STEEL TRACKS!

IN THE *WINTER* MONTHS, WHEN THE GROUND IS FROZEN SOLID, THE ENEMY WILL BE FORCED TO DIG HIS FOXHOLES IN THE *SNOW.* IF YOU COME UPON A SOLDIER WHO IS DUG IN ONLY IN SNOW--

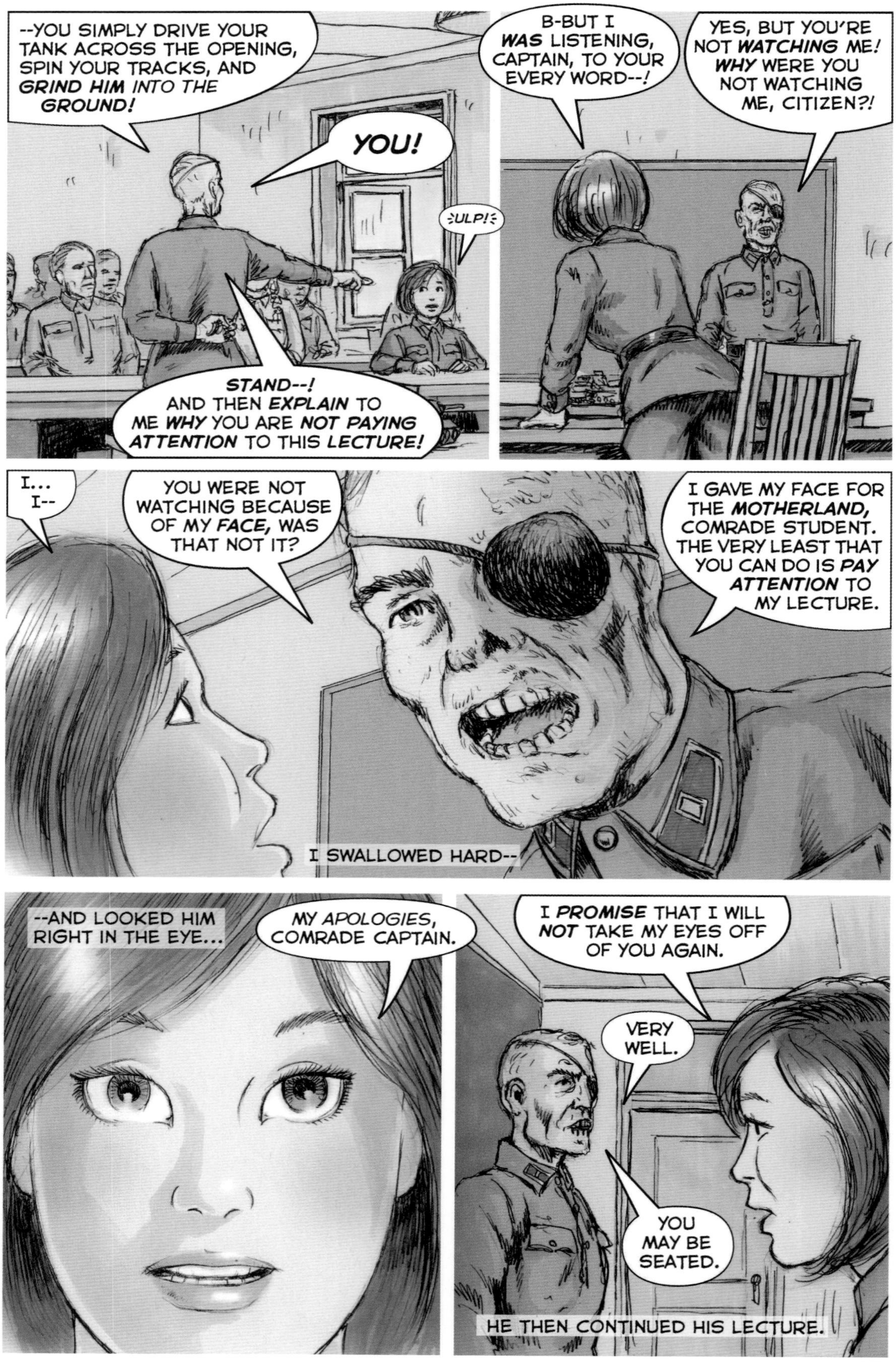
--YOU SIMPLY DRIVE YOUR TANK ACROSS THE OPENING, SPIN YOUR TRACKS, AND GRIND HIM INTO THE GROUND!
YOU!
ULP!
STAND--! AND THEN EXPLAIN TO ME WHY YOU ARE NOT PAYING ATTENTION TO THIS LECTURE!
B-BUT I WAS LISTENING, CAPTAIN, TO YOUR EVERY WORD--!
YES, BUT YOU'RE NOT WATCHING ME! WHY WERE YOU NOT WATCHING ME, CITIZEN?!
I... I--
YOU WERE NOT WATCHING BECAUSE OF MY FACE, WAS THAT NOT IT?
I GAVE MY FACE FOR THE MOTHERLAND, COMRADE STUDENT. THE VERY LEAST THAT YOU CAN DO IS PAY ATTENTION TO MY LECTURE.
I SWALLOWED HARD--
--AND LOOKED HIM RIGHT IN THE EYE...
MY APOLOGIES, COMRADE CAPTAIN.
I PROMISE THAT I WILL NOT TAKE MY EYES OFF OF YOU AGAIN.
VERY WELL.
YOU MAY BE SEATED.
HE THEN CONTINUED HIS LECTURE.

THE FIRST TIME I TRIED TO DRIVE A TANK, I WAS *EAGER.* I THOUGHT OF IT AS A FUN ADVENTURE.

WELL, *BIG* TYMOSHENKO DRIVES A TANK LIKE SHE WAS BORN TO IT!

NOW, LET'S SEE HOW *LITTLE* TYMOSHENKO DOES AT IT.

ALL *RIGHT.* NOW...

WHAT WAS IT MILLA TOLD ME...?

"JUST *EASE OUT* ON THE, CLUTCH"--

WHOO!

:WHOOPS!:

WHOA--!!

I WAS SO SORE THAT NIGHT THAT MILLA HAD TO HELP ME INTO BED.

:UURNGHK!:

AT EASE, COMRADES. WE'RE JUST CHECKING ON OUR TRAINING IN THE FIELD...

EVERY PERSON WHO HAS EVER WORKED ON A TANK, FOR WHATEVER ARMY OR COUNTRY, KNOWS TOO WELL THAT THE HARDEST JOB IS TRACK AND SUSPENSION REPAIR. IT IS VERY SLOW, DIRTY, HEAVY, AND *DANGEROUS* WORK.

AND HOW ARE THE TYMOSHENKO SISTERS DOING, NOW THAT THEY ARE WEAPONLESS?

"WEAPONLESS," COMRADE CAPTAIN? WE SIMPLY WERE ISSUED SOMETHING A LITTLE LARGER.

CAPTAIN, I HAVE A QUESTION. IN KIEV, I USED TO LISTEN ON MY RADIO TO THE LENINGRAD PHILHARMONIC. ITS PIANIST WAS NAMED NIKOLAI KOVCHENKO.

I HEAR YOU ARE ONE AND THE SAME.

YES, THIS IS TRUE.

OH, THIS IS AN HONOR! I WAS WONDERING... IF THERE'S A PIANO AROUND HERE--

--PERHAPS YOU WOULD GRACE US WITH A SMALL CONCERT...?

STILL SMILING, THE CAPTAIN PULLED HIS LEFT HAND FROM HIS POCKET...

I'M AFRAID MY CONCERT DAYS ARE OVER.

CAPTAIN KOVCHENKO WALKED OFF WITH HIS CLIQUE...

...LEAVING ME FEELING TWO INCHES TALL.

HOW DO YOU DO IT, KATUSHA?

JUST RUN ME OVER WITH THE TANK, MILLA.

DO NOT BE DISTRESSED, COMRADE TYMOSHENKO...

...KOVCHENKO IS NOT THE SORT OF MAN TO BE OFFENDED.

CAPTAIN RAMSKOV'S WORDS WERE EXTREMELY WELCOME.

IT WAS IN THE COMMUNICATIONS AND RADIO CLASSES THAT I HAD A CHANCE TO REALLY SHINE...

WHEN *NORDRIN'S BRIGADE* IS REFORMED, EVERY TANK WILL AT LEAST HAVE A RADIO RECEIVER. THAT SHOULD MAKE A *BIG* DIFFERENCE.

IN SOVIET RUSSIA, RADIO TECHNOLOGY WAS STILL PRIMITIVE, DOUBLY SO FOR ITS TANK UNITS.

ANY ADVANTAGES THE *T-34*S HAD WERE WASTED WHEN GERMAN UNITS COULD EASILY OUTPERFORM THEM WITH BETTER COMMUNICATIONS.

WE STAYED SO BUSY THAT TIME SEEMED TO PASS MUCH TOO QUICKLY...

NIGHTS ARE GETTING MUCH *COLDER*...!

YES-- WINTER IS COMING.

I HOPE TARAS IS *WARM*--AND *SAFE*...

EVERY SOVIET CITIZEN WAS WATCHING THE EVENTS UNFOLDING IN *STALINGRAD*. WE KNEW THAT IF GERMANY WON, IT'D BE ALL OVER. WE UKRAINIANS WOULD HAVE TO DECIDE WHETHER WE WERE TO LIVE UNDER FASCIST DOMINATION--OR REMAIN EXILES FROM EVERYTHING WE HAD EVER KNOWN AND LOVED.

FROM WASHINGTON TO LONDON, THE EYES OF THE WORLD WERE ALSO FOCUSED ON THE CITY ON THE VOLGA...

IN THIS YEAR, *1942*, IT COULD ALL BE CHANGING--IN NORTH AFRICA, IN THE NORTH ATLANTIC, IN THE SOUTH PACIFIC...BUT IT ALL HINGED ON *STALINGRAD*. WINSTON CHURCHILL UNDERSTOOD THIS WHEN HE CALLED IT THE *"HINGE OF FATE."*

IN SEPTEMBER 1942, POLITICAL COMMANDER NIKITA KHRUSHCHEV TURNED OVER THE COMMAND OF THE *62ND ARMY* TO GENERAL VASILY CHUIKOV.

COMRADE CHUIKOV, HOW DO YOU INTERPRET YOUR TASK?

WE WILL *DEFEND* THE CITY--

--OR *DIE* IN THE ATTEMPT.

THE FIRST THING CHUIKOV DID WAS PLACE *NKVD* GUARDS AT EVERY DEPARTURE POINT ON THE WEST BANK OF THE RIVER. ANYONE ATTEMPTING TO CROSS THE VOLGA TO SAFETY, UNLESS CARRYING PROPER PERMISSION OR BADLY WOUNDED, WAS TO BE SUMMARILY *SHOT*.

THE *GERMAN 6TH ARMY*, TRAINED AND EXPERIENCED IN OPEN MECHANIZED WARFARE, WAS NOT PREPARED FOR THE CLOSE-IN, HAND-TO-HAND FIGHTING IN STALINGRAD.

CHUIKOV MADE IT CLEAR HOW THE BATTLE WAS TO BE FOUGHT. "EVERY GERMAN MUST BE MADE TO FEEL THAT HE IS LIVING UNDER THE MUZZLE OF A RUSSIAN GUN," HE TOLD HIS MEN.

BECAUSE OF THE FEROCITY OF THE FIGHTING, THE DEAD ON EITHER SIDE SELDOM WERE RECOVERED OR BURIED.

THE BODIES SEEMED TO COLLECT IN LAYERS ON THE GROUND, LIKE GEOLOGIC STRATA.

CHUIKOV TOLD HIS STAFF: "EVERY MAN MUST BECOME ONE OF THE STONES OF THE CITY."

MEN ON BOTH SIDES LIVED AND FOUGHT IN CELLARS AND SEWERS. FOOD WAS SCARCE. PEOPLE TURNED TO EATING HORSES, DOGS, CATS--EVEN RATS. MEN FOUGHT TO THE DEATH OVER ACCESS TO SOURCES OF MARGINALLY CLEAN WATER.

THE CITY DEVELOPED A SOCIETY AND CULTURE OF ITS OWN. A SONG AROSE THAT BECAME POPULAR AMONG THE ENTRENCHED AND EMBATTLED SOVIET TROOPS:

"ZEMLYANKA" OR "THE DUGOUT"-- ALSO KNOWN AS "THE FOUR STEPS TO DEATH."

IT WAS CONDEMNED BY THE AUTHORITIES BECAUSE OF ITS PESSIMISM--BUT THE COMMISSARS LEARNED TO LOOK THE OTHER WAY.

"THE FIRE IS FLICKERING IN THE NARROW STOVE... RESIN OOZES FROM THE LOG LIKE A TEAR, AND THE CONCERTINA IN THE BUNKER SINGS TO ME OF YOUR SMILE AND EYES..."

IN MOSCOW, STALIN WAS EXASPERATED WITH THE SITUATION.

NO! YOU ARE *ALL* BEING FAR TOO *SHORTSIGHTED!*

HOW CAN YOU NOT UNDERSTAND THAT IF WE *SURRENDER STALINGRAD,* THEN THE SOUTH OF THE COUNTRY WILL BE *CUT OFF* FROM THE CENTER--?!

THIS WILL BE NOT ONLY A *CATASTROPHE* FOR STALINGRAD ITSELF--!

DEPUTY SUPREME COMMANDER *GEORGY ZHUKOV,* THE MAN WHO'D ENGINEERED THE DEFENSE OF LENINGRAD AND MOSCOW, WAS NOT LOOKING ONLY AT STALINGRAD ON THE MAP...

HMM...

--BUT WE'LL LOSE OUR MAIN WATERWAY...AND SOON OUR OIL SOURCE, TOO!

ZHUKOV WAS SCRUTINIZING THE GERMANS' THINLY DEFENDED FLANKS, MANNED MAINLY BY ROMANIANS AND ITALIANS...

...YES.

RIGHT THERE...

...AND THERE...

AS OCTOBER 1942 DREW TO A CLOSE, WINTER WAS ALREADY DESCENDING UPON THE BATTLEFIELDS OF THIS SPRAWLING WAR. A STRONG, CHILL WIND HAD BEGUN TO BLOW...

...LIKE THE WINDS OF FATE THAT WERE BLOWING ON THE MADLY SWINGING DOOR OF HISTORY...

...AND ONLY THE *HINGE OF STALINGRAD* WOULD DETERMINE ON *WHOM* IT WOULD *SLAM SHUT.*

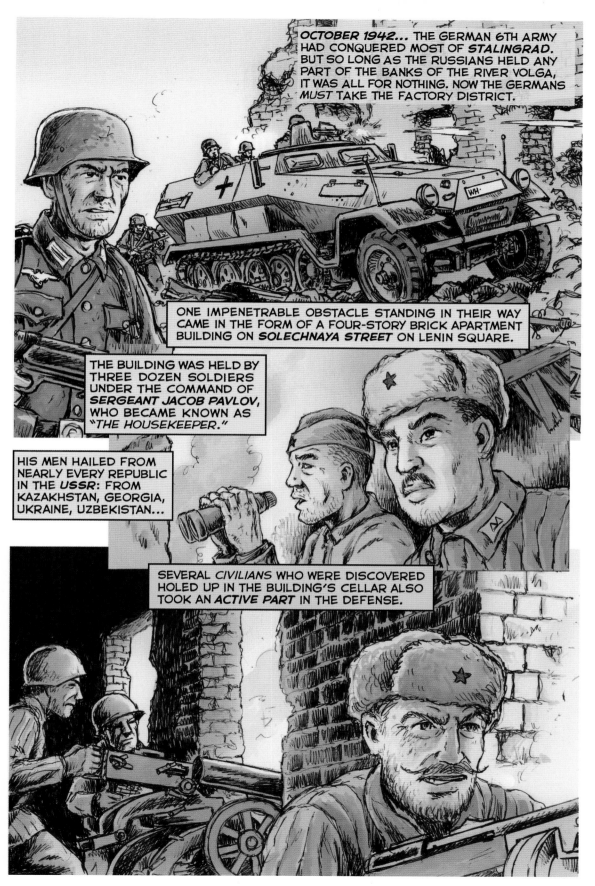

OCTOBER 1942... THE GERMAN 6TH ARMY HAD CONQUERED MOST OF *STALINGRAD*. BUT SO LONG AS THE RUSSIANS HELD ANY PART OF THE BANKS OF THE RIVER VOLGA, IT WAS ALL FOR NOTHING. NOW THE GERMANS *MUST* TAKE THE FACTORY DISTRICT.

ONE IMPENETRABLE OBSTACLE STANDING IN THEIR WAY CAME IN THE FORM OF A FOUR-STORY BRICK APARTMENT BUILDING ON *SOLECHNAYA STREET* ON LENIN SQUARE.

THE BUILDING WAS HELD BY THREE DOZEN SOLDIERS UNDER THE COMMAND OF *SERGEANT JACOB PAVLOV*, WHO BECAME KNOWN AS *"THE HOUSEKEEPER."*

HIS MEN HAILED FROM NEARLY EVERY REPUBLIC IN THE *USSR*: FROM KAZAKHSTAN, GEORGIA, UKRAINE, UZBEKISTAN...

SEVERAL *CIVILIANS* WHO WERE DISCOVERED HOLED UP IN THE BUILDING'S CELLAR ALSO TOOK AN *ACTIVE PART* IN THE DEFENSE.

SEARCHING THE BUILDING FOR USABLE ITEMS AND FOOD, A SOLDIER FOUND A WIND-UP *GRAMOPHONE* AND *ONE RECORD* WITH A PEELED-OFF LABEL...

IT PLAYED A TUNE NONE OF THEM RECOGNIZED.

DURING TIMES OF BOTH CALM AND MAYHEM, THEY PLAYED THE UNKNOWN TUNE...

THEY PLAYED IT UNTIL THE NEEDLE WORE THROUGH THE DISK.

DURING THE OCTOBER *PUTSCH*, THE GERMANS SENT FOUR TANKS AGAINST PAVLOV'S HOUSE. THEIR INTENTION WAS TO LEVEL THIS INFURIATING OBSTRUCTION.

PAVLOV SENT HIS MEN TO LOCATIONS IN THE BUILDING TO WHICH THE TANKS' GUNS COULD NOT ELEVATE.

YOU! *FOURTH* FLOOR!

THE *REST* OF YOU--DOWN IN THE *CELLAR!*

HE THEN SENT OUT A COMBAT PATROL WITH A *14.5MM PTRD* ANTI-TANK RIFLE.

THE COMBAT PATROL SUCCEEDED SO THOROUGHLY IN KNOCKING OUT ONE OF THE TANKS THAT THE REST *WITHDREW.*

FOR *58 DAYS,* PAVLOV'S HOUSE HELD AGAINST THE GERMANS... DURING THAT TIME, AS *GENERAL CHUIKOV* LIKED TO POINT OUT, THEY KILLED MORE GERMANS THAN IT TOOK TO TAKE *PARIS.*

ON THE 62ND ARMY'S HEADQUARTERS MAP, CHUIKOV'S CODE NAME FOR PAVLOV'S HOUSE WAS *"THE LIGHTHOUSE."*

JACOB PAVLOV FOUGHT ON TO BERLIN, AND BECAME A *HERO* OF THE SOVIET UNION. BUT SOMEWHERE ALONG THAT BLOODY ROAD, HE MET *GOD...*

...AND HE SPENT THE REST OF HIS DAYS AS AN *ORTHODOX PRIEST.*

ON *OCTOBER 22,* THE FIRST SNOWS BEGAN TO FALL AT STALINGRAD.

ALREADY? ARE WE GOING TO HAVE TO GO THROUGH ANOTHER RUSSIAN WINTER?

OH, GOD, NO!

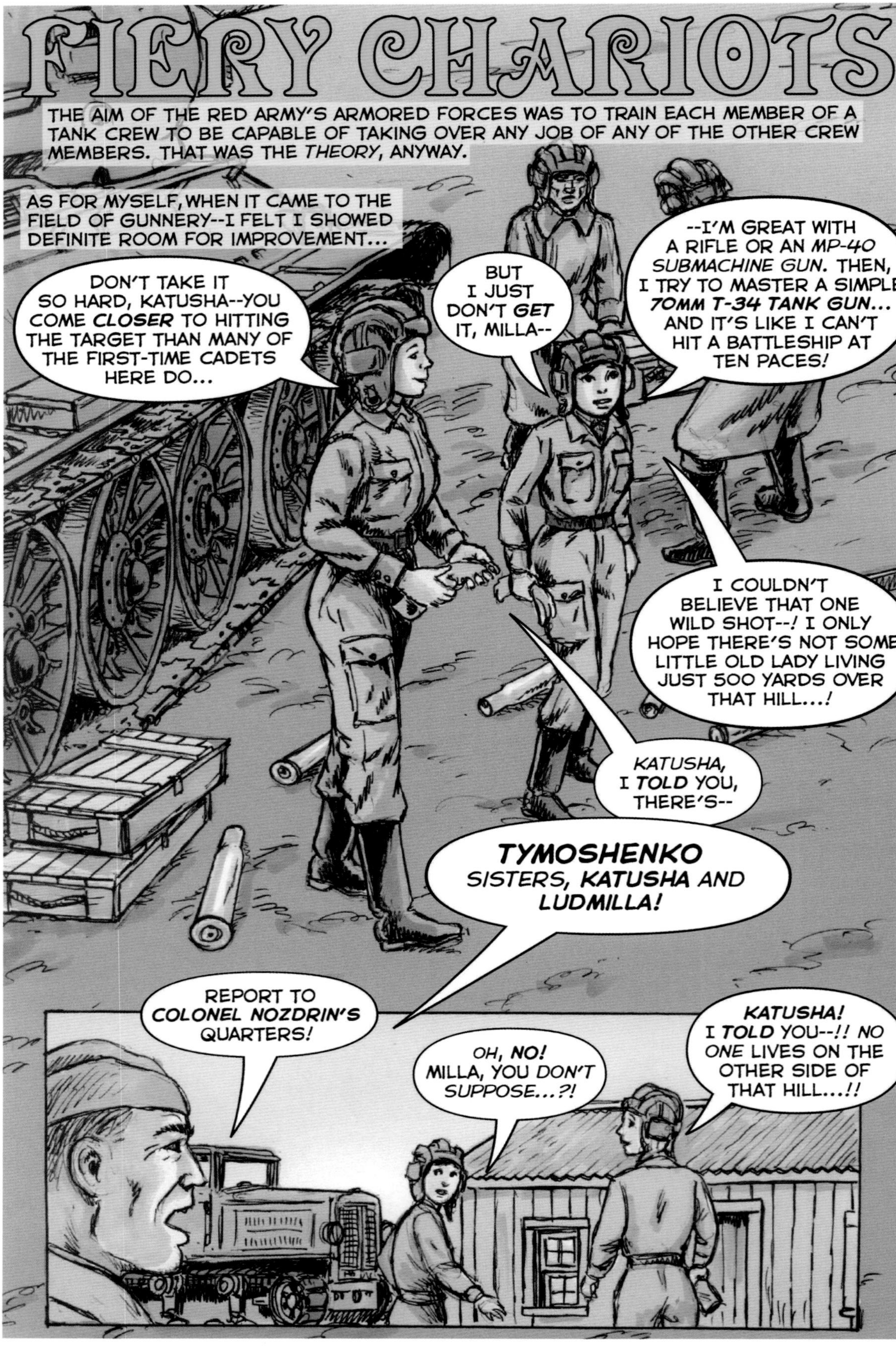
FIERY CHARIOTS
THE AIM OF THE RED ARMY'S ARMORED FORCES WAS TO TRAIN EACH MEMBER OF A TANK CREW TO BE CAPABLE OF TAKING OVER ANY JOB OF ANY OF THE OTHER CREW MEMBERS. THAT WAS THE *THEORY*, ANYWAY.
AS FOR *MYSELF*, WHEN IT CAME TO THE FIELD OF GUNNERY--I FELT I SHOWED DEFINITE ROOM FOR IMPROVEMENT...
DON'T TAKE IT SO HARD, KATUSHA--YOU COME ***CLOSER*** TO HITTING THE TARGET THAN MANY OF THE FIRST-TIME CADETS HERE DO...
BUT I JUST DON'T ***GET*** IT, MILLA--
--I'M GREAT WITH A RIFLE OR AN *MP-40 SUBMACHINE GUN*. THEN, I TRY TO MASTER A SIMPLE ***70MM T-34 TANK GUN...*** AND IT'S LIKE I CAN'T HIT A BATTLESHIP AT TEN PACES!
I COULDN'T BELIEVE THAT ONE WILD SHOT--! I ONLY HOPE THERE'S NOT SOME LITTLE OLD LADY LIVING JUST 500 YARDS OVER THAT HILL...!
KATUSHA, I ***TOLD*** YOU, THERE'S--
TYMOSHENKO *SISTERS,* ***KATUSHA*** AND ***LUDMILLA!***
REPORT TO ***COLONEL NOZDRIN'S*** QUARTERS!
OH, ***NO!*** MILLA, YOU *DON'T SUPPOSE...?!*
KATUSHA! I ***TOLD*** YOU--!! *NO ONE* LIVES ON THE OTHER SIDE OF THAT HILL...!!

TYMOSHENKO, REPORTING AS ORDERED!

AT EASE, COMRADES...

I UNDERSTAND THAT YOU HAVE BOTH SEEN COMBAT BEFORE...UNDER WHOSE COMMAND WAS THAT?

UNDER OUR UNCLE TARAS, SIR. WE WERE PARTISANS.

YES, IN A DIFFERENT KIND OF WAR.

FROM WHAT I HAVE HEARD--

--YOU'VE BEEN SHOT AT AND DRAWN BLOOD. THAT IS WHAT'S IMPORTANT. KATUSHA, YOU SHOW STRONG COMMUNICATIONS SKILLS.

AND MILLA, YOU WERE SINGLED OUT AS BEING A VERY GOOD DRIVER.

CONSEQUENTLY... I HAVE CHOSEN YOU TO CREW MY COMMAND TANK AS DRIVER AND RADIO OPERATOR.

THIS IS SENIOR SERGEANT MISHA BOVA. HE SERVED OUR BRIGADE WELL LAST WINTER. HE HAS JUST RETURNED FROM THE HOSPITAL.

HE WILL BE OUR GUNNER.

IN BATTLE, I WILL SERVE AS LOADER. SINCE MY COMMAND DUTIES WILL OFTEN KEEP ME AWAY FROM THE TANK-- KATUSHA WILL FILL IN FOR ME AS LOADER WHEN NECESSARY.

MILLA AND I WERE *WALKING ON AIR*...!

HOW IN THE WORLD DID WE MANAGE TO DO *THAT?*

SOMEONE HIGH UP LIKES US--AT LEAST THEY DON'T THINK OF US AS *"DUMB TUFTIES."*

UH-OH! OFFICERS COMING--!

IT WAS CAPTAINS KOVCHENKO AND RAMSKOV. IT SEEMED THEY WERE ALREADY AWARE OF OUR APPOINTMENT.

I'VE ONLY A MOMENT, BUT I WANTED TO OFFER MY HEARTY *CONGRATULATIONS* TO BOTH OF YOU!

THANK YOU, COMRADE CAPTAIN!

AND I, TOO, WISH YOU *WELL.*

THANK YOU ALSO, CAPTAIN RAMSKOV. *UH*, SIR...? I KNOW CAPTAIN KOVCHENKO IS AN INSTRUCTOR HERE AT THE SCHOOL, BUT WHAT CLASS DOES HE TEACH?

RAMSKOV'S DISFIGURED FACE DID NOT CHANGE-- BUT I SWEAR I ALMOST SAW THE TWINKLING OF A *SMILE* IN HIS ONE EYE...

CAPTAIN KOVCHENKO COMMANDS THE *INFANTRY BATTALION*--THE ONE THAT WILL RIDE YOUR BRIGADE'S TANKS INTO BATTLE.

HMM, WHAT DO YOU THINK OF THAT? I HEAR INFANTRY OFFICERS LIKE TO RIDE A TANK'S BOW MACHINE GUN...

YEAH, SO--?

THAT MEANS KOVCHENKO'S *BUTT* WILL BE SITTING JUST *INCHES* ABOVE YOUR HEAD!

MILLA?! JUST *SHUT UP*...!

WHEN WE WALKED BACK INTO THE BARRACKS, WE COULD JUDGE FROM THE FROSTY RECEPTION THAT THEY'D ALREADY GOT THE WORD, TOO.

MARUSYA POZHARSKY HAD GOOD WISHES TO GIVE US--BUT SHE WAS THE ONLY ONE OF OUR BUNKMATES WHO DID.

THAT'S *GREAT* NEWS!

THANKS, MARUSYA. WE WERE JUST *LUCKY*--

HA! "LUCK"?! 'S *THAT* WHAT THEY CALL IT BACK WHERE YER FROM, YA LITTLE TUFTY *GINCH?!!*

OXANNA PEREPELITSYN--! I *KNEW* IT...! THAT GIRL HAD A REPUTATION FOR BEING AS TOUGH AS THE *DEVIL*.

WE'RE *NOT IDIOTS!* ALL OF US KNOW DAMN WELL JUST *HOW* YOU BACK-COUNTRY SLUTS PAID OFF "OLD BULLET HEAD" FOR STINKIN' *PRIVILEGES*--

OXANNA HAD OBVIOUSLY BEEN BORN WITH A BAD HARELIP, *AND* A CHIP ON HER SHOULDER...

--WITH A NICE, FAT PIECE OF YOUR CUTE LITTLE "LUCK"!

I REALLY FELT SORRY FOR HER--EVEN THOUGH SHE WANTED TO WHIP MY BUTT.

OXANNA, THE ONLY THING I GIVE COLONEL NOZDRIN IS THE THE RESPECT DUE HIS RANK...

I'M SURE THAT YOU COULD DO JUST AS WELL AS I...

DON'T GIMME THAT CRAP! YOU WALTZ IN HERE *LATE*, RIGHT OFFA THE *FARM*, AN' GET *PROMOTED, BEFORE* THE *REST* OF US--?!

WELL, YER *NOT* GONNA "LUCK" YER WAY OUTTA *PAYING* FOR IT *HERE AND NOW*--!!

MILLA WAS ABOUT TO JUMP INTO THE SITUATION, UNTIL I SHOT HER A WARNING GLANCE. SHE STOOD DOWN--BUT I KNEW SHE HAD MY BACK.

THEN, VERY CALMLY, I TURNED BACK TO OXANNA...

OXANNA--NO MATTER *WHAT* I SAY, YOU'RE JUST GONNA GO *OFF*...

...SO *WHY* DON'T YOU *SHUT UP*, AND *GET TO IT*?!

OXANNA *CHARGED ME* LIKE AN ANGRY BULL.

I'M A SMALL TARGET, SO I JUST SIDE-STEPPED HER.

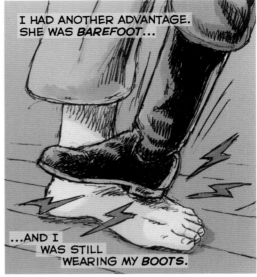

I HAD ANOTHER ADVANTAGE. SHE WAS *BAREFOOT*...

...AND I WAS STILL WEARING MY *BOOTS*.

I KNEW THAT'D BE JUST ENOUGH TO GET HER REALLY *MAD*...! SO AS SHE PASSED ME--

--I DROVE MY SKINNY LITTLE ELBOW INTO HER LOWER BACK!

AND THEN OXANNA *HIT THE FLOOR* LIKE A SACK OF BAD BEETS!

WHY, KATUSHA! TARAS WOULD BE *PROUD* OF YOU!

BUT OXANNA WASN'T DOWN FOR LONG...!

BECAUSE OF HER DISTORTED FEATURES, I REALLY *DIDN'T* WANT TO HIT OXANNA IN HER FACE...

...BUT I WASN'T GOING TO LET MY SENSE OF GOOD SPORTSMANSHIP--

--KEEP ME FROM *PROTECTING* MYSELF.

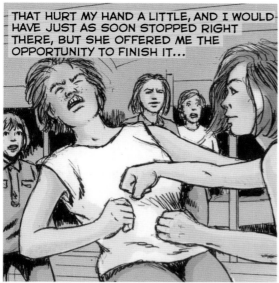

THAT HURT MY HAND A LITTLE, AND I WOULD HAVE JUST AS SOON STOPPED RIGHT THERE, BUT SHE OFFERED ME THE OPPORTUNITY TO FINISH IT...

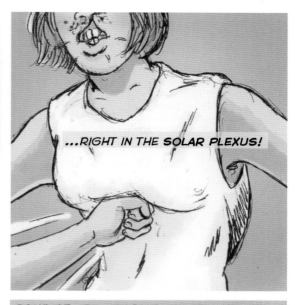

...RIGHT IN THE **SOLAR PLEXUS!**

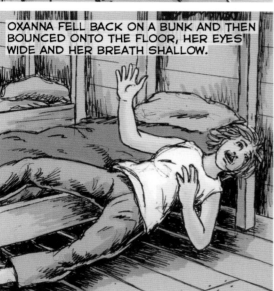

OXANNA FELL BACK ON A BUNK AND THEN BOUNCED ONTO THE FLOOR, HER EYES WIDE AND HER BREATH SHALLOW.

SOME OF HER ROUGH FRIENDS PICKED HER UP AND CARRIED HER TO HER BUNK, ALL OF THEM GIVING ME HARD GLARES.

HEY, **I** DIDN'T START THIS WHOLE THING. BUT I HOLD **NO GRUDGES.**

GETTING READY FOR BED THAT NIGHT, EVERYONE GAVE ME A **WIDE BERTH.**

WHAT IS IT ABOUT LIFE, WHERE A GOOD THING HAPPENS--THEN SOMETHING BAD ALWAYS COMES ALONG THAT KEEPS YOU FROM ENJOYING IT? I REMEMBER WHEN I WAS YOUNG THINKING THAT I SURELY WOULDN'T HAVE THESE BAD FEELINGS WHEN I GOT OLDER. DO I HAVE TO GROW OLDER STILL? DO I HAVE TO GROW ALL THE WAY UP?

WHAT IS MATURITY?

WHAT DOES BEING "MATURE" REALLY MEAN? DO WE EVER REACH FULL MATURITY? WILL I KNOW WHEN IT COMES?

I WAS SUDDENLY AFRAID WITH THE COMING OF MATURITY, I WOULD BE LOSING THE JOYS OF YOUTH. I DIDN'T WANT TO DO THAT...NOT **YET**...

221

SEVERAL DAYS LATER--ON *NOVEMBER 3RD,* IF I CAN REMEMBER CORRECTLY-- A MESSENGER CAME TO CAPTAIN RAMSKOV'S CLASS BEARING AN IMPORTANT NOTE.

STUDENTS... TRAINING HAS *ENDED.*

CREW ASSIGNMENTS ARE LISTED ON THE BOARD OUTSIDE EACH BARRACKS. BE PACKED AND READY TO MOVE OUT IN *6 HOURS.*

WHA--?!

CAPTAIN RAMSKOV STOPPED US AS WE LEFT THE ROOM.

COLONEL NOZDRIN PASSED ON A MESSAGE FROM YOUR *FATHER...*

"I WILL LOOK FOR YOU AT THE FACTORY."

THAT REALLY GOT OUR BLOOD FLOWING!

MISHA BOVA WAS WAITING FOR US WHEN WE CAME OUT.

SO--ARE THE TYMOSHENKO SISTERS ALL READY TO GO TO *WAR?*

WHAT-- *AGAIN?*

OH, HOW I *WISH* I'D BEEN KIDDING...

EVERYONE WAS ISSUED A PAIR OF FELT *VALENKI* BOOTS AND A BRAND-NEW SHEEPSKIN COAT.

EACH OF THE COMMANDERS WAS GIVEN A WRISTWATCH AND A FOUNTAIN PEN--AND SINCE WE WERE BOTH CREW MEMBERS OF THE BRIGADE COMMANDER'S TANK, MILLA AND I ALSO RECEIVED THEM.

MY FIRST *WATCH!*

WE WERE EACH ISSUED A SILK HANDKERCHIEF.

DON'T BLOW YOUR NOSE ON THAT!

IT'S FOR *FILTERING FUEL.*

THE TRUCKS WERE WAITING AND READY FOR US IN SIX HOURS...
MOST BRIGADES UP TO THAT TIME WERE A FIFTY-FIFTY MIX OF *T-34*s AND LIGHT TANKS LIKE THE LITTLE *T-70*s. BUT NOT US! WE WERE TO HAVE *THREE FULL BATTALIONS* OF *T-34*s—THAT'S *64 MEDIUM TANKS!* THAT IS A LOT OF POWER.

WE BOARDED THE TRUCKS AND HEADED IN THREE DIRECTIONS TO PICK UP OUR *T-34*s; THE *2ND BATTALION* TO THE *CHELYABINSK TRACTOR PLANT*, THE *3RD BATTALION* TO THE *SVERDLOVSK HEAVY MACHINERY FACTORY*, AND THE *1ST BATTALION*—AND OUR GROUP, THE *HEADQUARTERS SECTION*—WOULD HEAD TO THE *NIZHNIY TAGIL URAL CAR PLANT.*

THE TRUCK RIDE WAS LONG, ROUGH, AND BUMPY. WE WERE ALL TOO KEYED UP TO SLEEP.

BESIDES, THE VETERAN TANKERS KEPT US WIDE-EYED WITH HAIR-RAISING STORIES OF BLOODY BATTLES—ALL DESIGNED TO GIVE THE NEW TRAINEES *NIGHTMARES.*

IT WAS WELL AFTER DARK WHEN WE REACHED *NIZHNIY TAGIL*, BUT THAT DIDN'T MATTER BECAUSE THE HUGE FACTORY LIT UP THE NIGHT. IT BUZZED, CRACKLED, WHIRRED, AND SCREECHED WITH CONSTANT ACTIVITY.

IT WAS HARD TO BELIEVE THAT JUST A YEAR AGO, THIS HAD BEEN PEACEFUL FARMLAND.

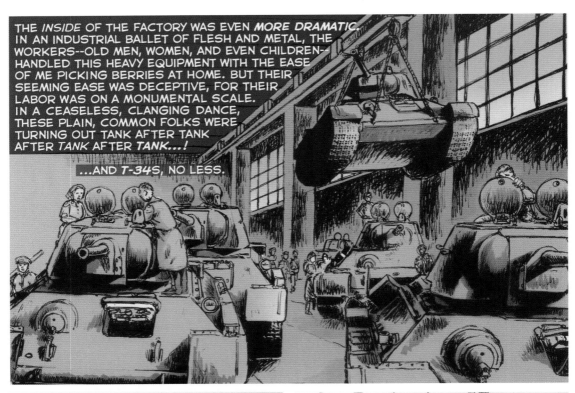

THE *INSIDE* OF THE FACTORY WAS EVEN *MORE DRAMATIC*. IN AN INDUSTRIAL BALLET OF FLESH AND METAL, THE WORKERS--OLD MEN, WOMEN, AND EVEN CHILDREN-- HANDLED THIS HEAVY EQUIPMENT WITH THE EASE OF ME PICKING BERRIES AT HOME. BUT THEIR SEEMING EASE WAS DECEPTIVE, FOR THEIR LABOR WAS ON A MONUMENTAL SCALE. IN A CEASELESS, CLANGING DANCE, THESE PLAIN, COMMON FOLKS WERE TURNING OUT TANK AFTER TANK AFTER *TANK* AFTER *TANK*...!

...AND *T-34*S, NO LESS.

THEY ASSIGNED US TO POSITIONS ON THE ASSEMBLY LINES, IDEALLY IN OUR AREAS OF EXPERTISE. THE GIRL WHO SHOWED ME HOW TO INSTALL THE 9R RADIO COULDN'T HAVE BEEN OVER FOURTEEN...!

MILLA WORKED WITH A FRAIL OLD MAN MOUNTING THE DRIVER'S ELECTRONIC DEVICES AND GAUGES.

NO ONE WATCHED THE CLOCK. WE KEPT AT IT, TIRED, COLD, AND HUNGRY... BUT NOT A SOUL COMPLAINED. THESE WERE THE SLEDS THAT WOULD CONVEY US TO WAR-- OUR *"FIERY CHARIOTS."*

WE WANTED THESE TANKS TO BE *PERFECT*. AND NONE OF US WANTED THE FACTORY WORKERS TO THINK THAT OUR STANDARDS WERE ANY LESS EXACTING THAN *THEIRS*.

FOR A CHANGE, PAPA FOUND *ME* BUSY WORKING ON MACHINERY. I COULD TELL HE WAS PROUD OF US. IT WAS WONDERFUL TO SEE HIS SMILE, ESPECIALLY AFTER HAVING TO LEAVE HIM BEHIND IN STALINGRAD.

AH! HERE COMES HALF OF MY TEAM! LET'S FIND MILLA--

--I HAVE SOMETHING TO SHOW YOU.

WELL, THERE SHE *IS*--! JUST AS *PERFECT* AS WE CAN MAKE THEM...

AND HOPEFULLY, SHE'LL PROVE HERSELF WORTHY ENOUGH TO TAKE MY GIRLS INTO *HARM'S WAY*--

--AND BRING THEM *BACK OUT* OF IT *SAFELY!*

WOW!

PAPA SURE HAD A KNACK FOR PICKING OUT *BIG PRESENTS!* FIRST, HE GAVE ME MILLA-- AND NOW, OUR VERY OWN *T-34* TANK!

I LAUGHED AND REACHED OUT TO STROKE MY NEW TOY--BUT AS I RAN MY HAND OVER THE ARMOR PLATING...

...THE FEEL OF THE COLD, HARD METAL AGAINST MY FINGERTIPS BEGAN TO GIVE ME THE *STRANGEST* SENSATION...!

YES, THIS TANK *WAS* A *SHE*--BUT WITH NO HEART, NO BRAIN, NO SOUL...! AND PERHAPS THAT WAS AS IT *SHOULD* BE.

I KNEW IN THAT INSTANT THIS MACHINE WOULD BE THE KIND OF IMPLEMENT THAT WOULD ALLOW US TO DO WHAT WE HAD TO DO--BECAUSE...

...SHE WAS A *REAL BITCH!*

WE EACH GAVE PAPA ONE LAST HUG AND KISS, THEN TURNED TO GO...

SOVIET TANK CREWS HOLD THE RANK OF JUNIOR SERGEANT OR ABOVE, SO UPON THE RECEIPT OF OUR TANK, MILLA AND I GOT AUTOMATICALLY *PROMOTED...!*

SO WE CLIMBED ABOARD OUR *T-34* AS *JUNIOR SERGEANTS.*

THE DIESEL ENGINE ROLLED OVER AND ROARED AT MILLA'S FIRST TRY.

*T-34*S ARE VERY LOUD-- BUT THAT WAS ALL RIGHT. WE WEREN'T PLANNING ON SNEAKING UP ON ANYONE.

THE TRACKS CLANKED ESPECIALLY LOUDLY, SINCE AT THAT TIME THERE WAS A SHORTAGE OF RUBBER. FEW ROAD WHEELS HAD RUBBER RIMS.

MILLA GUIDED US SMOOTHLY THROUGH THE BIG ROLL-UP DOORS. I TUNED THE RADIO IN CLEARLY, AND I HEARD COLONEL NOZDRIN AS HE DIRECTED US UP TO THE HEAD OF THE COLUMN.

HE WOULD BE THERE, IN HIS *GAZ67-B* FIELD CAR WITH HIS DRIVER, VERA FYODOROVICH.

WITH THE COLONEL OUT IN FRONT, AND US RIGHT BEHIND HIM...

...WE LED THE COLUMN DOWN A LONG, STRAIGHT, GRAVELLED ROAD.

WE HAD NOT SLEPT SINCE WE LEFT THE SCHOOL AT CHELYABINSK, BUT WE WERE STILL TOO KEYED UP TO BE BOTHERED. BACK THEN IN OUR YOUTH, WE WERE ABLE TO GO FOR MANY, MANY HOURS BEFORE FATIGUE FINALLY CAUGHT UP WITH US...

STILL, IT WAS COLD IN THE TANK-- AND THE ENGINE FANS IN THE REAR OF THE CREW COMPARTMENT PULLED A BRISK DRAFT OF ICY AIR THROUGH THE DRIVER'S HATCH.

OUR HEADLIGHTS GLEAMING, WE CONTINUED TO MOVE THROUGH HEAVY WOODS, KNOWING THAT THE NEAREST GERMAN PLANE WAS MANY HUNDREDS OF MILES AWAY.

A PINK DAWN SPREAD ACROSS THE SKY BEHIND US. THE DAYLIGHT BECAME MOST WELCOME WHEN WE TURNED OFF THE GRAVEL ROAD AND ONTO A NARROW DIRT PATH THAT MEANDERED THROUGH THE FOREST.

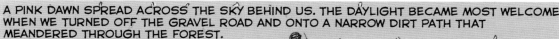

SINCE WE WERE AT THE HEAD OF THE COLUMN, THE DIRT SURFACE WAS FINE. BUT--THE MORE OF US THAT PASSED, THE MORE CHURNED UP IT BECAME.

A FEW TANKS TOWARD THE REAR OF THE COLUMN BEGAN TO BOG DOWN AND GET STUCK.

LUCKILY, THE VETERAN TANKERS KNEW HOW TO EXTRACT THEIR *T-34s* FROM THE MUD BY CUTTING DOWN SMALL TREES AND JAMMING THE LOGS UNDER THE TRACKS.

SINCE OUR PACE WAS NEVER MORE THAN 15 MPH, THOSE TANKS THAT SUFFERED THIS DELAY WERE ABLE TO KEEP UP.

THE SUN WAS DOWN BEYOND THE TREES WHEN WE REACHED A LARGE STUBBLED WHEAT FIELD NEAR A SMALL VILLAGE NEAR A LITTLE RIVER. THE TRUCKS OF OUR MAINTENANCE AND SUPPLY COMPANIES WERE ALREADY THERE, BUT OUR TWO OTHER TANK BATTALIONS HAD NOT YET ARRIVED.

PARK THEM ACCORDING TO PLATOON AND COMPANY, AND GET THE MAINTENANCE REPORTS COMPLETED.

THEN WE CAN POST SENTRIES AND LET EVERYONE TURN IN.

EACH TANK HAD A MAINTENANCE LOG, AND NONE OF ITS CREW COULD SLEEP UNTIL ALL PROCEDURES HAD BEEN FOLLOWED AND THE TANK DECLARED READY TO FIGHT AT DAWN.

THIS MIGHT BE A GOOD TIME FOR A LITTLE EXPLANATION.

SO FAR, YOU'VE SEEN A LOT OF WOMEN SOLDIERS AT THE CHELYABINSK TANK SCHOOL AND OTHER PLACES. BUT OUR BRIGADE NEVER WAS MORE THAN SIX PERCENT FEMALE. IN OUR TANKS, THERE WERE AROUND A DOZEN DRIVERS AND ASSISTANT DRIVERS.

LATER IN THE WAR, THERE WOULD BE SOME UNITS MADE UP ALMOST ENTIRELY OF GIRLS JUST LIKE ME.

A FEW WOMEN MANNED ANTI-TANK AND ANTI-AIRCRAFT BATTERIES, AND SEVERAL SERVED IN THE HEADQUARTERS STAFF.

BUT THE MEDICAL SECTION, INCLUDING DOCTORS, WAS PREDOMINANTLY FEMALE. YOUNG GIRL MEDICS WOULD DART OUT ONTO THE BATTLEFIELD UNDER FIRE TO DRAG WOUNDED SOLDIERS, OFTEN TWICE THEIR SIZE, TO AN AID STATION...

THESE VALIANT WOMEN WERE HELD IN UNIVERSAL RESPECT!

WE DID OUR MAINTENANCE, BUILT FIRES, AND HAD A SIMPLE BUT TASTY MEAL OF BREAD AND HORSE SAUSAGE THAT WE HAD RECEIVED BACK IN CHELYABINSK.

DO YOU LIKE HORSE SAUSAGE?

AS LONG AS I DIDN'T *KNOW* THE HORSE...!

THEN WE CURLED UP IN THE TARPAULIN THAT EVERY TANK CARRIED AND WENT TO SLEEP.

LATER IN THE NIGHT, I WAS AWAKENED BY A STRANGE SENSATION--THE EARTH WAS *SHAKING!*

--AAH...?!!

IS THIS WHAT AN *EARTHQUAKE* IS LIKE? I THOUGHT FOR A MOMENT...

THEN I REALIZED THAT THE VIBRATIONS WERE MERELY THE SOUNDS OF OUR 2ND AND 3RD BATTALIONS ARRIVING AT OUR MEETUP POINT.

THE SOUND OF 42 *T-34*S RUMBLING ACROSS THE EARTH AT ONCE WILL SHAKE YOU TO THE CORE. RECALLING IT REMINDS ME OF A LINE FROM A POEM I WAS TO HEAR LATER IN THE WAR...

"A WAR ISN'T FIREWORKS AT ALL-- JUST HEAVY DAILY LABOR..."

AND THE VETERAN TANKERS...?

GZZZKH

THEY SLEPT THROUGH THIS TUMULTUOUS ARRIVAL AS IF IT WERE NOTHING MORE THAN THE RISING OF THE MOON.

EARLY NEXT MORNING, THE WHOLE BRIGADE WAS UP AND READY FOR FIRING PRACTICE WITH THE NEW TANKS.

WE'VE GOT LOCAL CARPENTERS BUILDING TARGETS FROM OLD SLEDS AND WAGONS...

I WANT THE NEW MEN TO GO IN FIRST-- AND THEN THE VETERANS TO SHOW HOW IT'S REALLY DONE.

ON THE WAY TO OUR RANGE, I SAW SOME OF THE GUNNERY INSTRUCTORS FROM THE SCHOOL, AND TO OUR SURPRISE...

CAPTAIN RAMSKOV!

HELLO!

HIS POOR, BROKEN FACE COULD NOT SMILE, BUT HE GAVE ME A CRISP SALUTE.

THE NEW GUNNERS DID NOT DO BADLY AT ALL, PERFORMING THEIR DUTIES JUST AS THEY'D BEEN TAUGHT--

--"BY THE BOOK," AS THEY SAY.

THEN THE VETERANS TOOK OVER, AND WE WERE MOST IMPRESSED...!

I GUESS JUST THE FACT THAT THEY HAD SURVIVED THE FIRST YEAR OF THIS WAR REALLY SAYS IT ALL...

BUT THE REAL SURPRISE WAS OUR OWN GUNNER, MISHA BOVA. TIME AFTER TIME, HE HIT THE TARGET WHILE OUR TANK WAS MOVING--AND THE TARGET WAS BEING PULLED!

IF THE DRIVER CAN KEEP ME INFORMED ABOUT THE LAND AHEAD, AND THE TARGET IS LYING WITHIN ELEVEN O'CLOCK AND ONE O'CLOCK--

--I CAN HIT IT *EVERY* TIME!

I LOADED FOR MISHA DURING THE EXERCISE, AND THIS IS WHAT I DIDN'T LIKE ABOUT IT: THE FUMES FROM THE GUN CAN MAKE YOU PASS OUT. IT'S ALL RIGHT IF THE LOADER'S HATCH IS OPEN...

OTHERWISE, AFTER THREE OR FOUR SHOTS, YOU'LL BE ON THE FLOOR.

THREE DAYS LATER, WE WERE ON THE MOVE AGAIN-- THIS TIME TO A RAILHEAD 25 MILES AWAY.

ONCE THERE, WE FUELED OUR TANKS TO THE BRIM, THEN LOADED OUR STEEDS ON FLATCARS.

SO...IS THIS AS FAR AS YOU GO WITH US, CAPTAIN RAMSKOV?

YES, COMRADE TYMOSHENKO--THIS IS IT. I MUST NOW BE HEADING BACK TO CHELYABINSK.

CAPTAIN, I WISH TO THANK YOU FOR ALL THAT YOU'VE DONE FOR US...

I SHOWED MY APPRECIATION IN THE ONLY WAY THAT FELT APPROPRIATE....

--?!

YOU TAUGHT ME WELL, CAPTAIN--AND I PROMISE THAT I WILL MAKE YOU *PROUD.*

I KNOW YOU *SHALL.*

FAREWELL, COMRADE.

ON THIS TRIP, SOME OF THE NEWNESS AND WONDER HAD FINALLY BEGUN TO WEAR OFF...

...AND I SLEPT LIKE A BABY.

232

WE RODE THE TRAIN FOR FOUR DAYS. IT WAS GOOD WE HAD THE OPPORTUNITY TO REST ON THE TRIP, BECAUSE THE NEXT SEVERAL DAYS WOULD BE VERY HECTIC.

AT LEAST A DOZEN MORE TRAINS WERE FOLLOWING OURS, CARRYING THE REST OF OUR BRIGADE.

WE DISEMBARKED NEAR A LITTLE TOWN BESIDE A RIVER, WHICH TURNED OUT TO BE THE *DON*. THE FIRST THING I NOTICED WAS THE DOZENS OF LARGE FERRY BOATS AWAITING US.

DAY AND NIGHT, THEY FERRIED US ACROSS THE RIVER. IT TOOK TWO AND A HALF DAYS, AND THERE WERE NO MISHAPS OR ACCIDENTS. FORTUNATELY, THE WEATHER HAD TURNED BAD--CLOUDY SKIES AND THE STEADY SNOWFALL WOULD HELP COVER OUR MOVEMENTS IN CASE A GERMAN PLANE FLEW OVER.

AFTER WE GOT ACROSS, WE THEN MOVED OUR TANKS IN AND AROUND SEVERAL VILLAGES IN THE AREA.

A TRUCK CAME AROUND WITH BUCKETS OF WHITEWASH TO CAMOUFLAGE OUR TANKS.

MORE TRUCKS BROUGHT IN HAY. WE USED IT TO COVER OUR VEHICLES TO MAKE THEM LOOK LIKE HOUSES AND BARNS...

...AND WE ALLOWED THE POOR SKINNY LOCAL FARM ANIMALS TO EAT THEIR FILL.

LATER THAT DAY, OUR INFANTRY BATTALION MARCHED IN, ALL DECKED OUT IN NEW WHITE SNOW SUITS...

I JUST GOT WORD FROM HEADQUARTERS-- TOMORROW, THERE'LL BE A PERFORMANCE BY A MUSICAL TROUPE!

WOW! WHEN?

NOON, IN THE NEXT VILLAGE!

THE CONCERT WAS HELD IN A LITTLE BOWL-SHAPED AREA NEAR THE RIVER. THE ENTIRE BRIGADE--TANKERS, INFANTRY, AND SERVICE PEOPLE--COVERED THE SIDES OF THE BOWL. THE "STAGE" WAS A HAY-COVERED FLAT AT THE BOTTOM, WITH AN OLD BEAT-UP UPRIGHT PIANO AND ONE OF OUR TANKS FOR A BACKDROP. THE PERFORMERS WERE VERY GOOD. SIX GIRLS SANG, ACCOMPANIED BY THREE GUYS ON A BALALAIKA, AN ACCORDION, AND THAT PIANO, PLAYING POPULAR AND PATRIOTIC SONGS...

SUDDENLY, *CAPTAIN KOVCHENKO* STEPPED OUT IN FRONT OF THE CROWD...

...AND THE INFANTRY SOLDIERS WENT *WILD!*

NOT LONG AGO, SOMEONE ASKED ME IF I WOULD PERFORM A CONCERT. I REPLIED THEN THAT MY CONCERT DAYS WERE OVER...

BUT IN THIS COMPANY, I THOUGHT I MIGHT AS WELL GIVE IT A *TRY...*

THE CROWD ROARED ITS APPROVAL--AND THEN FELL UTTERLY *SILENT.*

HE BEGAN WITH "DARK EYES" THEN "MOSCOW NIGHTS"... DESPITE HIS DAMAGED HAND AND THE BEAT-UP PIANO, THE BEAUTIFUL STRAINS OF HIS MUSIC FLOWED UP AROUND US.

THE HUSHED AUDIENCE SWAYED ALONG IN TIME.

THE NEXT CHOICE SEEMED ODD AT FIRST, BUT IT MADE SENSE FOR THIS ASSEMBLAGE-- "THE SONG OF THE VOLGA BOATMEN."

THIS HOST OF BATTLE-HARDENED MEN HUMMED ALONG WITH STRENGTH AND CONVICTION.

I OVERHEARD THE TWO GIRLS BY US WHISPERING...

...HE'S ONLY TWENTY-SIX YEARS OLD...

...CHILD PRODIGY AT THE LENINGRAD CONSERVATORY...

...HIS WIFE IS A TALENTED VIOLINIST...

...DIMITRY SHOSTAKOVICH IS HIS GOOD FRIEND...

≤AAH!≥

THEIR LAST COMMENT HIT ME DEEP IN MY STOMACH.

KOVCHENKO ENDED HIS CONCERT WITH "MY COUNTRY." THE BRIGADE ROSE TO ITS FEET AND RESPONDED IN SONG. BUT AS I ROSE, I REFLECTED IN MY HEART...

THIS IS NOT *MY* COUNTRY. WHAT AM I DOING HERE?

ON THE WAY BACK, MILLA AND I WALKED IN SILENCE, AS WAS USUAL. BUT I COULD TELL THAT SHE KNEW SOMETHING WAS WRONG, AND WHAT IT WAS. FINALLY, SHE SPOKE UP...

YOU KNOW, KATUSHA...HE IS *RUSSIAN*.

AND WE WANT TO GO HOME TO *UKRAINE*.

YEAH...

THAT'S RIGHT...

I FELT MY FROSTY SILENCE THAWING...

...THEN IT ALL *BURST OUT*.

HOW DID WE EVEN GET HERE, MILLA? THE PATH THAT WE'VE TAKEN IS BEYOND BELIEF--!

--AND WHY IN THE WORLD IS *HE* THE ONE WHO MOVES ME?

DEAR, DEAR KATUSHA... YOU ARE *NOT* RESPONSIBLE FOR THE DIRECTION YOUR HEART PULLS YOU...

...YOU ARE ONLY RESPONSIBLE IF YOU *FOLLOW IT*.

THESE THINGS THAT I AM TELLING YOU SEEM SO INSIGNIFICANT-- EVEN SILLY. BUT THEY WERE NOT--THEY WOULD HAVE AN EFFECT ON MY WHOLE LIFE.

ASK YOURSELF--WHO CANNOT REMEMBER WHEN THEY FIRST FELL IN LOVE? EVERY ONE OF US CAN.

BUT--WHO CAN REMEMBER GREAT EARTHSHAKING EVENTS, LIKE THE *BATTLE OF STALINGRAD?*

I CAN REMEMBER THEM BOTH...

I CAN REMEMBER THEM BECAUSE I WAS *THERE.*

TIME: *7:30* ON THE MORNING OF *NOVEMBER 19, 1942.*

SOME 3,500 SOVIET ARTILLERY PIECES, MORTARS, AND ROCKET LAUNCHERS OPEN UP ON POSITIONS OF THE *ROMANIAN ARMY* TO THE NORTHWEST AND SOUTH OF STALINGRAD.

THE THIN FLANKS OF GERMANY'S *6TH ARMY* WERE BEING POUNDED TO PIECES.

NEAR THE VILLAGE OF BOLSHOY, OUR TANKS WERE ADVANCING THROUGH THE MURKY FOG...

CONDUCTOR, THIS IS THE 1ST CLARINET. *"THE DOOR HAS BEEN OPENED."*

VERY GOOD. "ADVANCE THE ENTIRE BRASS SECTION."

INFANTRY AND SAPPERS--AS WE CALLED THE ENGINEERS--HAD TAKEN OUT THE FORWARD OUTPOST AND CLEARED OUT THE MINEFIELDS.

THE TANKS ROLLED THROUGH.

CLINGING TO THE BACK OF EACH TANK WERE WHITE-CLAD RUSSIAN SOLDIERS, ALL ARMED WITH *PPSH-41* SUBMACHINE GUNS OR DESTYAREV LIGHT MACHINE GUNS.

ROMANIAN RESISTANCE HAD LITTLE EFFECT ON THE ADVANCE...

MANY RUSSIANS REMEMBER THIS DAY AS THE HAPPIEST DAY OF THE WAR.

THE VIOLATED MOTHERLAND AT LAST WAS AVENGING ITSELF.

THE TOWN OF *OSTROV*, LATE ON THE NIGHT OF *NOVEMBER 21*...

LOOK, COLONEL! HOW KIND OF THE GERMANS TO LEAVE THESE FOR US--AND IN SUCH GOOD SHAPE!

I BET WE COULD MAKE VERY GOOD USE OF THEM.

BELIEVE ME, WE *WILL*. I HAVE JUST BEEN GIVEN OUR ORDERS--

--THE BRIDGE OVER THE *DON* AT *KALACH*!

KATUSHA, GET ON THE RADIO. I NEED THESE DRIVERS--*ABARCHUK* AND *PERFILEV*.

YES, SIR!

MILLA--CAN YOU DRIVE THAT HALF-TRACK?

SURE!

ALL RIGHT. HERE'S WHAT WE'LL DO...

WE MOVED OUT JUST AFTER MIDNIGHT. IN THE LEAD WERE THE TWO CAPTURED GERMAN TANKS, THEIR HEADLIGHTS BLAZING...

BEHIND THEM CAME THE HALF-TRACK, WITH MILLA AT THE WHEEL AND KOVCHENKO AND SIX OF HIS MEN ON BOARD.

SIXTEEN *T-34*s FOLLOWED.

I WAS DRIVING OUR TANK, WITH COLONEL NOZDRIN AND MISHA BOVA IN THE TURRET.

THE LIGHT WAS DIM AS WE NEARED THE BRIDGE AT A LITTLE AFTER SIX IN THE MORNING. THE GERMAN SENTRY, COLD AND TIRED, DIDN'T NOTICE ANYTHING UNUSUAL AS HE WAVED THE TANKS RIGHT ACROSS.

THEN CAPTAIN KOVCHENKO, WEARING A GERMAN HELMET AND SMOKING A GERMAN CIGAR, STUCK HIS HEAD OUT OF THE TOP OF THE HALF-TRACK...

EH--?

...AND CAROMED THE HELMET OFF THE GUARD'S FACE AS WE OPENED FIRE!

‹UNNGH!›

BLANG!

THE UNSUSPECTING *FRITZES* WERE SURPRISED TO BE SHOT BY THEIR OWN *PANZERS!*

OUR SIXTEEN *T-34*s WERE LINED UP ON THE WEST BANK, FIRING ON ANYTHING THAT TRIED TO SUPPORT THE DEFENSE OF THE BRIDGE.

IT WAS SOON OVER. I LEAPT FROM OUR TANK, ELATED.

REMEMBER, KATUSHA? THIS IS THAT SAME BRIDGE WE CROSSED WITH TARAS LAST YEAR--!

AND WE'VE MANAGED TO TAKE IT WITHOUT LOSING A SINGLE MAN!

AH--IT *DID* SEEM FAMILIAR!

WHAT A DAY! WHAT A DAY!

AND WHAT DO *YOU* THINK ABOUT IT, LITTLE TYMOSHENKO?

WELL...THIS IS SURELY SOMETHING TO WRITE HOME ABOUT TO YOUR WIFE, CAPTAIN!

BUT THEN HIS FACE FELL, AS IF ALL THE LIFE HAD SUDDENLY WASHED OUT OF IT...

NO. YOU SEE... LAST WINTER, MY WIFE *DIED*--IN LENINGRAD...

SHE--AND OUR THREE DAUGHTERS-- STARVED TO DEATH.

NOVEMBER 23, 1942... THE SOVIET FORCES THAT HAD ATTACKED THE ROMANIAN ARMIES NORTHWEST AND SOUTH OF STALINGRAD HAD MET AT *KALACH.*

SEVEN ENTIRE ROMANIAN DIVISIONS HAD BEEN DESTROYED. BUT MORE IMPORTANT-- THE SOVIETS HAD SUCCESSFULLY COMPLETED THE ENCIRCLEMENT OF THE GERMAN *6TH ARMY.*

THE SOVIET TROOPS INVOLVED WERE JOYOUS, BELIEVING THEY HAD TRAPPED ABOUT 85,000 GERMANS, CUTTING THEM OFF FROM FOOD, FUEL, AND CONTACT WITH HOME.

BUT IN REALITY, THEY HAD TRAPPED NEARLY 300,000 MEN-- THE *6TH ARMY* AND ALSO PART OF THE *4TH PANZER ARMY.*

THOSE GERMANS WHO WERE TRAPPED IN THE "KESSEL" (BOILER OR CAULDRON) COULD NOT BE COUNTED OUT. THEY REFUSED TO BELIEVE THAT THEIR FÜHRER WOULD LEAVE THEM TO FREEZE AND DIE IN A FOREIGN LAND.

NEWS REACHED THEM OF THE PLANS OF FIELD MARSHAL ERICH VON MANSTEIN, THE COMMANDER OF ARMY GROUP SOUTH, TO SEND HIS ARMORED GROUP NORTHEAST FROM KOTELNIKOVSKI TO MEET THE 6TH ARMY, WHICH WOULD BE BREAKING OUT OF THE SOVIET ENCIRCLEMENT TO MEET THEM. ON THE BREATH OF EVERY MAN TRAPPED IN THE *KESSEL* WAS THE FAITHFUL AND HOPEFUL PHRASE: *"MANSTEIN IS COMING."*

ARENA

I CAN'T REMEMBER THE NAME OF THE TOWN--I DOUBT THAT ANY OF US COULD. I JUST REMEMBER IT AS "TWO CHURCHES" BECAUSE--WELL, THERE WERE TWO VERY PRETTY CHURCHES THERE...

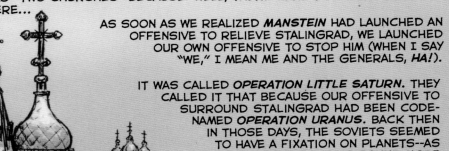

AS SOON AS WE REALIZED *MANSTEIN* HAD LAUNCHED AN OFFENSIVE TO RELIEVE STALINGRAD, WE LAUNCHED OUR OWN OFFENSIVE TO STOP HIM (WHEN I SAY "WE," I MEAN ME AND THE GENERALS, *HA!*).

IT WAS CALLED *OPERATION LITTLE SATURN*. THEY CALLED IT THAT BECAUSE OUR OFFENSIVE TO SURROUND STALINGRAD HAD BEEN CODE-NAMED *OPERATION URANUS*. BACK THEN IN THOSE DAYS, THE SOVIETS SEEMED TO HAVE A FIXATION ON PLANETS--AS IF IT COULD MAKE US SOUND MORE EDUCATED THAN WE REALLY WERE.

AHA...! SUKHANOV IS SIGNALLING.

HE SAYS CAPTAIN KOVCHENKO JUST CALLED DOWN FROM THE TOWER TO REPORT THERE ARE NO GERMANS--ONLY FIELDS AND BIRCH WOODS.

HA! I CAN SEE HIM!

WHAT'S HE DOING?

HERE-- LOOK FOR YOURSELF!

OH, MY HERO!

IF ONLY HE WERE WAVING AT *ME*...!

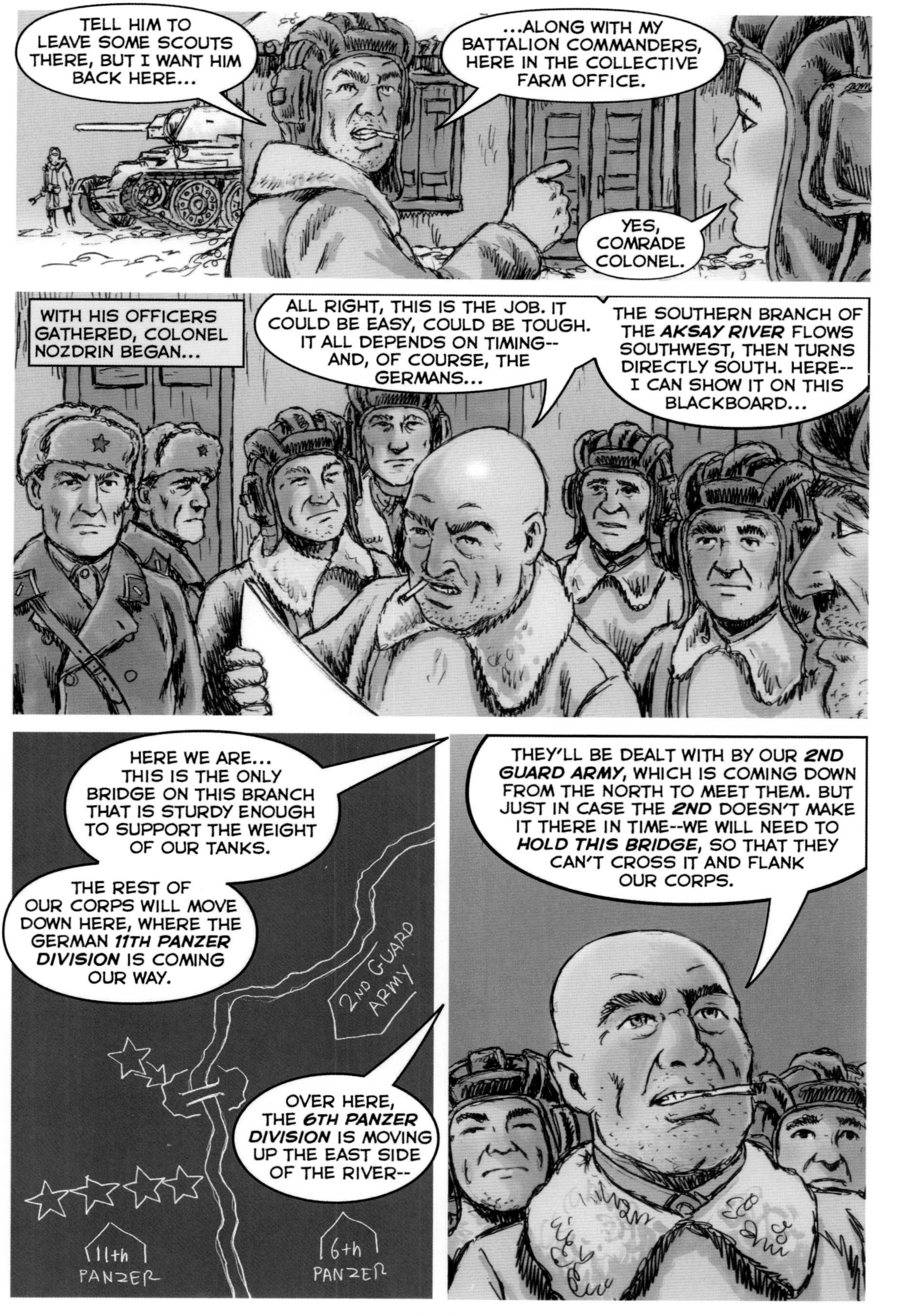

TELL HIM TO LEAVE SOME SCOUTS THERE, BUT I WANT HIM BACK HERE...
...ALONG WITH MY BATTALION COMMANDERS, HERE IN THE COLLECTIVE FARM OFFICE.
YES, COMRADE COLONEL.
WITH HIS OFFICERS GATHERED, COLONEL NOZDRIN BEGAN...
ALL RIGHT, THIS IS THE JOB. IT COULD BE EASY, COULD BE TOUGH. IT ALL DEPENDS ON TIMING--AND, OF COURSE, THE GERMANS...
THE SOUTHERN BRANCH OF THE AKSAY RIVER FLOWS SOUTHWEST, THEN TURNS DIRECTLY SOUTH. HERE--I CAN SHOW IT ON THIS BLACKBOARD...
HERE WE ARE... THIS IS THE ONLY BRIDGE ON THIS BRANCH THAT IS STURDY ENOUGH TO SUPPORT THE WEIGHT OF OUR TANKS.
THE REST OF OUR CORPS WILL MOVE DOWN HERE, WHERE THE GERMAN 11TH PANZER DIVISION IS COMING OUR WAY.
2ND GUARD ARMY
OVER HERE, THE 6TH PANZER DIVISION IS MOVING UP THE EAST SIDE OF THE RIVER--
11th PANZER
6th PANZER
THEY'LL BE DEALT WITH BY OUR 2ND GUARD ARMY, WHICH IS COMING DOWN FROM THE NORTH TO MEET THEM. BUT JUST IN CASE THE 2ND DOESN'T MAKE IT THERE IN TIME--WE WILL NEED TO HOLD THIS BRIDGE, SO THAT THEY CAN'T CROSS IT AND FLANK OUR CORPS.

NOGIN AND GUCHKOV--I WANT YOUR TANK BATTALIONS ACROSS THE RIVER AND INTO THE TOWN. DON'T DIG THEM IN--HIDE THEM INSIDE THE BARNS, HAYSTACKS--OR EVEN IN HOUSES. I'LL BE CHECKING ON THEM LATER.

MIRONOV, KEEP YOUR BATTALION UP HERE OVERLOOKING THE RIVER, BUT I WANT *YOUR* TANKS DUG IN.

KOLYA--ANY CIVILIANS LEFT IN TOWN?

I DIDN'T SEE ANY--BUT THERE ARE ALWAYS A FEW WHO STAY BEHIND.

I WANT TWO OF YOUR INFANTRY COMPANIES IN TOWN. DIG THEM INTO THE CELLARS. YOU KNOW WHAT I WANT.

RIGHT. IT MIGHT BE A GOOD IDEA TO PUT A FEW SCOUTS BACK IN THOSE BIRCHES OVER ON THE OTHER SIDE OF THE FIELD.

GOOD IDEA.

WHAT ABOUT *US*, COLONEL?

DIG THE TANK IN, BUT DON'T BOTHER MAKING ROOM UNDERNEATH IT. ONE MAN CAN STAY WITH THE TANK, AND ROTATE THE OTHERS INSIDE.

YES, SIR!

I REMEMBER HEARING A FAMOUS SOLDIER SAY THAT HE DID MORE SOLDIERING WITH A SPADE THAT HE DID WITH A GUN. I CAN CERTAINLY SWEAR TO THAT!

EVERY NIGHT WE HAD TO SPEND IN A COMBAT AREA, WE'D DIG OUR TANK IN TO A POINT JUST ABOVE THE TRACKS, AND THEN WE'D DIG A HOLE UNDERNEATH IT THAT WAS BIG ENOUGH FOR ALL OF US TO SLEEP IN. TONIGHT, WE WERE TO ROTATE SLEEPING INSIDE THE FARM BUILDING. BUT DESPITE WHAT COLONEL NOZDRIN SAID, WE DUG A HOLE BENEATH IT--ONE THAT'D BE DEEP ENOUGH TO HOLD ALL OF US.

IF THE GERMANS CAME, THIS WOULD BE THE COLONEL'S COMMAND POST. AND BY THEN, IT WOULD BE TOO LATE TO DIG THE HOLE DEEPER.

A FEW MILES TO THE SOUTH, GERMAN MECHANIZED INFANTRY WERE STEADILY MOVING THROUGH THE SLUSHY SNOW...

THESE MODERN CAVALRYMEN LONG AGO HAD LEARNED TO SLEEP ON THE MOVE, DESPITE BEING KNOCKED AGAINST THE STEEL HULL OR THEIR ALSO-SLEEPING FRIENDS...

THEY'D ALSO LEARNED TO IMMEDIATELY AWAKEN TO THE SOUND OF APPROACHING DANGER.

EH--?

WAS IST--?

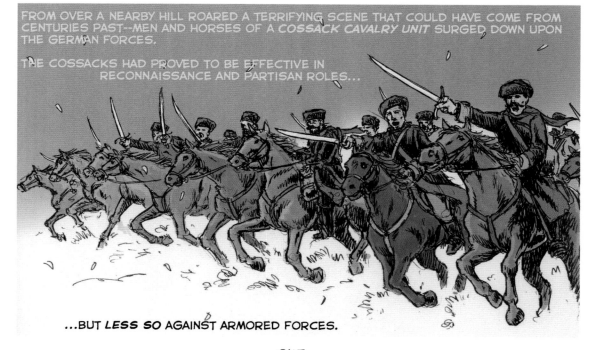

FROM OVER A NEARBY HILL ROARED A TERRIFYING SCENE THAT COULD HAVE COME FROM CENTURIES PAST--MEN AND HORSES OF A *COSSACK CAVALRY UNIT* SURGED DOWN UPON THE GERMAN FORCES.

THE COSSACKS HAD PROVED TO BE EFFECTIVE IN RECONNAISSANCE AND PARTISAN ROLES...

...BUT *LESS SO* AGAINST ARMORED FORCES.

THE *PANZERGRENADIERS* IMMEDIATELY DISMOUNTED AND FORMED A LINE WITH THEIR VEHICLES, WHICH THEY TURNED TO FACE THE ONSLAUGHT.

THE GERMANS PREPARED THEIR WEAPONS...

...AND CALMLY WAITED FOR THE ENEMY TO COME INTO RANGE...

THEN--

--THEY UNLEASHED A RAIN OF *LEADEN HELLFIRE!!*

SUDDENLY...

...ANOTHER ELEMENT CAME INTO PLAY!

THE GERMANS WERE JUBILANT TO SEE THEIR *PANZERS* ARRIVE!

WITH THEIR SUPERIOR FIREPOWER...

...THE TANKS MADE SHORT WORK OF IT.

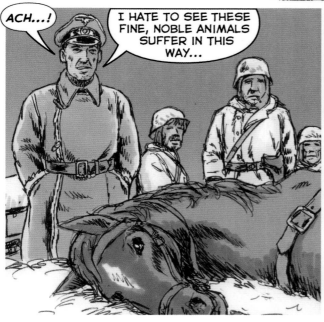

ACH...!

I HATE TO SEE THESE FINE, NOBLE ANIMALS SUFFER IN THIS WAY...

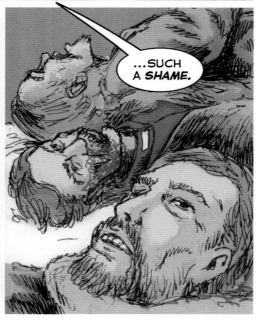

...SUCH A *SHAME.*

KATUSHA! WAKE UP!

:MMRF...?:

...YOU'RE EARLY--HOW COME?

WHY QUESTION GOOD FORTUNE? YOU CAN GO **INSIDE** NOW, WHERE IT'S NICE AND WARM.

MMMOKAY...

AH! COME ON **IN**, LITTLE TYMOSHENKO!

WHY... **THANK** YOU, COMRADE.

I MUST SAY, IT SEEMS YOU AND YOUR SISTER HAVE ADAPTED TO OUTDOOR LIFE BETTER THAN MOST OF MY INFANTRYMEN!

WELL, OUR UNCLE TARAS TAUGHT US HOW TO LIVE UNDER DIFFICULT SITUATIONS...

...BUT MORE IMPORTANT, HE TAUGHT US HOW IT JUST MAKES THINGS WORSE TO **COMPLAIN.**

HA! NOW **THAT** IS A LESSON FOR THE ARMY!

THE BRIGADE POLITICAL OFFICER SAT OFF IN THE CORNER. I WHISPERED TO KOVCHENKO...

AH, IT'S COMRADE **CHEKOV**...

HE'S ALWAYS SEEMED ODD TO ME--A BIT SCARY.

STEPHAN? OH, HE'S ALL RIGHT--A PRODUCT OF HIS ENVIRONMENT. THE POOR MAN IS AN ORPHAN OF THE REVOLUTION.

WHAT?

"HIS FIRST MEMORIES ARE OF BEING ALONE ON THE STREETS. HE KNOWS NOTHING OF HIS PARENTS--ALL HE EVER HAD OF HIS OWN WAS THE REVOLUTION...

Тульская Комсомольской

"HIS ONLY MOTHER IS RUSSIA... AND HIS FATHER IS THE PARTY."

OH. HOW SAD FOR HIM...

I...I WANT TO APOLOGIZE TO YOU, FOR WHAT I SAID ABOUT WRITING TO YOUR WIFE... YOU SEE...I--

--I HAD NO IDEA.

CAPTAIN KOVCHENKO DIDN'T SAY ANYTHING FOR A MOMENT.

WHEN HE SPOKE, HIS VOICE WAS HUSHED...

LARYISSA... WAS A RATHER FRAGILE GIRL... THE BIRTH OF OUR THIRD DAUGHTER TOOK A LOT OUT OF HER. SHE--SHE WAS MUCH TOO WEAK TO GO THROUGH THAT WINTER... AND-- AND OUR LITTLE GIRLS--∛

THE WORDS CAUGHT IN HIS THROAT. HE SWALLOWED HARD--AND WENT ON...

YOU KNOW...I KNOW THEY ARE GONE. THOSE WHO TOLD ME WOULD NOT HAVE LIED TO ME. BUT DEEP DOWN--I JUST CANNOT BELIEVE IT!

HERE, WITHIN MY BRAIN--I KNOW THEY'RE GONE...BUT--!

BUT--YOU CANNOT BELIEVE IT IN HERE...

KOVCHENKO SIGHED SOFTLY AND NODDED.

251

SEVERAL DAYS BEFORE WE'D REACHED *TWO CHURCHES*, AN UNSEASONAL THAW HAD OCCURRED THAT FORTUNATELY AIDED US IN THE "DIGGING-IN" PROCESS. IT LEFT THE EARTH SOFT AND WET.

THIS WAS A MAJOR HELP TO OUR INFANTRYMEN DIGGING BUNKERS UNDER HOUSES AND TO OUR TANKERS LOWERING THE TELLTALE SILHOUETTES OF THEIR VEHICLES.

THEN, AS IF BY MAGIC--THE FRIGID NORTH WIND RETURNED, FREEZING THE GROUND AND HARDENING OUR ARTIFICIAL BARRIERS.

AH, HAHAHA! YES!

THIS IS WHAT MAKES IGLOOS SO STRONG!

COLONEL NOZDRIN TRULY HAD AN EYE FOR THE LAND. HE PREPARED OUR POSITION SO WE'D BE READY FOR A LONG, DIFFICULT DEFENSE-- OR A QUICK PULLOUT.

HE WOULD STAND AROUND HOLDING A LONG STICK AS HE TALKED WITH SOLDIERS ABOUT ANYTHING AND EVERYTHING.

BUT WHILE HE TALKED, HIS MIND WAS WORKING...

...ROLLING THINGS OVER...

...ASKING HIMSELF QUESTIONS...

...AND SOLVING PROBLEMS.

TWO DAYS LATER, A SMALL VEHICLE APPROACHED OUR CAMP FROM THE EAST.

WE ALREADY KNEW OF ITS COMING BEFORE IT WAS IN SIGHT--ONE OF OUR SCOUTS UP IN THE BIRCH WOODS SAW IT AND SIGNALLED THE NEWS TO US WITH A FLASHLIGHT.

IT WAS A SMALL GERMAN HALF-TRACK, A *SDKFZ 250.*

THERE WERE FIVE MEN IN IT. THEY DROVE INTO THE VILLAGE AS IF THEY WERE TOURISTS LOOKING FOR A SUITABLE HOTEL ON THE PRYMORSKY BOULEVARD IN ODESSA.

THEY HAD NO IDEA HOW MANY *GUNS* WERE TRAINED ON THEM.

HMM...I DON'T SEE ANYBODY.

WELL, I SEE SMOKE FROM A FEW CHIMNEYS. *HA,* WE'RE JUST IN TIME FOR *BREAKFAST!*

LOOK! HERE COMES AN OLD MAN WITH A BASKET OF TREATS FOR US!

KURT, CAN'T YOU THINK OF ANYTHING BUT *FOOD?*

HOLD UP, OLD MAN! WHAT DO YOU HAVE THERE IN YOUR BASKET?

THE OLD MAN STOPPED AND TURNED, APPARENTLY FRIGHTENED...

THE GERMAN CALLED *KURT* WRESTED THE BASKET FROM THE OLD MAN'S HAND...

NO! THERE'S NOT ENOUGH FOR *ALL* OF YOU!

BUT THERE'S JUST THE *FIVE* OF US, OLD MAN*!*

JUST *FIVE* OF YOU!

THE OLD MAN'S LOUD STATEMENT WAS A FACT--NOT A QUESTION.

THEN, FROM OUT OF NOWHERE...

FOUR SHOTS RANG OUT SO FAST THEY SOUNDED AS *ONE.*

KURT TURNED...

...AND SAW HIS FOUR COMPANIONS LYING IN THE SNOW--ALL *DEAD* WITHIN AN INSTANT.

HE LOOKED BACK AT THE OLD MAN--AND SAW HIM SUDDENLY STANDING SEVERAL METERS AWAY FROM WHERE HE HAD BEEN.

HUH...?

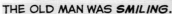

THE OLD MAN WAS *SMILING.*

KURT HAD NO INKLING THIS "OLD MAN" WAS REALLY OUR *SENIOR SERGEANT GENRIKH DYATLONKO,* RECIPIENT OF THE ST. GEORGE'S CROSS DURING THE GREAT WAR.

KURT LOOKED DOWN AT THE BASKET IN HIS HAND IN DAWNING *HORROR...*

THE LAST THOUGHT THAT KURT EVER HAD--

?

--WAS THAT SOMEONE HAD TAKEN HIS BASKET.

EXCELLENT WORK, GENRIKH!

HEH!

NOW--GET THOSE BODIES OUT OF HERE.

PETROV, DRIVE THEIR HALF-TRACK UP THE HILL AND PARK IT BEHIND THE FARM OFFICE.

IN JUST A FEW MINUTES...

...NOT A TRACE REMAINED TO SHOW THAT ANYTHING UNUSUAL HAD HAPPENED IN THE VILLAGE SQUARE.

NOW IT WAS TIME TO WAIT...

COLONEL NOZDRIN POSITIONED HIMSELF OUTSIDE, WHERE HE COULD DIRECT THE ACTION. HE KEPT ME BY THE RADIO, JUST IN CASE. I SAT IN THE DRIVER'S SEAT SO I COULD SEE OUT THE FORWARD HATCH.

MILLA STOOD UP IN THE TURRET WITH MISHA BOVA, PREPARED TO ACT AS HIS LOADER, IF NECESSARY.

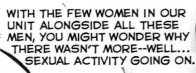

WITH THE FEW WOMEN IN OUR UNIT ALONGSIDE ALL THESE MEN, YOU MIGHT WONDER WHY THERE WASN'T MORE--WELL... SEXUAL ACTIVITY GOING ON.

AT THE FRONT, COMBAT UNITS WERE KEPT EXTREMELY BUSY. SLEEP--TRULY *DEEP* SLEEP--WAS A VERY ELUSIVE LUXURY.

SO IN REALITY, THERE JUST WASN'T ENOUGH *TIME.* BESIDES, PEOPLE OFTEN WERE JUST TOO DOG-TIRED TO EVEN *THINK* ABOUT IT.

BUT... IT *DID* HAPPEN.

MANY HIGH-LEVEL OFFICERS KEPT WHAT WERE CALLED "CAMP WIVES." TAKE, FOR INSTANCE, THE COLONEL'S DRIVER, *VERA FYODOROVICH...*

COLONEL NOZDRIN WAS MARRIED, IN FACT-- AND HAD A SON WHO WAS A PILOT. BUT IT WAS QUITE OBVIOUS TO ALL OF US THAT VERA SERVED AS HIS "CAMP WIFE." OF COURSE, NOBODY EVER SPOKE OF IT ABOVE A WHISPER--STILL, WE ALL ACCEPTED IT.

EVERYONE LOVED THE GIRL MEDICS. WHEN OUR GALINA MIKHAYLOVA PULLED ALEX FOMICHEVA FROM HIS BURNING TANK, HE SWORE TO HER HIS LOVE FOREVER...

...AND HE KEPT THAT VOW, TOO--ALEX FOMICHEVA WAS KILLED AT PROKHOROVKA.

I FELT A LITTLE SORRY FOR MISHA--HE CLEARLY LIKED MILLA. BUT MILLA ONLY HAD FEELINGS FOR UNCLE TARAS.

I GUESS THAT'S JUST THE WAY THINGS ARE.

BUT NOBODY AS YET HAD BOTHERED *ME.*

I WAS ONLY BOTHERED BY MY *OWN* FEELINGS.

NEAR NOON, SCOUTS IN THE BIRCH WOOD HEARD ROARING MOTORS AND CLANKING TRACKS.

SOON WE SAW ABOUT A DOZEN GERMAN HALF-TRACKS WHEELING INTO OUR VIEW. THEY TRUNDLED ACROSS THE SNOWY FIELDS... AND THEN--

--HEADED STRAIGHT FOR *TWO CHURCHES.*

WELL, HERE THEY COME--I HOPE EVERYONE IS *READY...!*

I KNEW CAPTAIN KOVCHENKO WAS READY... HE WAS *ALWAYS* READY FOR COMBAT.

THIS GROUP DID NOT ROLL IN FULL OF BRASH OVERCONFIDENCE LIKE OUR PREVIOUS VISITORS HAD. THESE HALF-TRACKS MOVED INTO A STAGGERED-LINE FORMATION--

--AND THEN THEY *STOPPED.*

THE *PANZERGRENADIERS* WERE DISGORGED FROM THE VEHICLES TO FORM A BATTLE LINE ACROSS THE WIDTH OF THE VILLAGE.

...THEN, PROMPTED BY A SIGNAL BLOWN ON A WHISTLE, THEY BEGAN THEIR *ADVANCE.*

WAIT TILL THEY GET CLOSER SO THE MACHINE GUNS IN THE HALF-TRACKS CAN'T DEPRESS...

WAIT...

...NOW.

OUR CONCEALED *DEGTYAREV* ANTI-TANK RIFLES OPENED UP ON THE HALF-TRACKS.

ONE ROUND DRILLED RIGHT THROUGH AN ENGINE BLOCK--AND CUT THE DRIVER IN TWO!

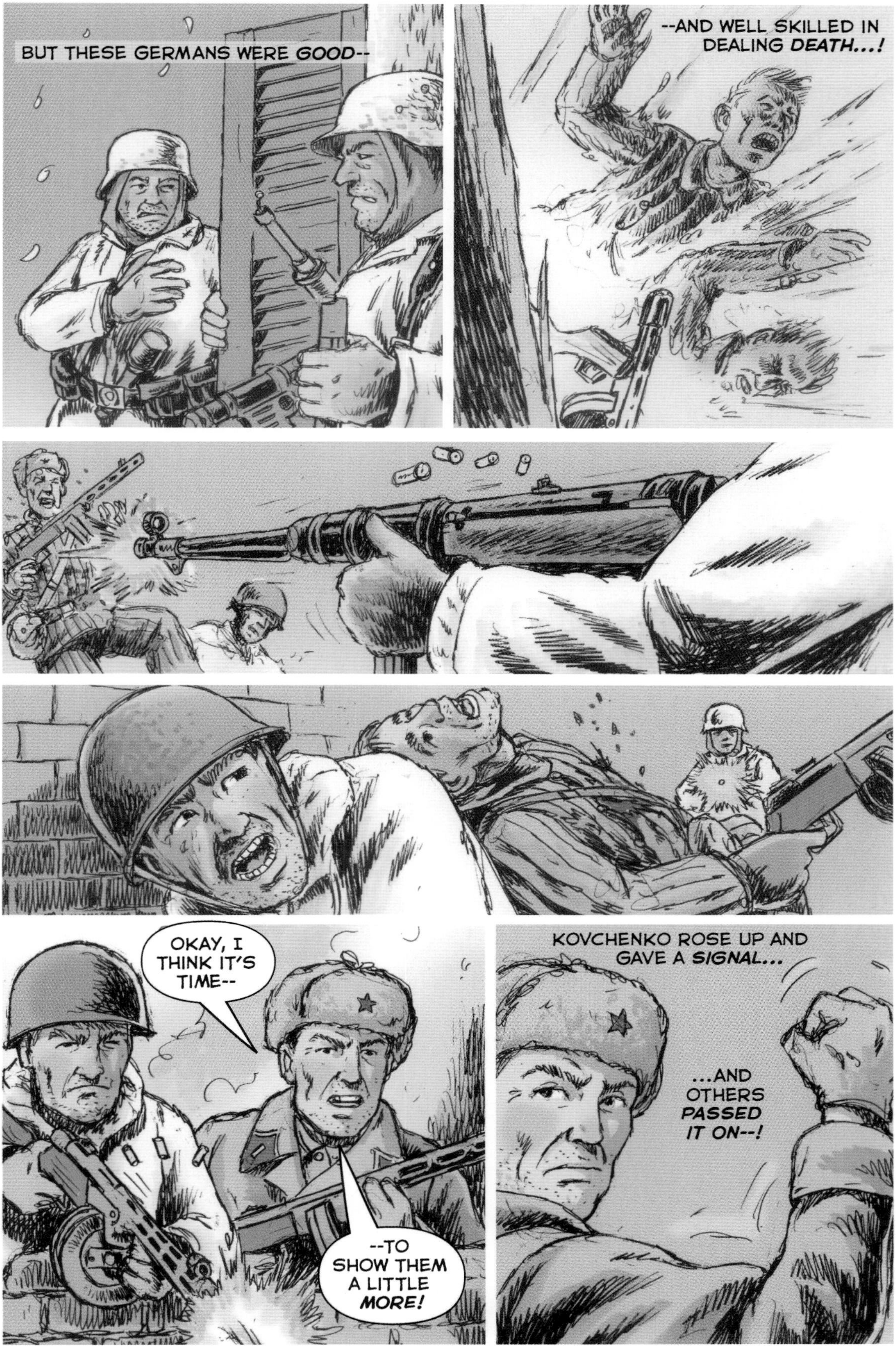
BUT THESE GERMANS WERE GOOD--
--AND WELL SKILLED IN DEALING DEATH...!
OKAY, I THINK IT'S TIME--
--TO SHOW THEM A LITTLE MORE!
KOVCHENKO ROSE UP AND GAVE A SIGNAL...
...AND OTHERS PASSED IT ON--!

A SINGLE *T-34* TANK ROLLED OUT FROM BEHIND A BUILDING...

...TWO MORE EXPOSED THEMSELVES FROM BENEATH THE HAYSTACKS...

THEY DROVE INTO THE FIELD AND FORMED ALONG THE GERMANS' FLANK...

...AS *THREE MORE* PULLED OUT ONTO THE FAR SIDE...!

UH--?!

ACH, SCHEISSE!!

...AND THEN THEY ENGAGED THEIR *STUNNED ENEMIES!*

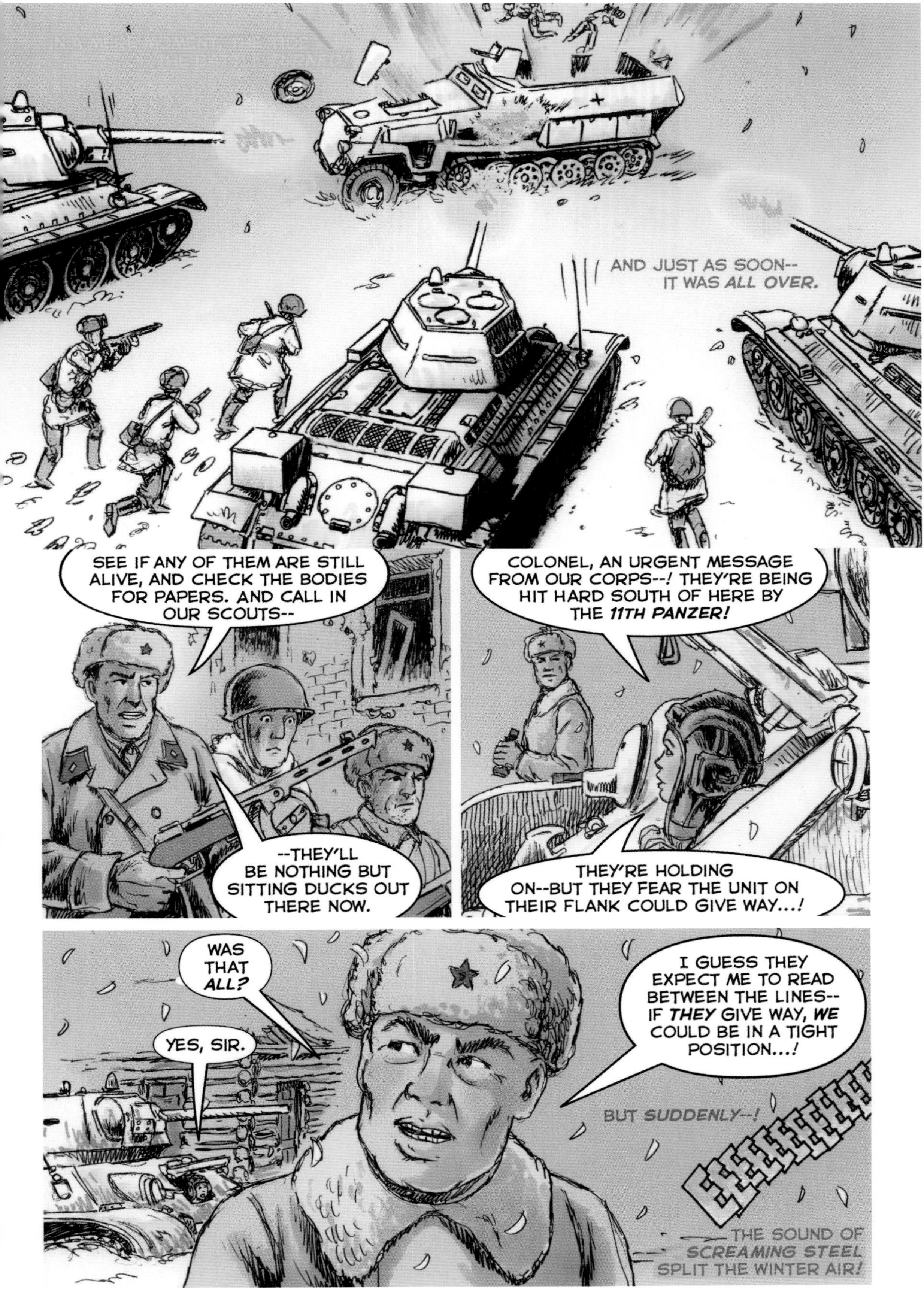
AND JUST AS SOON--
IT WAS ALL OVER.
SEE IF ANY OF THEM ARE STILL ALIVE, AND CHECK THE BODIES FOR PAPERS. AND CALL IN OUR SCOUTS--
--THEY'LL BE NOTHING BUT SITTING DUCKS OUT THERE NOW.
COLONEL, AN URGENT MESSAGE FROM OUR CORPS--! THEY'RE BEING HIT HARD SOUTH OF HERE BY THE 11TH PANZER!
THEY'RE HOLDING ON--BUT THEY FEAR THE UNIT ON THEIR FLANK COULD GIVE WAY...!
WAS THAT ALL?
YES, SIR.
I GUESS THEY EXPECT ME TO READ BETWEEN THE LINES-- IF THEY GIVE WAY, WE COULD BE IN A TIGHT POSITION...!
BUT SUDDENLY--!
--THE SOUND OF SCREAMING STEEL SPLIT THE WINTER AIR!

I'LL GET UNDER THE TANK! YOU CLOSE UP THAT HATCH!

AS I SHUT THE HATCH, I THANKED MY LUCKY STARS I'D DUG OUT THAT BUNKER BENEATH OUR TANK!

MOVE IT! QUICK!!

-I'M TRYIN', I'M TRYIN'--!!

THE BUNKERS UNDER THE HOUSES AFFORDED GOOD PROTECTION...

...BUT UNFORTUNATELY--*NOT* IN THE EVENT OF A *DIRECT HIT!*

THE BOMBARDMENT ENDED JUST AS QUICKLY AS IT HAD BEGUN.

EVERYBODY UP! CLEAR YOUR FIELDS OF FIRE--THEY'LL BE RIGHT *ON US!*

GET THE *WOUNDED* BACK UP THE HILL!

QUICKLY! BEFORE ANOTHER *BARRAGE BEGINS!*

WHERE'S *SHIRAKOV?*

HE'S *DEAD!* SHELLS CAUGHT US OUT IN THE OPEN--!!

CAPTAIN, I SAW MORE *TANKS!* THEY'RE BEHIND THOSE TREES, HEADING THIS WAY!

THEY'RE RIGHT ON *MY HEELS*--!!

SERGEYEV! GET THIS MAN UP THE HILL, WITH THE REST OF THE WOUNDED!

HEAR THAT *SOUND*, CAPTAIN--?! SHOULD WE GET OUR TANKS BACK UNDER COVER?

DON'T BOTHER, GENRIKH--IT'S FAR *TOO LATE* TO TRY TO FOOL THEM *NOW.*

OUT OF THE SMOKE AND BLOWING SNOW EMERGED GERMAN TANKS CAMOUFLAGED WITH JAGGED, ANGULAR LINES. AS WE HAD DONE WITH OUR TANKS, THESE WERE RANDOMLY SPLATTERED WITH WHITE PAINT TO PROVIDE CONCEALMENT IN THE WINTER LANDSCAPE-- BUT ALL IT ACCOMPLISHED WAS TO MAKE THEM LOOK LIKE EVEN MORE FEARSOME AND PROFICIENT INSTRUMENTS OF MURDER.

EH? THOSE *PANZER IV*S SEEM TO HAVE LONGER CANNONS...?!

OUR INFANTRYMEN INSTINCTIVELY BACKED OFF INTO THE VILLAGE, WHILE OUR TANKS ROLLED OUT TO MEET THE ENEMY.

ANY DISCUSSION OF CANNON-MUZZLE VELOCITY OR ARMOR STRENGTH WAS BESIDE THE POINT HERE...

...AT A RANGE THIS CLOSE, ALL ORDNANCE WAS *DEADLY*--

--AND *ALL* ARMOR *FAILED*.

BOTH SIDES WERE EXPLOITING THE LAYOUT OF THE BUILDINGS, AS IF THE WHOLE TOWN WERE SOME GIANT MAZE...

THE COLONEL SEEMED TENSE AND RIGID, BUT ABSOLUTELY FOCUSED ON THE JOB AT HAND.

THEY REALLY WANT TO TAKE THAT BRIDGE...

WELL, THEN, WHY DON'T WE JUST *BLOW* IT *UP?*

MUCH TOO LATE, I BIT MY TONGUE. IMAGINE LOWLY ME, ADVISING THE BRIGADE COMMANDER--! I FULLY EXPECTED COLONEL NOZDRIN'S RIGHTEOUS WRATH TO POUR DOWN UPON ME. INSTEAD, HE REPLIED IN A CALM, SOOTHING VOICE...

NO, KATUSHA. WE HAVE GOT TO *DEFEND* THE BRIDGE, NOT BLOW IT UP.

BUT I COULD SEE TENSION PULL THE MUSCLES OF HIS NECK AS HE WATCHED THE CAULDRON BELOW...

...THEN HE'D LOOK TO THE SOUTH, AS HE WONDERED WHETHER HIS CORPS WERE HOLDING OUT AGAINST THE *11TH PANZER*...

...THEN HE WOULD LOOK TO THE NORTHEAST, CURSING UNDER HIS BREATH--

--*WHERE* IS THE *2ND GUARD ARMY*...?!!

I LOOKED DOWN AT THE BOILING KETTLE BELOW... AND REFLECTED THAT IF IT COULD BE FROZEN IN TIME, AND IF THE UNIFORMS AND MOUNTS AND WEAPONS EXCHANGED, THIS AWFUL TABLEAU COULD BE REPRESENTATIONAL OF *POLTAVA* OR *BORODINO*--OR, EVEN FARTHER FLUNG, OF *WATERLOO* OR *GETTYSBURG*...

...OR EVEN *HELL!*

IT WAS UNBEARABLY *NOISY,* TOO. AUTOMATIC WEAPONSFIRE COMPETED WITH HIGH-VELOCITY CANNON BLASTS, AND WHATEVER SHORT PAUSE IN BETWEEN THAT COULD BE CALLED A LULL WAS FILLED WITH SCREAMS AND CURSES.

TANKS FOUGHT SO CLOSE TOGETHER THAT THE BLAST OF ONE GUN WAS INDISTINGUISHABLE FROM THE IMPACT ON ITS TARGET.

FROM THE TOP OF THE HILL, I COULD SEE MEN GETTING BLOWN APART--

--ONLY TO HEAR THE SOUND OF THE KILLING WEAPON AS IT REACHED MY EARS A SPLIT SECOND LATER.

GIANT ARMORED BEETLES LOCKED HORNS, SPITTING FIRE AND SMOKE, GRUNTING AND GROANING AND DIGGING INTO THE EARTH THAT THEY HAD REFUSED TO RELINQUISH.

AROUND THEIR CLAWING, DEADLY FEET, THE WARRIOR ANTS STRUGGLED--

--THEIR ENDEAVORS NO LESS *HELLISH.*

:GRR!:

:RNGH!:

AND, AS IN NATURE--

AAAIIEE!!

--*DEATH* MADE NO DISTINCTION.

THEN, THE THUNDER BEGAN TO ROLL AWAY. THE HATED INVADER BEGAN TO WITHDRAW INTO THE SMOKE AND FOG...

COLD STEEL COULD WITHSTAND THIS INFERNO--

--BUT FLESH AND BLOOD *COULD NOT.*

WITH THE CACOPHONY OF EXPLOSIONS AND SCREAMS STILL RINGING IN THEIR EARS, THE DEFENDERS LOOKED AROUND, BLINKING, AMAZED THAT THEY WERE NOT THE ONLY ONES STILL STANDING. GRADUALLY, THEIR SENSES RETURNED...

SLAVA, FIND THE COMPANY COMMANDERS AND BRING THEM ALL HERE.

GENRIKH--SEND SCOUTS BACK UP TO THE WOODS, TO WATCH IN CASE THEY TRY IT AGAIN.

SO WE PREPARED FOR ANOTHER ATTACK...

...AS THE MEDICS BEGAN TO AID THE WOUNDED--

--AND SOLDIERS COLLECTED THE DEAD.

THEY BROUGHT THE WOUNDED TO THE KOLKHOZ'S MEETING HALL. MANY HAD SUFFERED GHASTLY, LIFE-SHATTERING WOUNDS THAT WOULD SCAR THEM ALL THEIR LIVES--*IF* THEIR LIVES LASTED THAT LONG. THE MOST GREVIOUSLY INJURED ONES HELD SUCH TENUOUS HOLDS ON LIFE THAT THEIR PASSAGE TO THE OTHER SIDE WAS SCARCELY DETECTABLE.

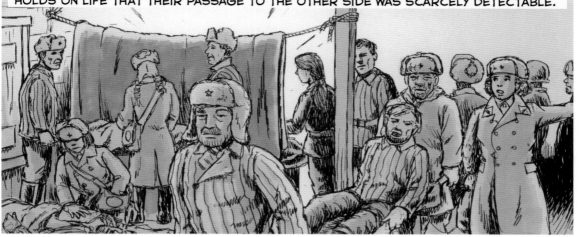

I HELPED THE MEDICS AS BEST I COULD, WISHING I HAD SPENT MORE TIME LOOKING OVER THE SHOULDER OF MY NURSE MOTHER... BUT MANY WERE BEYOND HELP.

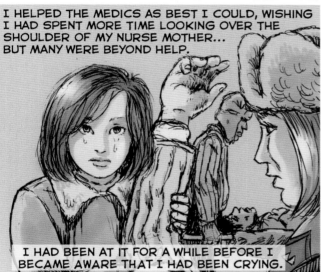

I HAD BEEN AT IT FOR A WHILE BEFORE I BECAME AWARE THAT I HAD BEEN CRYING.

THEN I LOOKED UP--AND SAW THAT COMMISSAR STEPHAN CHEKOV WAS WATCHING ME INTENTLY. HIS COLD, BLACK EYES DID NOT BLINK ONCE.

HE CONTINUED TO STARE UNTIL I TURNED AWAY.

BUT--THE MOST SHOCKING EVENT OF THAT DAY WAS COLONEL NOZDRIN'S ASSESSMENT OF THE HUMAN COST OF THE BATTLE...

SO, WE LOST 12 TANKS AND 37 CREW MEMBERS...

...AND AS OF RIGHT NOW, THE TOTAL IS 17 INFANTRYMEN DEAD AND 42 WOUNDED.

SO, I'D SAY THAT WE HAVEN'T DONE BADLY AT *ALL.*

"...WE HAVEN'T DONE BADLY AT ALL!"

MANSTEIN'S OFFENSIVE SOON PETERED OUT, BUT NOT BECAUSE HE DIDN'T HAVE THE STRENGTH TO CONTINUE OR THE WILL TO DEMAND THE SACRIFICE--SUCCESS HAD ALL ALONG DEPENDED ON THE GERMAN **6TH ARMY** MOUNTING AN OFFENSIVE OF THEIR OWN TO BREAK OUT OF THE RING AT STALINGRAD. BUT THOSE GERMAN TROOPS MAROONED INSIDE STALINGRAD HADN'T ENOUGH FUEL FOR THEIR VEHICLES TO GO TWENTY MILES.

NOR DID THEY HAVE THE STRENGTH-- BECAUSE BY NOW THEY WERE **STARVING.**

BUT THE **MAIN** REASON THEY WERE TRAPPED WAS **HITLER**--HE WOULD NOT ALLOW THEM TO BREAK OUT. HIS ENORMOUS EGO MADE HIM REFUSE TO GIVE UP THE CITY AFTER HAVING INVESTED SO MUCH IN CAPTURING IT. IN THE END, THE GERMAN **6TH ARMY** SUCCUMBED NOT ONLY TO THE BLOWS OF THE RED ARMY OR BITTER WINDS OF THE RUSSIAN WINTER-- BUT TO THE SHORTSIGHTED TREACHERY OF ITS **OWN LEADER.**

WHEN THE LAST GERMAN HOLDOUTS SURRENDERED ON **FEBRUARY 3, 1943,** THEY WERE BARELY RECOGNIZABLE AS THE STERLING PROFESSIONALS WHO'D ONCE TAKEN PARIS AND KIEV. THERE WERE ONLY **91,000** OF THEM LEFT, RAGGED AND STARVING...

LOOK, ALL OF YOU! **LOOK!**

THIS IS WHAT YOUR **BERLIN** WILL SOON LOOK LIKE!

IN THE NEXT FEW MONTHS, HALF OF THESE MEN WOULD DIE IN A TYPHUS EPIDEMIC. THE LAST OF THEM WOULD RETURN TO GERMANY IN **1955**--ONLY **6,000** STRONG.

WHEN THOSE FEW CIVILIAN SURVIVORS FINALLY CRAWLED FROM THE RUBBLE THAT HAD BEEN STALINGRAD, THEY FOUND THEIR CITY WAS A SMOKING RUIN, ITS SHATTERED STREETS CHOKED WITH SOME *200,000* CORPSES. BUT BESIDES THIS GRIM HARVEST, THEY DISCOVERED SOMETHING ELSE...

THEY NO LONGER REGARDED THOSE GERMANS WHOM THEY ONCE DREADED AND FEARED AS FORMIDABLE *SUPERMEN.*

THEY ALSO HAD BEGUN TO REALIZE THAT THE SOVIET UNION COULD WIN-- ALTHOUGH THE TIME REQUIRED AND THE PRICE TO BE PAID WERE YET UNDETERMINED.

WE HELD THE LINE AT *TWO CHURCHES* FOR A MONTH, BUT SAW NO FURTHER STRIFE. WE BURIED OUR DEAD, LUBED OUR TRACKS, CLEANED OUR GUNS, TUNED OUR ENGINES-- THEN RODE NORTH TO A RAILHEAD TO BE LOADED ONTO TRAINS AND SHIPPED WEST TO FOLLOW THE BATTLE.

COULD I PERHAPS RIDE UP TOP?

SURE!

THE COLONEL'S IN HIS *GAZ* WITH HIS DRIVER. BUT YOU'D BEST HANG ON--! MILLA AND I ARE IN A HURRY TO GET BACK TO *UKRAINE.*

I WAS JUST WATCHING COMMISSAR CHEKOV OVER THERE AT THE GRAVESITES...

IS THAT THE GRAVE OF A SOLDIER WHO WAS SOMEONE SPECIAL TO HIM?

HE WAS A PEASANT BOY FROM ULYANOVSK--STEPHAN WAS TEACHING HIM TO READ.

DURING THE ATTACK, THE BOY GOT SCARED AND TURNED TO RUN...

...SO STEPHAN SHOT HIM *DEAD.*

ANY FURTHER CONVERSATION BECAME IMPOSSIBLE AS OUR SQUEALING DIESEL ENGINES ROARED TO LIFE. THE COLONEL STOOD BESIDE HIS *GAZ* JEEP AND EYED HIS WARRIORS WITH PRIDE BEFORE HE WAVED HIS ARM AND SETTLED INTO HIS SEAT FOR A LONG MARCH.

OUR CLANKING, BANGING TANK TRACKS DISTURBED A HANDFUL OF SKINNY CHICKENS THAT HAD BEEN SEARCHING FOR ANY FORGOTTEN CRUMBS ON THE BARREN SOIL. THEY FLED AS WE GROUND DOWN THE BROWN-BLACK PATH, SLINGING NEW MUD INTO OLD. THE INFANTRYMEN RIDING ON THE BACKS OF THE *T-34*s GRABBED THE HANDRAILS TIGHTLY TO PREVENT BEING SLUNG OFF WHILE THEY ATTEMPTED TO GRAB SOME SMALL MEASURE OF ELUSIVE SLEEP.

I SLID DOWN INTO MY REGULAR SEAT BESIDE MILLA, AND AS SHE DROVE, I FOLDED MY ARMS UNDER MY SHEEPSKIN COAT AND TRIED TO STAVE OFF THE ICE-BOX COLD OF OUR TANK'S INTERIOR. I WEDGED MY SHOULDER AGAINST THE RADIO SET SO I COULD HALF-LISTEN TO THE SCRATCHY STATIC MUMBLING THAT PERHAPS COULD BE MY MASTER'S VOICE.

THE THROBBING OF THE ENGINE MUFFLED BY MY LEATHER HELMET WAS ENOUGH TO LULL ME TO SLEEP. I DRIFTED OFF INTO A SWEET SLUMBER, JUST AS IF I WERE A NAPPING CHILD ROCKED IN HER MOTHER'S ARMS.

FEBRUARY, 1943. THE SOVIET WINTER OFFENSIVE WAS STILL ROLLING. RUSSIAN FORCES WERE BEATING AGAINST THE GERMANS OF *ARMY GROUP A,* WHO WERE TRYING DESPERATELY TO HOLD ONTO THE CITY OF *ROSTOV-ON-DON.* IF ROSTOV FELL, ALL THE GERMAN FORCES IN THE CAUCASUS WOULD BE CUT OFF.

OUR BRIGADE HAD REJOINED OUR CORPS, AND WE WERE ADVANCING ACROSS THE DONETS RIVER TOWARD *KHARKOV...*

MANY AMONG US WERE EXCITED TO BE RETURNING TO *UKRAINE.*

THE COLONEL WAS ABOUT TO GIVE THE COMMAND FOR OUR BRIGADE TO ADVANCE WHEN HE NOTICED A GROUP OF JOURNALISTS FROM THE ARMY PAPER *KRASNAYA ZVEZDA* (RED STAR) STANDING NEARBY. ONE OF THEM WAS THE RENOWNED POET AND WRITER *VASILY GROSSMAN*--SO THE COLONEL DECIDED TO TRY SOMETHING A LITTLE MORE DRAMATIC.

INTO THE LAIR OF THE *FASCIST BEAST--!*

--ADVANCE!!

TEE HEE! HA HA! HA HA HA!! HEE HEE HEE! ⌐GIGGLE!⌐ ⌐SNORT⌐

VORONEZH AND KURSK WERE LIBERATED. IN MID-FEBRUARY, ROSTOV WAS TAKEN, BUT NOT BEFORE THE GERMANS HAD WITHDRAWN FROM THE CAUCASUS.

FOR THE MOST PART, THESE PRIZES WERE DEPOPULATED AND SHATTERED, THEIR POWER AND WATER SYSTEMS WRECKED.

IN EVERY CITY OR TOWN, SEARCHERS DISCOVERED SOME REMNANT OF THE POPULATION WHO STILL PERSEVERED.

COME OUT-- OR GET A GRENADE IN YOUR LAP--!

DON'T, PLEASE!

WE'RE COMING OUT--!

AT FIRST, THE SURVIVORS WERE FEARFUL--BUT EVEN THE POPULACE WHO'D BEEN PERSECUTED BY THE COMMUNISTS BECAME OVERWHELMED WITH JOY TO SEE THEIR SOLDIERS RETURN.

WE'RE YOUR PEOPLE!

AH! COME OUT INTO THE SUN, MOTHER! YOUR CITY IS SAFE!

IT WAS THESE CHILDREN OF THE WAR WHO RETAINED THE CLEAREST IMAGE OF THEIR SAVIORS: THE GRITTY SHUFFLE OF THEIR HEAVY BOOTS, AND THEIR DEEP VOICES, SPEAKING RUSSIAN WITHOUT FEAR...

YOU MEAN... THE GERMANS ARE--?

YES! ALL GONE!

WE CHASED THOSE DEVILS BACK TO HELL!

TO THEM, THESE RED ARMY SOLDIERS WERE HEROES OF A GREAT EPIC.

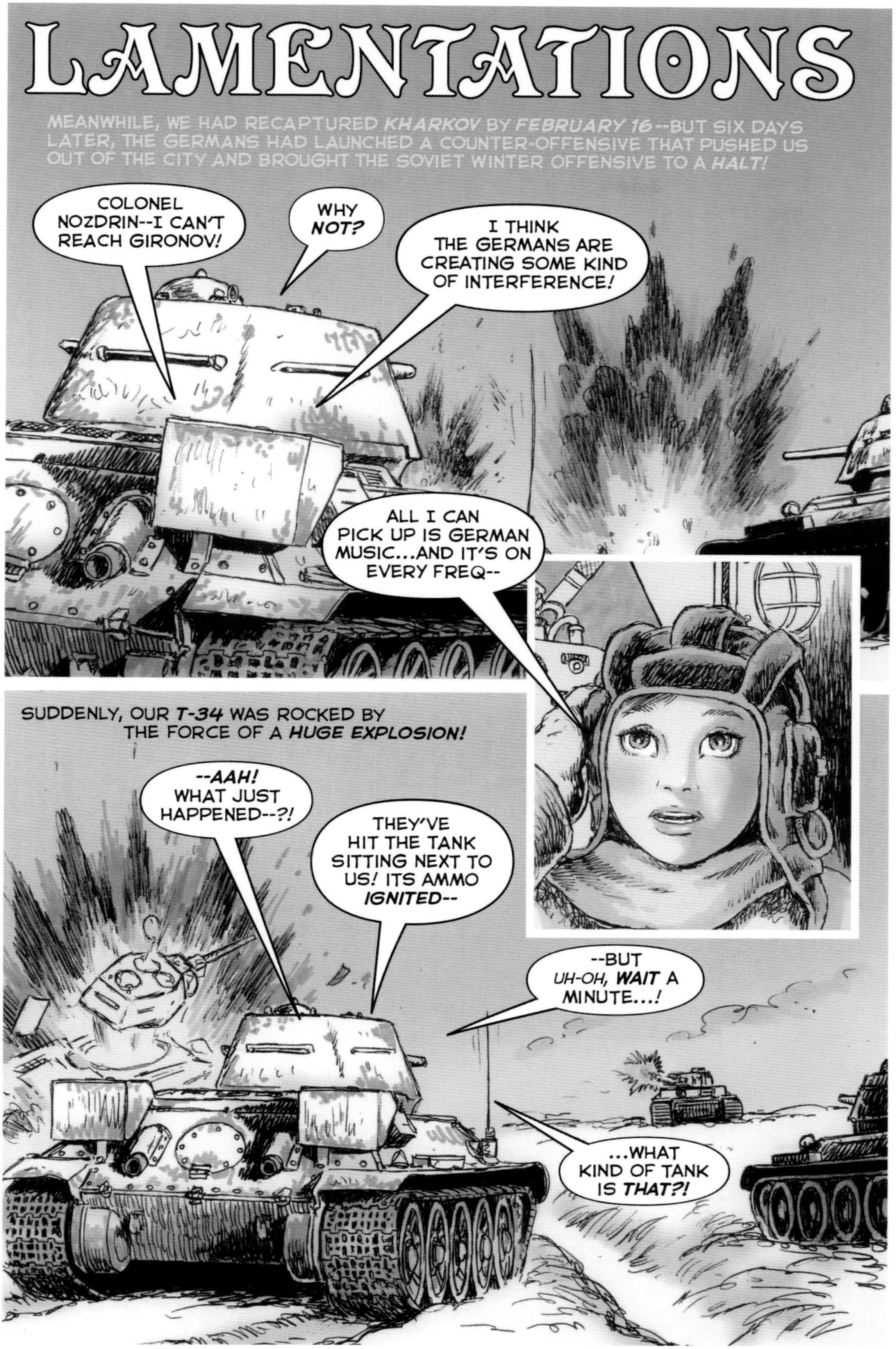
LAMENTATIONS
MEANWHILE, WE HAD RECAPTURED KHARKOV BY FEBRUARY 16--BUT SIX DAYS LATER, THE GERMANS HAD LAUNCHED A COUNTER-OFFENSIVE THAT PUSHED US OUT OF THE CITY AND BROUGHT THE SOVIET WINTER OFFENSIVE TO A HALT!
COLONEL NOZDRIN--I CAN'T REACH GIRONOV!
WHY NOT?
I THINK THE GERMANS ARE CREATING SOME KIND OF INTERFERENCE!
ALL I CAN PICK UP IS GERMAN MUSIC...AND IT'S ON EVERY FREQ--
SUDDENLY, OUR T-34 WAS ROCKED BY THE FORCE OF A HUGE EXPLOSION!
--AAH! WHAT JUST HAPPENED--?!
THEY'VE HIT THE TANK SITTING NEXT TO US! ITS AMMO IGNITED--
--BUT UH-OH, WAIT A MINUTE...!
...WHAT KIND OF TANK IS THAT?!

THE BIG GRAY-AND-WHITE BEAST SAT BOLDLY OUT IN THE OPEN, MAKING NO EFFORT TO HIDE ITS PRESENCE OR SEEK ADDITIONAL PROTECTION.

THIS WAS THE FIRST TIME OUR CREW HAD EVER SEEN A *TIGER TANK*, BUT IT ALSO MARKED ANOTHER FIRST FOR US--

--BEING *HIT* BY ONE!

THE SHELL STRUCK THE FRONT OF OUR LEFT TRACK, SHATTERING IT AND TAKING OUT ALL FIVE ROAD WHEELS--IN SHORT, EFFECTIVELY CRIPPLING OUR TANK'S MOVEMENT! THERE WOULD BE NO MORE ADVANCING FOR *US...*

BUT NOT SO FOR ANOTHER OF OUR *T-34*S. JUST THEN, IT ROARED BY ON OUR RIGHT SIDE--HEADING STRAIGHT AT THE *TIGER!*

IT WAS FIRING ON THE MOVE, ITS SHOTS GOING WILD...BUT THE BRAVERY OF OUR COMRADES-IN-ARMS BOUGHT US THE VALUABLE TIME THAT MILLA NEEDED. USING ONLY THE RIGHT TRACK...

...SHE MANAGED TO STEER US OVER A SHALLOW DITCH!

EVERYONE OUT THE FLOOR HATCH!

I HAD ALWAYS SAID MY SISTER COULD GET THE MOST OUT OF THE LEAST--BUT I'D HAD *NO IDEA.*

THE T-34 THAT HAD PASSED US WAS UNDER THE COMMAND OF YAKOV PETESKY, A YOUNG SERGEANT FROM NOVGOROD WHO'D ALWAYS HAD A REPUTATION FOR RECKLESSNESS. YAKOV'S NOBLE SACRIFICE GAVE US ENOUGH TIME TO GET OUT OF OUR TANK, SLIP DOWN INTO THE DITCH, AND MAKE A RUN FOR IT.

BUT MISHA BOVA'S YEAR-OLD LEG WOUND HADN'T PROPERLY HEALED, AND HE HAD A HARD TIME KEEPING UP. COLONEL NOZDRIN AND I HELPED HIM ALONG...

...BUT THE EVER-PRACTICAL MILLA BECAME IMPATIENT WITH OUR SLOW PACE.

HERE--TAKE THE *GUN*, KATUSHA. IF I HELP, WE CAN MOVE FASTER!

WE HAD SCARCELY GONE A HUNDRED YARDS-- BEFORE I FOUND A PERFECT USE FOR IT.

I WAS THANKFUL THE AWFUL NOISE OF THE BATTLE HELPED MASK ANY SOUND OF OUR APPROACH...

≥YAAGGH!≤

JUST BECAUSE I COULD *DO* IT *DIDN'T* MEAN THAT I WAS *USED* TO IT.

I KNELT TO COLLECT THE AMMO FROM THE BODIES--BUT WHEN I FOUND THAT THEY HAD NONE LEFT ON THEM, I LET OUT A CURSE THAT WAS WORTHY OF COLONEL NOZDRIN HIMSELF.

I STOOD THERE A MOMENT, SHOCKED AT MYSELF...AND THEN I RACED TO CATCH UP WITH THE OTHERS.

MEANWHILE, OUR BRIGADE HAD LOST MANY TANKS, AND THE INFANTRY HAD SUSTAINED HEAVY CASUALTIES. THEY'D BEEN FORCED BACK, BUT MANAGED TO WEAVE THEMSELVES INTO A STRONG LINE HELD BY A VETERAN RIFLE DIVISION FRESH FROM THE CONFLICT AT *STALINGRAD.* AS THE BATTLE RAGED, THEY TRIED TO ASSESS THE SITUATION...

GUCHKOV'S BATTALION LOST THE LEAST--HE STILL HAS ELEVEN TANKS...

DID ANYONE HAPPEN TO SEE WHAT BECAME OF *COLONEL NOZDRIN'S* TANK?

I SAW ONE OF THOSE *TIGERS* BLOW HIS TRACK OFF!

NO--! DID YOU SEE IF THEY BAILED OUT? AND DID THEY *ALL* GET AWAY?

I BELIEVE SO, CAPTAIN KOVCHENKO...

I SAW FOUR PEOPLE RUN DOWN THAT LONG DITCH THAT CUTS ACROSS THE PLAIN...

IT LOOKED LIKE IT WAS THE *COLONEL,* HIS GUNNER *BOVA*--

--AND BOTH OF THE *TYMOSHENKO* SISTERS.

WHICH DIRECTION DID THEY GO?

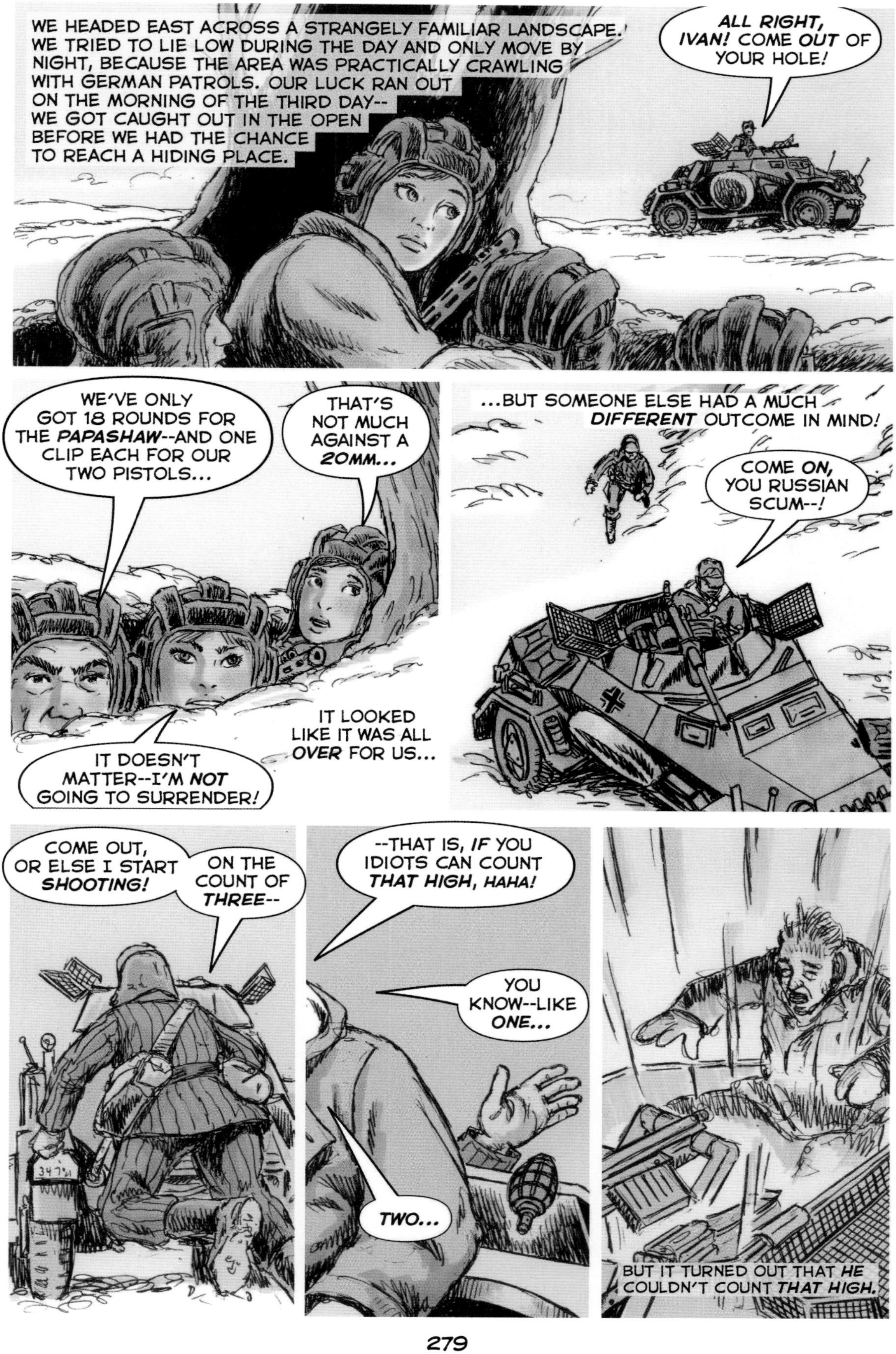

WE HEADED EAST ACROSS A STRANGELY FAMILIAR LANDSCAPE. WE TRIED TO LIE LOW DURING THE DAY AND ONLY MOVE BY NIGHT, BECAUSE THE AREA WAS PRACTICALLY CRAWLING WITH GERMAN PATROLS. OUR LUCK RAN OUT ON THE MORNING OF THE THIRD DAY-- WE GOT CAUGHT OUT IN THE OPEN BEFORE WE HAD THE CHANCE TO REACH A HIDING PLACE.
ALL RIGHT, IVAN! COME OUT OF YOUR HOLE!
WE'VE ONLY GOT 18 ROUNDS FOR THE PAPASHAW--AND ONE CLIP EACH FOR OUR TWO PISTOLS...
THAT'S NOT MUCH AGAINST A 20MM...
IT DOESN'T MATTER--I'M NOT GOING TO SURRENDER!
IT LOOKED LIKE IT WAS ALL OVER FOR US...
...BUT SOMEONE ELSE HAD A MUCH DIFFERENT OUTCOME IN MIND!
COME ON, YOU RUSSIAN SCUM--!
COME OUT, OR ELSE I START SHOOTING!
ON THE COUNT OF THREE--
--THAT IS, IF YOU IDIOTS CAN COUNT THAT HIGH, HAHA!
YOU KNOW--LIKE ONE...
TWO...
BUT IT TURNED OUT THAT HE COULDN'T COUNT THAT HIGH.

HAVE YOU TWO FORGOTTEN *EVERYTHING* I TAUGHT YOU?

≋GASP!≋

AAH!!

HAHAHA!

WE PASSED A BEAT-UP LITTLE TOWN ON OUR WAY HERE. WE'LL HOLE UP THERE UNTIL WE SEE WHICH WAY THE WIND IS BLOWING...

WHATEVER YOU SAY, UNCLE TARAS!

NOW WAIT A MINUTE! I SHOULD HAVE SOMETHING TO SAY ABOUT THIS--!

...AND WHO IN *HELL* ARE YOU...?

I AM *LIEUTENANT COLONEL RUSLAN NOZDRIN*--!

--AND THESE SOLDIERS ARE UNDER *MY* COMMAND!

WELL, HOW LUCKY FOR YOU. SINCE I'M TAKING THEM TO SAFETY, I'LL ALLOW YOU TO TAG ALONG...

...*OR* YOU CAN STAY *HERE.* IT HARDLY MATTERS TO ME.

I TOOK OVER HELPING MISHA SO THAT MILLA COULD WALK ALONG AHEAD OF US WITH UNCLE TARAS. I COULD HEAR THE COLONEL GRUMBLING UNDER HIS BREATH-- BUT HE DIDN'T KEEP IT UP FOR VERY LONG.

I'M AFRAID THAT THE CHURCH IS QUITE TORN UP, TOO. BUT SEE THAT *SMOKE* RISING UP OVER THERE...?

WHOEVER THEY ARE, I JUST HOPE THEY'RE FRIENDLIES...

UNCLE TARAS TOLD US ABOUT HIS TWO COMPANIONS...

"*ANATOLY* WAS IN PRISON FOR PETTY THIEVERY. THEY LET HIM OUT TO JOIN THE ARMY...

"*BATAAR* IS A KALMYK WHO'D BEEN FALSELY ARRESTED AS A COLLABORATOR. I TALKED THE *NKVD* INTO RELEASING HIM..."

I COULD JUST IMAGINE *HOW* UNCLE TARAS DID *THAT*...!

ALL WE FOUND IN THE CHURCH WAS AN OLD, SICK PRIEST AND A FEW OLD WOMEN WHO WERE TAKING CARE OF HIM.

BATAAR, WHY DON'T YOU FIND THE HIGHEST WINDOW AND KEEP AN EYE OUT...

UNCLE TARAS, THIS LADY COULD USE OUR HELP.

WE MUST HAVE A *FUNERAL* THIS AFTERNOON. IT IS THE THIRD DAY...

WE TRIED TO DIG THE GRAVE, BUT WE COULD NOT--THE GROUND IS FAR TOO *FROZEN!*

I THINK WE CAN DO THAT, SISTER-- WE'LL BE *HAPPY* TO HELP YOU GOOD LADIES OUT.

COLONEL NOZDRIN--SINCE YOU ARE NO DOUBT A PARTY MAN, AND AS SUCH ARE UNFAMILIAR WITH THE RITUALS OF THE ORTHODOX CHURCH...

...WHY DON'T YOU GO UPSTAIRS AND KEEP WATCH WITH OUR BUDDHIST FRIEND?

UNCLE TARAS LOOSENED UP THE FROZEN SOIL USING A COUPLE OF GRENADES...

THERE! NOW, LET'S DIG OUT THE LOOSE DIRT.

UNCLE TARAS--? I REALLY WISH THAT YOU WOULDN'T ANTAGONIZE COLONEL NOZDRIN...

HE TRULY *IS* A VERY GOOD COMMANDING OFFICER...

I *KNOW* THAT, KATUSHA-- I COULD IMMEDIATELY TELL HE WAS. I SIMPLY WANTED TO IMPRESS ON HIM THE GREAT *IMPORTANCE* OF TAKING THE BEST CARE OF YOU AND MILLA...

BUT *DON'T* FRET. I'LL BE SURE TO INCLUDE HIM IN ALL OUR IMPORTANT SURVIVAL DECISIONS...

...LIKE WHERE TO DIG A *LATRINE.*

THAT AFTERNOON, THEY BROUGHT OUT THE BODY OF THE MAN WHO WAS TO BE BURIED, APPARENTLY THE LAST MALE LEFT IN TOWN AFTER THE PRIEST. HE WAS VERY OLD-- IN HIS LONG LIFE, HE'D HAD TWO WIVES, ALONG WITH MANY CHILDREN AND GRANDCHILDREN...BUT HE HAD OUTLIVED MOST OF THEM.

COLONEL NOZDRIN, TOO, CAME OUT WITH US. BUT HE SEEMED A BIT UNCOMFORTABLE AND OUT OF PLACE, GIVEN THE CIRCUMSTANCES.

JUST AS THE PRIEST BEGAN TO SPEAK, AN OLD WOMAN WRAPPED IN A BLACK SHAWL BEGAN TO WAIL AND WRING HER HANDS. SHE FLUNG HERSELF ONTO THE SNOW, CRYING OUT LIKE ALL THE DEATHS OF THE WORLD WERE PUSHING HER DOWN.

I COULD TELL THAT THE COLONEL WAS UNNERVED BY HER DISPLAY...

...AND THEN THE OTHER WOMEN JOINED HER.

JUST WHAT IS *WRONG* WITH THESE WOMEN?

THEY ARE *MOURNING*, COLONEL.

UNCLE TARAS FIXED HIM WITH A GLARE AS SHARP AS A PAIR OF KNIVES.

THIS IS ABOUT *LOSS*. IT'S WHAT THEY DO WHEN THEY LOSE A HUSBAND OR SON OR DAUGHTER. THEY BELIEVE THIS MAN'S GOING TO A BETTER PLACE.

BUT THEY MOURN HIS DEPARTURE, AND FOR THE HARD LIFE HE'S LIVED.

THE PRIEST WENT ON, NOT AT ALL BOTHERED BY THE WOMEN'S UNEARTHLY POETRY OF LAMENT.

WITH THE SAINTS, LET THE SOUL OF THY SERVANT GO IN PEACE, O CHRIST, WHERE THERE IS NEITHER PAIN NOR SORROW NOR LAMENTATION, BUT ETERNAL LIFE...

WHEN I WAS LITTLE, I ONCE QUESTIONED MY MOTHER ABOUT THE SAME THING--WHY DO THESE WOMEN PROJECT SUCH AGONY AND PAIN?

SHE TOLD ME THAT WE CANNOT KNOW. WE UNDERSTAND NEITHER WHAT THESE WOMEN HAVE LIVED THROUGH, NOR THE HARDSHIPS THAT THEY HAVE EXPERIENCED.

SHE SAID THAT ONE DAY, WHEN I WAS OLDER, I WOULD UNDERSTAND. AND THEN SHE SAID--

--"NEVER JUDGE SOMEONE ELSE'S JOYS OR SORROWS."

SO, COLONEL--I IMAGINE ALL THAT WAS PROBABLY A NEW EXPERIENCE FOR YOU...

WELL, COMRADE TYMOSHENKO...

AS A COMMUNIST, I *AM*, OF COURSE, AN *ATHEIST*--

--BUT... NOT SO VERY *STRONGLY.*

THAT EVENING, SOME OF THE VILLAGE WOMEN CAME TO THE CHURCH WITH FOOD FOR US. IT WAS OBVIOUS THEY HAD BUT LITTLE...BUT WE WERE HUNGRY AND GRATEFUL.

UNCLE TARAS HAD NOTICED THE LOOKS MISHA BOVA GAVE MILLA.

I SEE THAT BOY HAS A THING FOR YOU...

WELL, TOO BAD FOR HIM--HE CAN *KEEP* IT.

HAS IT BEEN VERY BAD HERE UNDER THE GERMANS?

OH, YES! THEY WERE JUST LIKE THE *CHEKA* WERE, LONG AGO...!

...THEY KIDNAPPED OUR YOUNG ONES FOR SLAVE LABOR, OR KILLED WHOEVER THEY WISHED.

WE HAD HOPED THEY'D DISSOLVE THE *KOLKHOZES.* BUT THEY DECIDED TO USE THE SYSTEM FOR THEIR OWN BENEFIT--

BUT *WHY* WOULD YOU WANT THEM TO DISSOLVE THE *KOLKHOZES?* THAT IS A GREAT SYSTEM!

COLLECTIVE FARMS BROUGHT *SOCIALISM* TO THE COUNTRYSIDE!

EVERY EYE IN THE ROOM TURNED TO LOOK AT COLONEL NOZDRIN...

SO...I AM ASSUMING YOU'RE A CITY MAN, ARE YOU NOT...?

YES--FROM MOSCOW, AS WERE MY FATHER, AND HIS FATHER BEFORE HIM...

ALL RIGHT. LET ME POSE A QUESTION...

...LET'S SAY YOUR GRANDFATHER WORKS ALL HIS LIFE MAINTAINING A LITTLE SHOP TO SUPPORT HIS FAMILY. HE PASSES THE SHOP DOWN TO YOUR FATHER, AND THEN *HE* PASSES IT DOWN TO *YOU*... THEN THE SHOP BECOMES *YOUR* LIFE'S WORK, HOW YOU FEED YOUR WIFE AND CHILDREN.

THEN ONE DAY, SOME MEN COME TO SAY THAT YOU NO LONGER OWN YOUR SHOP, OR ANYTHING IN IT...

...THAT IT'S BEING TAKEN AWAY "FOR THE STATE," FOR THE "GOOD OF THE PEOPLE." AND IN THE PROCESS, ALL YOUR FOOD IS TAKEN FROM YOU--

--ALONG WITH EVERY VESTIGE OF YOUR ABILITY TO PROTECT AND FEED YOUR FAMILY.

BUT--COLLECTIVIZATION *WAS* FOR THE GOOD OF THE PEOPLE! IT WAS INSTITUTED TO DESTROY CAPITALISM AND ESTABLISH SOCIALISM THROUGHOUT THE COUNTRY...!

COLLECTIVIZATION WAS ALSO USEFUL IN GETTING RID OF THE WORST OFFENDERS OF THE CAPITALISTS, THE *KULAKS*--!

IT ENABLED US TO *ELIMINATE* THE *KULAKS* AS A SOCIAL CLASS...

BUT AT THAT, MILLA EXPLODED IN *RAGE!*

WHO WERE THE *KULAKS?* YOU HAVE NO IDEA--! THE "RICH PEASANTS," YOU CALL THEM...?!!

MY FAMILY WAS *NOT* RICH--YET MY OWN FATHER WAS *CONDEMNED* BY YOUR GLORIOUS *SOCIALIST STATE*--!

WHA--?

AND *WHY*--?

--BECAUSE HE WORKED HARD! HE MANAGED TO PUT A TIN ROOF ON OUR TINY HOUSE, WOODEN PLANKS OVER THE DIRT FLOOR...AND JUST BECAUSE WE HAD A LITTLE MORE THAN OTHERS HAD--

--MY FATHER WAS *ARRESTED,* THEN *SHOT*...AS A *"KULAK"!*

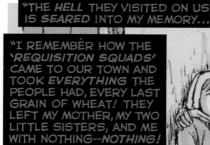

"THE *HELL* THEY VISITED ON US IS *SEARED* INTO MY MEMORY...

"I REMEMBER HOW THE *'REQUISITION SQUADS'* CAME TO OUR TOWN AND TOOK *EVERYTHING* THE PEOPLE HAD, EVERY LAST GRAIN OF WHEAT! THEY LEFT MY MOTHER, MY TWO LITTLE SISTERS, AND ME WITH NOTHING--*NOTHING!*

"THEY LEFT US TO STARVE...

"...AND STARVE, WE *DID.* MY BABY SISTER DIED FIRST. MY MOTHER HAD NO CHOICE--TO KEEP US ALIVE...SHE FED US OUR *SISTER'S FLESH.*

"BUT THAT DIDN'T LAST. MY OTHER SISTER DIED--AND MY MOTHER JUST LOST HER MIND FROM *DESPAIR.*

"SO...MAMA *HANGED HERSELF.*

"I WAS LEFT ALONE WITH HER. AND FOR DAYS, I SURVIVED, ONLY BY-- BY LIVING OFF--*OHH, GOD*--!!"

"I CAN'T RECALL LEAVING. ALL OF A SUDDEN, I WAS OUT WANDERING IN THE SNOW, FREEZING..."

"IF KATUSHA'S FATHER HADN'T FOUND ME DIGGING IN THE GARBAGE TO FIND FOOD, I SURELY WOULD HAVE *DIED*.

"OR EVEN *WORSE*--I WOULD HAVE GONE ON LIVING AS I HAD..."

MILLA STOPPED SPEAKING, AND SILENCE FELL UPON US LIKE A PALL. SHE STOOD THERE FOR A MOMENT, IN MUTE AGONY...

...THEN SHE TURNED AND WALKED OUT OF THE ROOM.

IT SEEMED LIKE AN ETERNITY PASSED BEFORE WE COULD SPEAK AGAIN.

KATUSHA...HAS MILLA EVER TOLD YOU OF THIS BEFORE--?

NO, NOT A WORD! I'VE *NEVER* HEARD ANY OF THIS BEFORE JUST NOW...!

UNCLE TARAS GOT UP AND FOLLOWED MILLA.

THAT NIGHT, I DIDN'T SLEEP WELL. I DON'T THINK ANY OF US DID.

I KNOW COLONEL NOZDRIN *DIDN'T*.

I HAD NO TROUBLE GETTING UP FOR THE LAST WATCH UPSTAIRS.

IT WAS ABOUT TWO HOURS FROM SUNRISE WHEN I SPOTTED THEM...

UH-OH!

UNCLE TARAS! GET UP HERE... QUICK!

EH--?

LIGHTS! COMING FROM THE WEST!

OKAY! GET EVERYBODY UP AND MOVING!

THERE IS A STONE BARN DOWN BY THE STREAM THAT WOULD BE A GOOD PLACE TO HIDE OUT...

BATAAR! YOU AND ANATOLY FIND A SAFE PLACE TO WATCH THEM, THEN COME REPORT TO ME.

WE DID OUR BEST AT ERASING ANY EVIDENCE THAT WE HAD BEEN IN THE CHURCH, THEN WE HEADED DOWN TO THE BARN. FROM THERE, WE WOULD DECIDE WHAT OUR OPTIONS WERE.

THERE'S ONE SMALL HALF-TRACK WITH FIVE MEN AND A MACHINE GUN, THEN TWO BIG HALF-TRACKS WITH SIX MEN EACH. WE ALSO SAW TWO *88MM* FIELD GUNS, AND WHAT LOOKS LIKE PLENTY OF AMMO.

WELL--THERE IS STILL ENOUGH DARK TO SLIP OFF TO THE EAST...

BUT--

"BUT" *WHAT,* COLONEL?

THOSE TWO 88'S ALONE COULD TAKE OUT *DOZENS* OF OUR TANKS IF THEY CAUGHT THEM CROSSING THE OPEN GROUND TO THE EAST...!

WE *MUST* DO SOMETHING TO DISABLE THEM!

UNCLE TARAS RELUCTANTLY AGREED WITH THE COLONEL TO RECONNOITER THE SITUATION BEFORE COMMITTING TO ANY ACTION. TO HIS CREDIT, THE COLONEL DIDN'T TRY "PULLING RANK" ON HIM--HE AGREED TO ABIDE BY TARAS' DECISION.

OKAY...

"THE GUNS ARE ON THE EDGE OF TOWN. THESE ARTILLERY MEN ARE PROBABLY NOT READY TO DEAL WITH A SMALL, SWIFT ATTACK.

"THE TWO MEN IN THE CHURCH WITH A PHONE LINE STRUNG TO THE GUNS ARE NO DOUBT ARTILLERY OBSERVERS.

"THREE MEN ON A MACHINE GUN WILL BE COVERING THE ARTILLERY'S RIGHT FLANK-- WE WILL HAVE TO TAKE THEM OUT FOR SURE.

"AT LEAST THERE'S A STRONG WIND TONIGHT. IT WILL HELP COVER UP OUR MOVEMENTS..."

BETWEEN US, WE HAVE FOUR PISTOLS, FOUR *PPSH'S*, AND SIX GRENADES. I'D RATHER WE HAD MORE. PERHAPS YOU GIRLS SHOULD STAY HERE--

NO! WE WILL DO OUR PART, AS WE ALWAYS HAVE!

I HAD EXPECTED NO LESS OF YOU. ALL RIGHT--

HERE'S HOW WE'RE GOING TO DO IT...

WITH THE UTMOST STEALTH, MISHA, MILLA, AND I CREPT UP TO A POSITION NEAR THE MACHINE-GUN NEST AND WAITED...

ON THE STREET BEHIND THE GERMAN GUNS, BATAAR AND ANATOLY TOOK POSITION TO DELIVER THE MOST FIRE ON THEM WHEN THE RIGHT TIME CAME...

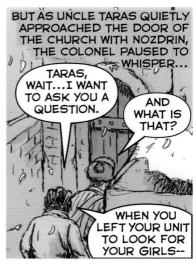

BUT AS UNCLE TARAS QUIETLY APPROACHED THE DOOR OF THE CHURCH WITH NOZDRIN, THE COLONEL PAUSED TO WHISPER...

TARAS, WAIT...I WANT TO ASK YOU A QUESTION.

AND WHAT IS THAT?

WHEN YOU LEFT YOUR UNIT TO LOOK FOR YOUR GIRLS--

--WHAT DID YOU TELL YOUR SUPERIORS?

EH--? I TOLD THEM *NOTHING*!

I FIGHT *FIRST* FOR THOSE THINGS THAT I CARE ABOUT-- STALIN AND THE MOTHERLAND ARE WAY ON DOWN THE LIST. BATAAR AND ANATOLY CAME ALONG BECAUSE THEY OWE *ME*---NOT THE STATE.

WELL...I CAN'T *APPROVE* OF WHAT YOU DID--

--BUT ALL THE SAME, I AM *GLAD* THAT YOU DID IT.

THEY SLIPPED IN AS QUIETLY AS THE CHURCH'S MICE. UNCLE TARAS SET ABOUT WORKING ON THE GERMAN OBSERVERS' PHONE CORD WITH HIS KNIFE--

--SLITTING IT HALFWAY THROUGH.

HELLO... *HELLO*--! *BLAST* IT!

THE COMMUNICATION WITH THE GUNS KEEPS BREAKING UP! CHECK THE LINE FOR A SHORT.

WELL, CHECK IT *AGAIN*!

BUT-- I *ALREADY* CHECKED IT!

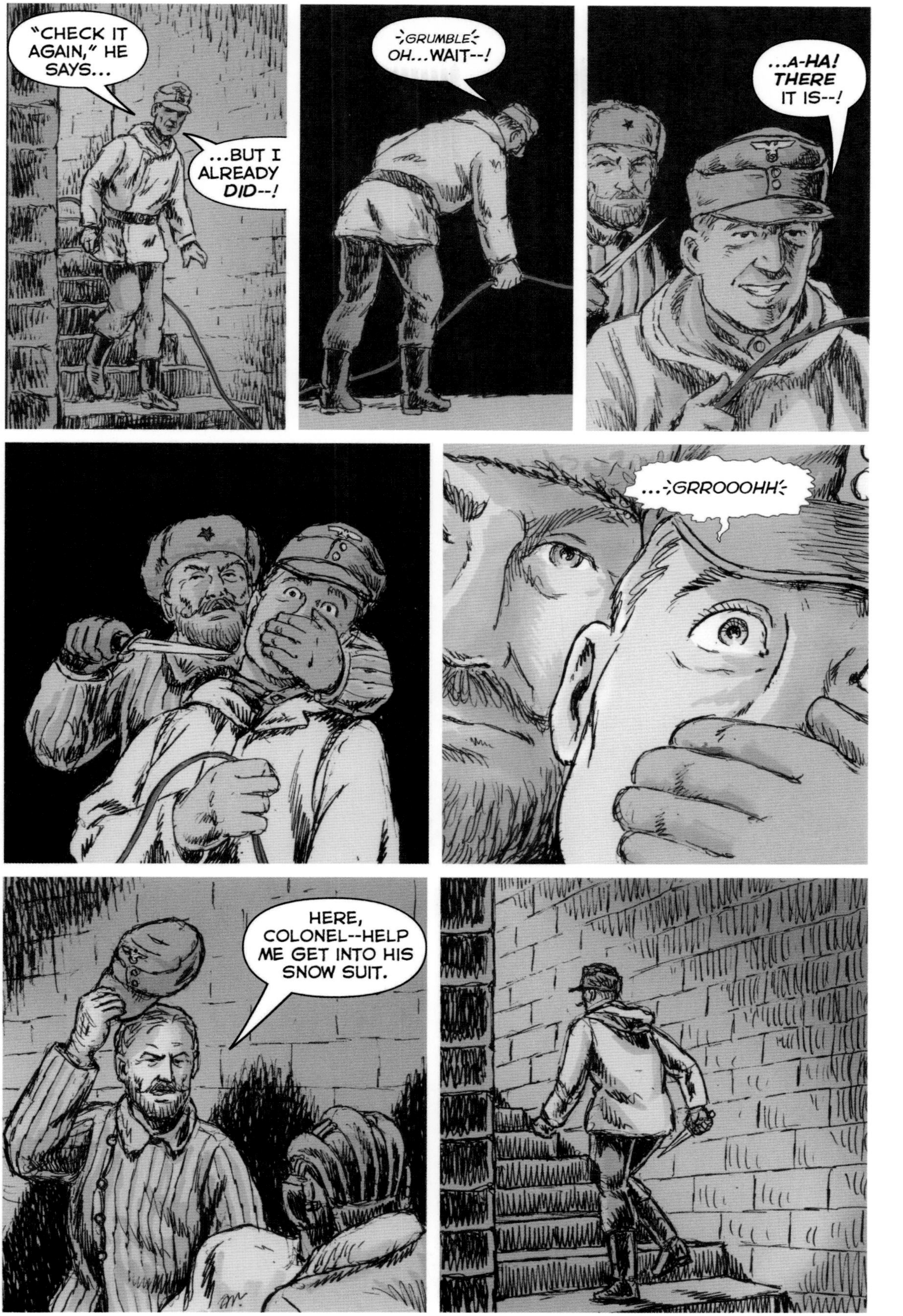
"CHECK IT AGAIN," HE SAYS...
...BUT I ALREADY DID--!
GRUMBLE OH...WAIT--!
...A-HA! THERE IT IS--!
...GRROOOHH
HERE, COLONEL--HELP ME GET INTO HIS SNOW SUIT.

DID YOU FIND THE PROBLEM?

IT'S ON *YOUR* END.

WHA--?

:AAAG--:

:--MMRF:

THE COLONEL DONNED THE OTHER SNOW SUIT, AND THEY LOADED UP THE GERMANS' EQUIPMENT...

THIS SHOULD EVEN THINGS UP, *EH?*

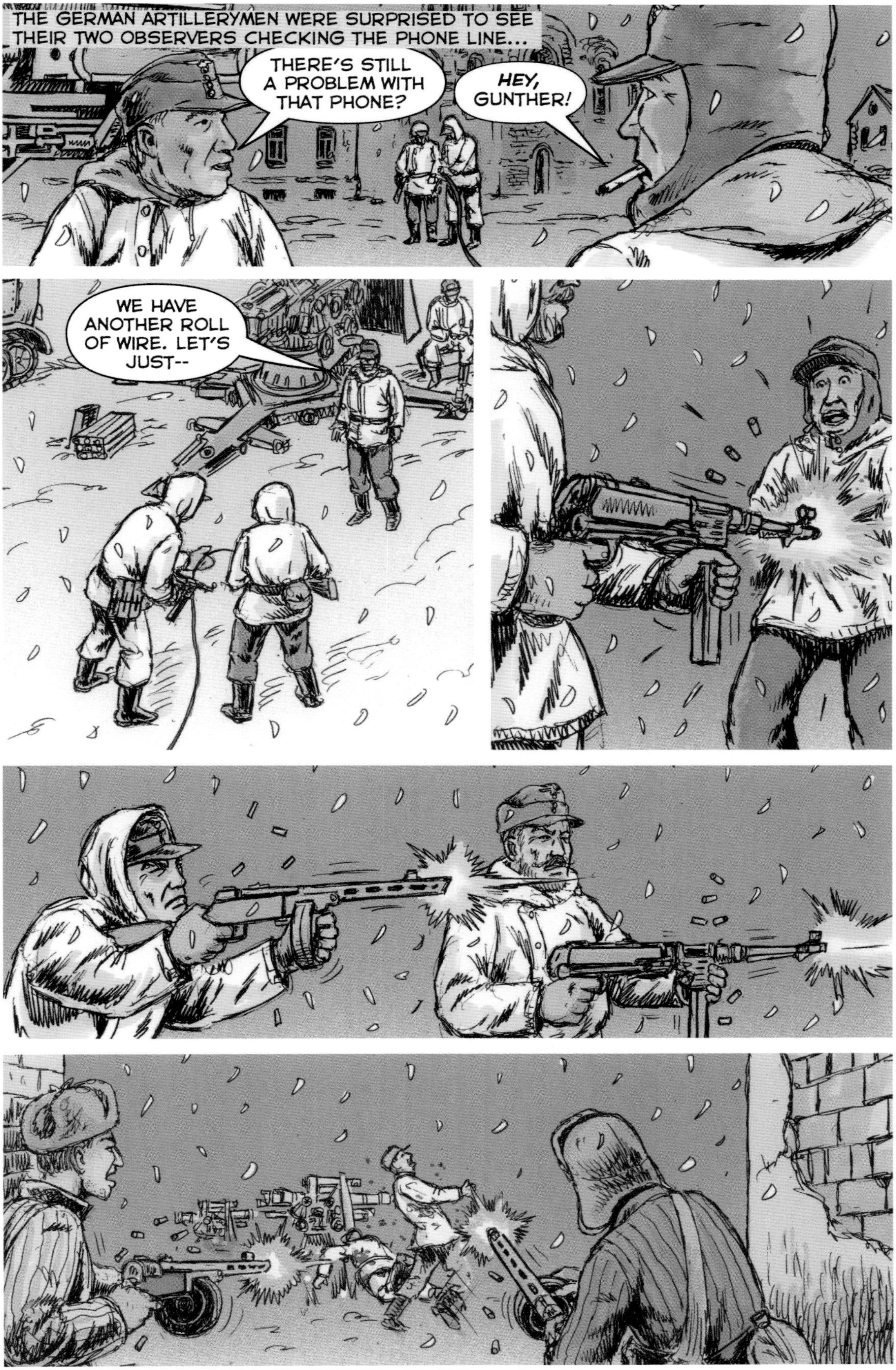
THE GERMAN ARTILLERYMEN WERE SURPRISED TO SEE THEIR TWO OBSERVERS CHECKING THE PHONE LINE...
THERE'S STILL A PROBLEM WITH THAT PHONE?
HEY, GUNTHER!
WE HAVE ANOTHER ROLL OF WIRE. LET'S JUST--

THAT'S OUR SIGNAL!

PULL AND THROW!

FIND ANY *WEAPONS* YOU CAN-- THEN LET'S GO HELP THE OTHERS!

MANY OF THE ARTILLERYMEN WERE CAUGHT OUT IN THE OPEN AND KILLED--BUT OTHERS GRABBED WEAPONS AND TOOK COVER AROUND THEIR GUNS!

LET'S MOVE TO THE LEFT TO TRY TO GET BEHIND 'EM!

SEEING UNCLE TARAS AND THE COLONEL MOVING GAVE TWO GERMANS THE IDEA TO TRY A SIMILAR MANEUVER...

...BUT THEY RAN RIGHT INTO *MILLA!*

IT HAS ALWAYS AMAZED ME HOW SO MANY PEOPLE LACK BOTH IMAGINATION AND COMMON SENSE. A PERFECT EXAMPLE WAS THE GERMAN WHO DECIDED TO CLIMB ATOP HIS OWN AMMO-LADEN HALF-TRACK IN ORDER TO THROW A GRENADE...!

297

THE GRENADE FELL IN AMONG THE BOXES OF *88MM* AMMO-- RIGHT BETWEEN TWO CANS OF GASOLINE AND A TELLER MINE!

UNCLE TARAS SAW IT LAND--BUT COLONEL NOZDRIN, DISTRACTED BY THE GUNFIRE, DIDN'T NOTICE IT!

OH, NO--!!

EH--?

--RUN!

WHAT DID YOU-- ⸗ERK!⸖

RUN!!

THE HORRIFIC BLAST EFFECTIVELY PUT AN END TO THE FIGHT AS THE GERMAN ARTILLERYMEN WERE PULVERIZED OR SHREDDED WHEREVER THEY STOOD...

...AND A HUGE *FIREBALL* LIT UP THE PRE-DAWN SKIES!

⌇GASP⌇ *GOD...!*

UNCLE TARAS AND COLONEL NOZDRIN LAY SPRAWLED ON THE GROUND, NICKED AND BLEEDING, THEIR GERMAN SNOW SUITS PRACTICALLY RIPPED FROM THEIR BODIES...

⌇UHHN...⌇

...BUT THEY WERE *ALIVE!*

THEN UNCLE TARAS FLASHED HIS BIG SMILE AT MILLA...

...AND MILLA SMILED BACK.

THEN UNCLE TARAS ROSE--BUT HIS MOTIONS WERE SHAKY, HIS LEGS WOBBLING UNDER HIM...

...HE DROPPED HIS WEAPON...

THE LOOK ON HIS FACE WAS ONE I HAD NEVER SEEN BEFORE--AND TO THIS DAY, ONE THAT I CANNOT FULLY UNDERSTAND.

THEN, BEFORE WE COULD REACH HIM--HE FELL BACK, ONTO THE HARD, COLD SNOW.

WE SAW HIS RIGHT SIDE WAS RIDDLED WITH SHRAPNEL AND SEEPING BLOOD. HE LET OUT A WEAK CHUCKLE...

HEH... CHEWED-- ⟩KOFF⟨ --BY WOLVES...

PANTING WITH OUR DESPERATION, WE ALL GATHERED CLOSE AROUND HIM AS WE TRIED TO DETERMINE WHAT TO DO...

...WHEN THERE WAS NOTHING AT ALL THAT WE *COULD* DO.

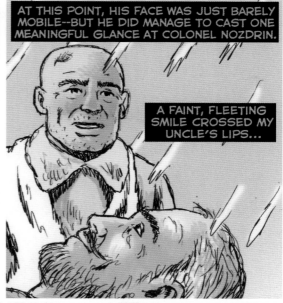

AT THIS POINT, HIS FACE WAS JUST BARELY MOBILE--BUT HE DID MANAGE TO CAST ONE MEANINGFUL GLANCE AT COLONEL NOZDRIN.

A FAINT, FLEETING SMILE CROSSED MY UNCLE'S LIPS...

MILLA HOVERED OVER HIM, NOT BLINKING, NOT BREATHING, AS HER WHOLE LIFE HUNG BY SOMEONE ELSE'S THREAD...

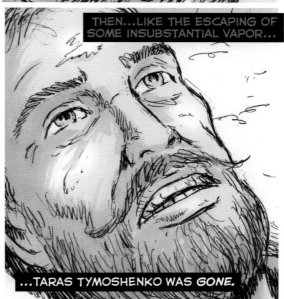

THEN...LIKE THE ESCAPING OF SOME INSUBSTANTIAL VAPOR...

...TARAS TYMOSHENKO WAS *GONE*.

AS WE REMAINED THERE IN STUNNED SILENCE, A THIN VEIL OF PINK WASHED OVER US FROM THE EASTERN SKY. THE ONLY SOUNDS WERE THE CRACKLING OF FIRES AND THE WHISPER OF THE FRIGID WIND.

THE OLD WOMEN OF THE VILLAGE, FORGOTTEN IN THE HEAT OF BATTLE, NOW CAME FORTH FROM THEIR HOMES.

THEN--MILLA ROCKED BACK ON HER HEELS, ROLLED HER EYES TO THE SKY, AND LET OUT A SHRILL CRY OF ANGUISH THAT CUT US ALL TO THE CORE.

HER LONG SHRIEKS BROKE ONLY LONG ENOUGH FOR HER TO SUCK IN MORE OF THE COLD AIR TO FUEL ANOTHER HEART-RENDING HOWL OF PAIN.

I FELT MY CHEST QUAKE AND FLUTTER UNCONTROLLABLY AS MY TEARS WETTED THE FRONT OF HIS *TELOGREIKA* JACKET.

THE WOMEN OF THE VILLAGE FELL TO THE GROUND BESIDE US, THEIR WAILING LAMENTS FILLING THE ICY AIR LIKE SOME ANCIENT, PRIMAL SONG.

THE MEN STOOD BY IN AWKWARD HELPLESSNESS, THEIR FACES TIGHTENING INTO MARBLE AS THEY GRIPPED HARD ON THEIR WEAPONS, THEIR TEETH BARING CURSES AND OATHS.

UNCLE TARAS HAD ALWAYS SO VALUED THE GUIDANCE OF HIS OLD MENTOR, *SEMEN KALASHNIKOV*...WAS HE LISTENING TO HIS VOICE NOW? I REMEMBERED THE WAY UNCLE TARAS HAD STOOD OVER SEMEN'S GRAVE IN KROVROT, LISTENING SO INTENTLY...WHEN ALL *I* COULD HEAR WAS THE WIND.

BUT ALL I KNEW WAS ANOTHER PRECIOUS HUMAN VOICE HAD BEEN FOREVER SILENCED...

...BUT NOT THE WIND...

SPRING, 1943. ALL ALONG THE 1,750-MILE FRONT, WHICH STRETCHED FROM LENINGRAD TO NOVOROSSIISK, THE SNOW WAS MELTING.

THE BUDS OF THIS SPRING OF 1943 WERE VERY MUCH LIKE THOSE OF THE SPRING OF 1942: HARD, DARK, AND RUSTY. THEY GAVE NO GREAT PROMISE OF A HARDY PLANTING SEASON WITH A BOUNTIFUL HARVEST TO COME.

BUT *MOTHER RUSSIA* YIELDED A HARVEST OF A KIND...

...A HARVEST OF CORRUPTION. A HARVEST TO FEED THE CROWS AND THE SCAVENGERS...

...AND ONLY *GOD* KNOWS WHAT ELSE.

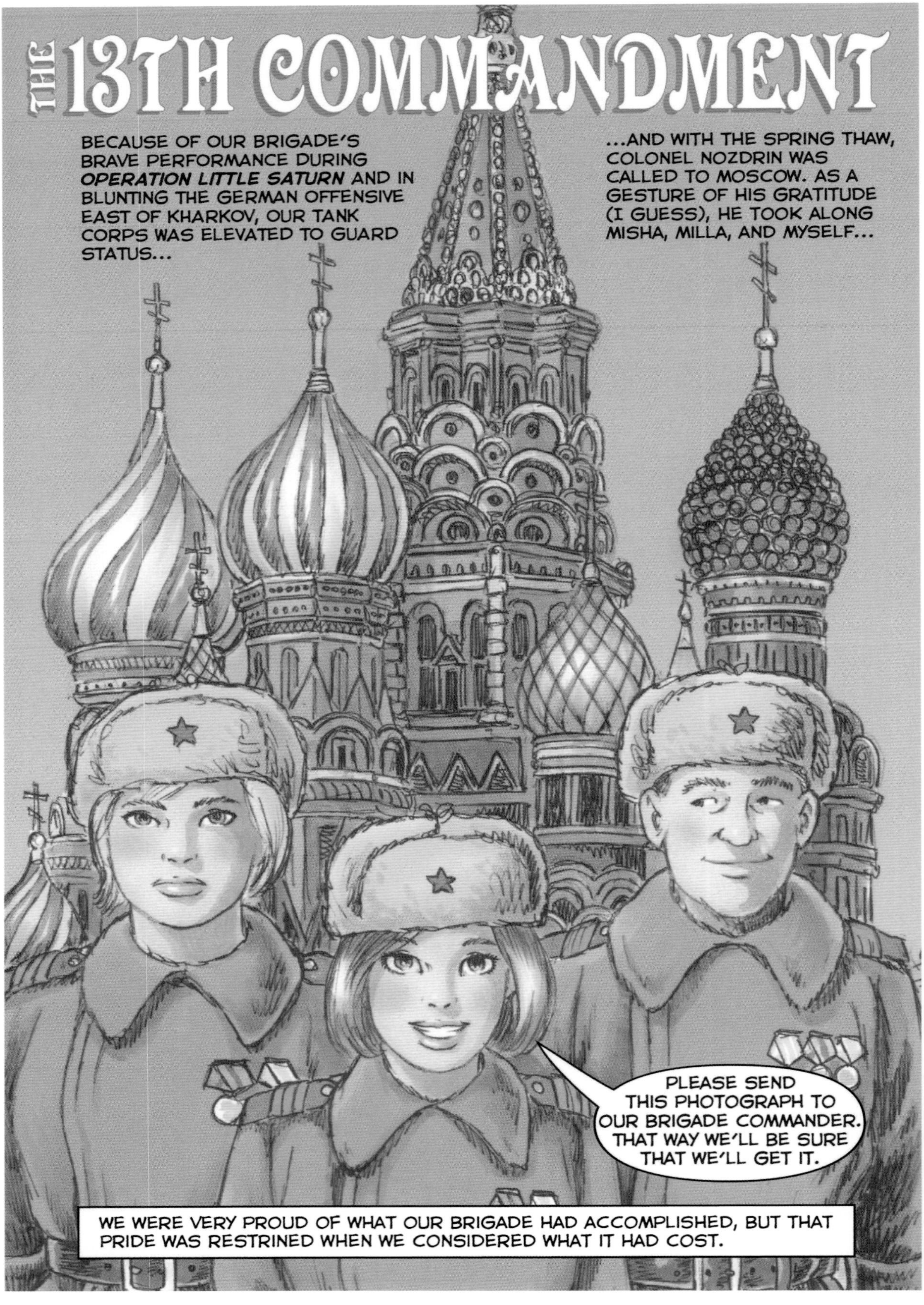
THE 13TH COMMANDMENT
BECAUSE OF OUR BRIGADE'S BRAVE PERFORMANCE DURING *OPERATION LITTLE SATURN* AND IN BLUNTING THE GERMAN OFFENSIVE EAST OF KHARKOV, OUR TANK CORPS WAS ELEVATED TO GUARD STATUS...
...AND WITH THE SPRING THAW, COLONEL NOZDRIN WAS CALLED TO MOSCOW. AS A GESTURE OF HIS GRATITUDE (I GUESS), HE TOOK ALONG MISHA, MILLA, AND MYSELF...
PLEASE SEND THIS PHOTOGRAPH TO OUR BRIGADE COMMANDER. THAT WAY WE'LL BE SURE THAT WE'LL GET IT.
WE WERE VERY PROUD OF WHAT OUR BRIGADE HAD ACCOMPLISHED, BUT THAT PRIDE WAS RESTRINED WHEN WE CONSIDERED WHAT IT HAD COST.

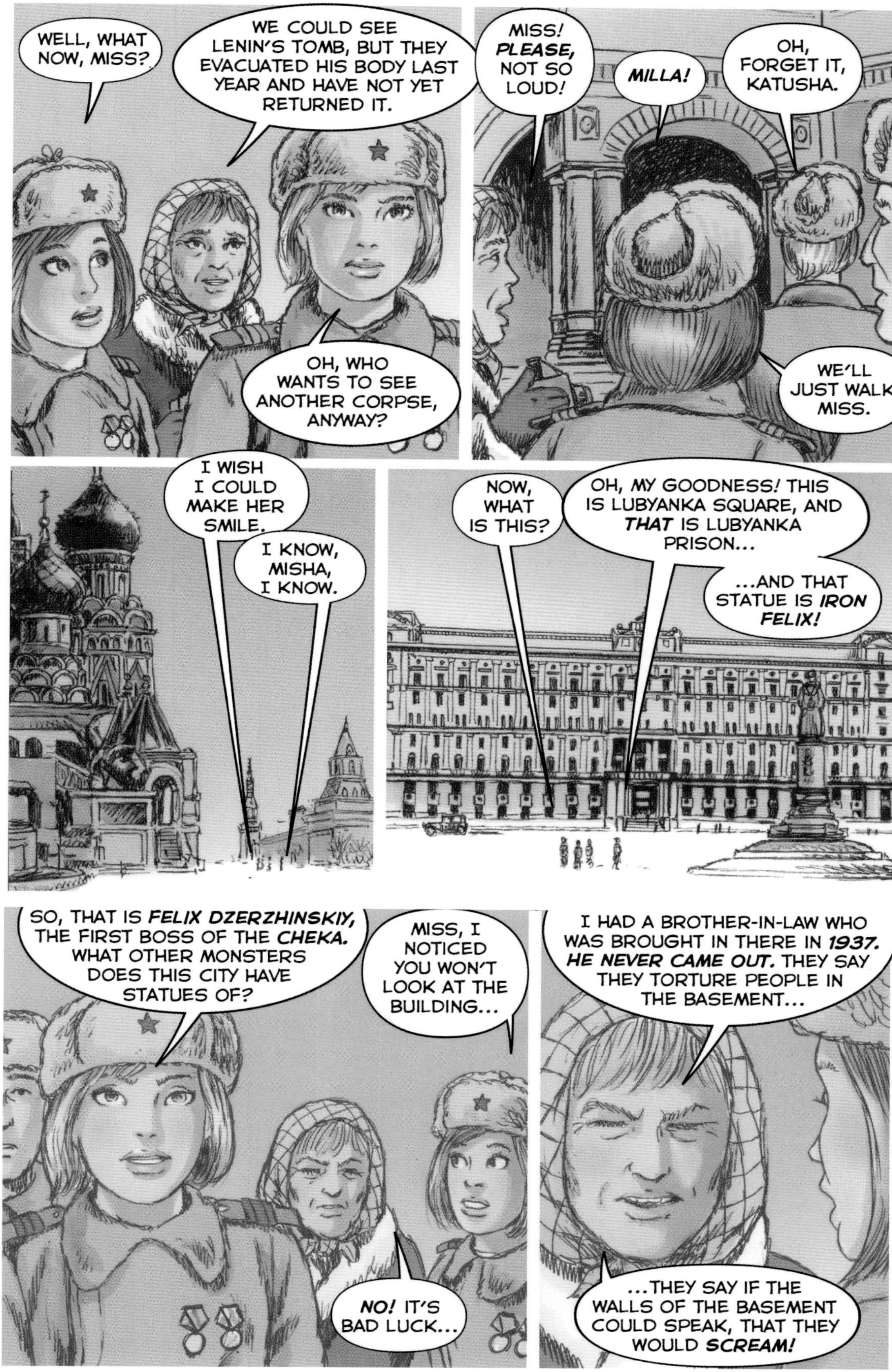
WELL, WHAT NOW, MISS?
WE COULD SEE LENIN'S TOMB, BUT THEY EVACUATED HIS BODY LAST YEAR AND HAVE NOT YET RETURNED IT.
OH, WHO WANTS TO SEE ANOTHER CORPSE, ANYWAY?
MISS! *PLEASE,* NOT SO LOUD!
MILLA!
OH, FORGET IT, KATUSHA.
WE'LL JUST WALK, MISS.
I WISH I COULD MAKE HER SMILE.
I KNOW, MISHA, I KNOW.
NOW, WHAT IS THIS?
OH, MY GOODNESS! THIS IS LUBYANKA SQUARE, AND *THAT* IS LUBYANKA PRISON...
...AND THAT STATUE IS *IRON FELIX!*
SO, THAT IS *FELIX DZERZHINSKIY,* THE FIRST BOSS OF THE *CHEKA.* WHAT OTHER MONSTERS DOES THIS CITY HAVE STATUES OF?
MISS, I NOTICED YOU WON'T LOOK AT THE BUILDING...
NO! IT'S BAD LUCK...
I HAD A BROTHER-IN-LAW WHO WAS BROUGHT IN THERE IN *1937. HE NEVER CAME OUT.* THEY SAY THEY TORTURE PEOPLE IN THE BASEMENT...
...THEY SAY IF THE WALLS OF THE BASEMENT COULD SPEAK, THAT THEY WOULD *SCREAM!*

COMRADES, AS WE ALL KNOW, THE SPRING THAW HAS BROUGHT ALMOST ALL OF OUR OPERATIONS TO A HALT. HOWEVER, OUR INTELLIGENCE UNITS HAVE BEEN WORKING OVERTIME, AND THEIR RESULTS HAVE BEEN EXTRAORDINARY.

CONSEQUENTLY, WE HAVE CONFIRMED THAT HITLER HAS ALREADY ORDERED A MAJOR NEW OFFENSIVE, TO BEGIN NOT BEFORE *MAY 1* OF THIS YEAR.

WE ALREADY KNOW WHERE THE ATTACK WILL OCCUR...

...HERE, AT THE *KURSK SALIENT.* THIS BULGE IN THE LINE EXTENDS ONE HUNDRED MILES INTO GERMAN-OCCUPIED TERRITORY. WE BELIEVE THE BLOW WILL FALL BELOW OREL IN THE NORTH AND ABOVE BELGOROD IN THE SOUTH.

THEIR INTENT IS TO CUT OFF OUR TROOPS IN THE SALIENT, THEN GO FOR MOSCOW.

AND WE MEAN TO LET THEM TAKE THEIR BEST SHOT. YES! WE WILL NOT INTERRUPT THEIR OFFENSIVE WITH ONE OF OUR OWN. WE SHALL LET THEM BREAK THEIR BACKS UPON OUR DEFENSES--THEN, WE WILL *ATTACK!*

HERE IS WHY THIS WILL WORK: FOLLOWING OUR VICTORY AT STALINGRAD, THE GERMAN TANK FORCES ARE IN TERRIBLE SHAPE. THEY HAVE LESS THAN 500 TANKS ON THE WHOLE FRONT. AS GOOD AS THEY MIGHT BE, THEIR NEW *TIGER TANKS* ARE FAR TOO EXPENSIVE AND TAKE THEM TOO LONG TO QUICKLY CONSTRUCT.

WE ESTIMATE THAT REBUILDING THESE FORCES COULD TAKE THEM UNTIL THE END OF JUNE.

RIGHT NOW, OUR FACTORIES IN THE URALS ARE TURNING OUT *ONE THOUSAND T-34S A MONTH!* SO...THE LONGER IT TAKES THE GERMANS TO PREPARE FOR THEIR OFFENSIVE--

--THE STRONGER *WE* BECOME!

THE SPRING SUN WAS ONLY AN ANTICIPATION AS OUR BRIGADE BEGAN ROLLING TOWARD THE FRONT.

WE LOADED UP OUR FEW REMAINING BATTERED TANKS ON FLATCARS, AND OFF WE WENT...

THIS IS MUCH BETTER THAN OUR TRIP TO THE URALS, *HUH*, MILLA?

WELL, AT LEAST OUR BATHROOM ISN'T AN OIL CAN...!

WE WERE ALL WELL RESTED, AND OUR SPIRITS WERE HIGH.

WE REACHED A POINT WHERE SEVERAL RAILROAD LINES CONVERGED. THERE, RIGHT BEHIND US, WAS A TRAINLOAD OF SHINY NEW GREEN *T-34S*--NOT EXACTLY SOMETHING THAT WOULD EXCITE A YOUNG GIRL, BUT I COULDN'T HAVE BEEN HAPPIER THAN A CHILD WHO'D BEEN GIVEN A NEW DOLL.

SOME OF THESE TANKS HAD NEW FEATURES, WHICH HAD BEEN CAST AT THE SVERDLOVSK PLANT. AND THE *TURRETS--?* WELL...

...THEY REMINDED US OF *COLONEL NOZDRIN.*

THERE WERE NEW RECRUITS, MALE AND FEMALE, WHO NEEDED PROPER TRAINING IN DRIVING AND FIGHTING IN THE TANKS.

EACH TANK *MUST* HAVE A TARPAULIN. THE FIRST TIME IT RAINS--

--YOU'LL FIND OUT *WHY.*

I'D TURNED 18 THAT APRIL AND FELT QUITE THE OLD HAND AS I EXPLAINED HOW TO PATCH AND PRUNE AND STROKE THESE STEEL CREATURES AND HOW TO CURL UP WITH THEM AT NIGHT TO SLEEP.

AND THERE WERE *KV TANKS* AND *76MM* AND *57MM ANTI-TANK GUNS*, AND *KATYUSHA ROCKETS*, AND MOUNTAINS OF AMMUNITION AND SUPPLIES...

...ALL OF IT STREAMING UP FROM SEAPORTS IN PERSIA, BROUGHT IN OR PULLED ALONG BY *STUDEBAKER* AND *GMC* TRUCKS FROM AMERICA.

AND THERE WAS *FOOD*--CANNED VEGETABLES, FRUIT, AND MEAT!

THIS *"SPAM"*...WHAT SORT OF FARM ANIMAL IS IT MADE FROM?

I DUNNO...BUT I'M NOT SURE JEWS CAN EAT IT.

OUR DAYS OF SHORTAGES WERE OVER.

THEN OUR INFANTRY BATTALIONS CAME BACK, FULL OF FRESH NEW FACES, FAMILIAR OLD HANDS--AND SPECIAL ACQUAINTANCES.

WELL, IF IT ISN'T LITTLE TYMOSHENKO! HOW WAS MOSCOW?

WELL, CAPTAIN...IT WAS NOT *KIEV*.

AH, TRULY...NOTHING COMPARES TO *HOME*, DOES IT? I AM SO GLAD TO SEE YOU WELL.

UH... COLONEL NOZDRIN TOLD ME OF WHAT HAPPENED--ABOUT YOUR UNCLE...

PLEASE ACCEPT MY CONDOLENCES.

WELL, WE ALL MUST BEAR OUR LOSSES.

I GUESS IT GIVES US ALL THE MORE REASON TO HATE THE GERMANS.

HIS COMMENT SURPRISED ME.

BUT MY RESPONSE SURPRISED ME *MORE*.

I THINK MILLA FEELS THAT WAY, BUT...NO, I *CANNOT*.

UNCLE TARAS WOULDN'T WANT ME TO THINK LIKE THAT.

HE WASN'T THAT KIND OF MAN.

CAPTAIN KOVCHENKO WAS SILENT FOR A MOMENT, AS IF BAFFLED BY WHAT I SAID.

AH. WELL--MY INFANTRY BATTALION IS BEING PULLED OUT OF THE BRIGADE AND PLACED IN ONE OF THE DEFENSIVE LINES...

...AND COLONEL NOZDRIN'S TANKS ARE ASSIGNED TO THE 5TH GUARD ARMY, IN A RESERVE POSITION.

WHERE WILL *THAT* BE?

LET'S SEE... IT'S A LITTLE TOWN BELOW KURSK...

ITS NAME IS *PROKHOROVKA*.

THE WORK IN PREPARING FOR THE GERMAN OFFENSIVE WENT ON WITHOUT A BREAK FOR WEEKS ON END. THOUSANDS OF CIVILIANS, MOSTLY WOMEN AND CHILDREN, WERE FREIGHTED IN TO DIG HUGE ANTI-TANK DITCHES.

MILLIONS OF MINES WERE LAID, AND THOUSANDS OF MILES OF BARBED WIRE STRUNG.

BUNKERS AND PILLBOXES WERE BUILT.

ANTI-TANK GUNS WERE PLACED IN THE FOUNDATIONS OF HOUSES, AND GUNNERY POSITIONS WERE CAMOUFLAGED TO RESEMBLE SOMETHING THAT THEY WERE *NOT.*

AND EVERY SOLDIER WAS SET TO WORK DIGGING TRENCHES FOR THEIR OWN POSITIONS...

REMEMBER WELL THE *13TH COMMANDMENT...*

"IT IS FAR BETTER TO DIG 10 METERS OF *TRENCH--* THAN A 3-METER *GRAVE.*"

MAY PASSED INTO JUNE, AND MORE AND MORE MEN FILED INTO THE LINE. ON EACH SIDE, MORE THAN A MILLION MEN HAD BEEN COMMITTED TO THE BATTLE.

WHEN THE GERMANS FINALLY GOT THE TANKS THAT HAD BEEN PROMISED FROM THEIR FACTORIES, THERE WOULD BE NEARLY 3,500 OF THEM.

THE SOVIETS HAD AROUND 6,000 TANKS.

IN THE SKIES ABOVE KURSK, ALMOST 5,000 AIRCRAFT WOULD BE ENGAGED.

ON *JULY 3*, IT WAS ANNOUNCED THAT WE SHOULD "EXPECT THE GERMAN ATTACK WITHIN THE NEXT THREE DAYS."

ON *JULY 4, 1943*, A SOVIET PATROL WENT OUT IN SEARCH OF SOME "TONGUES."

THEY RETURNED WITH A CAPTIVE SLOVENIAN PRIVATE TAKEN FROM A GERMAN ENGINEER PLATOON.

HE TOLD HIS INTERROGATORS THAT THE ATTACK WOULD BEGIN AT *0300* THE NEXT MORNING. THE WORD WAS QUICKLY PASSED THROUGH EVERY ECHELON OF THE SOVIET FORCES.

WITHIN THE GERMAN LINES, THE EARLY MORNING HOURS OF *JULY 5* WERE TENSE, BUT QUIET...

BUT RUSSIAN ARTILLERY GOT IN THE FIRST PUNCH--

--AS SOVIET AIRCRAFT HIT THE WAITING GERMAN ASSAULT FORCES!

THIS SHOCK THREW OFF THE GERMAN TIMETABLE SO THOROUGHLY THAT IT WASN'T UNTIL *0430* THAT THEY FINALLY OPENED UP THEIR ARTILLERY...

...BUT OPEN IT UP THEY DID!

THE GERMAN SHELLS FELL AMONG THE FRONTLINE TRENCHES, DRIVING THE RUSSIANS DEEP INTO THEIR WELL-PREPARED SHELTERS.

AT *0500*, BEFORE THE SMOKE COULD CLEAR, THE TANKS AND INFANTRY BEGAN THEIR ADVANCE, COMING ON IN BIG, POWERFUL WEDGES OF STEEL AND FIRE.

THE SOVIETS HAD SITUATED THEIR ANTI-TANK DITCHES AND MINEFIELDS TO CHANNEL THE ADVANCE INTO KILLING ZONES--

--WHERE THE UNPROTECTED INFANTRY COULD BE SAVAGELY MAULED.

THE PANZERS WERE TAKEN ON BY HEAVY ANTI-TANK MINES, ANTI-TANK GUNS...

...AND BY BRAVE MEN WIELDING MOLOTOV COCKTAILS.

ABOVE THE BATTLEFIELD OF KURSK, HUNDREDS OF PLANES FOUGHT FOR CONTROL OF THE SKIES...

THE GERMAN *JUNKERS 87 "STUKA"* HAD BECOME OBSOLETE AS A DIVE BOMBER...BUT ARMED WITH TWO *37MM ANTI-TANK GUNS--*

--IT MADE A PERFECT "TANK CRACKER."

WITH THIS COMBINED POWER, THE GERMANS WOULD CLOSE IN ON THE RUSSIAN TRENCHES...

DURING THE EARLY DAYS OF THIS BATTLE, WE HEARD THE THUNDER AND RUMBLING AND SAW THE CLOUDS OF DUST AND SMOKE. AT NIGHT, THE WESTERN SKIES GLOWED LIKE THE RISING OF AN UNEARTHLY SUN.

WHAT'S THE NEWS, COLONEL?

ON THE NORTHERN SIDE, THE GERMANS HAVE DRIVEN FOUR TO FIVE MILES INTO OUR LINES, BUT ARE STILL PRETTY MUCH CONTAINED...

WELL, THAT'S GOOD...

HERE ON THE SOUTH SIDE, THEY HAVE NOT ADVANCED AS FAR... BUT THEIR PRESSURE SEEMS TO BE MORE CONSISTENT--AND MORE VIOLENT.

WE HAVE KILLED A LOT OF GERMANS-- BUT THEY HAVE KILLED MANY OF US, TOO.

DAY AFTER DAY, THE GERMANS HAMMERED AWAY AT THE SEEMINGLY UNENDING LAYERS OF RUSSIAN TRENCHES, LEAVING IN THEIR WAKE THE SCORCHED HULKS OF THEIR TANKS AND THOUSANDS OF THEIR DEAD.

SOME OF THEIR NEW TANKS THAT WERE SPECIALLY DESIGNED FOR THIS OFFENSIVE PROVED TO BE LESS THAN SATISFACTORY. THE NEW PANTHER COPIED MANY OF THE FEATURES OF THE SOVIET *T-34*, AND EVENTUALLY WOULD BECOME A GREAT FIGHTING VEHICLE.

HOWEVER...

...THE FIRST OUT OF THE FACTORY HAD SO MANY MECHANICAL PROBLEMS THEY BROKE DOWN BEFORE REACHING THE FRONT LINES.

BUT THE REAL JOKE WAS THE *FERDINAND.*

DESPITE ITS POWERFUL *88MM* CANNON, IT HAD NO MACHINE GUNS TO PROTECT IT FROM AN INFANTRY ASSAULT.

A SINGLE BRAVE RED ARMY SOLDIER COULD EASILY BLOW OFF ONE OF ITS TRACKS WITH A GRENADE AND THEN FINISH IT OFF WITH A MOLOTOV COCKTAIL.

BUT THE *TIGER TANK* RULED THE BATTLEFIELD.

AT OVER 500 METERS DISTANCE, NO RUSSIAN TANK COULD STAND UP AGAINST THE GERMAN TIGER--

--AND GETTING THAT CLOSE ON THE OPEN FIELDS AROUND KURSK WAS A VERY DIFFICULT MANEUVER.

ON *JULY 10*, THE GERMANS REACHED THE *PYSOL RIVER*, THE LAST NATURAL BARRIER TO THEIR LINKUP WITH THE GERMAN FORCES COMING DOWN FROM THE NORTH.

THEY KNEW THE LARGE SOVIET ARMORED FORCES TO THEIR EAST MIGHT POSSIBLY STRIKE THEIR FLANKS, CUTTING OFF THEIR SUPPLIES, COMMAND, AND CONTROL...

RATHER THAN CONTINUE ALONG THEIR AXIS OF ADVANCE, THEY DECIDED INSTEAD TO CHANGE DIRECTION...

...SO THE *2ND SS PANZER CORPS* WHEELED TO THE RIGHT--AND HEADED TOWARD *PROKHOROVKA.*

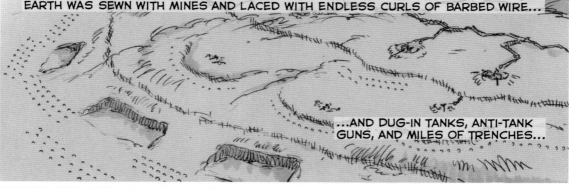

IN THEIR WAY LAY A LOW, FLAT HILL, GUARDED BY SEVERAL DEEP TANK DITCHES. THE EARTH WAS SEWN WITH MINES AND LACED WITH ENDLESS CURLS OF BARBED WIRE...

...AND DUG-IN TANKS, ANTI-TANK GUNS, AND MILES OF TRENCHES...

...TRENCHES THAT WERE MANNED BY *CAPTAIN KOLYA KOVCHENKO'S* INFANTRY BATTALION.

OUR WAITING IS JUST ABOUT OVER, BOYS. THE DEVIL HAS FINALLY ARRIVED.

317

COMING TO MAKE THEIR ACQUAINTANCE WAS A STEEL WEDGE--TIPPED WITH *TIGER TANKS!*

BEHIND THE TIGERS WERE OTHER GERMAN ARMORED VEHICLES--*PANZER IIIs* AND *IVs*, *STURMGESCHÜTZ IIIs*, AND *SCHÜTZENPANZERWAGEN 251* HALF-TRACKS--AND, OF COURSE, HORDES OF *WAFFEN SS INFANTRYMEN* CLAD IN CAMOUFLAGED SMOCKS!

RUSSIAN MORTAR CREWS WENT RIGHT TO WORK, SEPARATING THE INFANTRY FROM THE PANZERS...

...WITH *DEADLY EFFECT!*

DUG-IN *T-34s* OPENED FIRE ON THE LEAD TANKS...

...ONLY TO HAVE THEIR ROUNDS BOUNCE OFF THE TIGER'S TOUGH SKIN!

NOT WANTING TO WASTE THEIR EFFORTS, THEY WENT AFTER SOFTER TARGETS...

...WITH SOME SUCCESS--

--BUT IT WASN'T LONG BEFORE THE *88s* ENTERED THE DUEL...!

BUT THE BETTER-HIDDEN GUNS HAD FAR GREATER LUCK...

HA! AT UNDER 300 YARDS, THOSE TIGERS BURN AS WELL AS *ANY* TANK!

SEEING THIS SUCCESS, OTHER SOVIET TROOPS SOUGHT THEIR FAIR SHARE OF THE FUN AND GLORY...

THE GERMANS CHANGED THEIR APPROACH IN AN ATTEMPT TO AVOID THE HIDDEN ANTI-TANK GUN...

...ONLY TO BE HINDERED BY ANOTHER!

GERMAN INFANTRY POURED OUT OF THEIR HALF-TRACKS...

...CLOSELY COVERED BY THEIR STEEL CHARIOTS.

THE GERMAN ADVANCE WAS VERY COSTLY...

...BUT THEY WERE HAVING SUCCESS.

ONE TANK HELD BACK FROM THE POINT OF THE FRAY--A TIGER WITH A RED BANNER AND THREE ANTENNAS.

AN UNIDENTIFIED RUSSIAN SOLDIER CAME UP OUT OF A TRENCH BEARING TWO LIT MOLOTOV COCKTAILS...

A GERMAN SERGEANT, PROFESSIONAL AND QUICK TO REACT, GAVE HIM A QUICK BURST OF HIS *MP40*...

WHAAA--!?

--AAAA!!!
⸮WAAAGGHH!⸮

⸮RRRRAAAAAWWWW WAAAGGHHH!!⸮

⸮RAAAWGGH!!⸮

⸮YAAARRGHH!!⸮

⸮AAAIIIIEEE!!⸮

WITH THAT, AN EARTH-SHAKING, BARELY HUMAN ROAR EMITED FROM THE RUSSIAN TRENCHES...

...AND WITH IT, MANY OF THE INFANTRY ON THE HILL SPILLED OUT ONTO THE INVADERS...

...OH, LARYISSA... OH, MY GIRLS...I COME TO YOU NOW!

WHEN A MAN IS SHOULDER TO SHOULDER WITH HIS FRIENDS, HE CAN FACE ODDS THAT WOULD NORMALLY SEEM INSURMOUNTABLE.

HE FEEDS ON THE STRENGTH OF HIS FRIENDS--AND THEY, IN TURN, FEED UPON HIS...

BUT--WHEN ENGULFED BY SMOKE AND DUST AND DARKNESS, IT IS HARD TO TELL WHO IS FRIEND AND WHO IS FOE...

THE ENEMY THAT WAS WEAK AND CONFUSED AND ON THE ROPES SUDDENLY BECOMES STRONG AND PURPOSEFUL AND BELLIGERENT...

...AND THE SINGLE, SOLITARY SOLDIER, WHO BUT A MOMENT BEFORE WAS PART OF THE BRAVE, MOTIVATED "WE"--

--BECOMES THE TIMID, FRAIL "I." *

* HOMAGE TO VASILY GROSSMAN'S *LIFE AND FATE.*

THE COUNTERATTACK, WHICH HAD BEEN VERY COSTLY FOR THE DEFENDERS, FELL APART. BUT IT DID MANAGE TO DEMORALIZE THE GERMANS ENOUGH TO DISSIPATE THEIR STRENGTH. THE ASSAULT ON THE HILL WAS HALTED FOR THE NIGHT.

BY NOW, THE NIGHT OF *JULY 10-11,* THE FULL STRENGTH OF THE *FIFTH GUARD TANK ARMY* WAS MOVING FORWARD--AND WE WERE MOVING WITH IT.

COLONEL NOZDRIN, WE HAVE A MESSAGE FROM THE CORPS COMMANDER...

GENERAL ROTMISTROV IS SETTING UP A FORWARD HEADQUARTERS UP AHEAD, AND HE REQUESTS YOUR PRESENCE.

WE PULLED PAST THE HEAVY MORTAR UNIT TO FIND THE HEADQUARTERS IN AN OLD BARN NEXT TO A WINDMILL.

JUST HANG ON HERE--WE HAVE COMMUNICATIONS SET UP INSIDE, BUT KEEP READY IN CASE I NEED YOU.

WELL, I GUESS THAT LEAVES US OUT OF IT...!

YOU WON'T HEAR *ME* COMPLAIN ABOUT THAT.

WELL, I WILL!

I'M GETTING TIRED OF BEING LITTLE MORE THAN THE BOSS' CHAUFFEUR!

THAT NIGHT, ATOP WHAT I ALWAYS CALLED "KOLYA'S HILL," OUR MEN DID THEIR BEST TO EVACUATE THE WOUNDED AND PROVIDE WHAT COMFORT THEY COULD FOR THE DYING...

CAPTAIN KOVCHENKO!

MANY MEN ARE APPROACHING FROM OUR REAR!

IT'S RUSSIAN *PARATROOPS!*

AH! ARE WE EVER GLAD TO SEE YOU, COMRADE!

HOW MANY OF YOUR MEN STILL REMAIN, CAPTAIN?

LESS THAN 300--TODAY'S ATTACK WAS COSTLY...

...AND TOMORROW WILL BE A LOT *WORSE.*

CONTINUE TO HOLD THE CREST. I WILL PLACE MY THREE COMPANIES AROUND YOU.

DOBRY VYECHER, SERGEANT! WOULD YOU PERHAPS LIKE A LITTLE INFANTRY SUPPORT FOR YOUR GUN?

WHY, THANK YOU, LIEUTENANT! IF YOU DON'T MIND, COULD YOU GET YOUR BOYS TO SWEEP ME A CLEAN PATH OUT FRONT?

I NOTICED BEFORE THE SUN SET THAT OUR VIEW WAS BLOCKED BY FASCIST TRASH...!

AT THE CRACK OF DAWN ON *JULY 11*, GERMAN PLANES BEGAN TO RAIN HELL DOWN UPON THE RUSSIAN LINES.

ON THE HILL BELOW, KOLYA, HIS MEN, AND THE NEWLY ARRIVED PARACHUTISTS HUGGED THE BOTTOM OF THEIR TRENCHES AND FOXHOLES...

...WHILE THE BOMBS RATTLED THEM AROUND LIKE DICE IN A TIN CUP.

FROM HIS POSITION ATOP THE CREST OF THE HILL, KOLYA KOVCHENKO COULD SEE THE BATTLE BEGINNING TO TAKE FORM IN THE VALLEY BELOW THEM...

TWENTY-ONE HEAVY *KV TANKS* ROLLED FORWARD TO MEET THE ENEMY. THESE TANKS, ONCE REGARDED AS THE BEST THE RED ARMY HAD, WERE NOW OBSOLETE.

THIS FIGHT WAS TO BE THEIR SWAN SONG.

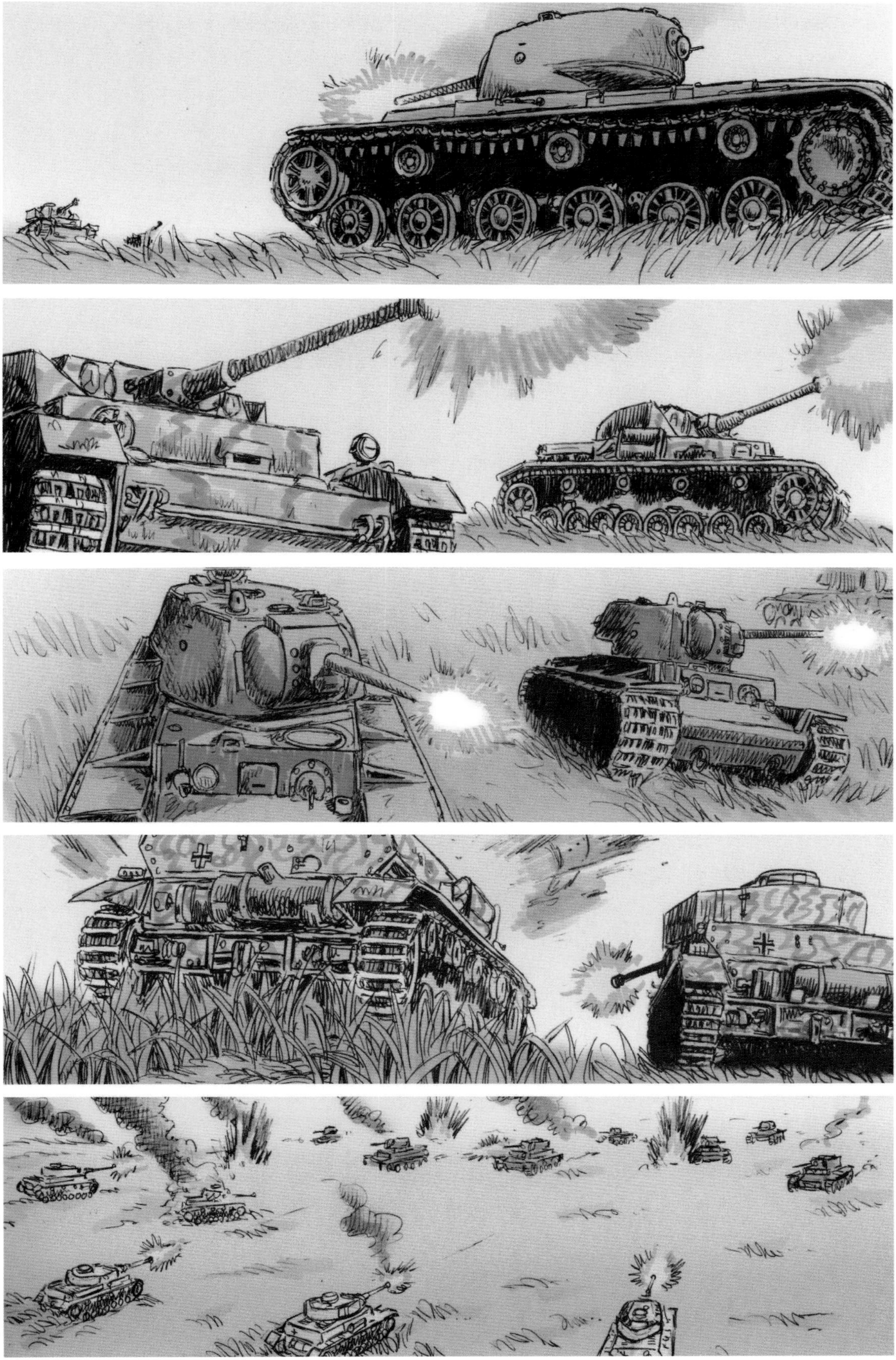

NOW, SUFFICIENTLY REINFORCED, THE GERMAN TANKS ROLLED UP THE HILL...

CAN'T YOU KEEP THAT AMMO COMING ANY FASTER?

I'M SORRY, SERGEANT.

I'M AFRAID THAT I'M THE ONLY LOADER LEFT--

HUH--?! WHAT HAPPENED TO GRISHIN?

OH... WAS THAT HIS NAME?

HE WAS HIT JUST A MOMENT AGO...

HE LOOKED KIND OF OLD. HAD YOU KNOWN HIM LONG--?

YES. ALL MY LIFE...

...HE WAS MY FATHER...

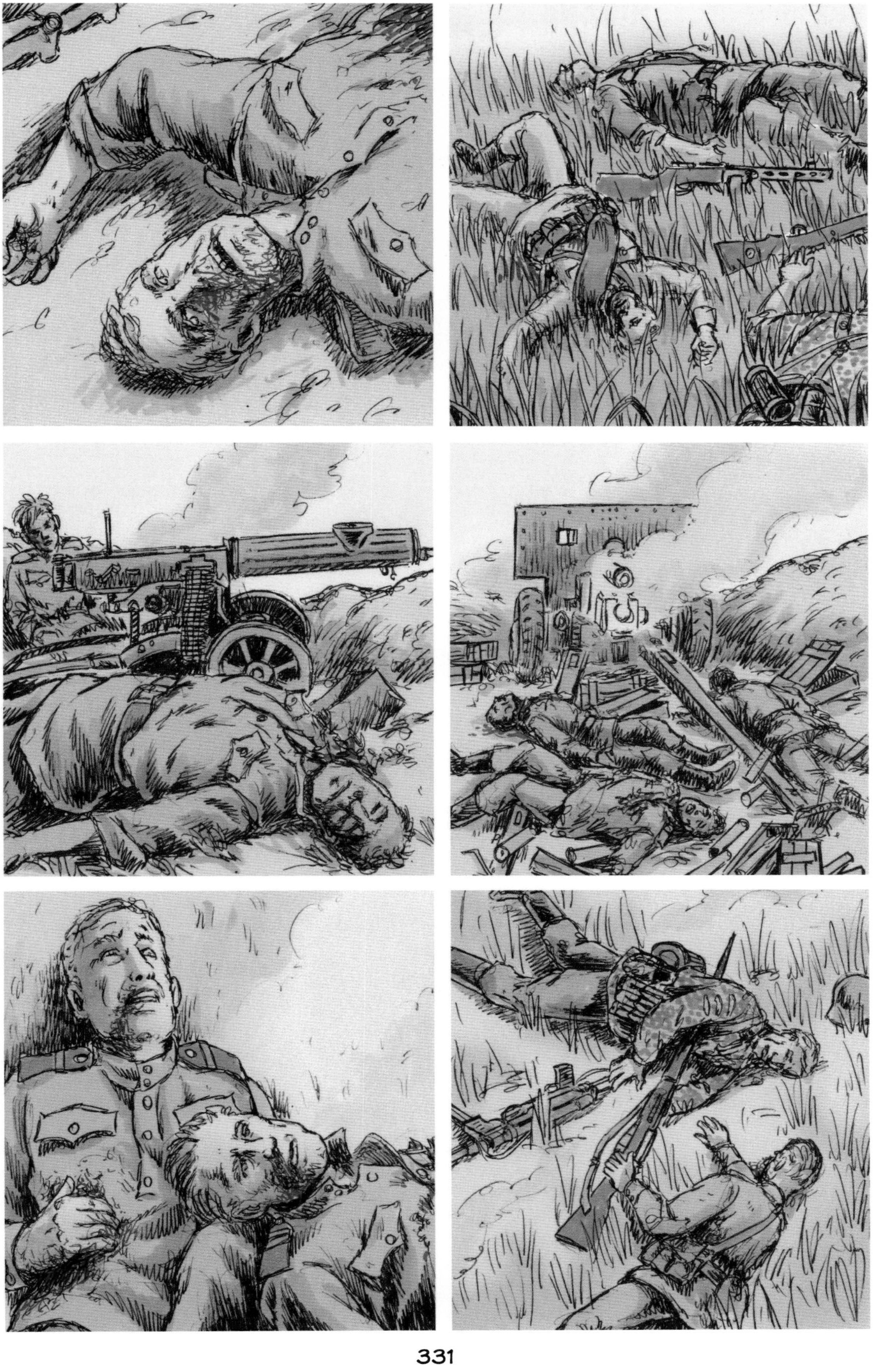

BUT WE WERE STILL WAITING BACK AT LIEUTENANT GENERAL ROTMISTROV'S HEADQUARTERS. FINALLY, *MARSHAL A. M. VASILEVSKY* ARRIVED WITH STRICT ORDERS FROM STALIN HIMSELF. THE DAY WAS WANING BEFORE COLONEL NOZDRIN RETURNED.

I AM TO KEEP MY BRIGADE IN RESERVE UNTIL THE LAST MINUTE...

...SO WE WILL REMAIN HERE UNTIL FURTHER NOTICE.

SO--ARE WE GOING TO *MISS* THIS FIGHT, COLONEL?

DON'T BE RIDICULOUS, MILLA! WE MUST SIMPLY BIDE OUR TIME, FOR STRATEGY'S SAKE.

FROM UP HERE, WE'LL BE ABLE TO SPOT THE GERMANS WITH THE NAKED EYE...

THE SETTING SUN WAS A GREAT RED BALL BURNING ITS WAY THROUGH THE DUST.

SOMEWHERE OUT THERE, A COLOSSAL HAMMER WAS BEATING ON AN ANVIL...

...AND IT WAS DRAWING CLOSER AND CLOSER TO *US*...

AS THE LEGEND GOES...IN 1295, A LONE PEASANT WANDERING THROUGH A FOREST ON THE BANKS OF THE KHAN BATU RIVER FOUND IT WITHIN THE TRUNK OF A TREE.

IT WAS CALLED THE *KURSK MADONNA.*

A MONASTERY WAS BUILT ON THE SITE OF THE DISCOVERY TO COMMEMORATE THE HOLY EVENT.

WHEN THE BOLSHEVIKS CAME INTO POWER, THEY ENDED THE MONASTIC CREED AND TURNED THE MONASTERY INTO A HOLIDAY CAMP FOR THE *NKVD.*

THE MADONNA WAS *LOST...*

THEN, IN *1943,* THE *NKVD* GAVE THE CHURCH A REPLACEMENT MADONNA--SO THAT THE FAITHFUL COULD PRAY FOR THE VERY SAME GOVERNMENT THAT HAD ENGINEERED THEIR PERSECUTION IN THE FIRST PLACE.

333

HARVEST AT PROKHOROVKA

THE DAWN CAME IN CLEAR AT *0230, JULY 12, 1943.* RAIN CLOUDS SOON ROLLED IN, OBSCURING THE SOVIETS' VIEW OF 600 GERMAN TANKS AS THEY BEGAN TO RUMBLE EAST.

TWO DAYS EARLIER, ON JULY 10, BRITISH AND AMERICAN FORCES HAD MADE A SUCCESSFUL LANDFALL ON THE MEDITERRANEAN ISLAND OF *SICILY.* HITLER WAS NOW FIGHTING A TWO-FRONT WAR.

IT WAS AN *ALL-OR-NOTHING* PROPOSITION.

TODAY, IF HITLER'S CAMPAIGN IN THE EAST WERE TO SUCCEED, A BREAKTHROUGH HAD TO BE MADE. HE WOULD HAVE TO SEND HIS TROOPS TO DEFEND THE SOFT UNDERBELLY OF EUROPE.

THIS WOULD BE THEIR LAST GREAT ATTACK IN THE EAST... GERMANY'S *LAST BLITZKRIEG.*

WE STOOD IDLE AT THE EDGE OF A FIELD OF SUNFLOWERS, AWAITING COLONEL NOZDRIN'S INSTRUCTIONS. I WALKED BACK ONE HUNDRED YARDS BEHIND US TO THE MORTARS SECTION TO CHECK THEIR FREQUENCY IN CASE WE HAD TO CALL THEM. WHEN I GOT BACK, MISHA WAS ALONE WITH THE TANK...

WHERE IS MILLA?

SHE WENT OUT TO CHECK THE FIELD--IN CASE WE HAVE TO CROSS IT, I GUESS...

...OR MAYBE SHE JUST DOESN'T CARE FOR MY COMPANY.

DON'T TAKE IT PERSONALLY, MISHA--MILLA HAS HER OWN DEMONS. I'VE LEARNED TO ACCEPT HER THE WAY SHE IS.

LET'S SEE...THIS FIELD IS ABOUT 150 YARDS WIDE...

...ABOUT 500 YARDS DEEP...

...WITH THE PSEL RIVER ON THE RIGHT, IRRIGATION CANAL ON THE LEFT...

...A DRY DITCH, ABOUT FOUR FEET DEEP...

335

THE GERMAN TANKERS HAD STOPPED IN THE HIGH GRASS TO ALSO WAIT. THEY ATE BREAKFAST, NAPPED, AND RELIEVED THEMSELVES, AS THEIR COMMANDERS GATHERED ONE MORE TIME TO GO OVER THE MAPS.

THEN, AT *0830,* THE *LUFTWAFFE* CAME SCREAMING OVERHEAD.

THAT'S *IT!* EVERYBODY MOUNT UP!

AGAIN THE PANZERS WERE ON THE MOVE, WITH THEIR COMMANDERS IN THEIR FANCY BLACK UNIFORMS, SITTING IN THE TURRETS AND SCANNING THE HORIZON FOR THE ENEMY...

SO FAR-- NOTHING.

THEN, FROM BEHIND EVERY HILL AND RIDGE, FARMHOUSE AND TREE--THE SOVIET FORCES BEGAN TO EMERGE. JUST A FEW TANKS TO BEGIN WITH...

...BUT SOON, THEY COVERED THE EARTH LIKE ANTS.

THERE WERE LIGHT *T-70*S AMONG THEM, EVEN A HANDFUL OF BRITISH-MADE LEND-LEASE *CHURCHILLS*, BUT THE GREAT MAJORITY WERE *T-34*S. ALL WERE MOVING AT TOP SPEED.

THEIR STRATEGY WAS TO REACH THE GERMANS AS QUICKLY AS POSSIBLE AND MIX IN WITH THEM UP CLOSE, MAKING THE PANZERS LOSE THE ADVANTAGE OF THEIR POWERFUL GUNS AND STRONG ARMOR.

THIS WAS *ROTMISTROV'S FIFTH GUARD TANK ARMY,* ALONG WITH EVERY RESERVE HE COULD MUSTER. THE GERMANS WERE FACING NEARLY 900 TANKS--

--ALL OF WHICH WERE COMMITTED TO THIS GAMBLE.

AS SOON AS THE GERMANS IN THE TIGER TANKS SAW WHAT WAS HAPPENING...

...THEY STOPPED IN THEIR TRACKS AND BEGAN TO TAKE AIM.

THEY FIRED OFF A FEW PREMATURE, WILD SHOTS--

--BUT NOT MANY.

THE GERMANS, WELL TRAINED AND PROFESSIONAL, KEPT THEIR NERVE...

...BUT SO DID WE!

MANY OF OUR TANKS WERE LOST BEFORE THEY COULD GET WITHIN LETHAL RANGE OF THE TIGERS...

...BUT ONCE THEY DID, ALL BETS WERE OFF!

ONE SIDE WAS NO DEADLIER THAN THE OTHER.

SOME TIGERS WERE TAKEN OUT AT UNBELIEVABLY CLOSE RANGE...

BUT OTHERS--

--WELL, THEY MAY HAVE FALLEN VICTIM TO THEIR OWN EXCITEMENT.

IN THE CONFUSION, FIVE TIGERS AND TWO HALF-TRACKS SLIPPED DOWN INTO A GULLY THAT CUT DEEP INTO OUR REAR...

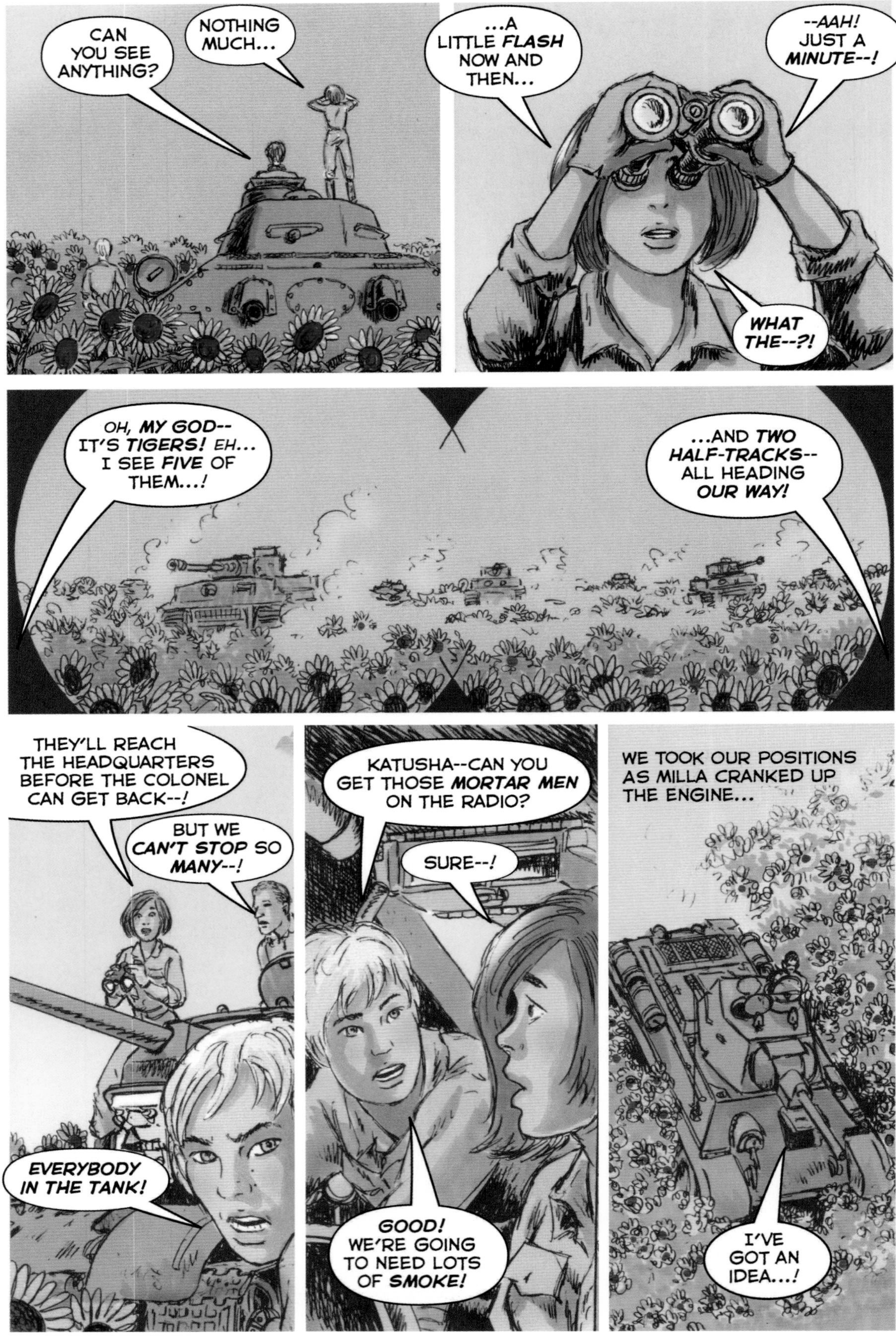
CAN YOU SEE ANYTHING?
NOTHING MUCH...
...A LITTLE FLASH NOW AND THEN...
--AAH! JUST A MINUTE--!
WHAT THE--?!
OH, MY GOD-- IT'S TIGERS! EH... I SEE FIVE OF THEM...!
...AND TWO HALF-TRACKS-- ALL HEADING OUR WAY!
THEY'LL REACH THE HEADQUARTERS BEFORE THE COLONEL CAN GET BACK--!
BUT WE CAN'T STOP SO MANY--!
EVERYBODY IN THE TANK!
KATUSHA--CAN YOU GET THOSE MORTAR MEN ON THE RADIO?
SURE--!
GOOD! WE'RE GOING TO NEED LOTS OF SMOKE!
WE TOOK OUR POSITIONS AS MILLA CRANKED UP THE ENGINE...
I'VE GOT AN IDEA...!

LET'S SEE... RIVER ON THE RIGHT, THE CANAL IS TO THE LEFT--

WHAT DO YOU HAVE IN MIND, MILLA?

I'LL SHOW YOU, KATUSHA...

OKAY, THERE'S THE *DITCH.* I'LL PULL DOWN INTO IT.

IT'S A GOOD HULL-DOWN POSITION, BUT I CAN'T SEE VERY WELL--!

I'LL BE YOUR EYES, MISHA.

I'M GOING OUT *FRONT.*

KATUSHA, YOU LOAD FOR MISHA, AND KEEP AN EYE OUT UP TOP. I'VE GOT THE PAPASHAW, EXTRA AMMO, AND A HALF DOZEN GRENADES...

...AND I HAVE THIS *SIGNAL FLAG.* I'LL WAVE IT WHEN I AM RIGHT IN THEIR LINE OF FIRE, SO THEN, YOU JUST *BLAST AWAY...!*

AND YOU BE SURE *YOU* GET *OUT OF THE WAY!*

YOU CAN *COUNT* ON *THAT!*

OKAY, YEVGENY! START GIVING US SMOKE--AND *DON'T STOP* UNTIL WE TELL YOU!

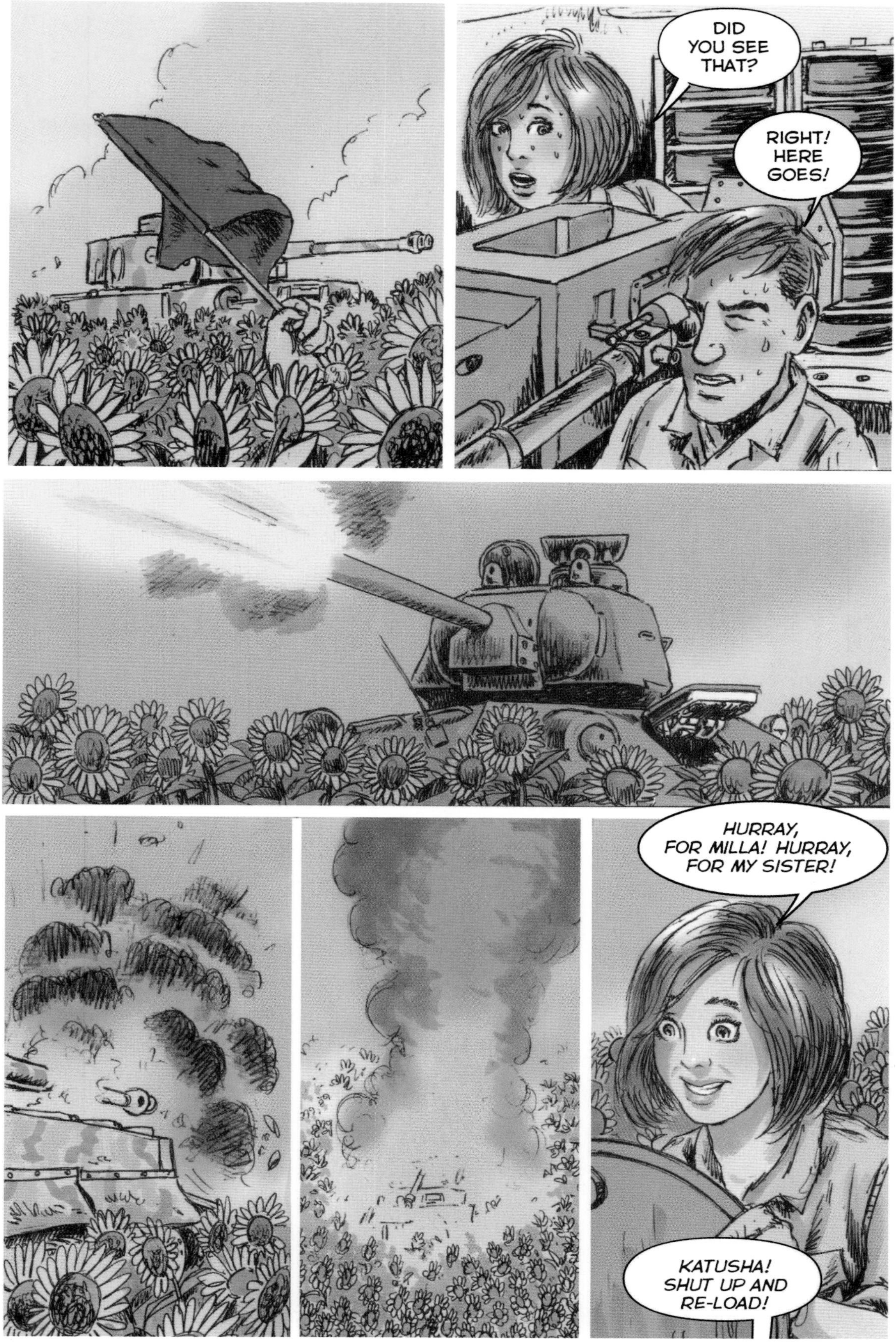
DID YOU SEE THAT?
RIGHT! HERE GOES!
HURRAY, FOR MILLA! HURRAY, FOR MY SISTER!
KATUSHA! SHUT UP AND RE-LOAD!

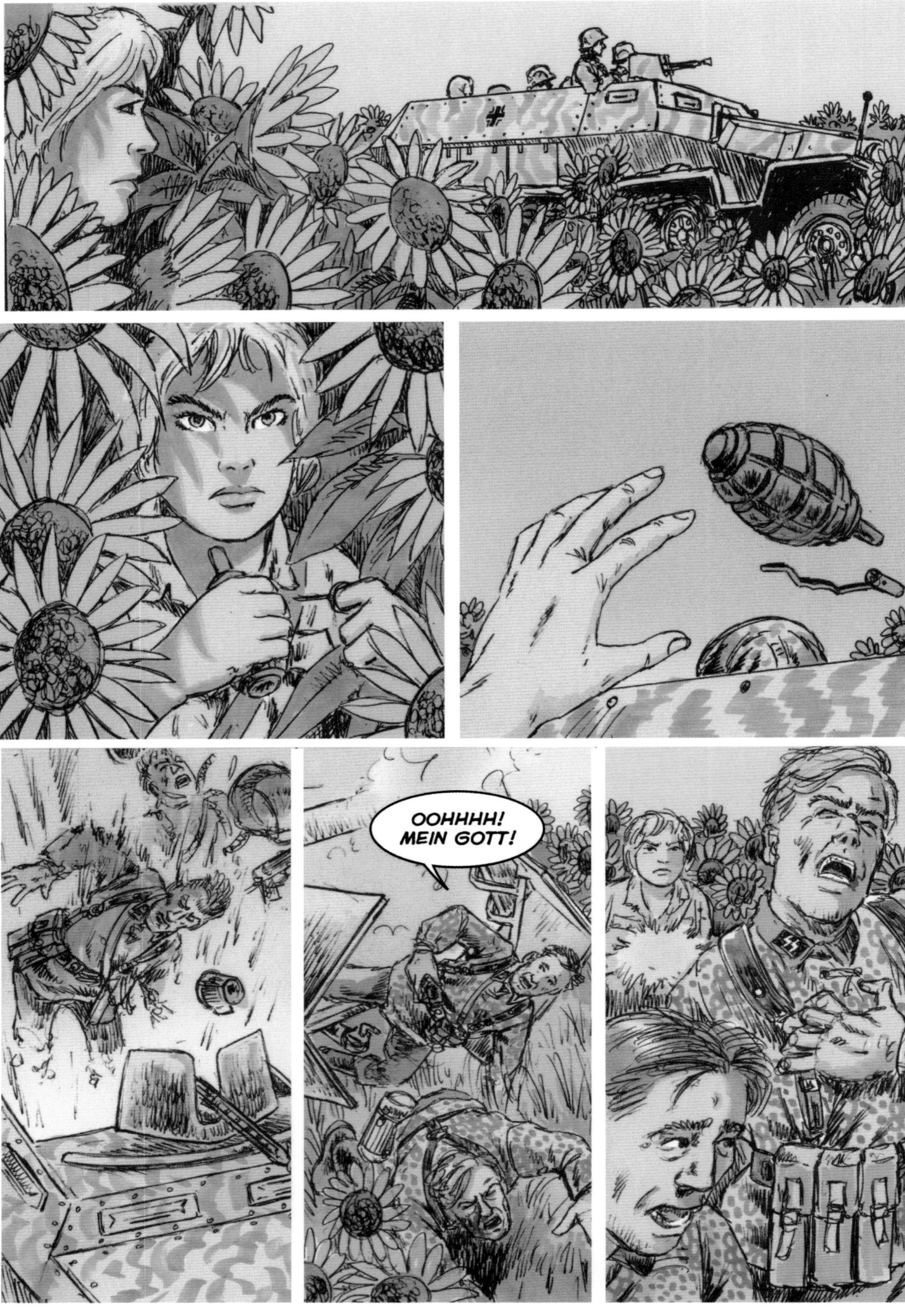
OOHHHH!
MEIN GOTT!

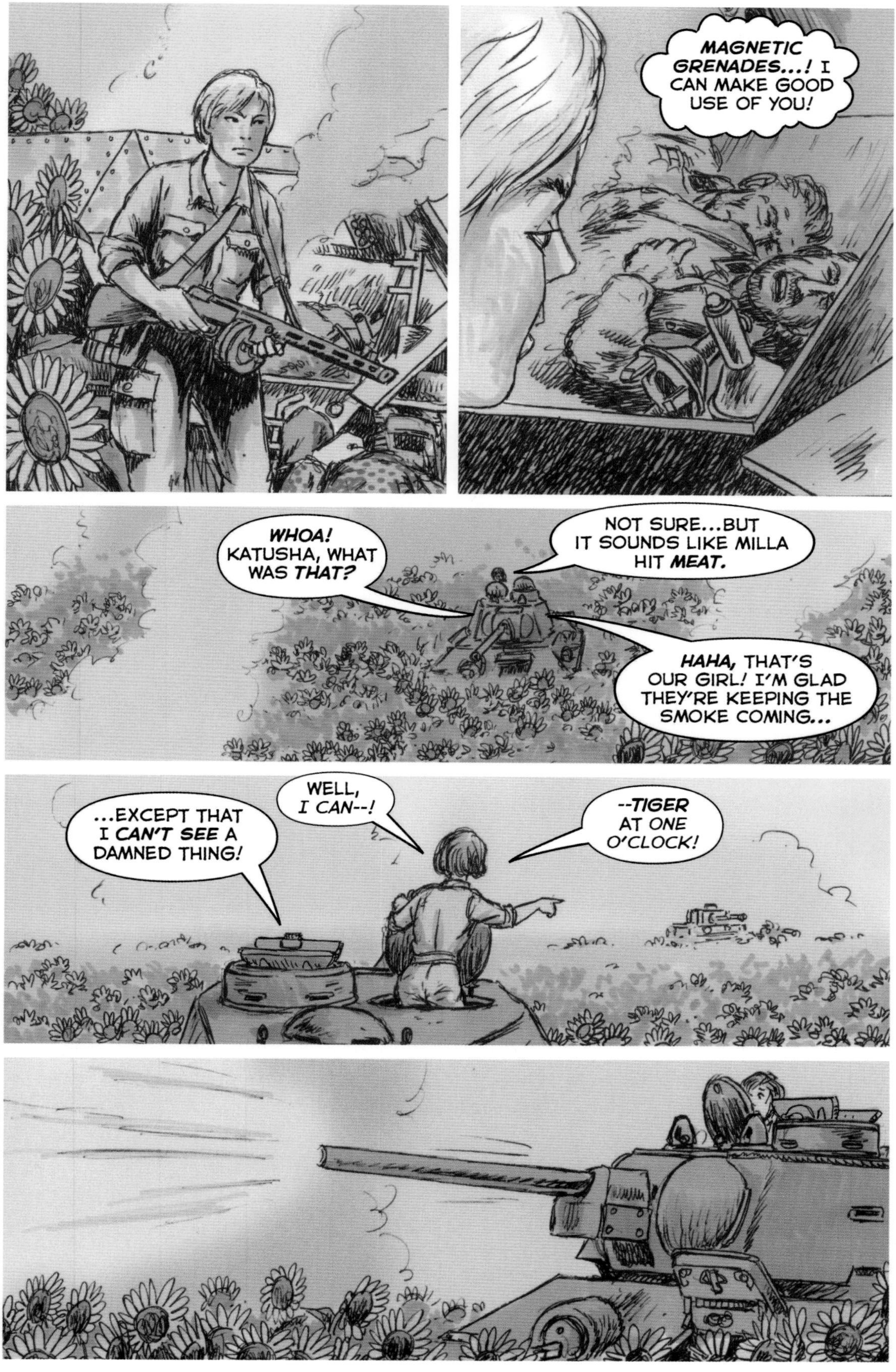
MAGNETIC GRENADES...! I CAN MAKE GOOD USE OF YOU!
WHOA! KATUSHA, WHAT WAS THAT?
NOT SURE...BUT IT SOUNDS LIKE MILLA HIT MEAT.
HAHA, THAT'S OUR GIRL! I'M GLAD THEY'RE KEEPING THE SMOKE COMING...
...EXCEPT THAT I CAN'T SEE A DAMNED THING!
WELL, I CAN--!
--TIGER AT ONE O'CLOCK!

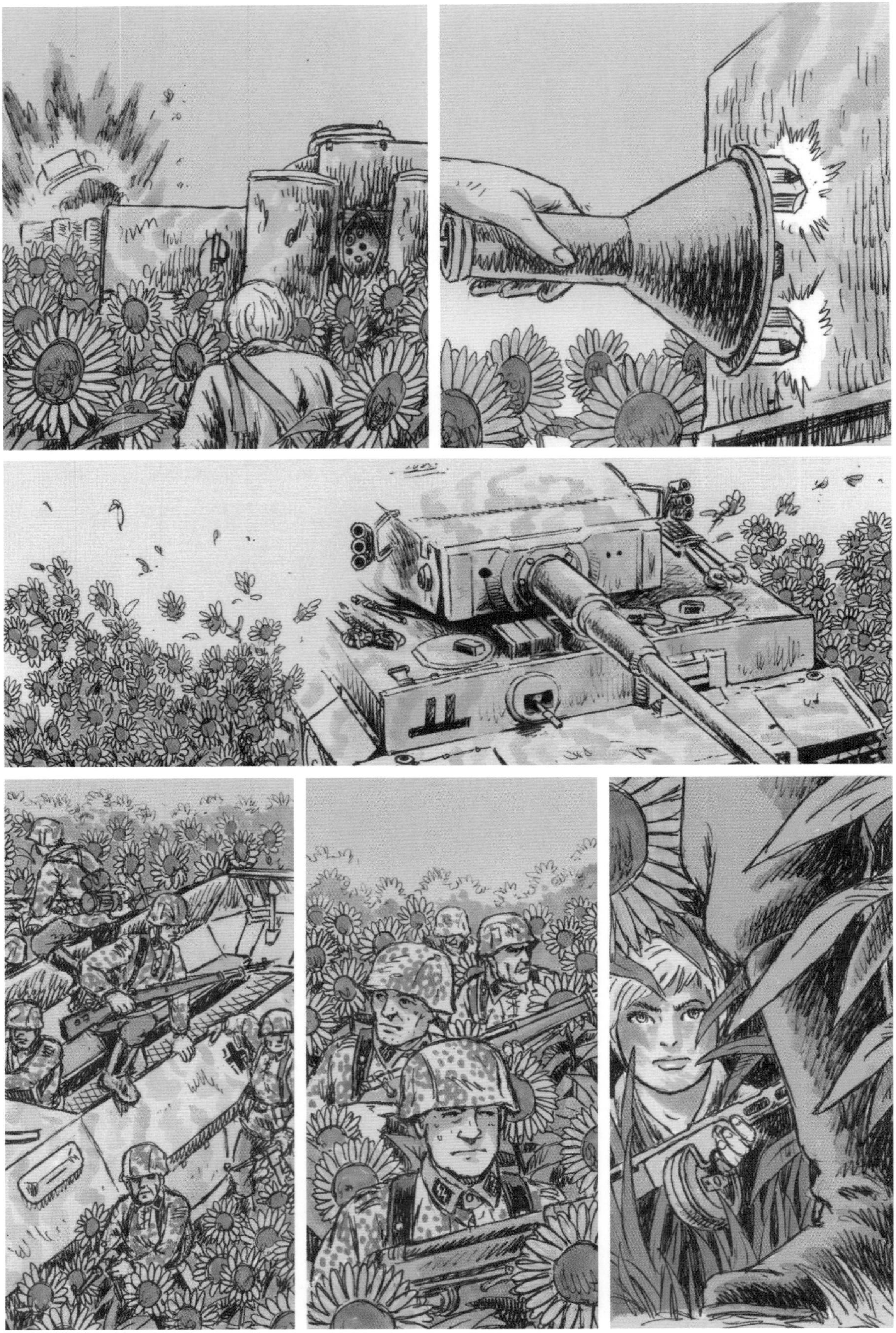

:AWK!:

:OOOF!:

:RAARR-AGHH!:

:AAGGHHK!:

DUMBKAUFT--!

--TO BE KILLED BY *YOUR OWN* MEN!

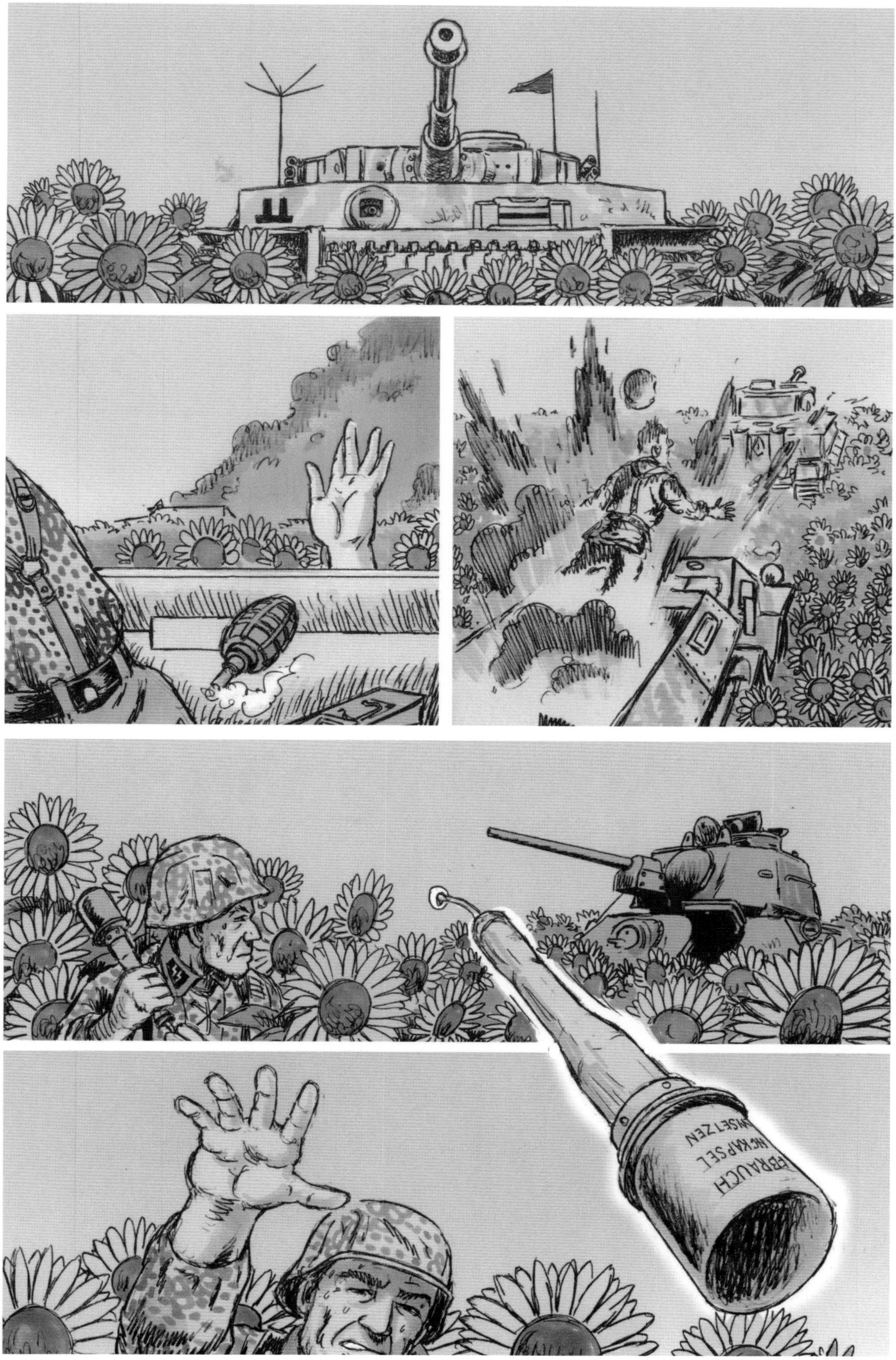

THE GRENADE BOUNCED OFF OUR TANK--

--BUT IT DIDN'T MISS US BY *FAR ENOUGH!*

;AAAGGHH!;

KATUSHA--! I'M *HIT BAD*--IN BOTH LEGS!!!

AAH!!

HANG *ON,* MISHA!

MISHA! ANOTHER *TIGER*-- RIGHT AT *TWO* O'CLOCK--!

YOU HIT THE TURRET RING! YOU'RE *RELOADED,* MISHA...!

...YOU'VE *GOT* TO HOLD ON!

YOU HIT THE TRACK!

BUT-- THEY'RE STILL IN THE FIGHT, MISHA...

...MISHA?

≷URRGHH≷

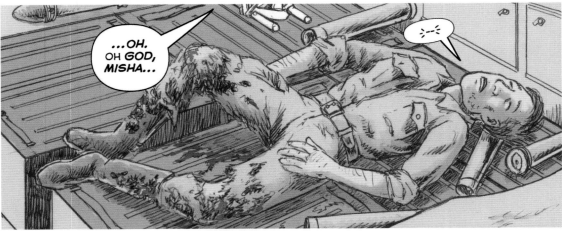

...OH. OH GOD, MISHA...

≷--≷

I IMMEDIATELY CLIMBED INTO THE GUNNER'S SEAT...

LET'S SEE-- I DID RELOAD. DIDN'T I--?

≷AAAAUGH!≷

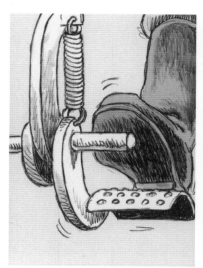

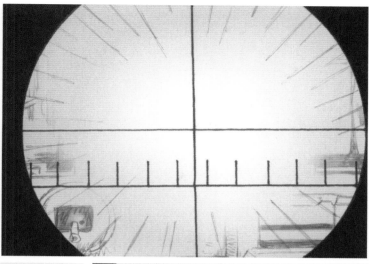

I WAS SUDDENLY AWARE OF THIS LOUD RINGING IN MY EARS--BUT I HAD NO IDEA WHERE IT COULD BE COMING FROM...

...THEN I REALIZED THAT WHAT WAS CAUSING IT WAS THE *DEAD SILENCE!*

I HAD MANAGED TO SCORE A HIT--

--RIGHT IN THE TIGER'S *GUN BARREL!*

SUDDENLY, I WASN'T ALONE--COLONEL NOZDRIN CAME ROARING UP IN HIS *GAZ*, AND THE MORTAR MEN CAME RUNNING UP, EMBARRASSED LOOKS PLAYING ACROSS THEIR FACES.

KATUSHA--!

SORRY, LITTLE TYMOSHENKO--! WE RAN OUT OF SMOKE SHELLS!

THAT'S ALL RIGHT--BUT THERE IS A *WOUNDED MAN* IN HERE...!

THERE, BOVA, YOU DID *WELL.* IT'S GOING TO BE ALL RIGHT...

⁻⁺OHHH⁺⁻

BUT-- WHERE IS *MILLA?*

I LOOKED ACROSS THE SHATTERED FIELD WHERE MILLA WAS WANDERING AMONG THE GERMAN DEAD.

SHE SEEMED TO BE LOOKING FOR SOMETHING...

WELL, I HOPE *GENERAL ROTMISTROV* IS SAFE AND SOUND...

ARE YOU KIDDING? HE NEVER SHOWED UP HERE.

WHA...?

HERE SHE COMES. WHAT DOES SHE HAVE THERE?

I THINK SHE'S BEEN COLLECTING HER OWN MEDALS.

OH, I THINK WE CAN DO BETTER THAN THAT.

THE GROUND AROUND PROKHOROVKA WAS LITTERED
WITH THE MANGLED BODIES OF THE DEAD
AND THE TWISTED, BURNING HULKS OF TANKS...

THE GERMANS HAD INFLICTED GREAT DAMAGE UPON US.

BUT THEY HAD NOT BROKEN THROUGH.

THEY HAD DONE THEIR WORST...AND HAD *FAILED.*
GERMAN TROOPS WOULD NEVER AGAIN ADVANCE INTO RUSSIA.

AND ONCE THE RED ARMY, NOW THE LARGEST FORCE EVER KNOWN IN WAR,
BEGAN TO MOVE...

...IT WOULD NEVER STOP.

OUR FORCES BURST FORTH LIKE A COILED SPRING. ON *AUGUST 5,* MEN CLAD IN DUSTY BOOTS AND SUN-BLEACHED SHIRTS ENTERED THE CITY OF *OREL...*

ON THAT SAME DAY, THEY LIBERATED *BELGOROD.*

SO MUCH WAR WAS YET TO BE FOUGHT, BUT IT HAD BECOME A TIME OF PRAISE. EVEN COMRADE STALIN FOUND IN HIS COLD HEART THE NEED TO MAKE A GESTURE OF GRATITUDE.

"TONIGHT AT TWENTY-FOUR HUNDRED HOURS, ON *5TH AUGUST,* THE CAPITAL OF OUR COUNTRY, MOSCOW, WILL SALUTE WITH TWENTY ARTILLERY SALVOES FROM 120 GUNS THE VALIANT TROOPS THAT LIBERATED OREL AND BELGOROD. I EXPRESS MY THANKS TO ALL THE TROOPS THAT TOOK PART IN THE OFFENSIVE... ETERNAL GLORY ON THE HEROES WHO FELL IN THE STRUGGLE FOR THE FREEDOM OF OUR COUNTRY. DEATH TO THE GERMAN INVADERS."

357

THERE WAS INDIVIDUAL PRAISE, TOO...

OUR BRIGADE HAD AGAIN DONE WELL.

COLONEL RUSLAN NOZDRIN WAS COMMENDED AND DECORATED.

HE ACCEPTED HIS AWARD WITHOUT COMMENT OR EXPRESSION.

CAPTAIN NIKOLAI KOVCHENKO AND THE MEN WHO SURVIVED THE BATTLE FOR *HILL 221* WERE PROPERLY REWARDED. KOLYA HAD AGAIN BEEN WOUNDED, WHICH AMOUNTED TO A FEW NICKS AND CUTS.

I RECEIVED A MEDAL FOR OUR ACTION IN THE SUNFLOWER FIELD. IT WAS NICE, AND IT MADE ME FEEL GOOD.

BUT IT WAS NOT *MY* AWARD THAT GAVE ME THE MOST PRIDE...

LUDMILLA TYMOSHENKO, IT IS WITH GREAT PRIDE AS THE COMMANDER OF THE *5TH GUARD TANK ARMY*--

--THAT I PRESENT YOU WITH THE HIGHEST DISTINCTION ANY SOVIET CITIZEN CAN RECEIVE.

I BESTOW UPON YOU THE TITLE...*HERO* OF THE *SOVIET UNION*.

BUT THERE WERE THOSE OF US WHO HAD PAID THE HIGHEST PRICE FOR VICTORY--

--WHO WOULD NEVER SEE THEIR JUST REWARDS...

I'M LOOKING FOR SERGEANT MISHA BOVA.

LET'S SEE... RIGHT OVER THERE. ROW *D*, BED SIX.

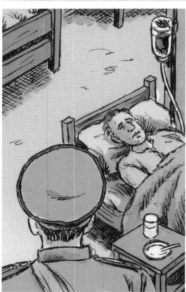

THE BAD, BLOODY DAYS OF DEFEAT WERE OVER...

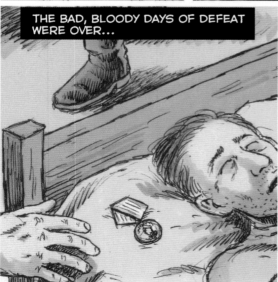

...AND THE BAD, BLOODY DAYS OF VICTORY WERE ABOUT TO BEGIN.

OVER THOSE HILLS, OVER RIVERS AND PAST VILLAGES AND FARMS, LAY *UKRAINE*...AND *HOME*, AND OUR HEARTS WERE FILLED WITH APPREHENSION AND HOPE.

SHARP COMMANDS FROM COLONEL NOZDRIN CRACKLED OVER OUR RADIO SETS...

...WE WERE ON THE MOVE AGAIN...

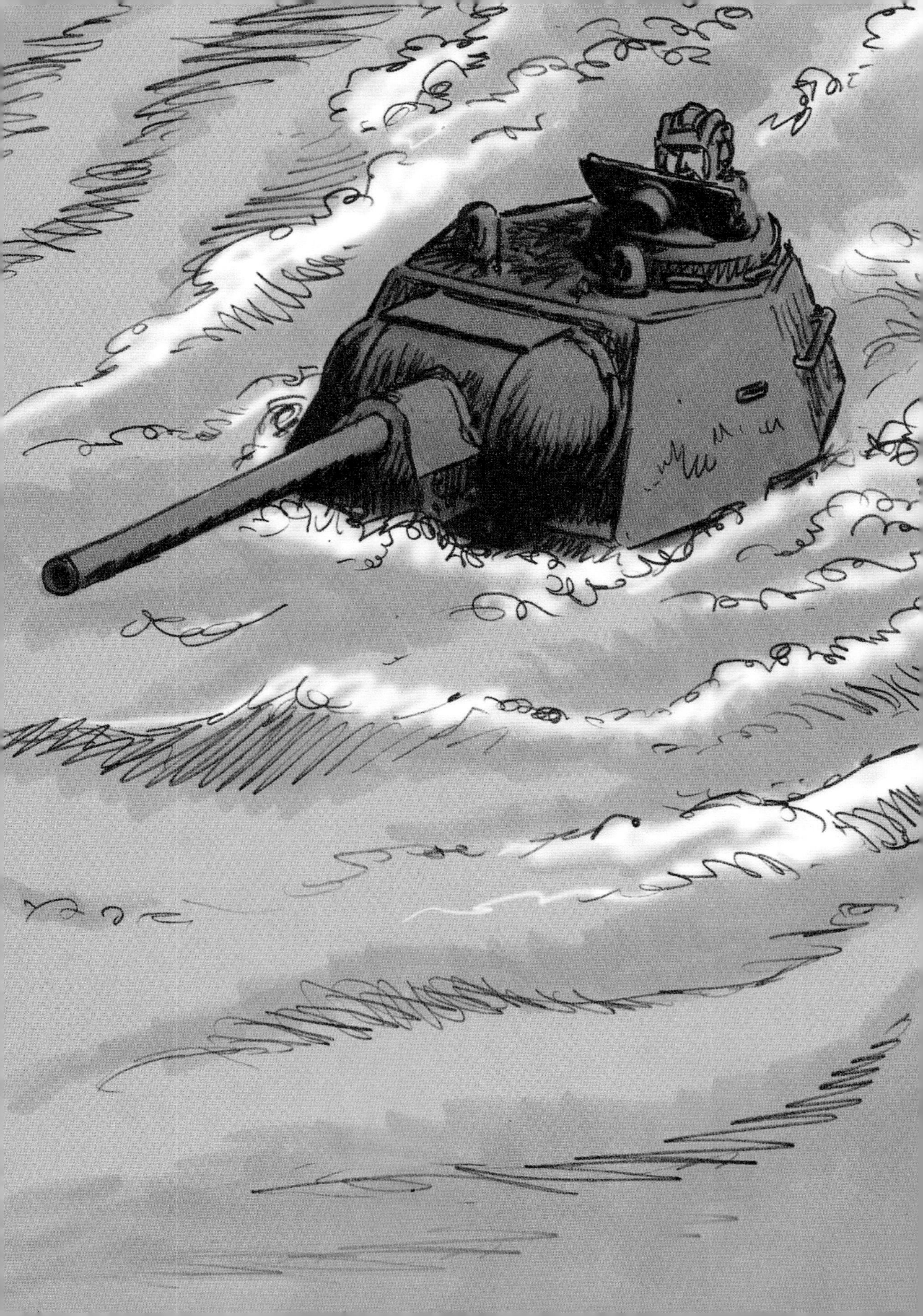

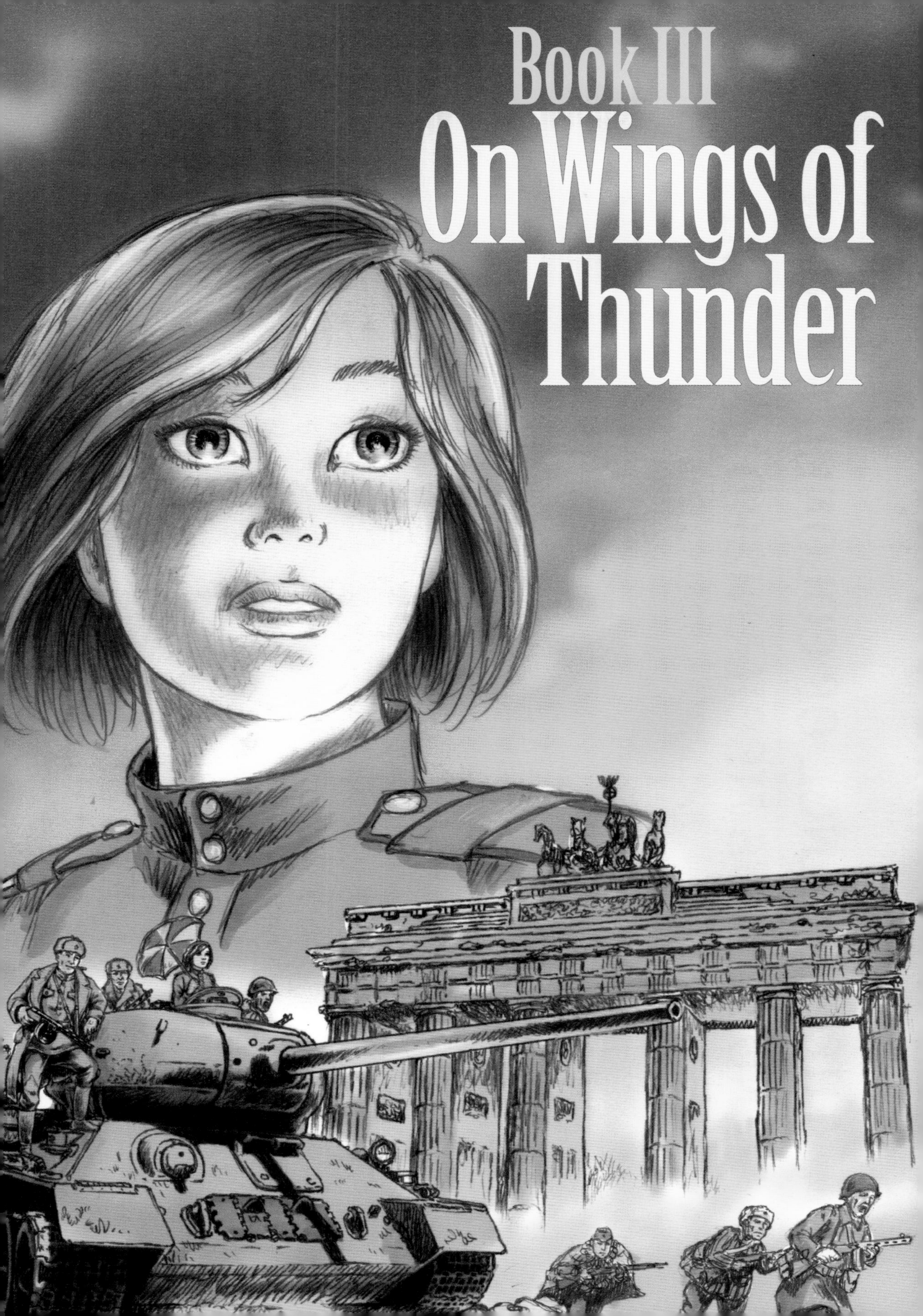
Book III
On Wings of Thunder

THE ADVANCE OF COLONEL RUSLAN NOZDRIN'S MECHANIZED BRIGADE

FALL 1943 - SPRING 1945

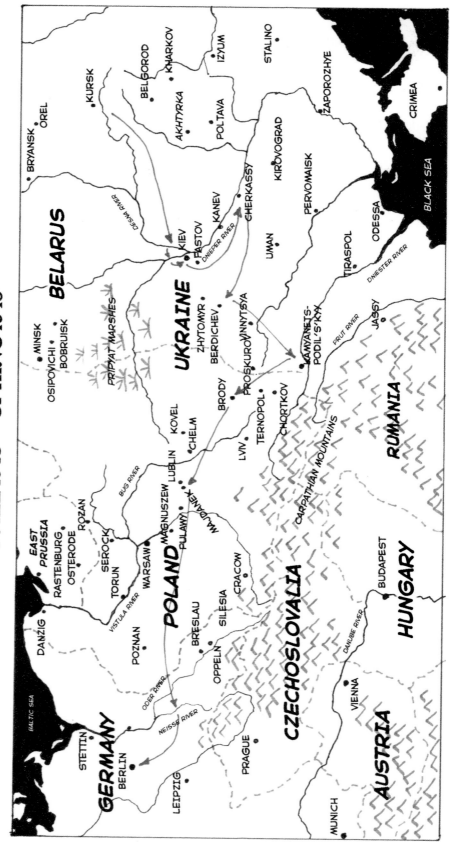

BY THE LATE SUMMER AND EARLY FALL OF *1943*, GERMAN FORCES IN RUSSIA WERE IN FULL RETREAT.

ALTHOUGH THE GERMANS STILL WERE A TOUGH AND PROFESSIONAL OPPONENT, THEIR NUMBERS HAD FINALLY SLIPPED FAR BELOW THOSE OF THE SOVIETS.

THE NAZIS STILL HAD *THREE AND A HALF MILLION* TROOPS IN THE EAST--BUT THEY WERE NOW FACING A RED ARMY OF *SIX MILLION.*

IN TANKS, THE GERMANS WERE OUTNUMBERED BY THREE AND A HALF TO ONE; IN PLANES, BY TWO AND A HALF TO ONE; AND IN ARTILLERY, TWO TO ONE.

FROM *FIELD MARSHAL ERICH VON MANSTEIN* TO THE LOWLIEST GERMAN PRIVATE, ONE THOUGHT OCCUPIED THEIR MINDS:

CROSS THE DNIEPER!

GET BEHIND THE MIGHTY RIVER, DIG IN--AND DEFEND YOURSELF!

IN THIS MATTER OF SURVIVAL, IT WAS THE ONLY ESCAPE FROM SLAVIC VENGEANCE.

IN THE MIDST OF THE DREADFUL RETIREMENT, HITLER ADDED AN ESPECIALLY DRACONIAN ELEMENT: *OPERATION SCORCHED EARTH!* HE ORDERED HIS ARMIES TO STRIP THE LAND FROM THE DONETS TO THE DNIEPER OF EVERYTHING USEFUL TO THE ENEMY...

ALL LIVESTOCK WERE TO BE TAKEN WITH THEM: 200,000 HEAD OF CATTLE, 150,000 HORSES, AND 270,000 SHEEP WERE HERDED WEST IN AN EFFORT TO DENY FOOD TO THE ONCOMING SOVIET ARMY.

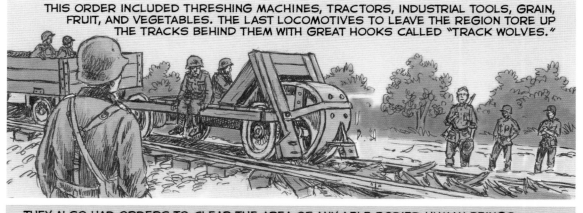

THIS ORDER INCLUDED THRESHING MACHINES, TRACTORS, INDUSTRIAL TOOLS, GRAIN, FRUIT, AND VEGETABLES. THE LAST LOCOMOTIVES TO LEAVE THE REGION TORE UP THE TRACKS BEHIND THEM WITH GREAT HOOKS CALLED "TRACK WOLVES."

THEY ALSO HAD ORDERS TO CLEAR THE AREA OF ANY ABLE-BODIED HUMAN BEINGS. THOUSANDS OF WOMEN, CONSIDERED POTENTIAL WAR WORKERS FOR THE RUSSIANS, WERE UPROOTED AND FORCE-MARCHED WESTWARD.

I HAD SO WANTED TO RETURN TO *KIEV*...

...BUT I DIDN'T THINK IT WOULD BE *THIS WAY.*

AS CLEAR AS TEARS

SEPTEMBER 1943. THE DESNA RIVER FLOWS SOUTHWEST AND RUNS INTO THE DNIEPER A FEW MILES BELOW KIEV. OUR TANK BRIGADE REACHED THIS BODY OF WATER, AND SINCE WE WERE NOT SUBMARINES, WE STOPPED THERE.

THIS RIVER, WHICH I HAD NEVER GIVEN MUCH THOUGHT TO BEFORE, NOW SEEMED LIKE THE BEST GIFT THIS SIDE OF PARADISE--THAT AND A BAR OF ROSE-SCENTED SOAP SENT TO US FROM COLONEL NOZDRIN BY WAY OF HIS DRIVER AND BEDMATE, *SENIOR SERGEANT VERA FYODOROVICH.*

OOOHHHH, THAT FEELS SO *GOOD!* ALL I'VE HAD TO USE ON MY HAIR WAS THAT BLACK "K" SOAP.

RUSLAN LETS ME LOOK FOR TREE MOSS SOMETIMES. NEXT TIME I GO, I'LL GET YOU SOME...

...FOR ALL OF US TO ENJOY. YOU KNOW, YOU GIRLS ARE SPECIAL TO HIM.

FROM VERA'S SEEMINGLY BOTTOMLESS BAG OF GOODIES CAME ANOTHER SURPRISE...

YOU TWO HAVE TOOTHBRUSHES?

THEY WORE OUT A FEW HUNDRED MILES AGO.

WELL, JUST WET YOUR INDEX FINGER, AND I'LL PUT SOME OF THIS ON IT.

RRAAOOOWW! WRAAT'S RUNDERFALL!

ISN'T IT? IT'S TOOTH POWDER-- IT CAME FROM THE AMERICANS.

THINK WE'LL BE PUSHING ACROSS THE DNIEPER SOON?

I DON'T THINK SO...

RUSLAN SAYS THE MAIN EFFORT WILL BE MADE FARTHER SOUTH, ON THE BURKIN BEND.

I'D SURE LIKE TO SEE HOME. THE WAY THINGS ARE, I DON'T REALLY EXPECT TO FIND ANYONE THERE...

BUT...YOU NEVER KNOW.

YOU'RE NOT ALONE, KATUSHA.

EVERY UKRAINIAN IN THE BRIGADE HAS BEEN HANGING AROUND HEADQUARTERS, WAITING FOR THE ORDER TO CROSS.

ARE THOSE DRY, MILLA?

NO. BUT THEY'RE GOOD AND CLEAN.

NOT EVERYBODY WAS WAITING ON ORDERS TO CROSS. CAPTAIN NIKOLAI KOVCHENKO SENT A COMPANY OF HIS INFANTRY ACROSS THE DESNA, WHERE THEY SET UP SEVERAL OBSERVATION POSTS TO MONITOR THE GERMANS ON THE OTHER SIDE OF THE DNIEPER.

BUT ONE OF KOLYA'S OFFICERS WAS NOT SATISFIED WITH WAITING...

SGT. MAJOR *GENRIKH DYATLONKO*, A JEW FROM BERDYCHIV, SEIZED A LARGE FISHING BOAT ONE NIGHT.

HE ORDERED TWENTY OF HIS MEN TO CROSS THE DNIEPER AND TAKE UP POSITIONS ON A CLIFF ON THE RIGHT BANK. IT WAS CLEAR HE PLANNED ON STAYING--HE TOOK ALONG TWO HEAVY MACHINE GUNS AND PLENTY OF AMMO.

THEN HE *CALLED* KOLYA ON HIS USED AMERICAN-MADE *SRC300* RADIO.

WE'RE OVER THE DNIEPER NOW, CAPTAIN... CARE TO JOIN US?

DAMN IT, GENRIKH!

THAT WASN'T OUR PLAN!

WELL, THEN... PERHAPS YOU WOULD WISH TO MAKE A SPECIAL REQUEST OF *COMRADE STALIN*, WHILE I HAVE HIM ON THE LINE?

SURE!

TELL 'IM TO SEND US OVER A COUPLE OF *MORTARS*...

...BECAUSE I'M STARTING TO SUSPECT THE GERMAN ARMY'S THINKING ABOUT *ATTACKING* US.

DESPITE HIMSELF, KOLYA LAUGHED.

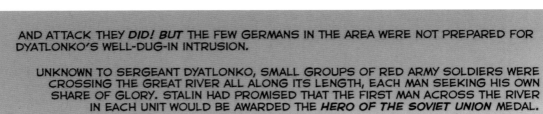

AND ATTACK THEY *DID! BUT* THE FEW GERMANS IN THE AREA WERE NOT PREPARED FOR DYATLONKO'S WELL-DUG-IN INTRUSION.

UNKNOWN TO SERGEANT DYATLONKO, SMALL GROUPS OF RED ARMY SOLDIERS WERE CROSSING THE GREAT RIVER ALL ALONG ITS LENGTH, EACH MAN SEEKING HIS OWN SHARE OF GLORY. STALIN HAD PROMISED THAT THE FIRST MAN ACROSS THE RIVER IN EACH UNIT WOULD BE AWARDED THE *HERO OF THE SOVIET UNION* MEDAL.

BY MID-*1943*, SOME 300,000 SOVIET PARTISANS RAGED BEHIND THE GERMAN LINES, KILLING MILITARY PERSONNEL, BLOWING UP BRIDGES AND MILITARY INSTALLATIONS, AND GATHERING INFORMATION FOR THE RED ARMY.

BUT ONE OF THEIR JOBS WAS TO REMIND THOSE UNDER GERMAN RULE THAT THEY WERE STILL SUBJECT TO SOVIET LAW.

BRUNO AND OKSANA KOROLYOV, YOU HAVE BEEN CHARGED AND FOUND GUILTY OF PROVIDING PHYSICAL AID TO THE FASCISTS...

BUT--THEY *STOLE OUR TWO COWS! WHAT* COULD WE HAVE *DONE* ABOUT THAT?

WE HAD KEPT THE COWS *HIDDEN* IN THE WOODS...!

I WOULD MILK THEM EVERY MORNING AND THEN SHARE THE MILK WITH OUR NEIGHBORS!

HOW COULD WE HAVE KNOWN THE GERMANS FOUND OUR HIDING PLACE?!

ONE MORNING, I WENT TO MY COWS AND COULD NOT FIND THEM!

I DIDN'T KNOW THE GERMANS TOOK THEM--I'M STILL NOT SURE OF IT!

YOU SHOULD HAVE PLANNED FOR THE EVENTUALITY OF THE GERMAN THEFT BY KILLING THE ANIMALS.

THE SENTENCE FOR THIS CRIME IS DEATH--BY HANGING.

CARRY OUT THE SENTENCE IMMEDIATELY!

FOUR HOODED FIGURES CAME OUT FROM BEHIND A CANVAS BLIND.

EVERYONE KNEW WHAT THEY WERE THERE TO DO.

GOD, I HATE THIS! WE ALL KNOW THE OLD COUPLE IS INNOCENT!

YOU SAY THEY ARE INNOCENT, VASILY?

BY THEIR FOOLISH ATTITUDE, THEY HAVE AIDED OUR ENEMY.

AND FOR THAT--

--THEY MUST BE PUNISHED.

ZHENYA SURE HAS GROWN HARD, HASN'T SHE?

YES.

SHE CERTAINLY HAS.

OH, GOD--!

THERE *IS NO* GOD.

I'VE HAD ENOUGH OF THIS. THIS IS *NOT* THE ROUTE ON WHICH UNCLE TARAS STARTED US.

I THINK SOME NIGHT I MIGHT JUST--

IF YOU LEAVE, VASILY... THEY WILL JUST COME AFTER YOU.

I KNOW. I HEAR THERE ARE NATIONALIST PARTISANS TO THE WEST. THAT MAKES MORE SENSE TO ME.

TO *ME*, ALSO.

I'LL PRAY FOR YOUR DECISION.

FATHER ZAPOLYE, THANK YOU FOR YOUR PRAYERS.

THANK *YOU*, VASILY. YOU ARE THE ONLY FRIEND I HAVE WHO REMINDS ME...

...HOW I WAS ONCE A PRIEST.

372

MEANWHILE, THE RUSSIAN CROSSING OF THE DNIEPER AT THE BURKIN BEND WAS NOT GOING WELL. TO GET MORE TROOPS OVER THE RIVER IN A HURRY, SOME 7,000 SOVIET PARATROOPERS WERE DROPPED.

BUT THE ASSAULT WAS A DISASTER!

THEY CAPTURED NO ENEMY POSITIONS, AND ONLY 2,300 SURVIVED TO LINK UP WITH THE PARTISANS.

KOLYA MANAGED TO GET A REINFORCED COMPANY ACROSS THE RIVER TO JOIN UP WITH SERGEANT DYATLONKO, STRENGTHENING THEIR POSITION...

...BUT WHAT THEY REALLY NEEDED WAS *ARMOR*.

SO COLONEL NOZDRIN AND HIS STAFF WENT TO WORK ON HOW TO GET THE TANKS ACROSS.

HERE--IT'S 300 YARDS WIDE, BUT ONLY SEVEN FEET DEEP.

AND A *T-34* STANDS SEVEN FEET, TEN INCHES HIGH...

BUT--IS THAT WITH OR WITHOUT THE *COMMANDER'S CUPOLA?*

IN MY LIFE, I HAVE MET GOOD PEOPLE AND BAD PEOPLE...

BUT MOSTLY THERE HAVE BEEN GOOD PEOPLE WHO HAVE DONE *BAD THINGS*--AND BAD PEOPLE WHO HAVE DONE *GOOD*.

MAMA HAD RE-ENTERED KIEV ACROSS THE CHAINE BRIDGE AND DOWN RUINED KHRESCHATYK STREET TO TOTOLSTOGO L'VA, NOT TOO FAR FROM OUR HOME DISTRICT OF ZALIZHYCHNY.

BABUSHKA WAS NOT FEELING WELL, AND MAMA DESPERATELY WANTED TO GET HER MOTHER HOME SO SHE COULD REST.

ONCE THEY GOT THE CIVILIANS ACROSS THE DNIEPER, GERMAN SECURITY BECAME VERY LAX, AS IF THEIR MAIN CONCERN HAD BEEN TO GET THEM OUT OF THE REACH OF THE RUSSIANS. A FEW BRAVE SOULS HAD ALREADY SLIPPED AWAY...

...BUT THE GERMANS DIDN'T SEEM TO CARE.

ONE OF THEIR GUARDS WAS A GERMAN SERGEANT OF ABOUT 50 YEARS OF AGE. HE TREATED THEM KINDLY AND HAD EVEN LET BABUSHKA REST OFTEN.

STRUGGLING WITH THE FEW GERMAN WORDS SHE KNEW, MAMA TRIED TO COMMUNICATE HER WISH TO TAKE BABUSHKA TO OUR HOME.

TO THEIR GREAT SURPRISE, THE GERMAN PICKED UP THEIR MEAGER BURDENS...

...AND FOLLOWED THEM HOME.

A 45-MINUTE WALK BROUGHT THEM TO OUR HOUSE.

IT HAD BEEN TWO YEARS SINCE MAMA HAD LEFT HOME.

IT PAINED HER TO SEE THE WEEDS GROWN UP TO THE WINDOWS AND HER TIDY GARDEN ALL OVERGROWN AND WILD.

AT SOME TIME, OUR HOUSE HAD BEEN LOOTED. THE MATTRESSES AND SOME COOKWARE WERE GONE, AND IT WAS ALL FILTHY--BUT IT WAS *HOME*.

AND MAMA'S ICON WAS STILL ON THE WALL.

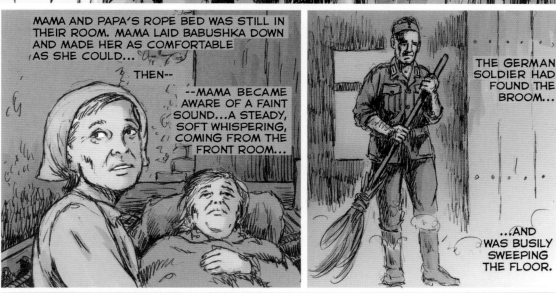

MAMA AND PAPA'S ROPE BED WAS STILL IN THEIR ROOM. MAMA LAID BABUSHKA DOWN AND MADE HER AS COMFORTABLE AS SHE COULD...

THEN--

--MAMA BECAME AWARE OF A FAINT SOUND...A STEADY, SOFT WHISPERING, COMING FROM THE FRONT ROOM...

THE GERMAN SOLDIER HAD FOUND THE BROOM...

...AND WAS BUSILY SWEEPING THE FLOOR.

HE LEFT AND RETURNED TWO HOURS LATER, CARRYING SOME BLANKETS AND A BURLAP SACK WITH CANNED FOOD, BREAD, AND SAUSAGE. HE BUILT A FIRE IN THE STOVE WITH SCAVENGED WOOD, DREW WATER FROM THE WELL, AND SERVED THEM A HEARTY DINNER.

THAT NIGHT, BABUSHKA AND MAMA SLEPT SOUNDLY ON THE ROPE BED, WRAPPED IN THE WARM BLANKETS.

THE OLD SERGEANT CHOSE TO STRETCH OUT ON THE HARD FLOOR IN THE FRONT ROOM.

SOON HIS LOUD SNORES FILLED THE HOUSE, A SIGNAL OF SAFETY FOR THE TWO WOMEN.

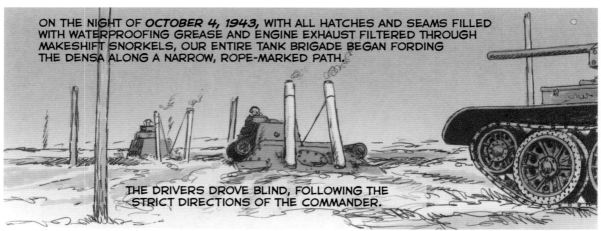

ON THE NIGHT OF *OCTOBER 4, 1943,* WITH ALL HATCHES AND SEAMS FILLED WITH WATERPROOFING GREASE AND ENGINE EXHAUST FILTERED THROUGH MAKESHIFT SNORKELS, OUR ENTIRE TANK BRIGADE BEGAN FORDING THE DENSA ALONG A NARROW, ROPE-MARKED PATH.

THE DRIVERS DROVE BLIND, FOLLOWING THE STRICT DIRECTIONS OF THE *COMMANDER.*

YOU KNOW, WE'VE BEEN IN SOME TIGHT SPOTS--BUT I DON'T THINK I HAVE *EVER* SEEN THE COLONEL SO *NERVOUS!*

WELL, IT'S FOR GOOD REASON...

"...HE *CAN'T SWIM.*"

WITHOUT SERIOUS MISHAP--

WELL, EXCEPT FOR A FEW PEOPLE GETTING SOMEWHAT *WET...*

...OUR BRIGADE MADE IT ACROSS.

BEHIND US, ELEMENTS OF A PONTOON BRIDGE WERE FLOATED ACROSS. BEHIND *THAT* WAS A SWARM OF SUPPLY TRUCKS AND ARTILLERY AND AMMUNITION...

...AND LOTS AND LOTS OF TROOPS.

THE NEXT NIGHT, UNDER THE COVER OF A COLD, HEAVY RAIN, WE STARTED ACROSS THE DNIEPER, USING TWO LARGE BARGES THAT THE GERMANS HAD STUPIDLY LEFT BEHIND. CARRYING THREE TANKS AT A TIME, BY MORNING WE HAD SIXTY *T-34s* ON THE RIGHT BANK OF THE GREAT RIVER.

OUR PART IN THIS OFFENSIVE WAS SMALL INDEED.

MANY CROSSINGS OCCURRED UP AND DOWN THE RIVER, INVOLVING UNTOLD THOUSANDS OF RED ARMY TROOPS--MAKING THIS ONE OF THE LARGEST OPERATIONS OF THE WAR.

ASSAULTS ACROSS THE RIVER WOULD GO ON UNTIL THE END OF THE YEAR.

WE THEN MOVED INTO THE LINE WITH OUR INFANTRY, WHO HAD BEEN HOLDING ON EVER SINCE SERGEANT DYATLONKO HAD MADE HIS UNAUTHORIZED FORAY.

377

THE GERMAN SERGEANT WENT ABOUT HIS DUTIES WITH HIS COMRADES, BUT STILL...

...EVERY COUPLE OF DAYS HE WOULD STOP BY TO CHECK ON THEM AND BRING THEM FOOD.

HE EVEN PATCHED UP THINGS HE FOUND AROUND THE HOUSE IN NEED OF REPAIR.

ONE NIGHT, MAMA NOTICED BABUSHKA WAS RESTLESS AND COULDN'T SLEEP. SHE ASKED WHAT WAS WRONG.

AY, THAT LOVELY EASTER CAKE...PLEASE, BRING ME SOME OF IT...

BUT-- MAMA, EASTER IS *SIX MONTHS* AWAY....!

SOMETHING ABOUT MY GRANDMOTHER'S EXPRESSION BOTHERED MAMA. SHE PUT HER HAND ON HER FOREHEAD...

POOR BABUSHKA WAS BURNING UP WITH FEVER.

MAMA TRIED AS BEST SHE COULD TO COMFORT HER MOTHER, GIVING HER SIPS OF WATER FROM THE WELL AND HOLDING A COOL, WET TOWEL TO HER FOREHEAD.

THE NEXT DAY, WHEN THE GERMAN SAW HOW SICK BABUSHKA WAS, HE WAS *MOST DISTRESSED*.

HE LEFT, APPARENTLY WITH SOME PURPOSE...

A WHILE LATER, HE BROUGHT A GERMAN MEDICAL ORDERLY PLUS A LOCAL UKRAINIAN WOMAN WHO WAS ABLE TO UNDERSTAND GERMAN.

THE MEDIC SAYS HE MOSTLY DEALS WITH WOUNDS, BUT HE WILL DO WHAT HE CAN.

THE MEDIC GAVE HER SOMETHING FOR FEVER, BUT THE OLD WOMAN'S CONFUSED MUTTERING CONTINUED...

〈WHAT IS IT SHE ASKS SO MUCH?〉

〈IT'S EASTER CAKE.〉

〈SHE SAYS SHE WOULD LIKE SOME.〉

THE SERGEANT AND THE TRANSLATOR SPOKE FOR A WHILE...

...AND THEN HE LEFT.

WHEN HE RETURNED THAT EVENING, HIS BURLAP SACK WAS BULGING WITH ITEMS. IMMEDIATELY, HE AND THE TRANSLATOR WENT TO WORK IN MAMA'S KITCHEN.

THEY BUILT A WOOD FIRE IN THE STOVE, THEN BROKE OUT THE INGREDIENTS: *FLOUR, SUGAR, POPPY SEEDS, VANILLA EXTRACT, A CAN OF EVAPORATED MILK...*

THE OLD SERGEANT EVEN HAD A SMALL SACK OF HARD RAISINS, WHICH HE SOFTENED UP BY SOAKING THEM IN WATER.

THEY FOUND A FEW SMALL, EMPTY CANS--A PERFECT SIZE, SINCE THERE WASN'T ENOUGH FOR MORE THAN THAT--AND POURED THE BATTER INTO THE CANS TO BAKE.

SHE WATCHED THE SERGEANT AS HE HANDLED THIS TASK WITH A NATURAL TALENT AND AFFECTION. THAT WAS WHEN MAMA REALIZED HE WAS NO COMBAT SOLDIER...

...BUT A *COOK*.

HE PULLED FOUR LITTLE CAKES FROM THE OVEN...

...AND COVERED THE TOPS IN ICING HE MADE FROM THE MILK, SUGAR, AND VANILLA.

THEN...

...HE PRESENTED THE FINEST CAKE TO BABUSHKA...

BABUSHKA SNIFFED THE CAKE, OPENED HER EYES, AND SMILED.

CHRIST IS RISEN!

MAMA HAD THE STRANGE FEELING BABUSHKA WAS LOOKING STRAIGHT THROUGH THEM AT SOMETHING OR SOMEONE NOT EVEN IN THE ROOM.

HE IS RISEN INDEED...

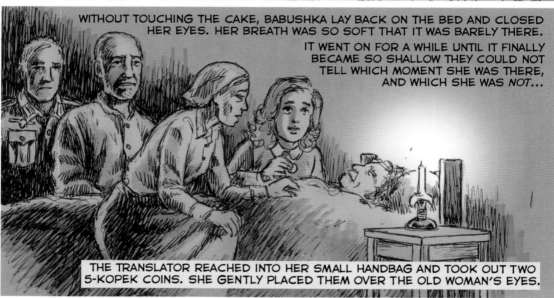

WITHOUT TOUCHING THE CAKE, BABUSHKA LAY BACK ON THE BED AND CLOSED HER EYES. HER BREATH WAS SO SOFT THAT IT WAS BARELY THERE.

IT WENT ON FOR A WHILE UNTIL IT FINALLY BECAME SO SHALLOW THEY COULD NOT TELL WHICH MOMENT SHE WAS THERE, AND WHICH SHE WAS *NOT*...

THE TRANSLATOR REACHED INTO HER SMALL HANDBAG AND TOOK OUT TWO 5-KOPEK COINS. SHE GENTLY PLACED THEM OVER THE OLD WOMAN'S EYES.

THE SERGEANT WENT OUT ONTO OUR DARK LITTLE PORCH...

...WHERE HE *WEPT*.

THE NEXT MORNING, THE SERGEANT WENT TO WORK GATHERING WOODEN DOORS FROM ABANDONED HOUSES AND BARNS...

HE WAS BUILDING A PROPER COFFIN FOR BABUSHKA.

THE ONLY PAINT HE HAD WAS GERMAN ARMY GRAY...

...BUT IT WAS FINE.

THERE WERE NO VILLAGE MEN TO ACT AS PALLBEARERS, SO THE SERGEANT GOT THREE OF HIS OWN MEN TO HELP. THE GERMANS CARRIED MY GRANDMOTHER'S COFFIN TO THE *ZALIZNYCHNY MASYV*, WHERE THEY HAD ALREADY CAREFULLY DUG A TIDY LITTLE GRAVE.

SEVERAL WOMEN WERE WAITING THERE TO MOURN.

THE TRANSLATOR, WHO MAMA FOUND OUT WAS NAMED LENA KRYSAN, WALKED ALONG ARM-AND-ARM WITH HER.

THE GERMAN SERGEANT HAD EVEN FOUND AN ORTHODOX PRIEST TO PERFORM PROPER FUNERAL RITES.

MAMA RECALLED THE SAD DAY OF HER FATHER'S FUNERAL...

...AND HOW OUR OWN GOVERNMENT REFUSED TO LET A PRIEST OFFICIATE AT HIS SERVICE.

THE IRONY OF IT HELD A BITTERSWEET TANG...

IT HAD TAKEN A KINDLY ENEMY TO CONFER THE GRACE OF COMMON HUMAN DECENCY.

STALIN AND HIS *STAVKA*, THE RED ARMY COMMAND HEADQUARTERS, CONCENTRATED ALL THEIR EFFORTS ON THE BUKRIN SECTOR. BUT ONE POLITICAL COMMISSAR CONSIDERED THE LYUTEZH BRIDGEHEAD TO BE A BETTER STRATEGY--*GENERAL NIKITA KHRUSHCHEV.*

WHY DO THEY IGNORE US...?

WELL, THE *GERMANS* SURELY WON'T-- NOT FOR LONG.

INDEED, THEY *DIDN'T!* THE GERMANS THREW A WALL OF PANTHER TANKS ACROSS OUR PATH TO BLOCK OUR ADVANCE OUT OF THE BRIDGEHEAD. AT *KURSK*, THE PANTHERS HAD PERFORMED POORLY--BUT THE *PANZERTRUPPEN* HAD WORKED OUT THE BUGS.

THEY WERE NOW A DEADLY WEAPON.

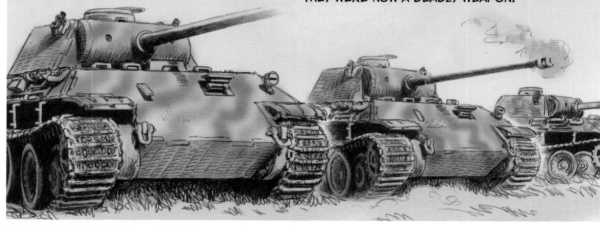

IN OUR BRIGADE'S COMMAND TANK, MILLA AND I BORE WITNESS TO COLONEL NOZDRIN'S FRUSTRATION AS WE STRUGGLED TO GET THE UPPER HAND...

BLAST IT! THERE AREN'T ENOUGH OF US TO STRIKE THEM AT MORE THAN ONE POINT AT A TIME!

HOW MANY TIMES HAD COLONEL NOZDRIN SEEN HIS MEN AND TANKS SHATTERED AGAINST THE IRON PROFESSIONALISM OF THE *WEHRMACHT?* HIS FACE REMAINED AS HARD AS IT EVER WAS--BUT I KNEW TOO WELL THAT INSIDE, HIS GUTS WERE TWISTING.

OUR *T-34s* PROBED FOR A WEAK SPOT, BUT THE CRESCENT-SHAPED LINE OF PANTHERS HAD EVERY APPROACH COVERED.

SOON, THE SLOPE WAS DOTTED WITH BURNING HULKS--

--AND THE CHARRED, SMOLDERING FORMS OF THEIR LOST CREWS.

THE GERMAN GUNNERS WERE CALMLY PERFORMING THEIR GRIM WORK...

...WHEN SUDDENLY--!

FROM THE SOUTH CAME A GRINDING, RUMBLING MASS OF *SU-152s*, SQUAT ASSAULT GUNS THAT WERE MORE THAN A MATCH FOR THE PANTHERS, OR EVEN THE TIGERS. THAT'S WHY WE CALLED THEM *ZVEROBOY,* OR "BEAST KILLERS."

AN ASSAULT GUN BRIGADE! TALK ABOUT PERFECT TIMING!

WHOO-RAAAHHH!

THE *SU-152s* TORE INTO THE PANTHERS!

THE GERMAN LINE COLLAPSED.

THEN THE RAINS OF AUTUMN BEGAN AND SLOWED DOWN JUST ABOUT *EVERYTHING.*

WELL, IF IT ISN'T THE *TYMOSHENKO TWINS!* DO JOIN US...WE HAVE PLENTY OF ROOM OVER AT THE BANQUET TABLE.

WHY, THANK YOU VERY MUCH, CAPTAIN KOVCHENKO!

HAVE YOU HEARD THERE'S NOW A PONTOON BRIDGE ACROSS THE DESNA? SOON, ONE WILL CROSS THE DNIEPER!

REALLY?

AND COMRADE STALIN HAS DECIDED TO SHIFT THEIR EFFORTS FROM *BUKRIN...*

...TO *HERE!*

THAT'S *GREAT!* I SURE WOULD LIKE TO SEE KIEV AGAIN...

WOULDN'T YOU, MILLA?

I GUESS.

YOU DON'T REALLY EXPECT THINGS TO BE JUST LIKE THEY *WERE,* DO YOU?

WHAT DO YOU MEAN?

DON'T BE SO *NAIVE!*

YOU WON'T FIND EVERYONE WAITING THERE LIKE SOME BIG HAPPY REUNION!

WELL... I GUESS I CAN *HOPE.*

"*HOPE*"?!

I GAVE UP ON HOPE A LONG TIME AGO.

385

FOR THE NEXT SEVEN NIGHTS, IT RAINED--AND THE RED ARMY USED THIS TO COVER THE MOVEMENT OF TENS OF THOUSANDS OF MEN TO THE *LYUTEZH BRIDGEHEAD.*

THEY TOOK FOUR ROUTES, MOVING BY NIGHT AND RESTING DURING THE DAY.

TANKS AND CANNON WERE MOVED ACROSS ON PONTOON BRIDGES, THEN CAMOUFLAGED UNDER TREES, HAYSTACKS, BARNS--UNDERNEATH ANYTHING THAT COULD CONCEAL THEM.

SOME 2,000 ARTILLERY PIECES AND 500 ROCKET LAUNCHERS WERE PLACED NEAR THE PERIMETER OF THE BRIDGEHEAD.

THE AREA BECAME VERY CROWDED, VERY *FAST.*

SIX RIFLE DIVISIONS WERE BROUGHT IN. IT WAS NECESSARY THAT AS MANY MEN AS POSSIBLE WERE TO RIDE ON THE TANKS.

I DECIDED THAT THE *T-34s* NEEDED MORE HANDRAILS.

ONE DAY, I WAS WITH COLONEL NOZDRIN AS HE DISCUSSED THE WEATHER WITH A FEW OFFICERS.

IF ONLY WE HAD 24 TO 48 HOURS WITH NO RAIN, WE COULD GET THIS OFFENSIVE MOVING...!

WELL, ANYWAY-- CALL ALL COMPANY OFFICERS TO TODAY'S MEETING AT 1600. *DISMISSED.*

SERGEANT TYMOSHENKO... MAY I--*EH*, HAVE A QUICK WORD WITH YOU?

YES, SIR?

YOU KNOW...WE DON'T KNOW WHAT SHAPE KIEV WILL BE IN WHEN WE GET THERE, BUT-- WELL, I WAS WONDERING...

YES?

D'YOU SUPPOSE, IF WE COULD FIND ANYTHING THERE LIKE, SAY, A RESTAURANT--

A... WHAT?

UH, IF WE HAD TIME, WE COULD--YOU KNOW, CLEAN UP A BIT, THEN GO OUT FOR A NICE MEAL...

I MEAN, *UH*...NOT AS A SERGEANT AND CAPTAIN, BUT--

LIKE COMRADES?

YES! EH-- NO, *NO.* MORE LIKE--*EH*...

LIKE A *MAN* AND A *WOMAN.*

OH, YES! *EXACTLY* LIKE THAT.

WELL, I'M OFF TO THE MEETING. WE WILL SPEAK LATER. THINK ABOUT IT...

CAPTAIN KOVCHENKO...?

I WOULD *LOVE* TO.

FINALLY, THE RAIN STOPPED...

THE GROUND BEGAN TO DRY, AIDED BY A COLD NORTHERN WIND.

WINTER WAS RETURNING.

AT DAWN ON *NOVEMBER 3,* OUR ARTILLERY AND ROCKETS OPENED UP ON THE GERMANS. AT THAT MOMENT, I REMEMBERED A SONG WE ONCE SANG...

"OH, DNIEPER, DNIEPER, YOU FLOW FAR AWAY... AND YOUR WATER IS AS CLEAR AS TEARS..."

WELL, WE WERE OVER THE DNIEPER NOW. OUR ENGINES ROARED AND THROBBED...

EVERYONE *ABOARD WHO'S* COMING!

I WAS ON MY WAY HOME.

THROUGH SMOKE AND FLAMES, WE POURED AHEAD.

SOME INITIAL RESISTANCE CAME FROM WELL DUG-IN ENEMY POSITIONS...

...BUT THEIR ADVANTAGE DIDN'T LAST VERY LONG.

THAT WAS AN *88!*

KATUSHA, COME UP HERE--

--AND TAKE THE *GUNNER'S* SEAT!

ANOTHER ONE OF OUR TANKS WAS HIT...!

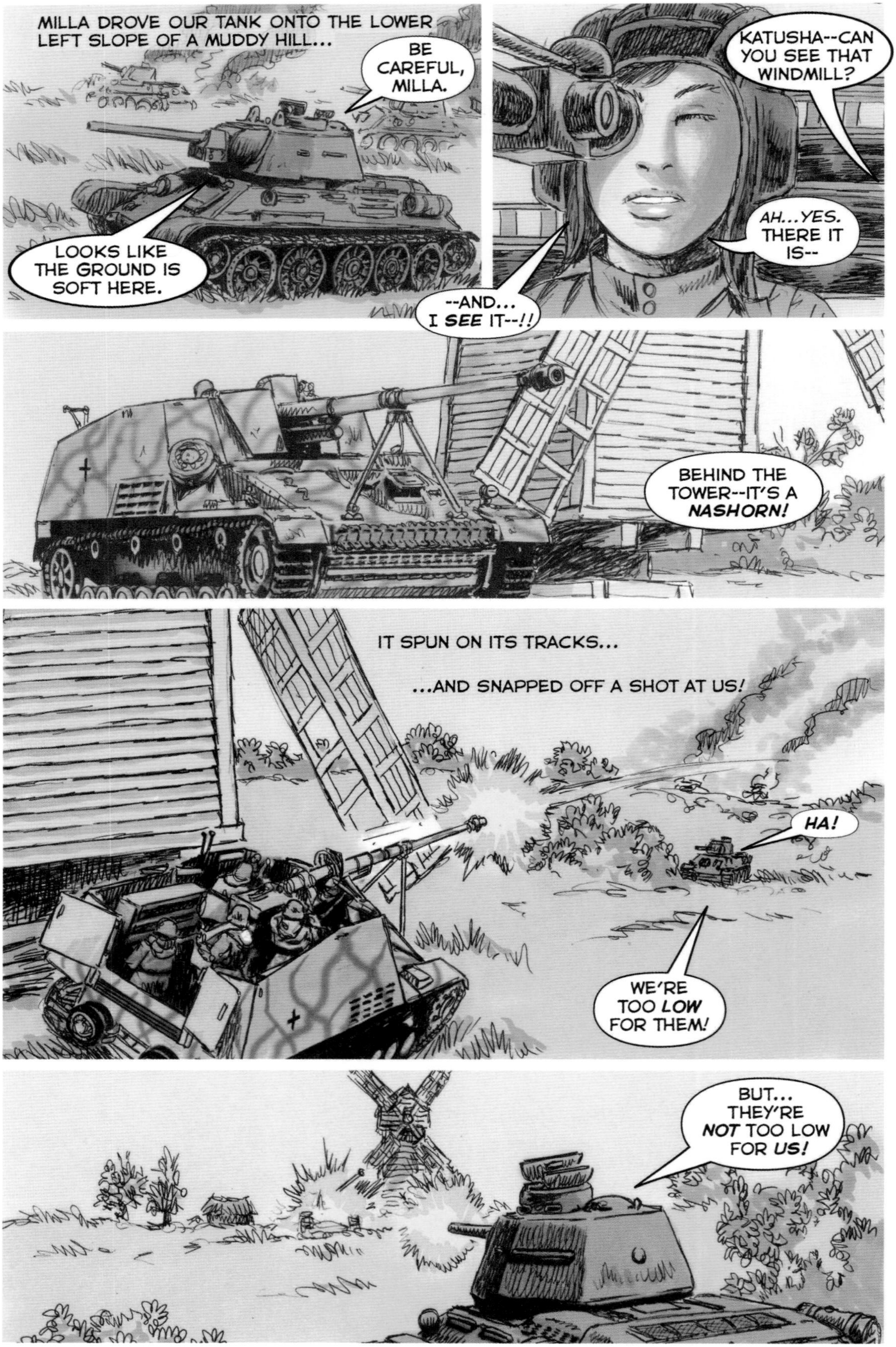
MILLA DROVE OUR TANK ONTO THE LOWER LEFT SLOPE OF A MUDDY HILL...
BE CAREFUL, MILLA.
LOOKS LIKE THE GROUND IS SOFT HERE.
KATUSHA--CAN YOU SEE THAT WINDMILL?
AH...YES. THERE IT IS--
--AND... I SEE IT--!!
BEHIND THE TOWER--IT'S A NASHORN!
IT SPUN ON ITS TRACKS...
...AND SNAPPED OFF A SHOT AT US!
HA!
WE'RE TOO LOW FOR THEM!
BUT... THEY'RE NOT TOO LOW FOR US!

HEY! THAT WAS A GREAT SHOT, PAPA NOZDRIN!

HA! BUT IT WASN'T ME--IT WAS *LITTLE* TYMOSHENKO!

PLEASE, COLONEL-- *DON'T* CREDIT ME!

THE ONLY SHOT I WILL EVER BRAG ABOUT MAKING WILL BE MY *FINAL* ONE.

I LOOKED DOWN--AND SAW BLOODY CUTS ON CAPTAIN KOVCHENKO'S CHEEK.

WHAT HAPPENED TO YOU?

EH, NOTHING. I WAS JUST RIDING THE FIRST TANK TO GET HIT.

SUDDENLY, I WAS ANGRY.

YOU SHOULDN'T DO THAT!

KOLYA AND HIS MEN ALL LAUGHED AT THIS, AS IF I'D MADE A JOKE--

BUT I *WASN'T* KIDDING.

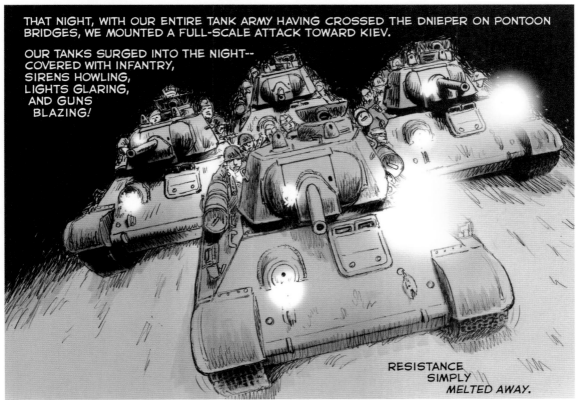

THAT NIGHT, WITH OUR ENTIRE TANK ARMY HAVING CROSSED THE DNIEPER ON PONTOON BRIDGES, WE MOUNTED A FULL-SCALE ATTACK TOWARD KIEV.

OUR TANKS SURGED INTO THE NIGHT-- COVERED WITH INFANTRY, SIRENS HOWLING, LIGHTS GLARING, AND GUNS BLAZING!

RESISTANCE SIMPLY *MELTED AWAY.*

EARLY THE NEXT MORNING, MAMA HEARD A KNOCK ON HER DOOR...

IT WAS THE OLD GERMAN SERGEANT.

OH! GOOD MORNING.

BITTE... SIE MÜSSEN *GEN WESTEN* GEHEN.

MAMA SAW LENA KRYSAN AT THE GATE, WITH SUITCASE IN HAND.

THEY HAVE ORDERED ALL THE ABLE-BODIED TO GO WEST.

THE LOOK ON THE GERMAN'S FACE WAS ONE OF APOLOGETIC MISERY.

HE BOWED AWKWARDLY TO MAMA, THEN HELD OUT A SMALL PAIR OF GERMAN ARMY BOOTS...

BITTE, LIEBE DAME...ICH GEBE IHNEN DIESE *STIEFEL.*

I'LL HAVE TO WRAP SOME RAGS AROUND MY FEET FOR THESE...

COULD I HELP YOU PACK ANYTHING?

IF YOU'D LIKE, BUT THERE ISN'T MUCH...

YOU KNOW...HE IS VERY MUCH ASHAMED ABOUT ALL THIS.

WELL, I WOULDN'T WANT HIM TO BE OVERJOYED...

LENA, I MUST LEAVE MY FAMILY A NOTE. DO YOU HAVE A PEN AND PAPER?

LENA ASKED THE SERGEANT, WHO HANDED MAMA HIS PEN AND A 5-REICHSMARK NOTE.

THIS WILL HAVE TO DO...

SHE PLACED IT ON A LITTLE TABLE UNDER THE ICON...ALONG WITH SOMETHING ELSE.

ONE OF *THESE* WAS LEFT OVER. SOMEHOW IT SEEMS RIGHT TO LEAVE IT HERE...

...LIKE AN OFFERING.

THEY JOINED A LIVING RIVER OF CIVILIANS ON THE ROAD.

SO, YOU ARE GOING, TOO...?

:SIGH: I MIGHT AS WELL...

ALTHOUGH I REALLY DIDN'T DO ANYTHING DIFFERENTLY THAN OTHERS DID...

...I WOULD BE CONSIDERED BY MANY A *COLLABORATOR.*

AS DID EVERYONE ELSE, I DID WHAT I HAD TO DO...TO *SURVIVE.*

SINCE I LEFT MY HOME THE FIRST TIME, I'VE LOST A *DAUGHTER,* A *GRANDSON,* AND NOW, MY *MOTHER...*

I PRAY I *DON'T LOSE* ANYONE *ELSE.*

393

KIEV. EARLY IN THE MORNING HOURS OF *NOVEMBER 6, 1943,* THE RED FLAG AGAIN FLEW ATOP THE OLD DUMA BUILDING ON KHRESHCHATYK BOULEVARD.

HERE, THE DESTRUCTION WAS TERRIBLE.

BUT THE TRUTH IS THAT IT WAS THE *RUSSIANS* WHO HAD BLOWN UP THIS STREET BEFORE THEY LEFT.

...AND NOW ALL I CAN THINK IS "WHERE'S MAMA?" AND IF SHE WILL COME BACK--!

A MOMENT, KATUSHA...YES, COLONEL NOZDRIN?

WE'RE DEAD ON OUR FEET--ABOUT OUT OF GAS AND AMMO. I JUST GOT WORD WE'LL BE GOING NOWHERE FOR AT LEAST A WEEK....

IN THE MEANTIME, I WANT YOU AND SERGEANT TYMOSHENKO TO TAKE MY *GAZ* AND TRY TO INITIATE CONTACT WITH THE NATIVES.

ESPECIALLY THOSE WHO MAY ALSO BE NAMED *TYMOSHENKO.*

YES, COMRADE COLONEL! *DELIGHTED,* COMRADE COLONEL!

ARE YOU READY TO ROLL?

I'LL GO GET *MILLA!*

MILLA, COME ON--WE'RE GOING TO THE HOUSE! LET'S SEE IF ANYBODY IS HOME!

THAT'S FINE, KATUSHA. YOU GO AHEAD. I HOPE YOU FIND SOMEBODY THERE.

DON'T YOU *WANT* TO GO?

I DON'T THINK SO.

IT'S NOT AS IF THEY ARE *RELATIVES* OF MINE.

MILLA! YOU'RE MY *SISTER--!!*

KATUSHA, I AM NOT RELATED TO ANYONE ON THIS EARTH.

LOOK, GO AHEAD. I HOPE YOU FIND EVERYTHING YOU ARE LOOKING FOR.

I'LL BE ALL RIGHT.

MILLA'S NOT COMING?

NO.

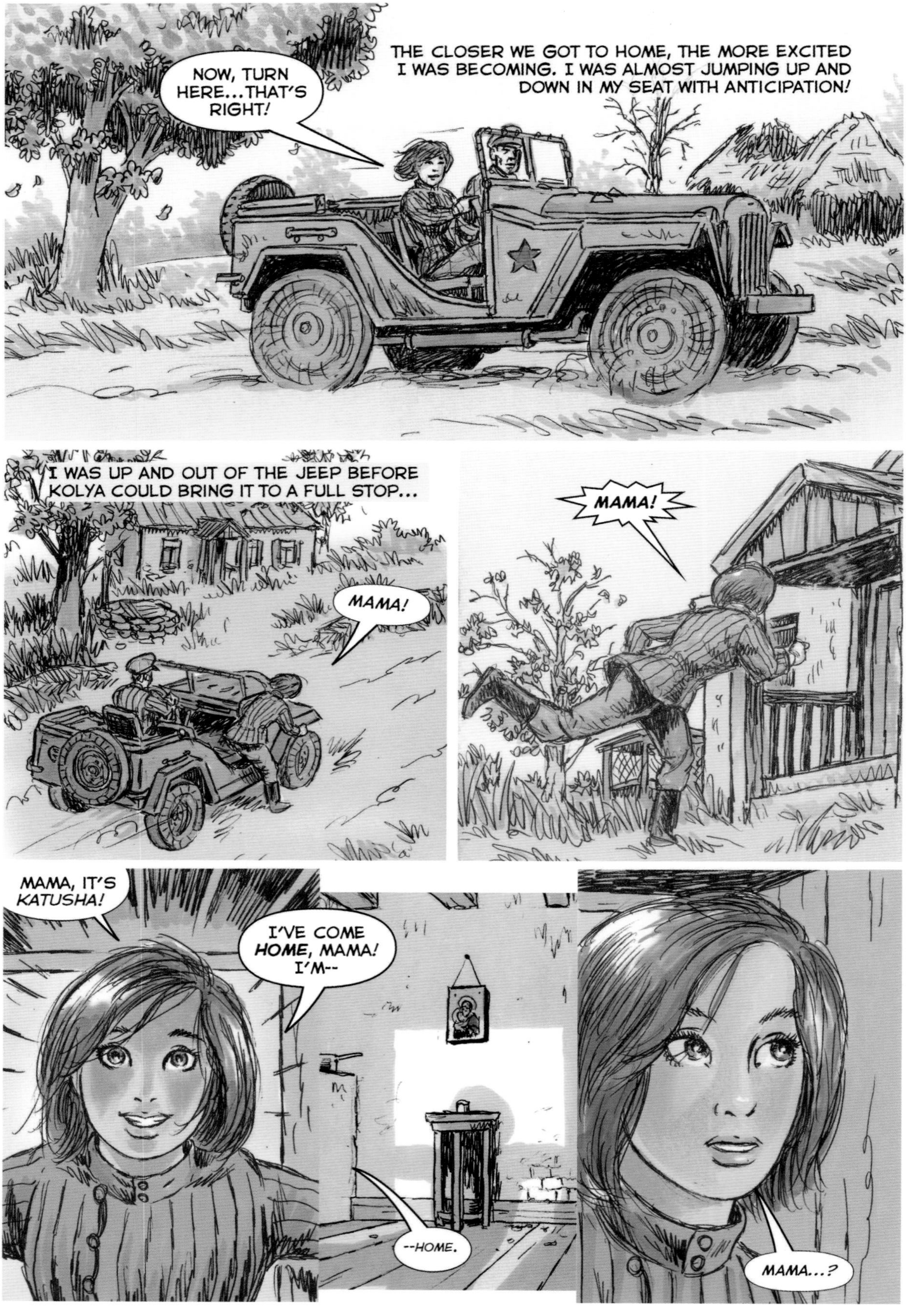
THE CLOSER WE GOT TO HOME, THE MORE EXCITED I WAS BECOMING. I WAS ALMOST JUMPING UP AND DOWN IN MY SEAT WITH ANTICIPATION!
NOW, TURN HERE...THAT'S RIGHT!
I WAS UP AND OUT OF THE JEEP BEFORE KOLYA COULD BRING IT TO A FULL STOP...
MAMA!
MAMA!
MAMA, IT'S KATUSHA!
I'VE COME HOME, MAMA! I'M--
--HOME.
MAMA...?

THEN I SAW WHAT SAT ON THE TABLE BELOW THE ICON...

WHA--?

GERMAN MONEY...AND AN *EASTER CAKE*--?

BUT--? THIS CAKE IS ALMOST *FRESH*...!

AND SOMETHING'S WRITTEN ON THE MONEY...?

"MY LOVING FAMILY, I HAVE BEEN HERE AND WILL RETURN, IF POSSIBLE. I PRAY THAT I WILL FIND YOU HERE.

"MAY GOD PROTECT US ALL. --MAMA."

SOMEHOW, ON THE WAY HERE, I HAD EXPECTED TO FIND EVERYTHING JUST THE WAY IT HAD ALL BEEN BEFORE...

...MAMA AT THE STOVE...

VASILY AND MILLA IN THE GARDEN... NATASHA AND PAPA PLAYING WITH DIMA...

I EVEN IMAGINED COLONEL NOZDRIN SAYING TO ME, "STAY HOME, KATUSHA. YOU'VE DONE ENOUGH. YOU HAVE PAID THE PRICE...

"YOUR WAR IS *OVER.*"

I HELD MAMA'S ICON AND RAN MY FINGERS ACROSS ITS WORN GOLD LEAD...

MY GOD, KOLYA...

...HOW I *HATE* THIS WAR...!

IS THERE ANY WAY OUT OF THIS WAR--BESIDES VICTORY?

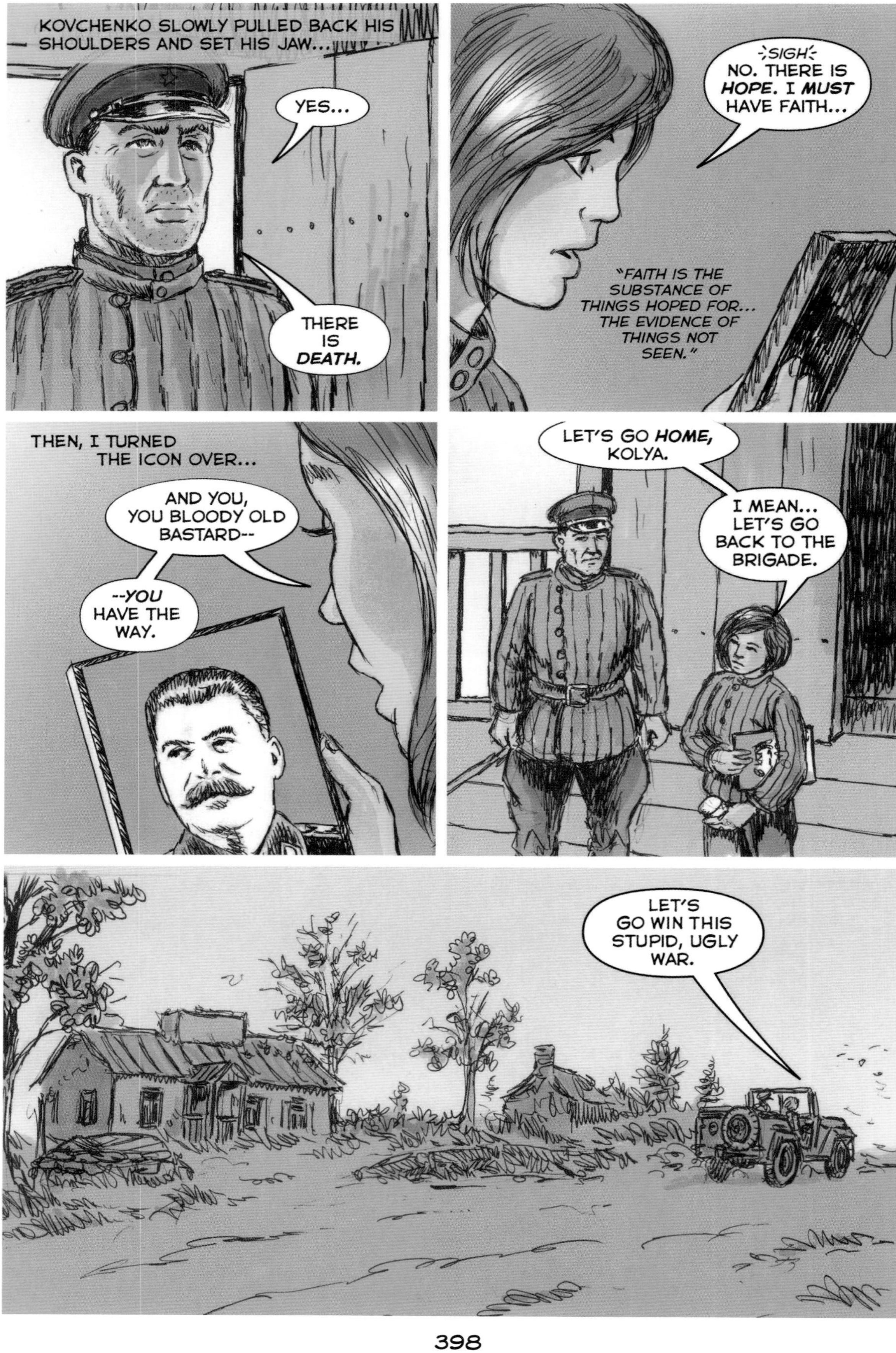
KOVCHENKO SLOWLY PULLED BACK HIS SHOULDERS AND SET HIS JAW...
YES...
THERE IS *DEATH.*
SIGH
NO. THERE IS ***HOPE.*** I ***MUST*** HAVE FAITH...
"FAITH IS THE SUBSTANCE OF THINGS HOPED FOR... THE EVIDENCE OF THINGS NOT SEEN."
THEN, I TURNED THE ICON OVER...
AND YOU, YOU BLOODY OLD BASTARD--
--***YOU*** HAVE THE WAY.
LET'S GO ***HOME,*** KOLYA.
I MEAN... LET'S GO BACK TO THE BRIGADE.
LET'S GO WIN THIS STUPID, UGLY WAR.

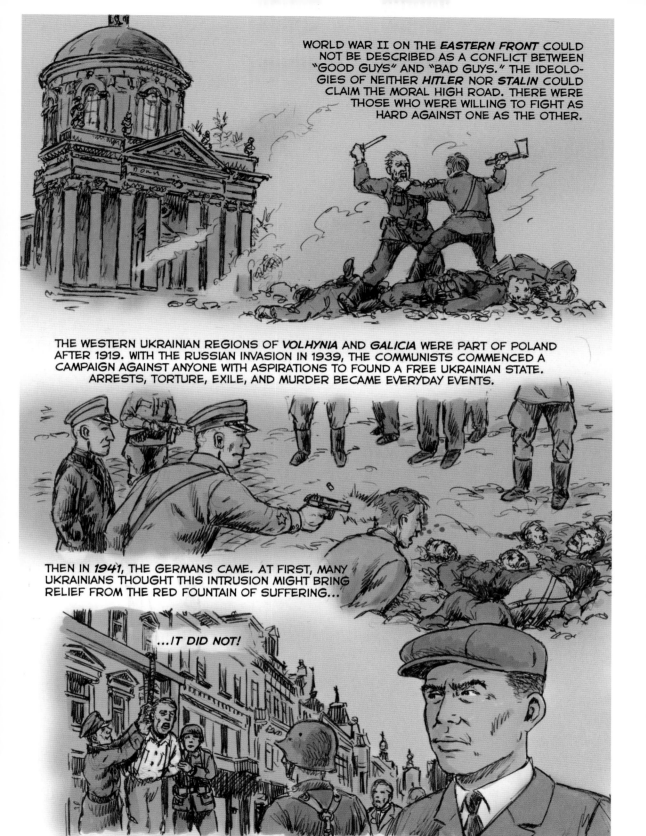

WORLD WAR II ON THE *EASTERN FRONT* COULD NOT BE DESCRIBED AS A CONFLICT BETWEEN "GOOD GUYS" AND "BAD GUYS." THE IDEOLOGIES OF NEITHER *HITLER* NOR *STALIN* COULD CLAIM THE MORAL HIGH ROAD. THERE WERE THOSE WHO WERE WILLING TO FIGHT AS HARD AGAINST ONE AS THE OTHER.

THE WESTERN UKRAINIAN REGIONS OF *VOLHYNIA* AND *GALICIA* WERE PART OF POLAND AFTER 1919. WITH THE RUSSIAN INVASION IN 1939, THE COMMUNISTS COMMENCED A CAMPAIGN AGAINST ANYONE WITH ASPIRATIONS TO FOUND A FREE UKRAINIAN STATE. ARRESTS, TORTURE, EXILE, AND MURDER BECAME EVERYDAY EVENTS.

THEN IN *1941*, THE GERMANS CAME. AT FIRST, MANY UKRAINIANS THOUGHT THIS INTRUSION MIGHT BRING RELIEF FROM THE RED FOUNTAIN OF SUFFERING...

...*IT DID NOT!*

THOSE WHO POSSESSED THE WILL AND THE ABILITY TO DO SOMETHING ABOUT THIS PROBLEM KNEW THEY COULD NOT SIMPLY PICK ONE SIDE OVER THE OTHER... *THEY HAD TO FIGHT BOTH!*

SO WAS BORN THE *UKRAINIAN INSURGENT ARMY*, COMMONLY KNOWN AS THE *UPA*.
THE SOLDIERS OF THE *UPA* WERE WELL TRAINED AND DISCIPLINED, AND FOUGHT
A DEFENSIVE *AND* OFFENSIVE WAR AGAINST THE GERMANS.

BUT SOON, THE *UPA* WAS ENGAGING IN RUNNING GUN BATTLES WITH *RED PARTISANS!*
IN AN ATTEMPT TO WIPE OUT THE *UPA,* COMMUNIST GUERILLA LEADER *SIDOR KOVPAK*
LED HIS PARTISANS SOUTHWESTWARD ACROSS UKRAINE.

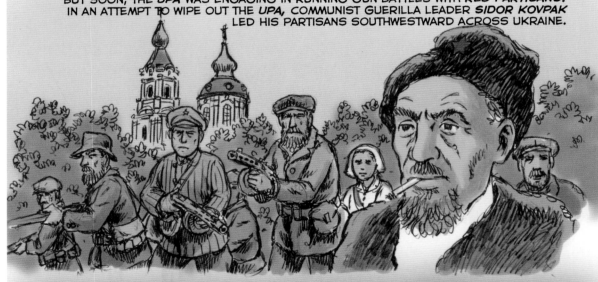

BUT THE *UPA'S* INTELLIGENCE NETWORK WAS EXCELLENT, AND THEY FREQUENTLY
KNEW THE RED PARTISANS' ROUTE OF ADVANCE LONG BEFORE SEEING THEM.

:YEAAGGHH!!!:

A COUPLE GOT AWAY...

THEN LET'S GET THEIR WEAPONS AND GET OUT OF HERE.

HEY!

THIS ONE'S STILL ALIVE!

HE'S NOT HURT BAD--JUST STUNNED BY A GRENADE.

HE'S ONLY A KID.

WELL, LET'S TAKE HIM WITH US....

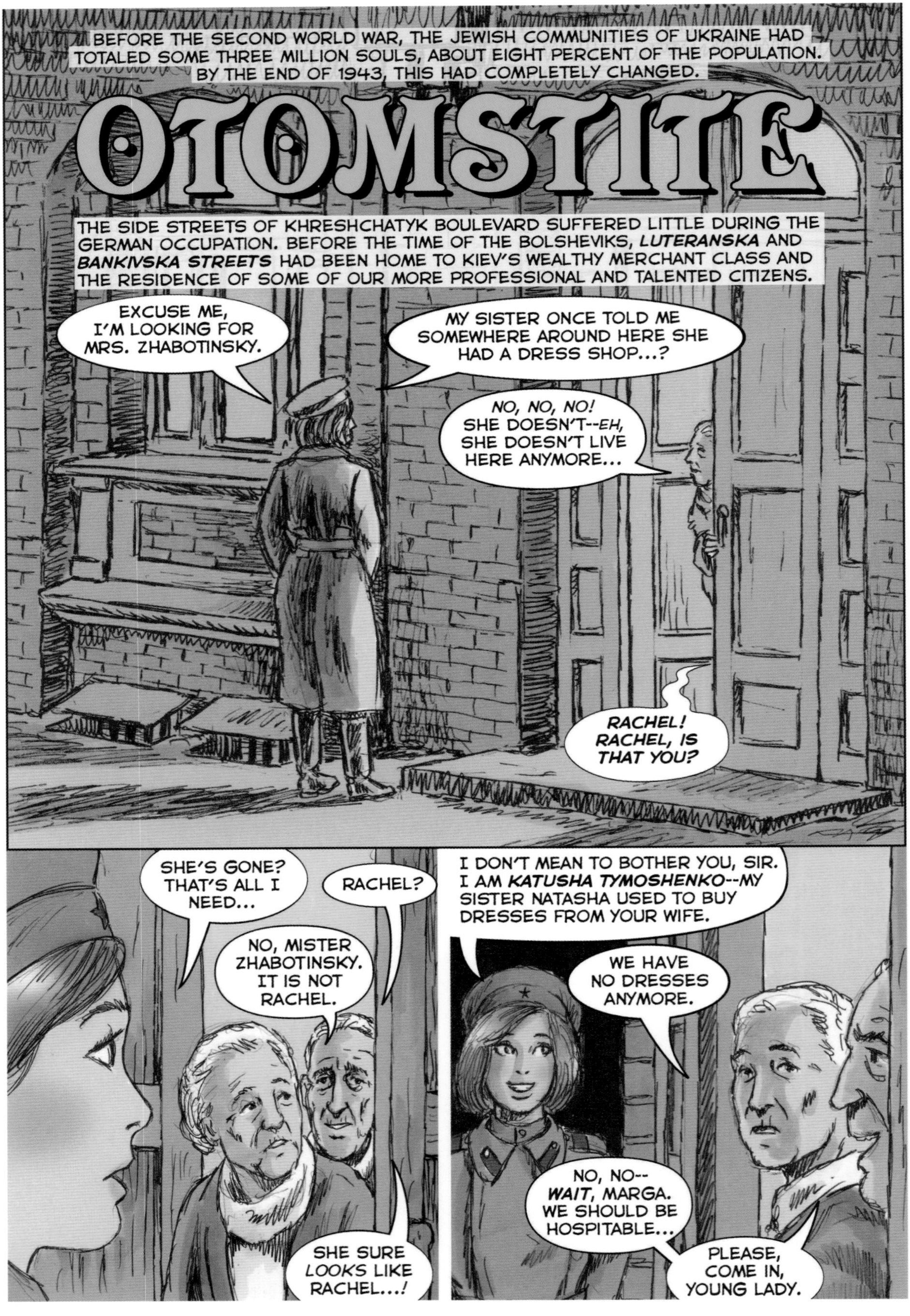
BEFORE THE SECOND WORLD WAR, THE JEWISH COMMUNITIES OF UKRAINE HAD TOTALED SOME THREE MILLION SOULS, ABOUT EIGHT PERCENT OF THE POPULATION. BY THE END OF 1943, THIS HAD COMPLETELY CHANGED.
OTOMSTITE
THE SIDE STREETS OF KHRESHCHATYK BOULEVARD SUFFERED LITTLE DURING THE GERMAN OCCUPATION. BEFORE THE TIME OF THE BOLSHEVIKS, *LUTERANSKA* AND ***BANKIVSKA STREETS*** HAD BEEN HOME TO KIEV'S WEALTHY MERCHANT CLASS AND THE RESIDENCE OF SOME OF OUR MORE PROFESSIONAL AND TALENTED CITIZENS.
EXCUSE ME, I'M LOOKING FOR MRS. ZHABOTINSKY.
MY SISTER ONCE TOLD ME SOMEWHERE AROUND HERE SHE HAD A DRESS SHOP...?
NO, NO, NO! SHE DOESN'T--*EH,* SHE DOESN'T LIVE HERE ANYMORE...
RACHEL! RACHEL, IS THAT YOU?
SHE'S GONE? THAT'S ALL I NEED...
RACHEL?
NO, MISTER ZHABOTINSKY. IT IS NOT RACHEL.
SHE SURE *LOOKS* LIKE RACHEL...!
I DON'T MEAN TO BOTHER YOU, SIR. I AM ***KATUSHA TYMOSHENKO***--MY SISTER NATASHA USED TO BUY DRESSES FROM YOUR WIFE.
WE HAVE NO DRESSES ANYMORE.
NO, NO-- ***WAIT***, MARGA. WE SHOULD BE HOSPITABLE...
PLEASE, COME IN, YOUNG LADY.

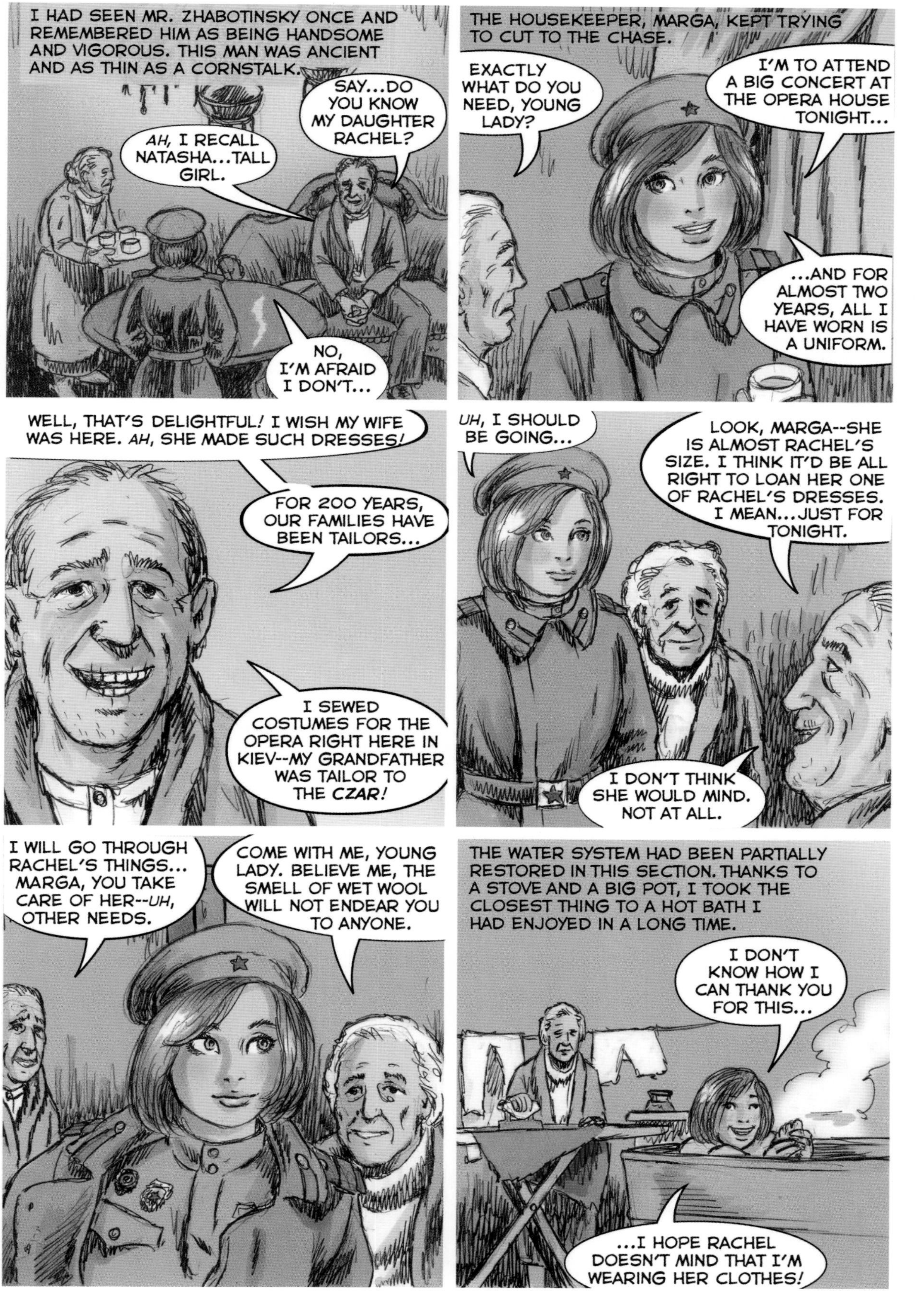
I HAD SEEN MR. ZHABOTINSKY ONCE AND REMEMBERED HIM AS BEING HANDSOME AND VIGOROUS. THIS MAN WAS ANCIENT AND AS THIN AS A CORNSTALK.
SAY...DO YOU KNOW MY DAUGHTER RACHEL?
AH, I RECALL NATASHA...TALL GIRL.
NO, I'M AFRAID I DON'T...
THE HOUSEKEEPER, MARGA, KEPT TRYING TO CUT TO THE CHASE.
EXACTLY WHAT DO YOU NEED, YOUNG LADY?
I'M TO ATTEND A BIG CONCERT AT THE OPERA HOUSE TONIGHT...
...AND FOR ALMOST TWO YEARS, ALL I HAVE WORN IS A UNIFORM.
WELL, THAT'S DELIGHTFUL! I WISH MY WIFE WAS HERE. AH, SHE MADE SUCH DRESSES!
FOR 200 YEARS, OUR FAMILIES HAVE BEEN TAILORS...
I SEWED COSTUMES FOR THE OPERA RIGHT HERE IN KIEV--MY GRANDFATHER WAS TAILOR TO THE CZAR!
UH, I SHOULD BE GOING...
LOOK, MARGA--SHE IS ALMOST RACHEL'S SIZE. I THINK IT'D BE ALL RIGHT TO LOAN HER ONE OF RACHEL'S DRESSES. I MEAN...JUST FOR TONIGHT.
I DON'T THINK SHE WOULD MIND. NOT AT ALL.
I WILL GO THROUGH RACHEL'S THINGS... MARGA, YOU TAKE CARE OF HER--UH, OTHER NEEDS.
COME WITH ME, YOUNG LADY. BELIEVE ME, THE SMELL OF WET WOOL WILL NOT ENDEAR YOU TO ANYONE.
THE WATER SYSTEM HAD BEEN PARTIALLY RESTORED IN THIS SECTION. THANKS TO A STOVE AND A BIG POT, I TOOK THE CLOSEST THING TO A HOT BATH I HAD ENJOYED IN A LONG TIME.
I DON'T KNOW HOW I CAN THANK YOU FOR THIS...
...I HOPE RACHEL DOESN'T MIND THAT I'M WEARING HER CLOTHES!

MARGA PAUSED, HER EYES SAD...

LISTEN, CHILD. TWO YEARS AGO, MR. ZHABOTINSKY AND HIS FAMILY WERE TAKEN TO *BABI YAR*...

HE WAS THE ONLY ONE TO *RETURN*.

THIS NEWS HIT ME LIKE A SLAP IN THE FACE.

OH, THAT POOR OLD MAN...

...AND I'LL BE WEARING A DEAD GIRL'S CLOTHES.

ALL YOU NEED TO KNOW IS THAT THIS MAKES THE OLD MAN HAPPY.

LET US JUST LEAVE IT AT THAT.

I HOPE YOU LIKE THE TRADITIONAL UKRAINIAN STYLE. IT'S SILK. MY WIFE WORKED THREE YEARS ON IT, ON AND OFF.

OH, IT'S *GORGEOUS!*

HER EMBROIDERY IS *AMAZING!*

I MADE THIS CLOAK FOR A PERFORMANCE OF *BORIS GODUNOV*. WHILE IT SEEMS AN ODD COMBINATION...

...I THINK IT WILL DO NICELY.

AND THESE EARRINGS BELONGED TO MY GYPSY GRANDMOTHER.

THANK YOU BOTH SO MUCH! I'LL BE BACK AFTER THE PERFORMANCE.

TAKE YOUR TIME, DEAR.

I'LL LEAVE THE DOOR UNLOCKED FOR YOU.

I WENT TO THE CORNER OF *SOFIYSKA* AND *NEZALEZHNOSTI* WHERE I WAS TO MEET KOLYA AND SAT DOWN ON A BENCH.

WHEN HE WALKED RIGHT BY ME WITHOUT A GLIMMER OF RECOGNITION, IT WAS ALL I COULD DO TO KEEP FROM LAUGHING.

FOR A WHILE, HE STOOD AT THE CORNER, WAITING IMPATIENTLY...

THEN SUDDENLY...

IT WAS LIKE A DREAM.

KOLYA WAS WALKING ON AIR AS HE ESCORTED ME INTO THE RESTAURANT. COLONEL NOZDRIN'S EYES NEARLY POPPED OUT OF HIS HEAD, AND OUR CORPS COMMANDER AUTOMATICALLY ROSE TO HIS FEET.

I HAD ALWAYS WANTED TO BE AS GLAMOROUS AS NATASHA. THAT NIGHT, FOR THE FIRST TIME IN MY LIFE, I TRULY FELT BEAUTIFUL.

NOT EVEN THE ARMY COOKS COULD SPOIL SUCH A MAGICAL EVENING. AFTER THE MEAL, THE *OPERA* AWAITED...

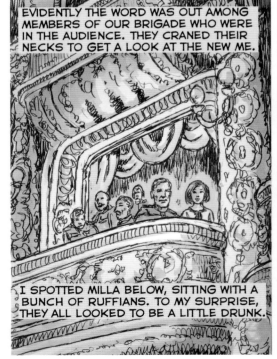

EVIDENTLY THE WORD WAS OUT AMONG MEMBERS OF OUR BRIGADE WHO WERE IN THE AUDIENCE. THEY CRANED THEIR NECKS TO GET A LOOK AT THE NEW ME.

I SPOTTED MILLA BELOW, SITTING WITH A BUNCH OF RUFFIANS. TO MY SURPRISE, THEY ALL LOOKED TO BE A LITTLE DRUNK.

THE CONCERT, PERFORMED BY TRAVELING ENTERTAINMENT TROUPES AND MILITARY BANDS, WAS PLEASANT, THOUGH IT HAD A LITTLE TOO MUCH MARTIAL MUSIC FOR ME. THE SINGERS WERE GOOD, AND I ENJOYED THE SING-ALONG.

TOWARD THE EVENING'S END, THE ORCHESTRA PLAYED A SELECTION FROM DIMITRY SHOSTAKOVICH'S *SEVENTH SYMPHONY*, ALREADY BEING CALLED THE *LENINGRAD SYMPHONY.*

WRITTEN DURING THE VERY FIRST WINTER OF THE WAR, MANY OF THE MUSICIANS WHO PRACTICED IT STARVED TO DEATH BEFORE IT WAS FORMALLY PERFORMED...

...KOLYA'S WIFE WAS ONE OF THEM.

IT WAS A WONDERFUL EVENING! I WAS SHOWERED WITH A GREAT DEAL OF ATTENTION. VERA FOMICHEVA TOLD ME SHE THOUGHT WE WERE THE MOST HANDSOME COUPLE THERE.

I CAUGHT A GLIMPSE OF MILLA...

...WITH THE STRANGEST LOOK ON HER FACE.

AS WE WALKED THE QUIET STREETS ARM-IN-ARM...

I MUST STILL CARRY THIS DRESS BACK TO MISTER ZHABOTINSKY...

WELL, THEN...

...BEFORE YOU TURN BACK INTO A PUMPKIN...?

IT'S RIGHT HERE. MARGA PROMISED ME SHE WOULD LEAVE THE DOOR UNLOCKED.

THE FIRST THING I HEARD AS WE ENTERED WAS THE SOUND OF SOMEONE *WEEPING*.

MARGA--? WHAT'S THE MATTER?

POOR MISTER ZHABOTINSKY..! HIS DESPAIR HAS BEEN SO, SO *GREAT*... BUT *STILL*--

SHE TURNED TOWARD A SLIM RAY OF LIGHT COMING FROM A NEARLY CLOSED DOOR...

--I DID NOT THINK HE WOULD DO *THIS*...!

KOLYA AND I ENTERED THE ROOM...

BACK AT THE PARTISAN CAMP...

THE LEADERS HAVE MADE THEIR *DECISION,* ZAPOLYE.

I'M GOING TO TELL YOU WHAT IT IS, BUT YOU KEEP IT TO YOURSELF.

ALL RIGHT.

THEY KNOW THAT VASILY HAS BEEN CAPTURED BY THE *UPA.* KOVPAK HAS A SPY PLACED WITH THE BANDERITES IN *IVANO FRANKIVSK...*

...THEY FEAR THAT VASILY MAY KNOW HIM--SO THEY'RE SENDING THE DAMNED FOUR EXECUTIONERS TO KILL HIM!

WHAT!? THEY CAN'T DO THAT!

YES, THEY *CAN!* AND REMEMBER, YOU DIDN'T HEAR IT FROM ME, PRIEST.

YOU AND I ARE *EVEN.*

I CANNOT LET THAT HAPPEN, ZHENYA--I OWE *TARAS TYMOSHENKO* TOO MUCH.

BUT--I CAN'T SEE *HOW* YOU CAN STOP IT FROM HAPPENING.

I'VE SENTRY DUTY AT 0400. I'LL SLIP OUT THEN. BUT... ZHENYA--

--I DON'T SEE HOW *YOU* WILL BE ABLE TO FACE KATUSHA...

...UNLESS *YOU* DO SOMETHING.

HE'S CRAZY! WHAT COULD WE POSSIBLY DO?

ON THE WAY BACK TO HER ENCAMPMENT, ZHENYA PASSED THE HEADQUARTERS TENT JUST AS FOUR INDIVIDUALS CAME OUT...

MY GOD! IT'S *PRIKIP HONSHAR!*

...AND *HE* IS ONE OF THE FOUR EXECUTIONERS!

HOW DID THAT COME ABOUT?

AT ABOUT 0430 THE NEXT MORNING, FATHER ZAPOLYE PICKED THAT TIME TO SLIP AWAY...

IT'S GOOD AND QUIET. NO ONE WILL MISS ME UNTIL...

CARE TO HAVE A TRAVELING COMPANION?

ZHENYA! WHAT MADE YOU DECIDE TO JOIN ME?

NEVER YOU MIND...

...JUST BE GLAD THAT YOU HAVE SOMEONE TO COVER THE REAR.

ON THE MORNING OF *FEBRUARY 17, 1944,* THE GERMAN FORCES TRAPPED WITHIN THE *CHERKASSY-KORSUN POCKET* WERE DESPERATELY TRYING TO EXTRACT THEMSELVES.

A LARGE FORMATION OF THESE TRAPPED TROOPS REACHED THE *GNILOY TIKICH RIVER.* IT WAS A SMALL BARRIER, ONLY TWENTY FEET WIDE AND TEN FEET DEEP. BUT IT WAS VERY SWIFT, AND THE TEMPERATURE WAS *TEN DEGREES BELOW ZERO.*

THE GERMANS DROVE A 17-TON HALF-TRACK INTO THE WATERS TO MAKE A BRIDGE, BUT IT WAS SWEPT AWAY.

MAYBE WE CAN MAKE A *HUMAN CHAIN...*

EVERYONE HANG ON TIGHTLY...

WHAT'S *THAT...?*

UM GOTTES WILLEN!

RUSSIAN TANKS! THE IVANS ARE HERE!

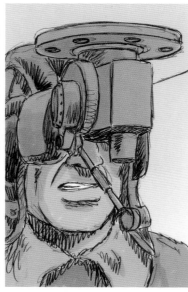

SOME MEN SWAM ACROSS THE RIVER, BUT BEFORE THEY COULD GET A HUNDRED YARDS BEYOND IT, THEIR CLOTHES FROZE SOLID. OTHERS STRIPPED AND TRIED TO THROW THEIR UNIFORMS ACROSS BEFORE SWIMMING.

THE UNLUCKY ONES FAILED TO GET THEIR BUNDLES ACROSS. THE LUCKY ONES WERE SIMPLY CUT DOWN BY THE MURDEROUS FIRE.

THAT'S IT, MEN...HOLD YOUR FIRE!

LET'S SAVE SOMETHING FOR THE INTELLIGENCE BOYS TO INTERROGATE.

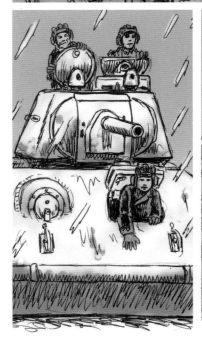

LORD...

413

SERGEANT DYATLONKO, PICK A TEAM TO CHECK THE BODIES FOR PAPERS OR DOCUMENTS.

YES, CAPTAIN KOVCHENKO.

ANATOLY AND BATAAR HAD STAYED WITH OUR BRIGADE AFTER UNCLE TARAS WAS KILLED.

SINCE ANATOLY WAS A PROFESSIONAL THIEF, A JOB LIKE THIS WAS PERFECT FOR HIM.

IT SEEMS ALMOST EVERY GERMAN SOLDIER OWNS A CAMERA. WHAT DO THEY TAKE PICTURES OF?

THEY TREATED THE TRIP TO RUSSIA AS SOME BIG SAFARI--AND THEY WANTED SNAPSHOTS OF THEIR TROPHIES.

WELL, IT'S NOT SUCH A FUN ADVENTURE FOR THEM ANYMORE...

THEY ALSO SEEM BENT ON RECORDING THEIR OWN CRIMES.

CAMERAS GO UP THE CHAIN OF COMMAND TO INTELLIGENCE-- THEY DEVELOP THE FILM AND EXAMINE IT ALL CLOSELY. ANY PHOTOGRAPHS WE FIND GET PASSED ALONG, TOO.

BUT I ALWAYS LIKE TO TAKE A PEEK FIRST.

WHAT CRIMES DID *THIS* YOUNG FELLOW CHOOSE TO KEEP IN HIS LITTLE PICTURE BOOK?

SHALL WE HAVE A LOOK...?

OH, GOD...!

I BET THESE WERE TAKEN AT *BABI YAR*..

NO! NO! I *DON'T* WANT TO SEE *ANYMORE!*

WHAT KIND OF PERSON WOULD CARRY SOMETHING LIKE *THAT* AROUND WITH THEM?

WELL, YOU'VE HEARD OF *KOPELEV?* LOOK AT HIS TANK.

HE HAS A HUMAN SKULL ON EACH FENDER. THEY SAY HE'S KNOCKED OUT 17 GERMAN TANKS, INCLUDING *THREE TIGERS!*

FACE IT... SOME PEOPLE *LIKE* WHAT THEY ARE DOING.

HE'S WON PRAISE FOR HIS FIGHTING ABILITY.

IS THAT NOT WHAT THEY GIVE *MEDALS* FOR?

"PRAISE FOR FIGHTING ABILITY!" COURAGE! BRAVERY!

BUT THE PICTURES IN THAT GERMAN'S PHOTO BOOK... I SAW *CRIMES! MURDER!*

TELL ME... WHERE IS THE *DIFFERENCE?*

THAT EVENING...

SORRY...SHE'S PAST FIELD REPAIR. THE TURRET RING IS WARPED. HALF THE TRACK LINKS ARE CRACKED. I'D SAY SHE'S ONLY GOOD FOR A FACTORY REBUILD.

HER TRANSMISSION'S SO FULL OF SHAVINGS THAT THE FLUID SPOONS OUT LIKE A BOWL OF KASHA.

WELL, IT'S JUST BEEN THE TWO OF US WORKING ON IT, AND NO ONE COULD HAVE DONE BETTER.

IT'S JUST THAT SHE IS LIKE ME...

...OLD AND TIRED.

HEY, LITTLE TYMOSHENKO. COLONEL NOZDRIN WANTS TO SEE YOU THIS EVENING, BUT NO HURRY...

SURE... I'LL GO RIGHT OVER.

DOBRY VYECHER, SGT. DYATLONKO! WHATEVER HAS YOU IN SUCH DEEP THOUGHT?

I WAS JUST THINKING THAT TODAY IS *FRIDAY...*

...AND WONDERING HOW MANY TIMES I'VE MISSED THE SABBATH SINCE I JOINED THE ARMY...

MY BEST FRIEND AT HOME WAS JEWISH, BUT NOT VERY RELIGIOUS.

MY WIFE, GOD REST HER SOUL, WAS A RABBI'S DAUGHTER...WHILE SHE YET LIVED, WE WERE IN BEFORE EVERY FRIDAY'S SUNSET.

SHE'S BEEN GONE NINE YEARS NOW. AFTER THAT, I BECAME A TRAVELING INSPECTOR WORKING FOR THE RAILROAD.

I UNDERSTAND YOUR FATHER IS A RAILROAD MAN.

YES, HE IS.

WELL, SINCE MY DEAR WIFE HAD GOT ME IN THE HABIT, I CONTINUED TO KEEP THE SABBATH...

I FOUND FAMILIES ALL OVER UKRAINE WHO'D TAKE ME IN WHEN I WAS IN THEIR AREA ON FRIDAYS. MY REVERENCE MADE ME A POPULAR MAN WITH THE FAITHFUL.

AS I TRAVELED THE RAILS, I WAS GREETED AS IF A SAINT--LIKE *A GOD IN ODESSA,* AS THEY SAY.

MAYBE SOON YOU'LL BE ABLE TO KEEP THE SABBATH *AGAIN,* GENRIKH.

WELL... THE MASTER AWAITS.

THE COLONEL LOOKED TIRED. I NOTICED HE AVOIDED LOOKING ME IN THE EYE...

I HEAR YOUR TANK IS WORN OUT...

YES, SIR. WORD SURE GOT AROUND FAST ON THAT.

I'LL GET RIGHT TO THE POINT...

MILLA HAS ASKED FOR COMMAND OF HER OWN TANK.

WHAT!?

I COULDN'T TURN HER DOWN. WHAT COULD I SAY? SHE WON THE *HERO OF THE SOVIET UNION* MEDAL!

IN FACT-- YOU'RE BOTH TOO EXPERIENCED FOR YOUR PRESENT DUTIES. SO...

...I'M GIVING YOU *BOTH* COMMAND OF YOUR *OWN TANKS!*

THESE ARE THE *NEW T-34/85* TANKS.

YOU'LL NOTICE THE BODY'S PRETTY MUCH THE SAME. BUT NOTE THE TURRET NOW HAS AN *85MM GUN*-- AND THE TANK HOLDS *THREE CREW MEMBERS!*

THREE?!

YES... GUNNER, LOADER, AND COMMANDER! HE--OR, EXCUSE ME, LADIES, *SHE* DOESN'T HAVE TO DOUBLE AS GUNNER ANYMORE. THE COMMANDER CAN FINALLY *COMMAND!*

THAT'S FOR ME!

MANY OF YOU DRIVERS CAN COMMAND FROM THE DRIVER'S POSITION, AND WE CAN WIRE THE INTERNAL COMMUNICATION THAT WAY.

418

SINCE CREWS WERE BEING KILLED FASTER THAN THEY CAME OUT OF SCHOOL, VOLUNTEERS WERE SCARCE.

SO YOU'RE *KOPELEV*... I'VE BEEN HEARING A LOT ABOUT YOU.

AND YOU'RE *BIG TYMOSHENKO.* HEARD A LOT ABOUT *YOU*, TOO.

I HEAR YOU JUST LOST YOUR LAST TANK.

I HAVE ONE OF THE NEW 85s. INTERESTED?

NO MORE COMMAND CRAP! ALL I WANT IS TO *SHOOT.* HELL, IF WE BURN, I'LL GET MY OWN HIDE OUT. I DON'T WANT ANYONE ELSE TO WORRY ABOUT...

NO PROBLEM.

I'LL HANDLE THE COMMAND... YOU JUST *SHOOT.*

I'VE LOST FIVE TANKS... AND I'M THE ONLY ONE WHO WALKED AWAY.

I SHOULD HAVE *DIED* A LONG TIME AGO.

I KNOW EXACTLY HOW YOU FEEL.

VERA FYODOROVICH HAD PROMISED TO PUT THE WORD OUT AMONG OUR SISTER BRIGADES THAT I NEEDED A CREW. I WONDERED IF I WOULD GET ANY VOLUNTEERS...

ER...EXCUSE ME, SERGEANT TYMOSHENKO?

EH--?

JUNIOR SERGEANT *PEREPELITSYN*... I'M REPORTING FOR DUTY.

OXANNA?

THE ONE AND ONLY! I HOPE YOU DON'T MIND THAT I'M HERE. I MEAN...

...AFTER THAT HELLACIOUS FIGHT WE HAD IN THE BARRACKS BACK AT TANK SCHOOL AND ALL.

OXANNA, I COULD NOT BE HAPPIER-- YOU'RE MY FIRST VOLUNTEER!

I WON'T BE THE LAST...

...I HEAR ANOTHER FACE FROM OUR PAST MAY BE SHOWING UP.

SHE WAS RIGHT! THE NEXT DAY, MARUSYA POZHARSKY, A GREAT FRIEND FROM THE TANK SCHOOL, REPORTED AS DRIVER.

BUT WE WOULDN'T BE AN *ALL-GIRL* CREW.

WE WERE SENT TWO YOUNG MEN STRAIGHT FROM TRAINING: *SLESAREV*, AN ASSISTANT DRIVER/RADIO OPERATOR/BOWGUNNER AND THE ONLY ONE YOUNGER THAN I...

HAS HE EVEN BEEN WEANED?

HA, I'LL FIND OUT TONIGHT.

...AND *RZEPECKE*, OUR LOADER, WHO WAS A WELL-EDUCATED POLE.

MEANWHILE, MUCH FARTHER WEST...

THEY'RE MOVING FAR TOO LEISURELY. WE MUST TAKE CARE NOT TO CATCH UP WITH THEM.

FATHER ZAPOLYE, I WAS WONDERING...

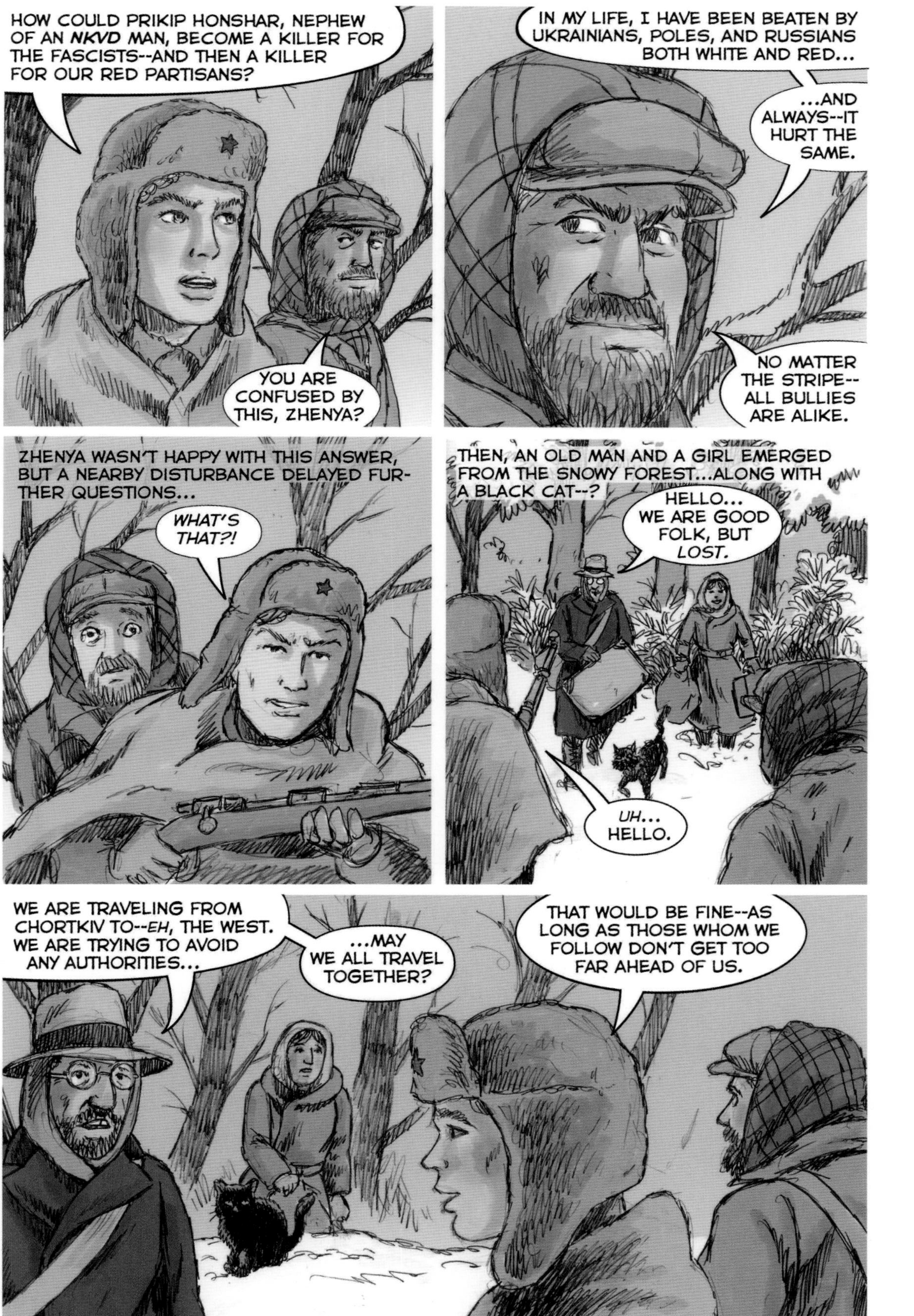
HOW COULD PRIKIP HONSHAR, NEPHEW OF AN NKVD MAN, BECOME A KILLER FOR THE FASCISTS--AND THEN A KILLER FOR OUR RED PARTISANS?
YOU ARE CONFUSED BY THIS, ZHENYA?
IN MY LIFE, I HAVE BEEN BEATEN BY UKRAINIANS, POLES, AND RUSSIANS BOTH WHITE AND RED...
...AND ALWAYS--IT HURT THE SAME.
NO MATTER THE STRIPE--ALL BULLIES ARE ALIKE.
ZHENYA WASN'T HAPPY WITH THIS ANSWER, BUT A NEARBY DISTURBANCE DELAYED FURTHER QUESTIONS...
WHAT'S THAT?!
THEN, AN OLD MAN AND A GIRL EMERGED FROM THE SNOWY FOREST...ALONG WITH A BLACK CAT--?
HELLO... WE ARE GOOD FOLK, BUT LOST.
UH... HELLO.
WE ARE TRAVELING FROM CHORTKIV TO--EH, THE WEST. WE ARE TRYING TO AVOID ANY AUTHORITIES...
...MAY WE ALL TRAVEL TOGETHER?
THAT WOULD BE FINE--AS LONG AS THOSE WHOM WE FOLLOW DON'T GET TOO FAR AHEAD OF US.

THE WAR THUNDERED ALL ALONG THE FRONT. FOR US, IT THUNDERED LOUDEST AT THE SMALL CITY OF *BERDYCHIV,* SOMETIMES CALLED THE JEWISH CAPITAL OF UKRAINE.

AS WE NEARED THE OUTSKIRTS, WE WERE GREETED BY A LINE OF SQUAT, UGLY *STUG III ASSAULT GUNS* SITUATED BETWEEN THE OUTLYING BUILDINGS.

OUR INFANTRY DISMOUNTED AND TOOK COVER BEHIND US.

FOR SOME REASON, I FELT ESPECIALLY BOLD AS A NEW TANK COMMANDER.

ALL RIGHT...

...LET'S JUST SEE WHAT THIS THING WILL DO.

PEEL OVER TO THE RIGHT.

THIS IS COLONEL NOZDRIN! LET THE 85mms GO FORWARD!

MAKE WAY FOR THE 85s!

THE ONLY WAY I COULD SEE BETTER WAS WITH MY HEAD STICKING UP OUT OF THE COMMANDER'S CUPOLA. I WASN'T USED TO FEELING SO EXPOSED.

PULL UP INTO THAT DRAW, MARUSYA.

TRY TO GET US INTO A HULL-DOWN POSITION!

MEANWHILE, MILLA WAS QUICKLY CLOSING THE GAP BETWEEN HER TANK AND THE ASSAULT GUNS.

IN THE EXCITEMENT, TWO *T-34-76*s FOLLOWED ALONG, BLAZING AWAY WITH THEIR LESS-POWERFUL WEAPONS.

MILLA'S GUN, MANNED BY THE STEELY-EYED KOPELEV, TOOK OUT ONE OF THE *STUGS*.

SHE THEN STEERED HER TANK BEHIND A STURDY STONE BARN.

ANOTHER *STUG* WENT AFTER THE MOST CONVENIENT TARGET...

CAN YOU GET A GOOD SHOT, OXANNA?

IF HE JUST STICKS OUT HIS NOSE A LITTLE FARTHER...

...THERE!

YOU GOT ANOTHER ONE, OXANNA! GOOD SHOOTING!

LET'S MOVE IN, MARUSYA.

MILLA TURNED AND CUT DOWN A NARROW STREET, LEAVING THE PURSUING *T-34/76* WIDE OPEN...

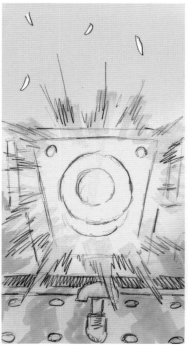

BOTH MILLA'S AND MY TANKS PULLED ONTO A MAIN STREET AT ALMOST THE SAME MOMENT. GERMAN TROOPS WERE RUNNING EVERYWHERE--FIGHTING, TRYING TO SURRENDER, OR JUST TRYING TO GET OUT OF THE WAY.

AND THERE, IN THE MIDDLE OF IT, WAS YET ANOTHER *STUG III*--WITH HIS REAR END POINTED IN THE WRONG DIRECTION.

AS THE REST OF OUR TANKS AND INFANTRY PUSHED PAST US INTO THE TOWN, MILLA CLIMBED OUT OF HER TANK, GRINNING WITH EXCITED TRIUMPH.

WOW! FIVE *STUGS* BETWEEN THE TWO OF US!

I LOOKED BACK TOWARD THE BURNING HULKS OF THE TWO TANKS THAT HAD FOLLOWED MILLA INTO TOWN.

WELL... IT WAS NOT WITHOUT ITS *COST.*

I COULDN'T HAVE DONE ANYTHING FOR THEM. I HAD MY HANDS FULL.

BUT, STILL...

WELL...WHAT WOULD *YOU* HAVE DONE?

I DON'T KNOW-- PROVIDE COVERING FIRE FOR THEM OR SOMETHING...?

UHH...

YOU'RE RIGHT. THERE WAS NOTHING YOU COULD DO.

I'LL SAY ONE THING FOR YOU, KATUSHA. YOU SURE DO KNOW HOW TO KNOCK THE SATISFACTION RIGHT OUT OF EVERYTHING I DO.

YOU'RE TWO OF A KIND, YOU AND YOUR DAMNED MOTHER!

AS MILLA STALKED OFF, I FELT SHOCKED AND HURT BY HER CONTEMPT FOR MAMA.

BUT THEN I CONSIDERED WHAT MILLA HAD SAID...AND I DECIDED TO TAKE IT AS A COMPLIMENT. EVEN IF SHE HADN'T MEANT IT THAT WAY.

THAT'S JUST WHAT *MAMA* WOULD DO.

THAT EVENING, AS OUR INFANTRY WAS STILL PUSHING ON THROUGH BERDYCHIV, WE SETTLED IN TO DO SOME MAINTENANCE.

AH, IT SURE FEELS GOOD HAVING SOME FRESH HANDS TO HELP DO THE WORK--

SERGEANT TYMOSHENKO!

EH? YES, CAPTAIN!

HAVE YOU SEEN SERGEANT DYATLONKO?

427

NO, NOT TODAY...

HE WENT LOOKING FOR SOME PEOPLE HE KNEW HERE FROM BEFORE THE WAR, AND HE HASN'T COME BACK...

I'M BECOMING WORRIED.

YOU KNOW, SERGEANT TYMOSHENKO--WE CAN DO THE MAINTENANCE WITHOUT YOU.

THAT'S RIGHT. GO HELP THE CAPTAIN LOOK FOR THE SERGEANT.

WE DROVE THROUGH THE STREETS OF BERDYCHIV, SEEING A FAIR NUMBER OF CIVILIANS. WE ASKED THEM WHERE THE JEWISH SECTION WAS, ONLY TO GET NERVOUS LOOKS AND COMMENTS LIKE "ZHIDS ALL GONE." WE FINALLY HAPPENED UPON SERGEANT DYATLONKO.

HE WAS SITTING BY HIMSELF ON A CURB, LOOKING DESPONDENT.

ARE YOU ALL RIGHT, GENRIKH? ARE YOU HURT?

I CANNOT UNDERSTAND IT. NOT AT ALL...

THIS PLACE--IS MY HOME...

SO MANY PEOPLE HERE--I KNOW THEM. SOME JUST WELL ENOUGH FOR A WARM GREETING...

...BUT SOME, I KNOW WELL ENOUGH TO SHARE GREAT FAMILY JOYS AND SORROWS...

AND *NOW*...THEY ARE *NO LONGER HERE!* SOME OF THEIR HOUSES SIT *EMPTY*--

--AND OTHER HOMES HAVE *STRANGERS* LIVING IN THEM!

ONCE, THESE STREETS *RANG* WITH THE SOUNDS OF MY NEIGHBORS PASSING BY...!

...GREETING ONE ANOTHER, OR EXCHANGING WORDS BOTH SIGNIFICANT AND TRIVIAL--SO MANY PEOPLE!

A MAN WHO WAS A PRINTER AND BOOKBINDER KEPT A SHOP RIGHT OVER THERE. HE WAS A FINE CRAFTSMAN WHO LIVED UPSTAIRS WITH HIS WIFE AND SON...

I REMEMBER THE WOMAN WHO'D PUSH HER LITTLE CART BY HERE. SHE SOLD TASTY BUNS, AND STRUDEL SHE MADE FROM APPLES AND NUTS...

"A SURGEON AND A PROSTHETIST WHO WERE BEST FRIENDS WOULD WALK TOGETHER TO THEIR JOBS AT THE CITY HOSPITAL EVERY DAY...

"THE DRIVER OF THE STREETCAR, ALSO A NEIGHBOR, WOULD LOOK OUT FOR THEM, AS THEY WOULD BE LOST IN SUCH DEEP CONVERSATION THEY'D WALK OUT IN FRONT OF HIS STREETCAR WITHOUT A GLANCE..."

AND A NIGHT WATCHMAN WHO, AS HE MADE HIS WAY HOME FROM WORK EACH MORNING, WOULD PASS HIS DAUGHTER ON HER WAY TO SCHOOL...AND HE'D ALWAYS PAUSE TO GENTLY KISS HIS LITTLE ONE ON THE FOREHEAD.

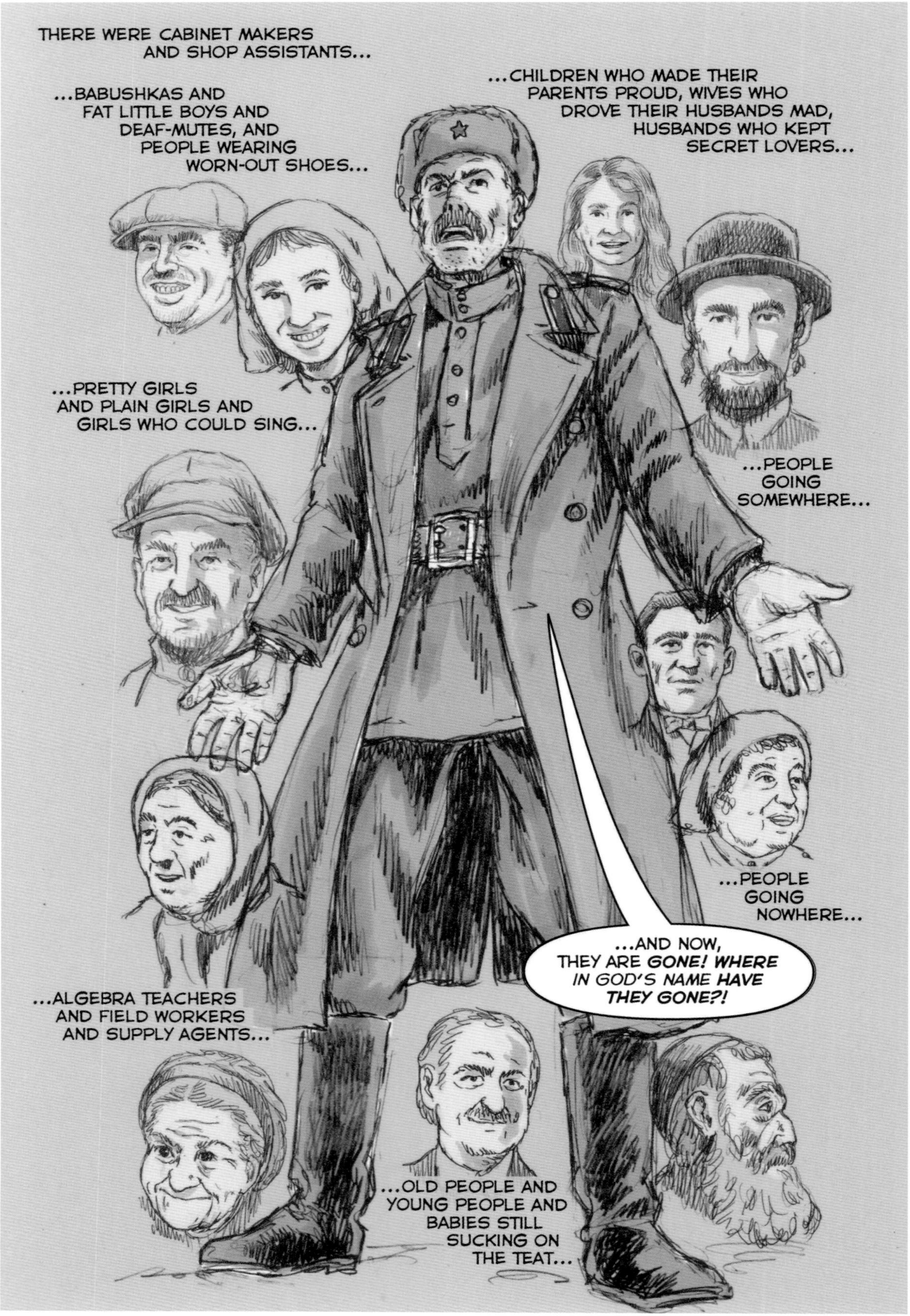
THERE WERE CABINET MAKERS AND SHOP ASSISTANTS...
...BABUSHKAS AND FAT LITTLE BOYS AND DEAF-MUTES, AND PEOPLE WEARING WORN-OUT SHOES...
...CHILDREN WHO MADE THEIR PARENTS PROUD, WIVES WHO DROVE THEIR HUSBANDS MAD, HUSBANDS WHO KEPT SECRET LOVERS...
...PRETTY GIRLS AND PLAIN GIRLS AND GIRLS WHO COULD SING...
...PEOPLE GOING SOMEWHERE...
...PEOPLE GOING NOWHERE...
...AND NOW, THEY ARE *GONE! WHERE* IN GOD'S NAME *HAVE THEY GONE?!*
...ALGEBRA TEACHERS AND FIELD WORKERS AND SUPPLY AGENTS...
...OLD PEOPLE AND YOUNG PEOPLE AND BABIES STILL SUCKING ON THE TEAT...

SERGEANT DYATLONKO SUDDENLY DISPLAYED THE FACIAL EXPRESSION OF SOMEONE MAKING A GREAT DISCOVERY.

HE TURNED HIS HEAD TO LOOK DOWN A SIDE STREET...

...AND SUDDENLY, HE WAS *OFF!*

BUT-- *WHERE IS HE* GOING?

I DON'T KNOW--BUT WE'RE FOLLOWING!

THE SERGEANT'S HEADLONG PATH LED US TO A PLACE WHERE HE MUST HAVE FELT HE COULD FIND A POSSIBLE ANSWER TO HIS PAINFUL QUESTIONS...

...A SYNAGOGUE.

GENRIKH THREW OPEN THE FRONT DOORS WITH A CRASH.

THERE WAS NO ONE THERE.

THE ALTAR HAD BEEN *SMASHED*, THE *TORAH BURNED*...

...AND THE FLOOR WAS LITTERED WITH THE WRECKAGE OF THE VIOLENCE.

THERE WAS AN UNDERTONE OF OLD, DRIED BLOOD IN THE MUSTY AIR. KOLYA'S RUNNER, SLAVA VENGROVA, NOTED THE REASON WHY.

LOOK AT THE WALLS--BULLET HOLES, ALL OVER...

FROM THE PATTERN, I'D SAY THOSE ARE FROM MACHINE GUNS.

MY EYES HAD TO ADJUST TO THE DIM LIGHT BEFORE I NOTICED SOMETHING ELSE...

IS THAT...?

YES! I CAN MAKE OUT FAINT *WRITING* IN PENCIL ON THE WALLS... IT'S EVERY PLACE I LOOK--!

MESSAGES HAD BEEN SCRAWLED *EVERYWHERE*.

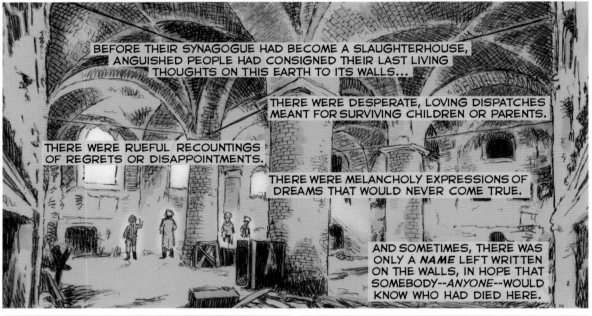

BEFORE THEIR SYNAGOGUE HAD BECOME A SLAUGHTERHOUSE, ANGUISHED PEOPLE HAD CONSIGNED THEIR LAST LIVING THOUGHTS ON THIS EARTH TO ITS WALLS...

THERE WERE DESPERATE, LOVING DISPATCHES MEANT FOR SURVIVING CHILDREN OR PARENTS.

THERE WERE RUEFUL RECOUNTINGS OF REGRETS OR DISAPPOINTMENTS.

THERE WERE MELANCHOLY EXPRESSIONS OF DREAMS THAT WOULD NEVER COME TRUE.

AND SOMETIMES, THERE WAS ONLY A *NAME* LEFT WRITTEN ON THE WALLS, IN HOPE THAT SOMEBODY--*ANYONE*--WOULD KNOW WHO HAD DIED HERE.

I FELT LIKE AN INTRUDER, READING THESE MOST PRIVATE AND PERSONAL MOMENTS.

SERGEANT, WHAT'S THIS WORD? I CAN'T QUITE MAKE IT OUT...

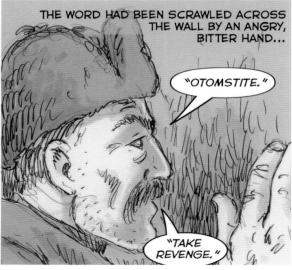

THE WORD HAD BEEN SCRAWLED ACROSS THE WALL BY AN ANGRY, BITTER HAND...

"OTOMSTITE."

"TAKE REVENGE."

432

ZHENYA'S GROUP DECIDED TO HOLE UP FOR THE NIGHT IN AN ABANDONED HOUSE IN A VILLAGE ALONG A ROCKY RIDGE. THERE'D BEEN NO CONTACT WITH THE GERMANS, BUT THEY HAD LOST SIGHT OF THE FOUR EXECUTIONERS THEY'D BEEN TAILING.

I GUESS THEY'VE OUTPACED US--THERE'S BEEN NO SIGN OF THEM SINCE THE DAY BEFORE YESTERDAY...

DO FORGIVE US FOR SLOWING YOU DOWN--

NO! DON'T SAY THAT.

IT WOULD'VE BEEN FAR WORSE TO CATCH UP WITH THEM.

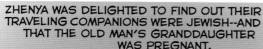

ZHENYA WAS DELIGHTED TO FIND OUT THEIR TRAVELING COMPANIONS WERE JEWISH--AND THAT THE OLD MAN'S GRANDDAUGHTER WAS PREGNANT.

WHAT'S IN THE SUITCASE?

UHH...

WELL... *MONEY.* OF A SORT.

MY GRANDFATHER'S A PRINTER. HE PRINTED MONEY FOR THE UKRAINIAN INSURGENT ARMY. IF WE PURCHASE ANYTHING FROM THE PEOPLE, WE PAY THEM IN THIS SCRIPT. IT'S WORTHLESS NOW--

--BUT ONE DAY, IT MIGHT *NOT* BE.

THE *BANDERITES?!* I'VE HEARD THEY *KILL* JEWS!

NONE OF THE ONES I KNOW DO THAT, BUT I HEAR THERE ARE SOME THAT HAVE.

MY FATHER'S A DOCTOR WITH THE *UPA*-- MY HUSBAND IS A SOLDIER. WE MET IN *KAMYANETS-PODILSKY* AFTER WE FLED FROM *VINNYTSYA.*

THAT'S WHERE YOU ARE FROM? TELL ME--

--WHAT HAPPENED THERE?

433

THE *HORROR* OF VINNYTSYA! FIRST OFF, THE GERMANS KILLED SOME 5,000 JEWS, AND THEN BUILT HITLER'S FORWARD HEADQUARTERS THERE! AFTERWARDS, THE 10,000 SLAVE LABORERS AND RUSSIAN P.O.W.s WHO BUILT IT WERE KILLED-- AND THEN, 9,000 MORE BODIES WERE FOUND BURIED IN A FRUIT ORCHARD--!

WHO WERE *THEY?*

WHY DID THE GERMANS KILL THEM?

OH, BUT THE GERMANS DIDN'T KILL THEM. THEY WERE VICTIMS OF THE *RUSSIANS!* THE *NKVD* DID IT, BACK IN THE '30s.

SO...WHY DID THEY KILL THEM? THEY DIDN'T LIKE THEM, I GUESS.

YOU KNOW... *"ENEMIES* OF THE *PEOPLE."*

ER-- I GUESS I OUGHT TO-- UM...

...GO AND TAKE LOOKOUT DUTY.

LOOK, ZHENYA... I UNDERSTAND YOU ARE FEELING VERY TROUBLED ABOUT ALL THIS, BUT--

OF *COURSE NOT! OH, NO--* I'M SURE YOUR *GOD* WILL HAVE SOMETHING COMFORTING TO SAY ABOUT EVERYTHING!

TELL ME, FATHER...

WHAT DOES *YOUR GOD* HAVE TO SAY ABOUT *THIS?*

FATHER ZAPOLYE CLOSED HIS EYES IN DEEPLY SILENT THOUGHT FOR A FEW LONG MOMENTS...

ZHENYA...TO BE PAINFULLY HONEST--? OF LATE, *MY* GOD HAS SAID *VERY LITTLE* TO ME.

OH, YES, I HAVE SOUGHT HIM--I HAVE LISTENED, AND PRAYED, AND READ HIS WORD...

I CAN ONLY TAKE SOLACE IN KNOWING THAT HE *HAS* SPOKEN TO ME BEFORE. I WILL TELL YOU WHAT HE SAID...

"GOD SAW THAT THE WICKEDNESS OF MAN WAS GREAT IN THE EARTH...

"...AND THAT EVERY IMAGINATION OF THE THOUGHTS OF HIS HEART WAS ONLY *EVIL*, CONTINUALLY...

"...AND IT REPENTED THE LORD THAT HE HAD MADE MAN ON THE EARTH...

"...AND IT GRIEVED HIM AT HIS *HEART*."

MANKIND IS EVIL, ZHENYA. I HAVE TRIED SO HARD TO SEE GOOD IN HIM--

--AND EVERY TIME, MAN HAS *FAILED* ME.

AND BECAUSE OF HIS EVIL NATURE, I'VE SOMETIMES BELIEVED OUR WORLD IS COMING TO AN END...

"...AT LEAST, OUR PART OF IT..."

IT WAS A BEAUTIFUL DAY, WITH HUGE WHITE CLOUDS FLOATING OVER THE DNIEPER LIKE SAILING SHIPS. VASILY AND DIMA PLAYED BAREFOOT ON THE SANDY SOIL WHILE NATASHA LOOKED ON AND LAUGHED IN DELIGHT.

MAMA AND I PREPARED CHICKEN AND PICKLED CUCUMBERS AND MUSHROOMS. I CUT UP BIG, SWEET STRAWBERRIES WE HAD JUST PICKED IN THE NEARBY WOODS.

UNCLE TARAS SLEPT IN THE GRASS. MILLA SPRAWLED BESIDE HIM, WATCHING HIS CHEST RISE AND FALL AS HE SNORED.

WE ALL ATE OUR FILL, AND THEN WE SANG SONGS UNTIL WE BECAME SLEEPY IN THE SUMMER SUN.

I LAY MY HEAD IN MY MOTHER'S LAP, AND SLEPT LIKE A YOUNG CHILD AS SHE STROKED MY HAIR...

...AND THEN, I AWOKE IN *HELL*.

A WORLD OF CROWS

KAMYANETS-PODILSKY, MARCH 1944. THE 11TH CENTURY SETTLEMENT BUILT ON A SHARP BEND OF THE SMOTRYCH RIVER. LEGEND HAS IT THAT WHEN TURKISH SULTAN OSMAN SAW IT IN 1621, HE ASKED WHO HAD BUILT IT. "ALLAH," ONE OF HIS GENERALS ANSWERED. "THEN LET ALLAH TAKE IT," SAID THE SULTAN, AND RETREATED WITH HIS ARMY.

BUT THE RED ARMY KNEW NO SUCH RESTRICTIONS. AS LONG AS THEY HAD ARTILLERY AND PLANES TO BOMBARD THE ROOFS, AND TANKS TO BREAK ITS WALLS, AND SOLDIERS TO DIG OUT THE GERMANS, NO OBJECTIVE SEEMED TOO DIFFICULT OR COSTLY.

KATUSHA?

HUH...? WHAT?

TIME TO SHOOT AGAIN.

WELL, THEN--GO AHEAD AND SHOOT! YOU DON'T HAVE TO TELL ME EVERY SINGLE TIME, RZEPECKE!

HEY!

DON'T GIVE HIM SUCH A HARD TIME, KATUSHA!

I WAS HAVING THE CRAMPS AND WAS IN A ROTTEN MOOD.

HAND ME THE SPADE. I GOTTA GO DIG OUT A TOILET.

HERE.

AND TAKE YOUR PISTOL.

THAT PISTOL LOOKS A LITTLE RUSTY. YOU SHOULD CLEAN IT.

I'M NOT AIMING TO ASSAULT THE GERMAN ARMY BY MYSELF! MY PISTOL WILL DO FINE.

RATHER THAN FACE THE BATTALION LATRINE WITH ITS SQUALOR AND LACK OF PRIVACY, I AMBLED DOWN THE SLOPE OF THE HILL AND AWAY FROM OUR TANKS.

I HAD NOTICED EARLIER THAT THE MANY MIGRATORY BIRDS AROUND HERE SEEMED TO BE IN A STATE OF CONFUSION. THEY'D NO DOUBT JUST RETURNED FROM THE SOUTH, I FIGURED...

...AND FINDING THIS LAND SO TORN UP SINCE LAST SUMMER, THEY MUST BE UNCERTAIN IF THEY HAD ARRIVED AT THEIR DESTINATION.

BUT THE CROWS SHOWED NO SUCH PERPLEXITY. WHAT THEY WERE LOOKING FOR WAS AVAILABLE AND PLENTIFUL.

I'D SCARCELY BEGUN RELIEVING MYSELF WHEN I BECAME AWARE OF A RUSTLING SOUND IN THE NEARBY BRUSH...

438

I FUMBLED WITH MY PANTS AS I DREW MY PISTOL FROM ITS HOLSTER...

THEN I SAW THEM.

TWO GERMAN SOLDIERS, EACH CARRYING TWO *PANZERFAUST*, WERE CREEPING THROUGH THE TALL GRASS...

IT WAS IMMEDIATELY CLEAR THAT THE VERY LAST THING THEY WERE EXPECTING WAS *ME*.

I HAD TO SEIZE THE ADVANTAGE AND STRIKE FIRST BEFORE THEY WOULD BE ABLE TO REACT...

...AND I *DID*!

THE *7.62MM* ROUND HIT ONE OF THEM SQUARE IN THE THROAT, WHICH WAS ENOUGH.

HOWEVER--HIS PARTNER WAS RAISING HIS *MP-40*!

I FIRED AGAIN, BUT AS I DID...

...I FELT MY GUN JAM SOLID!

MY SHOT HIT HIS WEAPON JUST ABOVE THE TRIGGER, MAKING IT AS USELESS AS MY *TOKAREV*.

439

HE SNARLED AS HE THREW DOWN HIS WEAPON AND PULLED A SMALL KNIFE FROM HIS BELT, THEN CAME AFTER ME WITH A LOOK OF RESOLVE AND EXCITEMENT.

I FLUNG MY PISTOL AT HIM, WHICH HE DODGED WITH LITTLE EFFORT.

I HAD NO OTHER WEAPON. ALL I HAD WAS MY SPADE.

AS I WIELDED IT AND CHARGED HIM, I LET OUT THE WILD RUSSIAN WAR CRY!

OOO-RAAWWW!!!

SURPRISED, HE FALTERED...

...AND I *STRUCK!*

AAAGGHH!!!

440

ALERTED BY THE TWO GUNSHOTS AND MY WAR CRY, MY COMRADES CAME RUNNING. SERGEANT DYATLONKO WAS THE FIRST ONE TO REACH ME...

WHAT IN THE NAME OF **GOD?!**

OKAY! *OKAY!* YOU CAN RELAX... IT'S *OVER.*

KATUSHA... PULL UP YOUR *PANTS.*

BY THE NAMES OF ALL THE SAINTS--!

THESE TWO MEANT TO KNOCK OUT SOME OF OUR TANKS! LUCKY FOR US YOU SPOTTED THEM.

UNLUCKY FOR *THEM.*

YOU'LL GET A MEDAL FOR THIS!

HUH?!

OHHH, *NO, NO, NO!* DON'T TELL ANYONE ABOUT THIS!

ANYBODY WHO TELLS ANYONE ABOUT THIS WILL GET HIS EYES CLAWED OUT!

...DOES EVERYBODY GET THAT?!!

I THEN REALIZED I WAS SOBBING, MY TEARS WASHING RUTS INTO THE BLOOD ON MY FACE. MY COMRADES STOOD THERE A MOMENT IN SHOCK AND EMBARRASSMENT...

THEN EACH SLOWLY TURNED AND WALKED AWAY.

AFTER SEVERAL DAYS OF SILENCE BEYOND THEIR EXPECTED DELIVERY DATE, THE *UPA* SENT OUT A MOUNTED PATROL IN SEARCH OF THE PRINTER AND HIS DAUGHTER.

ON THE ROCKY RIDGE AHEAD OF THEM, THE PATROL SPOTTED AN ABANDONED VILLAGE. WHIFFS OF SMOKE TRAILING FROM IT COMPELLED THEM TO INVESTIGATE.

LEADING THE PATROL WAS *VIKTOR YAROELAV,* THE COMMANDER OF A COMPANY-SIZED UNIT OF THE *UPA.*

RIDING WITH THEM WAS ONE OF THEIR NEWEST RECRUITS, *VASILY TYMOSHENKO.*

ZHENYA!

VASILY!

WHAT ARE *YOU* DOING HERE?

JUST TAKING CARE OF POOR *FATHER ZAPOLYE...*

...AND LOOKING AFTER THIS "MONEY" UNTIL SOMEONE COULD TAKE IT OFF MY HANDS.

THEN A FORLORN YOUNG SOLDIER CAME FORWARD.

BUT... WHERE IS *REBECKA?*

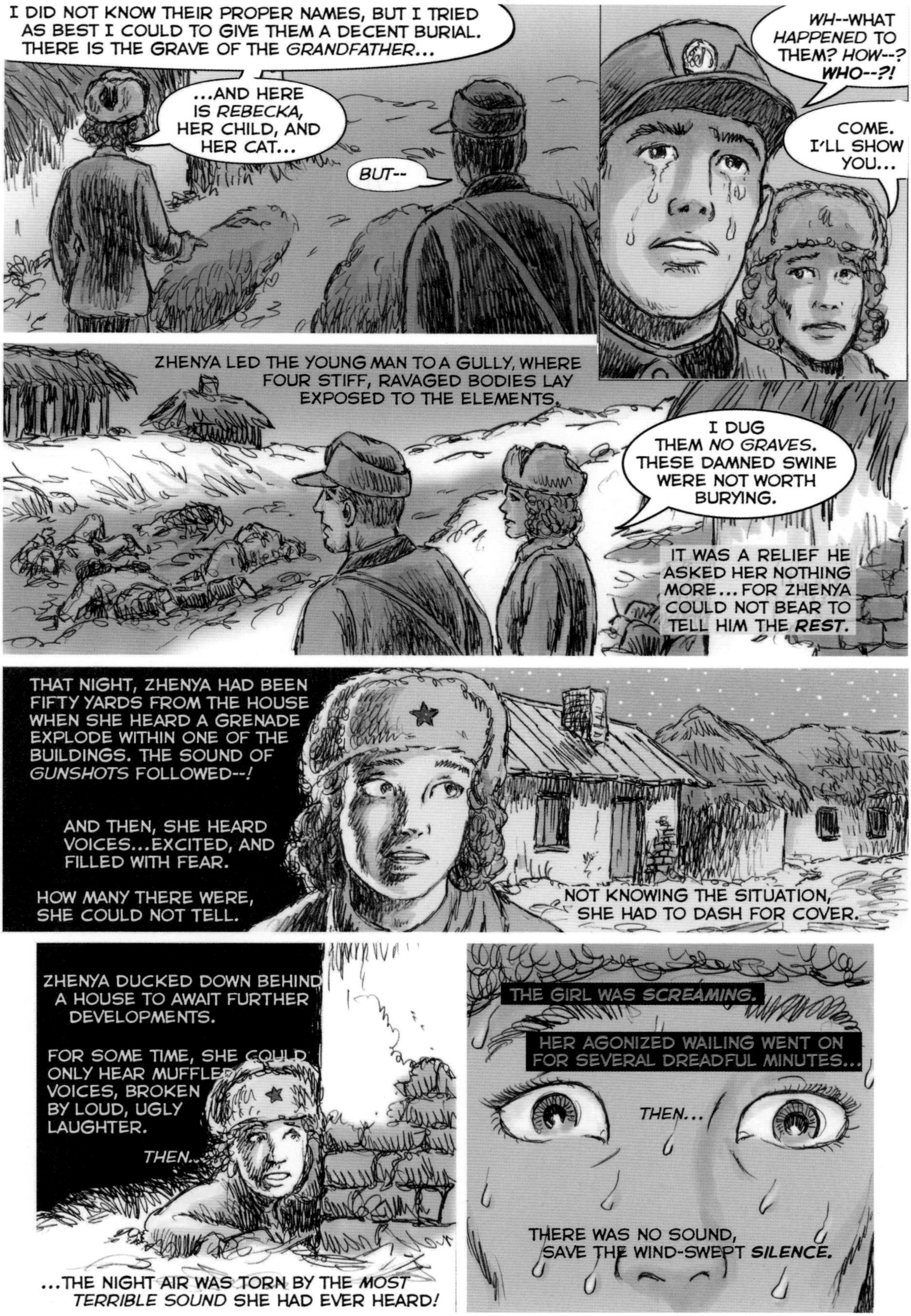
I DID NOT KNOW THEIR PROPER NAMES, BUT I TRIED AS BEST I COULD TO GIVE THEM A DECENT BURIAL. THERE IS THE GRAVE OF THE *GRANDFATHER*...
...AND HERE IS *REBECKA*, HER CHILD, AND HER CAT...
BUT--
WH--WHAT *HAPPENED* TO THEM? *HOW--?* ***WHO--?!***
COME. I'LL SHOW YOU...
ZHENYA LED THE YOUNG MAN TO A GULLY, WHERE FOUR STIFF, RAVAGED BODIES LAY EXPOSED TO THE ELEMENTS.
I DUG THEM *NO GRAVES*. THESE DAMNED SWINE WERE NOT WORTH BURYING.
IT WAS A RELIEF HE ASKED HER NOTHING MORE... FOR ZHENYA COULD NOT BEAR TO TELL HIM THE ***REST***.
THAT NIGHT, ZHENYA HAD BEEN FIFTY YARDS FROM THE HOUSE WHEN SHE HEARD A GRENADE EXPLODE WITHIN ONE OF THE BUILDINGS. THE SOUND OF *GUNSHOTS* FOLLOWED--!
AND THEN, SHE HEARD VOICES...EXCITED, AND FILLED WITH FEAR.
HOW MANY THERE WERE, SHE COULD NOT TELL.
NOT KNOWING THE SITUATION, SHE HAD TO DASH FOR COVER.
ZHENYA DUCKED DOWN BEHIND A HOUSE TO AWAIT FURTHER DEVELOPMENTS.
FOR SOME TIME, SHE COULD ONLY HEAR MUFFLED VOICES, BROKEN BY LOUD, UGLY LAUGHTER.
THEN...
...THE NIGHT AIR WAS TORN BY THE *MOST TERRIBLE SOUND* SHE HAD EVER HEARD!
THE GIRL WAS *SCREAMING*.
HER AGONIZED WAILING WENT ON FOR SEVERAL DREADFUL MINUTES...
THEN...
THERE WAS NO SOUND, SAVE THE WIND-SWEPT ***SILENCE***.

THEN, WITH HER SUSPENSE SO GREAT SHE COULD WAIT NO LONGER, SHE BEGAN SPRINTING BACK TO THE BUILDING...

...AND RAN HEADLONG INTO A LARGE MAN, ONE OF THE FOUR PARTISAN KILLERS!

THE IMPACT MADE HER DROP HER RIFLE.

ZHENYA KNEW IF HE SAW HOW SMALL SHE WAS, HE WOULD SOON OVERCOME HER.

SO SHE JAMMED A SPLINTERED STICK INTO HIS LEFT EYE.

SHE PRESSED ON IT UNTIL HIS CONVULSING ENDED, AND HE FINALLY BECAME STILL.

ZHENYA RECOVERED HER WEAPON, THEN CREPT UP ON THE THREE REMAINING THUGS. THEY HAD BUILT A SMALL FIRE AND WERE LAUGHING AS THEY WORKED TO FORCE OPEN THE LOCK ON THE SUITCASE.

UNNOTICED, SHE SLIPPED INTO THE HOUSE THEY HAD OCCUPIED.

INSIDE IT, SHE FOUND FATHER ZAPOLYE, UNCONSCIOUS AND BADLY BEATEN.

THE OLD JEWISH PRINTER LAY CLOSE BY...

...HIS BODY BULLET RIDDEN AND *DEAD*.

THEN...

...SHE FOUND THE *GIRL*.

444

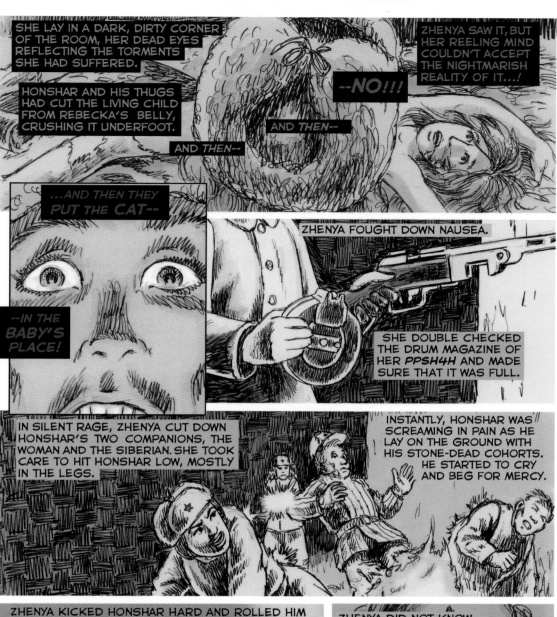

SHE LAY IN A DARK, DIRTY CORNER OF THE ROOM, HER DEAD EYES REFLECTING THE TORMENTS SHE HAD SUFFERED.

HONSHAR AND HIS THUGS HAD CUT THE LIVING CHILD FROM REBECKA'S BELLY, CRUSHING IT UNDERFOOT.

AND THEN--

AND THEN--

--NO!!!

ZHENYA SAW IT, BUT HER REELING MIND COULDN'T ACCEPT THE NIGHTMARISH REALITY OF IT...!

...AND THEN THEY PUT THE CAT--

--IN THE BABY'S PLACE!

ZHENYA FOUGHT DOWN NAUSEA.

SHE DOUBLE CHECKED THE DRUM MAGAZINE OF HER *PPSH4H* AND MADE SURE THAT IT WAS FULL.

IN SILENT RAGE, ZHENYA CUT DOWN HONSHAR'S TWO COMPANIONS, THE WOMAN AND THE SIBERIAN. SHE TOOK CARE TO HIT HONSHAR LOW, MOSTLY IN THE LEGS.

INSTANTLY, HONSHAR WAS SCREAMING IN PAIN AS HE LAY ON THE GROUND WITH HIS STONE-DEAD COHORTS. HE STARTED TO CRY AND BEG FOR MERCY.

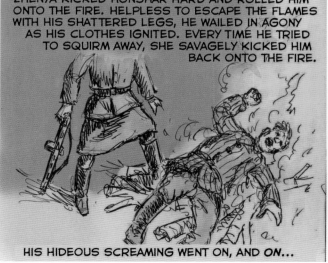

ZHENYA KICKED HONSHAR HARD AND ROLLED HIM ONTO THE FIRE. HELPLESS TO ESCAPE THE FLAMES WITH HIS SHATTERED LEGS, HE WAILED IN AGONY AS HIS CLOTHES IGNITED. EVERY TIME HE TRIED TO SQUIRM AWAY, SHE SAVAGELY KICKED HIM BACK ONTO THE FIRE.

HIS HIDEOUS SCREAMING WENT ON, AND *ON*...

ZHENYA DID NOT KNOW HOW LONG IT LASTED...

BUT IT WASN'T ENOUGH.

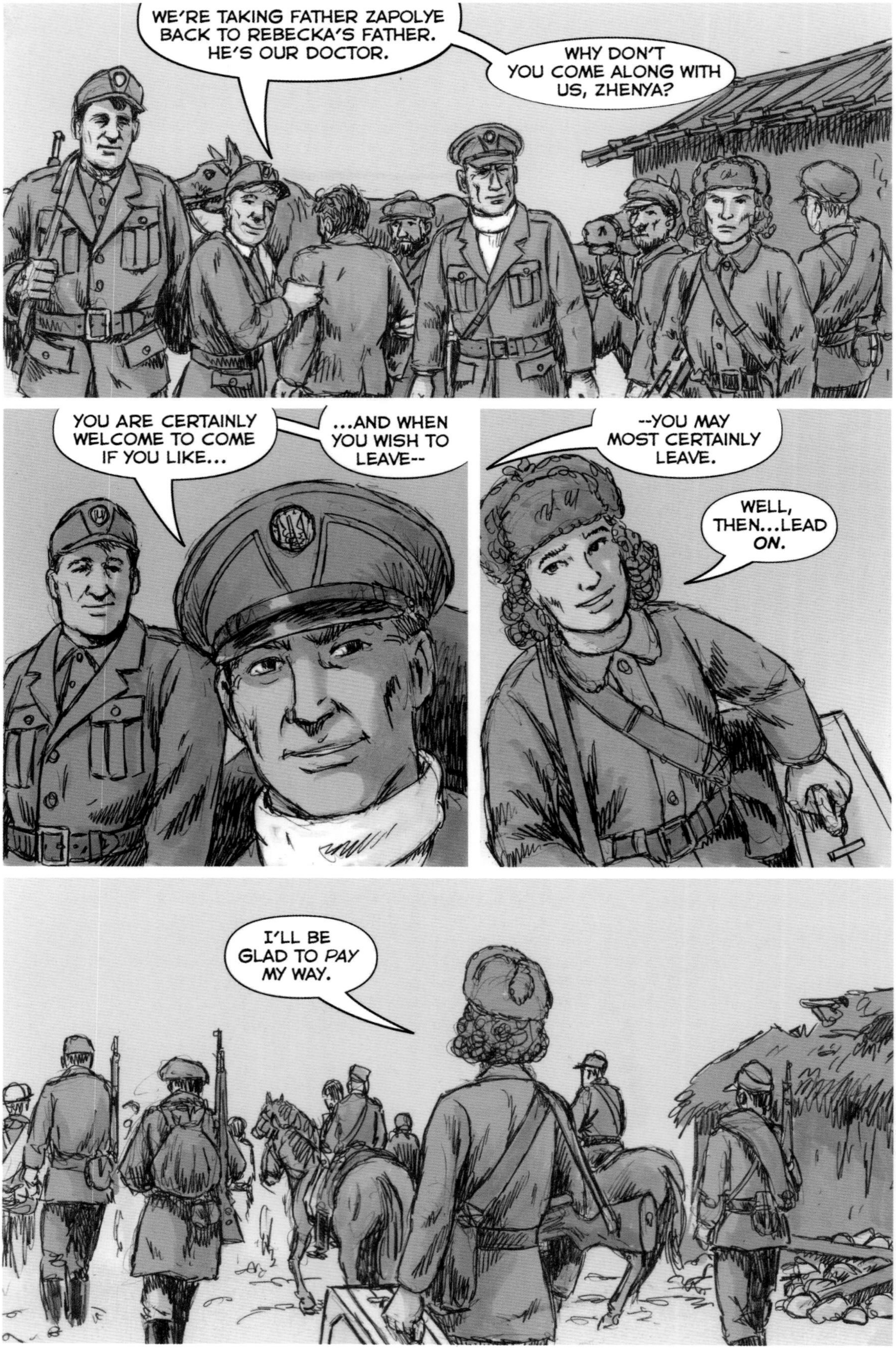
WE'RE TAKING FATHER ZAPOLYE BACK TO REBECKA'S FATHER. HE'S OUR DOCTOR.
WHY DON'T YOU COME ALONG WITH US, ZHENYA?
YOU ARE CERTAINLY WELCOME TO COME IF YOU LIKE...
...AND WHEN YOU WISH TO LEAVE--
--YOU MAY MOST CERTAINLY LEAVE.
WELL, THEN...LEAD *ON*.
I'LL BE GLAD TO *PAY* MY WAY.

BY LATE MARCH, THROUGH HEAVY SNOW, THE GERMAN 1ST PANZER ARMY WAS ABLE TO EXTRACT ITSELF FROM THE KAMYANETS-PODILSKY POCKET.

BUT ONE PANZER BATTALION WAS ALL BUT WIPED OUT BY SWARMS OF RUSSIAN GROUND-ATTACK AIRCRAFT.

AMONG THE GERMANS TRAPPED IN KAMYANETS-PODILSKY'S OLD TOWN WERE THREE MEMBERS OF AN *SS-EINSATZGRUPPE*, ALONG WITH THEIR TWO UKRAINIAN *SCHUMA* "HELPERS." EVERYONE HAD GATHERED IN THE OLD TOWN SQUARE TO WATCH AS THE *NKVD* MADE QUICK EXAMPLES OF THEM.

MILLA HAD GROWN DISTANT. THOUGH I HARDLY SAW HER ANYMORE, WHENEVER GOOD FORTUNE CAME AROUND, I STILL LIKED TO SHARE IT WITH HER.

AH! THERE YOU ARE!

LOOK WHAT I'VE GOT!

WHAT IS IT?

IT'S MOLDOVAN WINE AND RED CRIMEAN CHAMPAGNE-- RECOVERED FROM A GERMAN SUPPLY COLUMN!

WOW!

I SHARED CHAMPAGNE WITH KOPELEV, EVEN THOUGH I DIDN'T LIKE HIM.

I'M GOING TO POKE AROUND FOR WHAT ELSE I MIGHT FIND. WANT TO GO WITH ME, MILLA?

NO, THANKS. I WANT TO SEE THIS.

MILLA WAS EAGER TO SEE THE HANGING, BUT I TURNED TO GO. BUT THEN I GLANCED AT THE MEN ON THE GALLOWS...

SOME OF THE CONDEMNED MEN WERE MAKING LAST-MINUTE APPEALS FOR MERCY--A WASTE OF TIME, SINCE THEY SPOKE IN GERMAN AND NOBODY UNDERSTOOD THEM. BUT I GUESS ALL THEY HAD WAS TIME.

THEN ONE OF THEM CAUGHT MY EYE...

YOU! I KNOW YOU. YOU ARE HARTMUTH PULZER, ARE YOU NOT?

WHAT?

DO YOU REMEMBER ME?

REMEMBER HOW YOU CALLED ME A "UKRAINIAN ROSE"?

AND HOW YOU DESTROYED THE VILLAGE OF KROVROT?!

WHAT?

BUT HE WAS OVERWHELMED BY A TERROR SO GREAT HE COULD NOT COMPREHEND A WORD I WAS SAYING.

WHAT?!

WHAT?!!

ARE YOU REALLY SO SELF-CENTERED THAT YOU CANNOT GRASP THE IMMENSITY OF YOUR OWN CRIMES?

PULZER'S BLANK STARE WAS ENOUGH OF AN ANSWER. AS I TURNED AWAY, A RUSSIAN SOLDIER STANDING NEARBY TRIED TO BE OBLIGING...

COMRADE, IF YOU WISH, YOU COULD DRIVE THE TRUCK OUT FROM UNDER HIM...

NO, THANK YOU.

AS I WALKED AWAY, IT TOOK ALL OF MY STRENGTH NOT TO BREAK INTO A RUN. I HEARD THE TRUCK'S ENGINE TURN OVER, THE CLASH OF ITS GEARS, AND THEN...

I COULDN'T GET OUT OF EARSHOT BEFORE THE HORRIBLE CREAKING OF THE ROPES BEGAN.

MEANWHILE, ON THE STREETS OF THE TOWN...

SO, WHAT IS IT WE ARE LOOKING FOR, COMRADE SERGEANT?

NEVER YOU MIND, PRIVATE TEMKIN.

THERE IS AN OLD FRIEND OF MINE WHO LIVES AROUND HERE, SOMEWHERE...

SERGEANT DYATLONKO HAD ALSO SUCCESSFULLY SOUGHT OUT THE LOCAL WINE, BUT HE KEPT ON SEARCHING...FOR SOMETHING ELSE.

SMERSH, A SPECIAL SECTION OF THE NKVD, ARRIVED THE NEXT DAY, AND THERE WAS AN INVESTIGATION. ON THE THIRD DAY, THE WHOLE BRIGADE WAS CALLED OUT TO OBSERVE A VERY QUICK COURT MARTIAL. IT DIDN'T MATTER THAT DYATLONKO HAD FOUGHT BRAVELY IN TWO WORLD WARS, A REVOLUTION, AND A CIVIL WAR. IT ALSO DIDN'T MATTER THAT HIS ENTIRE FAMILY HAD BEEN KILLED BY THE ENEMY.

I AM COMPLETELY GUILTY OF THE CHARGES, AND I MAKE NO EXCUSES. HOWEVER, MY YOUNG FRIEND HERE WAS AN INNOCENT BYSTANDER. I PLEAD FOR MERCY FOR HIM.

PRIVATE TEMKIN... YOU ARE SENTENCED TO 25 YEARS OF SERVICE IN A PENAL BATTALION.

SERGEANT DYATLONKO...

...YOU ARE SENTENCED TO BE *EXECUTED*--IN FRONT OF THE ENTIRE BRIGADE.

SENTENCE TO BE CARRIED OUT *IMMEDIATELY*.

COLONEL NOZDRIN STEPPED OUT, AND IN A VOICE THAT WAS TIGHT AND HARSH, BARKED AN ORDER...

CAPTAIN KOVCHENKO.

YOU WILL NOW CARRY OUT THE *EXECUTION*.

KOLYA STOOD ROOTED IN A STATE OF SHOCK, AS DID THE REST OF US.

HE DID NOT--*COULD NOT*--MOVE...

...UNTIL NOZDRIN HAD GIVEN THE ORDER A *SECOND* TIME.

ON YOUR KNEES.

IT'S ALL RIGHT, KOLYA...

...I HOPE TO SAY HELLO TO YOUR GIRLS.

FORGIVE ME, BROTHER.

WE PUSHED ON WEST INTO *GALICIA*.

HISTORICALLY, GALICIA HAD NOT BEEN SOVIET, AND ITS PEOPLE SEEMED, IN MANY CASES, NO MORE HAPPY TO SEE US THAN THEY HAD BEEN TO SEE THE GERMANS.

AS WE FOUGHT AND DIED CROSSING THEIR LAND, WE SAW THE MANY CATHOLIC CRUCIFIXES THEY'D PUT UP BESIDE THE ROAD. THESE MAY HAVE BEEN A COMFORT TO SOME...

BUT TO MANY, IT SIMPLY MEANT "YOU ARE NOT WELCOME HERE."

KOLYA WENT ABOUT HIS JOB WITH THE SAME PROFESSIONALISM THAT HE ALWAYS HAD SHOWN...

...BUT CLEARLY, SOMETHING HAD GONE OUT OF HIM.

THEN ONE DAY IN JUNE WHEN WE WERE COILED UP IN AND AROUND A SMALL VILLAGE, KOLYA SENT WORD FOR ME TO MEET HIM ON THE EDGE OF TOWN AT A LITTLE HOUSE WHERE A LOCAL WOMAN WITH THREE DAUGHTERS WAS PREPARING A MEAL FOR US.

AS I PASSED BY A GROUP OF OUR INFANTRY, I HEARD A LOVELY SOUND...

SOMEWHERE NEARBY, A BOY WITH AN ACCORDION WAS PLAYING *PLAISIR D'AMOUR.* IT PUT ME IN A MELLOW, CONTENTED MOOD.

THE MAYOR OF THIS LITTLE TOWN SWEARS THIS LADY IS THEIR BEST COOK. AND *YOU,* WITH MORE WINE...?

ACTUALLY, I'M TRYING TO CUT DOWN--BUT IT'S A '37 MOSEL.

AH, THAT'S HER YOUNGEST GIRL. SHE'S FOND OF ME--I GAVE HER MAMA SIX CANS OF SPAM AND A SACK OF POTATOES.

TEN GUESSES WHAT'S ON OUR MENU TONIGHT...

AH, SUCH EXQUISITE SPAM AND POTATOES! TRULY, OUR COOK IS A MAGICIAN.

SO...THE BRITISH AND AMERICANS HAVE LANDED IN FRANCE! WE NOW HAVE A SECOND FRONT.

THINK IT'LL HELP US?

I WOULDN'T BE SURPRISED. WORD IS THE GERMANS ARE PULLING UNITS AWAY FROM OVER HERE TO MEET THE THREAT.

453

IN FACT, AT THAT VERY MOMENT 17 MILES TO THE WEST, THE GERMANS WERE PREPARING TO ABANDON ONE OF THEIR AIRFIELDS DUE TO RED ARMY PRESSURE.

BUT BEFORE THEY DID, A HANDFUL OF PLANES WERE GOING TO TAKE ONE MORE CRACK AT *IVAN!*

TWO *STUKA* "TANK CRACKERS" AND SIX *FW190s* WERE LOOKING FOR TROUBLE...

THEY CAME IN LOW, HUGGING THE GROUND TO AVOID HIGH-FLYING *YAKS.*

...AND MANAGED TO REACH THE VILLAGE WITHOUT BEING SPOTTED BY ANYONE.

ONE TANKER, FILLING UP THE COMPRESSED AIR TANKS IN THE NOSE OF HIS VEHICLE, MANAGED TO SOUND HIS HORN BEFORE BEING BLOWN TO ATOMS...

UH-OH! WHAT WAS THAT?

DOWN! BEHIND THE WALL!

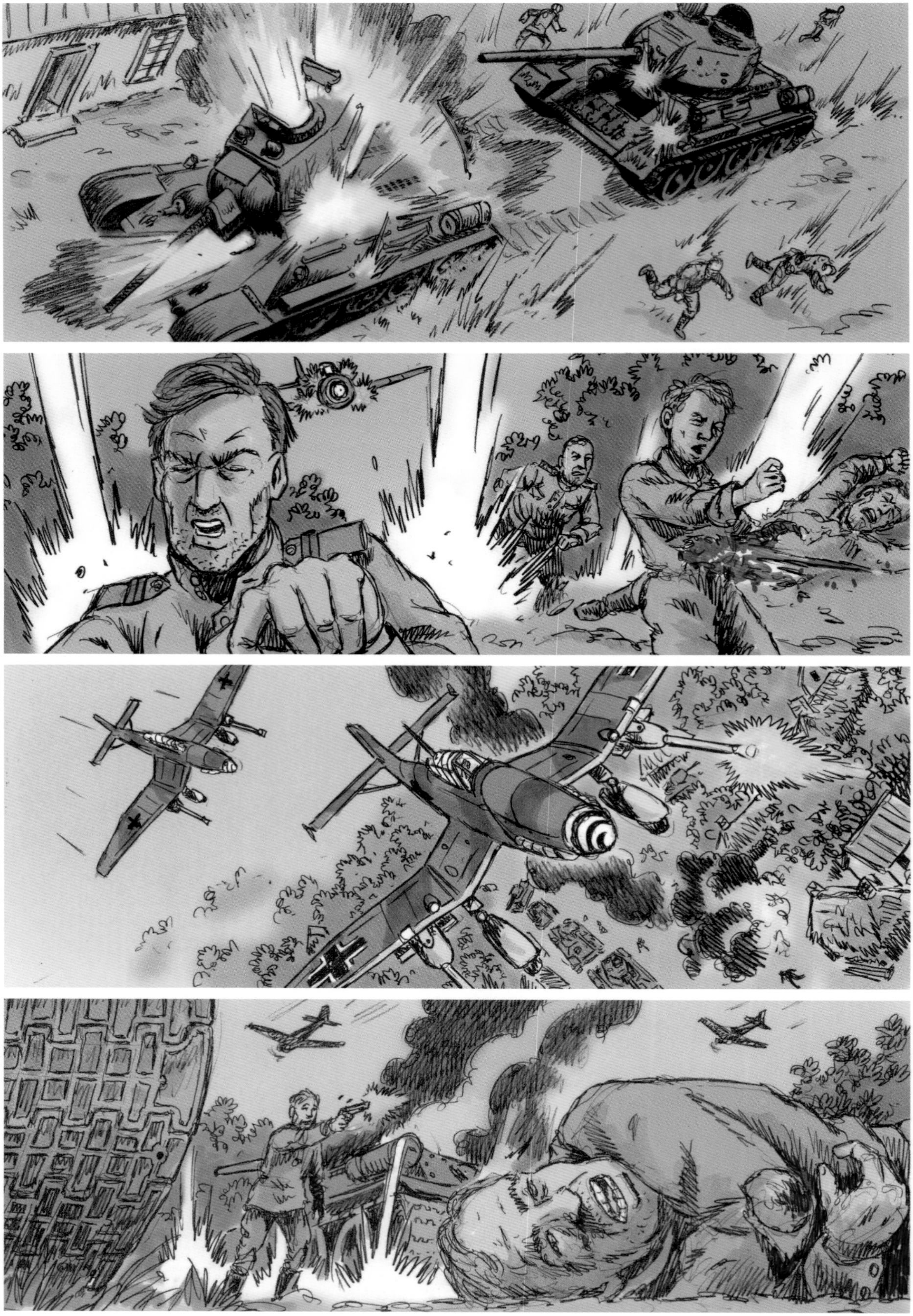

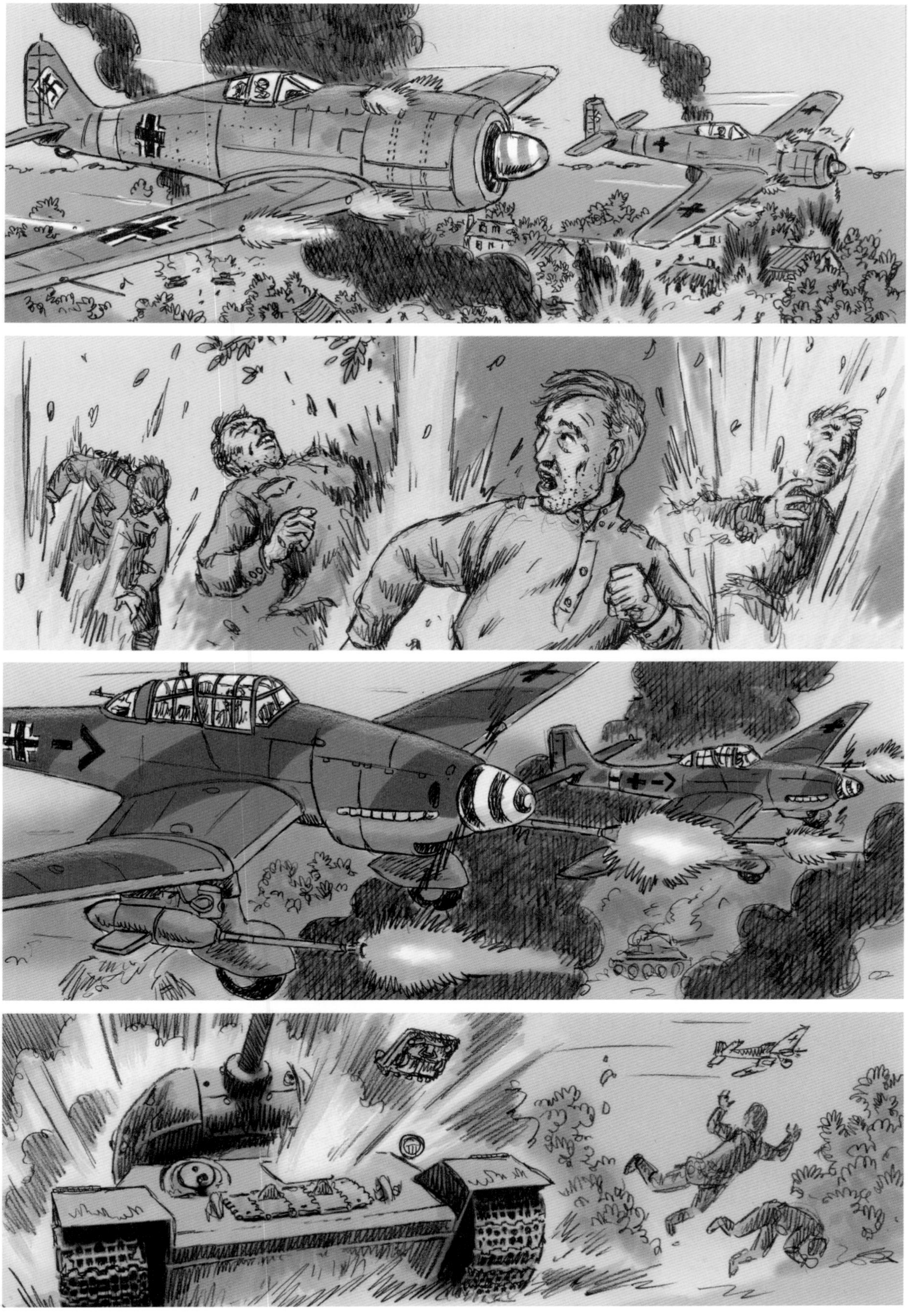

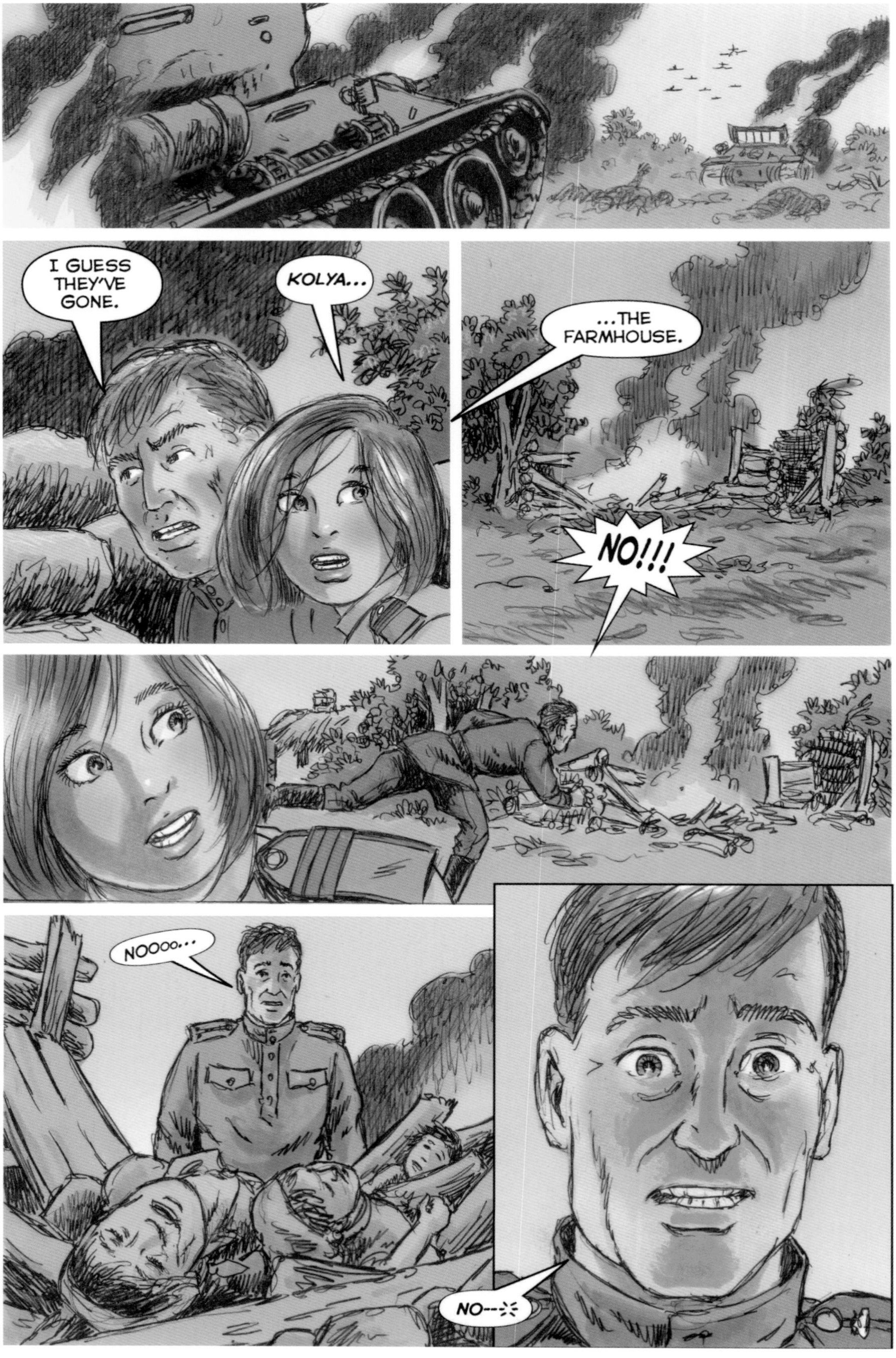
I GUESS THEY'VE GONE.
KOLYA...
...THE FARMHOUSE.
NO!!!
NOOOO...
NO--

THERE, IN FRONT OF THIS SLAUGHTERED FAMILY, KOLYA FELL TO HIS KNEES...

...AND BEGAN TO SOB LIKE I'VE NEVER HEARD ANYONE SOB BEFORE.

HE'D ONCE TOLD ME THAT THE DEATHS OF HIS WIFE AND DAUGHTERS WERE FIRMLY RECORDED IN HIS MIND, BUT THE REALIZATION HAD NOT YET TOUCHED HIS HEART...

TODAY, IT *DID.*

KOLYA WAS INCONSOLABLE. HE COULD NOT STOP CRYING, EVEN WHEN HIS MEN CAME WITH A TRUCK TO CARRY HIM TO THE FIELD HOSPITAL.

WE'LL TAKE CARE OF HIM.

THANK YOU, GREGORI.

LATER, I WENT TO CHECK ON HIM...

AH! KATUSHA...

YELENA, IS CAPTAIN KOVCHENKO ANY BETTER?

*UH...*HE'S NOT HERE.

WHY NOT?

WELL, HE WASN'T REALLY WOUNDED, SO HE WAS TAKEN SOMEWHERE ELSE--

WHERE?

UH...

WHO TOOK HIM?

I...I THINK IT WAS THE *NKVD.*

I STORMED RIGHT INTO COLONEL NOZDRIN'S HEADQUARTERS.

VERA SAW MY ANGER AND TRIED TO STOP ME, BUT I IGNORED HER.

KATUSHA!

NO!

THE COLONEL WAS DEEP IN DISCUSSION WITH HIS COMMANDERS OVER A MAP. IN MY SINGLE-MINDED PURPOSE, MY STUPIDITY, I DIDN'T EVEN NOTICE.

WHERE HAVE THEY TAKEN HIM?!

WE'VE COVERED ALMOST EVERYTHING. I WILL BE SPEAKING WITH EACH OF YOU INDIVIDUALLY TOMORROW.

THE OFFICERS STOOD UP AND FILED OUT OF THE ROOM IN AWKWARD SILENCE, THE LAST ONE SLOWLY CLOSING THE DOOR BEHIND HIM.

I DIDN'T SEE IT COMING.

AAKGH!

I FELT LIKE I HAD BEEN HIT BY A *122*MM.

WHEN I OPENED MY EYES, I SAW THE COLONEL STANDING OVER ME WITH A FACE THAT WAS HARD AND UNYIELDING.

LISTEN TO ME, SERGEANT. IT IS ONLY THE FEAR OF HAVING *TARAS TYMOSHENKO* HAUNTING ME THROUGHOUT ETERNITY THAT KEEPS ME FROM HAVING YOU TAKEN OUT AND *SHOT*.

COMMISSAR CHEKOV IS WITH HIM NOW. IF ANYONE CAN GET KOVCHENKO OUT OF THESE DIFFICULTIES, IT WILL BE *HIM*...

...BUT REMEMBER THIS...

...THE RED ARMY DOES NOT MAKE ALLOWANCES FOR WOUNDS THAT ARE "IN HERE."

NOW *GET* OUT!

HIS WOUND IS NOT "IN THERE."

VERA CRINGED WHEN SHE SAW MY SWELLING FACE, BUT SHE DIDN'T SEEM TO BE AT ALL SURPRISED BY IT.

DON'T JUDGE HIM TOO HARSHLY, KATUSHA.

THAT'S EASY FOR YOU TO SAY.

NO...PLEASE *LISTEN* TO ME. BACK IN KAMYANETS-PODILSKY--

--THE NIGHT AFTER HE'D HAD TO ORDER SERGEANT DYATLONKO'S EXECUTION...

...RUSLAN FOUND A ROOM AND LOCKED HIMSELF IN.

HE WOULDN'T LET ANYONE IN, NOT EVEN ME. AND THROUGH THE DOOR, I COULD HEAR HIM. HE WAS *WEEPING*.

KATUSHA... *HE SOBBED ALL NIGHT LONG.*

I TOOK A BREATH TO CALM MYSELF, THEN TURNED TO LEAVE.

EVERYONE HAS SOME SORT OF WOUND, KATUSHA...

YES. AND SOME OF US WILL *DIE* OF THEM.

AS I WALKED BACK TO MY TANK, I FELT SICK TO MY GUT WITH DISGUST FOR WHAT I WAS DOING AND THE CAUSE I WAS SERVING. *THIS WAR WILL RUIN US ALL, I THOUGHT, AND EVERY NOBLE TENDENCY WE CARRY...*

I WISHED TO *GOD* FOR SOME GREAT HEART I COULD TURN TO FOR COMFORT, TO SOOTHE MY SOUL AND TEND MY WOUNDS. I WISHED FOR UNCLE TARAS TO TALK TO, OR BETTER YET, MAMA...

ON *JUNE 22, 1944*, THE THIRD ANNIVERSARY OF THE GERMAN INVASION OF THE SOVIET UNION, THE RED ARMY BEGAN A SERIES OF ATTACKS AGAINST THE *GERMAN FOURTH* AND *NINTH ARMIES* IN BELORUSSIA.

THESE ATTACKS WERE SPREAD OUT OVER THREE DAYS...

...WHICH IS WHY THE GERMANS DID NOT IMMEDIATELY SEE A PATTERN.

IF THEY HAD FOLLOWED THE PARTISAN ACTIVITY, THEY MIGHT HAVE FOUND A CLUE.

DURING THIS PERIOD FROM THE 22ND THROUGH THE 24TH, MORE THAN 10,500 PARTISAN ATTACKS OCCURRED BEHIND THE GERMAN LINES. THEIR TARGETS WERE TELEPHONE LINES, RAILROAD TRACKS, ROADS, AND BRIDGES.

IT SOON BECAME CLEAR THAT THE RUSSIANS WERE MOUNTING A MAJOR OFFENSIVE.

THE RED ARMY'S *OPERATION BAGRATION* WAS DESIGNED TO DO NOTHING LESS THAN SPLIT *ARMY GROUP CENTER* AND PROPEL THE RED ARMY MORE THAN A HUNDRED MILES ACROSS THE POLISH BORDER.

IN THE END, IT WOULD DO QUITE A BIT *MORE* THAN THAT.

THIS WOULD GO DOWN AS THE GREATEST GERMAN DEFEAT IN HISTORY, EVEN GREATER THAN STALINGRAD. A 250-MILE HOLE WAS TORN IN THE CENTER OF THE GERMAN LINE.

TWENTY-EIGHT GERMAN DIVISIONS WERE DESTROYED, AND NEARLY 350,000 GERMAN SOLDIERS WERE KILLED OR CAPTURED.

IN JULY, WE WERE MOVED NORTH TO TAKE PART IN THE OFFENSIVE AGAINST *L'VIV*. WE WERE LUCKY TO BE ABLE TO MOVE PART OF OUR BRIGADE BY TRAIN TO **KREMENETS.**

YOUR CITY IS QUITE BEAUTIFUL. THAT'S A LOVELY CHURCH.

WHY, THANK YOU! WE CERTAINLY THINK IT IS.

I WAS A TEACHER HERE FOR MANY YEARS. WOULD YOU LIKE A LITTLE HISTORICAL TOUR?

THE OLD MAN LED ME ON A WALKING TOUR OF THE TOWN...

...AND THIS IS THE *OLD SYNAGOGUE*. IT HAS STOOD EMPTY EVER SINCE THE GERMANS CAME.

ONCE, THERE WERE 16,000 JEWS LIVING HERE IN *KREMENETS*. NOW, AS BEST AS I CAN FIGURE, WE HAVE *NONE*.

THE OLD TEACHER WAS WELL INFORMED ABOUT THE HISTORY OF THE WHOLE REGION. NOW WHEN WE WERE ADVANCING WEST, I WASN'T SURPRISED AT WHAT WE ENCOUNTERED.

KATUSHA, LOOK--*MORE* DERELICT TANKS! WHAT WENT ON HERE?

AH, YES! MY TOUR GUIDE BACK IN KREMENETS TOLD ME ABOUT THIS...

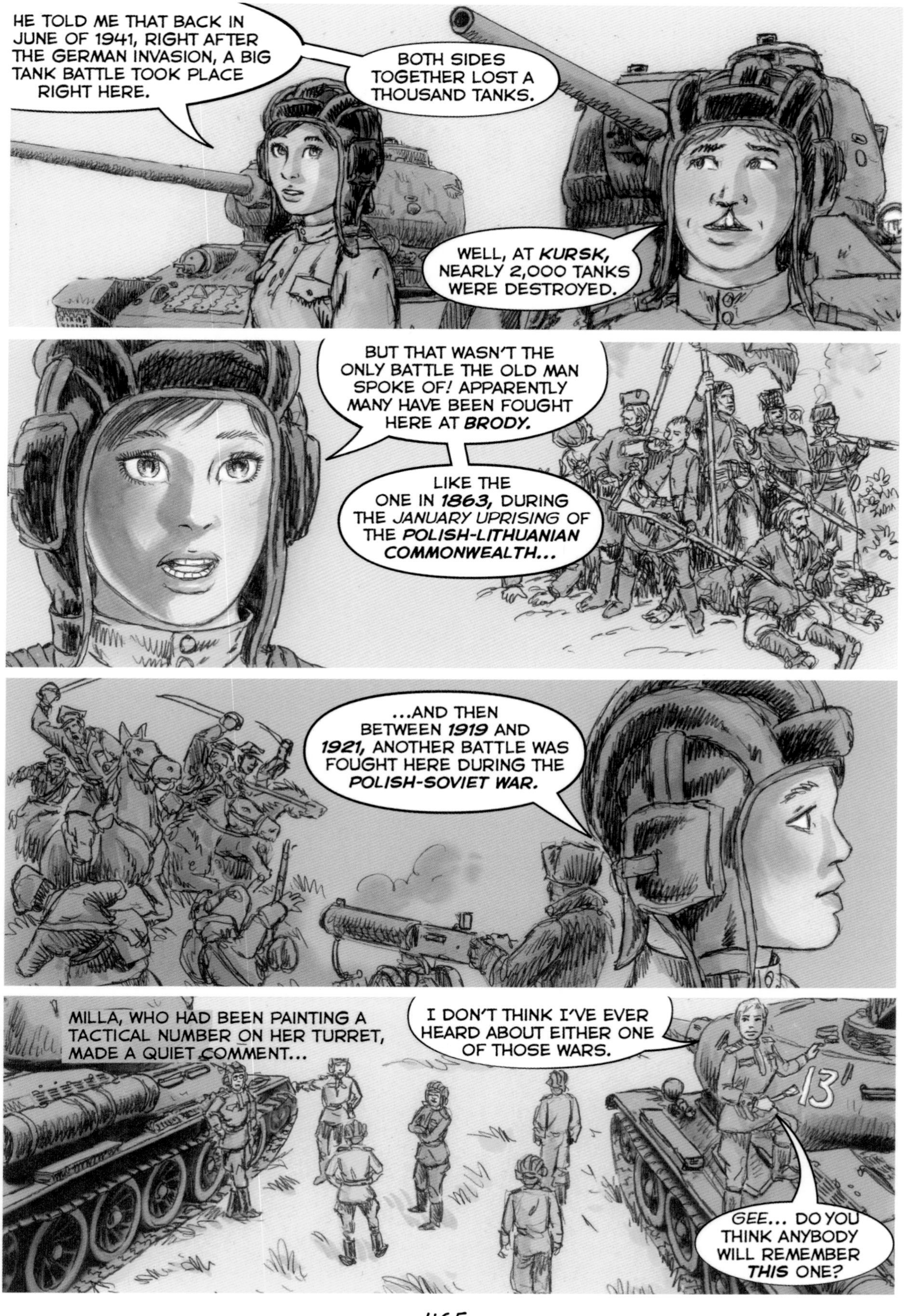
HE TOLD ME THAT BACK IN JUNE OF 1941, RIGHT AFTER THE GERMAN INVASION, A BIG TANK BATTLE TOOK PLACE RIGHT HERE.
BOTH SIDES TOGETHER LOST A THOUSAND TANKS.
WELL, AT KURSK, NEARLY 2,000 TANKS WERE DESTROYED.
BUT THAT WASN'T THE ONLY BATTLE THE OLD MAN SPOKE OF! APPARENTLY MANY HAVE BEEN FOUGHT HERE AT BRODY.
LIKE THE ONE IN 1863, DURING THE JANUARY UPRISING OF THE POLISH-LITHUANIAN COMMONWEALTH...
...AND THEN BETWEEN 1919 AND 1921, ANOTHER BATTLE WAS FOUGHT HERE DURING THE POLISH-SOVIET WAR.
MILLA, WHO HAD BEEN PAINTING A TACTICAL NUMBER ON HER TURRET, MADE A QUIET COMMENT...
I DON'T THINK I'VE EVER HEARD ABOUT EITHER ONE OF THOSE WARS.
13
GEE... DO YOU THINK ANYBODY WILL REMEMBER THIS ONE?

ON *JULY 13, 1944*, THE *1ST UKRAINIAN FRONT* OPENED THE *LVOV-SANDOMIERZ OFFENSIVE*. THEIR AMBITIOUS OBJECTIVES WERE NOTHING LESS THAN THE BORDERS OF POLAND AND RUMANIA.

BY THE SECOND DAY, SOVIET ARTILLERY HAD ALREADY SHATTERED TWO GERMAN INFANTRY DIVISIONS, SENDING THEIR SURVIVORS STREAMING BACK IN DISARRAY.

IN AN ATTEMPT TO PLUG THE HOLE, THE *1ST* AND *8TH PANZER DIVISIONS* WERE FLUNG INTO THE GAP.

ACCOMPANYING THEM WERE 11,000 MEN OF THE *14TH SS PANZER GRENADIER DIVISION*, ALSO KNOWN AS THE *GALICIA DIVISION*. THEY WERE UKRAINIANS WHO HAD VOLUNTEERED TO COUNTER GERMAN SUBJUGATION AND TO FIGHT THE RED ARMY. THEIR VERY PRESENCE MADE MANY OF MY COMRADES SEETHE WITH ANGER.

466

BUT THEY WERE GOOD FIGHTERS, NOT PRONE TO ATROCITY.

THEY FOUGHT FOR THEIR CONVICTIONS-- AND AS I, THEY FOUGHT FOR *UKRAINE*. THEY FOUGHT AGAINST *COMMUNISM*, AND I CAN'T ARGUE WITH THAT.

THE MEN OF THE GALICIA DIVISION WERE SENT IN TO RECAPTURE SOME LOST GROUND...

...AND RAN RIGHT INTO A SOVIET BRIGADE OF BRAND-NEW *IS-2 TANKS*.

THAT PUT AN END TO THEIR ADVANCE.

BY *JULY 22,* OF THE 11,000 UKRAINIANS WHO HAD MARCHED INTO BATTLE...

...ONLY *3,500* REMAINED.

THE GERMANS ALWAYS FOUGHT BITTERLY TO AVOID AN ENCIRCLEMENT, AND THIS TIME WAS NO DIFFERENT.

HOLD IT RIGHT HERE, MARUSYA. WE HAVE A LITTLE EARTH TO COVER OUR HULL...

OXANNA, HOW DOES IT LOOK FOR YOU?

GOOD!

WE OPENED UP, JOINED BY SEVERAL MORE OF OUR TANKS.

...WITH GOOD RESULTS.

JUST THEN, COLONEL NOZDRIN'S VOICE CRACKLED FROM THE RADIO SPEAKER...

THEY'RE PULLING BACK INTO THOSE LITTLE VALLEYS-- WE CAN'T REACH THEM, AND THEY CAN STILL KEEP OUR INFANTRY PINNED DOWN!

FIRST AND SECOND PLATOONS OF *2ND COMPANY*-- BREAK OFF AND TAKE THE ROAD BY THAT MILL. SEE IF YOU CAN GET IN BEHIND THEM!

THAT MEANT US--SIX OF US, THREE *T-34* TANKS WITH *85mm* GUNS, AND THREE WITH *76mm* GUNS. MILLA'S TANK, NO. 13, WAS IN THE LEAD.

THE GERMANS WERE EXPECTING SOMETHING OF THIS NATURE.

AHEAD OF US, I SAW SOMETHING SO STRANGE...

IT WAS A STORK'S NEST ATOP AN OLD TREE-- NOT AN UNUSUAL SIGHT IN ITSELF. I COULD MAKE OUT THE MOTHER STORK'S HEAD STICKING UP FROM HER NEST. BUT CIRCLING OVERHEAD...

...I SAW HUNDREDS OF CAWING CROWS, JUST HANGING IN THE AIR AS IF WAITING FOR A MEAL.

MILLA! THE ROAD GOES TOWARD THE *RIGHT!*

I DON'T SEE HOW IT WILL GET US IN BEHIND THE GERMANS...

ALL RIGHT.

WELL, THEN... LET'S JUST MAKE OUR OWN ROAD!

MILLA DIRECTED HER TANK TO THE LEFT...

...AND BLAZED A TRAIL, CUTTING THROUGH THE UNDERBRUSH AND CRUSHING SMALL TREES BENEATH THE RELENTLESS TRACKS OF HER MACHINE.

WHEN WE EMERGED INTO THE OPEN, MY CHIN DROPPED.

THERE AHEAD OF US WAS AN OLD GRAY YET STILL BEAUTIFUL CASTLE.

I'D SEEN POSTCARDS OF SUCH SCENES...

BUT SEEING IT FOR REAL, IN A SITUATION LIKE THIS, WAS PURE ABSURDITY.

UNLIKE ME, *MILLA* WAS PAYING NO ATTENTION TO THIS BEAUTIFUL AND OUTLANDISH SCENE.

SHE WAS MORE INTERESTED IN A COLUMN OF PANTHER TANKS THAT WERE MOVING ALONG ON THE SLOPE BELOW US, AS IF WITHOUT A CARE IN THE WORLD.

TWO OF THE PANTHERS BURST INTO FLAMES BEFORE THEY EVEN KNEW WE WERE THERE!

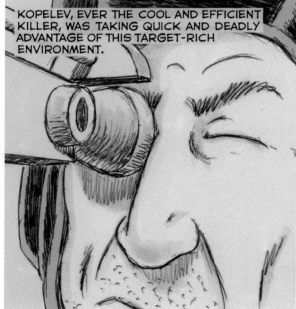

KOPELEV, EVER THE COOL AND EFFICIENT KILLER, WAS TAKING QUICK AND DEADLY ADVANTAGE OF THIS TARGET-RICH ENVIRONMENT.

OUR TANKS LINED UP IN FRONT OF THE CASTLE AND BEGAN TO BLAST OUR ENEMY.

SOME OF THE GERMAN CREWS PANICKED AND FLED THEIR TANKS BEFORE BEING HIT.

BUT ONE OF THE PANTHERS AT THE END OF THE COLUMN PULLED UP ALONG THE GRADUAL RISE, GIVING HIM THE OPPORTUNITY TO SEEK VENGEANCE ON THESE INTRUDERS WHO HAD STARTED THIS DANCE OF DEATH.

AH--!

"DEATH IS ALREADY CHALKING THE DOORS WITH CROSSES...

"AND CALLING THE RAVENS, AND THE RAVENS ARE FLYING IN..."

--ANNA AKHMATOVA

"HELLO, PAPA. THIS LETTER IS FROM YOUR LOVING DAUGHTER EKATERINA. IT IS WITH GREAT SADNESS THAT I INFORM YOU THAT LUDMILLA HAS FALLEN IN BATTLE. I WAS NEAR WHEN IT HAPPENED, AND I CAN ASSURE YOU THAT SHE FELT NO PAIN..."

"SHE WAS A FINE SOLDIER, MUCH BETTER THAN I, AND SHE FOUGHT VERY HARD. I SOMETIMES THINK THAT SHE TOOK THIS WAR A LOT MORE PERSONALLY THAN I..."

"I THINK IT WAS BECAUSE OF UNCLE TARAS' DEATH. WE BOTH LOVED YOUR BROTHER... BUT MILLA HAD SPECIAL FEELINGS FOR HIM.

"AFTER THAT, I SAW HER FILL WITH HATE--AND IT GAVE HER A SPECIAL STRENGTH THAT I SOMETIMES WISH I HAD.

"I HAVE ONLY KNOWN ONE GERMAN BY NAME IN THIS WAR, AND I RECENTLY SAW HIM DIE. IT WAS A JUST DEATH, AND I APPRECIATE THE RIGHTNESS OF IT...BUT IT GAVE ME NO PERSONAL SATISFACTION."

"I KNOW THAT I HAVE REASON TO HATE, WITH NOT KNOWING WHERE MAMA, NATASHA, DIMA, VASILY, AND BABUSHKA ARE...BUT I DID WRITE TO YOU ABOUT THE NOTE SHE LEFT AT HOME.

"WELL, THAT GETS ME BACK TO WHERE I WAS, ABOUT HATE. IF HATE IS THE ONLY REASON TO FIGHT THIS WAR, WE ARE GOING TO BE IN A PICKLE WHEN IT'S OVER...

"IF HATE IS ALL WE HAVE, WE WILL HAVE TO FIND ANOTHER WAR TO QUENCH THAT HATE...

"I REMEMBER ONCE READING WHAT TOLSTOY HAD TO SAY ABOUT WAR.

'WAR IS NOT A POLITE RECREATION, BUT THE VILEST THING IN LIFE. OUR ATTITUDE TOWARD THE FEARFUL NECESSITY OF WAR OUGHT TO BE STERN AND SERIOUS...WE SHOULD NEVER GO TO WAR EXCEPT FOR SOMETHING WORTH FACING CERTAIN DEATH FOR.'

"WOULDN'T IT BE SOMETHING IF WE WENT TO WAR FOR WHAT WE *LOVED*, RATHER THAN FOR WHAT WE *HATED*?"

LEDGERS of REVENGE

LATE JULY, 1944. IN WESTERN EUROPE, THE BRITISH AND AMERICANS WERE TRYING TO BREAK OUT OF NORMANDY SO THEY COULD ADVANCE TO PARIS AND THE GERMAN BORDER. THIS TITANIC CAMPAIGN WAS NOTHING COMPARED TO WHAT WAS GOING ON IN THE EAST. FROM THE BALTIC TO THE BALKANS, THE RED ARMY WAS IN FULL OFFENSE MODE. BULGARIA AND RUMANIA WERE IN THE PROCESS OF CHANGING SIDES. THE GERMANS WERE BEING BEATEN OUT OF ESTONIA, LATVIA, AND LITHUANIA, WHILE RUSSIAN CRUISERS BOMBARDED THEM FROM THE SEA. OUR TROOPS WERE CROSSING MOLDAVIA AND RUTHENIA ON THEIR WAY TO PRAGUE. AND WE WERE ENTERING POLAND.

WHAT IN *HELL* IS THAT?

I'D SAY IT WAS A MESSAGE FROM THE LOCAL UKRAINIAN NATIONALISTS.

IT'S AN OLD SYMBOL OF HOSTILITY: "A POLE, A JEW, AND A HOUND." IT ISN'T MEANT TO MAKE US FEEL WELCOME.

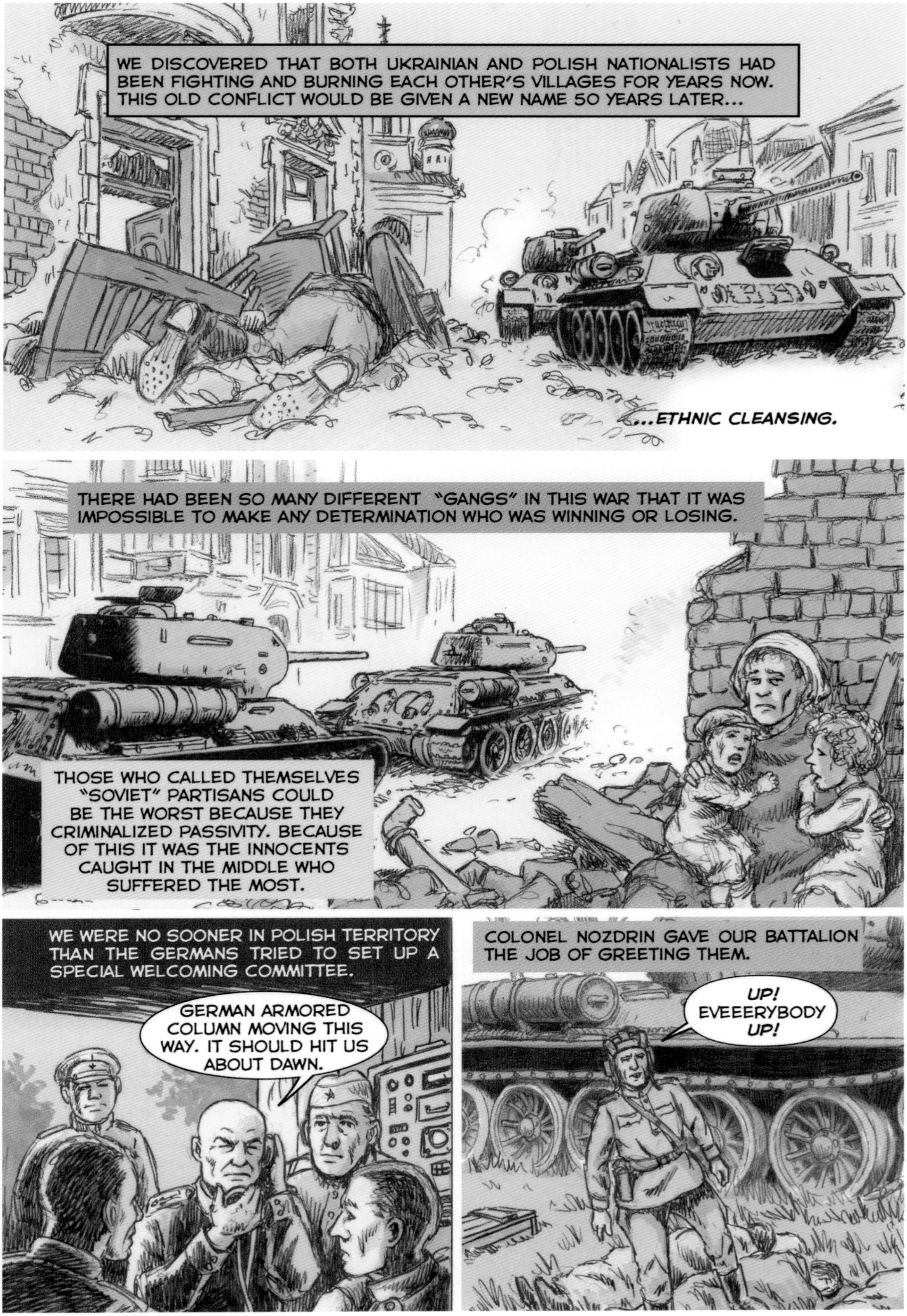
WE DISCOVERED THAT BOTH UKRAINIAN AND POLISH NATIONALISTS HAD BEEN FIGHTING AND BURNING EACH OTHER'S VILLAGES FOR YEARS NOW. THIS OLD CONFLICT WOULD BE GIVEN A NEW NAME 50 YEARS LATER...
...ETHNIC CLEANSING.
THERE HAD BEEN SO MANY DIFFERENT "GANGS" IN THIS WAR THAT IT WAS IMPOSSIBLE TO MAKE ANY DETERMINATION WHO WAS WINNING OR LOSING.
THOSE WHO CALLED THEMSELVES "SOVIET" PARTISANS COULD BE THE WORST BECAUSE THEY CRIMINALIZED PASSIVITY. BECAUSE OF THIS IT WAS THE INNOCENTS CAUGHT IN THE MIDDLE WHO SUFFERED THE MOST.
WE WERE NO SOONER IN POLISH TERRITORY THAN THE GERMANS TRIED TO SET UP A SPECIAL WELCOMING COMMITTEE.
GERMAN ARMORED COLUMN MOVING THIS WAY. IT SHOULD HIT US ABOUT DAWN.
COLONEL NOZDRIN GAVE OUR BATTALION THE JOB OF GREETING THEM.
UP! EVEEERYBODY UP!

OUR TANKS GROUND AND CLANKED THROUGH THE NIGHT.

CAPTAIN GUCHKOV, OUR BATTALION COMMANDER, WAS NO GREAT BRAIN, OR POLISHED LEADER OF MEN...

...NOR WAS HE MUCH TO LOOK AT.

BUT HE HAD PLENTY OF COMMON SENSE AND HAD A BRILLIANT UNDERSTANDING OF THE LAY OF THE LAND.

ON A HILL SOUTH OF THE ROAD WAS A BROAD FIELD OF TALL GREEN CORN. HE DIRECTED US TO MAKE OUR WAY THROUGH SOME THIN WOODS AND TO ENTER THE CORNFIELD FROM THE TOP OF THE HILL.

ABOUT A THIRD OF THE WAY DOWN, WE PARKED OUR TANKS AT STAGGERED INTERVALS. WE WERE CAMOUFLAGED WITH CUT CORN. THE LOWER SLOPES OF THE HILL, UNMARKED BY OUR TANK TRACKS, WOULD BE OCCUPIED BY OUR INFANTRY.

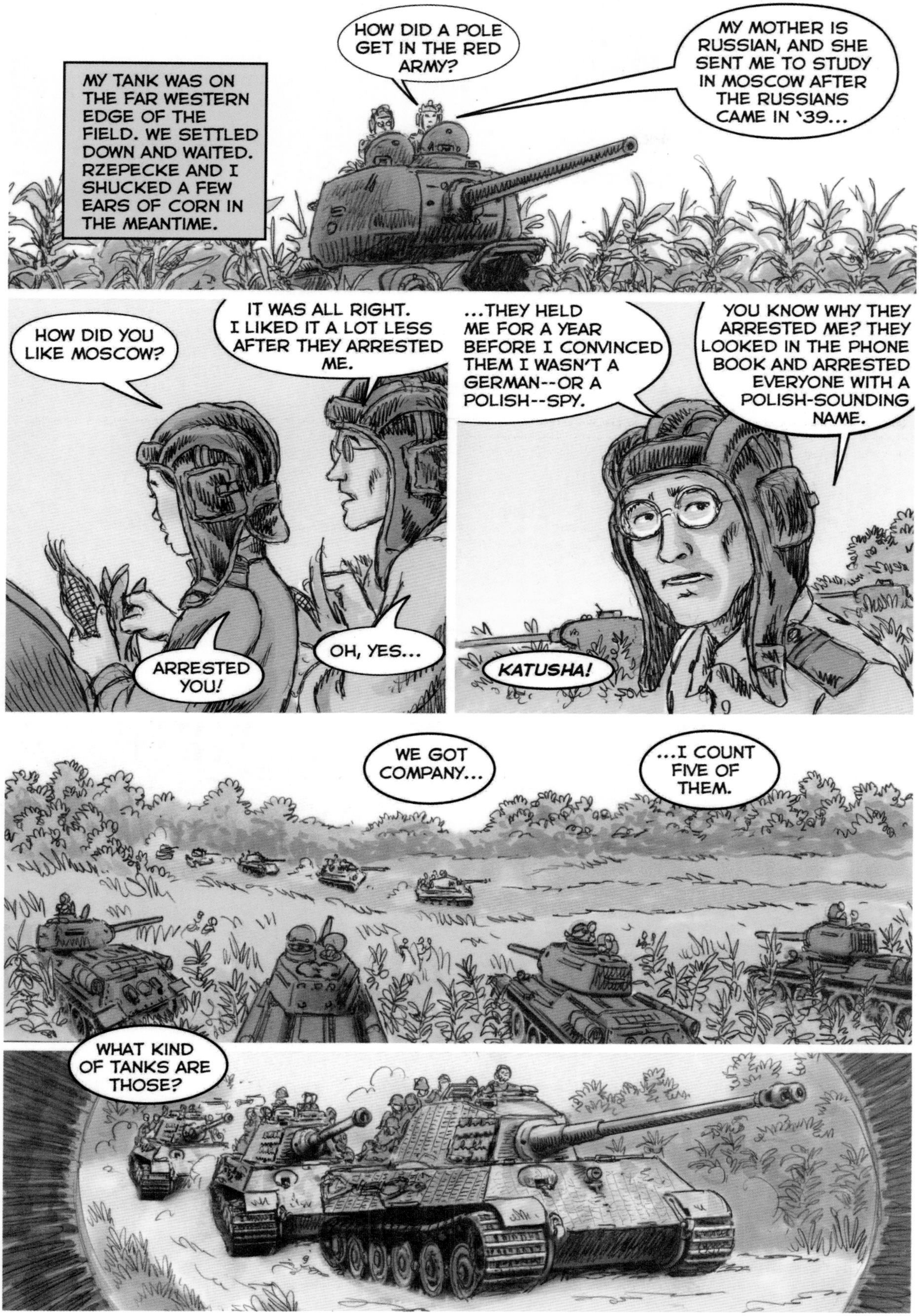
MY TANK WAS ON THE FAR WESTERN EDGE OF THE FIELD. WE SETTLED DOWN AND WAITED. RZEPECKE AND I SHUCKED A FEW EARS OF CORN IN THE MEANTIME.
HOW DID A POLE GET IN THE RED ARMY?
MY MOTHER IS RUSSIAN, AND SHE SENT ME TO STUDY IN MOSCOW AFTER THE RUSSIANS CAME IN '39...
HOW DID YOU LIKE MOSCOW?
IT WAS ALL RIGHT. I LIKED IT A LOT LESS AFTER THEY ARRESTED ME.
ARRESTED YOU!
OH, YES...
...THEY HELD ME FOR A YEAR BEFORE I CONVINCED THEM I WASN'T A GERMAN--OR A POLISH--SPY.
YOU KNOW WHY THEY ARRESTED ME? THEY LOOKED IN THE PHONE BOOK AND ARRESTED EVERYONE WITH A POLISH-SOUNDING NAME.
KATUSHA!
WE GOT COMPANY...
...I COUNT FIVE OF THEM.
WHAT KIND OF TANKS ARE THOSE?

THEY WERE NEW *KING TIGERS*, AND WE WERE FEELING A LITTLE OUTCLASSED.

THERE ARE TWELVE OF *US!* EVERYONE FIRE IN YOUR ZONE UNTIL YOUR TARGETS ARE *DEAD!*

THEN HELP OUT WITH WHAT'S LEFT OF 'EM!

WE ALL OPENED UP WHEN CAPTAIN GUCHKOV FIRED...

ALL OF OUR SHOTS WERE RIGHT ON TARGET. THE GERMAN INFANTRY RIDING THE TIGERS WERE SCATTERED ALL OVER THE PLACE, WHOLE AND IN PIECES.

BUT WE WEREN'T PENETRATING THE TIGER'S ARMORED HIDE.

FIRE AGAIN! KEEP FIRING!

THE TURRET HITS BOUNCED OFF AGAIN, BUT THE SHOTS HITTING ON THE BULKHEAD BESIDE THE ENGINE HIT GASOLINE.

THEN THEIR BIG GUNS SLOWLY TURNED OUR WAY...

480

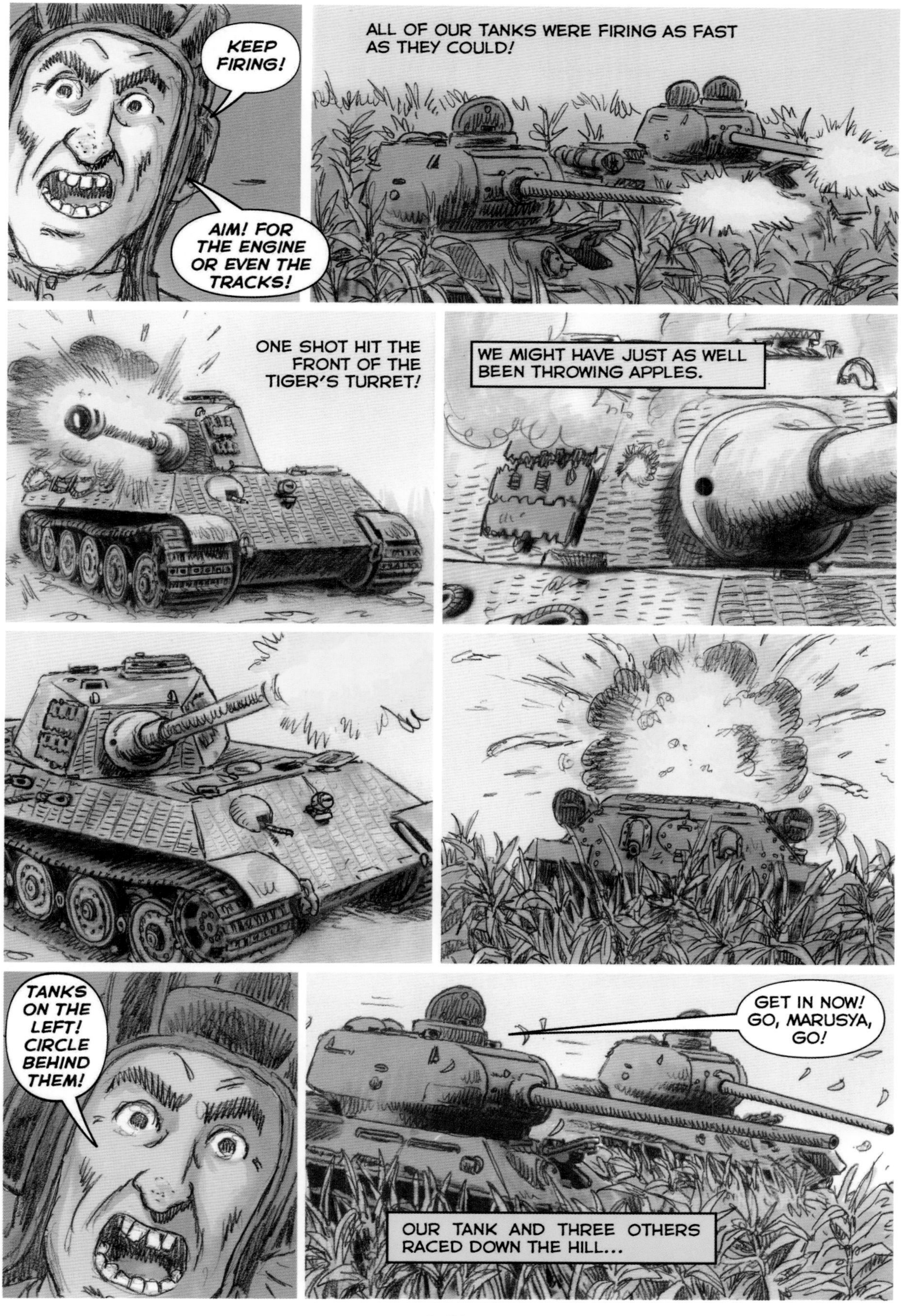
KEEP FIRING!
AIM! FOR THE ENGINE OR EVEN THE TRACKS!
ALL OF OUR TANKS WERE FIRING AS FAST AS THEY COULD!
ONE SHOT HIT THE FRONT OF THE TIGER'S TURRET!
WE MIGHT HAVE JUST AS WELL BEEN THROWING APPLES.
TANKS ON THE LEFT! CIRCLE BEHIND THEM!
GET IN NOW! GO, MARUSYA, GO!
OUR TANK AND THREE OTHERS RACED DOWN THE HILL...

LUCKILY, OUR INFANTRY IN THE CORNFIELD EXPECTED THIS MOVE, AND WERE SURE THEY WERE OUT OF OUR WAY...

...THEY CONTINUED TO FIRE THEIR WEAPONS AT THE TIGERS. THEIR GUNS DID NO GOOD, BUT I LIKED TO THINK THEY KEPT THE GERMANS RATTLED.

ANOTHER TIGER CAUGHT FIRE AND EXPLODED, BUT SEVERAL OF HIS BROTHERS HAD TURNED THEIR TOUGH FRONTS TO THE *T-34S* ON THE HILL AND...

WE PULLED OUT ONTO THE ROAD, FIRING AS WE WENT...

482

FIRE AGAIN! FIRE AGAIN! KEEP FIRING!

THE TWO REMAINING TIGERS WERE MAKING MINCEMEAT OF OUR TANKS IN THE CORNFIELD.

THESE NEW TIGERS WERE POWERFUL, BUT WERE SLOW AND LACKED MANEUVERABILITY...

...AND THEIR CREWS MUST HAVE BEEN FORGETFUL...

...BECAUSE THEY FORGOT ABOUT US.

WE HAD LOST HALF OF OUR TANKS. SOME OF THE DEAD CREW MEMBERS I BARELY KNEW, BUT OTHERS I HAD KNOWN FOR WHAT SEEMED LIKE AN ETERNITY.

WE WERE LUCKY! IF WE HAD BEEN OUT IN THE OPEN, THEY WOULD HAVE WIPED US OUT!

CAPTAIN GUCHKOV'S FATHER HAD BEEN AN EMBALMER, AND HE HAD ALSO BEEN TRAINED IN THE ART. HE COULD HAVE TAKEN A JOB IN THE ARMY IN THAT FIELD, BUT HE SAID HE WAS TIRED OF "HANDLING BODIES..."

I WANT TWO OF OUR TANKS ON THAT KNOLL WITH INFANTRY SUPPORT...

...THE REST OF THE BRIGADE SHOULD BE HERE WITHIN AN HOUR.

NOW, LET'S TAKE CARE OF OUR COMRADES...

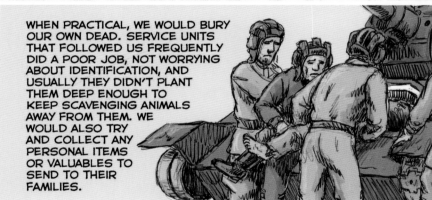

WHEN PRACTICAL, WE WOULD BURY OUR OWN DEAD. SERVICE UNITS THAT FOLLOWED US FREQUENTLY DID A POOR JOB, NOT WORRYING ABOUT IDENTIFICATION, AND USUALLY THEY DIDN'T PLANT THEM DEEP ENOUGH TO KEEP SCAVENGING ANIMALS AWAY FROM THEM. WE WOULD ALSO TRY AND COLLECT ANY PERSONAL ITEMS OR VALUABLES TO SEND TO THEIR FAMILIES.

THE *T-34 TANK* WAS THE MOST ROBUST AND SUCCESSFUL ARMORED VEHICLE OF THIS WAR, BUT IT DID HAVE A FEW PROBLEMS. THE DIESEL ENGINES DID CUT BACK ON FUEL FIRES, BUT IT DID NOT STOP THEM ALTOGETHER.

ALSO, THE LOW NICKEL CONTENT OF THE STEEL MADE IT VERY BRITTLE. AN ARMOR-PIERCING ROUND COULD MAKE IT SHATTER INTO HUNDREDS OF PIECES OF SHRAPNEL.

MANY A TANKER DIED TORN TO SHREDS BY THE STEEL OF HIS OWN TANK.

485

THIS WAS NOT A JOYOUS ACTIVITY, BUT ALL OF US DID OUR PART. WE HOPED THAT WHEN OR IF ANY OF US WERE IN THE SAME CONDITION, THAT WE WOULD RECEIVE TREATMENT JUST AS THOUGHTFUL AND CARING. IT ALSO GAVE US EACH A SOMBER ATTITUDE CONCERNING OUR OWN MORTALITY.

SOON THE REST OF THE BRIGADE ARRIVED, AND WE WERE ON THE ROAD AGAIN.

IT WON'T START! I DON'T KNOW WHY. WE DO OUR MAINTENANCE BY THE BOOK!

WE CAN'T FIND ANYTHING WRONG.

...WE BREAK OUR BACKS FOR THESE MONSTERS, AND THE HEADACHES GO ON AND ON...

YOU DON'T HAVE TO TELL ME. IF I SURVIVE THIS WAR, I WILL NEVER OWN A VEHICLE.

GET A HORSE.

THE FARTHER AND FARTHER WEST WE MOVED INTO POLAND, WE FOUND THAT THE HOMES WERE BETTER BUILT AND MORE COMFORTABLE. EVERYTHING SEEMED MORE ADVANCED. WE WERE ALWAYS TOLD THAT IN THE SOVIET UNION WE LIVED BETTER THAN EVERYONE ELSE. COULD THIS BE A LIE?

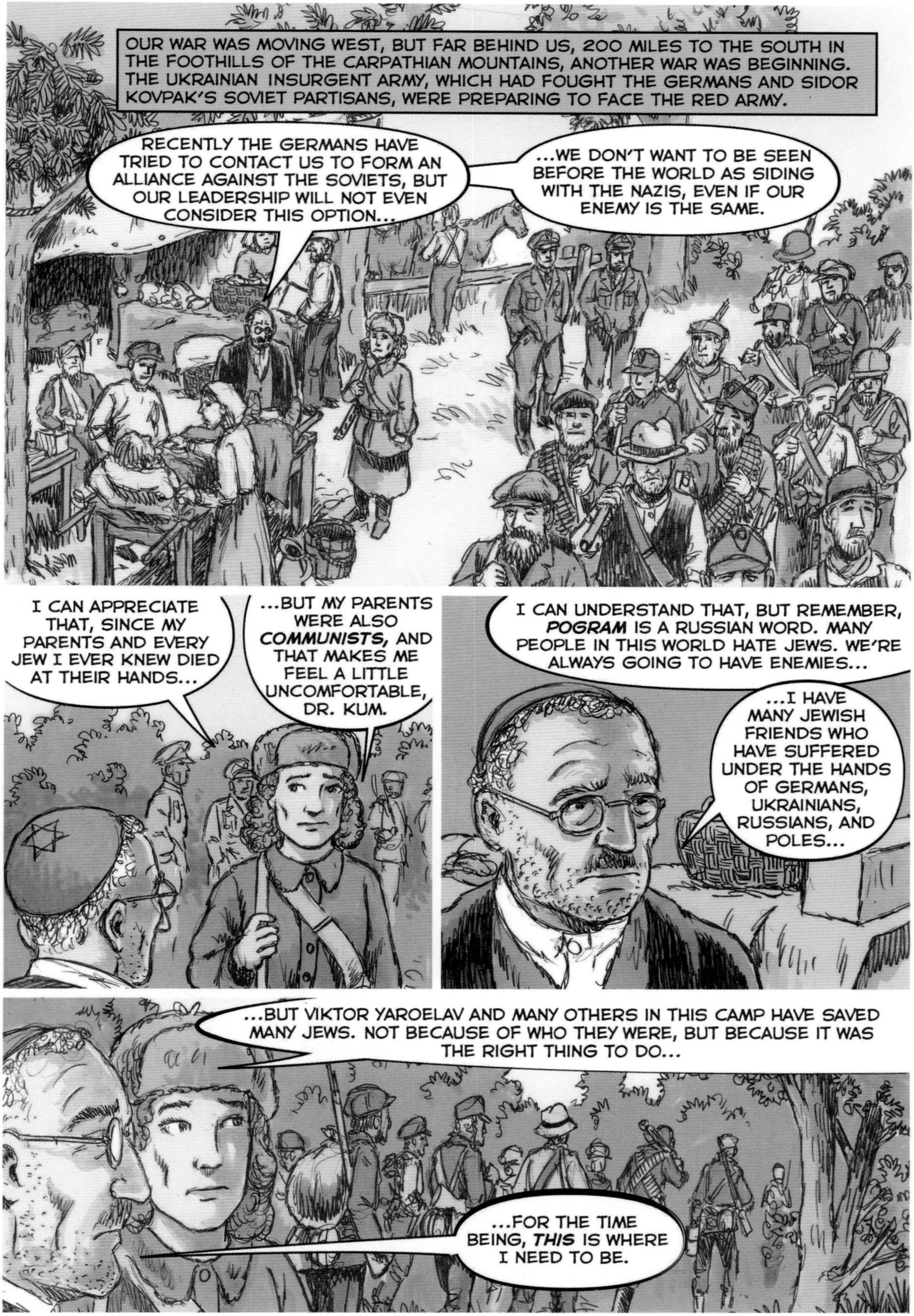

OUR WAR WAS MOVING WEST, BUT FAR BEHIND US, 200 MILES TO THE SOUTH IN THE FOOTHILLS OF THE CARPATHIAN MOUNTAINS, ANOTHER WAR WAS BEGINNING. THE UKRAINIAN INSURGENT ARMY, WHICH HAD FOUGHT THE GERMANS AND SIDOR KOVPAK'S SOVIET PARTISANS, WERE PREPARING TO FACE THE RED ARMY.
RECENTLY THE GERMANS HAVE TRIED TO CONTACT US TO FORM AN ALLIANCE AGAINST THE SOVIETS, BUT OUR LEADERSHIP WILL NOT EVEN CONSIDER THIS OPTION...
...WE DON'T WANT TO BE SEEN BEFORE THE WORLD AS SIDING WITH THE NAZIS, EVEN IF OUR ENEMY IS THE SAME.
I CAN APPRECIATE THAT, SINCE MY PARENTS AND EVERY JEW I EVER KNEW DIED AT THEIR HANDS...
...BUT MY PARENTS WERE ALSO *COMMUNISTS,* AND THAT MAKES ME FEEL A LITTLE UNCOMFORTABLE, DR. KUM.
I CAN UNDERSTAND THAT, BUT REMEMBER, ***POGRAM*** IS A RUSSIAN WORD. MANY PEOPLE IN THIS WORLD HATE JEWS. WE'RE ALWAYS GOING TO HAVE ENEMIES...
...I HAVE MANY JEWISH FRIENDS WHO HAVE SUFFERED UNDER THE HANDS OF GERMANS, UKRAINIANS, RUSSIANS, AND POLES...
...BUT VIKTOR YAROELAV AND MANY OTHERS IN THIS CAMP HAVE SAVED MANY JEWS. NOT BECAUSE OF WHO THEY WERE, BUT BECAUSE IT WAS THE RIGHT THING TO DO...
...FOR THE TIME BEING, *THIS* IS WHERE I NEED TO BE.

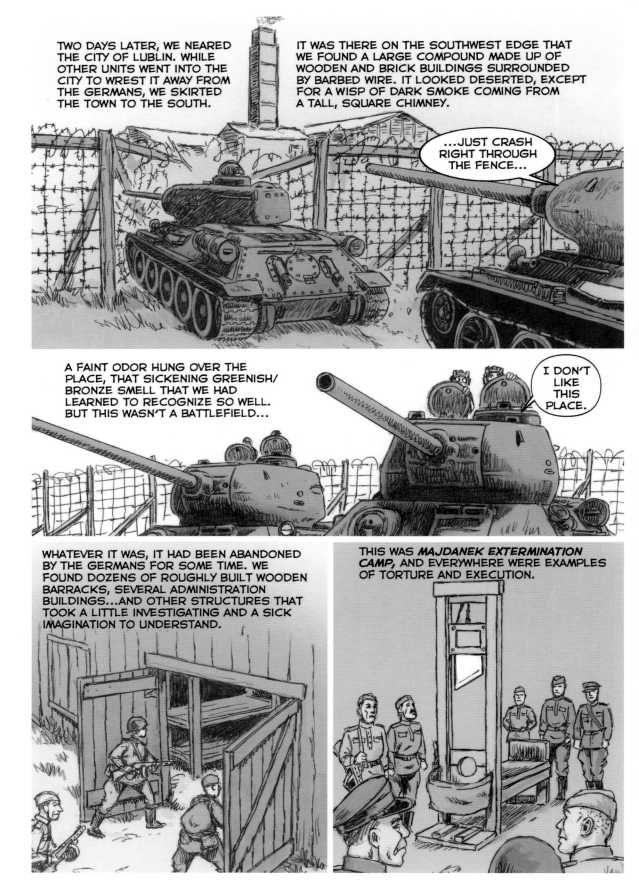

TWO DAYS LATER, WE NEARED THE CITY OF LUBLIN. WHILE OTHER UNITS WENT INTO THE CITY TO WREST IT AWAY FROM THE GERMANS, WE SKIRTED THE TOWN TO THE SOUTH.

IT WAS THERE ON THE SOUTHWEST EDGE THAT WE FOUND A LARGE COMPOUND MADE UP OF WOODEN AND BRICK BUILDINGS SURROUNDED BY BARBED WIRE. IT LOOKED DESERTED, EXCEPT FOR A WISP OF DARK SMOKE COMING FROM A TALL, SQUARE CHIMNEY.

...JUST CRASH RIGHT THROUGH THE FENCE...

A FAINT ODOR HUNG OVER THE PLACE, THAT SICKENING GREENISH/ BRONZE SMELL THAT WE HAD LEARNED TO RECOGNIZE SO WELL. BUT THIS WASN'T A BATTLEFIELD...

I DON'T LIKE THIS PLACE.

WHATEVER IT WAS, IT HAD BEEN ABANDONED BY THE GERMANS FOR SOME TIME. WE FOUND DOZENS OF ROUGHLY BUILT WOODEN BARRACKS, SEVERAL ADMINISTRATION BUILDINGS...AND OTHER STRUCTURES THAT TOOK A LITTLE INVESTIGATING AND A SICK IMAGINATION TO UNDERSTAND.

THIS WAS *MAJDANEK EXTERMINATION CAMP,* AND EVERYWHERE WERE EXAMPLES OF TORTURE AND EXECUTION.

ALL WE FOUND OF THE INMATES WERE DECOMPOSED REMAINS OF THOSE THEY HAD NOT HAD TIME TO BURN IN THE HUGE INDUSTRIAL OVENS. MOST OF THE LIVING SURVIVORS HAD BEEN MARCHED WEST.

BUT WE DID FIND 1,500 FORMER RUSSIAN SOLDIERS. THESE MEN HAD SWITCHED SIDES AND FOUGHT FOR THE GERMANS, EITHER FOR FOOD OR CONVICTION. THEY HAD BEEN WOUNDED IN BATTLE FIGHTING THE COMMUNISTS AND WERE RECOVERING IN A HOSPITAL HERE...

...ONE CAN ONLY IMAGINE THEIR FATE AT THE HANDS OF THE *NKVD*.

SERGEANT TYMOSHENKO...

I CAME TO ATTENTION WHEN COMRADE NOZDRIN CALLED. BEING THIS FORMAL, I LET HIM KNOW THAT I WAS STILL ANGRY ABOUT THE BLACK EYE HE HAD GIVEN ME.

YES, COMRADE COLONEL.

BUT, HE COULD SEE RIGHT THROUGH ME...

SO, IT'S LIKE THAT...

...WELL. I THOUGHT YOU WOULD LIKE TO KNOW THAT CAPTAIN KOVCHENKO IS TEACHING TACTICS TO INFANTRY OFFICERS NEAR SMOLENSK.

REALLY?! AND HE'LL BE SAFE THERE? HE'LL NO LONGER BE IN DANGER?

THAT'S RIGHT. HE CAN KEEP THAT POSITION FOR AS LONG AS HE WISHES.

THANK YOU FOR TELLING ME, COLONEL.

I COULD NEVER STAY MAD AT ANYONE VERY LONG.

WELL, THAT CERTAINLY WAS A STRANGE WAY TO ACT.

UH-HUH! IF SOMEONE TOLD ME THAT MY SWEETIE WAS 500 MILES AWAY, I WOULDN'T BE SO CHIPPER.

WHAT DID YOU SAY?!

ADMIT IT, KATUSHA. YOU'RE HAPPY BECAUSE HE'S SAFE.

THE FACT IS, YOU LOVE HIM. AND EVERYBODY KNOWS IT.

YOU'VE BOTH LOST YOUR MINDS!

EVERYONE IN THIS BRIGADE CAN TELL YOU: IT MAY BE A CLOUDY DAY, BUT WHEN KATUSHA AND KOLYA MEET, THE CLOUDS OPEN UP AND A RAY OF SUNSHINE POINTS RIGHT AT THEM.

I DIDN'T KNOW WHAT TO SAY. I WAS ANGRY AND EMBARRASSED AT THE SAME TIME.

IT DOESN'T MATTER. HE'S THERE AND I'M HERE...

...I'LL PROBABLY NEVER SEE HIM AGAIN.

MARUSYA AND OXANNA PUT THEIR ARMS OVER MY SHOULDERS LIKE THE FRIENDS THEY WERE.

NO! DON'T THINK OF IT THAT WAY...

...DON'T YOU REALIZE HOW LUCKY YOU ARE?

DO YOU REALIZE HOW FEW MEN ARE GOING TO BE LEFT AFTER THE WAR? THE AVERAGE GIRL WILL NEVER BE ABLE TO FIND A HUSBAND... WILL NEVER HAVE CHILDREN.

MY CHANCES WERE BAD ALREADY.

WHEN OXANNA SAID THAT, I HURT TO THE HEART FOR HER.

SO, I FIRMLY BELIEVE, I KNOW, THAT THERE IS HOPE FOR YOU IF THERE IS HOPE FOR ANYONE...

...ALL YOU HAVE TO DO IS STAY ALIVE!

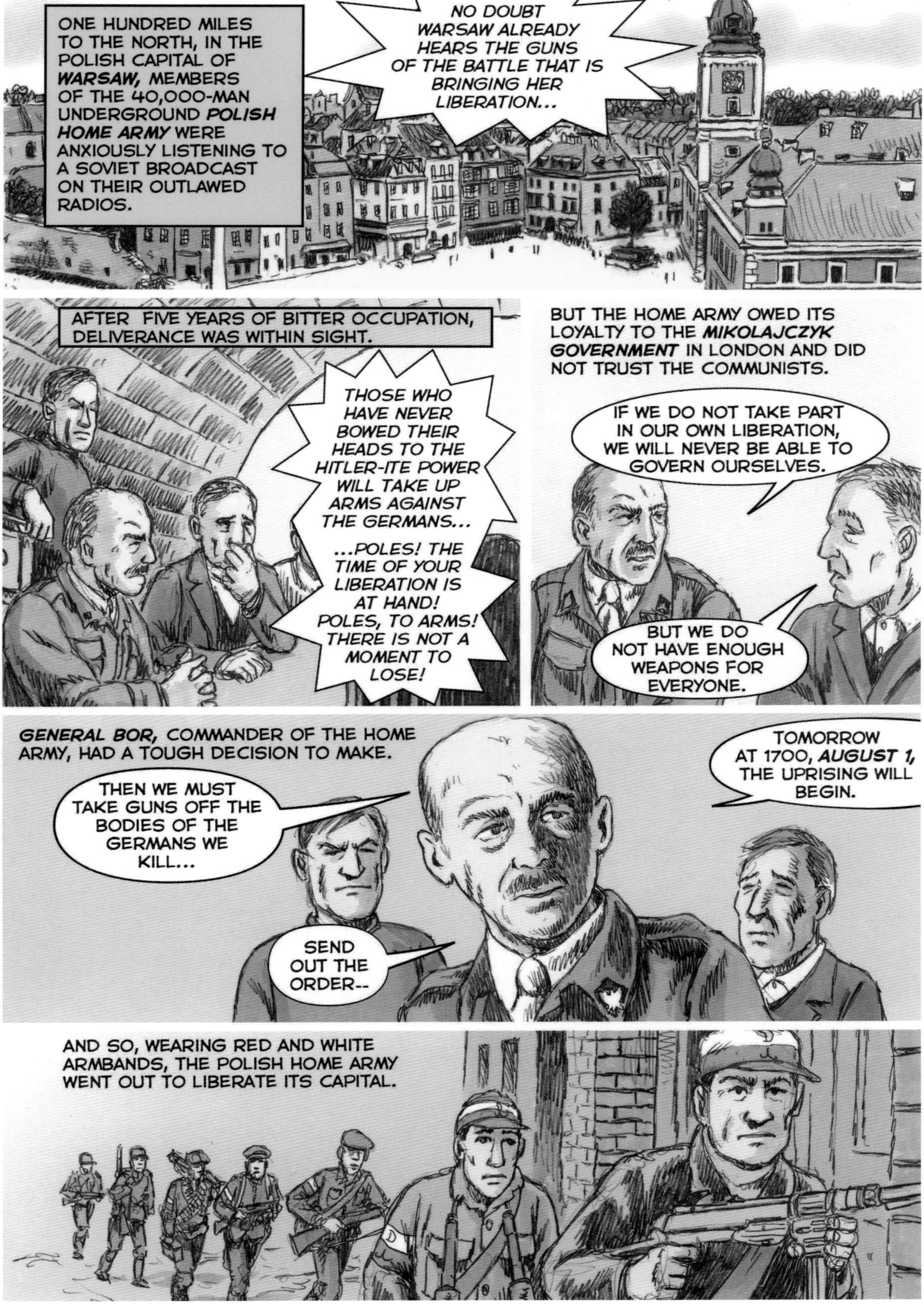
ONE HUNDRED MILES TO THE NORTH, IN THE POLISH CAPITAL OF ***WARSAW,*** MEMBERS OF THE 40,000-MAN UNDERGROUND ***POLISH HOME ARMY*** WERE ANXIOUSLY LISTENING TO A SOVIET BROADCAST ON THEIR OUTLAWED RADIOS.
NO DOUBT WARSAW ALREADY HEARS THE GUNS OF THE BATTLE THAT IS BRINGING HER LIBERATION...
AFTER FIVE YEARS OF BITTER OCCUPATION, DELIVERANCE WAS WITHIN SIGHT.
THOSE WHO HAVE NEVER BOWED THEIR HEADS TO THE HITLER-ITE POWER WILL TAKE UP ARMS AGAINST THE GERMANS...
...POLES! THE TIME OF YOUR LIBERATION IS AT HAND! POLES, TO ARMS! THERE IS NOT A MOMENT TO LOSE!
BUT THE HOME ARMY OWED ITS LOYALTY TO THE ***MIKOLAJCZYK GOVERNMENT*** IN LONDON AND DID NOT TRUST THE COMMUNISTS.
IF WE DO NOT TAKE PART IN OUR OWN LIBERATION, WE WILL NEVER BE ABLE TO GOVERN OURSELVES.
BUT WE DO NOT HAVE ENOUGH WEAPONS FOR EVERYONE.
GENERAL BOR, COMMANDER OF THE HOME ARMY, HAD A TOUGH DECISION TO MAKE.
THEN WE MUST TAKE GUNS OFF THE BODIES OF THE GERMANS WE KILL...
SEND OUT THE ORDER--
TOMORROW AT 1700, ***AUGUST 1,*** THE UPRISING WILL BEGIN.
AND SO, WEARING RED AND WHITE ARMBANDS, THE POLISH HOME ARMY WENT OUT TO LIBERATE ITS CAPITAL.

AT FIRST, THE REVOLT TOOK THE SMALL GERMAN GARRISONS BY SURPRISE. THE INSURGENTS MOVED FORWARD AND TOOK CONTROL OF SEVERAL IMPORTANT STREETS AND DISTRICTS. BUT THEY WERE UNABLE TO CAPTURE THE WEAPONS AND AMMUNITION THAT THEY NEEDED TO HOLD THEM.

THE GERMANS, SELDOM CAUGHT OFF GUARD FOR LONG, REINFORCED THE CITY'S GARRISON WITH SEASONED COMBAT UNITS.

THEY ALSO SENT SEVERAL UNITS THAT HAD FOUGHT AGAINST PARTISANS IN THE BRYANSK FOREST OF NORTHERN RUSSIA. MANY CRIMES WERE COMMITTED AGAINST CIVILIANS THERE.

ON AUGUST 5, THE GERMANS LAUNCHED THEIR OFFENSIVE AGAINST THE WARSAW INSURGENTS. THEN, SOMETHING EVEN MORE IMPORTANT HAPPENED...

STALIN ORDERED THAT THE RED ARMY ADVANCE ON WARSAW BE *HALTED!*

THE MESSAGE WAS CLEAR: THE INSURGENTS WERE LOYAL TO THE WESTERN-LEANING POLISH GOVERNMENT IN LONDON, AND STALIN CONSIDERED POLAND NOT A COUNTRY TO BE LIBERATED BUT TERRITORY TO BE CONQUERED.

THROUGH DIPLOMATIC CHANNELS FROM LONDON, WINSTON CHURCHILL BEGGED STALIN TO SEND RELIEF.

IN 1939 WE WENT TO WAR FOR POLAND. NOW WE MAY BE SEEING THEM JUST TRADE ONE DICTATOR FOR ANOTHER.

HE ALSO ASKED FOR ACCESS TO AIRFIELDS IN SOVIET TERRITORY SO THE WESTERN ALLIES COULD AIRDROP SUPPLIES TO THE POLES. STALIN DENIED PERMISSION FOR THIS ALSO.

FINALLY, BRITISH LANCASTER BOMBERS FLYING FROM BASES IN ITALY BEGAN DROPPING SUPPLIES TO THE POLES.

BUT SINCE THE GERMANS HAD PUSHED THE POLES INTO SUCH A SMALL AREA, THE SUPPLY PACKAGES MOSTLY FELL WITHIN THE GERMAN LINES. ALSO, FLYING SO FAR FROM THEIR BASES, ALMOST 30 PERCENT OF THE BRITISH PLANES WERE SHOT DOWN. THE AIRLIFT WAS DISCONTINUED.

THE INSURGENTS FINALLY SURRENDERED TO THE GERMANS ON OCTOBER 1, 1944.

NEARLY 200,000 CITIZENS OF WARSAW HAD PERISHED. IN AN ODD EXAMPLE OF NAZI JUSTICE, THEY TREATED THOSE WHO SURRENDERED LIKE PRISONERS OF WAR AND SENT THEM TO P.O.W. CAMPS.

THEN, USING EXPLOSIVE CHARGES AND FLAME THROWERS...

...THE GERMANS DESTROYED WHAT WAS LEFT OF WARSAW.

THAT FALL WE REMAINED IN GARRISON IN LUBLIN FOR SEVERAL WEEKS. DURING THAT TIME, WE TOOK IN NEW MEN TO REPLACE OUR DEAD AND RECEIVED NEW TANKS AND EQUIPMENT, GETTING BACK TO FULL STRENGTH.

ONE NIGHT, THEY SHOWED US A MOVIE IN ONE OF THE OLD BARRACKS AT MAJDANEK CONCENTRATION CAMP.

IT WAS A MUSICAL CALLED "AT 6PM AT THE END OF THE WAR."

TOWARD THE END OF THE FILM, THE GIRL IS SINGING TO HER LOVER AS HE MOUNTS A HORSE AND RIDES BACK TO THE BATTLE ALONG A WOODED HILLSIDE.

WHEN THE FILM WAS OVER, A COMMISSAR CAME ONTO THE STAGE AND GAVE A SHORT HISTORY LESSON ABOUT THE GERMANS IN OUR COUNTRY.

THEY WERE COMPLETELY SHAMELESS, THE WAY THEY TREATED OUR WOMEN AND OUR PRISONERS. OUR LIVES WERE NOTHING TO THEM...

...I TELL YOU, WE MUST COLLECT TWO EYES FOR EACH EYE!

IT WAS TURNING INTO A HATE MEETING, AND THE CROWD WENT WILD.

I'M TELLING YOU. COMRADES. MAKE YOUR LEDGER OF REVENGE, AND EXACT FROM THE GERMANS EVERY ITEM ON IT.

WE WALKED BACK TO OUR QUARTERS IN A DRENCHING DOWNPOUR.

IS THAT THE NEW HEAVY STALIN TANK?

YES. OFFICIALLY IT IS THE *IS2M.* I UNDERSTAND THAT WE'LL HAVE A WHOLE BATTALION OF THEM, PLUS OTHER NEW VEHICLES.

THE WOMEN OF OUR BRIGADE MANAGED TO ROPE AND BLANKET OFF A SECTION OF THE BARRACKS SO WE COULD GET A LITTLE PRIVACY.

I WENT RIGHT TO BED. IN NO TIME I WAS HAVING A STRANGE DREAM, THAT WAS VERY MUCH LIKE THE MOVIE I HAD SEEN THAT EVENING.

IN THE DREAM, THERE WAS A SCENE OF FAREWELL JUST LIKE IN THE MOVIE, BUT IT WAS KOLYA AND I SAYING GOODBYE...

...BUT IN MY "MOVIE" IT WAS I WHO WAS JUMPING UP ON A HORSE, AND IT WAS I WHO WAS GOING BACK INTO BATTLE.

IT WAS THE STRANGEST THING...

...AS I RODE ALONG THE RIDGE, I COULD SEE THREE FIGURES WAVING AT ME FROM THE EDGE OF THE WOODS.

...AS I RODE CLOSER, I COULD TELL THEY WERE SMILING, BECKONING ME ON WITH FRIENDLY ASSURANCE...

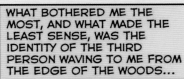

...SUDDENLY, I COULD MAKE OUT WHO TWO OF THEM WERE...

...IT WAS MILLA AND UNCLE TARAS.

I WOKE UP WITH A JOLT, DRENCHED IN A COLD SWEAT. FEELING AS IF...

...AS IF I HAD BEEN BECKONED FROM THE GRAVE.

WHAT BOTHERED ME THE MOST, AND WHAT MADE THE LEAST SENSE, WAS THE IDENTITY OF THE THIRD PERSON WAVING TO ME FROM THE EDGE OF THE WOODS...

...IT WAS PAPA!

AS THE YEAR 1944 CAME TO A CLOSE AND WE PREPARED FOR OUR NEXT ADVANCE, WE HEARD RUMORS OF A GREAT BATTLE TAKING PLACE NEARLY A THOUSAND MILES TO THE WEST. HITLER, IN AN ATTEMPT TO STOP THE AMERICAN DRIVE INTO GERMANY, MOUNTED AN OFFENSIVE USING ALL HIS BEST PANZER DIVISIONS. THE AMERICANS WERE DESTROYING THESE DIVISIONS AT GREAT COST TO THEMSELVES. OTHERWISE, THESE TANKS WOULD BE FACING US ACROSS THE VISTULA. I REMEMBER BEING GRATEFUL FOR THESE YOUNG AMERICANS FIGHTING OUR ENEMY THAT WINTER IN A BATTLE THAT THEY CALLED THE "BEND" OR THE "SWELL" OR SOMETHING.

IN JANUARY, WE WERE BACK TO FULL STRENGTH AND BEING MOVED ACROSS TO A BRIDGEHEAD ON THE VISTULA. IT WAS SLOW GOING ON THOSE SNOWY ROADS FILLED WITH TANKS AND INFANTRY.

ONE DAY WHILE WE WERE PLODDING ALONG, WE HEARD A LOUD COMMOTION FROM THE REAR. AT FIRST IT WAS THE BLOWING OF HORNS, AND THEN THE LOUD CHEERS OF MEN.

THEY WERE CHEERING A GROUP OF MEN RIDING IN AN AMERICAN-MADE JEEP...

...AS THE JEEP GOT CLOSER...

...THE CHEERING GOT LOUDER...

...UNTIL...

...MY GOD! IT WAS KOLYA!

497

HE WAS COMING BACK TO THE BRIGADE. COLONEL NOZDRIN WAS DRIVING, WEARING A GRIN FROM EAR TO EAR. IN THE BACKSEAT WAS COMMISSAR CHEKOV AND KOLYA'S RUNNER, VENGROVA.

THEY DROVE BY US AND STOPPED ABOUT TWENTY FEET AHEAD, AMONG ALL THE INFANTRY OFFICERS. KOLYA GOT OUT AND HUGGED AND PATTED THE BACKS OF THE OLD HANDS.

THE NEW "GREEN" OFFICERS AND MEN STOOD AROUND WITH CONFUSED EXPRESSIONS, UNTIL SOMEONE EXPLAINED WHO THIS HANDSOME SOLDIER WAS. ON HEARING THIS, THEY STRAIGHTENED THEIR BACKS AND LOOKED ON IN AWE.

COMMISSAR CHEKOV, LOOKING VERY SATISFIED WITH HIMSELF, STEPPED OUT OF THE JEEP AND STARTED LOOKING AOUND. I REMEMBER WONDERING WHAT THIS SCARY BOLSHEVIK WAS LOOKING FOR.

THEN HIS EYES CAME TO REST ON *ME*, AND *STOPPED!* HE SMILED, AND GAVE ME A LITTLE NOD.

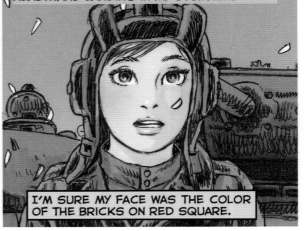

I SWALLOWED HARD AND RETURNED THE NOD TO BE POLITE. ALL KINDS OF EMOTIONS AND FEELINGS WERE RUNNING THROUGH MY HEAD...AND LANDING IN MY STOMACH!

I'M SURE MY FACE WAS THE COLOR OF THE BRICKS ON RED SQUARE.

SEVERAL HUNDRED MILES TO THE SOUTHEAST, ANOTHER WAR WAS BEGINNING. DESPITE THE FACT THAT THIS WAR AGAINST THE GERMANS WAS NOT YET OVER, STALIN WAS SENDING *NKVD* TROOPS INTO THE CARPATHIAN MOUNTAINS OF SOUTHWESTERN UKRAINE TO DESTROY THE UKRAINIAN INSURGENT ARMY...

THESE SECURITY MEN CONSIDERED THIS INCURSION A LARK. AFTER ALL, AFTER THE GERMANS, HOW BAD COULD A BUNCH OF DUMB UKRAINIAN HILLBILLIES BE?

FIRE!

WITHIN THE SPACE OF A FEW DAYS, MORE THAN 300 *NKVD* MEN WERE *DEAD,* AND MANY MORE WOUNDED. THIS WAR WOULD BE LONG AND BLOODY, AND MANY YEARS WOULD PASS BEFORE THERE WOULD BE A RESOLUTION FOR ANYONE.

LATE ON THE NIGHT OF *JANUARY 11*, WE WERE MOVING UP TO OUR POSITION FOR THE UPCOMING OFFENSIVE. WE WERE NOT TO BE IN THE INITIAL ASSAULT BUT WERE PREPARED TO FOLLOW UP WHEN NEEDED. WE WERE SITTING ON A SNOWY ROAD WITH HALF A DOZEN INFANTRY ON OUR BACKS. I HAD LET THEM UNFOLD OUR TARP TO COVER THEMSELVES AND CATCH THE HEAT FROM THE ENGINE. SUDDENLY, AN OFFICER IN A GREATCOAT CAME RUNNING TO OUR TANK AND CLIMBED UP. RIGHT AWAY I KNEW WHO IT WAS.

HELLO, THERE! I'M SORRY I HAVEN'T HAD THE CHANCE TO GET BY TILL NOW.

I SAID NOTHING, JUST LOOKED AT HIM WITHOUT SMILING.

WHAT'S WRONG?

WHY DID YOU COME BACK? YOU DIDN'T HAVE TO. YOU WERE SAFE THERE...

WHY DID YOU COME BACK?

THERE WAS NOTHING FOR ME THERE...

...BECAUSE I BELONGED HERE.

AREN'T YOU GLAD TO SEE ME?

I HAVE NEVER BEEN HAPPIER TO SEE ANYONE IN MY LIFE...

...BUT WHAT ABOUT LENINGRAD? IS THERE NOTHING FOR YOU THERE?

NO. I UNDERSTAND THAT NOW...

...I UNDERSTAND IT *HERE*.

WE JUST LOOKED AT EACH OTHER FOR AT LEAST A FULL MINUTE. DESPITE THE COLD AND WIND, I HAD A WARM FEELING AND FELT PERFECTLY CONTENT.

WELL, *GOD* HELP US.

AT *0435* ON THE MORNING OF *JANUARY 12,* THE ARTILLERY OF THE *1ST UKRAINIAN FRONT* OPENED UP. THEY HAD 300 GUNS FOR EVERY KILOMETER OF FRONT.

HOUSES WERE IMMEDIATELY REDUCED TO DUST. BUNKERS AND PILLBOXES CAVED IN ON THEIR OCCUPANTS. STUNNED AND TRAUMATIZED SURVIVORS LAY HELPLESS UNDER THE SOVIET CACOPHONY.

AT *0500,* SOVIET PENAL BATTALIONS MOVED FORWARD. THESE WERE PETTY THIEVES, POLITICAL PRISONERS, MEN WHO HAD FLED FROM BATTLE OR WERE WAR PROFITEERS. NOW THEY CLEARED MINE FIELDS AND PERFORMED "RECONNAISSANCE BY COMBAT."

THERE WOULD BE NO MEDALS FOR THESE MEN. IF CRIPPLED, THEIR RECORDS WOULD BE EXPUNGED. IF THEY DIED, THEIR DEBT TO THE STATE WOULD BE "PAID IN FULL."

AT *1000,* A SECOND BARRAGE BEGAN, REACHING A DEPTH OF SIX MILES AND LASTING FOR TWO HOURS.

THIS HORRIFIC FIRE DESTROYED 60 PERCENT OF THE GERMAN ARTILLERY AND KILLED, WOUNDED, OR VAPORIZED 25 PERCENT OF THEIR MEN.

IT ALSO DESTROYED THE HEADQUARTERS OF THE *FOURTH PANZER ARMY.*

ONE TIGER TANK BATTALION, IN THE MIDDLE OF FUELING THEIR VEHICLES WHEN THE BOMBARDMENT HIT, WAS COMPLETELY DESTROYED. THEY WERE PART OF *THE 17TH PANZER DIVISION*, ONE OF THE UNITS WE HAD FOUGHT AT STALINGRAD.

BY LATE MORNING, THE FIRST MECHANIZED UNIT WAS WAVED FORWARD. IT ROARED THROUGH THE SNOW AT TOP SPEED.

FORTY MINUTES LATER, WE WERE GIVEN THE COMMAND TO CRANK OUR ENGINES. ON THAT DAY, ALL OF OUR TANKS STARTED, AND THE ROAR OF THE DIESELS SHOOK THE SNOW FROM THE TREES.

TEN MINUTES LATER, THE TANK IN FRONT OF US BOLTED FORWARD. WE WERE RIGHT BEHIND THEM.

WE ROLLED ACROSS THE SNOWY LANDSCAPE ALL DAY AND INTO THE NIGHT. OUR INTELLIGENCE WAS SO GOOD THAT THERE WERE FEW DELAYS...

...BUT THERE WERE ENOUGH OF THEM TO MAKE GOOD BATHROOM STOPS.

BEING A POLE, RZEPECKE HAD BEEN A LITTLE DEPRESSED FOR THE LAST SEVERAL DAYS, BECAUSE OF WHAT HAD HAPPED IN WARSAW AND THE RED ARMY'S GENERAL HEAVY-HANDEDNESS IN HIS COUNTRY. HE SUDDENLY CHEERED UP.

WELL, IT COULD BE A LOT WORSE...

HOW'S THAT?

I COULD BE FROM GERMANY.

THERE WAS SOMETHING THAT WE HAD LEARNED SINCE STALINGRAD AND KURSK: THE GERMANS HAD NEVER GIVEN UP ON THE IDEA THAT THEY WOULD WIN THE WAR TO ACHIEVE THE "FINAL VICTORY."

THEY WERE SO ARROGANTLY SURE IN THEIR GREATNESS THAT THEY THOUGHT THAT IF THEY SOMEHOW LOST THE WAR, OR FAILED TO WIN IT, THAT THEY COULD JUST GO HOME TO GERMANY, PUT ON THEIR LEDERHOSEN, SMOKE THEIR PIPES, AND TALK ABOUT WHAT A GOOD CAMPAIGN IT HAD BEEN.

THE IDEA THAT WE WOULD BE FOLLOWING THEM HOME DIDN'T SEEM TO SINK IN UNTIL WE WERE BEATING ON THE DOOR.

THE LEFT FLANK OF THE *1ST UKRAINIAN FRONT* LIBERATED *KRACOW* AND DISCOVERED THE NEARBY DEATH CAMP OF *AUSCHWITZ*. THE OVENS HAD BEEN COLD FOR TEN DAYS, BUT THE EVIDENCE LEFT PROVIDED PROOF THAT A MILLION PEOPLE--BOTH JEWS AND NON-JEWS--HAD DIED THERE.

WHEN THE AVERAGE RUSSIAN SOLDIER WAS TOLD ABOUT IT, HE SEETHED FOR VENGEANCE. *MARSHALL KONEV* SHOWED NO EMOTION AT ALL WHEN TOLD. PERHAPS HE WAS TOO USED TO STALIN'S MASS MURDERS.

THE FIGHTING WAS HARD, BUT SPORADIC. WE WERE HEADING TOWARD THE INDUSTRIAL AND MINING REGION OF UPPER SILESIA, AN AREA STALIN WANTED TAKEN INTACT.

THEN, ON *JANUARY 20*, IT HAPPENED...

...GERMANY!

кермания

A BARBARIAN ARMY HAD ENTERED CENTRAL EUROPE!

FOR A TIME YEARS LATER, "POLACK" JOKES
WERE POPULAR IN SOME CIRCLES. THIS COULD
ALSO BE SAID FOR "ITALIAN" JOKES, AND MANY
OTHER ETHNIC GROUPS. I'VE EVEN HEARD
RUSSIANS TELL UKRAINIAN JOKES.

THESE JOKES USUALLY MAKE FUN OF A NATIONALITY'S INTELLIGENCE OR CULTURE
OR CLEANLINESS. WELL, ALLOW ME TO TELL A *REAL* POLISH JOKE: IT GOES, "THE
POLES ARE ATTACKED BY THE GERMANS AND THE RUSSIANS AT THE SAME TIME.
WHICH ONE DO THEY FIGHT FIRST?"

AND THE PUNCH LINE IS: "FIGHT THE RUSSIANS
FIRST--BUSINESS BEFORE PLEASURE."

...NOT FUNNY, HUH?

AS WE ADVANCED ACROSS POLAND, THE *NKVD* CAME IN OUR WAKE.
ANYONE WITH THE SLIGHTEST CONNECTION WITH THE *POLISH HOME
ARMY* AND ITS LONDON-BASED LEADERS WAS ARRESTED.

POLISH JEWS, EVEN THOSE STILL WEARING THEIR CONCENTRATION CAMP
STRIPES, WERE TAKEN INTO "PROTECTIVE CUSTODY." THE SOVIETS HAD HEARD
OF THE PLANNED *POLISH JEWISH COUNCIL* SOON TO MEET IN THE UNITED
STATES. ANY INFLUENCE FROM OUTSIDE THE SOVIET SPHERE WAS SUSPECT.

MANY POLES SERVING IN THE RED ARMY DESERTED TO JOIN *ARMY KRAJOWA,* AN UNDERGROUND ORGANIZATION THAT FOUGHT THE GERMANS AND WERE NOW FIGHTING THE SOVIETS.

A VARIATION ON THE OLD JOKE.

THE SAME THING WAS HAPPENING IN WESTERN UKRAINE AS THE FOLLOWERS OF *STEPHAN BANDERA* WERE BEGINNING THEIR GUERILLA WAR AGAINST THE COMMUNISTS.

IT WOULD LAST INTO THE 1950S.

RIGHT AND *WRONG* CAN SOMETIMES BE VERY DIFFICULT TO DEFINE. DID I FIGHT AGAINST EVIL? MOST ASSUREDLY! DID I FIGHT *FOR* EVIL? I MUST CONFESS THAT IN A WAY I DID. BUT DON'T JUDGE ME UNTIL YOU WALK THOSE MANY MILES IN MY SHOES...

FRITZ 75MM! AND IN A GOOD POSITION, TOO.

...OR AT LEAST RIDE IN THEM.

YOU'RE RIGHT OUT IN FRONT OF HIM BEFORE YOU CAN SEE HIM...

...MARUSYA, I'M GOING TO STEP OUT AND SEE IF I CAN SEE WHERE IT IS...

LILY AMONG THORNS

GERMANY, MARCH 1945. AN EARLY THAW HAD TURNED THE ROAD TO VICTORY INTO A SEA OF MUD, AND GERMAN RESISTANCE WAS AS TOUGH AND DETERMINED AS EVER.

AAGGHHH!!

HANG ON, KATUSHA! WE'RE PULLIN' UP TO GET HIM!

ANOTHER FIGHT WON, AND WE'RE SAFE FOR THE MOMENT. HOWEVER, I WAS IN NO MOOD TO CELEBRATE.

HE WAS HARD TO GET... KATUSHA? WHAT HAPPENED TO YOU?

HIS LAST SHELL HIT THE FAMILY TOILET!

KATUSHA! YOU'RE COVERED IN...IN SHIT!

HA, H...

WHAT'S SO FUNNY?!

YOU'RE NOT GOING TO GET BACK IN THE TANK, ARE YOU?

I WAS AFRAID THAT THE NEWS ABOUT THIS WOULD TRAVEL ALL OVER THE BRIGADE IN NO TIME AT ALL. AND THEN, OF ALL PEOPLE, COLONEL NOZDRIN WALKED UP.

WELL...

DON'T SAY ANYTHING, COLONEL. PLEASE, DON'T SAY ANYTHING.

THE COLONEL HELD BACK A SMILE AND TURNED TO ONE OF HIS STAFF OFFICERS...

FIND SERGEANT TYMOSHENKO A CLEAN UNIFORM...

...KATUSHA, WE'RE STAYING HERE OVERNIGHT TILL THE AMMO TRUCKS REACH US TOMORROW...

...FUEL TRUCKS WILL BE HERE BY NOON.

CONSIDER YOURSELF ON LEAVE UNTIL WE MOVE OUT TOMORROW AFTERNOON...

...*PLEASE!* TAKE YOUR TIME. I'M SURE YOUR CREW CAN SEE TO ANY MAINTENANCE TONIGHT.

THANK YOU, COLONEL.

DOES THE COLONEL HAVE ANY IDEA WHERE I COULD CLEAN UP?

THAT HOUSE OVER THERE SHOULD HAVE EVERYTHING YOU NEED. I'LL PUT THE WORD OUT THAT IT IS *OFF LIMITS* TO EVERYONE, SO YOU WON'T BE BOTHERED. I WILL HAVE THE CLEAN UNIFORM DELIVERED THERE.

THANK YOU VERY MUCH, COLONEL.

I CAN UNDERSTAND WHY NO ONE WANTED TO BE AROUND ME AT THAT MOMENT. I COULD BARELY STAND MYSELF...

...BUT, IF I COULD FIND CLEAN WATER--WELL, EVERY CLOUD HAS A SILVER LINING...

MY, MY! THIS IS REALLY SOMETHING!

I WAS AMAZED THAT THE FRONT DOOR WAS UNLOCKED, BUT AFTER THAT, AMAZEMENT FOLLOWED AMAZEMENT. I THOUGHT THAT THIS MUST BE THE HOME OF A HIGH NAZI OFFICIAL. IN RUSSIA, ONLY THE HIGHEST RUNG OF THE PARTY LIVED IN A PALACE SUCH AS THIS.

I WANTED TO EXPLORE, BUT IN MY FOUL CONDITION I WAS TOO UNCOMFORTABLE. I FOUND AN OLD BURLAP BAG IN A CLOSET AND STRIPPED DOWN RIGHT THERE AND PUT MY FILTHY UNIFORM IN THE BAG. I THEN PUT THE BAG BACK INTO THE CLOSET, TO DISCARD OR LATER CLEAN IF NECESSARY.

THEN IN MY UNDERWEAR AND BOOTS, AND WITH UNCLE TARAS' LUGER, I WENT LOOKING FOR SOMEWHERE TO WASH.

THE HALLWAY UPSTAIRS WAS DARK, BUT WITH AMAZEMENT #8 I FOUND THAT THE ELECTRICITY WAS STILL ON, SO I TURNED ON AN OVERHEAD LAMP.

WHEN I OPENED THE FIRST DOOR ON THE RIGHT I SAW A BEAUTIFUL MARBLE SINK WITH FANCY FAUCETS BELOW AN OVAL MIRROR. I TURNED ON ONE OF THE FAUCETS AND WAS NOT ONLY SURPRISED TO SEE WATER, BUT *HOT* WATER AT THAT. THERE WERE CLEAN TOWELS HANGING FROM A HANDLE ON THE WALL. I THOUGHT HOW NICE IT WOULD BE IF I HAD MOTHER'S WASH TUB HERE.

THEN I SAW *AMAZEMENT #10.*

AT FIRST I THOUGHT IT WAS A BEAUTIFUL WHITE BOAT, BUT THEN I SAW THE FAUCETS AT ONE END, AND I KNEW WHAT IT WAS.

I STARTED LETTING WATER INTO THE CON-TAINER, FIRST USING HOT ONLY, THEN USING THE COLD FROM LETTING IT GET TOO HOT.

ON THE SHELF NEXT TO IT I FOUND SEVERAL BARS OF COLORFUL AND SWEET-SMELLING SOAPS. THERE WERE ALSO PERFUMED POW-DERS THAT MADE BUBBLES WHEN I MIXED HANDFULS OF THEM WITH THE WATER...

...IT WAS MORE WONDERFUL THAN WORDS.

THE RAPTURE OF THE HOT, SOAPY WATER WAS INTERRUPTED BY THE SOUND OF FOOTSTEPS COMING UP THE STAIRS. I REACHED FOR THE LUGER.

THERE WAS A SOFT KNOCK ON THE DOOR, AND I DELAYED MY REPLY UNTIL THERE WAS A SECOND, HARDER INQUIRY.

WHO IS IT?

THE DOOR SLOWLY OPENED...

IT'S ME.

IT WAS KOLYA!

ALL I COULD SEE OF HIM WAS THE FRONT OF HIS CAP AND THE TIP OF HIS NOSE.

I BROUGHT YOUR UNI-FORM...

OH! THANK YOU!

...I'LL LEAVE IT RIGHT HERE.

YOU COULD TELL HE WAS FIGHTING AN UNCONTROLLABLE URGE TO PEEK AROUND THE CORNER.

IT WAS LIKE LIGHTING BOLTS WERE SHOOTING BACK AND FORTH THROUGH THE DOOR.

IS THERE ANYTHING ELSE I CAN DO FOR YOU?

MY THROAT WAS DRY AND MY HEART WAS RACING. I SWALLOWED HARD...

...WELL...

...YOU COULD SCRUB MY BACK.

GREAT, EARTH-SHAKING EVENTS...

...WHAT EPISODE OF PROMINENCE WILL *GOD* PLACE NEXT TO THIS TO KEEP IT IN MY MEMORY?

WHAT IMMENSE AFFAIR OF STATE WILL VIE WITH THE MEMORIES OF A YOUNG GIRL FOR *WEDNESDAY, MARCH 21, 1945?*

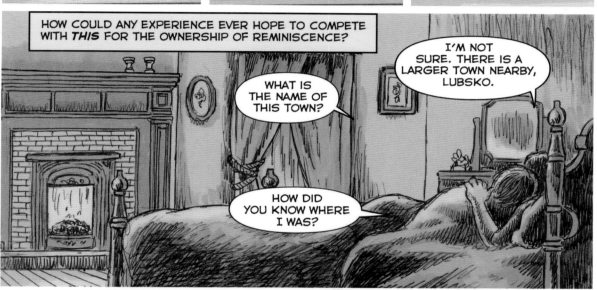

HOW COULD ANY EXPERIENCE EVER HOPE TO COMPETE WITH *THIS* FOR THE OWNERSHIP OF REMINISCENCE?

WHAT IS THE NAME OF THIS TOWN?

I'M NOT SURE. THERE IS A LARGER TOWN NEARBY, LUBSKO.

HOW DID YOU KNOW WHERE I WAS?

STEPHAN CHEKOV HEARD COLONEL NOZDRIN ORDER ONE OF HIS STAFF TO BRING YOU A CLEAN UNIFORM...

...STEPHAN FIGURED IF ANYONE SHOULD INVADE YOUR PRIVACY, IT SHOULD BE ME!

COMMISSAR CHEKOV THOUGHT OF *THAT?*

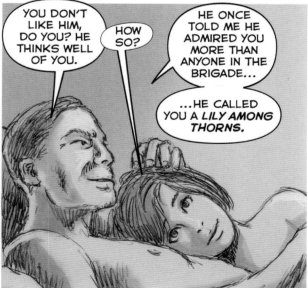

YOU DON'T LIKE HIM, DO YOU? HE THINKS WELL OF YOU.

HOW SO?

HE ONCE TOLD ME HE ADMIRED YOU MORE THAN ANYONE IN THE BRIGADE...

...HE CALLED YOU A *LILY AMONG THORNS.*

STEPHAN IS A HARD MAN. SO IS COLONEL NOZDRIN AND THE OTHERS... KILL THE ENEMY AND BURY THE DEAD...

...THERE'S NOT MUCH TIME FOR ANYTHING ELSE.

STEPHAN CANNOT SHED TEARS, EVEN IF HE WANTED TO, BUT HE ONCE TOLD ME...

"LITTLE TYMOSHENKO CAN CRY. I HAVE SEEN HER! EVEN IN THE HEAT OF BATTLE, I HAVE SEEN TEARS FLOW DOWN HER CHEEKS..."

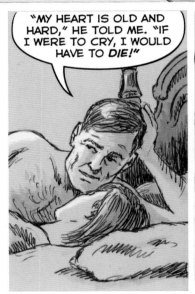

"MY HEART IS OLD AND HARD," HE TOLD ME. "IF I WERE TO CRY, I WOULD HAVE TO *DIE!*"

"TOO MUCH BLOOD," HE WENT ON. "TOO MUCH DEATH. WHEN IT SEEMS IT WILL OVER COME ME, I JUST SAY, 'LITTLE TYMOSHENKO WILL CRY FOR THEM...'

"HER HEART IS SO MUCH BIGGER, SO MUCH *BETTER* THAN MINE."

AND HE'S RIGHT, YOU KNOW...

YOU'RE PROBABLY THE SMALLEST SOLDIER IN THE BRIGADE, BUT YOU HAVE THE BIGGEST HEART.

IT CAN BREAK, YOU KNOW.

I'LL DO ALL I CAN DO TO PROTECT IT.

WHEN THE RED ARMY ENTERED GERMANY THEY DISCOVERED CAMPS HOLDING HUNDREDS OF THOUSANDS OF SOVIET PRISONERS OF WAR. BECAUSE OF *STALIN'S ORDER NO. 274*, THEIR LOT DID NOT IMPROVE. MOST OF THEM WERE PUT RIGHT ONTO TRAINS FOR THE GULAGS OF SIBERIA.

THEY ALSO FOUND MANY RUSSIANS, UKRAINIANS, AND OTHER SOVIET PEOPLES WHO HAD SERVED THE THIRD REICH BECAUSE OF CONVICTION OR JUST IN ORDER TO SURVIVE.

MANY OF THESE WERE IMMEDIATELY DISPATCHED.

EVEN THOSE WHO HAD BEEN TAKEN TO GERMANY AGAINST THEIR WILL TO BE USED AS SLAVE LABOR HAD A VERY SHORT-LIVED CELEBRATION WHEN LIBERATED.

YOU LAZY *BITCHES!* YOU'VE BEEN HERE LIVING IN THE LAP OF LUXURY WHILE WE'VE BEEN FIGHTING FOR THE LIBERATION OF THE MOTHERLAND...

EH?

...YOU COULD HAVE DONE LIKE THOSE THOUSANDS OF OTHERS AND FLED TO THE FOREST...

...AND FOUGHT AS PARTI-SANS...

...YOU COULD HAVE JOINED THE RED—

...WHAT IS IT YOU WANT, WOMAN?

YOU DON'T REMEMBER ME AT ALL, DO YOU, SASHA?

COME ON, GIRLS...

THE MOST AMAZING THING OF ALL, WAS THAT HE NEVER ASKED ABOUT NATASHA OR DIMA...

...LET'S GO HOME.

...BUT MAYBE THAT WASN'T SO AMAZING AFTER ALL.

IN THE MORNING, AFTER KOLYA HAD GONE BACK TO HIS BATTALION, I ROAMED THROUGH THE HOUSE, GATHERING A FEW THINGS WE COULD USE. I ONLY TOOK THINGS THAT I DIDN'T THINK THEY WOULD MISS, OR PERISHABLE THINGS THAT WOULD GO BAD ANYWAY. AFTER ALL, THIS WASN'T MY PROPERTY.

I WENT BACK TO THE CLOSET WHERE I HAD LEFT MY UNIFORM. I THOUGHT IT BEST THAT I THREW IT AWAY OUTSIDE. IF THE OWNERS OF THE HOME RETURNED, I DIDN'T WANT TO DISGUST THEM.

IN THE BACK OF THE CLOSET, IN A WOODEN BOX I FOUND FRAMED PHOTOGRAPHS OF WHO MUST HAVE BEEN THE FORMER RESIDENTS.

ONE WAS THE PICTURE OF A FAMILY, WITH SEVERAL GENERATIONS SHOWN. IT DIDN'T HAVE TO SHOW A MENORAH IN THE PICTURE FOR ME TO KNOW THEY WERE JEWISH.

I KNEW THEN THAT I HAD WITNESSED A PERSONAL HUMAN TRAGEDY.

THIS WAS A FINE, BEAUTIFUL HOME. WHO COULD JUSTIFY STEALING IT FROM SOME-ONE ELSE? IT WAS THEFT, ANY WAY YOU LOOKED AT IT.

OH, LOOK! HARD-BOILED EGGS!

THAT HOUSE HAD AN *ELECTRIC* ICEBOX. SO THEY'RE STILL GOOD AND FRESH...

...WHERE IS RZEPECKE?

GONE! HE DISAPPEARED LAST NIGHT.

JOINED POLISH PARTISAN GROUPS, I GUESS.

I'M NOT SURPRISED. HE WASN'T HAPPY WITH THE WAY THINGS HAD GONE IN POLAND. SLESAREV, I GUESS YOU'VE GRADUATED TO LOADER.

WELL, HAVE YOU HEARD? WE'VE GOT OUR MARCHING ORDERS. OUR WHOLE ARMY IS TURNING AND ROLLING *NORTH.*

THAT'S RIGHT, STRAIGHT TO *BERLIN!*

THEN LET'S GET ON WITH IT.

...OH, I ALSO FOUND THIS IN THE HOUSE...

PERFUME! THAT WILL MAKE THE TANK SMELL GOOD!

...THAT'S NOT ALL...

I UNBUTTONED MY *COVERALLS* DOWN TO MY NAVEL AND OPENED IT UP...

IT'S JUST BEAUTIFUL...

WHAT'S IT CALLED?

IT'S CALLED A *BRASSIERE.*

520

APRIL 1945. NAZI GERMANY WAS BEING CRUSHED FROM BOTH SIDES. OUR WESTERN ALLIES WERE STREAMING ACROSS THE RHINE, AND THE AMERICANS HAD SURROUNDED AND FORCED THE SURRENDER OF MORE THAN 300,000 GERMANS IN THE RUHR VALLEY.

GENERAL EISENHOWER INFORMED MARSHAL STALIN THAT HE HAD NO INTENTION OF TRYING TO REACH BERLIN, LEAVING THAT PRIZE FOR THE RUSSIANS.

BUT STALIN DIDN'T BELIEVE HIM. CONSEQUENTLY, HE SET UP A COMPETITION BETWEEN HIS TWO TOP GENERALS ON WHICH WOULD REACH THE CITY FIRST. HE WAS DETERMINED THAT THE AMERICANS WOULD NOT GET THERE FIRST.

Р. ДЛЕР

БЕРЛИН

ФРАНКФУРТ-НА-

ЛИГ

ДРЕЗ

GENERAL ZHUKOV, NOW COMMANDING THE 1ST BELORUSSIAN FRONT, WOULD BE CROSSING THE RIVER ODER AND ATTACKING BERLIN FROM THE EAST.

COMING UP FROM THE SOUTHEAST, AFTER CROSSING THE NEISSE RIVER, WOULD BE *IVAN KONEV'S* 1ST UKRAINIAN FRONT, TO WHICH WE WERE ATTACHED.

521

WE HAD ALREADY ESTAB-
LISHED BRIDGEHEADS
ACROSS THE NEISSE
AND WOULD LAUNCH
OUR OFFENSIVE FROM
THEM. BY THE MIDDLE OF
THE MONTH, THE MUDDY
ROADS WERE PACKED
WITH TANKS, TRUCKS, AND
TROOPS MOVING UP FOR
THE ASSAULT. SINCE WE
WERE FREQUENTLY UNDER
THE FIGHTER UMBRELLA
OF THE BRITISH AND
AMERICANS, WE WERE
ORDERED TO PAINT A
WHITE STRIPE AROUND
OUR TANK TURRETS AND
A WHITE CROSS ON TOP.

HAPPY
BIRTHDAY,
BEAUTIFUL!

GOD! THAT MADE ME FEEL GOOD!

SO, YOUR
BIRTHDAY IS
APRIL 15! HOW
OLD ARE YOU?

I'M TWENTY,
OXANNA.

KATUSHA!
LOOK AT
THAT!

IT WAS THE FAMOUS *KUZNECHIK,* THE CAMEL
THAT HAD ACCOMPANIED THE *308TH RIFLE
DIVISION* ALL THE WAY FROM STALINGRAD.

THE END WAS NEAR. WE HAD ONE BIG BATTLE
LEFT TO FIGHT. BUT MANY OF US WOULD
DIE IN THE PROCESS. I PRAYED THAT I AND
THOSE CLOSEST TO ME WOULD SURVIVE.

IN SOUTHWESTERN UKRAINE, THE *NKVD* WAS GOING AFTER THE UKRAINIAN INSURGENT ARMY WITH A VENGEANCE. THE PREVIOUS SPRING, GENERAL NIKOLAI VATUTIN, THEN COMMANDER OF THE 1ST UKRAINIAN FRONT, WAS KILLED IN AN AMBUSH BY THE *UPA*.

DAMN! MORE OF THEM ON THE LEFT!

TOO MANY OF 'EM...

...BREAK OFF AND RE-ASSEMBLE YOU-KNOW-WHERE!

THIS IS GETTING TO BE A BAD HABIT.

WELL, AT LEAST WE CAN FALL BACK.

I'M AFRAID ONE DAY THEY'LL BE BACK THERE, TOO.

AT *3AM*, ON THE MORNING OF *APRIL 16, 1945,* 42,000 RUSSIAN GUNS OPENED UP ON THE DEFENDERS OF BERLIN.

SOVIET AIRCRAFT, WHICH HAD COMPLETE COMMAND OF THE AIR, BEGAN THE FIRST OF THOUSANDS OF BOMBING AND STRAFING SORTIES.

HUNDREDS OF SEARCHLIGHTS, MANY OF WHICH HAD BEEN PART OF THE AIR DEFENSE OF MOSCOW, TURNED THE NIGHT INTO DAY. MOST OF THESE LIGHTS WERE MANNED BY RUSSIAN GIRLS.

THEN THE LEADING ELEMENTS OF TWO AND A HALF MILLION SOVIET TROOPS SPRANG FORWARD.

FOR STALIN AND THE MOTHERLAND!

IN ZHUKOV'S SECTOR, THE **SEELOW HEIGHTS** WERE HIS MAIN DIFFICULTY. MANNED BY THE TOO YOUNG AND THE TOO OLD, THE GERMAN TRENCHES HELD OUT AGAINST WAVE AFTER WAVE OF ATTACKERS.

IN KONEV'S SECTOR, THERE WERE DEEP WOODS WITH SOFT MARSHY GROUND TO STALL OUR TANKS. WITHIN THE GERMAN FORCES WERE OLD MEN WHO HAD JUST RECENTLY BEEN DRAFTED INTO THE WEHRMACHT. THESE MEN WOULD USUALLY MAKE TOKEN RESISTANCE AND THEN SURRENDER. BUT THE MOST DEADLY DEFENDERS WERE THE **HITLER YOUTH,** 14- AND 15-YEAR-OLD BOYS WHO HAD BEEN RAISED ON THE REICH'S POISON.

THE DAYS OF ENDURING WAVE AFTER WAVE OF GERMAN PANZERS WERE OVER. THE GERMANS HAD FEW TANKS LEFT, AND THEIR CREWS HAD LITTLE EXPERIENCE...

...BUT THEY HAD PLENTY OF **PANZERFAUST,** WHICH COULD BE FIRED BY ANYONE FROM BEHIND A TREE.

HOWEVER, OUR BRIGADE WAS STUCK IN THE BIGGEST TRAFFIC JAM I HAD EVER SEEN. IT WAS BUMPER TO BUMPER AND MOVING AT A SNAIL'S PACE. A LOT OF PEOPLE WERE IN A BIG HURRY. ACTUALLY, I WAS HAPPY WHERE WE WERE.

GIVE ME A HAND UP, BOYS.

GLADLY, CAPTAIN KOVCHENKO.

IT ALWAYS AMAZED ME HOW KOLYA COULD CALL ALL HIS MEN BY THEIR FIRST NAMES...

HOW ARE THINGS, PYOTR? VLAD, LEONID...

...THIS RIDE WILL HELP YOUR BLISTERS, ALEKSEY.

...BUT HE COULD ALSO RECALL THE NAMES OF THE DEAD.

AND HOW ARE YOU, "LITTLE" TYMOSHENKO?

FINE! ENJOYING THE SLOW PROGRESS.

I AGREE. THIS IS THE YOUNGEST, GREENEST BUNCH WE'VE EVER HAD...

I WOULD HATE TO TAKE THEM INTO THE KIND OF FIGHT THAT THEY'RE HAVING UP AHEAD.

OH, *MY!* WHAT HAPPENED HERE?

GERMAN SS UNITS ARE ROAMING THE COUNTRYSIDE AND HANGING ANYONE WHO LEAVES HIS POST OR TRIES TO SURRENDER.

WHAT DOES THE SIGN SAY?

I BELIEVE IT SAYS SOMETHING LIKE, "I TRIED TO DEAL WITH THE BOLSHEVIKS," OR SOMETHING LIKE THAT.

ICH HABE VERSUCHT, MIT DEN BOLSCHEWIKI UMZUGEHEN

HUM! I GUESS THEIR *SS* IS A LOT LIKE OUR *NKVD*.

WELL, IN A WAY, I WISH WE HAD A LITTLE MORE POLICE PRESENCE RIGHT NOW.

WHY'S THAT?

THOUSANDS OF RAPES HAVE OCCURRED --SOME SAY ENCOURAGED BY OUR COMMANDERS.

I HAVE STATED STRONGLY TO MY MEN THAT I WOULD NOT TOLERATE IT, BUT IF YOU HEAR ANY RUMORS LET ME KNOW.

OKAY! WHAT'S GOING ON OVER THERE?

OH, CHEKOV AND HIS MEN CAUGHT A BUNCH OF RUSSIANS WHO WERE FIGHTING FOR THE GERMANS...

...YOU KNOW, *VLASOV'S MEN.*

DO THEY SHOOT THEM OR HANG THEM?

NEITHER...

...THEY KICK THEM TO DEATH.

ON THE EVENING OF **SATURDAY, APRIL 21**, THE TANKS OF ZHUKOV'S 1ST BELORUSSIAN FRONT ENTERED THE EASTERN OUTSKIRTS OF BERLIN. HE HAD WON THE GREAT RACE. HOWEVER, THE FIGHT WAS FAR FROM OVER.

BY THAT TIME, OUR BRIGADE HAD REACHED THE FRONT AND WAS FIGHTING THROUGH THE FOREST SOUTH OF THE CITY. SINCE WE HAD CROSSED THE NEISSE, WE HAD TRAVELED MORE THAN A HUNDRED MILES BUT HAD NOT YET REACHED THE SOUTHERN SUBURBS.

THE SOLDIERS WE WERE FIGHTING WERE A MIX OF HITLER YOUTH, REGULAR WEHRMACHT TROOPS, AND WAFFEN SS. MANY OF THE REGULARS SEEMED MORE INTERESTED IN BREAKING THROUGH TO THE WEST AND SURRENDERING TO THE AMERICANS.

THE OLD RESENTMENT BETWEEN THE WEHRMACHT AND THE SS WAS COMING OUT IN A BIG WAY. IF WE WERE NOT THERE TO OCCUPY THEM, THEY PROBABLY WOULD HAVE FOUGHT EACH OTHER.

DESPITE THE WEATHER BEING RATHER WET, THE FOREST WAS BURNING AND THE AIR WAS FULL OF SMOKE. WEAPONS FIRE CAME FROM EVERY QUARTER, AND OUR EARS ACHED FROM EXPLOSIONS AND THE SCREAMS OF THE DYING.

SUDDENLY, WE WERE HIT FROM THE RIGHT BY SEVERAL TANKS AND HALF TRACKS.

OUT OF THE HALF TRACKS CAME SHRIEKING GERMAN GIRLS DRESSED IN BLACK WITH **SS** RUNES ON THEIR COLLARS.

THEY WERE ALL YOUNG AND SCREAMING LIKE SOME SORT OF EVIL WITCHES...

WE SCREAMED BACK.

THE FOREST FLOOR WAS COVERED WITH THE BLASTED AND CRUSHED BODIES OF THE DEAD AND DYING, HARDLY RECOGNIZABLE AS HUMAN. HELL COULD NOT HAVE BEEN SO UGLY.

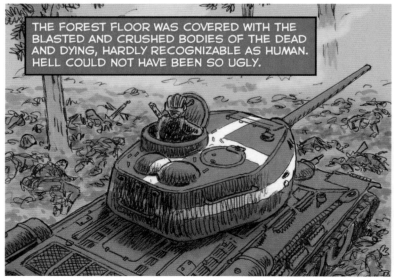

OCCASIONALLY I WOULD NOTICE THE GLIMMERING GOLD OR SILVER OF A WEDDING BAND.

WE REACHED A LITTLE PLACE CALLED *LICHTERFELDE,* WHICH WAS A SUBURB OF BERLIN. WE HAD FINALLY REACHED THE CITY.

I WAS TOO TIRED TO GET EXCITED.

CAPTAIN GUSHKOV'S VOICE CAME OVER THE RADIO...

YOU CAN GET OUT OF YOUR TANKS, BUT DON'T GO FAR...

KATUSHA, I WAS WONDERING. I'VE NOTICED YOUR PICTURE OF COMRADE STALIN...

...AND I NOTICED THAT THERE IS AN ICON ON THE BACK...

WELL, OXANNA, THE TRUTH OF THE MATTER IS, THERE'S A PICTURE OF STALIN ON THE BACK OF MY MOTHER'S ICON.

DO YOU PRAY, KATUSHA?

AS WE TALKED, I SAW MOVEMENT IN A NEARBY ALLEY...

YES, BUT I DON'T FEEL LIKE I'VE GOTTEN VERY GOOD RESULTS. MY PRAYERS SEEM TO ONLY GO TO THE ROOF OF THE TANK...

NOW, MY MOTHER KNEW HOW TO PRAY! I BET SHE COULD GET GOD ON OUR RADIO!

SHE SOUNDS NICE. I WISH I KNEW WHO MY MOTHER WAS...

531

I THINK SHE TOOK ONE LOOK AT ME AND DROPPED ME OFF AT THE ORPHANAGE.

UH-OH! THAT'S TROUBLE.

WHAT'S TROUBLE?

MARUSYA! YOU AND SLESAREV STAY WITH THE TANK...

...OXANNA, YOU COME WITH ME!

HEY! HEY! YOU MEN, COME BACK HERE!

I SAID COME BACK HERE!

I MAY HOLD THE RANK OF A SENIOR SERGEANT, BUT MY ABILITY TO IMPOSE MY WILL ON OTHERS WAS CERTAINLY LACKING...

DON'T DO THAT!

EEEEEEE!

I SAID, STOP IT!

532

GET OFF OF HER, I SAID!

AAAGGG!

YOU MEN SHOULD BE ASHAMED OF YOURSELVES! SHE'S ONLY A CHILD!

SHE'S THE SPOILS OF WAR...AND WHAT'S CAPTAIN KOVCHENKO'S *CAMP WIFE* DOING LECTURING US?

WHOA! DID THAT EVER MAKE ME *MAD!!!*

YOU WOULDN'T BEGRUDGE US OUR FAIRLY EARNED BOOTY, WOULD YOU?

AND I DON'T THINK YOU WOULD KILL ME, WOULD YOU, COMRADE?

I TRIED TO CALM MYSELF, AND LOWERED MY PISTOL...

NO, I WOULDN'T KILL YOU...

...COMRADE.

BUT IT DOESN'T BOTHER ME AT ALL CRIPPLING YOU...

...COMRADE!

YYEEEEOOOOO!

MY VICTIM ROLLED AROUND ON THE GROUND IN AGONY. I HAVE TO ADMIT, HE WAS RATHER FUNNY.

YOU MEN! GET HIM TO AN AID STATION!

...UUURRGG!

THE YOUNG GIRL, WHO COULDN'T COMMUNICATE A SINGLE WORD IN MY LANGUAGE, LOOKED UP AT ME WITH PURE GRATITUDE.

IT'S ALL RIGHT. YOU GO BACK TO YOUR HIDING PLACE.

I FOUND IT MORE SATISFYING THAN DESTROYING A HUNDRED OF HER NATION'S TANKS.

EVERYONE LEFT...EXCEPT FOR ONE DISAPPOINTED-LOOKING SOLDIER.

WHAT'S THE MATTER WITH YOU?

I WAS HOPING TO LOSE MY VIRGINITY...

DON'T BE GONE TOO LONG, OXANNA...

UH, OKAY, KATUSHA...

OUR TANK COMPANY BUILT A BONFIRE IN A HUGE BOMB CRATER. WE WERE AMAZED HOW MUCH DAMAGE HAD BEEN DONE BY THE AMERICAN AND BRITISH BOMBERS BEFORE WE GOT HERE. WE HEATED RATIONS ON A FIRE AND HUMMED A FEW SONGS AS THE FIGHTING WENT ON NEARBY.

KOLYA SHOWED UP WITH A SERIOUS EXPRESSION ON HIS FACE.

AM I IN TROUBLE?

NOT AS FAR AS I'M CONCERNED. THEY LIED ABOUT WHAT HAPPENED. THEY SAID THEIR FRIEND GOT SHOT IN THE FOOT BY A SNIPER...

HAVE YOU EVER HEARD THE LIKE?

SNIPERS DO GO FOR TANK COMMANDERS, THOUGH. I'D FEEL BETTER IF YOU WERE WEARING THIS WHEN YOU HAVE YOUR HEAD OUT.

ALL RIGHT. BUT I NEVER SEE YOU WEARING ONE.

I'M THE BATTALION COMMANDER...

...MY MEN HAVE TO RECOGNIZE ME.

YOU TAKE CARE OF YOURSELF. DON'T DO ANYTHING FOOLISH AT THIS LATE DATE.

THE SAME FOR YOU, LITTLE TYMOSHENKO.

AFTER HE LEFT, OXANNA AND I SAT BY THE FIRE IN SILENCE. WE NOW HAD A SECRET POINT OF REFERENCE "NOT TO TALK ABOUT," AND IT WAS NICE.

WHERE ARE YOU FROM, OXANNA?

KIRZHACH, 50 MILES EAST OF MOSCOW. UGLY TOWN, UGLY PEOPLE.

MY HEART WENT OUT TO HER AND I IMAGINED WHAT A HARD LIFE SHE HAD.

THEN YOU WON'T BE GOING BACK AFTER THE WAR.

HA! NOT LIKELY.

YOU KNOW, I WENT TO SCHOOL WITH A BOY NAMED NATAN. HE PLAYED THE BANDURE--OH-SO BEAUTIFULLY. HE ALSO HAD A BEAUTIFUL SINGING VOICE. BUT, HE WAS BLIND, YOU SEE...

...IF NATAN SURVIVED THE WAR, I WOULD VERY MUCH LIKE YOU TO MEET HIM...

...I THINK YOU TWO WOULD LIKE EACH OTHER VERY MUCH.

I COULD SEE OXANNA'S EYES BROADEN IN THE FIRE LIGHT AND SPARKLE WITH MOISTURE.

REALLY?

REALLY.

YOU JUST COME HOME WITH ME. I'LL INTRODUCE YOU TO NATAN AS MY SISTER.

OXANNA SAID NOTHING FOR SEVERAL MINUTES, SOAKING IN ALL I HAD SAID. THEN, SHE SPOKE CLEARLY, SO THE HEAVENS WOULD MAKE THE MOMENT.

THIS HAS BEEN THE MOST WONDERFUL DAY OF MY LIFE.

WE SAT THERE TOGETHER IN THE SHELL HOLE, THE SMOKE AND SCENT OF DEATH FILLING OUR NOSTRILS. A HUNDRED YARDS AWAY, PEOPLE WERE FIGHTING AND DYING BY THE THOUSANDS. BUT AT LEAST FOR ONE PERSON...

APRIL 27, 1945, WOULD NOT BE ABOUT DEATH, BUT ABOUT HOPE.

ALL THE NEXT DAY OUR TANKS, TOGETHER WITH UNITS OF MOBILE ARTILLERY, BOMBARDED THE BUILDINGS ON THE OTHER SIDE OF THE *LANDWEHR CANAL.* THERE WERE SEVERAL TRANSPORTATION STATIONS IN FRONT OF US, AND WE UNDERSTOOD THAT THE ENEMY WAS USING THE UNDERGROUND RAILROAD AS BUNKERS.

THE *BERLIN PHILHARMONIC* WAS ALSO IN OUR SIGHTS. GUNS PROVIDED THE ONLY MUSIC.

IN THE PRE-DAWN OF *APRIL 29...*

EVERYBODY READY? NOW!

FOLLOW ME!

OOOORRRAAAAAA!

537

HOW MANY MORE TIMES DO I HAVE TO TWIST MY GUTS IN PRAYER AS I WATCH HIM SPRINT INTO SOME RIDICULOUS AND SUICIDAL ATTACK? HOW MANY MORE CHANCES MUST HE TAKE?

OUR MEDICS QUICKLY REMOVED OUR DEAD AND WOUNDED OFF THE BRIDGE BEFORE OUR TANKS CROSSED. I AM ALWAYS GRATEFUL FOR THIS. I HAVE HAD TO RUN OVER OUR OWN MEN BEFORE.

WELL, I HOPE YOU'RE HAPPY! IF WE DON'T END THIS SOON, I'LL TURN GRAY.

GERMAN BULLETS DON'T SEEM TO LIKE ME.

I KEPT A STERN FACE AND TIGHT LIPS.

I DON'T LIKE JOKES LIKE THAT.

THE COCKY GRIN FADED FROM HIS FACE, REPLACED BY A VERY SERIOUS EXPRESSION.

I LOVE YOU, EKATERINA.

HE HAD NEVER SAID IT BEFORE. HE HAD INFERRED IT, AND I HAD BEEN HAPPY WITH THAT.

WHY DID YOU SAY THAT? NOW?

HE QUICKLY TURNED AND WALKED TOWARD WHERE HIS MEN WERE GATHERING ON THE NORTHERN SIDE OF THE BRIDGE.

IN CASE...

JUST IN CASE...

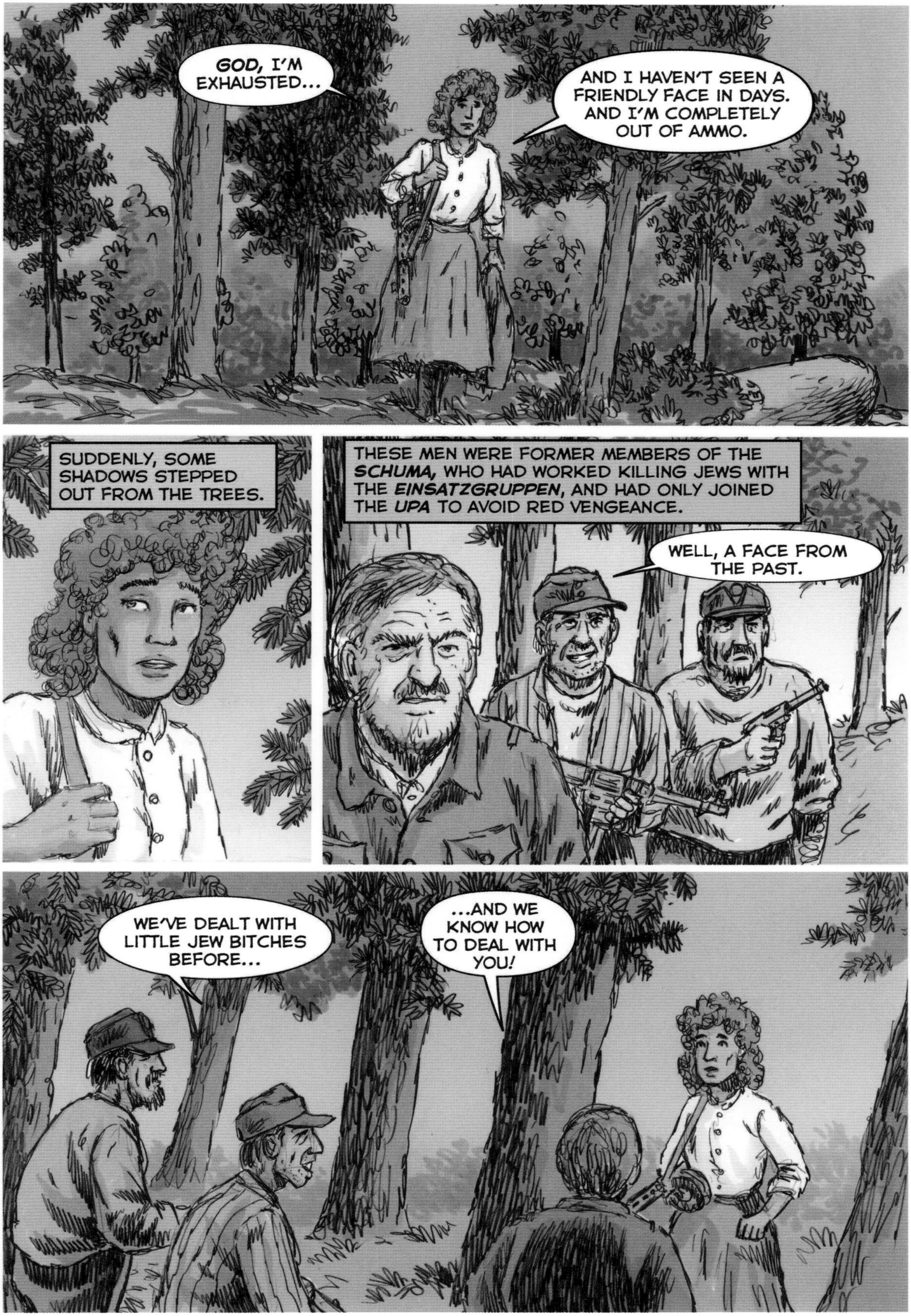

GOD, I'M EXHAUSTED...
AND I HAVEN'T SEEN A FRIENDLY FACE IN DAYS. AND I'M COMPLETELY OUT OF AMMO.
SUDDENLY, SOME SHADOWS STEPPED OUT FROM THE TREES.
THESE MEN WERE FORMER MEMBERS OF THE SCHUMA, WHO HAD WORKED KILLING JEWS WITH THE EINSATZGRUPPEN, AND HAD ONLY JOINED THE UPA TO AVOID RED VENGEANCE.
WELL, A FACE FROM THE PAST.
WE'VE DEALT WITH LITTLE JEW BITCHES BEFORE...
...AND WE KNOW HOW TO DEAL WITH YOU!

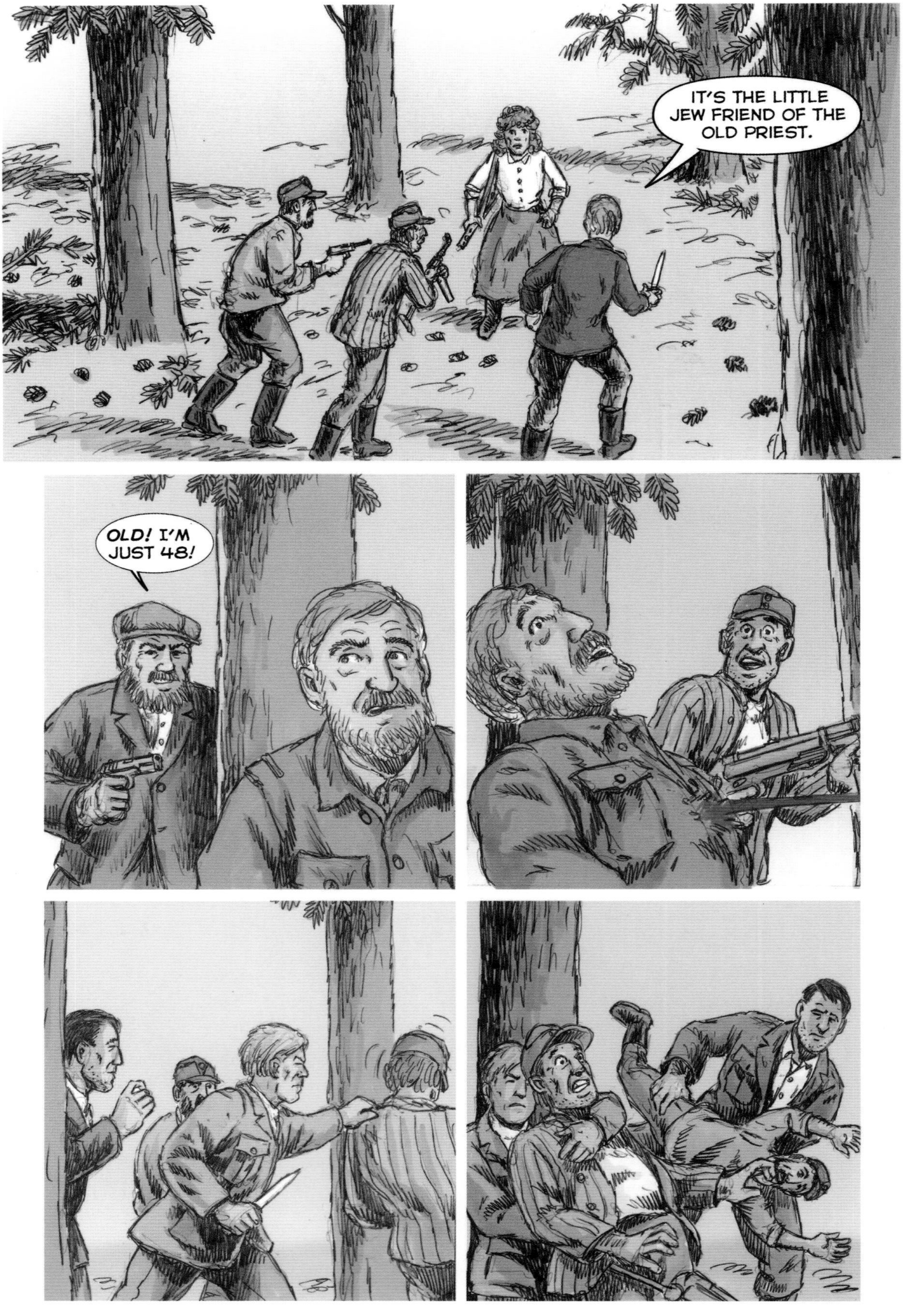
IT'S THE LITTLE JEW FRIEND OF THE OLD PRIEST.
OLD! I'M JUST 48!

KRACK!

VASILY, WHAT LUCK WE RAN INTO EACH OTHER!

LUCK? LUCK HAD NOTHING TO DO WITH IT. WE'VE BEEN LOOKING FOR YOU.

YOU ONCE CAME LOOKING FOR ME, ZHENYA...

...IT'S NATURAL AND RIGHT THAT WE SHOULD COME LOOKING FOR YOU.

WHO ARE THE HEROES? WHO ARE THE VILLIANS? MAYBE IT'S JUST THOSE WHO SURVIVE AND THOSE WHO DON'T. THE LIVING AND THE DEAD.

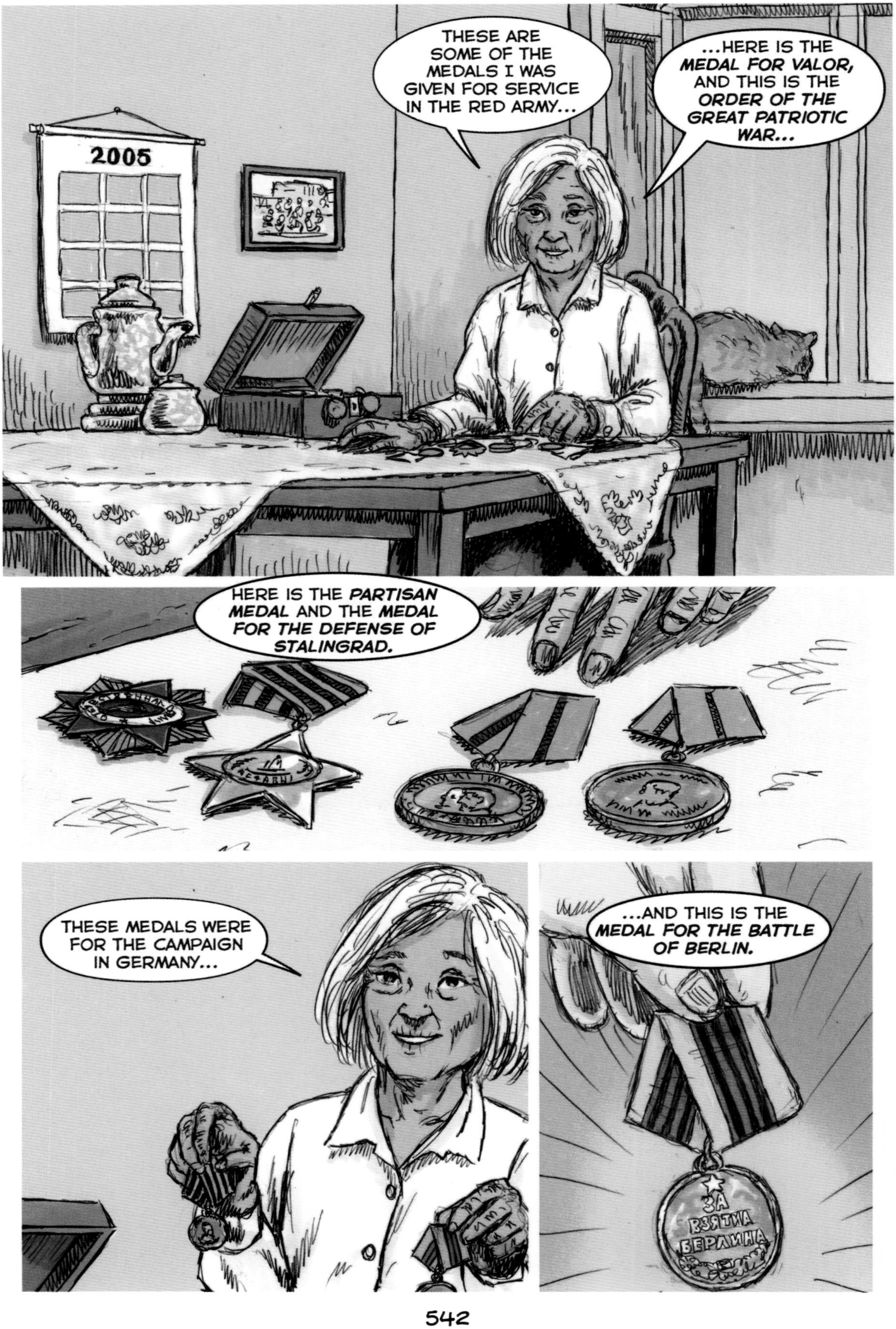

2005
THESE ARE SOME OF THE MEDALS I WAS GIVEN FOR SERVICE IN THE RED ARMY...
...HERE IS THE *MEDAL FOR VALOR,* AND THIS IS THE *ORDER OF THE GREAT PATRIOTIC WAR...*
HERE IS THE *PARTISAN MEDAL* AND THE *MEDAL FOR THE DEFENSE OF STALINGRAD.*
THESE MEDALS WERE FOR THE CAMPAIGN IN GERMANY...
...AND THIS IS THE *MEDAL FOR THE BATTLE OF BERLIN.*

REMEMBER ME

APRIL 30, 1945. THE THIRD REICH IS IN ITS LAST AGONIES. BOYS, SOME NO OLDER THAN 14, ARE SACRIFICING THEMSELVES FOR A LOST CAUSE, AND FOR A MAN WHO CARES NO MORE FOR THEM THAN MY LEADER CARES FOR ME.

WHY DO THEY DO IT, KOLYA?

THEY KNOW WHAT THEIR ARMIES DID IN RUSSIA, AND THEY KNOW THAT THERE WILL BE A STIFF PENALTY TO PAY.

BUT THEY ALSO SWORE AN OATH TO HITLER. THAT MEANS A LOT TO THEM. THEY WILL KEEP THEIR WORD NO MATTER WHAT...

...THE GERMANS ARE RATHER FUNNY THAT WAY.

ARE YOU ALRIGHT, KATUSHA? YOU LOOK A LITTLE PALE.

I'M FINE.

GGHHAKK!

GOSH, KATUSHA! I WOULD HAVE THOUGHT YOU'D SEEN ENOUGH OF THIS...

"AUNT OXANNA!" I LIKE THE SOUND OF THAT.

TELL NO ONE!

DO YOU THINK THIS STEEL MESH WILL HELP AGAINST THE PANZER-FAUST?

THE THEORY SEEMS RIGHT. I SURE HOPE SO.

WE WERE ADVANCING DOWN A FAIRLY WIDE STREET WITH BUILDINGS OF THREE TO FIVE STORIES ON EACH SIDE.

A SQUAD OF OUR MEN WOULD ADVANCE DOWN EACH SIDE OF THE STREET, CHECKING OUT THE BUILDINGS AND EVERY NOOK AND CRANNY AS THEY WENT.

THIS WAS A VERY STRESSFUL JOB.

TWO TANKS WOULD FOLLOW ABOUT A HUNDRED FEET BEHIND THEM, ONE ON THE FAR RIGHT WITH ITS TURRET TURNED SLIGHTLY TO THE LEFT AND ONE ON THE FAR LEFT WITH ITS TURRET TURNED TO THE RIGHT. THEY WOULD COVER THOSE ADVANCING AND PROVIDE FIRE SUPPORT WHEN NEEDED.

THE BULK OF OUR INFANTRY FOLLOWED THE TANKS, READY TO DEPLOY ON A MOMENT'S NOTICE.

OTHER GROUPS SUCH AS THESE ADVANCED ON PARALLEL STREETS. THEY KEPT IN CONTACT BY RADIO AND THROUGH THE ALLEYS WHEN POSSIBLE.

WE WAITED BEHIND THE INFANTRY. WE WERE TO TAKE UP A LEAD POSITION IF ANYTHING HAPPENED TO ONE OF THE TWO LEAD TANKS...

THE INFANTRY MADE A PATH FOR US AS WE PASSED THROUGH. KOLYA TRIED TO SMILE.

SOME OF OUR SOLDIERS MADE WAGERS ON HOW MANY METERS WE WOULD GO BEFORE DESTRUCTION.

THE WEATHER WAS COOL, BUT ALL OF US IN THE TANK SWEATED...

THE *PANZERFAUST* HAD BECOME A MORE FEARED WEAPON THAN THE TIGER TANK...

ANY IDIOT COULD AIM AND FIRE IT.

THE "BED SPRINGS" WORKED.

WELL, IT DID THAT TIME.

THE INFANTRY WENT INTO THE BUILDING WHERE THE SHOT CAME FROM. A HALF-HOUR FIGHT ENSUED. WHEN IT WAS OVER, ONLY TWO-THIRDS OF OUR MEN CAME OUT.

MORE INFANTRY WOULD MOVE UP TO TAKE THE PLACE OF THE CASUALTIES...

...AND THE KILLING WENT ON.

FEW OF OUR SOLDIERS WHO HAD SURVIVED THE "STREET FIGHTING UNIVERSITY" AT STALINGRAD STILL REMAINED. WE HAD FORGOTTEN HOW OUR SOLDIERS HAD USED THE SEWERS TO MOVE IN BEHIND THE ENEMY. THE GERMANS WERE LATE TO LEARN THIS LESSON...BUT LEARN, THEY DID.

AS KOLYA HAD ADVISED, I WORE MY HELMET. I HAD ALWAYS FOUND THAT I COULD BEST PERFORM MY DUTIES AS TANK COMMANDER WITH MY HEAD OUTSIDE THE HATCH, WITH TARAS' PISTOL CLOSE AT HAND.

ON THIS DAY, I KEPT A *PAPASHAW* AT THE READY AT ALL TIMNES.

THE HELMET DID MAKE IT DIFFICULT TO SEE STRAIGHT UP.

FROM BEHIND US, AMID THE CHATTER OF AUTOMATIC FIRE, I HEARD A HOLLOW BOOM. IT WAS THE DESTRUCTION OF ONE OF OUR WAITING RELIEF TANKS, AGAIN BY *PANZERFAUST*. WE WERE BEING CUT OFF FROM OUR REAR SUPPORT.

SUDDENLY FIRE RAINED FROM EVERY QUARTER. THE GERMANS HAD LET US ADVANCE INTO A TRAP. KOLYA'S INFANTRY WAS TAKING FIRE FROM WHAT SEEMED LIKE EVERY WINDOW.

OXANNA BEGAN FIRING THE COAXIAL MACHINE GUN, SO I TURNED TO SEE GERMAN INFANTRY ADVANCING ON US FROM OUR FRONT. THEY WERE WILD EYED AND DETERMINED LOOKING. I FIRED INTO THEM WITH THE *PAPASHAW*.

MARUSYA! BACK UP! BACK UP!

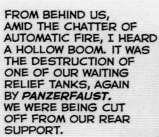

549

AS WE BACKED UP, WE DID NOT NOTICE THE MANHOLE COVER RIGHT BELOW US...

...AND WE FAILED TO SEE THE MENACE IT HELD...

I WAS BLOWN FROM THE HATCH LIKE THE CORK FROM A CHAMPAGNE BOTTLE.

I BOUNCED OFF THE ENGINE DECK AND THEN FELL TO THE PAVEMENT WITH A JOLT...

THE TANK-- MY TANK-- KEPT ROLLING

I ROLLED OUT OF THE WAY OF THE TRACKS.

THE TANK CLIMBED ACROSS A SIDEWALK AND BACKED INTO THE CORNER OF A BUILDING. THE ENGINE SPUTTERED AND THEN WENT DEAD.

I CRAWLED BACK INTO THE TURRET AND RELUCTANTLY LOOKED INSIDE.

AGSK!

THROUGH THE SMOKE I COULD SEE THAT THE *PANZERFAUST* HAD DONE ITS JOB. ITS SHAPED CHARGE HAD BURNED A HOLE THROUGH THE LOWER FRONT STEEL PLATE. IT SHATTERED THE CRUDELY FORGED STEEL INTO HUNDREDS OF RED-HOT SPLINTERS THAT COULD SHRED HUMAN FLESH. ONLY THIS RAVAGED FLESH WAS MY BEST FRIENDS.

I REACHED INTO THE REAR OF THE TURRET AND RETRIEVED MAMA'S ICON. SOME PEOPLE CAN DEVELOP A CERTAIN KINSHIP WITH A NON-LIVING PIECE OF MACHINERY. I CANNOT. TO ME THIS WAS A COLD, LIFELESS HUNK OF IRON...

...BUT ITS CREW WAS SOMETHING ELSE.

I PLACED THE ICON IN A HAVERSACK AND HUNG IT OVER MY SHOULDER. SUDDENLY, NEW ROUNDS BEGAN PINGING OFF THE SIDE OF THE TURRET.

THE FIGHT WAS NOT YET OVER.

THE SONIC SHOCK OF THE HIT WAS STILL RINGING IN MY EARS, BLOCKING OUT EVERYTHING ELSE. THE CARNAGE AROUND ME EXPLAINED WHAT A REVERSAL HAD OCCURRED.

I RETRIEVED MY PISTOL AND *PAPASHAW* AND HID BEHIND THE TANK. ONCE THEY REALIZED I WAS HERE, A GRENADE WOULD QUICKLY ERASE THEIR PROBLEM.

THEN I HEARD AUTOMATIC FIRE FROM BEHIND ME AND THE TRADITIONAL RUSSIAN WAR CRY...

IT WAS KOLYA! HE CAME RUNNING OUT OF THE SMOKE FIRING FROM THE HIP, BREAKING UP THE GERMAN ADVANCE...

HERE! HAVE A FRESH DRUM!

THAT SLOWED THEM DOWN A LITTLE. BUT WE NEED TO HURT THEM MORE...

...IF WE RUN FOR IT NOW, THEY'LL GET US!

THE ENEMY CAME AT US, BUT WE FOUGHT OFF THEIR POORLY ORGANIZED ATTACKS WITHOUT MUCH DIFFICULTY. BUT WHEN KOLYA RAN OUT OF AMMO, HE MADE THE MISTAKE OF WITHDRAWING A GRENADE FROM HIS POCKET WITH HIS DAMAGED LEFT HAND.

HE HAD NO SOONER PULLED THE PIN THAT IT SLIPPED FROM HIS THUMB AND TWO FINGERS...

I WAS COMPLETELY IGNORANT OF ITS PRESENCE, AS IF THAT MATTERED.

KOLYA FLUNG HIMSELF ON TOP OF ME, WHICH I MISTOOK AS TOTALLY SPONTANEOUS AND POORLY TIMED AFFECTION.

THE LAST TWO GERMANS PEERED THROUGH THE SMOKE TO SEE IF WE WERE FINISHED. I FINISHED THEM WITH THE LAST TWO ROUNDS IN MY LUGER.

I SLOWLY ROLLED KOLYA OVER AND OPENED HIS OVERCOAT.

IT WAS BAD...*VERY BAD.*

I USED EVERYTHING I COULD, INCLUDING HIS HAT, TO TRY AND SLOW THE BLEEDING, AND STRAPPED HIS OVERCOAT ON AS TIGHT AS I COULD.

LET'S SEE IF I CAN PICK YOU UP...

...OH...

HE WAS TWICE MY WEIGHT. THERE WAS NO WAY I COULD CARRY HIM TO A MEDIC.

...LEAVE ME, KATUSHA...

SHUT UP.

I GOT HIM INTO AN OLD WHEELBARROW AS BEST I COULD.

I WON'T MAKE IT, KATUSHA...

...YOU SHOULD LEAVE ME...

YOU CAN FORGET THAT!

NO CHILD OF MINE IS GOING TO GROW UP NOT KNOWING ITS FATHER!

"DO NOT CALL ME, FATHER, DO NOT SEEK ME;

"DO NOT CALL ME, DO NOT WISH ME BACK.

"WE ARE ON A ROUTE UNCHARTED,
FIRE AND BLOOD ERASE OUR TRACKS."

"ON WE FLY ON WINGS OF THUNDER,
NEVER MORE TO SHEATHE OUR SWORDS,

"ALL OF US IN BATTLE FALLEN,
NOT TO BE BROUGHT BACK BY WORDS.

"WILL THERE BE A RENDEZVOUS? I KNOW NOT.
I ONLY KNOW WE STILL MUST FIGHT.

"WE ARE SAND GRAINS IN INFINITY, NEVER MORE
TO MEET, NEVER MORE TO SEE LIGHT.

"FAREWELL THEN, MY SON, FAREWELL THEN
MY CONSCIENCE, MY YOUTH AND MY
SOLACE, MY ONE AND MY ONLY.

"AND LET THIS FAREWELL BE THE END
OF A STORY, OF SOLITUDE VAST
IN WHICH NONE IS MORE LONELY."

"IN WHICH YOU REMAIN, BARRED FOREVER AND EVER...

"FROM LIGHT AND FROM AIR WITH YOUR DEATH PANGS UNTOLD.

"UNTOLD AND UNSOOTHED, NOT TO BE RESURRECTED.

"FOREVER AND EVER AN EIGHTEEN-YEAR-OLD...

"FAREWELL THEN. NO TRAINS EVER COME FROM THOSE REGIONS,

"UNSCHEDULED OR SCHEDULED. NO AIRPLANES FLY THERE."

"FAREWELL, THEN, MY SON, FOR NO MIRACLES HAPPEN...

"AS IN THIS WORLD DREAMS DO NOT COME TRUE.

"FAREWELL. I WILL DREAM OF YOU STILL AS A BABY,

"TREADING THE EARTH WITH LITTLE STRONG TOES;

"THE EARTH WHERE ALREADY SO MANY LIE BURIED.

"THIS SONG TO MY SON IS COME TO ITS CLOSE."

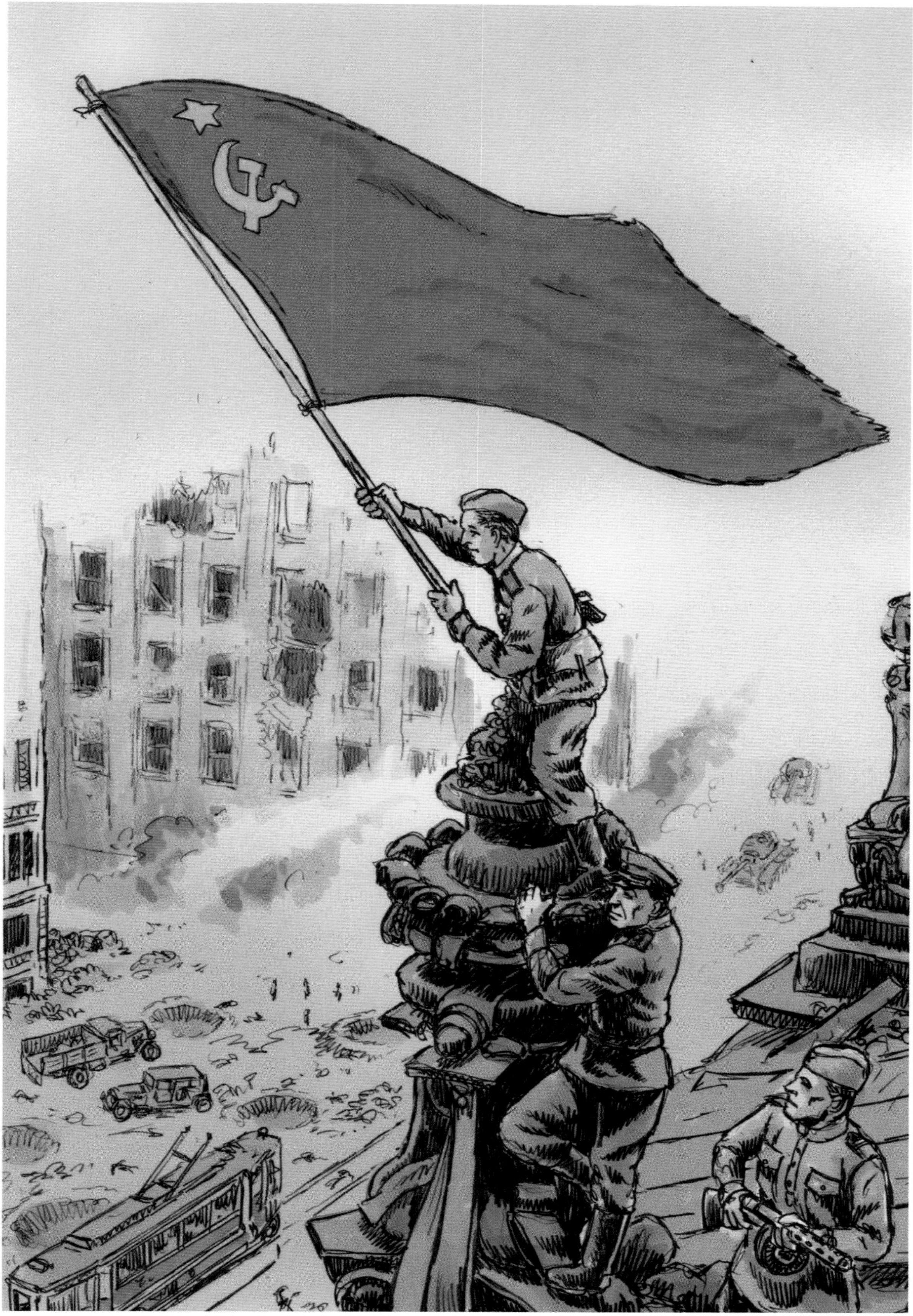

OCTOBER 1945.

I'VE BEEN AWAKE SINCE DAWN, AND I HAVEN'T SEEN A SINGLE BUILDING OR HOUSE THAT HADN'T BEEN SHATTERED...

...ALL I'D SEEN WERE OLD WOMEN AND SCARECROW CHILDREN, AND FEW, SO FEW, MEN.

AH! SERGEANT TYMOSHENKO. I WAS JUST COMING TO SEE YOU.

COLONEL NOZDRIN PULLED A YELLOW ENVELOPE FROM HIS POCKET....

I HAD TO CRACK A FEW SKULLS TO GET THIS THROUGH. IT'S WORTH *36,000 RUBLES...*

...YOUR BOUNTY FOR *18 GERMAN TANKS.* YOU PROBABLY GOT MORE, BUT THAT'S ALL I COULD VERIFY.

YOU CAN CASH THIS WITH THE MILITARY AUTHORITY IN KIEV.

WHAT ABOUT MILLA? AND MISHA BOVA? AND OXANNA? AND MARUSYA? AND...

LOOK! I CAN DO NOTHING FOR THEM. *WHO CAN?* YOU TAKE IT. *YOU* LIVE FOR THEM.

THAT'S A BIG RESPONSIBILITY.

YOU ARE A VERY RESPONSIBLE GIRL.

OH, I HAVEN'T SEEN VERA. WHERE IS SHE?

HA! YOU HAVEN'T HEARD?

SHE MET AN AMERICAN MAJOR. SHE'S GOING TO MARRY HIM AND MOVE TO THE U.S. OF A.

ME? I'M GOING BACK TO MY WIFE AND FAMILY.

WILL YOU FIND IT STRANGE THAT THERE ARE THINGS ABOUT THIS WAR THAT WE WILL MISS?

NO...

561

I WENT TOWARD THE REAR OF THE TRAIN, INTO THE MEDICAL CARS. I WALKED PAST THE SHATTERED LIMBS AND FACES, NEITHER LOOKING LEFT NOR RIGHT.

THERE HE IS! HOW ARE YOU FEELING?

BETTER. MUCH BETTER.

IT'S ABOUT 40 MINUTES TO KIEV. I HAVE PERMISSION TO STAY HERE TILL THEN.

COLONEL NOZDRIN WAS JUST HERE, TELLING ME I SHOULD MAKE YOU AN HONEST WOMAN.

HE'S RIGHT, OF COURSE. BUT I WANT YOU *STANDING* AT OUR WEDDING.

HE TOLD ME ABOUT YOUR FATHER, TOO. WHEN DID IT HAPPEN?

THE LETTER FROM THE FACTORY SAID EARLY LAST SPRING. HE WORKED HIMSELF TO DEATH, THEY SAY...

YOU KNOW, I HAD A PREMONITION ABOUT IT. A DREAM. I DIDN'T KNOW WHAT IT MEANT AT THE TIME.

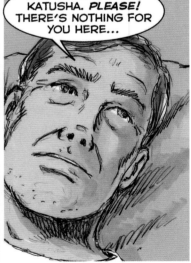

STAY ON THE TRAIN, KATUSHA. *PLEASE!* THERE'S NOTHING FOR YOU HERE...

YOU DON'T KNOW THAT, AND NEITHER DO I. BUT I'VE GOT TO FIND OUT. IF THERE'S NO ONE HERE, THEN...WELL, WE'VE STILL GOT EACH OTHER...

...BUT I'VE GOT TO KNOW ABOUT MY FAMILY, KOLYA.

I'VE GOT TO KNOW...

...HERE.

KIEV! POVITROFLOTS'KY PROSPECT!

KIEV WAS NOT NEARLY AS TORN UP AS A LOT OF PLACES I HAD BEEN, BUT IT STILL SEEMED LIKE A GHOST TOWN.

I SAW FEW PEOPLE...

...AND THEY MOVED LIKE GHOSTS.

AS I NEARED THE ZALIZNYCHNY DISTRICT, I NOTICED A SMALL GROUP OF PEOPLE SITTING AROUND A BONFIRE.

WHO IS IT? WHAT DO YOU WANT?

I MEAN NO HARM. DO YOU KNOW IF ANYONE IS LIVING IN ZALIZNYCHNY?

THE OLD WOMAN WAS OBVIOUSLY OUT OF HER HEAD.

WHY DO YOU LOOK FOR THE LIVING AMONG THE DEAD?

I STARTED TO WALK AWAY, BUT I NOTICED SOMETHING STRANGE ABOUT THEIR FIRE...

WHAT IS THAT YOU'RE BURNING?

BIBLES.

WHAT?!

I SAID, BIBLES. WE FOUND A WAREHOUSE OF THEM THAT THE BOLSHE-VIKS HAD TAKEN AWAY FROM PEOPLE A LONG TIME AGO...

...THEY BURN REAL WELL...

564

THE RAGGEDY LITTLE MAN HELD ONE OUT FOR ME.

HERE! TAKE ONE!

I NUMBLY TOOK IT, FEELING LIKE A LOWLY THIEF.

I THEN TURNED AND WENT ON MY WAY.

I STUMBLED ON DOWN THE DUSTY, GUTTED STREET, VAGUELY AWARE THAT IT WOULD BE AFTER DARK BEFORE I REACHED MAMA'S HOUSE.

WHAT WOULD I DO IF I REACHED IT IN THE DARK AND THERE WAS NO ONE THERE? WHAT WOULD I DO? WHERE WOULD I GO?

WHEN I REALIZED THAT I WAS CRYING, I STOPPED AND SAT DOWN BY THE CURB.

I HELD UP THE BIBLE THAT I HAD TAKEN TO THE FADING AUTUMN LIGHT. IT WAS MADE OF DUSTY BLACK LEATHER...

...ON THE COVER WAS THE SHADOW OF AN OLD CROSS THAT HAD ONCE ADORNED IT. PERHAPS THE CROSS HAD BEEN MADE OF SILVER, OR EVEN GOLD.

I OPENED UP THE FRONT COVER OF THE BIBLE...

...AND LOOKED INSIDE...

THERE WAS AN INSCRIPTION IN UKRAINIAN THAT READ:

"THIS BIBLE IS A GIFT FROM GOD, AND FROM YEVGENIAA GRIGOREVICH TUGUSOV, TO MY HUSBAND, SEMEN STEPANOVICH KALASHNIKOV, ON OUR WEDDING DAY, 14 AUGUST, 1891."

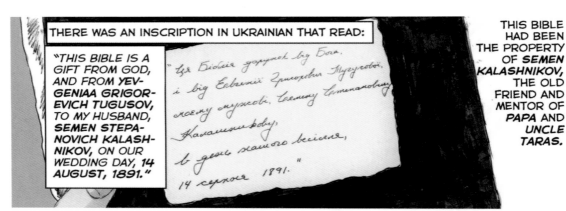

THIS BIBLE HAD BEEN THE PROPERTY OF **SEMEN KALASHNIKOV**, THE OLD FRIEND AND MENTOR OF **PAPA** AND **UNCLE TARAS.**

MY TEARS FELL ON THE PAGES OF THE BIBLE LIKE RAIN. I SAT THERE AND CRIED FOR WHAT HAVE MUST HAVE BEEN AN HOUR.

THEY WERE TEARS OF GRIEF AND LOSS, BUT ALSO TEARS OF HOPE.

FINALLY, CRIED OUT, I STOOD UP AND CONTINUED ON MY JOURNEY.

IT WAS WELL AFTER DARK AS I WALKED DOWN THE DUSTY LITTLE ROAD ON THE WESTERN OUTSKIRTS OF KIEV. ALL THE HOUSES WERE DARK AND LOOKED DESERTED. THEN I SAW A VERY DIM GLOW FROM A FAMILIAR WINDOW.

...MY HEART HELD BACK, BUT MY FEET SPED UP UNCONTROLLABLY.

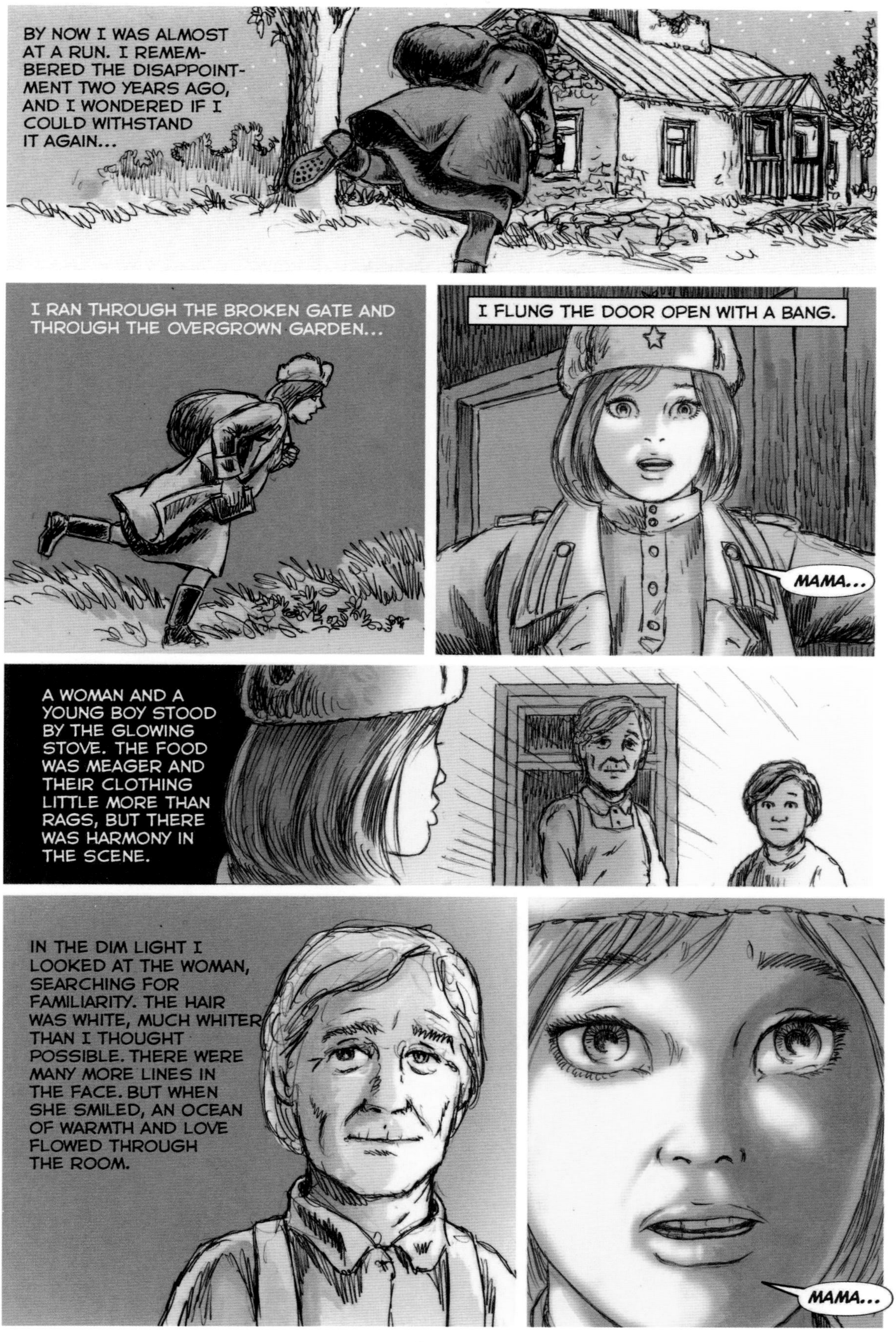
BY NOW I WAS ALMOST AT A RUN. I REMEMBERED THE DISAPPOINTMENT TWO YEARS AGO, AND I WONDERED IF I COULD WITHSTAND IT AGAIN...
I RAN THROUGH THE BROKEN GATE AND THROUGH THE OVERGROWN GARDEN...
I FLUNG THE DOOR OPEN WITH A BANG.
MAMA...
A WOMAN AND A YOUNG BOY STOOD BY THE GLOWING STOVE. THE FOOD WAS MEAGER AND THEIR CLOTHING LITTLE MORE THAN RAGS, BUT THERE WAS HARMONY IN THE SCENE.
IN THE DIM LIGHT I LOOKED AT THE WOMAN, SEARCHING FOR FAMILIARITY. THE HAIR WAS WHITE, MUCH WHITER THAN I THOUGHT POSSIBLE. THERE WERE MANY MORE LINES IN THE FACE. BUT WHEN SHE SMILED, AN OCEAN OF WARMTH AND LOVE FLOWED THROUGH THE ROOM.
MAMA...

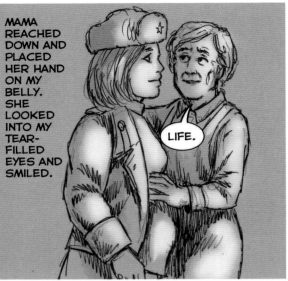

MAMA REACHED DOWN AND PLACED HER HAND ON MY BELLY. SHE LOOKED INTO MY TEAR-FILLED EYES AND SMILED.

LIFE.

THE LITTLE BOY, WHO LOOKED TO BE ABOUT EIGHT, WALKED UP BESIDE ME AND PUT HIS HAND ON MY ARM.

HE SMILED WARMLY. IT WAS THEN THAT I NOTICED THE WOODEN CROSS AROUND HIS NECK THE CROSS THAT HAD ONCE HUNG ON THE NECK OF BABUSHKA'S DOG. THIS LITTLE BOY WAS MY NEPHEW DIMA. THE DOG'S NAME HAD BEEN MUKHTAR. I HAD FORGOTTEN THIS, BUT DIMA, NEVER WOULD.

MOTHER HAD FOUND HIM IN A HOME FOR CHILDREN ORPHANED BY THE WAR. HOW HE HAD SURVIVED ALONE, WE'LL NEVER KNOW, BECAUSE HE NEVER TALKED ABOUT IT.

THE WAR WAS OVER.

THERE WAS MUCH WORK TO BE DONE. WHEN I WAS ABLE, I WENT TO WORK AS AN ELECTRICAN. I WIRED MANY OF THE BEAUTIFUL BUILDINGS THAT NOW LINE KHRESHCHATYK BOULEVARD.

IN THE 1960S, I WENT TO WORK MAKING TELEVISIONS, BLACK-AND-WHITE, OF COURSE.

KOLYA ARRIVED IN KIEV IN 1946, AFTER RECOVERING FROM HIS WOUNDS AND CLOSING HIS AFFAIRS IN LENINGRAD.

WE WERE MARRIED IN WHAT I THINK IS THE MOST BEAUTIFUL CHURCH IN KIEV, *ST. ANDREWS,* AND BEGAN OUR LIVES TOGETHER. AS WELL AS OUR SON, WE RAISED TWO DAUGHTERS TOGETHER.

KOLYA TAUGHT MUSIC AND PIANO IN OUR LOCAL SCHOOL. IN SOME FORM OR OTHER, ALL THREE OF OUR CHILDREN FOLLOWED HIM IN THIS FINE PROFESSION.

LIFE WAS GOOD.

BUT KOLYA HAD GREAT DIFFICULTY DEALING WITH THE GHOSTS OF THE WAR. WE BOTH DID, BUT I THINK I DEALT WITH IT BETTER THAN HE.

MY BROTHER VASILY SURVIVED THE WAR, BUT I NEVER SAW HIM AGAIN. HE SURRENDERED TO THE AMERICANS IN AUSTRIA WITH MEMBERS OF THE GALICIA DIVISION. AFTER TWO YEARS OF SCRUTINY IN A CAMP IN NORTHERN ITALY, HE WAS ALLOWED TO EMIGRATE TO CANADA. HE MARRIED AND RAISED A FAMILY THERE.

About the Author

For more than 30 years **Wayne Vansant** has been writing and illustrating comics and graphic novels on historic and military subjects, beginning with Marvel's *Savage Tales* and *The 'Nam*. Since then he has produced *Days of Darkness*; *Battron: The Trojan Woman*; *Blockade*; *The War in Korea*; *Stephen Crane's The Red Badge of Courage*; *Normandy*; *Grant vs. Lee*; *Bombing Nazi Germany*; *The Battle of the Bulge*; *The Red Baron*; and others.

NO ONE THAT I KNOW EVER HEARD WHAT HAPPENED TO FATHER ZAPOLYE. ALTHOUGH THE COMMUNISTS SLIGHTLY LOOSENED THEIR STRANGLE-HOLD ON RELIGION DURING THE WAR, THEY NEVER RELEASED IT ALTOGETHER. MEMBERS OF THE CATHOLIC AND GREEK CATHOLIC CHURCHES IN WESTERN UKRAINE WERE IMPRISONED AND SOMETIMES MURDERED UP UNTIL THE 1980S.

I HAVE SEEN MANY THINGS IN MY LIFE. I HAVE SEEN THE PASSING OF *COMRADE STALIN* (AND YES, I CRIED, BUT I DON'T KNOW WHY). I SAW THE FALL OF THE SOVIET UNION, SAW THE INDEPENDENCE OF UKRAINE, AND WITNESSED OUR NATION'S FIRST BABY STEPS TOWARD DEMOCRACY...

BUT...THERE WILL ALWAYS BE THOSE WITH A LUST FOR POWER WHO WANT TO HAVE CONTROL OVER THE LIVES OF OTHERS...

NOW KOLYA'S GONE, MAMA'S GONE, AND DIMA'S GONE. BUT I STILL HAVE MY CHILDREN, MY GRANDCHILDREN, AND MY GREAT-GRANDCHILDREN.

WAS THIS STORY TRUE, YOU ASK? OR WAS IT JUST AN OLD WOMAN'S BLURRY MEMORY OF A YOUNG GIRL WHOSE LIFE WAS CHANGED FOREVER ON THAT TERRIBLE SUNDAY IN JUNE 1941? MORE THAN 70 YEARS HAVE PASSED SINCE THAT DAY, AND THOSE WHO SHARED ITS HORRORS AND HOPES WITH ME ARE NOW GHOSTS. THE ONLY TANGIBLE TRACES THAT REMAIN ARE A FEW MEDALS AND AN OLD MOTH-EATEN WOOLEN UNIFORM, STORED AWAY IN A MOLDY OLD TRUNK.

ONE THING THAT I STILL HAVE FROM THOSE DAYS IS MY MOTHER'S ICON...

...IT REMAINS PERMANENTLY NAILED AND GLUED TO THE WALL OF MY FLAT...

...THE DAY MY SON WAS BORN, I PROMISED *GOD* THAT I WOULD NEVER TURN IT OVER AGAIN.

SLAVA UKRAYINI!